BAZO

A Saga Novel

D. Randall Faro

This book is a work of fiction. References to real people, events, establishments, organizations, or locales are intended only to provide a sense of authenticity and are used fictitiously. All other characters and all incidents and dialogue are drawn from the author's imagination and are not to be construed as real.

This novel is dedicated to my wife, Mary Elizabeth, our children David and Katherine, and to the memory of our daughter, Jeniffer.

Synopsis

Born to Norwegian missionaries in Zimbabwe and raised within the culture of the Ndebele tribe, Jedediah Bazo immigrates to the United States where he becomes a USMC officer.

After the Marines and years of travel, the core values he discovers lead him into the ministry. Eventually he abandons the institutional church to work with street people on Seattle's south side. Known as Father Jed, he encounters much of the seedier side of life, including the atrocity of human trafficking. USMC skills and an expertise in the martial arts serve him well when confronted with raw evil.

Edge-of-your-seat action scenes find Bazo repeatedly faced with the question of when violent force can be justified. His faith-based attitudes nudge him in one direction, but life or death decisions arise when others play by different rules.

A richly developed cast of characters spanning three continents and five decades make this an exciting literary journey. The reader will come to champion Jedediah Bazo, and to wrestle with the same ethical issues he does.

Foreword

Jedidiah Bazo was born in my mind around the advent of the 21st century. The characters and storyline were developed and refined on Washington mountains, in coffee shops, logging highway miles on my touring motorcycle, lying in hospital beds, and in a little man-cave writing shack hidden among Douglas Firs high above the Chehalis River. The in-mind writing journey took me around the world, both to places where life beat me into shape and to locales I hope yet to explore.

The novel is in no way autobiographical, but my experiences in the United States Marine Corps, the Lutheran ministry, and many of the various story locations provided a context for putting the saga together. Some surnames in the book are drawn from reality, but no character is meant to represent any actual person, living or dead.

Along with the goal of weaving an enlivening story, I endeavored to use words and style in a way that resulted in both readability and a presentable use of the English language. My hope is that the reader not only enjoys the tale, but thinks, “That was a good way to string words together.”

While the last-page remarks acknowledge the assistance by those without whom this would never have gone to market, any mistakes – historical, geographical, grammatical – are mine alone. If any are noted in the reading, I'd be happy to be notified at drfaro.author@gmail.com in order to make corrections.

If you found Bazo an enjoyable read, it would be much appreciated if you would give it a good star rating, write a favorable review, and recommend it to your friends. Self-published authors depend in large part on the support of their readership. Thanks.

Jedediah and company carry on.

Look for the sequel, GUNNAR, in the coming year.

"You go to church and pray to God, and everything after that sort of depends on where you stand, how you look at it, right and wrong. You know, sometimes you have to squint."

Pleading Guilty, Scott Turow

"There just comes a time when a man says: Enough!"

Black Cross, Greg Iles

Prologue

May 2005 - North Bend, Washington

A substantial portion of his life had been spent in wilderness areas. Yet the sound that woke him at the beastly hour of four a.m. was something out of a horror movie. Barely above the subconscious level in his post-REM sleep cycle, he clearly heard a hellish screech that stood every hair on his body at attention. In his soporific state of mind, Bob's first thought was that he had never heard anything quite like it before. A mystifying question quickly followed: was he dreaming or was the sound an actual cry in the dark? A glance at the fuzzy digits on the nightstand clock informed him that it was several hours yet until dawn, a realization which supported the nocturnal fantasy conclusion.

But just as he dismissed the rude awakening and began to slip back into what he hoped was a better dream, Bob almost levitated as a hideous and extended howl seemed to fill the cavity of their bedroom. There was no mistaking reality this time

An animal-like shrieking, it was one he couldn't identify amidst the grogginess of his rational senses struggling to come up for air. It was close enough to be clearly heard, but didn't fit any category of wildlife sounds with which Bob was familiar. The semi-scream would crescendo, drop off to nothing, and then recycle beginning with a kind of muffled keening that communicated serious distress.

"Judy, did you hear that?" Bob asked as he gently elbowed his wife. Generally experiencing a deeper diurnal cycle, Judy slowly came to the surface and heard the unnerving discord.

"What in the world?" she exclaimed with a bit of anxiety.

And then they both heard the pawing, scratching on what sounded like their front door. A couple of hours before dawn was not a time one wished for surprises of this nature.

Bob and Judy Taskins had lived the majority of their married lives in metropolitan areas. Bob was an aerospace engineer who had worked his way up the management ladder in Lockheed Martin, Northrop Grumman, and Boeing. His vacation and earned-time-off days were spent almost exclusively in the bush hunting, fishing, and climbing. Such activities were as intrinsic to Bob's nature as flying was to the eagles he loved to watch. Judy knew and accepted this need for wildness, even accompanying him on some of his less ambitious expeditions.

When Bob retired at age sixty-two they looked for a home outside of but near a metro area. They couldn't go too far afield because the contract work he continued to do for a variety of aerospace corporations necessitated accessibility to a major airport. North Bend, Washington was the ideal situation.

North Bend is just short of forty miles east of SeaTac Airport, yet nestled between the South and Middle Forks of the Snoqualmie River in the western foothills of the rugged North Cascade Mountains. The Seattle metro area was less than an hour away, and, more importantly, the property they found was on the western edge of the kind bush Bob loved. Thousands of square miles of bona fide wilderness lay to the east, and the Taskins' property was pleasantly isolated at the end of the trail. Mt. Si Road crossed the only bridge over the Middle Fork Snoqualmie and then 434th snaked north alongside the river, dead-ending in a cathedral-like stand of cedar and fir. With only a couple of other secluded residences on the way to road's end, the property provided the privacy and rough setting which suited the Taskins' desires to a T.

They built a custom log home down a long driveway, hidden from the public roadway. Landscaped with rhododendrons and the area's ubiquitous ferns to blend in with the terrain, it was both a quiet sanctuary for the couple as well as a beautiful retreat for their children and friends, all of whom they enjoyed entertaining. In the fourth year at their foothills paradise, they were comfortable in their relative isolation and thoroughly familiar with the flora and fauna of their environs.

Which made the early morning screeching and scratching confusing in the extreme, and cause for some alarm.

"Bob. Bob! Go see what that is!"

"I'm going, but I'm picking up my rifle on the way. I don't know what's making that racket, but I'm not going to find out barehanded."

"Well, be careful. Don't just go charging out the front door." Which was a normal admonition for Judy to utter since it was in Bob's nature to go charging out of front doors.

As Bob made his way to the gun cabinet in their study, the intermittent noise continued albeit the crescendos seemed less intense. A low-intensity yard light leaked some illumination onto the home entrance, but not enough for Bob to make out what was creating the racket. A moderately heavy fog also reduced visibility. He could tell it was on the other side of the front door, but the peephole did not allow him to determine what the balled up creature at the threshold might be. He turned on the lights to the full-house-wraparound deck and proceeded to the back door. He stealthily crept along the side of the house, cartridge in the chamber and safety off. As he approached the corner, he could hear that the creature had not moved toward him but was still groveling in front of the door.

Very slowly and cautiously he slid the barrel of his .300 Savage Remington Gamemaster around the corner, followed by his line-of-sight gaze. And froze.

Lying in a fetal position was a crumpled heap of tawny, scrawny, bruised and bleeding skin and bones. Bob's realized presence precipitated ear-piercing wails accompanied by a hesitant groveling in his direction. Bob was startled by its appearance and found it impossible to ascertain gender or ethnicity. His volume level easily carried through the door as he bellowed:

"Judy, call the sheriff!"

Chapter 1

July 1946 - Matopos Hills, Rhodesia

Jumbles of towering boulders, some which twenty men could not encompass with their arms and washed crimson, umber and ecru by the evening sun, dominated the landscape. A gentle breeze rustled the mopani leaves with the resulting effect of thousands of huge green butterflies trying to escape the branches. Yips and growls and bird shrieks fitting for any Tarzan movie provided a sonorous background for the momentous event.

Surrounding the Fjelstad family, one hundred and fifty Ndebele warriors in full battle dress stood with assegais poised to strike. Wearing only loincloths and the traditional tall feather headdress, they chanted the ancient victory song while swaying their elongated shields in sync. Powerful drum beats, intimidating guttural intonations, and unified menacing scowls seemed to leave no doubt as to their intentions.

A rainbow of hues formed a backdrop for the warriors in the form of scores of Ndebele women in ceremonial finery. Their bright, multi-colored robes seemed to blend into one shimmering mass as they swayed in unison to the incantations of the men. The *imlingakobe*, strands of beads draped from their heads, swung with their movements, and the brass rings jingling around their necks, arms, and legs added to the surrealistic nature of the happening. The anticipation and tension the Fjelstads felt was conspicuous.

"Arvid, is this real?" she asked with quivering voice.

"Look around, Bergitta. We couldn't change things now no matter how much we might want to."

"Who would have thought our prayers would bring us to this?"

"We had no idea, did we? But now we must be bold and brave and steadfast."

The Matopos Hills was an area of granite kopjes and wooded valleys south of Bulawayo in southwestern Rhodesia. Formed billions of years ago, the kopjes eroded to produce smoothly rounded features called dwalas, the land between them interspersed with boulders and thickets of vegetation. Mzilikazi, founder of the Ndebele nation, gave the area its name, meaning "Bald Heads."

The Ndebele were descendants of the Zulus in South Africa. In the late 1830s Mzilikazi led some twenty thousand of his tribe north from South Africa and established a new nation he called Mthwakazi, but which later Europeans labeled Matabeleland. Mzilikazi formed the Ndebele nation from a multitude of locals which included the Nguni, Sotho, Tswana, Kalanga, Shona, Venda and Tonga tribal groups. He organized this ethnically diverse conglomerate into a militaristic system of regimental towns, his capital named Bulawayo, or "the place of killing." Anyone observing the ferocious host that surrounded the Fjelstads would have easily surmised that more death was about to be added to the tradition.

No one knew how many Ndebele populated the area, but it was indisputable that the Fjelstads were the only white people within hundreds of square miles. The Matopos Hills had been their home for the past six years. In February 1940 they left their beloved Norway for the unknowns of the Rhodesian interior. The Norwegian Missionary Society, founded in 1842 in Stavanger with its goal being the spread of the Christian message, primarily in Africa, commissioned Arvid and Bergitta for service in the southern part of the continent. Idealistic and passionate, the recently married couple excitedly headed for Africa and the tribal lands of the Ndebele. Their early days were full of apprehension and wonder as they adjusted to topography, flora, fauna, and cultural norms as different from Norway as one could possibly imagine.

Early in their adopted land they were confronted with the kinds of challenges that would characterize their new life. Walking westward from their primitive hut on the Mtshabezi River west of the regional center of Gwanda, they followed a barely discernable track toward a village to which they were given sparse and fuzzy directions. Bergitta stopped underneath one of the ubiquitous ironwood trees.

"Look, Arvid. I never cease to be amazed at the wonders of this land." Cradling several of the bifoliate leaves in her palm she noted, "It's no wonder they call it the butterfly tree. It looks like all the branches are about to fly away."

As Arvid came closer to examine her find, he suddenly froze in place and whispered to Bergitta, "Don't move. Do not even blink." In spite of the quietness of his command, she could sense that he was deadly serious. Movement in her peripheral vision revealed the reason.

Less than a soccer field away, a black rhinoceros eyed them studiously. It looked to Arvid like a Landsverk L-120 tank with an attitude. They had no idea from where it had come or how long it had been observing them. But Arvid knew they were in extreme danger. Only three weeks ago a village elder had been trampled to death by a rhino when he was caught walking alone across the savanna. The scrub Mopani were not tall enough to climb, and he knew there was no chance of outrunning a charging rhino.

Arvid whispered again, "Remember that they have very bad eyesight. If we don't move a muscle he'll likely think we're just part of the landscape and move on."

Just as Bergitta was about to mouth a hushed reply, the rhino lowered his massive head, snorted what looked to them like smoke, and charged straight at them. Arvid grabbed his wife as she reflexively started to bolt. "Freeze!" he blurted quietly but forcibly. "It's our only chance." Keeping one's composure with a charging rhinoceros bearing down would be a test of anyone's grit, but Arvid and Bergitta stood their ground, each one murmuring what they thought would probably be their last prayer. Thirty yards from the doomed couple the rhino thudded to a stop, but kept looking at them with beady little eyes. Arvid and Bergitta could see nothing through their own tightly shut eyes.

Since one loses an accurate sense of time in situations of crisis such as this, Arvid couldn't later estimate how long the magnificent beast stood there contemplating their future. But eventually, and as suddenly as had been his charge, the rhino turned ninety degrees and trotted off between two kopjes, apparently deciding the skinny couple wasn't worth his time and energy.

"Do you want to faint first or can I?" Bergitta exhaled.

"Are you trying to tell me you were worried?" Arvid replied with manufactured bravado.

"Worried! I was scared to death! And by the way, what's that liquid running down your leg?"

"Just sweat, my dear. I knew he'd stop if we didn't move."

"Next time you know something like that, let me in on the secret so I don't have a near-stroke."

Taking a deep breath to calm his heart rate, Arvid said, "Part of the reason we're here is for excitement, isn't it?"

"Yeah, well, dying isn't very exciting, so I'll thank you to keep a closer look out for rhinos and such."

Arvid promised to increase his vigilance and they

continued westward with one more vivid account to record in their ongoing journal.

Six years later they felt almost as much at home in the Matopos Hills as in their native Norway. A commitment to the Ndebele people had solidified for both of them, and they had formed deepening relationships as a result of their respect for and affirmation of the people and their customs. The Ndebele sensed their genuine care, and many had come to embrace them as family.

The one thing that the couple began to wonder about was the lack of a child. It wasn't because they eschewed the physically intimate aspect of their relationship, but month after month there was no hint of pregnancy. They were willing to raise a family in the southern African bush with all of its attendant risks, but Bergitta's apparent barrenness made that seem more and more unlikely.

Until that October day.

Bergitta approached Arvid with a coquettish smile that quickly earned his attention.

"Honey, I have some news that I think you're going to like."

Arvid had no idea what was coming when Bergitta revealed that for the second time she missed her monthly flow and was without doubt with child. Hearing this announcement he wasn't sure which was more intimidating, a charging rhino or an impending child. But then he swept his beaming wife into his arms as they together thanked their God for the blessing.

Local intra-tribal rivalries combined with occasional marauding incursions from the Tswana in neighboring

Bechuanaland created a measure of instability in the area. An added complication for the Fjelstads was the fact that their presence was not universally accepted by the Ndebele, some of the hardcore traditionalists resenting the advent of a religion that seemed at odds with the beliefs to which their ancestors had adhered. But by and large they enjoyed the hospitality of the majority, and most importantly that of numerous esteemed village chieftains. Aware of the somewhat fragile nature of their situation, Arvid and Bergitta nevertheless prepared for the coming child with all the enthusiasm of first-time parents. They continued their mission work, but always checking their backs for the possibility of hostility.

The Ndebele warriors and their gyrating female backups closed in on the Fjelstads. A circle of campfires surrounded the embracing couple as the drumbeat gained momentum and volume, and the metal-tipped assegais gleamed ever closer in the light of the flames. The Ndebele leader, Njabulo, resplendent in his chieftain's royal robes, raised his scepter high above the heads of Arvid and Bergitta and proclaimed in a thunderous voice: "*Indodana ozalwa* – A son is born!" Sharing the Fjelstads' elation and gratitude, the Ndebele welcomed this new child into their tribal community with the age-old ritual used to celebrate new life.

The drummers quickened the pace while the tribal cry of victory was uttered in raucous frenzy from the over four hundred gathered Ndebele. Suddenly the drums slowed and quieted the assembly to a low murmur. Arvid stood next to the chief in the center of the fire circle, lifted his son high above his head and shouted with joy: "His name is Jedediah!"

Chapter 2

December 1946 - Matopos Hills, Rhodesia

There was a mammoth difference between raising a child in Bergen and doing so in the Rhodesian bushveld. While the Fjelstads were faced with numerous challenges, they had acclimated so completely to life in southern Africa that many things which would appear threatening to the average Norwegian had become normal for them. Added to this was the incalculable joy that little Jedediah brought into their lives which simply overshadowed what might be considered hardships in other situations. Arvid's consistent efforts to provide a regular supply of fresh fruits and goat milk helped insure the nutritional value of Bergitta's breastmilk. The daily rigors of hauling water, cooking, washing, and parenting seemed to invigorate the new mother. After several months, Arvid felt comfortable enough with mother's and child's progress to continue with his forays to surrounding villages. Bergitta even went with him to a couple of the closer communities. The Ndebele, who treasured babies as gifts from God, be it the creator-god Zimu, the ancestral spirits, or the new Christian God, were captivated by this new little white one.

The Fjelstads were only the second white missionaries to come among the Ndebele. Their predecessor, a slight and somewhat fragile single man who never acclimated to either the climate or the culture, lasted only three years. He gathered a small following which, as he departed, he assured could expect a successor within a short time. He had communicated his imminent departure to the home Missionary Society, who realized that some individuals found idealized missionary work to be not so ideal, and felt the need to shorten the term of their service. There was generally a supply of individuals ready and waiting for an assignment. Arvid and Bergitta were among that supply.

They embodied classic Nordic features. Arvid was broad-shouldered and a shade over six feet tall, with Bergitta only two inches shorter. Both had blonde hair, blue eyes, and the characteristic elongated head with aquiline nose. Some Ndebele were indeed tall, but the flaxen hair and alabastrine skin of the Fjelstads seemed to mesmerize them. They were initially regarded with some reserve, but their congeniality, their affirmation of Ndebele traditions and ways of life, and their eagerness to learn and speak isiNdebele won the hearts of most.

Late one day they sat in front of their traditional wattle and daub hut watching the blaze-orange sun setting behind the kopje they had named Eric the Red because of its oxidized ferrous cap. The now-familiar whistlings of the bushshrikes and sugarbirds were soothing lullabies to the young family. Jedediah was cradled in Bergitta's arms while Arvid wrapped them all together in a wool blanket to ward of the evening chill. Their world was pervaded with a momentary sense of peace as they processed thoughts about how their life was unfolding.

"Would you have believed we could be so happy?" Bergitta sighed as the sun's last rays highlighted her stunning azure eyes.

"Indeed," Arvid replied, "our life here is more than anything we ever expected. I had some reservations about whether we could adjust or not, but it's startling how quickly I have come to feel this land and these people to be our own."

"And I as well. Maybe Jedediah has something to do with it. I was happy when it was just the two of us, but with our child's birth I've discovered a deepness of love I never knew existed. It feels like he was destined to be born here . . . and to bring us closer together."

"And you do not feel the urge to return to our homeland to raise Jedediah?" Arvid questioned.

"Someday that will happen, but we will teach him to

be Norwegian even as he becomes part Ndebele. Whatever length of time God wants us to remain here, imagine how valuable this experience will be as he matures. His world is already expanding far beyond that of most children back home."

Sorting his thoughts for several moments, Arvid reflected, "I already think of this as our home, and wonder if we'll ever want to return to Norway." Worrying how they would affect Bergitta, he regretted his words as soon as they came out of his mouth.

Seeing the look of concern on his face, she replied, "It is home for all three of us, my love. And the God who brought us here will surely direct our future. For now, we live and serve as we have been guided."

Her words comforted him as he gave inward thanks again for the gift of his wonderful wife. With the sun's temporary demise and the veld's concert of night sounds soothing them into a pleasant drowsiness, the tranquil couple retired into their dwelling and fell asleep with Jedediah surrounded by their warmth.

"*Livuke njani.* Good morning, my friends. We have far to travel today."

Jacob Bazo, the surname being the Ndebele word for axe, was not only their guide and mentor, but he and his wife Naomi had become cherished friends. Having acquired a rudimentary knowledge of Norwegian from the original mission founder as well as having come to embrace the Christian faith, the Ndebele couple took Arvid and Bergitta under their wings from almost the first day. As the relationship developed, it proved invaluable in both Jacob's uncanny ability to navigate anywhere in the region without map or compass, and in his serving as intermediary with the village chieftains as Arvid sought to establish relationships that would eventually welcome his sharing of the faith. When the two men went from village to village throughout the Motopos, Bergitta stayed with Naomi and learned the ways of the Ndebele. With the Fjelstads' eventual fluency, they used isiNdebele almost exclusively to communicate. The closeness of the two couples was cemented even more so when Naomi acted as the midwife for Jedediah's birth.

"Good morning to you, Jacob," Arvid replied as he stuck his head around the mat doorway. But Jacob immediately recognized an uncharacteristic concern on Arvid's face.

"Something is amiss. What is it, my brother?"

"It's Bergitta. Early this morning she awoke with a stiff neck and a headache. Now she has a fever as well that seems to be growing. I don't think this is a good day for me to travel."

"And Jedediah?" Jacob asked with growing apprehension.

"He seems fine at present, and I feel no different."

"Nevertheless," Jacob replied, "please let me take the child to Naomi until we figure out what the problem is and nurse Bergitta back to health."

While not wishing to alarm Arvid, Jacob secretly felt a stab of concern. The Bazos' niece with a four month old baby was currently living with them, and had wet nursed Jedediah several times. While most Norwegians would likely have been shocked at this, the Fjelstads were aware of the growing knowledge of antibodies and how the niece's milk could contain some that would be valuable for warding off a host of local diseases.

"You know Jedediah will be in good hands, and Thembelani has plenty of milk to share with him until Bergitta's fever passes."

Grateful for this caring gesture, Arvid asked him to wait while he wrapped the baby. Handing him to Jacob, he said, "I will be over in a while." Knowing he didn't need to ask, he did anyway. "And if it is not too much trouble, please send Naomi over to help attend to Bergitta's personal needs. Perhaps she will know what the problem is and suggest a remedy."

As Jacob carried Jedediah to his hut on the other side of the Mtshabezi, his concern deepened. During the past years, numbers of villagers had fallen prey to some malady of which they had no understanding. There had been a brief lull, but just last month two young adults had died in the neighboring village. His wife must act quickly.

By the time Naomi reached the Fjelstads' hut Bergitta's headache was worse than ever and she was retching violently. Cause for further alarm was the fact that now Arvid was beginning to feel poorly, complaining of nausea and neck stiffness. The nearest doctor, a British expat who seemed more at home with a flask instead of a stethoscope in hand, was hours away in Gwanda. As the day progressed and the Bazos wondered what to do, the Fjelstads' conditions went from bad to worse. By sundown neither could rise from their mats, and they were both racked with increasing temperatures, accelerated joint pain, splitting headaches, and an inability to keep down even liquids.

The Ndebele had no medical knowledge of meningococcal meningitis. To be sure, many had succumbed to the fast-acting disease, but tribal lore considered it either a scourge of the gods or it was recognized simply as part of the hard life one lived in Africa. They had local potions that sometimes mediated the symptoms, but they knew nothing of its cause, the bacterium *Neisseria meningitidis*, its prevention or cure. Jacob and Naomi were all too aware that what they were observing in their friends had led to tragic results with neighbors in a very short time.

By noon of the next day Arvid and Bergitta were each in a coma. By the setting of the sun they had both died.

Chapter 3

January 1960 - Salisbury, Rhodesia

Jedediah was on the cusp of a change in his life that was both exciting and terrifying. As he sat in the Trans World Airlines L-049 Lockheed Constellation listening to the four 18-cylind-er radial Wright R-3350 engines rev up for takeoff, he couldn't help but wonder if this was the right thing to do. The roar sounded louder than a hundred bull elephants in musth, and while he had certainly seen airplanes traverse the skies high above, it was unconceivable to him how this slug-shaped metal giant with three tails could get off the ground in the first place, much less soar with the eagles. He was flanked by Don and Ingrid who had told him airplanes were safe, yet at the moment he did not feel safe. But he had been taught to face fear with bravery, so with racing heart and clenched jaw Jedediah determined to meet this challenge with the same fortitude that imbued his character and brought him to this venture.

His father made this once-in-a-lifetime trip to Salisbury to accompany his son to the airport where the latter would journey to places which had been described to him yet exceeded his comprehension. Jedediah's flight would take him to London for a brief overlay and then to that faraway kingdom called America. Jacob believed this was best for the young man. After all, he would return home eventually, would he not? The Ndebele warrior did not dare to answer the question.

Having undergone the two-month Ndbele initiation rite of *ukuwela*, Jedediah had made the transition from boyhood to manhood. Most Europeans and Americans would not look upon a fourteen-year old as a man, but Jedediah Bazo knew he was made of steel. Like an axe. Yet he could not deny that of the five hundred species of butterflies native to Rhodesia, at least half were flitting around inside his stomach. The new and freshly starched western clothes he wore were a stark contrast to his native garb, but at least it would help him to blend into his new world

instead of sticking out like a scarecrow in his father's maize field.

Before Jedediah boarded the plane, Jacob spoke to him with an ache in his chest and a lump in his throat. "My son, you are a gift of God. Your mother and I are blessed by you, as you will also bless those with whom you go."

Choking back tears, Jedediah replied, "Father, I will return. I shall honor the Bazo name and remember all that you have taught me."

Jacob took from his pocket a leather thong from which hung a likeness of the African fish eagle which he had carved from mahogany. The eagle was a sign of strength and one of the most important symbols representing the Ndebele's precolonial past. He placed it around Jedediah's neck, put his hands on his shoulders, and said with husky voice, "To help you remember who you are."

Jedediah gripped the carving with both hands as the aircraft began lumbering down the runway. No tears wet his eyes, but his heart was crying.

When Arvid and Bergitta died, Jedediah was in the care of Jacob and Naomi. The five-month-old child felt at ease in both the home and the arms of the Bazos. There were also three older siblings, two boys and one girl, to care for him, along with the extended family in close proximity. The Ndebele embodied the African adage that it takes a village to raise a child. While Jedediah had begun to bond with his biological parents, intellectually processing their sudden absence was beyond his development. His tummy was kept full, his bottom kept dry, and he was loved as a child of the clan. He had no consciousness, of course, that his skin was white in contrast to his African family. But Jacob and Naomi were all too aware.

"When do you think they will come and take him?" Naomi asked after the funeral and grieving period.

"And who would that be?" Jacob replied.

Naomi had no answer. Having developed their close relationship with the Fjelstads, they had learned that both were only children and neither had living parents nor grandparents. With no immediate family, they supposed Jedediah might be claimed by the Missionary Society and exported back to Norway. The Society's main office in Salisbury had been notified of the Fjelstads' deaths, but the tribal representative who dictated the letter to Jacob for him to write in Norwegian failed to mention a surviving child. It simply escaped notice at the time, and later no one ever knew whether this was an oversight or done purposefully. While waiting for God to decide what should happen, the Bazos were committed to caring for the child as one of their own. A surprise awaited them.

The surprise was that no one came for Jedediah. The Ndebele are patient people who, in typical African fashion, know they cannot hurry events beyond their control. While the death and burial of the Fjelstads had been acknowledged, month after month passed without hearing anything from the office in Salisbury about Jedediah. What Jacob and Naomi did not know was that the Mission Society knew nothing of Jedidiah's existence.

Having grown accustomed to the slow pace of African life combined with reveling in their newfound family joy, the Fjelstads had not immediately sent notice of Jedediah's birth to Salisbury. Primitive communications and the isolation of the Matopos Hills made contact with the Rhodesian office of the Mission Society sporadic. The reporting procedures were complicated by the fact that the sole administrator in Salisbury had returned to Norway a month before Jedediah's birth, with his replacement not on station until early November 1946. That same month Arvid wrote a letter to the new mission head notifying him of their child's advent and requesting that he insure the birth be recorded in Norway. But an all-too-often occurrence in Rhodesia was that letters were lost in the postal system, and what the Fjelstads never knew was that Arvid's letter became one of those casualties.

There was also no formal recording of births in tribal areas such as the one in which the Fjelstads lived. In the 1940's there had never been a systematic census of the Ndebele in the Matopos Hills, and how many people inhabited the area was a good guess at best. The clans kept their family relationships and numbers recorded primarily in their memories.

The end consequence of these combined factors was that little Jedediah was a non-entity with respect to birth records. Month after month passed with no communications from Mission Society personnel. By the time a year had passed since the tragic deaths of his parents, Jedediah simply felt like a part of the Bazo family, and the feeling was mutual. As time progressed, Jacob felt no need to pursue any procedures that might lead to Jedediah's forced removal. In his mind, the child was his son.

Jedediah was on the path to become an Ndebele warrior. The fact that warring with other Bantu nations and the late 19th century conflicts with the British South Africa Company was in the distant past did not affect a young male's training. Respect for the nation's history and ancestors, along with a determination to preserve their traditions in spite of colonialism, mandated that Ndebele men learn the old ways from the elders. As an Ndebele, Jedediah participated with eagerness in the processes that would produce a man who embodied the Ndebele values of integrity, courage, and commitment to family and tribe.

To a pampered westerner it would have seemed an oppressive life. To the Ndebele it was simply a way of life. To be sure, a lack of modern conveniences and hard physical labor were normal parts of their existence. But rather than view such as misfortune, they accepted it as their lot in life and appreciated the character and strength spawned by the demands of daily living.

The Bazo family lived in a traditional home. A mud-walled rectangle with thatched roof, the exterior walls were covered with the house paintings for which the Ndebele were known. These colorful paintings, done by women, originated after losing the Boer Wars and the subsequent harsh punishments imposed by their conquerors. The wall paintings were seen as harmless cultural art by the Boer farmers, but they were in fact a secret code, known only to the Ndebele, which depicted their suffering, grief, and inward triumph. When Jedediah approached his abode he would generally stop and gaze at the symbolic patterns, reminding himself again how blessed he was to be an Ndebele.

In his younger years Jedediah enjoyed the pampering of his mother, Naomi, and his older sister, Sisasenkosi. His language became isiNdebele as he was assimilated into the life and culture of the people. His older brothers, Mandlenkosi and Thabani, tutored him in proper child behavior, which included respect for one's elders and taking part in family responsibilities. By the time he was eight, Jedediah helped with the management of the family's meager herd of cattle, and at ten years old he worked alongside his father and brothers in the maize fields. Hard labor along with his Nordic genetic heritage gave the growing child a stature and broad shoulders that surpassed his more slightly built peers. His physique and whiteness seemed to induce other boys to look to him as a leader.

Jacob was one of a minority of Ndebele who was a private landowner in contrast to most who managed parcels of communal land allocated by the village head. Passed down from his father, the four acres owned by Jacob was used for a mixture of growing maize and grazing cattle. It was a labor intensive occupation which provided sparse cash profits for essentials. But gardening, livestock, and hand-crafted clothes and utensils combined to produce a standard of living adequate for a family with Ndebele expectations.

Although most Ndebele gave their children traditional ethic names, many adults took Christian names upon baptism. A large percentage of the nation had become Christian with the influx of missionaries from the early 1800's onward. Such was the case with Jacob and Naomi, and they were happy to continue using Jedediah's given name.

One day in Jedediah's twelfth year while coming in from the field with his father, Jacob said, "The time has come, my son, for *ukuya eNgomeni*. Are you ready?" The rite of initiation from boyhood to manhood took place at various ages depending on the judgment of the father. Many had to wait until their thirteenth or even fourteenth year, but Jacob sensed that his son had reached a level of maturity and strength adequate for the traditional tests. In fact, Jedediah exhibited a level of knowledge, ability and self-confidence which exceeded that of most boys two or three years his senior.

"I am ready, my Father. I have listened to your teachings and observed how you live, and now I want to be a man."

The ancient ceremonial male rite of passage, also called *Ukuwela*, is typically held during the winter. Boys are sent into the chilly wilderness for two months with specific instructions meant to instill fortitude, resourcefulness, wisdom, and an indelible association with tribal customs and beliefs. Although embracing Christianity, many Ndebele continued to combine it with elements of ancestor veneration and the spiritual understandings of their forebears. It was easy to assimilate their ancient concept of *uNkulunkulu*, "the very high one," into the missionary-painted picture of an almighty God sitting high in the heavens. It was intended that during *ukuwela* a boy would commune with the spirits, and the culminating ceremony included circumcision.

"You will leave then after the next full moon. I will make the arrangements."

"Thank you, my Father. I will not disappoint you."

Jedediah indeed came back a man. While his prowess was recognized by both tutors and contemporaries alike, it was soon to be tested.

Lions are indigenous to the Matopos hills. With increased human population and the encroachment on habitat, the reduced lion numbers made the mauling or death of human beings a rarity. But the big cats could cause serious mischief, particularly in the form of livestock deprivation. Such was the case in the environs of the Bazo clan during Jedediah's thirteenth year. An old male rogue well past his prime hunting years had taken to preying on local farmers' cattle and goats, a task much easier on the joints than trying to chase down a gazelle. Something needed to be done, so the men of the community organized a hunt to rid themselves of this economically devastating scourge. Being a man, Jedediah was included in the hunting party.

As the first curvature of the rising sun appeared in the east, the hunters began following the tracks that led away from his latest kill, a prime milk cow pregnant with calf. One villager, a seasoned warrior named Elijah, carried the only firearm, an antiquated British .303 Lee Enfield. It was functional, and the head hunter was a reasonable marksman, but the trick was to herd the lion into a position where the elder could get a kill shot. The rest of the hearty troop were armed with assegais and hand drums.

The hills were interspersed with either lone or small stands of acacia and mopani trees and an occasional majestic baobab. The scrub between them was often chest or head high, dense, and thorny. The rogue's tracks disappeared into an enlarged area of such scrub where visibility was limited to several yards. The time-worn plan devised by the head hunter was for him to circle around to the far side of the scrub where he knew it opened up into a rocky field, and where he would wait while the beaters hopefully drove the lion out into the open. It was a perfect setup since Elijah would be to the east of the copse with the sun to his back.

The hunter-beaters lined up abreast and waited for the signal that Elijah was in place. Jedediah was on the far left side of the skirmish line where he would actually skirt the north edge of the bush. This was one of the safest positions in a hunt since if the lion saw someone in the open on the periphery he would generally stay to cover within the copse unless forced out the side away from the beaters. Upon hearing the cry of the fish eagle, the pounding of fifty hand drum beats resounded as the line moved slowly into the thick brush. They knew from experience that any lion would run from such cacophony, in this case hopefully into Elijah's sights.

Jedediah's adrenaline level had never been so high. This was the kind of excitement for which any young Ndebele male yearned, and although he knew the tactics of the hunt had been historically successful, he hoped for at least a glimpse of the royal beast in flight.

The stately king of the pride had not lived so long by accident. He had survived many a hunt and had learned what worked and what did not. Having a flank grazed by a shot on a similar drive several years back when he had fled the drums into the open, he now knew not to bolt in a direct line away from the beaters. As the skirmish line proceeded through the thorny bush, the drums became ever more loud and unnerving. The lion began to belly crawl northward, parallel to the advancing line. Learned behavior drove him toward the extremity of the threat, knowing that his chance of escape was better with one native on the end rather than surrounded by a host of chanting, beating hunters. The beaters were within thirty yards of where he now crouched but had not yet seen him. The lion could also see between the vegetation to the open country to the north. Waiting until the line was a mere ten yards away, he bolted.

At that precise moment Jedediah was mere steps from where the lion exploded out of the copse. In the face of danger a wild beast has the choice to fight or take flight. With enough distance between animal and the threat, flight is almost always the chosen option. The distance between Jedediah and the lion was not even close to being enough. The lion turned almost in mid-air and hurled himself at the young warrior.

In the space of one drumbeat Jedediah saw five hundred pounds of fury coming directly at him. Backlit by the sun, the lion's golden coat and jet black mane both seemed on fire. The three inch long canines glistened with saliva as a deafening roar came from his wide open jaws. In a movement of pure instinct, Jedediah dropped his drum, threw himself on his back, and with the butt end plowed into the ground, held his assegai with both hands at an upward angle. No sooner had the tip of the spear reached its zenith when the full weight of the lion came crashing down upon it. Whether by providence or Jedediah's guiding hand, the blade entered the feline's heart, effectively slicing it in two and causing instantaneous death. Having fallen to one side, roughly half the lion's weight pinned the hunter down, blood from the foul-smelling mouth dribbling onto the ground next to Jedediah's head.

Hearing the unmistakable roar, the other beaters rushed northwards and burst out of the bush. Upon seeing the blood-covered body of Jedediah and the lion with assegai protruding from its back, they assumed that there had been a dual death. But when the closest hunters heard him moan, they rushed to pull the lion off, revealing a shaken young man . . . but one who was alive. After a short recovery period,

Jedediah ascertained that he had nothing more than some claw scratches and several bruises, and perhaps a cracked rib or two. The lion was much the worse for wear.

Jedediah returned to the village a hero. The story of his courage and skill was told and retold, and his stature in the clan became one of awe and reverence. To his credit, Jedediah did not let all this go to his head. Even though the thought that any of his fellow warriors would have acted in like manner kept his self-importance in check, he secretly felt both proud and thankful. Those two feelings came from the way his family looked at him with love and pride. And this was by far the most important to him.

Chapter 4

January 1960 - Salisbury, Rhodesia

A variety of complications had resulted in the Fjelstads' replacements not arriving until 1951. After the death of Arvid and Bergitta, the Missionary Society was hesitant to send anyone else into that isolated situation until communication and medical care had progressed to the point where they had a greater degree of confidence about placing a missionary couple. No one from Norway felt the call to rural Rhodesia, but providence again smiled on the Matopos Hills.

A Norwegian-ancestry couple from America visiting Norway, Don and Ingrid Hofstad, became aware of the Society's search for missionaries to live in Rhodesia. While not an ordained clergyman, Don had an undergraduate degree in religious studies and a Master of Theology degree from the Lutheran seminary in St. Paul, Minnesota. He had discussed with Ingrid the possibility of overseas missionary service, and their interest was sparked upon learning of the Norwegian Missionary Society's need in Rhodesia. After exploring possibilities with the Society, they returned to the U.S. and subsequently formally applied for the position. Following a lengthy application and approval process and a half year of isiNdebele language training, the Hofstads found themselves headed for a new home and unknown adventures in the Matopos Hills.

When the Hofstads arrived at the mission station, the Fjelstads' old dwelling had been readied for them with a thorough cleaning, refurbished furniture, and new tribal paintings applied to the outside walls. A warm and joyous Ndebele welcome replete with traditional tribal wear, dance, and food, quickened in Don and Ingrid the sense of a loving community which acted as if it had found long lost children. With the obviously genuine sincerity evidenced by those gathered to receive them, any apprehensions they might have felt dissipated like smoke from a campfire.

But they were more than a little surprised to find a five-year-old white boy in the care of the Bazo family. In the days following, when Jacob related to them how this came to be, the Hofstads wondered what responsibility they might have to report the situation to Mission Society headquarters in Norway. As they pondered this, their own relationship with Jacob and Naomi grew, and they witnessed how little Jedediah was very much Ndebele and part of the Bazo family. They eventually concluded that his world was right as it was, and they would respect the situation that had evolved with the provision that the future might bring them to another perspective. For the present, they also covenanted to tutor the child in ways in which the Ndebele were not capable, which is how Jedediah came to learn English.

Rhodesia was still a colony of Great Britain at this time. Therefore had Jedediah been living in Salisbury or Bulawayo he could easily have gone to schools that taught English, but such opportunities did not exist in the Matopos Hills. Under the tutelage of the Hofstads, by the time he was twelve years old Jedediah could speak fluent English. He also enjoyed other parts of the world opened up to him by Don and Ingrid: mathematics, the sciences, world history, and western music and art. Jacob did not object to this; rather he encouraged it. He had a sense that someday his son would find these learnings useful.

Jedediah's education was bolstered and accelerated by a trait the Hofstads recognized early on: his memory. People have differing memory capabilities, some being exceptional in the extreme. Napoleon possessed such a skill, memorizing long number sequences, people, maps, and military movements to near perfection. Teddy Roosevelt would read two or three books a day and remember every detail. Pope John Paul II's semi-photographic memory enabled him to become fluent in twenty-one languages and one hundred dialects in his lifetime. Jedediah edged close to that kind of ability. This skill is largely genetic, and no one knew that one of Bergitta's uncles possessed the trait.

While there is no such thing as a truly photographic memory, there were times when this Rhodesian bush child caused wonder. One of the first manifestations was Ingrid beginning to teach Jedediah the multiplication tables when he was eight years old. She gave him a sheet with tables for numbers two through ten and asked him to try to memorize the table for two and three. A half hour later he came back and could perfectly recite the values for all nine tables. Repeated quizzing in the succeeding days and weeks proved that they were a permanent part of his memory. Flabbergasted at first, his mentors came to realize and accept that Jedediah's capacity for remembering was an attribute that made him an exceptionally gifted learner.

The Hofstads also had opportunity to help Jedediah explore what it meant that he was a Christian. While he had been baptized and the Bazos read from the Bible and prayed, there had essentially been no spiritual care for the clan since the Fjelstads' deaths. Now that resident missionaries were back, there was a resurgence of Christian practices . . . the meanings and relevance of which Jedediah wished to investigate. With Don and Ingrid's nurturing, their relationship also continued to deepen.

The Hofstads had been with the Ndebele for almost nine years. They were there when the lion hunt took place, and had assisted with Jedediah's healing. One evening some months after his fourteenth birthday, Jedediah was walking with Don alongside the Mtshabezi River. The flamingo-pink sky dotted with stratocumulus clouds, the gurgling sound of the crystalline stream over smooth river rocks, the verdurous banks of the river, and the soft croaking of the tree frogs imparted a sense that all was at peace. After savoring the wonder in silence for a time, Don risked a question over which he and Ingrid had prayed much, and which might put Jedediah in a situation of emotional conflict.

"Jedediah, what would you think of coming with us to America for a while?" Coming out of the blue, the question left Jedediah stunned and speechless. "This isn't something you need to answer right now," Don continued, "but Ingrid and I would like you to think about it."

Finding his voice, Jedediah said, "Do you mean for a visit? We would go together and then come back here?"

"That's not what we're thinking. Due to our parents' needs and some personal financial concerns, we will be leaving Rhodesia permanently in several months. Our years here have been wonderful, but it is time for us to return to our roots. We've been thinking that you might come live with us for several years to get the education that simply isn't available here in the Matopos. If you choose to do so, we will cover all expenses and if you at any time decide to return here we will honor that. Since we have no children, it would be our privilege and joy to have you live with us while you continue your studies."

Jedediah was considerably stunned with this surprise offer. He had never imagined that such an opportunity might present itself, and now that it did he had no idea how to react.

"I . . . I don't know what to think. I need some time,

and to talk with my father."

"Of course. And please know, Jedediah, that we will understand completely if your decision is to remain here. But we hope you will at least consider it prayerfully. We will need an answer within a couple of weeks since there are bureaucratic procedures that will have to begin immediately if this is to happen."

"Yes . . . yes, thank you. Right now my head is spinning, but I will talk with my family and then with you when I have made a decision."

The Hofstads had an additional motive for wanting Jedediah to come with them to America. While organized resistance to white supremacy in Rhodesia began in the 1920s, radical active opposition materialized in the 1940s. Because the Matopos Hills was an isolated rural area far south of the primary resistance activity around Salisbury, the growing tensions in the country were not as evident as in the turbulent north. But the Zimbabwe African People's Union had been formed, and the recruiting of young men for possible armed conflict was getting closer and closer to Gwanda. Don and Ingrid hoped to spare Jedediah from the guerrilla war that looked to be not far over the horizon.

The day's light was quickly fading as the village came within sight. It was all so familiar to Jedediah, and imparted a sense of security as the home and family he had known for fourteen years. As he and Don parted, Jedediah, the boy-man, walked to his home without any idea how he should respond.

Several days later Jedediah crossed the river bridge to the Hofstads' home. The discussion with Jacob had not been a long one. While he did not reveal this to his son, Jacob had been secretly hoping for an opportunity such as this. Sensing Jedediah's tremendous potential, Jacob also realized that he did not have the resources for his son to exploit it. Without financial benefactors, he did not even have the wherewithal to provide for advanced schooling in Bulawayo. While communicating that the decision was Jedediah's to make, he intimated that here was a marvelous opportunity of which virtually no Ndebele young man could dream. Jacob knew that to reject this offer might mean a lifetime as a peasant farmer for Jedediah. And he felt sure that his son was destined for more than that.

"So, have you decided what to do?" Don asked and then held his breath.

With mixed feelings, Jedediah replied, "I have, and I am honored to accept your gracious offer."

Slowly exhaling, Don continued, "Do you really feel this is the right path?" He knew this decision would not have been made without Jacob's blessing.

"It is my decision, and I feel it is the right one."

"Well then, my young friend, we have much to do. Let's get started.

There were documents to be procured such as passports and visas, all complicated by the lack of any official records for Jedediah. But they had jumped through all the bureaucratic hoops, aided by a dear friend who was a Minnesota senator, and were now starting the journey together to a new home in Minneapolis. As the wheels left the runway Jedediah felt much the same as when charged by the lion. Yet the African fish eagle gave him strength along with a growing sense that God just might use him in some important way. At the moment, he could not begin to imagine how.

And there was his name. It was who he was. It was what he was.

He was Bazo.

The Axe.

Chapter 5

May 1964 - Minneapolis, Minnesota

It was early morning the day of his high school graduation and Jed was walking the pleasant path around picturesque Lake Hiawatha in southeast Minneapolis. It hadn't taken him long to get used to his classmates and teachers shortening his name to Jed. It seemed to be the American way. He knew that Jedediah meant "loved by the Lord," and someone using an abbreviated nickname certainly didn't change that. The Jed part of the Hebrew name comes from the verb "to love" anyway, and he was happy to be reminded that this was how God wanted him to live. He would later find out just how difficult it can be to work out the practicalities in real life.

Alone on the roughly circular path on this crisp spring morning, the young man mused on how dramatically his life had changed from his formative years in Rhodesia.

The bustling city of Salisbury, with its population a bit under 200,000, had been a hefty shock to a 14-year-old who had never been out of the Matopos Hills, save one short trip to Bulawayo in his infancy. The two day overlay in London increased his astonishment. But finding himself ensconced in the teeming metropolis of Minneapolis-St. Paul was testing his mettle. From the vehicle-filled highways and byways to the 400-foot-plus Foshay Tower to grocery stores filled with an unimaginable variety and amount of foodstuffs, it bombarded the senses of an Ndebele country boy. Initially sticking to Don and Ingrid like beeswax, Jed quickly assimilated to life in the city. His facility with English increased exponentially with each passing week, and he became more and more comfortable in his new environment.

Advanced studies being a prime motivator, Jed's knowledge level and Intelligence Quotient were tested to determine his grade placement. His IQ was on the genius end of the scale. Due to the Hofstads' diligent instruction, the feeding of his voracious reading appetite, and his memory capacity, Jed's knowledge level was that of a gifted high school sophomore. In spite of this and because of his rural African background, it was counseled that he should enter as a first-year student to be on par with youngsters his own age. Thus began his U.S. education at Roosevelt High School in southeast Minneapolis, not far from their home on the shores of Lake Hiawatha.

His high school experience was productive in the extreme, and four years seemed to fly by with the speed of light. The huge three-story brick building was somewhat imposing at first, but Jed's adaptability and self-confidence enabled him to adjust with a minimum of emotional upheaval. It didn't take long before the scholastic scene was salted with the social one. Without a trace of fat on his honed six-foot-one frame and his handsome square-jawed face fringed with slightly wavy straw-colored hair, he rarely passed a knot of adolescent females without turning heads. Having been nurtured by the Ndebele clan mentality, social relationships came easily and before long Jed had developed a cadre of friends that included him in the plethora of school events. Another talent bolstered his acceptance. In Rhodesia where football, the version Americans call soccer, is ubiquitous, he was one of the best forwards in the Matopos Hills, scoring more goals than anyone in recent memory. Given his natural athletic abilities, he was able to make the adjustment to U.S. football and became a potent wide receiver who helped the team win the state championship in his junior year. His easy-going nature, combined with both his Ndebele and Christian values, resulted in congenial relationships with both students and staff. While he didn't tout it, his African background became general knowledge and his peers were fascinated by the stories they could occasionally pull out of him. Jed was someone you would want as a friend, but would not want as an enemy. As Big Al found out one day.

The nickname fitted Big Al because he was. An imposing six foot four, he topped two hundred and fifty pounds, although too much of it slopped over his belt buckle. He was a defensive tackle on the football team and prided himself on doing as much physical damage as he could to opposing team members. Al's size was intimidating, and he used it to his advantage. With his generally mean disposition added, Big Al was someone you either wanted on your side or wanted to avoid. And he didn't like the pretend-African new guy.

Crossing the practice football field on his way home after classes one day, Jed saw a small group of students shouting and gesturing as they surrounded Al and Bobby Risto, a smaller boy who sometimes had trouble controlling his mouth. The latter had said something Al didn't like, so he decided Smart Mouth needed a lesson in respect. Jed saw that Bobby was already bleeding copiously from his nose and that Al appeared to think additional damage was warranted. Although Jed was pacific and gentle by nature, Ndebele code included defending the weak if unjustly treated by oppressors. So Jed dropped his backpack and stepped into the circle.

The bully's back was to Jed when he heard, "That's enough, Al."

Surprised that anyone would challenge him, the big oaf turned to see who would be so foolhardy. Upon seeing who it was, he uttered something between a snort and a guffaw followed by the most menacing tone he could muster, "Well, well. If it ain't the African alien, Bazo. Oh, excuuuuuse me . . . I meant Bozo."

"Come on, Big Al." Jed used his egocentric nickname

in a feigned sign of respect. "You've done enough damage so why don't we call it a day."

"Well lookie who's telling who what to do. You keep your snotty nose outta somethin' that ain't none of yer business. Unless, that is, you want a different kind of nose too."

Jed looked around Al's massive frame and said, "Bobby, you go on home now."

Al's face began to resemble the color of a beet as he snarled over his shoulder, "Hey twerp, you move and you're dead meat." Then to Jed, "You asked for it, Bozo," as he balled his fists and took a step toward Jed, clearly intending to demonstrate who was the big man on campus.

Jed turned his back on Al, took two steps forward and began swaying from side to side in a low crouch. This shocked Al into a standstill.

The Bazo clan had been practicing capoeira as long as anyone could remember, the competitions generally being in the form of dance rituals where, to wild drumbeats, contestants exhibited their skill with pulled strikes to prevent actual damage. What his classmates did not know was that Jedediah was an advanced student of capoeira and had not lost a dance-match in his age group since he was eleven. Originating in Angola, this rare martial art depended more on flexibility and rapidity of movement rather than sheer strength. With swaying movements to keep the opponent off guard and feints to force an opening, strikes were made primarily with the legs or knees. Elbows rather than hands often completed a counter-strike against a determined assailant. Primarily defensive based on the principle of non-resistance, meaning avoiding an attack using evasive moves, it included offensive strikes if needed.

When Al signaled his attack with a guttural roar, Jed glanced quickly over his shoulder to fix his position. Then with a speed the onlookers would have thought impossible, Jed launched himself into a backflip and caught Al squarely in the solar plexus with both heels. As Al doubled-up and fell backward, Jed landed lightly on his feet and turned to face his nemesis. Al's body fat had absorbed a portion of the blow, but it still took him several moments to gulp air with some difficulty. Having never been bested and now enraged beyond reason, he struggled to his feet and charged Jed while bellowing like a wounded beast. Standing his ground, Jed easily swayed under the massive right fist swung in fury. As the attacker's drive carried him by, Jed used his own momentum to deliver his elbow to Al's right temple. If he had applied all his strength in the strike, Al would likely have died. But Jed pulled slightly at the last moment, yet with enough power that Al crumpled into an unconscious heap. Al's assembled support group stood dumbstruck. No one moved a muscle as Jed put his arm around Bobby and led him off the field.

True to the meaning of their name, the Bazos always cut their capoeira competitors down, which Jed aptly demonstrated in this encounter. Later, walking back to his house, he was very conscious of the Fish Eagle pressing against his chest.

There were three consequences to this encounter. The first was that as the story spread like an African bushfire through Roosevelt High School, Jed began to be viewed as something like a cross between Superman and The Hulk. The esteem for him that continued to grow was enhanced by the fact that Jed evidenced no bravado as a result of his exploit.

To the contrary, he continued to manifest his peaceful, humble character. The second result was that Big Al's bullying came to an end. In fact, bullying of any kind at the school was reduced significantly, especially if Jed was anywhere in the area. The third was that Jed was somewhat conflicted by what he had done. He knew that the discipline of capoeira was a defensive one that promoted peace and well-being, although one practiced in the art was equipped to do damage in extreme circumstances. So he questioned whether what he had done was justified. Could he, should he, have handled the situation in a less violent way? Little did he know at the time just how much soul-searching in this regard the future would bring.

The afternoon he crossed the podium to receive his high school diploma, his grade point average second only to the class valedictorian, Jed looked out at the beaming faces of Don and Ingrid. Their four years together had been mutually fulfilling ones, the Hofstads feeling like Jed was the child they were never able to conceive. At the conclusion of the ceremony, the mortar boards that filled the air brought to Jed's mind the flocks of black scarlet-chested sunbirds that were a normal sight on the Rhodesian bushveld. How far he had come, actually and psychologically, from his childhood home. How much he had come to think of America as home. And he wondered when, if ever, he would he return to his Ndebele family.

With the next steps of his life already set in motion, Jed could not consider a trip to Africa in the foreseeable future. In several weeks he would be off to college.

Chapter 6

July 1967 - Seattle, Washington and Quantico, Virginia

Jed had completed his third year at the University of Washington and was in the middle of a 10-week United States Marine Corps summer training program called Platoon Leaders Course (PLC) at the huge USMC base, Quantico, Virginia. This was one of the tracks that led to a commission as a Second Lieutenant in the Corps. Being in this position was something that might have seemed something at odds with his background, but given the circuitous route that led him here, it felt right.

Having initially been granted valid immigrant status in the U.S., by the end of his freshman year in college he had fulfilled the 5-year residency requirement needed to naturalize as a citizen. Don had encouraged this both for the permanency it offered if desired, and for various doors it could open that were not available to non-citizens. Time and distance had affected his felt connections to his Ndebele homeland, yet he did not feel that becoming a U.S. citizen was abandoning it since he really never felt Rhodesian. His allegiance was to family and clan rather than the nation. He thought of home as the Matopos Hills instead of Rhodesia. In addition, not only would citizenship enable applications for citizen-only financial aid, he had developed a strong sense of gratitude, and even allegiance, toward the country that had welcomed him and provided such a host of opportunities. So, on a fittingly bright summer day in 1965 Jed found himself with hand over heart reciting the United States Oath of Allegiance.

Being accepted into college was not an issue for Jed. His high school grades and extracurricular activities produced a host of recruiters knocking on his door. Having grown up in a southern African country was another valuable asset since many schools of higher learning sought qualified foreign students to add to the multi-cultural composition of their institution. Although not at all sure in what vocational direction he was headed, Jed's interests leaned toward the humanities. His Ndebele upbringing, four years of rapid and thorough inculcation into American society, and the Christian value system which still held sway over him yielded a harvest of interests and questions about the mind, heart and soul of human creatures. Quantum physics and integral calculus, as fascinating and useful as they might be, took second place to the philosophical and spiritual meanderings of Jed's ever-inquisitive mind. Thus his primary concern when contemplating post-secondary education was which school would combine the best financial package along with an excellent humanities program. It did not take long during his senior year for one school to stand out as fitting the bill.

The University of Washington in Seattle appeared to meet the desired requirements, and then some. Within the College of Arts and Sciences they had a humanities department that stressed diversity and critical thinking, both high on Jed's list. When he read the description of the purpose and philosophy of the department, he thought it had been created specifically for him:

Introducing students to the interrelation of ideas and society demonstrates the need to consider intellectual problems from many perspectives. The goal of the program is to provide the tools for critical thinking while engendering an attitude of personal engagement and creativity within students. We encourage them to think for themselves, and to utilize responsible ways to analyze the world and categories for understanding it.

Incentive was added when communication with department staff members emphasized their commitment to academic freedom and individual initiative in a student's pursuit of a course of study suited to his or her perceived needs. A tremendous additional drawing card was the best financial assistance package of any of the schools attempting to recruit him. Technically an orphan and with the Hofstads' in the lower middle class income bracket, Jed was in a position for the maximum grant money. Academic scholarships helped round out the figures, and the kicker that put the ball through the goal posts was the offer of an additional moderate football scholarship to play with the fabled Huskies.

When Don looked up from a study of all the documents sent by the university, Jed asked, "What do you think?"

"Well, Jed, the more important question is what do *you* think?"

"I think you know I'm inclined to accept their offer, but I guess I'm looking for some affirmation that this is the right decision. I mean, the U of M right here isn't too far behind."

Being a bit of a devil's advocate, Don replied, "True. But there's something to be said for exploring new territory."

Having taken to calling them Aunt and Uncle, Jed responded, "You mean it would be okay with you and Aunt Ingrid if I went so far away?"

"I'm not saying we wouldn't miss you, but the offer's top notch, and getting out from under our wings might just be good for you. And nothing's permanent. If it doesn't work out, I'm sure Minnesota would still be interested, and you know our home will always be your home."

Jed rolled these thoughts around in his head, a bit of a struggle going on between clinging to the security his close relationship with Don and Ingrid provided and the natural desire of a young man to explore new frontiers and put his self-sufficiency to the test. "I'm going to sleep on it for a couple of days and see what happens. Your support either way means more than you know."

Jed never regretted his decision to accept UW's offer. The bustling campus within a large multicultural metropolitan area and the excellence of his chosen course of study was fulfilling his desires and the Hofstads' hopes. Toward the end of his sophomore year he felt like an American more than ever, and he was, to no one's surprise, excelling in his studies. The Huskies Rose Bowl appearance during Jed's freshman year didn't materialize again until 1978, but as a wide receiver he helped the football team to an even win-loss record in 1965. It was after the win over Oregon State in November that a life-changing event happened.

He was leaving Husky Stadium after the post-game team meeting, heading for his on-campus dorm room. Most of the crowd had dissipated and the parking lot contained only a few stragglers. Although Jed was pumped from the win, he graciously declined some of his teammates' invitation to join them for self-congratulatory suds. Along with never having sampled an alcoholic beverage that tasted any better than turpentine, any loss of self-control was abhorrent to Jed. He had witnessed oftentimes the idiot behavior that accompanied over-imbibing, which seemed to be the point to many of his fellow students. He was not going to fall into that trap.

As he came upon a bus stop at the edge of the parking lot, he glanced at a young woman huddled against the November chill in the corner of the shelter. A fleece hood framed the most angelic face Jed had ever seen. She had gorgeous hazel eyes that even without makeup would stop any man in his tracks. This windblown fall afternoon they were puffy and reddened, but not from any irritating weather. It looked as if she had been crying. Jed was still pretty shy with girls even though most would consider selling their birthright if it would win his attentions, but something drew him to this beatific but sad-looking wallflower. With several deep breaths of the chill air and a compulsion he had never before felt, he approached to within several feet and said, "Hey, everything okay?"

"Yes . . . I mean . . . it's . . . I'll be fine." Although she didn't sound fine to Jed.

"Look, I don't want to intrude but . . . well, I just thought maybe . . ."

With an obvious tremor in her voice she said, "No, really. It'll be . . ." and then emitted an involuntary sob that started Jed and left him wondering what in the world to do now.

Daring to approach a little closer he offered, "I'm sorry. I mean, I wish I could do something to help." And then not knowing what else to say, "But I'll leave if I'm bothering you."

"That's okay. I don't normally do this, but sit down if you'd like." It wasn't her normal behavior to invite strange men into her space, but something about his countenance and what appeared to be a genuine concern triggered her reaction.

Sitting down on the bench but not too close, Jed asked, "Again, I don't want to stick my nose where it doesn't belong, but can I help with anything?" While speaking, Jed noticed her slender yet full figure covered by a merlot-colored light woolen coat that failed to hide her Betty Grable legs. He couldn't put his finger on why, but he started feeling a tightness in his chest.

"I don't know . . . I . . . I don't think so. But thanks for asking."

Out of the blue and surprising the life out of himself, he asked, "Do you live on campus? Can I walk you home?"

"That's very kind of you. Yes, I live in Hansee Hall, but I can take the bus."

"I'm heading over to Odegaard Libe anyway and I could use a walk to loosen up my legs after the game."

Suddenly the young woman realized who she was talking to. "Wait! You're Jedediah. Everybody knows you! You can't be sitting here talking to me!"

Jed was embarrassed and replied, "Well, maybe the Husky lovers know me, but other than that I'm just another guy on campus."

"I just saw you make that unbelievable touchdown catch that won the game for us. This is unreal . . . me sitting on a bus bench with you." It was obvious that she was a bit overwhelmed that one of the team stars was giving her the time of day, but for the moment it was taking her mind off of her situation.

"Well, glad to meet you. And since you know my name it would probably make sense for me to know yours."

"Oh, I'm sorry. Angela. I'm Angela Wyatt."

"A very fitting name, Angela. Now it would be my honor if you let me walk you back to your room. I promise not to bite and you don't have to tell me why you were crying if you don't want to."

As it turned out, Angela wanted to. In fact, the walk to

Hansee Hall was the beginning of a beautiful relationship.

The normally twenty minute trek took them an hour, a couple of side loops extending the distance purposefully. Jed had never encountered a woman with whom he could converse so easily. Angela, in turn, sensed in Jed a non-threatening genuineness that was markedly different from what she had experienced all too often, namely, campus studs captivated by themselves and looking to sweep delicious coeds off their feet and into bed. While generally somewhat reserved, by the time she and Jed were halfway to Hansee Hall she surprisingly found herself sharing her story, including details previously held privately in her heart. Jed was spellbound.

Angela had been a castaway. Born to a Seattle hooker, she never even knew who her father was. Her earliest childhood memories of her mother always had needles on the nightstand and a variety of unknown men on the bed. She never knew where home might be, Mom changing residences more times than she could remember. At five years old, one day she headed out to the neighborhood playground, or a garbage-strewn, broken-swing-set excuse for one, to which she was farmed out for most of her waking hours, and never saw her mother again. Hunger eventually brought her home to a rundown duplex awash in the flashing lights of police cars and ambulances. If they would have let her in, she would have seen her mother sprawled naked on the bed, dead of an overdose, and one of those strange men in a pool of blood on the floor. The very unlucky fellow had been gut-shot with two blasts from a Smith & Wesson .357 Magnum. One would have done the trick. After figuring out who the little waif was, authorities notified social workers who came and carted her away.

For years Angela bounced through a procession of a forgettable number of foster homes. Some were okay, most were not. Suffering a variety of physical, emotional, and sexual abuse, she often headed for the hills. But the hills didn't have much to offer in the way of food and shelter, so she would end up back on the street and eventually back under the auspices of the state child welfare services.

Then the unimaginable happened: a caring couple with their wits about them took her in. Peter and Florence Smith had experience with problem foster children previously, and profited from the sharp learning curve. Something between Angela and them clicked, and under their loving guidance she began to believe that life could actually be worth living. With decent clothes, healthy food, and the security of mother and father figures who she came to realize honestly cared for her, Angela took baby steps toward becoming a lovable and responsible teenager. Professional counseling and the knowledge that the Smiths were really going to be there for her resulted in Angela's grades improving measurably, and she started developing friendships with fellow students other than the ones just released from the juvenile detention center. The Smiths adopted her, and by the middle of her senior year in high school she received the absolutely shocking news that her application to the University of Washington had been accepted. Finances weren't an issue because the computer software industry had made Peter a wealthy man, but during her second year at UDub a large part of her world again came crashing down.

Hearing that barely a month before the Smiths had both died instantly in a head-on crash with a loaded logging truck whose driver had fallen asleep at the wheel, the only words Jed could think of were "I'm sorry."

"Yeah, me too . . . I mean, thank you, Jed. It's still all so fresh in my mind. I'm having trouble concentrating on my studies."

"Well, no wonder. Do you have friends to help support you here at school?"

"Not really. A lot of acquaintances, but between studies and spending time with my parents . . ." Then another heartbreaking sob burst out. "I've felt pretty much alone since . . ."

"Weren't you with friends at the game today?"

"A couple at the dorm asked if I'd like to come with them, but they were all, like, fun and giggles, and I just can't do that. But since I couldn't even keep a book in focus I decided to go watch the second half and hopefully get my mind on something else. Didn't work too well, although I did see your touchdown catch."

"Angela . . . do you ever go by Angie or is it always Angela?"

"I prefer Angela. It somehow makes me feel more grown up, and maybe more respectable."

"Okay, Angela it is." Then after a pause, "we have something in common." Jed then proceeded to give her a short version of his history which included losing his parents, albeit before he even knew them. Although there was a vast difference in circumstances, the common touch points engendered the beginning of a felt bond for both of them.

Arriving at her dorm sooner than he would have liked, Jed said with a discernable amount of trepidation, "I don't want to seem presumptuous or disrespectful, but can I see you again, Angela?"

With the first faint smile since their meeting, she replied, "I think I'd like that, Jed. I really appreciate your taking this time with me, and for listening. I haven't met very many people willing to do that."

With his heart rate up a couple of notches – a new feeling for Jed – he replied, "Well, okay. You can count on a call from me soon."

"I look forward to it, Jedediah Bazo. By the way, you told me the meaning of Jedediah, but what about Bazo?"

"It's a Ndebele word and to my knowledge my clan is the only one who claims it."

"And it means?"

"Axe. A man of the Bazo clan is an axe who can cut down anything in his way."

Jed and Angela did indeed see each other again. Often. Their relationship grew in leaps and bounds so that by the summer of 1967 when he headed east for the ten week Marine Platoon Leaders Course, they were struggling with the concept of being away from each other for so long. Both took comfort in their growing love relationship, one which they were committed to pursuing.

Moving up a forested Virginia hillside in ninety degree heat and loaded with fifty pounds of combat gear, Jed acknowledged to himself again that this was right where he should be. The demanding course was physically grueling and academically challenging, and his leadership skills were evident. Passing marks were necessary in all three areas to become a commissioned officer in the Marine Corps. While many of the aspirants struggled with various requisite exercises, Jed accomplished them all with relative ease. Reaching the summit well ahead of his brothers-in-arms, he mused over what had brought him here.

During his third year in college Jed felt a growing sense of gratitude for his adopted country, or rather the country that had adopted him. He had often thought about the line from the citizenship oath he had taken which said *I will support and defend the Constitution and laws of the United States of America against all enemies, foreign and domestic.* Oaths were sacred to the Ndebele, and Jed wanted to do more than just mouth the words. The Vietnam anti-war movement had not yet gained momentum, and President Johnson and company continued a mildly effective propaganda campaign to convince the American public of the necessity of the war. Operation Junction City from February to April, the largest U.S. airborne operation since WWII, was in the daily news and much discussed on campus. Even given his pacifistic leanings, the Ndebele mandate to help protect the weak, in this case the South Vietnamese with whom America was in an official military alliance, won over Jed's mind and heart.

Out of curiosity he visited the campus Naval Reserve Officers Training Corps unit one day and ran into the Marine on staff, Major Clint Reynolds. The day's conversation with the veteran leatherneck and the information pamphlets he was given led to several more visits over the ensuing weeks. By early May he had applied and was selected for the Platoon Leaders Course which, if successfully completed, would lead to his commissioning as a U.S. Marine 2nd Lieutenant on graduation day the following spring.

With two weeks left in the course, Jed was first in his PLC battalion in every category. As well as being liked for his congenial personality, he was respected as a leader by both peers and career Marines who knew leadership when they saw it. Sweat running down his back and feeling like he could tackle another mountain, Jed could already envision the gold bars being pinned to his epaulets.

Chapter 7

September 1967 - Seattle, WA and Quantico, VA

Back at the University of Washington for his senior year, Jed felt like the stars had lined up just for him. Not only lined up, but forming one of the Dippers and pouring sweet honey right into his lap.

He had completed the Platoon Leaders Course like he was born for it. Instructors couldn't remember an officer candidate who had achieved what Jed did. Physically and academically he left everyone in the dust, and his leadership capabilities topped the charts. He embodied the principles and values of a Marine Corps officer: honor, courage, commitment, and example. Exhibiting these traits consistently is what motivates enlisted men to follow you anywhere, and the tried-and-true NCO instructors at the PLC already knew they would not hesitate to go into battle with him.

One item in Jed's skill set left them literally speechless. Included in a Marine's training is hand-to-hand combat. Along with the standard pugil stick exercises was a rudimentary introduction to several martial arts such as judo and karate. The staff NCOs demonstrated some of the techniques, and then paired off the trainees for practice. When Jed was pitted against his fellow PLC candidates the result was something between confusion and mirth. He seemed to have developed his own unorthodox method of swaying and lightning-fast kicks and punches that bewildered his opponents, the latter looking like elementary school students fighting Muhammad Ali. One cocky lad who was a Chicago Jr. Golden Gloves champion whispered to the sergeant that he could make quick work of Jed, so they were put on the mat forthwith. Less than thirty seconds into the contest Mr. Golden Gloves was on his back with a bruised rib and struggling to maintain consciousness after a sidekick to his left temple. None of them, of course, had ever heard of the African art of capoeira.

Watching this from the side, Staff Sergeant Jim Causey thought that it was time to show Jed just how much he had yet to learn. Causey was a fourth degree taekwondo *dan*, or black belt, and a *Sabum* at a prestigious martial arts center off base. Commanding Jed to the mat, the sergeant went on the attack at the sound of the starting whistle. Without giving Jed time to begin his feinting swaying motions and intending the lesson to be a quick one, he hurled forward in an *ee dan ap chagi,* or jumping front kick, aimed at Jed's solar plexus. As fast as Sergeant Causey was, Jed was faster. He easily ducked under the attack, allowing the instructor to sail by while kicking thin air. Confused and somewhat angry, Causey turned to find Jed's back turn to him. Puzzled by Jed's seeming ignorance and arrogance, he knew it was time for the heart of the lesson. Taking one step forward, he initiated an *ap chagi* or front snap kick, aiming for the nerve junction at the base of the neck. He knew that too hard a blow would break Jed's neck but that pulling the kick at the last moment with a disciplined amount of pressure would only paralyze him momentarily.

Jed was waiting in a semi-crouch. Hearing the one step toward him, Jed powered himself high into the air into a backward flip. As Causey's leg came up for the *coup de grâce,* he saw Jed's body flying over his head. On the way down Jed administered a pulled kick to the back of the sergeant's head which put him flat on his face and semi-conscious. He then stood there for a counterattack which never came. The incident became a legend, many hearing it wishing someone had filmed it.

Jed took to the Marine Corps like a duck to water. But questions tickled the back of his mind. The USMC method of indoctrination works well, yet it cannot completely erase learned values and experiences that might seem somewhat at odds with that for which Marines are trained. Back at school, conflicting thoughts hovered behind his overt consciousness, like trying to see something through darkly-tinted glass. The odd glimpse would give him pause, but most of the time he was so tied up with studies and his ever-deepening relationship with Angela that he could ignore it.

But not always.

Jacob and Naomi's children held to the Christian faith within which they had been raised. Under the care of Don and Ingrid in Minneapolis the church was also an important part of Jed's life, and it was upon this foundation that he began his college career. He certainly never abandoned it completely, but academic pressures, newly discovered ways of thinking, and the options at hand for a young man experiencing initial independence made for less than regular church attendance. He knew his heart was in the right place but it didn't always make the connection with his feet. Now that the Marine Corps was in the mix, when Jed did allow for some introspection he frequently came up short of answers. With the Vietnam War not likely to end anytime soon and Jed very likely to find himself in the middle of it, the kinds of things he knew he would be called upon to do forced the issue to the fore.

He did have a casual relationship with the campus pastor, Darrell Lee, aka Pastor D, at the local Lutheran Student Center. So one day he arranged a meeting where he hoped some helpful guidance might accompany the thick brew in the center's continuously bubbling coffee machine.

Pastor Darrell, thirty-three years old and a stout fellow with full beard and goldilocks down to his shoulders, had seen some serious stuff in life. A Korean War Army veteran, he came to faith a bit later in life and was now serving as campus pastor after four years in a Nebraska congregation. He wore his usual clergy shirt with signature clerical collar because he said it helped people focus not on him but rather on what the collar represented.

In his bleached Levis and form-fitting Semper Fi T-shirt Jed looked every bit the budding Marine. He would have shined his running shoes if they'd have taken polish. After some introductory small talk, they got to the meat of the matter.

"Are you saying you wonder if a man can be both a Marine and a Christian?" the pastor queried.

"That's just the point, Pastor D. I'm having a hard time figuring out how they go together. I mean, how can I go over to kill people when I've always thought that taking human life is wrong? Do I just set aside my faith?"

After letting the question hang in the air for several moments, Lee responded, "Let me ask you a question, Son. How many colors are in the rainbow?"

Curious where this would lead, Jed answered, "Let's see, there are seven primary colors, along with the variety in the overlap areas. If you allow for mixing all seven primaries in whatever combination you want I suppose there would be hundreds of colors."

"Hundreds, huh? You didn't mention black and white."

"Because black is the absence of color and white light contains all of them," Jed answered with scientific authority.

"Okay, so you'd say a rainbow isn't black and white."

"Certainly not black, but white only because that's where all the colors come from."

Pastor D paused for a time to let Jed's mind process

the analogy and then said, "Jed, do you see life as white and black?"

He didn't take long before answering. "Not really. There's good and evil, right and wrong, although I think which is which can depend somewhat on the situation."

"Can you give me an example?"

He thought about using his encounter with Big Al years ago, but holding back, Jed replied, "I'd have to think about that for a while."

"Let me try one on you for size. Admittedly a dramatic example, but one to make a point. Do you have any sisters?"

"Yes. Two of them in my Ndebele family in Rhodesia."

"How old are they?"

"Sibongile, my older sister, is twenty-four and Zinhle is eighteen."

"Okay, let's say you came upon a fellow about to rape Zinhle and the only way to stop him was with lethal force, maybe even kill him. Would you do it?"

Without hesitation Jed replied, "Of course. I would be honorably protecting a defenseless woman and member of my family. To not act in that circumstance would be shameful."

"But as Christians are we not to turn the other cheek? To be men of peace instead of violence?"

"Well sure, but not every situation in life is so black and white." And then he realized what he had just said.

"I'm sorry, Jed, but there's no handbook, the Bible included, that provides an answer to everything that might happen," Pastor D went on. "Even though it's an overused example, we do have the case of Jesus using force to clear the temple of dishonest entrepreneurs, which one can misuse to justify anything one wishes. But I believe it points us to the multi-colored character of life that resists a rigid legalism."

"Legalism?"

"Living by the law, Jed, instead of by the gospel."

"So how do I figure out what the gospel would have me do in a given situation?"

"If you're looking for canned answers for all of life's questions and problems, you've come to the wrong guy. I'm afraid all a man can do is meet each one as they come and ask God's guidance and strength to do the right thing."

"And what if I do the wrong thing?"

"Jed, a good share of the time you won't know one way or the other when you do it. We generally find out sometime after the fact whether our decisions were right or wrong, good or bad. But we have to live life, which means making decisions . . . and acting on them. The alternative is to hide in a cave or curl up in some catatonic state of inaction."

Pastor Darrell could see these thoughts rolling around in Jed's head. Which he thought was good. It was healthy to be asking the questions, and he felt his task was simply to encourage individuals to wrestle with God and themselves, and to come up with their own answers. The best a good counselor could do was assist with the discovery of alternatives and information that might not have been previously considered.

"You've given me some food for thought, Pastor D. If I had to answer right now, I'd say it's possible for me to be both a good Christian and a good Marine."

"And it might be the same conclusion after a heap more thinking about it, Jed. Remember something else too. Jesus never condemned any of the soldiers that came to him . . . even healed one's daughter without a word of judgment about his profession. And who was the one that looked up at the dead Jesus on the cross and proclaim him as the Son of God? A soldier. A Roman centurion." A pause, then, "Just offering some brain fodder to add to the mix."

As they walked toward the door Jed said, "You got me thinking all right. Thanks for your time. And I just might be back."

"Any time, Jed. I sense you're in a good space, and the guidance will come if you keep looking in the right direction. By the way, you and that beauty Angela still an item?"

With an instantaneous ear-to-ear grin, Jed beamed, "Hundred percent, Pastor. In fact she's waiting for me right now."

During this last year in college Jed had an off-campus experience that was to prove formative later in life. As part of his effort to become ever more American, and simply out of curiosity, he would roam the various environs of the greater Seattle metropolitan area when time allowed. The glitzy parts always fascinated him due to their dramatic contrast with his Matopos Hills homeland, but he tended to gravitate to the more ethnically diverse areas and what locals called the "seedy" side of the city. Pike Place Market was a favorite, and from there he would branch out to neighborhoods like Pioneer Square, Belltown, and Rainier Valley. Even though Seattle was a relatively safe big city, folks warned him about kicking around these areas alone, especially after dark. While Jed didn't worry too much about that, one evening he had an encounter with a local resident that left a deep impression on him.

It was a chilly February day with the sun on the downhill slope toward its disappearance into the Pacific Ocean. Enjoying both the exercise and the up-close advantage of exploring on foot, he had spent most of the late afternoon investigating the docks, eateries, and neighborhoods on the south end of Lake Union. Before catching a bus back to the campus, he wanted a look at Denny Park since it was the oldest one in the Seattle system, established in 1884. It was an easy five block jaunt from the south end of the lake, and after a walkabout in the park he might even have time for a trip to the observation deck of the famous Space Needle that had been built for the 1962 World's Fair. One of his professors had told him that the view from the top was particularly spectacular when the nighttime lights turned the city into a sparkling fairyland.

When Jed reached the park he realized that it wouldn't take him long to traverse the two by four block green space. He entered it at the northeast corner of John Street and 9th Avenue and headed for the opposite southwest extreme. Two diagonal walking paths divided the rectangular park into four triangles, crossing at the center in a small circular area ringed with several benches. Jed reached the point where the paths intersected as the dusk was gently but quickly easing out the day's lambency. In the failing light he saw a crumpled pile of something behind one of the benches. Wondering what this unsightly lump was doing in an otherwise manicured park, he went over, accidently stepping on part of whatever it was, and bent down to discover a man lying on his side next to a pair of ancient crutches and clutching a damp paper bag with a green bottle poking out.

"I'm . . . I'm sorry," Jed softly apologized. "I didn't see you there."

Looking up with unfocused, bleary eyes, the man croaked a barely discernable, "No shit, Charlie Brown. Nobody does."

Wondering what else he could or should say, Jed responded, "Is there . . . can I help you with anything?"

"Sure, Champ. Wouldn't happen to have an extra five hundred bucks to spare, huh?"

"Well, not really," Jed replied weakly, "but could you use five for some food?" Jed had never come face-to-face with a homeless beggar so he wasn't sure what to do.

"Hell no . . . but I sure could use some cash for another jug of Thunderbird," said the human train wreck with his palm up at the end of an outstretched arm.

Jed didn't think that was what he wanted to do, so out of confusion and curiosity he asked the fellow how he had ended up in this sorry state. The man threw back the filthy blanket that lay over him to reveal one leg amputated above the knee and the other one ending in a club foot. He wore a soiled pair of ratty shorts and a Mariners sweatshirt that looked like a Salvation Army reject. Verbal communication becoming increasingly more difficult, the man's head was now bobbing as he struggled to maintain consciousness.

As Jed sat on his heels and wondered what to do next, a city cop appeared on the scene and looked down with obvious distain at the vagrant, booted the now prone man's club-footed leg, and gruffed, "C'mon, Sam. Get your lazy ass up and moving. You know you ain't supposed to spend the night here. I should haul your stink'n carcass down to the drunk tank right now."

Standing up to face the policeman, Jed asked, "Do you have to talk to him that way?"

"Damn right I do. He don't listen to nothing else. And what the hell business is it of yours anyway?"

Coming to the quick conclusion that it really wasn't his business anyway and not being one to challenge legitimate authority, Jed mumbled something about hoping the policeman could give the fellow some help and continued southwest toward Denny Way.

Deciding to save the Space Needle for another day, he turned for the bus stop to catch his ride back to the campus while mulling over what he had just experienced. Poor and crippled people were not unknown in the Ndebele community, but they always had family or friends to see to their needs. How, in a city as full of wealth as Seattle, could a disabled person obviously at the end of his rope be kicked out of a park like one might do to a stray dog? And why didn't *he* do anything more to help the guy? Should he have given him some money?

Back in his dorm room he was forced to push these thoughts to the back of his mind since there was some serious studying to be done for his Philosophy of Religions test on the morrow.

Angela and Jed had become thoroughly committed to one another. Even with the pressures of his last-year studies and football, they found time to be together. Remembering where it had begun two years earlier, they made a point of meeting in the Husky Stadium parking lot after each game. Losing four of their six home games in 1967, Jed could use the comfort as he licked his wounds. This was a particular need after the last game of his college career, the traditional Apple Cup battle with Washington State University. Not only did they lose by two points, but Jed only had three catches for twenty-seven yards, his lowest numbers for the year.

"It's humbling, Angela. Downright humbling."

"Well, Jed, as important as it might seem at the moment, it *is* only a game."

"Yeah, I know. I know. But it still stings."

"But your overall career was great. You've got nothing to be ashamed about there. So now it's on to bigger and better things. And besides, now you'll be able to concentrate more on your studies . . . and me," Angela said with a sexy smirk.

"Nothing wrong with that, my little angel," a nickname Jed used because she had surely become that to him.

"We've got to watch it though," she said with some amount of sarcasm, "since for Major Reynolds, Semper Fi is for the Corps and not for distracting coeds."

"Hey, the Corps might be the essence of life for him, but for me everything comes second to you."

Gazing into his with her beautiful hazel and tear-filled eyes, Angela said, "Jed, you *are* my life. And we need to talk about what to do with ours together."

It was a tough call.

Immediately upon graduation Jed would head back to Quantico, Virginia and The Basic School (TBS), a half-year training program that every Marine officer was required to complete. The PLC program was designed to be a physically demanding environment where sleep deprivation, military tasks, and memorization are constantly forced on candidates to test their ability to handle stress and the demands of command leadership. But TBS trained every single officer to command an infantry platoon whether eventually moving into artillery, tanks, supply, military engineering, or whatever. The reality was that with the infantry being the heart and core of an armed conflict, it was incumbent upon an officer in any supporting component to know both how his support was needed and, if necessary, how to command an infantry platoon. Jed also knew that he could pretty well bet the farm that once TBS was completed and after a short leave of absence, he would be heading for Nam. So the big question for the two young lovers was whether or not to get married before his deployment.

Angela was advocating for marriage right after graduation. She wasn't pushy about it, for she had learned that pushiness was not a technique that worked well with Jed. Besides, she really did trust his judgment more than her own.

Jed's we-should-wait viewpoint won the day. Angela had one more year of school to complete her degree, which would mean only a period of a few months after her graduation until his 13-month tour of duty overseas was completed. Unspoken, but in the back of Jed's mind and uncomfortable as it was, he also wanted her to be unencumbered in terms of possible future relationships in case he returned in a body bag.

As they fell ever more deeply in love but relatively comfortable with their decision to hold off on marriage, it was a joyous occasion for both of them as Jed crossed the stage and received his Bachelor of Arts degree. Instead of gown and mortar board like the majority of the graduating class, those being commissioned as officers in the armed forces wore uniforms. As Jed took the Oath of Office, his six foot two finely-honed physique cut a striking figure in Marine Corps dress whites. Jed spoke the words with passion:

I do solemnly swear that I will support and defend the Constitution of the United States against all enemies, foreign and domestic; that I will bear true faith and allegiance to the same; that I take this obligation freely, without any mental reservation or purpose of evasion; and that I will well and faithfully discharge the duties of the office on which I am about to enter. So help me God.

They reminded him of his citizenship oath a few years back, which now meant more to him than ever.

The celebration was enhanced by Don and Ingrid's presence. They and Angela had met only once for a brief time when they had visited Jed earlier in the year. But a growing mutual affection for and appreciation of one another was obvious.

During the two-week period before reporting for duty at Quantico, Jed took Angela to his home in Minneapolis. It gave him great pleasure to show her his old haunts and introduce her to a few friends with whom he had stayed in touch. After she flew back to Washington he spent a few more quality days with his honorary aunt and uncle, and then headed for his new life in the United States Marine Corps.

Chapter 8

May 1968 - Ap Bia Mountain, Republic of Vietnam

"Holy shit, Sarge, you gotta be kid'n me."

"Ain't never seen any shit that's holy, Wilson. An' I ain't kid'n you."

Looking at the slope in front of them, Corporal Billy Wilson said, "Whoever told you to send my squad up that hill is outta their freak'n mind. Or else they just like watching

Americans die."

"Why don't you go tell that to Lieutenant Olgivie. I'm sure he'd appreciate your advice," Sergeant Royer snapped. "Nobody likes being here, but here's where we are and you and me don't have the luxury of picking and choosing what orders we follow."

"But Sarge, this is plumb dumbass suicide! You might as well be asking me to pop our guys myself."

"Being in this godforsaken hellhole itself is dumbass. And, Corporal Wilson, I ain't asking anything; I'm telling. Get your squad in position NOW. When second squad is on your left flank I'll fire the flare and we'll move out. See you at the top."

"Ya, right . . . long as the top you're talking 'bout is heaven," Billy muttered as he moved laterally across the muddy slope to give his squad their orders.

Billy Wilson, twenty-one years old, should have been operating one of his dad's backhoes outside Four Corners, Montana. Thanks to the wisdom of Uncle Sam and the crap-luck of the draft lottery, here he was hunkered down in a torrential monsoon rainfall on the side of Ap Bia Mountain, or Hill 937 as the brass called it, in Viet-damn-Nam.

Ap Bia is in the rugged, jungle-shrouded mountains of South Vietnam barely a mile from the Laotian border. Rising from the floor of the western A Shau Valley, Ap Bia Mountain is a looming, solitary massif, unconnected to the ridges of the surrounding Annamite range. It dominates the northern valley, towering some 937 meters above sea level. Snaking down from its highest peak are a series of ridges and fingers, one of the largest extending southeast to a height of 3,000 feet, another reaching south to the same elevation. The entire mountain is a rugged, uninviting wilderness blanketed in double- and triple-canopy jungle, dense thickets of bamboo, and waist-high elephant grass that in some cases was taller than Sgt. Royer's six-foot-five height. Local Montagnard tribesmen gave it its name, which translates into English, "the mountain of the crouching beast." Official histories of the battle in which Billy was engaged refered to it as Hill 937 its elevation, but the American soldiers who fought there dubbed it "Hamburger Hill," a sad throwback to the Battle of Pork Chop Hill during the Korean War.

The battle of Hamburger Hill occurred during Operation Apache Snow, the sobriquet being somebody's idea of a joke in a tropical rainforest. The op was the second part of a three-phased campaign intended to root out North Vietnam Army forces in the remote A Shau Valley, a prime NVA infiltration route into South Vietnam. Since U.S. efforts to clear the valley had been consistently unsuccessful, the equivalent of two divisions augmented by substantial artillery and air support were amassed to hopefully accomplish the task. The NVA had moved three regiments into the area to recover from losses sustained during a previous U.S. Marine operation in February.

Wilson's platoon was part of Company B, 3rd Battalion, 187th Infantry Regiment, 101st Airborne Division. They had been involved in a variety of minor clashes in the hill country west of Hue, but nothing like what lay ahead as they formed a skirmish line and waited for the jump-off signal. Artillery and aerial bombardment was supposed to have laid waste the upper slopes, but nobody knew for sure how effective the prep had been as they stared through the rain into nearly impenetrable jungle. In fact, the NVA bunkers, constructed to take advantage of the terrain and with overhead cover, suffered little damage. They were so numerous and well-built that many could not be destroyed by indirect fire but had to be attacked directly with napalm, recoilless rifle fire, and dogged platoon and squad-level actions. This was hampered by the decentralized command of the American small units, resulting in a compromise of coordinating action. Close air support was often directed at the platoon level with aircraft at times missing intended targets completely, and in some cases hitting friendlies instead of the enemy.

When the red-orange glow of the signal flare could be seen beneath the heavy clouds, Billy shouted at his men to advance. In the first forty yards nothing happened. But as the nine-man squad step-crawled upward into a less dense patch of jungle, two Soviet RPD light machine guns opened up from an all-but-invisible bunker. Taking hits from guns firing six hundred and fifty rounds per minute, within seconds five of the squad were dead and the other four wounded. Billy's flak jacket saved his life from two shots he felt slam into his chest, but a third took a hefty chunk of flesh out of his left upper arm. The deafening staccato of small arms fire, the boom of motors exploding, and Huey Cobras screaming overhead in a futile attempt to provide covering fire, all drowned out Corporal Wilson's cries for help.

"Medic! Medic! Medic!" he screamed at the top of his bruised lungs.

He felt someone pulling on his legs and then Sergeant Royer's voice, "I gotcha, Billy," as he slid downhill into the camouflage of the foliage. "No medics nearby. How bad are you hurt?"

"I can hardly breathe and my left arm got the holy shit shot out of it."

"What's the condition of your squad?"

"Doesn't look good. The whole world blew up and I saw Rankin and Morrow go down hard. I don't know about anybody else. No damn thing could be alive up there. Am I alive?"

"You're gonna make it, Billy. It's not pretty but looks like just a flesh wound to me."

"Hurts like hell. Wha'da we do now?"

"I gotta check on the other squad. You in good enough shape to find your guys?"

"I don't know, Sarge. I feel like I'm gonna pass out," Billy grimaced.

Royer quickly put a compression bandage on his wound and said, "OK. Just hunker down here and stay out of sight. If you hear anyone else from the squad, try to get them over here with you. If I can find a medic in this shitstorm I'll send him your way."

As the sergeant slithered off to find second squad, the noise of the battle increased rather than slackened, and it was all Billy could do to maintain consciousness. He heard a rustling in the vegetation to his left and managed with some difficulty to train his M16 in that direction. With nerves on the edge of sanity, he was ready to let go on full automatic if anything resembling an NVA uniform came into view. Then he heard Jansen's raspy voice, "Billy! Sarge! Anybody! Need some help here."

"Over here, Oly. Can you crawl?" Billy hoarsely shouted as he lowered his rifle.

Moments later Private Olaf Jansen, a strapping farm

boy from South Dakota, made his way to Billy's side. He was without a rifle and the bottom three fingers on his right hand were missing. Seeing Billy's bloody shoulder he sputtered, "Sonsabitches. You hit bad?"

"Sarge says it didn't hit anything vital but it hurts like hell! What about the rest of the guys?"

"I was next to Rankin and he took one in the head. Then my damn hand got shot off and I couldn't tell who else got hit. Can you help me stop the bleeding?"

With some difficulty due to his arm wound and the onset of shock, Billy got a tourniquet on Oly's forearm and cinched it just enough to slow the blood flow to a trickle. Knowing they were no good for any more shooting, they covered themselves with a rain poncho and waited for either the battle to end . . . or to bleed to death. In a matter of minutes, Billy slipped into the black world of unconsciousness.

When he could see and hear again, fuzzy as both senses were, Billy was on a stretcher farther down the base of the hill. Arriving at the battle aid station, he was given morphine and hooked to an IV while awaiting chopper transport to a more secure field hospital. It was only when recovering in the 95th Evacuation Hospital at the base of the Marble Mountains south of DaNang that he learned he and Jansen were the only survivors of his squad. He also learned that Hamburger Hill had finally been taken on May 20th after horrendous casualties, only to be quietly abandoned on June 7th at the command of Major General John Wright. It was understandable that Wilson and the other survivors of the battle wondered, *What the hell? Over four hundred killed and wounded . . . for what purpose? Throw men at impossible defensive positions like you'd stuff beef into a meat grinder, take the high ground by some miracle, and then a few days later trot off like we didn't give a damn about the hill in the first place? Who was running this cockamamie war?*

Billy thought the bullet to his arm might be his ticket home. No such luck. It wasn't as bad as all the blood made it seem, so after a period of convalescence on an offshore hospital ship he was choppered back to Bravo Company which had been relocated to the Duy Xuyan District in Quang Nam province southwest of Hoi An. Really tired of this freak'n war and figuring he probably wouldn't make it home alive anyway, Billy dove headfirst into booze, pot, and sex when he could get it. Which is how he met Yuan Kao.

Yuan was a young Chinese-Vietnamese woman whose parents were part of the ethnic Chinese contingent that made up some five percent of the population. Now in her late teens, her mother died when she was twelve and she was soon after farmed out by her father to distant relatives. The war and economic hardships forced her to fend for herself by the time she was sixteen. There were few ways to garner enough income upon which to survive, but catering to the needs of horny GI's was one of them. Yuan could have been a hands-down winner in any beauty contests if they had had them. As it was, it simply insured that sex-starved soldiers would gravitate to her like bees to orchid blossoms. Which is exactly what Billy did.

Bravo Company stopped for the night along the Thu Bon River on the west side of Highway 1, the road bordering the coast for most of South Vietnam's length. Polluting the landscape was a dusty collection of shacks including what passed for the local bordello. Urine-yellow exterior walls pockmarked with bullet holes held up a rusty sheet metal roof that looked like it might dissolve if it rained too hard. Inside there were two rooms with sagging, soiled mattresses. To a hungry GI nothing more was required. Billy, feeling no pain with a combination of alcohol and THC in his bloodstream, paid the going rate for a pleasurable fifteen minutes with Yuan. She protested a bit when he didn't produce a condom, a standard practice for Yuan to prevent unwanted babies, a nasty social disease, or both, but had no choice when cornered by a brawny Montana cowboy who was in no mood for objections.

By the time Yuan was ready to deliver her baby, Billy was long gone, his 13-month tour of duty accomplished. She had informed him of her pregnancy and harbored the slight hope that he might want to facilitate her immigration to the U.S. as his beloved wife. But nothing Vietnamese was beloved to Billy, and he took pains to insure he never crossed paths with Yuan again before his departure. So it was with the assistance of a couple of girlfriends that on a star-filled night in a shack on the outskirts of Tam Ky, Yuan gave birth to her Amerasian child. She named him Bo, which in her mother tongue means *precious*. Time would reveal what a horrendous misnomer that would be.

Chapter 9

June 1968 - Quantico, VA and Camp Pendleton, CA

"Never seen any damn thing like it," marveled First Sergeant Jack Adams. Since enlisting at twenty years old, Adams was your ultimate Marine. He was a veteran of Chosin Reservoir in the Korean War, and three tours of duty in Vietnam including the first three months of the battle for Khe Sanh. In other words, not all that easy to impress. And he was impressed.

Captain Rick Leslie, Jed's TBS Company Commander, responded, "You've been around a lot longer than I have, Top, but this is a first for me too."

They had just watched Lieutenant Bazo shave fifteen seconds off the arduous obstacle course record, one which had not been bested for over a decade. He hardly seemed winded and could have been showered and sitting at the mess hall by the time the last candidate plodded through the demanding test.

"I do believe Colonel Hampton is going to want to talk to this boy."

"Are you thinking what I'm thinking?" Leslie queried.

"I am if you're thinking Recon."

"Great minds, Top. Great minds."

"Bazo has scored off the charts in just about every category we have here. Expert in both rifle and pistol, academically pert near a hundred percent, physically so far ahead of the rest that they quit trying to catch up, and he does land navigation like he don't even need a map and compass."

"And to boot," the captain added, "he seems to naturally command the respect of his peers. Could be a poster boy for Marine Corps leadership."

"I'll tell you another damn thing: if I'm heading into battle with a shavetail lieutenant, I hope it's Bazo."

"That's something coming from you, Top. Time to get the boys back to barracks. I'm going to see if I can catch the colonel. First thing we need to do is make sure he gets assigned to infantry."

As Jed handily met the challenges the months of TBS

presented, he felt more and more at home in the Marine Corps. When he tried to put his finger on why, it seemed to come down to a growing commitment to his new country along with the ease with which he acquired the skills required of a Marine officer. Sometimes he thought they went a bit overboard with the "gung ho" mentality, but the *esprit de corps* and leatherneck pride was working its way into his system. Part of his embracing this attitude, he mused, might be the pure Norwegian DNA of which he was composed. When he first entertained the idea of becoming a Marine, he did some research that led him to articles on the Norwegian equivalent called the Special Warfare Group, or Marinens Jegervåpen. The father of a fellow Norwegian student at UDub was an MJ, and Jed remembered some of the stories the son told of his dad's exploits.

His uneasiness with how being a Marine and a man of faith might conflict was largely pushed to the back of his mind. The alternative, he reasoned, was to do away with all armed forces, which seemed ludicrous to him in light of the evil that all too often manifested itself in this usually-not-black-and-white world. He hadn't heard anybody suggesting that we do away with the police. While the idea of killing another human being was abhorrent in and of itself, it was more abhorrent to let devils-incarnate like Hitler and Stalin have free reign.

He even went to church at the base chapel occasionally. One of these days, if time allowed, he just might have coffee with the TBS chaplain to kick around his ongoing philosophical questions.

Of one thing he became convinced, that he wanted to be an infantry officer, MOS 0301 (Military Occupational Specialty). They didn't call the infantry "grunts" for nothing, and wherever the grunt work was, that's where he wanted to be. The lion's share of the MOS quotas coming down from Headquarters Marine Corps were for infantry, and he was high enough in his class rankings to likely insure his preference. But if the gods of war stuck him in something like the supply corps he would have to do some serious lobbying, begging even, with the leatherneck hierarchy.

With three weeks to go, Captain Leslie called Jed into his office. "At ease, Lieutenant" Then getting right to it, "I see that you requested assignment to the infantry."

"Yes, sir," Jed responded in his starched utilities and spit-shined boots.

"Well, you've got it, Lieutenant. You've proved yourself beyond measure here at TBS. In fact I'm pleased to inform you that you are number one out of your class of two hundred and seven. Well done."

"Thank you, sir."

"One question, Lieutenant Bazo, about the CCRE." The Comprehensive Combat Readiness Exam was a three hour written examination to test a student's knowledge in weapons, military history, strategy and tactics, land navigation, and military leadership. It was composed of two hundred multiple choice, one hundred true-false, and fifty short answer questions. "You scored one hundred percent on the test, something nobody's ever done in the history of TBS. How did you do that? Are you just lucky or really that good?"

Jed looked him square in the eye and said, "I've got a good memory, sir."

Leslie figured nobody could have a memory *that* good,

but the score was what it was. So he went on, "Most of those assigned to infantry will be getting orders for Nam immediately. Our needs are steadily growing there and that doesn't look to change anytime soon."

"Yes, sir. Any idea, sir, how soon I'll be shipping out after Basic School?"

"Likely be around two weeks, give or take. Unless, that is . . . "

"Yes, sir? . . ."

"Colonel Hampton would like to talk with you."

A small tingle went up Jed's spine. It was not normal for a young second lieutenant to have an audience with the battalion commander. "Did I do something wrong, sir?"

"On the contrary, Bazo. You have excelled in so many areas that . . . Well, I'll let the Colonel explain."

"Yes, sir. May I ask, sir, when this meeting will take place?"

"In about five minutes, Lieutenant. He's waiting for you in his office the next floor up right now."

This was all a bit sudden, but when the battalion commander summoned you, there was no hesitation. After being dismissed by Captain Leslie, Jed headed for the stairwell and the second floor. He wasn't really worried, but his curiosity was at an all-time high.

Lieutenant Colonel Hampton was every bit a Marine's Marine. He believed in Corps, country, and God, in that order. His military achievements were evidenced by a chest full of medals that rivaled the rainbow. If not intimidating, he was the epitome of USMC inspiration poured into winter greens. His ramrod posture made him look as if he was at attention seated behind his desk.

"At ease, Lieutenant. In fact, please have a seat." Although surprised, Jed complied by sitting stiffly in one of the wooden chairs facing the colonel's desk. "I understand you requested and were assigned to the infantry."

"Yes, sir." Jed replied crisply.

"Well, I won't beat around the bush. Have you thought about Force Recon?"

Jed knew it existed, and that it had something to do with intelligence gathering. At this point all he had really thought about was being an infantry platoon commander. "Not really, sir. I've been pretty much oriented toward commanding an infantry platoon."

Hampton studied the young buck for a few moments and then went on, "It's the elite of the infantry, son. It means three more months of specialty training . . . airborne, scuba, special weapons, demolitions, and more. Recon goes in the farthest, sometimes behind lines, to gather intel for the infantry units. Highly trained, highly skilled, and willing to take risks the average fella doesn't want to touch. And they don't take just anybody."

"It sounds very interesting, sir."

"Are you interested, Lieutenant Bazo?" the colonel said with steel in his eyes.

What harm could interest do,? So Jed replied, "Yes, sir, I am interested. But I would be hesitant to make any commitment until I know more about what I'd be getting into."

"Understood. And no commitment is asked for right now." Handing Jed a manila folder packed with documents, he went on, "But I'd like you to look this information over and report back to me Saturday morning after PT."

"Yes, sir. Will do. And thank you, sir."

"We'll see, Lieutenant. I'm pretty skimpy with my recommendations for Recon. But, as I said, you look over that info and we'll talk again the day after tomorrow."

"Permission to ask a question, sir."

"Permission granted."

"Were you Force Recon, sir?"

The colonel's eyes squinted almost imperceptibly and an observant eye would have seen his chest expand just a bit more. He stood, paused several heartbeats and said, "Semper Fi. That's all Lieutenant."

Jed abruptly stood and snapped to attention. He did not salute since Marines only salute when wearing a cover, which they do not do inside unless they are under arms wearing a duty belt. After a perfectly executed about face, he walked out of the office with his curiosity definitely on the upswing.

After the rest of the day's duties were performed, Jed could hardly wait to examine the material the colonel had given him. When he read the following, most of the nerve cells in his body came to attention:

The Force Reconnaissance (FORCON), also known as Force Recon, is one of the United States Marine Corps' special operations capable forces (SOC) that provide essential elements of military intelligence to the command element of a Marine Air-Ground Task Force, supporting their task force commanders, and their subordinate operating units. Historically, the Force Recon companies performed both deep reconnaissance and direct action operations.

FORECON is responsible for operating independently behind enemy lines performing unconventional special operations in support of conventional warfare. The unit's various methods of airborne, heliborne, submarine and waterborne insertions and extractions are similar to those of the Navy SEALs and Army Special Forces.

The more he read of the history, mission, and operational capabilities of Force Recon, the more he felt drawn to it. It seemed like it had been designed for him, or vice-versa. He loved challenges, especially testing the limits of his own body, and he relished something that would do this to an even greater degree than TBS. He thought back to his explorations of the Norwegian military structure, and Force Recon seemed equivalent to Marinejegerkommandoen (MJK), the oldest and most elite of their special operations forces that branched off of their Navy's Marinens Jegervåpen. Throughout the western world's navies and marine forces, if one wore the MJK insignia it was well known that you wanted him on your side. Jed's Norwegian genes, Ndebele upbringing, and American military training combined to make Recon an obvious choice.

In addition, Force Recon was an infantry MOS but a specialized one that was essential to successful infantry ops. If so assigned, a side benefit would be several months of training at Camp Pendleton, CA . . . which hopefully meant that Angela could fly down at least once for some time together before his eventual deployment.

On Saturday morning Jed stood again before Lieutenant Colonel Hampton and expressed his desire to pursue the Force Recon option.

"You need to know, Lieutenant Bazo, that not all candidates accepted for Force Recon successfully complete the course."

With a spark in his eye that the colonel couldn't miss, Jed responded, "Sir, I'd be pleased to see you there for my graduation exercises."

That being exactly what Hampton wanted to hear, he came around his desk and said as he shook Jed's hand, "The assignment is yours, Lieutenant. Do the Marine Corps proud." Sensing the Fish Eagle underneath his uniform, Jedediah had complete confidence that he would.

Due to the pressured training schedule ahead, Jed came to realize that it would be senseless for Angela to come down to California. Instead, he went to Seattle before reporting in for Force Recon training. Angela met him at the airport looking like a bona fide movie star, and when they flew into each other's arms they both felt like they never wanted to let go.

"Jed, I didn't think it was humanly possible to miss someone so much."

"Knowing you were waiting for me gave every day its meaning," he responded. "Even during some of the toughest physical challenges, I pictured you there at the finish line and it pushed me harder than ever. I can't imagine life without you."

Since they had written each other with fanatical regularity, there was not much news to catch up on. Angela was well aware of his upcoming Recon training and subsequent deployment to Vietnam. Over meals and leisurely walks in the few days they had together, they mostly drank in each other, knowing the extended separation that was on the horizon.

Jed stayed with her in her new off-campus apartment. Her roommate had gone home to Montana for the summer, so they had complete privacy. After the first few nights of cuddling, Angela's demeanor and actions indicated that she wanted more . . . much more.

"Angela, you know we decided to wait until marriage to go all the way. I'd still like to honor that decision."

Her eyes moist, Angela replied, "But Jed, you know that day might never come. More of our men are being killed over there every day, and what if . . . I mean, I can't even force myself to think that maybe . . . Oh Jed, don't talk. Just hold me. I'm safe . . . it's OK . . . just hold me, Jed."

Two years of pent up passions plus the impact of what she was saying opened the floodgates. It would have been unbelievable to most of their contemporaries, but this was the first time for both of them. There was a bit of awkwardness, some fumbling, but they managed to express their love for each other in a way that neither could have imagined would be so fulfilling, so wonderful. Once the threshold had been crossed, they could not seem to get enough of each other. By the time Jed had to head south to California they felt even more so that their love had been cemented irrevocably. They felt like they had bestowed a wordless benediction on each other, one which they trusted would hold them together until Jed's return.

Three weeks later Jed reported for the Basic Recon Course at the School of Infantry in Camp Pendleton, CA. The ensuing nine weeks included training in limit-testing individual physical skills, ocean swims with fins, advanced land navigation, helicopter rope suspension training, communications and supporting arms, small unit tactics, mission planning, amphibious reconnaissance, boat operations and nautical navigation. As usual, Jed's memory capacity shocked and amazed his instructors. They gave him one test designed to humble any over-self-inflated recon Marine. No one had ever passed. He was led blindfolded into a room with an M16 rifle on a table disassembled down to the last spring and roll pin into its eighty-seven parts. He was told he had three minutes to reassemble the rifle into working order, the blindfold remaining on. Jed handed them a perfectly functioning rifle in two and a half minutes. When asked how he could do that, he replied that having done it without a blindfold at TBS he simply remembered how. Years later the incident was still being re-told around Camp Pendleton.

Upon successful completion of the course, the closing exercises at which Lieutenant Colonel Hampton could not be present but for which he sent a personal message of congratulations, Jed was posted immediately to the Army Airborne School at Fort Benning, Georgia, where he earned his jump wings. He thought floating down in a T-10 parachute was one of the most fun things he had ever done.

Early in May he was in another airplane, this one high over the Pacific Ocean on its way to Vietnam.

Chapter 10

November 1969 - North of Lao Bao, Republic of Vietnam

They can tell you anything. Everything. It's all just a hint. When your boots hit the ground in an actual combat zone, you realize that all the stories you've heard, everything you've read, all that you've imagined, has just been a peek or two at reality. Like someone telling you what it's like to make love . . . which is but an iota of the real deal. Except combat is to make war, not love. And making war is not what the movies tell you. It has nothing to do with glory or splendor or nobility. It has to do with kill or be killed. Survival at its basest level. What they told you was just a hint.

Jed's boots first hit the ground at Danang where he reported to the 1st Marine Division for his assignment to 1st Reconnaissance Battalion. A couple of nights there began his acclimation to artillery blasts and screaming F-4 Phantoms overhead in the neighborhood of 24/7. There were the obligatory orientation sessions, which included some critical "do's" and "don'ts." A heavy emphasis was put on "do kill" and "don't be killed."

Jed wasn't scared. At least not yet. Of course, the enemy was generally not taking pot-shots at troops around Division Headquarters in a basically secure area. As he approached the double-rotor CH-46 Sea Knight for transport to his field unit, he thought again of how these nimble flying beasts reminded him of two dragonflies procreating, except louder. The feeling he experienced wasn't fear; it was more an adrenaline rush than anything akin to angst or faintheartedness. He knew he would be seeing the dead and dying, which was nothing new since there had been plenty of that to go around back in his Matopos Hills homeland. The big difference would be that here, people, including him, would be purposefully trying to kill each other. Except for the firing ranges, all the preparatory war games stateside were done with blank rounds. Now when Jed pulled the trigger he would be sending a 5.56×45mm, 62-grain projectile at 3,100 feet per second to rip human flesh to shreds. While he intellectually knew this to be the case, his training was so ingrained that he no longer questioned its necessity. Bad guys were trying to kill good guys, and Marines were here to stop them. As sobering as introspection on the subject might be, so be it. An oath is an oath, and Jed still felt like he took it for the right reasons.

Bravo Company of 1st Recon Battalion to which Jed was assigned supported the 2nd Battalion of the 7th Marine Regiment. The 7th Marines were battle-hardened veterans, having been in-country since 1965 and heavily involved in the 1968 Tet offensive. Forward elements of the battalion were located in the rugged mountains of the Huong Hóa district in Quang Tr□ Province, part of their mission being to interdict and prevent traffic along the Ho Chí Minh trail. A key factor to enable the effectiveness of this mission was good intelligence. That's where 1st Recon Battalion came in.

After debarking from the Sea Knight, Jed found his way to Bravo Company and Captain Russ Frye. The commanding officer was older than he expected, and he later learned that the captain was a *mustang*, an officer who had come up through the enlisted ranks. Mustangs were a minority among commissioned officers, but they brought with them a wealth of experience from the enlisted man's side of the tracks. The lines on his face and the starch of his bearing bespoke a man who had been there, and for whom the Corps was serious business. He shook hands with Jed and offered coffee which was kept warm on a can of Sterno. "Welcome to Bravo Company, Lieutenant."

"Thank you, sir. Glad to be here . . . I guess."

"You'll find out soon enough. It's what we signed up for, and Uncle Sam spares no effort in making our stay comfortable."

Looking around at the imposing jungle and field accommodations, Jed replied, "That's very obvious, Captain. Looks like it doesn't get much better than this."

"Oh believe me, it doesn't. Unless, that is, you like turkey-size mosquitos, tigers, and snakes that'll kill you by spitting at you. Not to mention NVA."

"Like you said, sir, it's what we signed up for."

After refilling his canteen cup with muddy brew, Frye continued, "We don't get much detail out here, Bazo, but they told us you had good training reports – maybe the best. What made you pick Recon?"

"I like a challenge, sir. Regular infantry would have been fine, but when my TBS battalion commander explained what Recon does, it seemed made for me. I liked just about all the training, and did OK. So now I'm here to give back to my country."

Liking Jed's response, Frye continued, "Says in the report that you naturalized; that you grew up in Africa."

"Yes, sir. Rhodesia my first fourteen years."

"They speak English there?"

"Well, the Brits do. They colonized the place in the late 1800s, but in the rural areas tribal languages are the norm. My family speaks isiNdebele so I grew up with that as my native tongue."

"Your parents weren't native, I presume."

"Yes and no. My birth parents died when I was five months old and I was adopted and raised by a family of the Bazo clan which belongs to the Ndebele nation."

"That's a new one for me. So where did you get this good English? I hardly detect any accent."

"It's a long story, but missionaries from America came and I learned English from them for the next nine years. Then I went to Minnesota with them for high school. That ended up leading me to the University of Washington for another four years. Add all that up and it's a lot of years of speaking English. I also just like languages and words, so I've worked very hard to sound like an American when I speak it."

"And you do a good job of it. That's quite a history you have there. I'd like to hear more details when we have time."

"It would be my pleasure, sir. First, I'm pretty interested in what I'll be doing here."

"I'll give you a brief general picture and then take you over to introduce you to your platoon."

Captain Frye briefed Jed on their immediate situation and what he could expect in the near future. That near future included a reconnaissance patrol which he would be leading within forty-eight hours. Even with the pre-op preparations at hand, Jed made time for a quick letter to Angela which would go out with the resupply chopper the next day. Operations details, including locations, were strictly forbidden, but that made no difference to Jed since his aim was simply to tell her in at least ten different ways how much he missed her.

The reception by his platoon was warm and lukewarm. Warm because he was one of them and they knew he wouldn't be there unless he had proven himself well in the selection and training process. Lukewarm because he was green, and any newbie had to demonstrate his competence to earn complete trust. He started out on the right foot by acknowledging with his NCOs that he absolutely had to depend on them for their experience and expertise. He was their commander, but a commander who admitted he had a lot to learn.

By late afternoon of the second day after arriving, Jed found himself leading a patrol some nine miles west of base camp. They were in a mountainous region only several miles from Laos and the infamous Ho Chí Minh trail which meandered along the west side of the border. Arial recon indicated possible new NVA troop movements coming down from the north, and ground verification with greater detail would enable the 7th Marines to make them wish they had stayed home. Jed's seven-man patrol was to remain undetected and to bring back up-to-date intel.

They had been inserted in a northwest-by-southeast valley north of Lao Bao, the latter being a market center on the border with Laos. It was likely that any NVA units moving down the Ho Chí would have elements in this valley to protect their left flank. Observation of any flanking units would almost surely indicate a major intrusion from the north.

Platoon Staff Sergeant Red Baukus took the point. A career Marine who had been in-country nine months and knew what he was doing, he was built like an Angus bull, was just about as black, and exuded competence and self-confidence. While Jed was more than willing to rely on his sergeant's experience, he was also anxious to do the job for which he had been trained. Baukus seemed to realize both. Some sixth sense about this new shavetail lieutenant made him feel OK about his being their new leader.

About the only thing the Huong Hóa district had in

common with Virginia or California was that it was on planet Earth. The triple canopy jungle was wet, humid, and filled with critters that populate horror movies. *Hot* doesn't do it justice. Try a hundred and twenty degrees and raining. Poisonous centipedes a foot long and plants that bite you make sneaking through the underbrush something you'd like to reserve for your worst enemy. Then again, Jed thought to himself, nobody ever said Vietnam was a sugar-coated, candy-ass affair.

As the patrol kept to the foliage along the shallow stream they were following northwest, Sergeant Baukus gave the signal to stop and fade into the underbrush. Their camo gear and face paint made them essentially invisible. An almost inaudible metallic clink around a bend in the creek was the cause for alarm. Jed was in the middle of the line of march, followed by three patrol members front and back. Knowing that not being detected was paramount, he gave the sign for ultra-quiet to be passed up and down the line. Peering between vines and bamboo shoots covered with crystalline drops, all seven men could have been stone statues.

They all saw the NVA patrol round the bend. The gurgling water masked their sound somewhat, but Jed could hear the odd scrape of a boot on river rocks. It was a squad-sized unit of thirteen men which was very likely covering the flank of a company or battalion on the other side of the ridge that formed the south border of the valley. The North Vietnamese patrol had no idea Jed and his men were there, and eventually they disappeared to the southeast. After a safe period of time, Jed conferred over a map with Sergeant Baukus. They agreed that rather than following the NVA down the route from which they had just come, climbing to the top of the ridge at whose base they stood might give them a look at troop size and movements on the other side.

Scrambling up roughly fifteen hundred feet of jungle was nobody's idea of a picnic. The only saving grace was that the canopy was so high that the underbrush was not as thick in lower elevations. They had to move quietly and with hyper-vigilance in case there were other NVA on the slopes. They made it to the crest, which overlooked Lao Bao on the Sepon River. The height of the ground cover prevented adequate visibility, so Corporal Stanton was sent up a tree with binoculars.

"Anything worth looking at up there?" Jed asked after Stanton's return to earth.

"Yes, sir. Looks to be at least two companies parked between us and the town. Could be the rest of the battalion is still coming down the Ho, and they might just be fix'n for an assault on our base."

"OK. Good job, Corporal. Sergeant Baukus, what do you think?"

"Well Lieutenant, I think we need to get this info to Captain Frye ASAP so he can notify headquarters. We might as well bomb the shit out of these bastards while they're sitting there with their pants down."

The young lieutenant consulted his map again and said, "OK. Listen up. We've got about an hour of daylight left. That should be just about enough time to follow this ridge to its southern terminus where we'll hit the pass that the NVA patrol will likely follow back to their company. Once we're sure they're through, we'll cross to Hill 844 where we should get good radio contact to base. We can hunker down for the night listening to the artillery overhead sending the NVA to wherever they go when they die. But let's be very, very careful that we're not spotted by that patrol that went by us."

"I agree, Lieutenant" Baukus responded. "Boys, we'll use the same order of march . . . and step lightly. Move out now."

As the gods of war would have it, they reached the end of the ridge just in time to see the rear of the NVA patrol move through the pass to rejoin their unit for the night. They then slipped down the ridge, moved north through the pass, and topped Hill 844 just as the jungle darkness surrounded them. Jed made radio contact with Capt. Frye and relayed the exact coordinates for the center of the NVA encampment. As his men formed a tight defensive circle and took turns sleeping, the night sounds of the jungle mixed with 155mm howitzer shells screaming above and laying waste to a two square mile area north of Lao Bao. Jed and company were not there to see the results, but it was a good bet that the NVA battalion that had moved into the area had been significantly compromised in its operational capabilities.

The next morning at first light the glorious whump-whump-whump of a UH-1 Huey on the way to pick them up sounded from the east. The patrol descended to a plateau with enough landing room and lit a smoke grenade to guide the pilot. As the skids touched down and the patrol ran for the bird, the first bullet plowed into the ground next to Jed. Obviously some pissed-off NVA commander had deduced that the night artillery barrage had been directed by spotters, and had sent a unit back through the pass hoping to find them. They were at the extreme range of the enemy AK-s, but getting hit at any distance was still getting hit.

"Go! Go! Go!" Jed yelled as they all turned into Olympic sprinters. Per tradition and protocol, the troops boarded first and the officer was the last one in line. Jed was returning covering fire with his M16 on full automatic and saw at least two of the attackers go down hard. While the rest of the patrol was in or close to the chopper, Corporal Stanfield, the last man ahead of Jed, took a round in the back of his right thigh. It went to the side of his bone and missed the femoral artery, but he still went down like a rock. Forty yards from the chopper, Jed emptied his last magazine, scooped up the wounded Marine in a fireman's carry, and ran for the open door with bullets plowing the ground on both sides of him. Seeing what was happening and timing it just right, Baukus gave the lift-off signal to the pilot when Jed was ten yards away. With a foot of air between the ground and the chopper's skids, Jed literally threw Stanfield onto the deck and several hands pulled him aboard as the aircraft shot skyward and out of NVA range in a matter of seconds.

Back at base camp nobody pumped up what happened. They had done what they were trained to do. But the word spread, and the Marines of 1st Recon Battalion, to a man, knew they'd follow Lieutenant Bazo to hell and back.

Chapter 11

November 1969 - Annamite Range, Republic of Vietnam

Corporal Stanfield's leg wound was not life-threatening, but likely ended his overseas tour of duty. Jed spoke with him back in base camp just before he was loaded on the medevac chopper for transport out of the jungle.

"You're going to be OK, Corporal. Take more than one misplaced NVA bullet to keep you down."

"Damn right, sir. You might see me yet before your tour's up."

"I wouldn't count on that, but you get yourself healed up . . . we need men like you."

"Thank you, Lieutenant. Recon hasn't seen the last of me yet. And thank you too for saving my ass."

"That's what we do for each other, Marine. You're a credit to the Corps and I'd be honored to have you in my unit any day."

Trying not to grimace from the obvious pain, Stanfield replied, "The feeling's mutual, sir. Go out there and knock down some more for us." And as Jed shook his hand, "Semper Fi."

After the patrol north of Lao Bao, Jed and his platoon rested for close to a week in base camp. This gave him time to begin getting to know the enlisted men in his charge, as well as his fellow officers in both 1st Recon and the infantry units they supported. He also had the opportunity to be briefed more thoroughly on their area of operations and to familiarize himself with the layout of the land by studying the topo maps for hours. Jed was well-versed in land navigation with map and compass, but under Jacob's tutelage in Rhodesia he also honed what seemed to be an instinctual feel for direction and distance once familiarized with a geographical area. Psychologists say that we remember things that are important to us. It was important enough to Jed to virtually imprint the topographical maps on his brain.

Seven days after his first patrol Jed led a second, this one south of Khe Sanh where the Ho Chí Minh trail crossed a bump of Vietnam that pushes southwest into Laos. U.S.

incursion into this area had been sparse for the last couple of months in part due to the villages in the lowland areas being supportive of past American operations there. One village in particular, Thái Ba, had alerted an infantry platoon to NVA activity to the east which allowed their hasty withdrawal before being surrounded by a couple of enemy companies. Jed was told they might gain additional intel from the villagers, so a Vietnamese Marine interpreter accompanied them.

Slowly and quietly the patrol moved down a southward sloping ridge just north of the Sepon River floodplain on which Thái Ba was situated. The river there formed the Vietnam-Laotian border, but a few miles to the east the border shot northeast while the river continued its southward meandering. Jed had been cautioned to take care to not cross into Laos. As the patrol reached the lower, less-treed slopes of the chain of hills they had been following, the flood plain came into view, including the village of Thái Ba . . . or what was left of it. Sergeant Calloway, the lead NCO on this patrol, glassed the area and reported, "Looks like we're too late, Lieutenant."

After a solid hour of observing the seeable portions of the flood plain followed by short excursions both east and west along the ridge baseline to ensure no enemy presence, the patrol crossed the shortest exposed distance from the hills to the village for a close-up examination of what Calloway had seen with the binoculars. The village was not deserted. It was dead. Men, women, children, babies, elderly . . . everybody. Many had been massacred in their huts, some charred beyond recognition as their torched dwellings had collapsed upon them. Others that were strewn around the village had been torn apart by gunfire or hacked viciously with machetes. Or both. Under one shade tree Jed came upon two bodies . . . a very elderly woman with arms wrapped around what looked to be about a one-year-old boy. The baby had been shot in the head, the bullet then proceeding into the grandmother's heart. Scenes of similar carnage were throughout the now-extinct little community, the total body count amounting to fifty-two individuals. As they began a systematic search of the village, Jed cautioned his men to be on high-alert lookout for booby traps, a favored NVA/VC tactic that accounted for many injuries and lives.

Stores of rice and other foodstuffs were strewn everywhere and there was not a habitable dwelling left. As Jed was taking all this in and fighting a queasy feeling in his stomach, one of the corporals hand-signaled Jed to come have a look. On the exterior wall of a storehouse that had been spared fire someone had scrawled in blood *kephan boi*. Jed sent the corporal to find the Vietnamese translator who related its meaning: traitor. The village and all its inhabitants had obviously paid the price for their support of American troops.

As they prepared to resume their mission, Jed remarked to Sergeant Calloway, "You hear about it, Sarge, but it's worse than I thought it would be. How can human beings do this to each other?"

"Par for the course, Lieutenant. You get used to it."

But Jed didn't want to get used to it. He felt the beginning of a growing anger taking root, but didn't want to lose his cool in front of his men. "We'll see. We've still got some ground to cover so let's get those booby traps disabled and head for our night objective before we lose too much more light."

"Yes, sir. I'll have us ready to move out in fifteen minutes."

The next two days were uneventful and they were extracted without complications. After making his report to Captain Frye, Jed spent some time alone thinking about the vivid images from Thái Ba that were still fresh in his mind. His thoughts drifted toward the conclusion that men who would do such things needed to be stopped. You either chose to put a stop to their evil or tried to sleep at night picturing more babies shot in the head. Jed knew which was the right choice for him.

Although the artillery attack on the NVA encampment outside Lao Bao had done some damage, the extent was unclear and the brass' best guess was that a larger build-up was underway. Verifying intel was needed. High altitude spotter planes had acquired some grainy photos that appeared to indicate a considerable build-up of enemy forces north of the Sepon River on the Laotian side of the border. To be sure, U.S. ground forces were not allowed incursions into Laos. The last thing needed was a new front against a well-armed Pathet Lao, the Laotian equivalent of South Vietnam's Viet Minh, colloquially called Viet Cong. But clandestine cross-border patrols had taken place for quite some time, and what the American public didn't know didn't hurt them. An unspoken jarhead credo was, "if it saves Marine lives, do it."

After another five days' rest, Jed's third time out found his patrol farther north of Lao Bao than his first incursion. It was an eight-man patrol with Sergeant Baukus again the lead NCO. Fire Team One leader was Lance Corporal J.D. Lanceford, a lean-and-mean fighter who grew up on a ranch outside Waco, Texas, and had been in-country six months. His two other team members were Corporal Reggie Halloway, a high school football star from Pittsburgh who was on his second patrol, and Private 1st Class Luca Guarino, a demolitions specialist from the Bronx who was basically happy if he could be blowing things up. Fire Team Two was led by Corporal Hugo Sanchez. He grew up with his feet on both sides of the border around Nuevo Laredo, Mexico, and had proven himself repeatedly during his eleven months in The Nam as a communications expert. This would be his last patrol before rotating home. Jed's other fire team members were Private 1st Class Sammy Spees, a Wisconsin logger who looked like Paul Bunyan, and Lance Corporal Danny Bair, a wiry state champ wrestler from Iowa who was the platoon's expert sniper if needed. Except for Halloway, all had been seasoned by months of in-country experience that gave Jed confidence in this particular group.

Their mission was, as usual, intelligence gathering without being detected. The NVA were getting mighty tired of artillery and bombing attacks that rained on them with geographical precision, the accuracy largely a result of the due diligence of Force Recon units who provided reliable information on enemy positions. This particular foray was to investigate the spotter plane reports and return with more detailed intelligence to guide preemptive strikes.

Three Huey choppers lifted off at the first hint of light. Two were decoys that touched down halfway between Khe Sanh and Lao Bao. The one with Jed's patrol deposited them on a ridge about four miles north of Lao Bao and within sight of the Laotian border. The plan was to attain several high points on the Vietnamese side which would enable visual contact with a portion of the Ho Chí Minh trail that crossed a relatively open river plain. If needed, they were authorized to cross into Laos and stealthily proceed south to hills that might allow a better look-see at NVA troop strength. By 0600 on the first of a programmed five-day patrol they found themselves alone in the jungle, except for maybe a North Vietnamese division or two. Jed had the terrain firmly engrained in his mind, including the best communication locations and the extraction point. They were to be on extra high alert for NVA patrols that might be searching for Americans carrying out their precise mission.

Around mid-afternoon the Force Recon patrol was following a short upward-sloping defile that would take them to a mountaintop providing an advantageous view of the Laotian side of the border. Baukus was again on point and Spees anchored the team. Jed was in the middle, with radioman Sanchez right behind him. Ten yards separated each of them. Clothed in camo utilities and with faces and hands painted to match the shadows and colors of the surrounding jungle, they treaded quietly and with utmost care up the draw. They had not reckoned on the NVA determining this to be a likely enemy infiltration route, hence setting up a possible ambush on the small percentage chance that an American patrol actually chose this path. The gamble paid big dividends for Ho Chi Minh. For Jedediah and his men it was a disaster of the first magnitude.

Since the NVA were trained professionals who knew how to use demo, and the VC were ingenious at improvising crude but effective explosive devices out of captured or dud ordinance, American forces attempted in earnest to not let any of their armaments fall into enemy hands. It didn't always work out that way.

The M18 Claymore mine is a wicked weapon of war. It is command-detonated and directional, meaning it is fired by remote control and blasts a pattern of devastation in a sixty degree arc from where it is pointed. Enclosed in a convex plastic case and in front of a layer of C-4 explosive, seven hundred 1/8-inch-diameter steel balls set into an epoxy resin are propelled at 4000 feet per second in a fan-shaped pattern six feet high and fifty yards wide. The equivalency would be eighty-five 12-guage shotguns loaded with double-aught buck fired simultaneously. The optimum effective range is roughly fifty yards with a hit probability of thirty percent on a man-sized target at that distance. Jed's patrol was forty yards away when the designated soldier in the NVA squad depressed the M57 firing device.

Because the trigger man jumped the gun before Spees came into the kill zone, the initial blast missed him all together. Staff Sergeant Baukus died instantly when a spray of steel balls raked his face and neck. Following next, Lanceford and Halloway both went down with wounds from head to foot, unconscious and adding their lifeblood to the welcoming jungle floor. Guarino's legs were knocked out from under him and he belly-crawled into dense foliage away from the attacking NVA. The only reason Jed escaped a death blow was that he had knelt down with his nose to the ground examining a metal insignia on the trail that had caught his eye. Screaming hot metal tore off the top half of his rucksack and knocked his helmet flying. Sanchez and Bair, having strayed too close to each other, were both hit midsection and lay on the ground watching their internal organs spill out. Sanchez' radio had also been shattered by the blast.

It took a couple of seconds for Jed's head and vision to clear. Looking up and down the line he saw five Marines dead or dying and Guarino disappearing into the underbrush. As he scurried on hands and knees toward Guarino's concealed position, a severely pissed-off Spees came running up the draw firing his M16 on full automatic toward the direction from which the blast came.

"Down! Down! Spees, get your ass down!" Jed screamed as he reached the visual shield of ferns and bamboo. But no sooner had the words escaped his mouth when AK-47 rounds reduced the hulking Marine from Wisconsin to a writhing mass on the ground. Now that the smoke from the Claymore had cleared, fire from the Chinese-made Kalashnakovs ensured that the six patrol members they could see were absolutely dead. Then the shots began to be directed at the general vicinity where they thought two of the Marines had escaped.

"Guarino, how bad you hurt?" Jed whispered from five feet away. Bullets hit below them and to their sides, but it was obvious the NVA didn't know exactly where they were.

Guarino's voice communicated severe pain. "My left knee is blown all to hell and my right calf is bleeding like a stuck pig. No way I can move, Lieutenant."

Jed was fighting to control an unknown feeling: panic. "You have any idea how many there are?"

"Not a clue. Could be two or twenty. That was a damn Claymore, but all it takes is one to mash the trigger."

With his mind racing, Jed proffered, "Look, we've got lots of ground cover and if I can get you on my back we can make it to the top of this ridge and lose them."

"Wouldn't make it with my added weight, sir. You

know how steep and high this ridge is." His voice was getting weaker with the loss of blood and as shock began to set in.

"I can't leave you here, Guarino."

"No sense two of us dying, Lieutenant. I'm good as gone and you gotta let command know what's happening out here."

Even though the reasoning was correct, Jed didn't like it one stinking bit. But he knew what spades meant when they were dealt to you, so he said, "OK, Marine. You take my four grenades and hold them off as long as you can. If they take you alive, hang tough and we'll come get you before they have a chance to move you far." He knew how false his words sounded, but he didn't know what else to say. Both he and Guarino knew the risks Force Recon Marines were required to take, and they also both knew that mission accomplishment was paramount.

"Head out while you can. With eight frags I can hold 'em off long enough for you get over the ridge. And do me a favor, Lieutenant."

"What's that, Guarino?"

"Tell my folks that I did OK. Now you better get a move on."

"Will do, but don't give up just get. I plan on seeing you back at base before this is all over. God bless."

God bless? Nobody in the Marine Corps said God bless. But Luca appreciated it anyway, and gave a feeble wave as Jed started moving up the ridge as quickly and quietly as possible.

Jed thought he had travelled maybe five hundred vertical feet when he came to a rock cliff too steep to climb. He had heard sporadic enemy fire and the explosion of five

M26 fragmentation grenades before things went silent below him. He knew he'd been leaving a trail of broken and crushed vegetation, but now he was on a rock shelf and they wouldn't know whether he had gone left or right. Guessing that his pursuers would figure he would head toward his base to the right, Jed chose to go left toward Laos. He worked his way along the rocky bench careful to not dislodge loose stones or make scraping sounds. His shredded pack had lost most of its contents, but side pockets still contained some field rations and extra ammunition magazines for the M16 he carried.

After fifteen minutes he saw that the bare outcropping that hopefully obscured his trail petered out not far ahead and the jungle reclaimed the terrain. Once he reached the cover of the flora he would then head uphill again in the hope of passing over the ridge summit and disappearing on the other side. With no radio to contact his unit, Jed's only option was to cover the ten miles southwest until he reached either base camp or other friendly forces probing westward. Glancing eastward to make sure no one had followed him, he turned to traverse the last twenty yards to the concealment of the rainforest.

Facing him were three individuals, each pointing their rifles at his chest.

Chapter 12

November 1969 - Annamite Range, Republic of Vietnam

The leader of the NVA squad that ambushed Jed's patrol was no neophyte. He split the squad into three fire teams, one which would follow Jed uphill and the other two flanking to the left and right a half mile each before heading for the top of the ridge. The hope was that if the fleeing American veered laterally east or west, one of the flanking units would pick him up. Which is exactly what happened.

Jed's rifle muzzle was pointed at the ground and he knew that if he even began to raise it for a quick burst on full auto the odds were that he would be full of holes before moving it forty-five degrees. So he slowly set it on the ground and stood with his arms outstretched. Facing him with obviously itchy trigger fingers were three figures in NVA uniforms. Although Jed had trouble estimating the age of Asian people, he guessed one to be in his early 20s while the other two looked like they should be playing soccer for some high school in Hanoi. They were thin and appeared extremely nervous, but Jed figured he wasn't dead yet only due to an order to take him alive if possible. Sergeant Twenties barked something in Vietnamese and while he and Private Schoolboy One held their rifles steady, Private Schoolboy Two tied Jed's hands behind his back with a green vine they had harvested from the area. Their inexperience was evidenced by the fact that they divested Jed of his pack, rifle, Colt .45 and ammunition, but missed his Ka-Bar. When Jed started up the ridge, he had taken the sheathed knife off its thigh strap, stuck it in his right boot, and pulled his pant leg over to conceal it. At the moment it did not seem to him much of a match for three fully automatic high-powered rifles. Besides, as soon as they rejoined the larger group the knife was sure to be discovered. The older lad fired three rapid shots, some prearranged signal Jed assumed, and shoved him roughly down the route which they had ascended.

If there was anything to give Jed hope it was the fact that the green vine with which he was tied was damp and somewhat stretchy. Added to that was the lack of expertise with which the youngster had bound his wrists. As they plodded downhill under a double canopy and in fading light, Jed surreptitiously worked his wrists back and forth slowly loosening the knotted greenery. Jed was put in the lead with Twenties immediately behind him. Their anxiety seemed to lessen now that they had the big American disarmed and subdued, and they no doubt were anticipating hearty commendations from the higher ups. Reaching a narrow bench a couple of hundred feet above the valley floor, the leader roughly jerked Jed to a stop, knocked him to his knees with the butt of his rifle, and babbled something to the other two. When they had all refreshed from their canteens, offering none to Jed, Sergeant Twenties motioned to Jed to get on his feet. That's when several shots rang out.

The rearmost soldier took one in the back and pitched forward like a felled tree. The other lad in front of him was hit in the chest with two rounds which nearly lifted him off the ground. The leader whirled around looking for the shooter's location, saw the muzzle flash from behind a deadfall and kneeled to return fire. With no hint that he was about to receive any assistance, Jed had separated his hands behind his back while his captors were drinking. When the firing began, he pulled his Ka-Bar from his boot and covered in a single bound the six feet between himself and the team leader whose back was now to him. He plunged the huge blade into the base of the soldier's neck, severing the spinal cord and turning him into a limp rag.

This all happened within a matter of a few seconds. Jed had no idea from whom the rescuing shots came, but he figured that the old adage, *the enemy of my enemy is my friend* , worked for him. As he remained absolutely motionless to see what happened next, two young men emerged from the underbrush some thirty yards away. They were obviously Asian, wore the ubiquitous peasant dress dubbed "black pajamas" by U.S. troops, and carried AK-47s. But they were also obviously not Vietnamese. They approached Jed with rifle muzzles pointed downward and communicated with hand signs for him to follow them with haste. When Jed asked, also using hand signs, if it was OK to reclaim his weapons and ammunition, they nodded vigorously, adding whirling hand motions to indicate again the need to hurry.

Instead of continuing a descent to the defile, the two men proceeded westward along the hillside. They followed a trail of sorts that Jed would not likely have seen on his own, and after half an hour they drifted left onto another ridge that pointed due south. With the maps in his mind, Jed knew for sure that they were now in Laos. And while still having no idea who had saved him or why, he was more than content to be in this position rather than being tied up with a rifle pointed at the back of his head.

With fading light and increasing night jungle sounds, Jed wondered how long they were going to keep on the move. His question was answered as they followed a small stream to a forty foot waterfall at the base of which was a small campfire circle with six other well-armed men sitting around it. One of Jed's saviors had uttered a raucous bird call three times before coming into the view of the campers, who greeted them as comrades-in-arms. Although none of them spoke a word of English and Jed didn't even know what language they were using, they also greeted him and welcomed him into their circle. The presence of NVA in the area precluded a fire, but they had meager provisions of flatbread, dried vegetables of some kind, and something folks back home would call jerky even though it might be from dogs or rats. Jed gratefully ate what they offered and drank from the waterfall pool in spite of having lost his water purification tablets. As they curled up to snooze until first light, Jed fell asleep wondering who these men were and where they were planning on taking him. Having no better alternative, he figured he'd find out in the morning.

The ragtag but seemingly disciplined crew was up just as the night jungle sounds were fading, performed gastronomical and hygienic duties, and set off in a southerly direction as soon as the new day's faint rays allowed visual navigation. Unless he wanted to go it alone in mountainous jungles impregnated with North Vietnamese Army units, Jed thought he had better flow with the current program. They proceeded extremely cautiously, remaining in thick vegetation except for narrow valleys separating the series of ridgelines that crossed their path. At each dingle one man would cross alone after a time of careful observation, followed by the rest of the group after he was safely on the further slope. They travelled thus all morning until shortly after high noon the ridge on which they currently trod sloped gently down to a flood plain, the river in sight being about a half mile away.

Jed knew they had to be some distance into Laos, although he had no idea how far, and he guessed correctly that they were looking at the Sepon River on which the border town of Lao Bao was situated. He knew that the river flowed westward toward the Mekong from its source in the Annamite Range, but his knowledge of the area in general was insufficient for him to place in his mind where they were on the map. Of one thing he was very confident: between where he stood and his home base to the east there were beaucoup enemy of both NVA and VC stripes.

The apparent leader of this whoever-they-were group sent two of the men east to scout for enemy activity. Staying within the forest canopy to escape detection, the men returned two hours later and a group discussion ensued. Of course Jed couldn't understand a word, but he could feel a consensus as they all nodded and uttered approving grunts. It appeared to Jed that this was more of a democracy than a chain-of-command military unit. At any rate, more hand signs indicated that they were to hunker down until sundown before making a move. They were blessed with a cloud cover that brought an appreciated early and very dark night. Miming the footfalls of the tigers that prowl the Southeast Asian mountains at night, the men, spaced at twenty yard intervals, arrived at the bank of the Sepon in a little more than an hour. Knowing exactly where to look, they quickly located three dugout canoes hidden in the thick riverbank growth. They distributed themselves evenly among the watercraft and softly paddled off in a west-northwesterly direction. Only ears of the elephant or eyes of the Oriental bay owl could have detected their hushed meandering up the serpentine river. They didn't ask and Jed didn't offer to paddle since he was preoccupied with keeping his bulk from capsizing the tippy canoe, an event which he expected to happen at any given moment.

After many hours of paddling downriver, their progress affected by the darkness and about a million bends in the river's course, the pre-dawn revealed an approaching confluence with a larger river. They joined the southward flow of what Jed later learned to be the Banghiang River and immediately came to shore on the west bank. The land was flatter here as the river bisected a wide gap in the ridge that had formed the south bank of the Sepon on their night travels. The men seemed much less anxious at this juncture and broke out a breakfast fit for . . . well, men sneaking around the jungles of Laos. They even put together a small fire to brew some kind of local tea. One can only do so much with hand signs, but Jed tried to get them to convey where they were going and how long it would take. It appeared to him they were communicating that they would reach their destination before sunset. Which they did.

Several more hours of gently flowing alternately past low mountains and flat gaps between them, the river entered a narrow canyon with steep banks towering on both sides. They came to a cleft on the east bank which opened into a small lagoon where Jed saw other dugouts tied up at a trailhead. They debarked there, leaving one man to attend to some dockside duties of sorts, and motioned Jed to follow them uphill. Two hours of grueling switchbacks finally transitioned to a more gentle slope which then crested onto a broad plateau. Jed was astonished to see a bona fide village . . . women, children, animals, activities of all sorts.

As they approached the perimeter of the village proper, an officer of the United States Navy wearing his flight suit stepped out of a hut, extended his hand to Jed and said, "Welcome to Nhon Phat."

Chapter 13

November 1969 - Savannakhet Province, Laos

To say that Jed was dumbfounded would be an understatement. Giving thanks for being alive and not dodging bullets, yet wondering where he was and who these people were, the last thing in the world he expected was to be greeted by a fellow commissioned officer. Seeing the gold leaf of a lieutenant commander sewed on his flight suit, Jed grabbed the extended hand and said, "Hello, sir. Am I ever glad to see you and more than a little anxious to find out what's going on here."

The senior officer replied, "Come with me and we can fill each other in." He said a few words Jed didn't understand to the leader of the rescue group and then motioned Jed to follow him over to some log benches under a stand of teak trees.

"Name's Bud Beecham. Been flying from the Bonnie Dick until my A-4 got shot out from under me a month ago. I floated down west of Dong Hoi on the Laotian side. Lost my radio, enemy everywhere . . . thought I was a goner until these guys picked me up."

"Just exactly who are these guys? I'm more than a little confused."

Recognizing the USMC emblem, Beecham asked, "First off, who are you, Lieutenant?"

"Oh, sorry, sir. Jed Bazo. First Recon Battalion out of Fire Base Echo Tango."

"Not sure where that is, but what happened to get you here?"

Jed gave him a brief account of the ambush of his patrol and his subsequent capture and rescue. Then asked again, "So who are these guys and what are we doing here?"

"Ever hear of the Hmong, Lieutenant?"

"We had some sketchy briefing on them, but it didn't include a lot of details."

"Well that's who these guys are, and we're pretty damn lucky they're on our side." Beecham then proceeded to give Jed a short lesson in the geopolitics of the piece of earth on which they were sitting.

The Hmong people originated in southern China as a minority ethnic group that began migrating into Southeast Asia in the 18th century. They established communities in the high mountainous regions of Laos, and in the early 1960s the U.S. began to recruit and train them to fight against the invading North Vietnamese Army. During the Laotian Civil War the Hmong fought against the Pathet Lao, which was the Laotian communist equivalent of South Vietnam's Viet Cong and Cambodia's Khmer Rouge. Pathet Lao was organized, equipped, and even led by NVA forces. The Hmong's two-fold main mission was to help block the Ho Chí Minh trail and to rescue downed American pilots and isolated American ground troops. The Hmong exhibited strong support for the United States in its fight against the North Vietnamese and Laotian communist forces, and though their role was generally kept secret in the early stages of the conflict, they made monumental sacrifices to help the U.S. They were a small thorn in the NVA's flesh compared to the massive U.S. effort against them, so little attempt was made to locate and attack their villages hidden in the high country.

"So they pick up guys like you and me and try to get us back to our units when they can."

"How long have you been here, sir?" Jed asked.

"Today's the twenty-eighth day. That's not counting the four days of sneaking around it took us to get here."

Jed queried, "They issue you fellows emergency radios in case you have to eject, don't they?"

"Yeah, but mine somehow got dislodged in the jump and now's part of the scenery out there somewhere," Bud replied forlornly as he pointed to the jungle northward.

Gesturing toward a group of Hmong gathered around

a cookfire, Jed said, "Obviously these guys haven't made contact with any American units. How come it's taking so long to get you back to Nam?"

"These guys are small in number and damn careful with their resources. Ever since Tet '68 the North has stepped up the numbers and equipment they're moving south. They tell me the border area is literally crawling with NVA and trying to sneak me through right now would be impossible."

Wondering how they could tell him anything, Jed asked, "You speak their language, Commander?"

Beecham chuckled. "Hardly. Fella here who calls himself Kasa does some English. At least we can get our thoughts across. Best as I can tell he worked a while for a Navy group in the delta area guiding patrol boats up the Mekong. He picked up the lingo . . . kind of hard to understand most of the time, but enough to make do."

"Does he tell you anything about when he can get you out of here?" Jed asked hopefully.

"All I get is, 'No go now. We see. We see.' So in the meantime I'm glad enough to have three squares a day and not be in an NVA POW camp. Don't really have much choice but to accept the fact that I'm in their hands for now. Biggest problem is how to occupy my time while waiting. Speaking of which, let me show you around the vill; maybe we'll run into Kasa and I'll introduce you."

Beecham gave Jed a cursory tour of his temporary home. It had obviously been there for some time as there were cultivated gardens, community food storage huts, and rudimentary water and sewer systems. The commander told Jed he guesstimated that several hundred people lived there, although it was difficult to tell since there seemed to be constant movement in and out of the village. The huts, temporary as they might have looked to a Minnesota boy, appeared as if they had been lived in for a considerable period. They ended the walkabout back at the dwelling designated for lost Americans. It was a simple two-room affair with bamboo slat walls and thatched roof. It had four sleeping mats on a packed bare ground floor even with mosquito nets hanging over them. It also had a makeshift table against one wall with a crude bench. There was a lot of dirt, but it appeared to be clean dirt. Bud told him vermin were not much of a problem as long as you didn't count snakes. He didn't know whether it was because not many types lived this high up in the hills, or because of the Laotian proclivity to keep dogs and cats, that the numbers of unwanted critters was minimal. Either way was okay with him.

A daily rhythm of sorts was established, but time moved rather slowly for Jed while waiting for word of his impending extraction. He busied himself with two primary activities: physical fitness and trying to learn something of the Hmong language.

Being physically fit had always been one of Jed's passions. While exercise options were limited around the village of Nhom Phat, two opportunities were at his doorstep. The first was miles of jungle trails on which to run. The plateau on which the village was situated was no more than a half mile at its widest, but it extended laterally on the mountainside for several miles. Many years of hunting and foraging resulted in a maze of interlocking trails that provided challenging jaunts due to the mile-high altitude and the montane forest flora. The canopy of Fujian cypress, teak, and China fir towered one hundred feet or more skyward while the lower bamboo stands formed the trails into verdant tunnels. Gibbons and multi-colored winged creatures provided treetop choruses while a runner never knew when he might meet a muntjac or have to hop over a resting Malayan pit viper. Due to the undulating terrain with uncountable twists and turns it was difficult to judge distances, but Jed's two to three hour circuits kept the sweat pouring and both lungs and legs in tip-top condition.

The second part of his conditioning routine was climbing. The mountain continued for hundreds of vertical feet above the plateau upon which the village sat. In places the gradient was mild to semi-steep while in others it became serious rock climbing. One particular face was several hundred yards wide, about four hundred feet high, and with dozens of challenging routes to the top. The degree of difficulty went from easy scrambling to Class Four, or maybe even Five. Working his way up various avenues on this face gave Jed's arms, wrists, chest, and shoulders all the workout they needed to keep in top shape. In addition, the hours he spent conditioning his body made the days go a whole lot faster than sitting around the village brooding.

The village culinary spread was not typical Marine mess hall victuals. Copious amounts of rice was augmented by a variety of vegetables, fish and various dark meats, a description of the latter which Jed never quite grasped. Having had mildly unpleasant cases of the Vietnam two-step, meaning one did not want to be more than two steps away from a commode of sorts, he and Bud were adamant about boiling any water they used for consumption. Overall the table fare was both tasty and nutritional.

The Hmong language tested his ability with foreign tongues. He and Kasa struck up a friendship, the latter helping him pick up the most useful phrases such as thank you, good morning, may I help you, and when-am-I-going-to-get-the-hell-out-of-here. Jed was determined to give it some persistent effort, and as the weeks progressed, aided by his stupendous memory, he could understand and communicate at a rudimentary make-do level.

The two American guests did not want to exert undue pressure on their gracious hosts, but they hinted at every appropriate opportunity their desire to be guided back to an American unit, *any* American unit. Almost every week they would see an F-4 or A-4 fly high overhead, but with no way to send up a signal all they could do was gaze skyward while fighting down feelings of consternation. The weeks churned into months, and around the middle of his fifteenth week Jed asked Kasa directly, "When can you help us back to our units?"

The wiry veteran replied, "Not safe. Too many enemy. We die if try."

"We are thankful for your care," Jed offered sincerely, "but we need to get back to our bases."

"Not safe now. When NVA move away, we go. We watch and help when time good."

Kasa could sense Jed's and Bud's frustration, but he was not willing to undertake a fool's errand. He assured the officers that scouting patrols were keeping a close watch on NVA and Pathet Lao movements and they would be moved east to American installations as soon it would not be a suicide mission. Confident that they couldn't make it on their own, Jed and Bud had no alternative but to bide their time patiently. Well, somewhat patiently. Jed had concerns about Angela, Don and Ingrid not hearing from him for such a long time. The fact that none of them were officially related to Jed led him to wonder how much information they could access. If the Hofstads were to discover his MIA status, they would surely convey that to Angela, and she would be worried sick.

Then one day: “Jed, Jed, get over here quick! Hurry up!” Bud shouted to Jed who was just coming in from a run.

Jed sprinted to the hut entrance. Drenched in sweat but barely panting, Jed saw the sparkle in Bud’s eyes and asked, “What’s up?”

“Wait’ll I show you what Havika’s group brought in today. This could be our ticket out!”

Chapter 14

January 1970 - Seattle, Washington

Angela knew Jed had arrived safely in Vietnam when she received a short letter from him in June that was sent from Da Nang. She also knew that he could not tell her anything about his locations or operations in-country and that, due to the nature of his responsibilities, his ability to send correspondence would be limited. As the weeks wore on and no further letters came, she finally called the Hofstads to ask if they had heard from him. They also had received one letter from Da Nang and nothing more. Both were somewhat comforted by the fact that no Marine Corps officer had showed up at Don and Ingrid's with the dreaded worst news.

By September Angela's suspicions were confirmed, but she did not want to convey the news to Jed until she had heard from him again. Of course, keeping the knowledge all to herself severely mitigated a significant portion of the joy that normally accompanies pregnancy. Her roommate was her only real confidant, although as weeks turned into months it was impossible to visually hide from others what was happening. Then physiological complications intruded. Angela knew morning sickness was normal, but concern arose when she began to experience symptoms beyond the norm. Around the fourth month persistent swelling of her hands, feet, and face occurred, followed a month later by headaches and occasional fuzzy vision.

With very little money and no health insurance, Angela finally went in desperation to the King County Public Health Center downtown. After waiting for two and a half hours she was finally taken to an examination room and met by a harried and tired doctor who still worked hard at being compassionate. Some standard tests were administered with the primary finding of an abnormally high blood pressure. She was given some antihypertensive medications, advised to stay off her feet as much as possible, and told to come back in two weeks if symptoms continued. She returned to the apartment with her apprehensions slowly transforming into fear. Then came the phone call with the second most dreaded news.

It was Ingrid calling with the explanation for why no one had heard from Jed for four months. Since the Hofstads were his family of record, a major with the Twin Cities Marine Corps Recruiting Office showed up at their home with the news that Jed was missing in action (MIA). Details were sketchy, maybe because they did not have them or maybe because it was classified information, but all they knew was that a patrol he had been leading went off the radar. The bodies of his men had been recovered weeks after their failure to return, but Lieutenant Bazo had simply disappeared. They were told that they would be contacted with any new information as it was procured.

It was all Angela could do to keep from fainting. With tears streaming down her cheeks, she sobbed momentarily before being able to speak. She wasn't sure why she had withheld the news previously, but finally finding her voice she told Ingrid about her pregnancy. Again, what should have been an occasion for great rejoicing was dampened considerably by the news of Jed's disappearance. Responding to additional questions, Angela also revealed the medical complications she was experiencing. Ingrid immediately offered to fly her to Minneapolis either for some respite or to carry the baby to full term while with them. Angela expressed immense gratitude for the offer, but thought that she wasn't supposed to fly and that the symptoms seemed to be lessening somewhat. The conversation closed with the promise to stay in weekly contact, Ingrid adding that of course she would get ahold of her immediately if and when any news of Jed's situation was received.

Don and Ingrid had natural anxiety about Jedediah's whereabouts and well-being. While hoping it was not just wishful thinking, they clung to a conviction that the one who had become like a son to them was eventually going to be found and return home. Life experiences had inculcated in them a realization that things didn't always turn out the way one wished, but the balance between the ideal and the real was always a delicate one. Innate optimism and lifelong faith bolstered their conviction, and provided a modicum of peace and comfort amidst the disquiet to which they were tempted.

Some of their most meaningful support came from friends within their community of faith. For years they had participated in a couples' Bible study, and the evening after the phone conversation with Angela they gladly drove to the church for a regularly scheduled gathering of their support group.

Late morning the next day a good-friend neighbor came over to invite herself in for a cup of coffee. She noticed on the way that the morning paper was still in the middle of the driveway, and when she rang the doorbell it went unanswered.

Two weeks passed without a phone call from either of the Hofstads. Angela had not, in fact, been feeling any better, and was giving serious consideration to accepting Ingrid's offer. She finally decided to call and talk it over with Ingrid again. After several rings the answering machine came on . . . but with a voice message spoken by neither Don nor Ingrid. Confused, Angela hung up. She waited a couple of hours and tried again. This time an unfamiliar female voice answered.

"Hello?"

Wondering if she perhaps dialed the wrong number, Angela asked, "Is this the Hofstad residence?"

"May I ask who is calling please?"

"My name is Angela and I'd like to speak to Don or Ingrid."

"Angela, my name is Doris and I'm Ingrid's aunt. May I ask what your relationship to them is?"

An electric feeling crept up Angela's back and the room began slowly revolving. "Their honorary son, Jed Bazo . . . he's my fiancé. We're going to . . . what's wrong? Where's Ingrid? Did something happen?"

It then clicked for Aunt Doris who this young lady was and she replied, "I'm so very sorry to tell you this, Angela, but Don and Ingrid were killed in an automobile accident five days ago. The funeral was this morning. Again, I'm so sorry."

Angela began feeling lightheaded and didn't know what to say to this stranger. All that came out was, "I . . . I can't believe it. This really isn't . . . I'm sorry . . . I'm not feeling well. Maybe I can call back later."

"Of course, dear. Let me also give you my home phone number. I know this is a shock. Let's talk later today or tomorrow if you're up to it."

"Yes, yes. Thank you. Goodbye."

As soon as she hung up, Angle crumpled to the floor unconscious.

This couldn't be true. It couldn't happen again. Angela now felt as alone as she had when her adoptive parents died in a collision during her second year in college. With the Hofstads gone, her increasingly difficult pregnancy, and not knowing whether Jed was dead or alive, she teetered on the edge of despair.

Two days later she talked to Aunt Doris again to learn that a drunk driver doing 80 mph in a 30 mph zone plowed into them on Cedar Avenue about a mile and a half from their home as they returned from an evening church meeting. Ingrid was dead upon arrival at Methodist Hospital and Don expired the next morning. Since Angela felt like Jed's family was her family and had looked forward to enjoying a relationship with the Hofstads for many years, news of their deaths brought part of her world crashing down again. She couldn't help but wonder what she had done to deserve this hammer of God that crushed her life to bits even as it had become so promising. She knew MIA meant there was some hope, but deep inside she feared that she was alone forever.

Yet not really alone. She felt her extended belly and vowed to be strong for the child that would always be a part of Jed with her. But as she tried to work through her grieving for the Hofstads and her growing surety that Jed would not return, her health issues worsened.

By October, the sixth month, Angela began to experience periodic convulsions and extended periods of nausea and vomiting accompanied by what she interpreted as severe heartburn. On one of her trips to the Public Health Center the doctor mentioned the term preeclampsia and the possible need for hospitalization if her situation didn't improve. Angela thought she would research this when she could get to the campus library, but for the present it was all she could do to make it from bed to bathroom after forcing down a bit of unappetizing food.

In mid-December during her eighth month, Angela's roommate awoke one morning to find her unconscious on the floor and having contractions. Unable to arouse her, the roommate called an ambulance that rushed Angela to the University of Washington Medical Center. It was clear that the baby was not waiting any longer and that Angela's slip into a coma would not allow for natural childbirth. The specialist recognized a clear case of eclampsia, proceeded with a cesarean section, and the baby was successfully delivered. Angela hemorrhaged a tremendous amount of blood and suffered a massive tonic seizure. In spite of their best efforts, she died on the delivery table.

Because Angela had no next of kin, the biological father was MIA in Vietnam, and there was no one else to contact, the baby boy was immediately adopted by a young couple who had been on a waiting list for several years.

Chapter 15

January 1970 - Savannakhet Province, Laos

Jed couldn't believe his eyes when Commander Beecham pulled an ANC/PRC-90 survival radio out from behind his back. This was standard issue to combat pilots, and Jed guessed it was likely the model issued to Bud.

"Holy moly!" Jed exclaimed. "That your radio?"

"It is now," said Beecham, "but it's not the one I lost."

"So where'd this baby come from?"

Bud explained. "Havika was out with a four man scouting party that saw a pilot eject after his plane was hit by one of those damn NVA surface-to-air missiles, likely from a site just north of the DMZ. He disappeared in the trees on a mountainside about seven miles northeast of here. Our guys found him first, hanging about forty feet up a tree with his neck broken. One of them climbed up for his dog tags, pistol, and radio, which they brought to me. Air Force captain, probably from one of the fighter squadrons out of Da Nang. Likely never get his body back, but at least I'll be able to report what happened."

"Does the radio work?"

"Like brand new. And the batteries appear to be at full strength."

Having been schooled on the Prick-25 and never issued the 90, Jed asked, "What's its range?"

"Ground-to-ground about one mile. But line-of-sight from a hilltop it can reach up to fifty miles."

"Which means the next time we see one of our aircraft we should be able to make contact."

"That's the plan, Lieutenant. So from this moment on we keep our eyes peeled and ears tuned for one of our own."

"Does it have multi frequencies?" Jed inquired.

"Only has two. Generally it's set on 121.5, which is probably what the flyboys monitor."

"Can't the NVA listen in on that wave?"

"Yes they can, Jed . . . which is why we pre-program codes so they have no idea what we're talking about. I'll give an alpha-numeric code for the date of extraction and a color for the location. We change those regularly, but when the pilot radios the Bonnie Dick with my call sign and codes they'll simply go back to the week I was shot down to figure out where to pick us up. Our location is Hill 666. To get there we've got to keep going up the Banghiang about twenty miles past the Sepon. The hill is a short hike to the east with a rock table for a top that'll make for a nice LZ. I've got to talk to Kasa to see how long it'll take us to get there."

"I wonder how soon we'll be able to make contact," Jed mused, knowing it would just be a waiting game.

"Anybody's guess. But since there's a fair amount of night sorties, we better keep a round-the-clock watch."

Already feeling the adrenaline level accelerating through his system, Jed began to experience a sanguine excitement for the first time in weeks.

After several days of alternating watches, it was early evening when Jed yelled to Bud who was just dozing off to get some sleep before his midnight turn. His acute hearing caught the distant sound when it was barely audible, and within thirty seconds Jed knew it was unmistakably a U.S. fighter-bomber. Bud fired up the radio on the run while he sprinted to the clearing in the middle of the village. When he guessed the plane was within range, he tuned it to the distress signal and keyed the transmit button. His joy was indescribable when a voice came squawking back, "Delta Romeo 14. We copy your signal. Switch to voice mode. I say again, switch to voice mode. Over."

Quickly dialing to 121.5, Ben knew he had to talk fast before the aircraft flew out of range. "Echo Tango 7 copy. Echo Tango 7 request relay message to Bravo Hotel Romeo flight group. Copy? Over."

"Copy Echo Tango 7. Go ahead. Over."

"Foxtrot Zulu seven niner Sierra. Code Amber. Alpha Mike Bravo Echo Romeo. Copy? Over."

"Copy. Repeat: Foxtrot Zulu seven niner Sierra. Code Amber. Alpha Mike Bravo Echo Romeo. Over."

"Affirmative. Thanks for the help. Over."

"Our pleasure. Hang in there. Over and out."

All they had seen was an unidentifiable speck in the sky, but the message got through. And that speck provided them with a horizon-to-horizon scope of hope.

After looking over the map Commander Beecham had preserved, Kasa had told him that they could make it to the designated extraction point by early morning if they paddled all night. Hope was added by the fact that the Hmong scouts reported what seemed to be a movement of the major NVA units farther south, and the fact that the LZ was a good ten miles west of the Ho Chí Minh trail. The primary danger would be from Pathet Lao forces.

The brass on the Bon Homme Richard would be able to figure out that FZ79S meant the day after tomorrow. Which meant that Bud and Jed would be hiking down the trail to the dugouts in less than twenty-four hours.

Havika led the four-man patrol that would take them to Hill 666. There would be three men to each of the dugouts with the lieutenant and the lieutenant commander occupying the center position in each one. Beecham carried the radio and they made sure that their firearms were cleaned and in good working order. They both had mile-high aspirations for a smooth rescue with no enemy contact along the way.

With a couple hours until the daylight faded into murky night, they gathered in the center of the community and said *ua tsaug rau koj*, thank you, to every villager present. They then began descending the trail to the lagoon.

The trip upriver went without a hitch as they encountered no Pathet Lao or NVA night river patrols. The Banghiang was a fairly shallow river this far upstream but one to two hundred yards wide once they paddled out of the steep-walled canyon in which the lagoon was situated. They were blessed with a cloud cover in this post-monsoon season and kept to the middle of the waterway. This meant they could be spotted only by someone with a night vision scope. That would be unlikely since ambient light was needed for its functioning and there was total darkness as they glided north. The two Americans, who could hardly see their hands in front of their faces, were amazed at the owl-like vision of the Hmong.

Jed did not even notice when they passed the mouth of the Sepon, but he knew from his fluorescent compass readings that they were travelling roughly northeast. As the black night began turning smoky-gray, the river took a pronounced southeasterly jag and Jed remembered from the map that right before it turned northward again they would reach the closest point of access to Hill 666. The terrain on the west, south, and east sides of the hill was more open, so they needed to get up the slope and conceal themselves in the brush alongside the landing zone. There was no exact time for the extraction. The protocol was simply to be at the LZ beginning with daylight on the designated day and wait for the chopper to arrive.

All six of them were about one hundred feet from the

summit when they heard two things almost simultaneously. First was the familiar whump-whump of an approaching chopper. Second was the also familiar sound of small arms gunfire with rounds ricocheting all around them.

"Pathet Lao. *Mus! Mus*!" Havika shouted and then began coordinating his own men's shots in the direction of the enemy fire.

The Laotian communists, coincidently scouting the very area Bud and Jed planned for their deliverance, had received a radio message that a helicopter was headed in their direction. They calculated that Hill 666 was the likeliest LZ on the chopper's path, and laid in for an ambush, hoping for the best. And the best happened. What the maps did not show the American officers was that the final approach to the tabletop summit was another of the Annamite Range's familiar rock faces. The one they had just started up wasn't overly steep, yet demanded some mild scrambling. In a matter of seconds their mild scrambling became a mad dash for their lives. Since the Hmong did not need to go all the way to the LZ, they took up positions to lay down covering fire at what appeared to be three riflemen.

Bud was in the lead and about thirty feet from the lip when a 7.62 slug took out part of his left triceps. His Colt .45 clattered into a chasm as he fell back against a large boulder and began shouting into the radio he held in his right hand. "Taking fire. Come in from the north. I repeat, come in from the north. Copy? Over."

"Roger Echo Tango. Sixty seconds out. Pop a red smoke so we know it's you. Over."

"No have smoke. Just come in from the north and we'll be there. Over."

"Roger that. Get your ass up that hill."

Jed saw that Bud was hit and that his left arm was useless. He was twenty feet behind and propelled himself upward to assist. His second step happened to be on what looked like a solid rock but was in fact a garbage-can-lid-sized boulder that teetered on the edge of the crevasse into which Bud's gun had dropped. As Jed put his full weight on it and the rock began its tumble into the abyss, he threw his body downward and in the opposite direction. This saved him from a twenty or so foot drop, but as he fell backward his head smashed into another rock and his world turned black.

"Echo Tango, where are you? We're coming in but taking lots of fire from a ridge to the north. Get here now! Repeat, get here now!"

Bud looked down at Jed and realized that with only one arm he was helpless to carry the heavily muscled lieutenant thirty feet up a rock face. He made the split-second and rock-hard decision that one man being rescued was better than none. And, assuming Jed made it back to Nhon Phat, he could alert the Marines to Jed's position for possible extraction. As he cleared the lip of the summit the choppers skids were just touching down. A crewman manning the M60 machine gun was spraying the ridge several hundred yards to the north from which they were receiving automatic weapon fire. Leaving a trail of blood from his maimed arm, Bud raced to the Huey and literally dove in. Within seconds the bird lifted off and headed southeast, away from enemy incoming and toward home.

While Havika and one of his men crept through the underbrush on the Pathet Lao's left flank, he sent the other two uphill to assist Jed. There were, in fact, only three enemy firing upon Jed and Bud, and the Hmong managed to get in position behind them without being seen. They had clear shots on the Pathet Lao soldiers, and when Havika and his partner opened with their AK-47s on full automatic, all three enemy combatants saw their last light of day. Rounding the hill again to their previous climbing route they found their compatriots leading a dazed Jed back down. He had a goose egg sized lump on the back of his head but was otherwise none the worse for wear . . . physically. Emotionally he was experiencing a distinct downer as he acknowledged his predicament. In just a few moments he had gone from a Mount Everest of expectation to a Mariana Trench of disappointment. But he would deal with that later. The immediate concern was to get back to Nhon Phat without any more firefights.

After forty-eight hours of night paddling and daytime hunkering down in shoreline vegetation, Jed and the Hmong patrol slipped back into the hidden lagoon. While again thankful for being alive and in safe hands, on the trek back uphill to the village Jed could not help but wonder when and how he was ever going to make it back to his unit. Even drawing strength from the tactile sensation of the Fish Eagle medallion against his chest, he thought this was a hell of a way to celebrate the new year.

Chapter 16

June 1970 - Savannakhet Province, Laos

Days turned into weeks and weeks into months. Jed was feeling more and more like a prisoner than a guest. He realized this was not the intention or fault of his Hmong hosts, but that did little to mollify frustrations that bordered on anger. Kasa stressed repeatedly that with NVA and Pathet Lao forces building up almost daily there was virtually no realistic chance of moving Jed east to hook up with any American or South Vietnamese units. If Kasa had known what it meant, he would have said that to try would be a crap shoot with the NVA holding loaded dice.

Jed comforted himself with the fact that he wasn't languishing in one of the POW camps in Hanoi or west of the Vietnamese border in either Laos or Cambodia. It pained him somewhat that he was not doing what he was trained for or participating in any way in the war effort, but at the same time he had a plentitude of hours to contemplate the pros and cons of that very effort. Seeing what bullets, shrapnel and napalm do to living flesh causes a man – well, most men – to question whether this was the best, or even proper, way to solve differences. Having now killed personally and watched brothers-in-arms be killed, he could not help but do some mental gymnastics over the righteousness or unrighteousness of taking another human being's life. He was a trained Marine, but that didn't mean he gave up his own conscience and soul.

Thinking about Angela also produced a variety of intense emotions. Her love was indeed a sustaining force for Jed while simultaneously producing a heartache of longing. At times he could almost feel her physical presence; on other days she felt as far away as Pluto. He anguished over what he knew would be the fears she experienced by not having heard from him for so many months. He felt the same, but to a lesser degree, about his parents in Rhodesia and his guardians in Minnesota. The hopeful assumption was that Lieutenant Commander Beecham had provided news of his predicament to the Marine Corps, but he had no way of knowing whether or not that information had been relayed to the Hofstads, and hence to Angela.

After three and a half additional months at Nhon Phat, Jed asked Kasa to come to his hut for tea. Jed had now picked up enough Hmong that they talked back and forth in sort of a pidgin-English-Hmong conglomeration. Attempting to forge forcefulness with diplomacy, Jed said with an imploring tone in his voice that was unmistakable to Kasa, "I need to get back to my unit, Kasa. Is there not any way to try with a chance of succeeding?"

Kasa had sensed Jed's growing uneasiness, and had been thinking himself of an alternative that was extremely risky but that just might be feasible. The plan which he outlined to Jed involved taking the Banghiang south to its confluence with the Mekong River. "Mekong here is border with Thailand. We take to Cambodia and village there have boat to Saigon. Very danger. Cost beaucoup dollar."

Jed's eyes opened wide at this unexpected offering. He came back with rapid-fire questions. "How far? How long will it take? What are the chances? How soon could we leave?" Kasa answered them more or less in order.

"Many day. Maybe two week. Fish boat have secret floor and travel only in light. You come out night. We do once before."

"When can we go? I will get payment for them when we reach American troops."

"Rains come soon. We go now if ready." Kasa had obviously been thinking about this for a while. May generally brought the onset of the monsoon season when torrential rains raised river levels and complicated navigation of their waters, so if Jed was game, Kasa thought either now or there would be a lengthy wait.

“If tomorrow is okay, I can be ready,” Jed replied. “How far will you go with me?”

“I go all way. Fishmen no know delta so good. I know everything. Take you where to go.”

Jed drifted off to sleep that night with his nerves tingling with excitement. He had no way of calculating the degree of risk involved, but at this point he was willing to try almost anything. And Kasa did say this route had succeeded once, yes? He did know that much of the journey would be on the Mekong’s winding course through Cambodia. But the Ho Chí Minh trail was a fair distance east of the river and the NVA would not likely be looking for American servicemen to their west. But there was one other thing of which Jed was not aware. A major invasion of Cambodia by combined U.S. and South Vietnamese forces had commenced at the end of April in an attempt to weaken the enemy and disrupt traffic on the Ho Chí Minh. One consequence of this action was a retreat to the west by major NVA units.

He certainly knew of the mighty Mekong, but Jed had never imagined that its muddy waters would be his lifesaver. At least that was his aspiration as he lay stretched out listening to its lapping sounds on the other side of the bulkhead against which his head rested. Many hours were filled with wonderings about how his life’s journey had taken him from rural Rhodesia to the bubbling caldron of Southeast Asia. He knew he wasn’t out of hot water yet, but he felt confident. It wasn’t a foolhardy, thoughtless aplomb. His visionary optimism was always tempered with objectivity. To be sure, turmoil, tempest, and uncertainty boiled on the surface, but in Jed's innermost being there was a peace that his faith had always provided him. Without Kasa Jed was pretty sure he would already be a dead duck. As resourceful and imaginative as Jed might be, he knew there was no way he could have successfully navigated the barriers of language, culture, geography and ethnic rivalries, not to mention the convoluted maze of one of the mightiest rivers in all of Asia.

The trip down the Banghiang in the Hmong dugout had been uneventful. It emptied into the Mekong which then formed the border with Thailand. At the little hamlet of Banh Thong on the west bank, Kasa had engaged a distant relative with an eighteen foot fishing canoe to take them to the Cambodian border. During this part of the voyage Jed spent the daylight hours lying supine underneath a tangle of fishing nets that provided a modicum of camouflage. From the odor, he guessed they had been in service since perhaps the eighteenth century. The canoe was the necessary riverine conveyance this far north due to a major cataract, the Khone Falls, blocking larger fishing vessels from downstream. After winding on the Mekong through southern Laos and coming to Khone Falls on the Cambodia border, Jed stared at one of nature's wonders.

He had never seen anything like it in his life, and guessed that he was one of very few Americans who had ever been here. The only way to the south side of the Khone Phapheng Falls was a combination of running the rapids and portaging. Volume-wise the largest in Southeast Asia, it was actually a series of cascading waterfalls over a six-mile river stretch that was characterized by thousands of islands and countless waterways. Hence, the Laotians refered to the area as *Si Phan Don*, meaning The Four Thousand Islands. The highest falls reached almost seventy feet, but many channels had much smaller drops which allowed daredevil runs during the rainy season. Since it was the tail end of the dry season, Jed and Kasa had to accomplish numerous portages to reach the southern end where the river opened up into a smooth expanse.

Kasa steered them several miles downstream to the substantial river town of Siem Wat. This was the upper reach of the lower Mekong fishing vessels, one of which they hoped would transport Jed to the Delta. Since the languages of Southeast Asia formed a sprachbund, the Mon–Khmer of the Cambodians having much in common with Kasa's Hmong–Mien, the astute and seasoned veteran of many years on the south Mekong was able to communicate his need. Considering the cargo to be transported, subterfuge and the willingness to accept the attendant risk was part of that need. The pucker factor was enhanced, of course, by the geopolitical factors that ravaged the region.

Kasa figured the spirits of his ancestors were with him when he located the same vessel he had contracted previously. It was a fifty-foot, square-stern vessel with a three story super-structure. It was equipped with a Japanese-made diesel engine that provided on-board power for lighting, bilge pumps, and refrigeration for icing their catch until reaching market. It was in fact a working fishing vessel, but one with a carefully concealed hideaway that more than once brought in profits not related to the denizens of the deep. Kasa's guarantee that Jed would make good on the agreed price was all the captain needed. If Jed did not live up to his part of the bargain, Kasa's destroyed reputation would preclude any future river business for him.

"We go in three hour," Kasa told Jed. "You stay in bottom when light. If Khmer Rouge come, you go hide hole. I show you now."

He took Jed down to the lowest deck under which were bilge pumps and hydraulic lines. A forward trap door enabled access to a four foot high area that both looked and smelled like hell. Slimy fish drippings, oil, grease, and general scum adorned the space, making it a terrible place for a honeymoon but a perfect concealment for someone wishing to escape the notice of lackadaisical searchers. Jed thanked Kasa for showing him, but declined a closer look unless it became absolutely necessary.

The situation in Cambodia was in flux. In the early years of the war in Vietnam, Cambodia attempted neutrality under the leadership of Prince Sihanouk. As the Vietnam War raged, the prince's overriding concern was to prevent Cambodia from being drawn into wider regional conflict. But immense pressures from neighboring countries forced difficult choices in pursuit of the least dangerous course of action when neutrality became impossible. In 1965 the country entered a pact allowing the presence of permanent North Vietnamese bases in eastern Cambodia, and the use of Cambodian ports on the Gulf of Thailand to move military supplies from China to NVA and VC units. In the ensuing years, Sihanouk began commending communism and deepening his country's relationship with China. That collapsed with the extremes of the Cultural Revolution in China and led to the Cambodian Civil War in 1967. Sihanouk retained power, but in March 1970 while he was out of the country, Prime Minister Lon Nol convened the National Assembly and deposed the prince in a bloodless coup. The United States immediately recognized the new Khmer Republic and Sihanouk fled to Beijing where he began to support the fledgling Khmer Rouge, a rebel communist offshoot of the Vietnam People's Army from North Vietnam.

What this meant for Jed was that the trip from here on would be fraught with the possibility of being boarded by either NVA or Khmer Rouge looking for cargo or people supporting the South Vietnam effort. Kasa told him that they would put in at Phnom Penh for supplies and for appearance's sake, and that this is where he might get a taste of hideaway bilge water.

As it was, Phnom Penh was not a problem. As one of many fishing vessels that were inspected randomly, Jed's boat escaped scrutiny. He stayed below decks, but was never given the signal to dive into the picturesque bowels. What they did gain was information. A week before their arrival at Cambodia's capital, a massive joint U.S.-South Vietnamese force had invaded Cambodia. While they would be sailing directly into the advancing allied operation, they would also run the gauntlet of NVA units attempting to escape to the west. Kasa would be on high alert, of course, but told Jed that he thought this was a good sign because they might run into friendly forces sooner than he had expected. Late afternoon of the day they left Phnom Penh it wasn't friendlies that caused frantic action.

"*Nkaum*! *Nkaum*! You hide now. Fast go!" Kasa shouted down the ladder to Jed as the NVA patrol boat approached.

Having practiced the drill, Jed headed to the lowest deck, which was a fish cleaning area, and then to the trap door to the bilge. Crew members opened it for him and he let himself down into a world of stink and muck. When the door was set back in place, with light only from tiny slivers that snuck through the floorboards above him, Jed was glad he didn't have claustrophobia. Once the trap door was secured, the crewmen spread slimy fish innards around, and stomped all over them in rubber boots so that the hatch became indistinguishable from any other part of the deck. They then moved the cleaning table directly over the now-disguised opening.

An NVA party of four boarded with scowling faces and guns locked and loaded. Wearing fisherman's clothing, Kasa was indistinguishable from the other workers. It would not be unusual for a Hmong to be there since many of the larger vessels had multi-ethnic crews. The boarding party searched both upper and lower decks with required diligence, and seemed to be somewhat disappointed that they found no military equipment headed for the Army of the Republic of Vietnam. Kasa tensed a bit when the leader asked the captain of the ship where the opening to the bilges was. The captain took him to the lowest deck and to the stern of the ship. A trap door identical to the bow hatch was opened and a sweet stench as from Hades itself came wafting up. Holding his nose as with a vise grip, the NVA soldier lowered his head into the lightless enclosure and decided immediately that it would take more than he was getting paid for him to go crawling around that disgusting dungeon. Gratefully ascending back to fresh air, he inquired what his men who had been dispatched to the front lower decks had found. They reported that there was no access to the bilges from the bow, silently praying that they would not be sent crawling from stern to bow looking for any stowaways.

While all this was taking place, Jed was holding his breath and trying to not squirm as a few of the ship's rats scurried around him. After what seemed like an interminable time, he eventually heard footfalls and scraping sounds above him and the trap door finally opened. Kasa was grinning down at him and said, "You likee there, GI? Maybe bring chow and pillow."

"Just get me chop-chop outta here," Jed responded. "What happened while I was napping?"

Kasa recounted the above decks adventure and said he thought that meant they were safe, at least for a while. Jed had been wearing black peasant clothes over his nearly-worn-out Marine utilities, and he couldn't get the filthy, stinky things off fast enough. He then bathed over the side in chocolate river water while both his washed Marine gear and black pajamas dried in the evening air. Night fell like a dark canvass over them and they anchored in midstream about twenty-five miles from the South Vietnamese border according to the captain's calculations.

To appear normal, the crew had done some fishing along the way . . . with the added benefit of the profit the catch would bring at the Saigon markets. Early morning brought in a few more nets worth of finny produce, and by mid-day they were again steaming south with some dispatch. Jed was back in his utilities with black peasant coverings and lounging on the fish-cleaning deck with growing anticipation for his reunion with fellow Americans. He figured they must be not much more than ten miles from the border, which meant they were in the heart of contested territory. All morning aircraft were overhead and distant bombing and shelling could be heard.

Kasa again ran to the ladder leading to Jed's deck and yelled, "Jed, boat come fast. Maybe NVA. You ready go hide when I say."

Holy moly, crappoly, and downright bullshit, Jed thought. Do I really have to crawl into that hellhole again? But, of course, it was much preferable to becoming a guest of the People's Army of Vietnam, so he was ready to scramble at Kasa's signal.

Jed felt the ship slowing to a crawl and then the clunk of another vessel tying up alongside. He had heard no additional alarm call from Kasa, but he, along with a couple of the fishermen, stood by the opened trap door ready for him to bolt. Jed could hear loud voices up above but couldn't make out what they were saying. Just as Jed was about to lower himself into the abyss, Kasa came down the ladder with a sorrowful expression and said, "We too late. You come or we all die."

With no viable option, Jed followed Kasa up the ladder. Squinting into the bright sunlight as his head came out of the hatch, all he could see at first were the barrels of four rifles pointed at his head. He put his hands up and stepped into the circle. His vision adjusted and he found himself looking at a chief petty officer and three crewman wearing uniforms of the United States Navy. He then looked to the port side and saw tied up to their fishing boat one of the most beautiful sights he had seen in his entire life: a Navy River Patrol Boat with twin .50 cal machine guns forward and another on the stern, and M60s mounted on both port and starboard sides.

Kasa, grinning from ear to ear, then stepped forward and said, “We make joke.”

Chapter 17

June 1970 - Mekong River

Under other circumstances the joke might not have been received so graciously. But Jed felt a chuckle-inducing tingle from the soles of his feet to the top of his badly-needing-a-cut hair. In spite of the usually good-natured traditional antagonism between leathernecks and squids, at that moment the United States Navy was close to the top of his to-be-appreciated list. Rather than ruin his reputation by pursuing an inclination to kiss Petty Officer 1st Class Garrett King, Jed, Kasa and the sailors did a lot of smiling and back-slapping. Due to the unpredictability of the current combat situation, PO King said, "Lieutenant, I think it's in our best interest to make tracks downriver as soon as possible."

"Couldn't agree more," Jed replied. "Just give me a minute or two and I'll be with you."

It was a moment of more than a little emotion. Jed had spent the past ten months with Kasa, and the brave Hmong warrior had risked a considerable amount to protect his life and get him home. "Kasa, *ua tsaug rau koj* is so little for all you have done for me. No words can say how big my thanks are. I'll never be able to repay you."

"No pay. My happy to help. Maybe someday we see again."

"I would like that, Kasa. Please tell the people of Nhon Phat I am safe, and thank you again."

"Will do, Lieutenant Bazo. Now you go Yankee friends. Kick some NVA ass, OK."

As they parted, Jed promised to have the required funds for the ship's captain and crew delivered to the company office in Saigon. He then boarded the Navy patrol boat and the crew detached the lines that held the two watercraft together.

With the sun halfway from its zenith to the western horizon, Jed watched the trawler as his escort vessel headed south into friendly territory. Standing at the bow deck railing and holding a Marine Corps salute, Kasa was bracketed by the jade and emerald hues of the jungle that formed the river's banks. As the patrol boat rounded a bend and Jed lost sight of the craft he would have named Saving Grace, he inhaled the air of what seemed an awful lot like salvation, and exhaled a prayer of gratitude toward the Southeast Asian skies.

Speeding downriver at flank speed, Petty Officer King was at the wheel and the other crewmen manned the machine guns port, starboard, and stern. Back with Americans in a boat bristling with weapons and communications that could call in close air support if needed, Jed felt a security he had almost forgotten existed. In the middle of the river they were basically out of range of small arms fire, but one never knew when an NVA gunboat might come roaring out of a tributary. This far north they might even encounter other native fishing vessels commandeered by Khmer Rouge or VC forces that could fire upon them at much closer ranges. The Navy patrols had learned the hard way to exercise due diligence.

Jed joined King at the wheel and asked, "Where we going, PO, and how long will it take us?" He felt pretty secure on the patrol boat, but his chief interest was to get out of the area of the current operation and find a way back to his unit.

"Headed for Vinh Long, Lieutenant. There's an airfield there where you'll be able to pick up a chopper for Tan Son Nhut. From there you can get a flight to anywhere in-country. Where's your unit?"

"1st Marine Division out of Da Nang, and the last I knew my platoon was west of Khe Sanh. But that was ten months ago so who knows where they might be now."

"Ten months! What the hell you been doing, if I may ask?"

Jed gave him the short version of his recent escapades and then asked a question that had been puzzling him. "Why'd you stop and board that fishing boat I was on? Is that normal?"

"Only normal when we're looking for something specific, like you." King replied.

"What do you mean me? How would anybody have any idea I'd be coming down the Mekong?"

"Seems it came from a Lieutenant Commander Beecham on the Bonnie Dick. As the story goes, after a couple of months healing up he returned to his unit. By then another pilot who had been helped by the same Hmong group had been reassigned to his ship and told about being taken out on the Mekong. Beecham then apparently had the word passed to all the Navy units operating on the river to be on the alert for fishing trawlers that might be giving a repeat performance. We all figured it was a pretty long shot, but looks like we scored a bulls-eye with you, sir."

"Well, thank the Lord for long shots," said Jed. "Sure hope I have a chance to thank Commandder Beecham someday."

He then asked how long it would take to get to Vinh Long. "It's around seventy-five river miles," PO King answered. "We'll anchor for the night at one of our supply points once we cross back into Vietnam. Assuming we don't get waylaid by any of our slant-eyed friends, we should have you there by noon tomorrow. I don't really expect any trouble because since the Cambodian incursion started we've had the bad guys pretty much on the run."

Having been out of the information loop for so long, Jed asked, "You mean we're finally winning this thing?"

"Hardly, Lieutenant. Seems like there's more and more pressure back home to get us out of here. In fact, scuttlebutt is that a week or so ago at some college in Ohio there was a riot and some students got killed by trigger happy National Guardsmen. Fact is that some ground forces are already being reduced."

Wondering what that might mean for himself, Jed went on, "You ready to go home, Mr. King?"

"Damn right, sir. I thought at first that we were doing a good thing here, saving us and the world from the commies. Even went so far as to sign up for a second tour. I've got four months left and now I can't wait to get the hell out of here."

"What changed your attitude?" Jed inquired.

"Long story. But eyeballing the waste of lives and material over and over turned me around. That plus the fact that we ain't ever gonna win this thing. Not unless we nuke North Vietnam off the map and then bring half our country over here. Even then I'd wonder. You know how long these sonsabitches have been fighting? They got a whale of a lot more patience than our folks back home do. And think about it . . . would you quit if it was some foreign power that invaded our country?"

These thoughts, along with what had happened to his Recon patrol, played on Jed's mind as they sped toward their night's anchorage. His months of isolation had also provided a lot of time for contemplation during which he tried to figure out what might be a proper balance between his commitment to God, country, and Angela. Angela! It should be a matter of only a few days now before he could contact her in some way or another from Da Nang. But what then . . . back to the death-ridden jungles up by the DMZ? And he couldn't ignore any longer the question that wouldn't go away: for what purpose?

They had passed several other patrol boats the closer they got to the delta, and a couple were tied up at Vinh Long when they pulled in, as King had estimated, shortly before noon the next day. As it turned out, a CH-47 Chinook that had delivered artillery pieces that morning was heading for Tan Son Nhut within the hour. Upon hearing a sixty-second account of Jed's odyssey the Army airfield dispatcher declared that the Chinook wasn't leaving without him. Profusely thanking Petty Officer King and his crew for their able assistance, Jed boarded the chopper. The flight was not a long one, and by 1500 hours the rescued Marine was ensconced within a U.S. base that was considered the busiest airport in the world.

During his ten months at Nhon Phat, he had miraculously attained an old straight razor that enabled him to maintain a semblance of being clean shaven. Since shaving had not been an option on the river trip, he looked pretty grizzly when arriving at Tan Son Nhut. The length of his hair and utilities that barely hung together and still smelled of bilge grunge didn't enhance his appearance. Sticking with his Marine issue uniform since he wasn't about to dress in Army or Air Force fatigues, he was able to get a haircut and shave before boarding a Hercules C-130 the next morning for the sprawling base at Da Nang. He had managed to locate a communications unit who notified his command that he was on the way, so he was not going to show up unannounced. Almost a year after landing there the first time, Jed stepped onto the tarmac and looked for transportation to the 1st Marine Division headquarters.

If the division command was surprised that he had made it out alive, he was just as surprised to find that 1st Recon Battalion had been pulled out and shipped home. As history reveals, the Marines are first in and first out. With the inevitable drawdown in forces, the leading USMC elements were in the vanguard of the creeping withdrawal. Jed was informed that his battalion had been sent stateside the previous month and that he would be processed to join them at Camp Pendleton, California. When he inquired about who had been notified in the U.S. about his MIA status, the personnel officer said that he had no knowledge one way or the other. Communication channels were complex and often messages got lost in the mix, so Jed still had no idea if the Hofstads and Angela had been given any information of his status. He was given some travel allowance and told all his back pay could be recouped upon arrival in Pendleton.

On the trip east the plane stopped in Hawaii to refuel. They were going to be there several hours, so Jed ran for a phone. He dialed Angela's number from memory and held his breath. After three rings an automated voice announced that the number had been disconnected. He then called the Hofstads' number and got the same message. He checked with phone information services for both Washington and Minnesota and got negatives for Angela and the Hofstads respectively. Confused and somewhat agitated, he boarded the last leg of the flight to California wondering what his next step might be.

The day after his arrival, Jed sat in the office of Lieutenant Colonel Brad Murphy, the commanding officer of First Reconnaissance Battalion. He was a grizzled veteran of both Korea and Vietnam who was both respected and liked by his subordinates. His visage conveyed strength and compassion, and he looked at the young officer in front of him with the affection he held for all dedicated Marines. Jed's personal gear had been shipped back with the unit and he was now smartly dressed in freshly pressed summer khakis. He had filed a report relating the substance of what happened after his patrol was ambushed and was waiting to find out what the Marine Corps had in store for him now.

"I understand the need to locate your fiancée, Lieutenant. You also have some well-deserved time off coming. Take thirty days and go find that gal of yours. When you report back for duty we'll have figured out the financial matters and what your next assignment will be."

"Thank you, sir. I'd like to leave as soon as possible."

"Understood. You can plan to do so tomorrow, but not until the mid-morning awards ceremony. You need to be there in dress whites."

"Aye aye, sir. May I ask for what purpose?"

"You have been awarded the Silver Star for action on your first patrol in August of last year."

Although the thought of a medal had never crossed his mind, Jed said, "Thank you, sir. I hope my men were given commensurate awards as well."

"I'll check into that, Lieutenant Bazo. There will also, of course, be a formal inquiry into the circumstances of your last patrol, capture and escape. In addition to yours, we have a preliminary report on some of it from a Lieutenant Commander Beecham. In time there could be another ribbon or two for your chest."

"Not necessary, Colonel, but thank you. Now if I may be excused I have some duties to attend to before leaving tomorrow."

"That'll be all, Lieutenant. I'll see you on the parade ground at ten hundred tomorrow."

"Yes, sir," Jed said as he snapped to attention, executed a perfect about face and headed for the door.

As he was about to exit, Colonel Murphy called out, "One more thing, Marine."

"Sir?" Jed replied as he turned around.

"I'm proud to have you in my command, Son. You are a credit to your Corps and country."

Chapter 18

July 1970 - Camp Pendleton, California

Jed sat in an overstuffed and overused chair in his Bachelor Officer Quarters apartment at Camp Pendleton. The devastating events of the past month led him to an emotional precipice he had never experienced before. Feeling perplexed about life in general and the course of his in particular, the two things that kept him on a semblance of solid ground were God and Corps. And the understanding and meaning of both of those was somewhat up for grabs.

The first shock had come at the Los Angeles airport, followed by a repeat performance at the Seattle one. Traveling in summer "Charlies," or short-sleeve khakis, he was easily recognizable as a Marine, and one who likely had served in Vietnam. Whether he had actually been there or not, anyone in a Marine uniform was a ready-made target for impudent and insensitive anti-war protestors. Jed found this out when vitriolic epithets were hurled at him, occasionally accompanied by spittle if the hurler could get close enough. He held his head high in spite of the unexpectedness of these attacks. It occurred to him as he ran for a cab at the Seattle airport that dodging bullets in Nam was maybe less unpleasant than this.

Upon arriving at Angela's apartment he found a young couple living there who had no idea who had preceded them. He then tracked down the agency that managed the complex. The woman staffing the office checked the records and found that the present occupants had moved in the past February, but the former residents left no forwarding address and she had no idea where they might be. Jed checked into a motel near the campus and got a restless night's sleep. His tossing and turning was exacerbated by the fact that, despite his efforts, he could not find any way to contact Don and Ingrid. The next morning he went to the university registrar's office to see what he might learn.

When he revealed to the receptionist who he was and what information he sought, the latter asked him to have a chair. After a short while a matronly woman appeared and introduced herself as Virginia Thorsen, the university's registrar. She invited Jed into her office.

"Lieutenant Bazo, do I understand correctly that you and Miss Wyatt were engaged?" At her use of the past tense, Jed's heart rate began to spike.

"Yes ma'am. Can you please tell me where I can find her?" Jed asked with not a little anxiety.

"I'm very sorry to tell you this, Lieutenant, but Angela died this past January."

Struggling to maintain his composure, Jed felt like he had been hit in the chest with an AK-47 burst. He sat stone still for a minute and Mrs. Thorsen was sensitive enough to hold her words while Jed processed the initial shock. The color drained from his face and he worked to steady his breathing as he whispered, "What happened?"

Using the familiarity of his given name in the hope that it would produce a modicum of comfort, she said, "She died in childbirth at the Medical Center here on campus. I'm so sorry, Jed. I'm so sorry."

The news of a child hit him like a lightning bolt. Emotional shock can result in one either breaking down to some degree, or embodying the title of the old Simon and Garfunkel song, "I Am a Rock," even if the latter is a façade. It was not in Jed's nature to break down. But he did feel like his brain synapses were moving through molasses.

"How come no one told me?" he replied and then immediately recognized the irrationality of the question. They were not married and there was no public record of their engagement, and even if Angela's roommate had communicated the death to the Marine Corps they would not have been able to deliver the news since he was MIA. "I'm sorry.

That was foolish."

"Not at all, Jed. I know this all comes as a terrible shock."

Taking a deep breath and swallowing hard, Jed then asked, "Did the baby live? Was it full term? Do you know what happened to it?" His apprehension focused, of course, on how many months Angela had been pregnant when she died.

"My understanding," Thorsen went on, "is that she was only a couple of weeks from full term. The baby was adopted immediately. But, of course, the adoption society keeps those details strictly confidential."

Jed did the math in his head and realized that during their time together before he began Force Recon training he was responsible for Angela's pregnancy. Even though he knew it never would have happened, there was comfort in knowing that she had not given him up for lost and joined with someone else. Yet it was discomfiting to learn that a child he helped procreate and whose gender he didn't even know was out there somewhere . . . somewhere he would probably never discover.

After continuing the conversation for a few more minutes, Jed thanked her for sharing the information while at the same time wondering how you could be thankful to hear of your beloved's death. He left the building with no idea what to do or where to go. Walking around the campus for a while, he didn't realize at first that his wanderings had taken him to the Husky football stadium. He went over to the bus stop bench where he and Angela had first met and sat down. Not really caring whether anyone was around to see or not, for the first time since he was a child in the Rhodesian hill country, he cried like a baby.

The next day Jed flew to Minneapolis to try to find out what happened to the Hofstads. Renting a car at the airport, he drove to his old home on Lake Hiawatha. It was vacant with a for- sale sign in the front yard. He saw lights on at the Fords' home next door, so he went to see what he could learn from the long-time neighbors. When Juanita saw him standing on the stoop she burst into tears. Over supper she and her husband, Carl, revealed what had happened. Carl said that in spite of knowing Jed's MIA status, they had indeed informed the Marine Corps of Don's and Ingrid's deaths in case he turned up. They grieved together for several hours, and the Fords insisted that he stay with them for the night.

Having given it some thought through another restless night, Jed spent part of the next morning tracking down Darrell Lee, his former campus pastor. The events of the past forty-eight hours had rubbed his emotions raw to the point where they felt like an open wound bathed in salt. His sense of aloneness precipitated a desire to book the first flight he could to Salisbury, but Marine discipline caused him to take a step back and assess the situation first. Pastor D was the only confidant to whom he felt he could turn, so when he discovered that the pastor was presently serving a congregation in Madison, Wisconsin, he kept calling until the familiar voice finally came over the phone. After lunch, profusely thanking the Fords and promising to stay in touch, Jed was heading down Interstate 94 for the four hour drive to Madison.

"How do I make sense out of all of this, Pastor D?" Jed

asked. Their reunion was heartfelt and Jed felt warmed by someone who he sensed truly cared about him. Darrell had welcomed Jed into the parsonage in which he lived, and they were now walking side-by-side around beautiful Lake Mendota after supper.

"You don't, Jed. Might as well try to figure out what's on the other side of the stars. Since logic or reason isn't part of the equation, 'bout all we can do when crap like this happens is figure out how to weather the storm. And the storms don't get much nastier than this."

He let that roll around in his head for a bit as they walked on in silence. Then, "I felt that way back in Nam too. No sense whatsoever. People who didn't even know each other and having no argument I could figure out, slaughtering one another like it was the normal thing to do. I haven't even begun to get my mind wrapped around that and then get hit with the loss of three of the most important people in my life. It's all such a jumble that I'm starting to wonder what there really is to live for."

"It's understandable, Jed, especially since it's just been a matter of hours since you learned all this. My encouragement is to give it some time and keep talking to people who can help you process what's happened. And don't forget to ask the Lord's help with all of this."

"Well, that's another problem for me," Jed proffered. "I'm really wondering what kind of God does these kinds of things."

"Hang on there a minute, friend. Are you suggesting God's been manipulating these happenings? You think He pushed some heavenly button to cause Angela and Don and Ingrid to die?"

"When you put it that way, no. But God surely allows terrible things like war and the death of a beautiful young woman to happen. If He's all powerful, why doesn't He prevent these tragedies?"

"You mean control the world like some cosmic puppeteer? Just make everything perfect so that no one suffers anything, ever? Would you really want that, Jed?"

"Why not? What would be wrong with a world with no suffering?"

"Think about it. We've talked before, Jed, about the God revealed in the Bible being one who is love, start to finish. Does what you're suggesting sound like love?"

"Wouldn't it be loving to make everybody happy? Make everybody get along?"

"Okay, try this. If you could have *made* Angela love you – drugs, hypnotism, whatever – no choice in the matter . . . she *had* to love you . . . would you have done it?"

"Of course not," Jed answered.

"Why not?"

"I never would have known if she really loved me for me."

"Yeah, but you'd still have her. She would have been yours to love and cherish."

"But I would have had a robot. That's not love."

"Precisely," Pastor D affirmed. "So does it make sense that the God who is love wants a world full of robots?"

"Well, when you put it that way . . ."

"I don't know any other way to put it. God gives us life and then lets us live it. All too often we make bad decisions that screw things up for ourselves and often for others. Things like war and addictions and infidelities. The list is legion. And sometimes it's just unfortunate mistakes. Fellow misses a step on a ladder, falls twenty feet and breaks his neck. That's not God's doing. In fact, when I used to get frustrated and ask God why He didn't straighten out the horrible mess the world's in, I'd get the same answer back every time."

"What was that," Jed asked with honest curiosity.

"God would say, 'Darrell, I was just about to ask you the same thing.'"

"You're not saying you actually heard God . . . or are you?"

"No, no. To say we hear God telling us something is a figure of speech. I mean that through a continuing study of the Bible accompanied by serious thought and prayer I'd get a sense of what God wanted me to do. Sometimes you 'hear it' right; sometimes you don't. But in terms of what we're talking about, I'm convinced that the message is pretty clear."

As they continued on the path around the lake, Jed began to feel a tiny easing of the tensions that had him tied up in knots. He knew the healing journey ahead was likely going to be a long one, but he felt like Pastor Darrell's presence and thought-provoking words gave him a baby-steps start. As the city lights coming on with the approaching darkness sparkled around the lake perimeter, they returned to the parsonage. Before turning in, Darrell said, "Jed, you're welcome to stay here until your leave is up, if you wish. I appreciate your company and I've got a feeling some more walks around the lake will do us both some good."

Jed spent two more weeks with Pastor D before returning to Pendleton. Looking back some years later, he would say that those weeks preserved his sanity and pointed him toward a direction in his life's path that he never would have imagined.

Still in the initial stage of the grieving process, when Jed returned a bit early to Camp Pendleton he hung on for dear life to the concrete foundation upon which he could count: the United States Marine Corps. He attained the rank of 1st Lieutenant and was assigned a platoon in Alpha Company, 1st Recon Battalion. The day he took command he was also pinned with the Navy Commendation Medal for his meritorious service in Nam. Jed guessed they figured there must be some merit in playing hide and seek with the enemy for ten months and coming out alive.

Stateside duty means training, training, and more training. The battalion had to be in absolute readiness for deployment at any given moment. The young lieutenant was relentless in pursuit of his platoon's attainment of the highest standards in every area of military competence. He pushed his men to the limits of physical fitness, marksmanship with every weapon in their arsenal, land navigation expertise, employment of demolitions, and perfecting basic infantry techniques. They ran. They swam. They jumped from airplanes. The crawled through mud. They disassembled and reassembled weapons blindfolded. In short, they became a premier platoon in the battalion for which any commanding officer would sacrifice some teeth, or maybe even a finger, to have in his company.

In addition to demanding excellence in the unit's training program, Jed became obsessive about his own physical fitness to a degree no one at Force Recon could recall.

He would run twenty miles at six minutes per mile and stop only because of time constraints. At least four days a week he would spend an hour or two following a weightlifting regimen designed to add lean body mass to his already substantial physique. By the spring of 1971 his six-foot-two frame carried two hundred and ten pounds of mostly muscle. He was as much a poster-boy Marine as had ever worn the eagle, globe, and anchor. It was getting difficult to find anyone willing to match hand-to-hand combat skills with him anymore, and you definitely wanted Lieutenant Bazo on your side . . . especially if he was pissed off.

The directive that came down from USMC headquarters at "8th and I Streets" in D.C. was not totally unexpected, yet still caused some restless ruminating among the officer ranks. As the politicians saw the writing on the Vietnamese wall, bills cutting funds to the Department of Defense started being passed. Everyone with a whit of sense knew the end was in sight, and with the drawdown in forces already begun, Marines knew where the axe would first fall. Officers were given the opportunity to transition from active duty to reserve status earlier than original commitments would have allowed. Put simply, the drawdown would save money and begin to salve the conscience of a distressed and ever-more-belligerent populace.

Jed sat facing his company commander, Captain Carl Mason, who was required to discern what each of his subordinates might wish with respect to the offer of an early out.

"So what are you thinking, Jed? Are you disposed to stay or cut and run?" Mason asked.

"Cut and run makes it sound like a defeat, Captain."

"Sorry. I didn't mean it that way. But some of our colleagues will jump at the chance to trade in their uniforms for civvies again. I kind of figured you might be looking at the Corps as a career."

Jed had given this serious consideration in the beginning. But what he had experienced in Vietnam, along with the added trauma of the loss of Angela and the Hofstads, provoked a reexamination of his life and what he might want to do with it. When the headquarters' directive was published, it brought him to a cusp that he knew had been in the making. "At one time, yes. But what's happened in the past three years has changed a lot of things for me. I'm going to take the early out."

Caught by surprise, Mason raised his eyebrows and replied, "Never expected that, Bazo. You've really thought this through and sure about it?"

"Yes, sir," Jed responded. "The Corps has been good to me and I've tried to give it my all. But it's time to move on."

"You sound pretty sure about this. Mind telling me move on to what?"

"I was kind of hoping you'd tell me that, Captain," Jed joked. "Can't really say at this point. But it's going to be in some direction that doesn't include war again. At least if I can help it."

"I imagine you know that as a commissioned officer you can be recalled to active duty at any time by an act of congress."

"Sure do. If called, of course I'll be here, but I'm hoping we can find other ways to settle our differences."

"Well, Jed, it's been an honor to serve with you and I

wish you all the best. They want those who choose this option to muster out fairly quickly, so in the next day or two you need to get over to the battalion offices and fill out the paperwork. We expect the processing won't take more than a few weeks."

"Thanks, Captain. I appreciate your leadership and support this past year and feel good that the Corps has men like you to carry on." They shook hands and Jed headed out on a long, solitary run around the base to let what he had just done sink in.

Three weeks later Jed, with mixed emotions, said so-long to the Marine Corps as he caught the shuttle for the San Diego airport. With such dramatic changes in his life in such a short time frame, there was only one person to whom he felt he could turn as he contemplated a very uncertain future. As he buckled up in the Boeing 727 the stewardess announced, "Our flying time to Madison, Wisconsin, will be approximately four hours. If there is anything we can do to make the flight more comfortable for you, please let us know."

Chapter 19

July 1971 - Madison, Wisconsin

Since Jed was unsure what next direction in life he should head, Darrell told him that he was welcome to stay with him as long as he wished. In Jed's muddled mental state he hoped that his friend could provide some assistance in recognizing what the next step might be. With Jed due to arrive in Madison at the supper hour, Pastor D was unable to pick him up at the airport because of a church function. Jed said that he was fine with taking a taxi to the pastor's digs.

After debarking, Jed proceeded to the baggage claim area to recover his suitcase. He was now wearing civilian clothes – permanently – and he knew this was going to take some getting used to. It tweaked a nerve or two for him to see various armed forces personnel walking around the airport in uniform. After retrieving his duffle he headed outside to find a cab, and noticed some kind of commotion off to his right. There was a small crowd of demonstrators with anti-war signs, several of whom had a young man backed up against a wall. The fellow was wearing the insignia of a private first class on his U.S. Army uniform and looked to be all of eighteen years old. Jed sensed some serious harassment happening, and as he edged closer to the confrontation he saw that the six-to-one outnumbered young soldier was experiencing some serious anxiety.

"Baby-killer," "murderer," "rapist," and other epithets were being shouted at the lad accompanied by globs of spittle and phlegm. One of the protesters even started poking the private in his midsection with the butt end a stick on which the other end was a placard which read: "I Don't Give a Damn About Uncle Sam."

"Whoa, folks. Let's just calm down here, okay?" Jed interjected as he eased himself between the antagonists and their quarry. To do so he had to gently push back the fellow who had been doing the poking.

"Like, who the hell are you?" one of the group asked.

"I'm just a patriotic American like you," Jed replied, "who thinks we ought to respect men like this soldier here for doing his duty."

"Bull and horseshit," another shouted, the volume level rising. "His duty is to tell Nixon and his warmongers to go screw themselves. This jerk is a traitor for killing innocent people in a war we never declared and have no business fighting. Now get out of our freak'n way, asshole."

"Cool it, will you," Jed said with his temper rising and a taste of bile on the way up. "Parade around all you want, but let this young man go his way."

Obviously not registering that Jed was six feet two inches of solid muscle, one of the assailants who felt like Jed was raining on their party stepped forward, grabbed Jed's left wrist with his right hand and started yanking him away from the soldier and toward the larger group of demonstrators. Mistake. So fast that no one really saw what happened, Jed's rigid right hand came down hard on the inside of the fellow's right elbow. The arm was immediately paralyzed from the shoulder down, and the hapless agitator let out a piercing yelp.

Just as Jed was turning toward the soldier to escort him away from the scene, the one who didn't seem too enamored of Uncle Sam swung his sign in an arc aimed for the top of Jed's head. Second mistake. Seeing it coming, Jed twisted to the side so that it caught him a glancing blow on the shoulder. It ripped his shirt and broke the skin, along with pushing Jed's blood pressure toward the stratosphere. As one of the sign-swinger's comrades came rushing at Jed with a roundhouse punch intended for Jed's head, the ex-Marine and capoeira expert deftly ducked under the swing and plowed four knuckles into the neophyte's Adam's apple. A fair amount of restraint went into Jed's blow, but sufficient force was used that the recipient fell to his knees gasping for breath. The sign holder now stood aside waiting for someone with more bravado to jump in. A guttural roar sounded behind Jed and he turned to see a three hundred pound tub of a guy barreling at him like an NFL linebacker. When tubby was three feet away and a nanosecond from crashing into him with the force of an enraged bull, Jed simply dipped to the left and clipped the attacker's right ankle with his own right foot. A meek moan accompanied a splatting sound as his momentum carried the man forward into the brick wall against which they had pinned the soldier. He fell backward unconscious and with blood pouring out of his broken nose. Jed faced the now backed-up demonstrators, none of whom seemed to want to follow in their colleagues' steps.

There was shouting, screaming, people running and jumping up and down. But the standoff lasted only a matter of moments and a half dozen airport security personnel were on the scene with billy clubs and pistols in hand. With Jed standing there basically unharmed and three demonstrators littering the environs, it seemed obvious who had done the damage. Less than forty-eight hours after receiving an honorable discharge for meritorious service to his country, Jed found himself handcuffed and in a paddy wagon headed for the city police station.

"So, how was the chow?" Pastor D asked as he and Jed munched on "The World's Best Bratwurst" the next evening at Brat und Brau on Regent Street.

"Well, I'm not suffering from ptomaine yet, but the meals were a fair bit tastier in Nhon Phat."

Darrell didn't have to bail Jed out because by noon the following day he had been released with no charges pending.

No fewer than ten witnesses interviewed were adamant that Jed's actions had been in self-defense, and the wound-licking protestors mumbled that they weren't interested in pressing charges and then faded off into the sunset. After keeping him overnight while the investigation was completed, the following morning the police sergeant on duty gave him his walking papers with a surreptitious pat on the back for a job well done.

"Got a question for you," the pastor said as he wiped a dollop of mustard off the front of his shirt.

"Shoot," Jed replied.

"How do you feel about what you did back there at the airport?"

"I kicked that around somewhat during my hours in the lockup. Hard to say since I'm doing a juggling act between feeling okay and not okay about it."

Adding to his Friar Tuck girth with a couple slurps of a double-chocolate milkshake, Pastor D responded, "Do you remember the conversation we had back at UDub shortly after you signed on with the Marine Corps?"

"You mean when we talked about black and white, law and gospel?"

"That's the one. So now I want to ask you how you see what happened yesterday within that context."

A minute or so of silence followed during which Darrell simply waited. Finally Jed spoke. "I guess I'd put what happened in the gray area. If I had just ignored the whole scene and walked on by then that young soldier would have continued to be humiliated and maybe even injured. God knows that after what he likely experienced in Nam he didn't need personal attacks to be added to that. It just seemed like the right thing to do to help him out."

"And what about when they turned on you. Should you have just walked away?"

"Pastor D, it all happened so suddenly. When fists and bodies and boards came flying at me I just reacted instinctively. I didn't have time to think it all through at the moment, but if I would have hightailed out of there it could have left the soldier stranded with an even angrier mob."

"So do I hear you saying you were justified in doing what you did?"

"Well, not really . . ." and after a pause, "but then again, yes. The kid needed help and I gave it. Not my fault that the bullies turned on me."

"Does this seem like one of those gray areas where you're damned if you do and damned if you don't?"

"Absolutely. But I gotta say that even given the vagaries of the situation, I'd probably do the same thing if it happened again."

"Fair enough. But how do you balance this with where your faith might be pointing you?"

"Like you've said, Pastor D, faith doesn't give us a textbook answer for every situation in life. And I did remember the account of Jesus coming to the defense of that woman they were going to stone to death. He defended her, right?"

"Yes he did. But don't forget that he used just words and the attackers drifted away."

"Yeah, well, he was lucky it worked for him. Didn't turn out that way for me."

"So Jed, what do you think Jesus would have done if they had started physically assaulting him and the woman?"

Darrell could see the wheels spinning in Jed's head for a bit. Then Jed answered, "Your guess is as good as mine. But even if he would not have fought back and suffered a beating," then after some hesitation, "I'm not Jesus."

Jed spent the next two weeks with Pastor Darrell. Along with their many conversations in between the pastor's ministerial duties, Jed busied himself with his daily physical fitness routine. Something made him always want to push his body's limits, and it gave him a lot of pleasure when he reached a personal best for any particular activity.

He ran around Lake Mendota at least three times a week. The actual shoreline was guesstimated to be close to twenty-two miles, but private property forcing one to the surrounding streets made the run almost thirty miles on the nose. He had been averaging six-minute miles, or three hours for the circuit. He smiled to himself on the day his stopwatch read two hours and fifty-two minutes, or five minutes and forty-four seconds per mile, at the end of the run.

He complemented his runs with alternating daily workouts at a weightlifting gym and at a local martial arts center. Lifters at the gym were often amazed at the weights he used for his size, a number of them commenting to their buddies that if that brick shithouse bench-pressing four hundred pounds was ticked off, they wanted out of the way. The martial arts instructors knew nothing of capoeira and were very interested in Jed's demonstrations of the basic techniques. They thought they'd better explore this little-known skill after Jed defeated all comers who used karate, tai kwon do, judo, or Jiu-Jitsu in mock combat.

Jed didn't care whether anyone else knew of his personal bests. Part of his sense of well-being was tied to his physical prowess, and the only person with whom he was in competition was himself.

The idea had been simmering in the back of his mind since he found out he would be leaving the Corps, and now the decision had been made. Jed felt that he needed to travel to Rhodesia to spend some time with his Ndebele parents and family. Far from the madding crowd, Jed also knew he would have unlimited and unfettered time to consider his future. After booking an open-ended round trip to Salisbury, he felt more than ever that this was a prudent next step.

During their conversation the night before leaving, Jed thanked Pastor Darrell profusely for his generosity and guidance, adding, "The time here gave me a chance to sort of get my feet on the ground. I'm not sure where I would have gone or what I would have done if you hadn't been here for me."

"The pleasure has been mine, Jed. I'm glad you can go spend some time with your family, and I'll bet they'll be overjoyed to see you."

"Well, I'm sure anxious to get back; it's been eleven years since we've seen each other. I've written them fairly regularly and sent them pictures from time to time, but we've got a lot of catching up to do."

"How old are Jacob and Naomi now?"

"Funny, I can't really say. I never asked them and it's doggone hard to judge an Ndebele's age by looking. Guess I'll find out."

Although a little hesitant to ask, Darrell thought he'd do so anyway. "How you fixed financially? I'm in a position to help out if you need it."

"Thanks, Pastor D," Jed replied. "That's very gracious of you, but I'm okay. After Nam I received just about a year's back pay which I didn't need to use since I was back on the regular payroll. I just put it in a savings account which I've kept adding to because I didn't really spend much month-to-month. It'll go a long way in Rhodesia."

"Good deal. Sounds like you're set. But I'm kind of like you. With no family, I've managed to stockpile a fair bit, so if you ever find yourself short, don't hesitate to give me a shout."

"I'll remember that, Pastor. You've done so much for me already. It's hard to come up with words that adequately express my gratitude."

"It's been a two-way street, Jed." Then Darrell remembered something he wanted to ask but always had seemed to forget. "By the way, I've often wondered about your last name. Does it have an Ndebele meaning?"

"It does. Bazo means axe. Part of the meaning for us is that an axe can be used for cutting down evil. My parents taught me that to the Bazo clan it means nothing can stand in the way of doing what's right."

They talked the clock past midnight, and after several hours sleep and some last minute packing, Jed boarded an early morning flight for Africa. As the wheels left the runway, Jed remembered that first flight when the plane lifted off the Salisbury runway carrying an excited and scared fourteen year old toward America. How uncertain his future had been, and how much had happened in the interim. This time fear wasn't a factor, but the uncertainty about his future was as palpable as on that January day in 1960.

Once he had decided to return to Africa, Jed had sent a letter to Jacob and Naomi. Due to the unpredictability of the Rhodesian postal system, especially in the heartland rural areas, Jed had no idea if his family knew that he was arriving. After a night in Salisbury he took a bus to Bulawayo where he then transferred for the leg to Gwanda. His village was some ten miles west on the Mtshabezi River, just a bit upstream from its confluence with the larger Thuli, a major tributary of the famed Limpopo. A dirt track masquerading as a road ran north of the Mtshabezi, winding roughly in the same southwestly direction as the river. The Bazo clan was situated on the riverbank some four miles south of the track.

Travelling with only a newly purchased medium-sized backpack, Jed caught a ride from Gwanda in a rusty pick-up with bald tires and an engine that sounded a lot like the dying gasps of a man with smoker's lungs. It was going to a community only four miles down the road, so after thanking the driver and giving him what would be an Ndebele's day's pay for the ride, Jed continued on his way afoot. Which was fine with him. Memories came flooding back as he recognized more and more landmarks the farther west he traveled, and he had no problem recognizing the turnoff south onto the bush track that would take him home. With just a few miles to go, he felt a joyful spring creep into his steps.

Jedediah never quite knew how it happened, but news in the Rhodesian bushveld regularly traveled faster than people did. Therefore, Jacob and Naomi knew that Jed had left Gwanda and they calculated his rough arrival time. As he neared his village, Jed felt a choking sensation in his throat as a plethora of images from childhood ran through his mind. And then he heard it. Unseen lookouts had seen him and given the signal to begin. Floating on the air of the veld came the voices of his clan singing the Ndebele song of welcome. He rounded the last bend and was greeted by scores of his Bazo family dressed in their tribal finery and swaying to the beating drums as they lifted their voices in a joyful chorus. His parents were in the center of the semicircle, and as Naomi opened wide her arms Jed ran into them and had to be careful not to crush her ribs with his affectionate gorilla hug. Then it was Jacob's turn to embrace his long-lost son.

After the initial welcome by the whole clan, which included introductions to younger siblings and cousins whom he had not met but who had heard of his exploits, the men went to the gathering area in the center of the village to begin the trading of stories while the women continued preparation of the celebratory meal. Soon they were feasting on spiced goat, beef, biltong, chicken and springbok, supplemented with copious amounts of mealiepap, papaya, roasted squash, native greens and, one of Jed's favorites, sorghum flatbread dipped in syrup made from the same plant. As the sun settled in the far west, Jed was taken to a vacant hut that had been cleaned and prepped after receipt of the letter announcing his pending arrival. He drifted off to sleep that night with a juxtaposition of emotions dominated by the gladness of his reunion with family and the anguish that Angela was not by his side.

The ensuing days were filled with Jedediah and his family catching up on each other's lives. His amazing memory applied to isiNdebele so that from day one he was chattering along in his native tongue as if he had never left. Storytelling is intrinsic to Ndebele culture as a way to retain and pass on history with a flair that textbooks miss. Jed and various Bazo clan members traded verbal chronicles with force and glee. The Ndebele sat wide-eyed as they listened to Jed's animated accounts of his adventures in parts of the world they could barely imagine. Of course he embellished the narrations for effect, but that was an expectation built into the process. The cool morning sessions were always followed by generous table fare, which was then generally followed by snoozing in the warming winter sun.

The current missionaries in residence, The Rev. Gerhardt Sommerfeld and his wife, Greta, came by for introductions one day. They knew the substance of Jedediah's history with the clan and were interested to meet this celebrity-son who had returned. After exchanging greetings and customarily imbibing some maize-based, locally brewed beer, they agreed to share a meal together at the pastor's home in the not-too-distant future.

Resting one late afternoon in front of his brightly painted home, Jacob asked Jedediah, "What next, my son? What are the plans for your life now?"

"That is what I must decide, my father." Jedediah went on, "I am counting on God's guidance, but I knew that I must spend time with my family before taking the next steps."

"That decision has given us great joy. You know that you are welcome to stay with us for as long as you wish."

"Thank you, Father. I will help with the work, and I am also able to contribute to our financial needs."

"We are well, my son. But act as you see the need. We are simply happy to have you in our midst after such a long absence. The family now feels whole again." Even as he spoke these words, Jacob knew that Jedediah was not there permanently. Yet he would take whatever he could get, at the same time hoping that perhaps he might aid his son's quest for a new direction in life.

Chapter 20

August 1971 - Motopos Hills, Rhodesia

Later in life when he looked back, Jed would think of them as the lost years. Not that he felt lost himself, in spite of a feeling of abeyance regarding his own life journey. He still had a sense of being grounded, although faint tremors portended a possible seismic shift in the making. His self-confidence was firm as he sought new experiences which were always accompanied by introspective assessment. His being lost only applied to anyone looking for him. He was lost to the world at large while exploring the dimensions and character of his inner spirit. To everybody else, not that it mattered to many, he was gone. Vanished. Out of sight, out of mind.

Jed's wanderings, both actual and subjective, during these years were motivated by a quest to understand the human heart and mind, both in general and his in particular. *Lost* seemed like an appropriate concept to apply to a large percentage of the human species. Bullying in schoolyards; devising and using manifold weapons of war to maim and slaughter one another; screaming spit-laden curses instead of mutually respectful dialogue; skinning cats alive for fun; sexually abusing ten-year-olds. On and on and on. From where does all this come? Why do people do such things? What might change them for the better, or set them on the right path in the first place? How does a lost person find oneself? How does a lost society find itself?

Lost years, Jed would think. Years that produced some findings, some new directions. Surprising directions to places which Jedediah would never have guessed.

Jedediah stayed with his Bazo clan for almost a year and a half. Sharpening the axe. Living the simple life of a farmer-herder, he threw himself into the life of the community as if he had never left. He was not a village elder, but his size and worldly experiences commanded a great deal of admiration and respect. Adding to his cachet was Jed's humility, never lording it over other young men of the village who, in turn, felt respected and honored by him. He also embraced the Ndebele esteem of their elders, honestly and seriously seeking their wisdom and enlightenment.

Life in the Rhodesian bushveld was a physically demanding one which resulted in Ndebele men generally displaying bodily fitness. But they had never seen anything like Jedediah. His physique was beginning to develop when he left the village at age fourteen. Now at twenty-five, with his birth parents' genes and over-the-top training since he was eighteen, he was a tower of strength and stamina revered throughout the Matopos. As fit as they were, no Ndebele could hold Jed's running pace for more than ten miles. Once he recognized this, he adopted a canter which would not make them feel inferior. His reputation reached new heights when, on a solo outing, he made a round trip from the village to the old Antelope Mine and back in just under nine hours, a round-trip distance of sixty miles.

The Bazo clan practiced capoeira with as much gusto as ever. Some of the more experienced men put Jedediah to the test, and his knowledge of and expertise in this ancient martial art grew even more.

Another important development during this time with his family was the relationship Jedediah developed with Gerhardt and Greta Sommerfeld. They had only about ten years on him, but amidst their conversations he perceived in them a wisdom and depth of character to which he aspired. They spent hours in dialogue over rooibos tea laced with honey or, if later in the day, the home-brewed maize beer. Gerhardt, who insisted that Jed drop the pastor prefix, had grown up in Hacksburg, Alabama, and had fought his way out of a culture laden with racism and guns. His stories revealed that these two obsessions often strolled down country roads hand-in-hand. They discussed religion and violence and how the two are ethically related, or not. Greta's father, a Lutheran pastor, had found a burning cross on his front yard one night because he preached a sermon about God loving blacks as much as whites. Three weeks later his church fired him and booted him and his family out of the parsonage. Greta's insightful input was included in the three-way exchange of ideas. Gerhardt also gave Jed some copies of *The Catholic Worker*, a newspaper-type periodical published roughly every other month and edited by Dorothy Day. Little did Jed know at the time to where those issues would lead.

Early in 1973 Jedediah told his family that he was ready to see more of southern Africa, and that he would be leaving in a week or two. Although they knew this day would come, Jacob and Naomi, both beginning to show their age, inwardly grieved even as they voiced their blessings. In their hearts they knew that Jedediah would not spend the rest of his life with the clan in the Matopos Hills. Their sorrow was stirred together with joy at the success of their son and pride that he bore the Bazo name. They expressed the hope that he would return to their village for a final visit before moving on to . . . wherever that might be. Jedediah Bazo, the Axe, promised that he would.

He began his travels ten days later. One thing for which he was grateful was that financial pressures were not a problem. He had spent little to nothing while with his parents, and had established a substantial bank account in Bulawayo upon which to draw as he roamed from country to country. African living expenses were considerably less than those in America, so his resources stretched even further.

Using buses, trains, and his thumb, Jed meandered somewhat aimlessly through Bechuanaland, Mozambique, Swaziland, and South Africa. Due to colonization and trade, some English was spoken in many locales Jed traversed. IsiNdebele, a Bantu language in a linguistic group with over two hundred subdivisions characterized by some degree of mutual intelligibility, provided him with the means for communication in most areas where English was sparse or unknown.

Jed's appreciation of the bounty and beauty of nature, landscape, and ethnic diversity increased with each new location visited. While he savored local customs and cuisine, he always attempted to engage the people in meaningful discourse. He wanted to know what they thought about life, what their values were, and from where these came. As his travels progressed, he became more and more aware of something he had experienced only marginally in Rhodesia: racism. As a boy, his life was with the tribal community and contact with Caucasians was rare. Now, just about everywhere he went he observed the absolute dominance of white skin over black. It was a distinct minority of whites who viewed native Africans as having matching value in God's sight or were due commensurate human rights. In fact, a sizable percentage of the white power brokers actually believed that God ordained white superiority and black servitude.

In May 1974 Jed found himself sitting in the office of Professor John De Gruchy at the University of Cape Town. Formally established as a university in 1918, the facilities were located on the magnificent slopes of Devil's Peak on land ironically donated by Cecil Rhodes. Beginning in 1960 UCT became anathema to a majority of the white community for its sustained opposition to apartheid, a system of subjugation and oppression codified in the laws of South Africa. The university admitted its first black students in the 1920s and set a course for the deliberate internal transformation of South African society, particularly focusing on higher education.

Pastor Sommerfeld had alerted Jed to the anti-apartheid movement in South Africa and to De Gruchy's leadership within it. He encouraged seeking an audience with him if possible. When Jed appeared at his office with little realistic hope for a meeting, he was surprised and delighted when the secretary checked with the professor and came back to say he would be happy to entertain Jed the following day at 10:00 a.m.

At the age of thirty-five, De Gruchy was one of the youngest full professors on the faculty and a co-founder of the Department of Religious Studies at the university. Wearing wrinkled khakis and an open collared pale blue shirt, he exuded self-confidence and a warm, welcoming attitude. He invited Jedediah to sit in a worn but comfortable leather armchair across from his, and poured two cups from a tea service already laid out on the coffee table between them. He began by asking to what he owed the pleasure of this visit.

Jed wasn't quite sure where to begin, but launched into a short version of his history and his current situation in life. During a bit of back-and-forth question and answer, De Gruchy intuited some of the struggles this young man was having. With the second cup of rooibos tea the professsor said, "So, you think we can find a way to eradicate the evil in the world, eh?"

"No, sir," Jed replied. "But I think we can do better than we are. After all, aren't you engaged in the blacks' struggle for freedom here in your country?"

"Indeed I am, Jed. But I am also realistic about the degree to which that can be accomplished."

"What about the means to accomplish it?" Jed asked.

"Are you asking if violence or force is justified? De Gruchy responded.

"That's certainly part of what I'm trying to figure out. Nelson Mandela sits imprisoned for life on Robben Island a few miles from here for condoning and using violence. I'm not sure if that's right or wrong, either what he did or what the government is doing to him. May I ask your perspective on this?"

After a sip of tea and a pregnant pause, De Gruchy remarked, "My answer, Mr. Bazo, is that you have to discover your own answer to that question. I'm sure you've thought about the fact that absolute rights and wrongs often don't work so well in a world that is largely gray. And the gray areas to which you and I gravitate might be very different shades."

"Do you mean," Jed inquired "that whatever I decide is right makes it right?"

"By no means. But the fact of the matter is that an ungodly share of the time we cannot tell with any certitude what is really right or wrong. Yet we have decisions to make. We have to do something or not do something. Even the latter is a decision, and one which often simply supports the status quo. Others can help us discover things to put on the scales, but in the end each individual has to judge what weighs what and get a sense of which side goes down."

"Look where it led for Mandela," Jed tendered.

"I'm sure," De Gruchy said, "he would rather be where he is than to abrogate his convictions."

"And yet from what I've read, you seem to have chosen the non-violent path of resistance."

"While that is true, I do not condemn those who in good conscience choose otherwise."

After giving Jed some time to process these thoughts, the professor asked, "Have you been to Namibia, Jed?"

"Is that South-West Africa?"

"That's what most down here still call it. The natives of that country call it Namibia, to the consternation of the German colonialists, I might add."

"No, sir, I haven't been there, but it's on my itinerary. Why do you ask?"

"I'd encourage you to spend some time in the north. Lots and lots of Lutherans up there, and the native Africans are also engaged in a struggle for peace with justice. The church, I might add, is in the vanguard of the movement."

"Have they chosen an armed struggle?"

"Some have. Some haven't. It's not altogether safe, but if you're willing to take the risk, you just might gain some valuable insights from being in the midst of the caldron. There's also lots of people from your own Christian tradition with whom you can toss around your thoughts . . . in the heat of battle, so to speak."

After a short time wrapping up the conversation, Jed earnestly thanked the professor for his time. That evening sitting in an outdoor cafe on Riebeek Street in downtown Cape Town sipping an after-dinner espresso, Jed started making plans for northern Namibia.

Jed played the roving tourist at first. After flying to the capital of Windhoek he rented a camper version of a VW van so it could double as mobile motel room. He then spent several days each in Etosha National Park and the Caprivi Strip observing elephants, lions, leopards, hippos, buffalos, giraffes, antelope, the majestic gemsbok and the diminutive dik-dik.

One close encounter almost interrupted his sojourn, perhaps permanently. On his last night in the Caprivi, Jed parked his camper-van by Popa Falls on the Cubango River. Being an early riser, he crawled out of his sleeping bag with the first rays of morning sun which were warming both the ground and his metallic rolling home. Putting on his running outfit, he pushed open the sliding side door to the van. As he put his left foot forward to step down he noticed movement in his left peripheral vision. An image instantly registered in his brain: snake!

The puff adder's jaws were wide open with bared fangs headed for his calf. The venomous viper's morning sunning routine had been disturbed and the serpentine reflex was to strike. Fortunately Jed had almost all his weight yet on his right leg. In the split second that he realized what was about to happen, Jed accomplished a one-leg upward launch while pulling his left knee toward his chest. As he rocketed forward, his downward glance registered the snake's snout about a quarter inch from his skin. By the time he completed a somersault and turned around, the reptile had recoiled and was facing him. But he was far out of striking range at this point, so Jed found a stick with which to pin down the deadly head, picked up the innocent creature that was just doing what snakes do, and released it down by the water's edge where it might find a frog or some such thing for breakfast.

A lesson, Jed thought to himself. One must never let down one's guard when it comes to snakes.

Onni Kinnunen was the assistant headmaster of Oshigambo School. The high school was founded in 1960 by the Lutheran church which Finnish missionaries had established in the late 1800s. It was situated on the bank of an intermittent river some twenty miles east of Ondangwa in the Oshikoto region of Namibia's far north. It was about twenty-five miles to the Angola border across which armed fighters for Namibia's independence found sanctuary from the occupying South African military forces. Jed had been directed there by personnel at the headquarters of the Evangelical Lutheran Ovambo-Kavango Church in Oniipa, a dusty collection of buildings housing the administration of a church body of hundreds of thousands of adherents.

After receiving him warmly and giving him a thorough tour of the school facilities, Kinnunen invited Jed to spend the night with him in his humble bachelor's quarters on the school grounds. Visitors from America were few and far between, and the Finnish teacher-missionary was eager to educate one about the plight of the native people. Jed gratefully accepted, and after a simple supper they lounged on the veranda as the light of day faded into the opaqueness of the Namibian night. The metallic *piu-piu* of the arboreal pied cuckoo and the day-end clucking of the grazing chickens provided an evening serenade. The swaying palms and sandy soil reminded Jed of the Vietnamese coastal lowlands, and given the current wayfaring of his mind, it was not lost on Jed that he now sat within another war zone.

"May I ask what may be a delicate question?" Jed asked his host.

"Ask what you may," Onni responded, "but I doubt anything could be too delicate for our circumstances."

"Thank you, sir. My wonderings have to do with whether or not the church supports the armed part of the struggle against the South Africans."

After a couple of puffs on his prized meerschaum pipe, he fastened Jed with a bemused hint of a smile and said, "First, please dispense with the 'sir'. We are brothers in the fight for justice, and given your history, your question would seem to be a moot one."

"My history," Jed responded, "is what gives rise to the question. The struggle for justice you mention can be fought in various ways, not all of them involving violence."

"Do you know what SWAPO is, Jed?"

"I know that it has something to do with the resistance movement, but I couldn't say for sure what the acronym stands for or just what they do."

After another puff on his pipe Onni said, "It stands for South West Africa People's Organization. It's been around a dozen years or so and is both the political and military arm of the people in their battle to take back their own nation. South Africa has been here since the League of Nations way-back-when gave this land to them as a mandate to manage and prepare for eventual independence. Problem is, South Africa sees South-West Africa, which they refuse to call Namibia, as a de facto fifth province of their country subject to the apartheid laws that govern their own perverse society.

They have no plans to allow Namibians to govern Namibians."

"What about the international community? Can't it force South Africa to turn it over?"

"In your dreams, my boy. Countries like yours and mine benefit too much from their economic relations with Pretoria. Rock the boat and a lot of the cash might wash overboard. SWAPO and their supporters are tired of waiting for an event they don't see happening without it being forced."

"That force including bullets?" Jed asked.

"My experience is that all Namibians would highly prefer a negotiated peace. But a peace with justice which must include full citizenship for Namibians of any color or tribe without discrimination. The white tribe gives no sign of that even being on the negotiating table. On the contrary, they quash with an iron fist any attempts of the native Namibians to gain freedom and self-governance."

"So are you saying that this justifies seeking to attain the desired ends with armed force?"

"Even though I'm not toting guns around myself, I guess I'd have to admit that SWAPO has my support. If you lived here to see what South Africa is doing to these people, I dare say you might, with your expertise, even become an advisor to their military arm. Let me ask you," Kinnunen went on, "If some powerful country invaded the U.S. and held the people there in virtual slavery, no vote, only menial labor jobs, demanding you call the occupiers 'Boss,' what would you do?"

"We, meaning the American people, wouldn't stand for it. Guaranteed," Jed replied.

"So would you see that as justification for resorting to armed warfare if any and every other avenue proved hopeless?"

"I get your point, but my struggle is how to reconcile this with my Christian faith. The two seem pretty mutually exclusive."

"Jed, most members of SWAPO are also members of our churches. The ones I've talked to don't like at all what they're doing, but they see themselves in that in-between area where right and wrong get awfully hard to distinguish. When you see your father shot dead right in front of you or when you can barely feed your family enough to subsist, it tends to influence one's ethical perspectives."

So here Jed was again. Time after time he found himself floundering in the backwaters of theological and ethical uncertainty. His childhood concepts of an absolute God with absolute laws was more or less reinforced by his military training. The old Marine adage, "*Our is not to question why; ours is but to do or die*," made things so simple. Except that he kept running into real life situations where simplicity didn't work so well. Gray. Not black and white, but gray. That image, noted by more than one of his mentors, kept coming back to him.

Yet even with the questions and confusion swirling around between his ears, the deep-rooted, sense of peace that had sustained him thus far never left Jedediah.

Jedediah, loved by God. Bazo, the axe that cuts down evil. How the wedded meanings of his name would be played out in life was, at least at the moment, beyond his seeing.

The wanderer had returned to the Matopos Hills after three years of seeking and seeing. The experiences, readings, thoughts, discussions and prayers of those years had coalesced into a theological and ethical mosaic which was slowly taking a recognizable shape. Subconsciously, Jedediah's knowledge was morphing into wisdom. He wasn't sure where it was all leading in a practical sense, but he felt a much better grasp of his moral compass heading.

The night before his leaving, the whole village gathered at the council fire and conducted the same Celebration of Life ritual on this same spot that had welcomed his birth twenty-eight years before. His parents presented him with a cross carved by Jacob and painted by Naomi with vivid Ndebele colors. Pastor Sommerfeld blessed him with the sign of the cross, and every member of the Bazo clan touched his shoulder as they quietly asked God's blessings upon him with

"*Unkulunkulu abe nani.*"

It was a stoic and tearful farewell as Jedediah parted from his family in the Matopos Hills. Stoic because that was the Ndebele way. It was tearful, even if it was the crying of the heart, because both son and parents thought this could be their last time together. Jedediah knew that the life expectancies of his parents in the African bushveld meant the likelihood of not seeing them again.

The last sight Jedediah saw as he looked back toward the village from the bed of the pickup truck in which he sat was Jacob holding Naomi's hand while he lifted high his ceremonial assegai and pointed it toward the sun. Their son held tightly to the fish eagle around his neck.

Chapter 21

August 1974 - Indianapolis, Indiana

There are numbers of things in life that can engender terror. The prospect of losing your kid is one of them. Thinking you might never see your child alive again is one of them. Sonny and Linn Torkelson's son, Gunnar, was nowhere to be found and several possibilities threatened the worst.

The Riviera Club in north Indianapolis sits on the

banks of the White River. Established in 1933, it is a family-focused aquatic center that at one time claimed being the largest outdoor pool in the country. With its gigantic sectionalized main pool augmented by a kiddie pool, junior pool, diving tank, and water slides, it is a dream come true for water enthusiasts. In addition to the pool facilities, it boasts six tennis courts, a ballroom for dining and dancing, and a picnic area along the shaded banks of the White. The river was the cause of the terror.

The Torkelsons had spent several late afternoon hours in the main pool area trying to beat the temperature-soaring-humidity-dripping Indiana heat. Gunnar, a headstrong, vivacious, fear-nothing six-year-old, had taken swimming lessons during the preceding six weeks. He was on his way to becoming a competent swimmer, but, par for the course, he figured he was already good enough to set a new English Channel crossing record. Due to his proclivity to adventure and risk, Linn generally watched him like a mama bear. One of the reasons they joined the Rivi was the fact that lifeguards were stationed about every three feet around the pool. Well, lots of them, anyway. Gunnar loved standing on Sonny's shoulders in five feet of water and projecting himself into a backflip. Never mind that ten in a row were belly flops, Gunnar would paddle over for another try.

After pool time the family gathered at one of the riverside picnic tables to feast on Linn's world-class fried chicken and potato salad. Gunnar, still in his swim trunks, was cavorting with a bunch of other children at the playground area as Linn spread the table. Both in lawn chairs, Sonny was talking Hondas verses Harleys with a motorcycle buddy. As they thought back over the scenario, it had been probably only ten or fifteen minutes since Gunnar had gone to the playground about thirty yards away when Linn gave the all-ready call for supper. Sonny turned toward the swing sets to motion Gunnar over . . . except Gunnar wasn't there. It peeved Sonny a bit that his son would wander to the tennis courts or the horseshoe pits without asking first, but the self-assured independent streak he so often exhibited was nothing new. Dad told Mom he'd be right back with the wayward youngster and set off to find him. Except he didn't find him.

After a quick but thorough search of the club's facilities, the only thing left was the river bank. Too little too late, but one of the playmates came forward to say he had seen Gunnar heading toward the river, some thirty yards from the picnic grounds. Little footprints, which might or might not have been Gunnar's, were found on the muddy bank, but the child was nowhere to be found. A quickly assembled crew of volunteers went as much as a half mile both up and downstream but with no sign of the youngster. The river is a slow, muddy stream meandering lazily through the city on its way to the Wabash. It looks calm as a cucumber on the surface, but the main channel has undertows in places that could easily pull a six-year-old beginning swimmer down.

Concern turned to panic as the Riviera personnel suggested it would be prudent to contact the police river squad, which included divers. Then Sonny heard one of the lifeguards about a hundred yards downstream excitedly yelling his name.

Sonny had been a high school sprinter, and he probably beat his best time speeding down the riverbank to the calling volunteer. As he approached the fellow with trepidation he saw him pointing across the water. Feeling indescribable relief, Sonny saw Gunnar on the far bank, some forty yards away, waving meekly to the crew on the Rivi side. After finding his voice, Sonny yelled for his son to not move a muscle. Gunnar knew the tone. He didn't move a muscle. A rowboat commandeered from a residence just north of the club was called back from its position a bit downstream. It picked up the chagrined youngster and delivered him back to his parents on the east side of the waterway.

Clutching him in a three-way, mommy-and-daddy bear hug, Sonny said, "What in hells-bells were you thinking?"

"Daddy," Gunnar said, "I thought we weren't supposed to cuss."

"Fine. Sorry. But, Gunnar, what in the world were you doing?" At this point Linn was still too emotional to speak.

Gunnar related how he had run to the riverbank just for a quick look. What 6-year-old doesn't think rivers are neat? Knowing he shouldn't be there, he was just about to return to the playground when he saw on the opposite bank a mommy bunny with four little kits. After a few river sips, the furry family turned and hopped down a faint path into the trees. Confident of his newfound swimming abilities and excited about the possibility of up-close wildlife viewing, Gunnar slipped into the warm, chocolate water and paddled to the other side. He followed the bunnies, catching a glimpse now and then, and soon realized that he was more or less lost in the maze of trees and underbrush which extended for quite a distance on the west bank. Not really worried – "I'm brave, Daddy" – it took him close to half an hour to find his way back to the banks of the river. By this time he also knew that he had executed a rather major goof.

Although Sonny was inclined toward things like twenty lashes with a cat-o-nine-tails, he and Linn agreed that they would confer later about an appropriate consequence for Gunnar's escapade. They felt incalculable relief, and resolved to be somewhat – somewhat? Hell, world-class! – more vigilant when it came to the management of their son's headstrong independence.

If you were looking for a model American family, the Torkelsons would fit. Sonny, a graduate of Purdue University with a degree in mechanical engineering, was on the management team with TurboCraft, a growing aerospace company. He had been a second-string safety on the Boilermakers football team, not playing that much but relishing being on the squad. Now in his early thirties, he still kept himself in shape with cycling and racquetball. Linn was an RN and head nurse in the emergency department at Methodist Hospital. She was a blonde beauty with parental roots in both Norway and Sweden. They were a law-abiding couple who didn't cheat on their taxes, believed in hard work and respect for authority, owned their own home, and participated actively in their Episcopalian congregation. They kept their house and yard neat, were part of Neighborhood Watch, and would take care of the properties on either side of them when the owners were on vacation. Put simply, anyone would be overjoyed to have them living next door.

Gunnar was their only child. He didn't come along until they had been married six years, and they thought it best to stick with one and give him their all.

They couldn't have loved him more, but Gunnar was a

challenge. Linn kept her eyes open for a book on how to raise a strong-willed child. With much of his behavior, the parents might have thought Gunnar had seen the old Anacin commercial where the daughter shouts, "Mother, please, I'd rather do it myself!" Whether it was choosing what he wanted to wear or putting the sugar on his morning cereal, Gunnar was firm in his determination to make his own choices and carry his own weight.

At the same time the little tyke had a lively, cheerful spirit accompanied by a natural inclination toward helpfulness and compassion. Once when he was five, Linn ran into him leaving the house with some bandages and a bag of tools. When questioned, Gunnar explained that seven-year-old Shuchun down the block had crashed her bicycle and skinned both knees. He was on his way to patch her up and fix the bike.

The Torkelsons knew their son's IQ was off the charts, and they had their hands full satisfying his endless curiosity. At six years old he was reading books for fourth graders, and simple math functions were done with ease. For some unknown reason he took a special interest in things Asian. He loved reading books about China, and when they had visited the Pacific Asia Museum in Pasadena the previous summer, the only way to get him out had been for Sonny to pick him up in a fireman's carry. In addition, Gunnar had a passion to know how mechanical and electrical things worked. If he was playing quietly, there was a good chance they would find him dismantling either mom's mix master or dad's electric shaver. Lincoln Logs were way too easy, and only the most advanced Erector Sets suited Gunnar's talents.

"What are we going to do with that boy?" Sonny said that night after Gunnar had bathed off the White River scum and gone to bed.

"Well, for one thing," Linn responded, "we're going to watch him a whale of a lot more closely. If he pulls something like that again, *he* might not die but *I* probably will from a heart attack."

"Yeah. That was too close today. But I don't want to stifle the little guy's enthusiasm."

"Stifle is one thing. Being irresponsible parents is another."

"Granted. But I hope this was a learning lesson for him as well as for us. I hear what you're saying, but I'd still much rather control enthusiasm in a child than have to try to instill it," Sonny said.

Linn took his hand and said, "Instilling doesn't seem to be a problem with Gunnar. What we need to do is keep a hawkeye's watch on what he does with it."

In his cozy bedroom Gunnar could hear their distant voices but couldn't make out the words of his parents' discussion. Not that it would have made much difference. He was drifting off to sleep with a smile as he remembered the day's adventure. And then he was dreaming of following the tracks of tigers and elephants in faraway strange lands.

Chapter 22

May 1975 - Tam Ky, Republic of Vietnam

Being a single mom in war-torn Vietnam was no cakewalk. On a ten-point scale, ten being died-and-gone-to-heaven, Yuan's view of life was somewhere between one and two. Dragging an Amerasian brat around while scrapping to keep from starving to death or biting a stray bullet as the idiot Americans and the idiot Viet Cong so-called patriots fought for ever higher body counts tested the limits of her ingenuity and endurance. The ravages of her hardscrabble existence was taking its toll on her natural beauty, the damage being accentuated by whatever chemicals she could scrounge to dull the pain of reality. Every once in a while the survival instinct almost drove Yuan to jettison the burden of an unwanted child. But even amidst her drug-induced fogginess, the genetic disposition to motherhood prevented abandonment. Nevertheless, little Bo was the worse for wear, getting little to eat and even less affection.

After asshole-Billy successfully flew the Vietnam coop in a Boeing 707 freedom bird back to what Yuan thought of as Never-Never Land, life in the homeland went from bad to very bad. As the U.S. began troop withdrawals in the early '70s, she gravitated back to the Tam Ky area, the only place she remotely considered her home town. Fewer soldiers and Marines resulted in a dramatic reduction of the minimal sex trade income, although nighttime visits occasionally happened as horny NVA replaced the departing Americans. Payment often came in the form of a slap to the back of the head. Bo was often an innocent observer, but sometimes drugged so he'd stop his infernal wailing and *get to damn sleep*.

Yuan finally found a job for almost-subsistence pay working for an ethnic Chinese family who somehow managed to continue farming throughout the war. During her long days in the fields, Bo would either be strapped to her back or left in the care of the farmer's aged mother. The latter was hampered by a gimpy leg and a bad heart, so the inquisitive toddler was mostly left to his own devices. Which is why he became scarred for life.

The farm was about eight clicks to the west of what U.S. troops jokingly called Nam Interstate-1, the main coastal highway. In earlier years it had been a combat area from time to time, and the fields Yuan tended were not far from the base of Nui Yon Hill. In May of 1969, as Billy was fighting for his life on Ap Bia Mountain to the north, a ferocious battle took place in the Tam Ky area. In the wake of the '68 Post-Tet offensive, elements of the U.S. 1st Calvary fought to re-take a bump named Nui Yon after VC and NVA troops had overrun the South Vietnamese Army outpost there. The Americans came out on top in this engagement, but heavy air and artillery support, which literally blew off the top of the hill, resulted in a variety of unexploded ordinance in the soft earth. There was nothing unusual about this. Just as there was nothing unusual about Bo and a couple of other playmates one day stumbling across a dud 105mm artillery round. One of life's mysteries is why primed rounds did not explode when they were supposed to, but later did when children beat on them with rocks.

The farmer's two grandchildren were blown to kingdom come. Bo, fortuitously out of the main blast line, was knocked off his feet with a piece of shrapnel cutting a deep wound from just below his left eye through his upper lip. By the time Grandma's screaming elicited help and they got Bo to a crude aid center in Tam Ky, he had lost a fair amount of blood and was clinging to life. But live he did, although marked for life with a ragged scar across his face that would have qualified his visage for a horror movie. As he grew in years it gave him a fierce appearance, which came in handy more often than not.

By 1973 the Americans had tucked tail and had run for their lives, although it took two more years of ragged conflict for the North to finally unify the country again. Seeing the writing on the wall, the farmer for whom Yuan worked had fled with his family on a boat to wherever, leaving Yuan and Bo to fend for themselves as the Communists reorganized life among the rice paddies. Mother and child were again forced to the edge of survival. Then she met Thao.

Thao Ngô was a Viet Cong guerilla fighter who now had nothing to fight but his own demons. He had been hardened by an underprivileged childhood and by the war, and felt that the time had come to reap some personal benefits. He was appointed as an overseer on a nationalized pig farm on the edge of Tam Ky, never mind that he knew as much about hogs as he did nuclear physics. With the newfound stability and pay-check security, Thao had money for cheap homemade booze. When Americans came home with a host of head problems they called it post-traumatic stress syndrome. Vietnamese didn't call it anything, and it was often treated with chemicals smoked, injected, or imbibed. Thao's preference was liquid therapy, and when he got drunk, he got mean.

One night before the hellish side of his personality kicked in, Thao met Yuan at one of his favorite watering holes. Getting on in years, he had arrived at the conclusion that he needed a wife, specifically one who could give him children to care for him in his old age. Although Yuan was considerably younger, Thao was captivated by the beauty she had nursed partially back, and decided Yuan was a good candidate for marriage. Lured by his acceptable appearance and apparently stable income, Yuan received his advances.

Over the coming months Thao basically behaved himself as he wooed the one he wanted, and eventually convinced Yuan to marry him. The only drawback was the scar-faced runt she toted around, but he figured he could put up with that as long as more sons came along to provide old age security and to propagate his "excellent bloodline."

Little did he know how misguided was his thinking.

Chapter 23

January 1976 - New York, New York

Arriving back in the U.S., the first thing Jed did was call Pastor Darrell. He was still firmly ensconced in Madison and told the long-lost wanderer that he was more than welcome to come stay with him to debrief and contemplate his next move. It was the next move that Jed wanted to run by him. He thanked Darrell and told him that he had some sight-seeing of America to do first. He wasn't sure how long it would be but he'd stay in touch along the way. It took a little over a year.

Jed had landed at JFK in New York City and was anxious to get out of the metro area and on the road as soon as possible. One of the two things he wanted to purchase for his continuing travels was a camper van. While he still had a fair amount of reserves in the bank, his Namibia experience proved that taking your motel-on-wheels with you provided a great deal of flexibility, and was also eminently more economical than supporting the motels of America night after night.

He asked one of the cabbies where would be the best place to go for a concentration of car dealers. The cabbie said, "Hop in, Mac. I'll get you there the shortest route." After a fairly quick ride, Jed found himself walking Utica Avenue in Brooklyn, which was used-car heaven. After several hours of perusing, Jed settled on a 1970 VW Westfalia that was in great shape at an acceptable price. It took him the rest of the day to withdraw funds, complete the transaction, and stock up on some basic food and equipment, but by late afternoon he was motoring toward the island.

Jed's destination was St. Joseph House in Lower Manhattan. He had discovered in his readings that the property had been purchased by Dorothy Day and operated as a store-front soup kitchen, a house of hospitality, and the base for publishing *The Catholic Worker*. The second thing Jed wanted for the upcoming journey was more of Dorothy Day's writings. His African readings of *The Catholic Worker* had opened to him a heretofore unexamined aspect of the Christian faith, and piqued his curiosity. Day's writings often touched on his own mental wrangling with how religion and violence and peace and all fit together. Or didn't. He wanted to further pursue the thinking of this unusual woman.

At St. Joseph House Jed was gifted with three things. First, he was offered a bed for the night which he gratefully accepted. Second, he acquired a huge stack of old *Catholic Worker* issues, for which he gave a generous donation. Third and most unexpected, he had coffee with Dorothy Day. When the staff worker, a huge black man with a smile to match his vibrant affability, queried him and learned a bit about Jed's ambitions, he asked if Jed would like to meet the founder of the movement. Astounded with the opportunity, Jed stammered, "Sure." After supper, which Jed helped serve to eighty-seven hungry vagrants, he was led into the small, cluttered room where Dorothy did her thinking and writing.

After the introductory pleasantries and some get-to-know-you-a-bit small talk, Miss Day asked, "So, Mr. Bazo, do you feel good about what you did in Vietnam?"

Jed wasn't anticipating such an inquiry, but answered, "Yes and no. I've wrestled with that over the years, and always seem to end up feeling unsure which way the scales are tipping for me."

"You tell me you're a man of faith," Dorothy went on. "What happens when you bring that to bear on the question?"

Jed replied, "That's exactly the issue I've been struggling with, ma'am. Sometimes I feel like it's the teeter-totter itself. Even with faith as my foundation, I oftentimes feel like it's shifting beneath my feet, pushing me one way sometimes and the opposite at other times. To put it simply, I'm having trouble seeing force or violence as a black and white issue."

"Ah," Dorothy said with a sly smile, "the old gray area, huh?"

"Exactly. For me, identifying absolutes that fit nicely into every situation in life is increasingly problematic."

"Join the club, Jed. But aren't there *some* things that are absolutely right or wrong?"

"For instance?" Jed said.

"How about raping little girls," Dorothy offered.

"Okay, I'd agree that's absolutely wrong. But what means are justified to prevent it? Or what are we justified in doing to the rapists?"

"To get an answer to that don't you think we'd better ask what Jesus would do?"

"Two problems," Jed countered. "Who really knows what he'd do, and, second, even if we think we know the answer, are we ever justified in acting differently?"

Dorothy, her eyes characteristically burning with passion, said, "While we rightly wrestle together with those questions in community, the answers that guide your personal actions, Jed, can only be decided by you."

After chatting for a few more minutes Jed thanked her profusely for her time. She wished him well on his pilgrimage and presented him with a copy of her book, *The Long Loneliness*.

The next morning Jed headed for Mississippi.

Jed had never been in the deep south, at least the southeastern states that were infamous for their formation of the Confederacy and subsequent continuing segregation of and discrimination against Arican-Americans. Having served alongside many blacks who were outstanding Marines and good friends, he wanted to experience firsthand the societal consequences of the general prejudice against non-whites in the south. He knew, of course, that bias against people of color was alive and well in the north, but he didn't think it was on the same quantitative and qualitative scale as below the Mason-Dixon. He picked Philadelphia, Mississippi, as a target due to the infamous killing of the three civil rights workers there a decade earlier.

On his go-where-the-spirit-moves odyssey, Jed roved with no set agenda across Virginia, South Carolina, Georgia, Alabama, and Mississippi. He visited numerous historical sites such as Charleston Harbor where the first Civil War shots were fired, Woodrow Wilson's boyhood home in Augusta, Georgia, the slave-built and oldest-in-Alabama Hughes Mill Covered Bridge near Coldwater, and the Grand Village of the Natchez, a prehistoric village dating from around 1200 A.D. built by members of the Plaquemine culture. He purposefully traversed southern Mississippi first, saving the Meridian and Philadelphia areas for later.

After visiting the federal courthouse in Meridian where seven of the Freedom summer killers were convicted in 1967, Jed drove to Philadelphia to actually stand on Rock Cut Road where the three civil rights workers were murdered. He wanted to see the site on Old Jolly Farm where they had been buried at the base of an earthen dam. Having read accounts of the calamity, Jed wasn't sure why he wanted to put his boots on the ground of the actual events. Perhaps part of it was to get a visceral sense of how upstanding, patriotic, church-going Americans could perpetrate such evil. One paradoxical factor held his particular interest: how could a preacher of the gospel participate in such madness? Edgar

Killen, a local Baptist minister, was implicated in the proceedings, but was not convicted because one juror stated that she could never possibly find a minister guilty. A racist-murderer at large and in the pulpit every Sunday? Something was wrong with this picture. More grist for Jed's mental mill.

Along with his sight-seeing, Jed also took some pains to mingle with the local populace along the way. He ate in mom-and-pop cafes, met friendly people in parks, and sat around fires in campgrounds with locals now and then. He purposely ventured into the economically depressed areas of various towns and became accustomed to the fact that they were disproportionately populated with black people. At first, most of them were somewhat wary of his size and color, but often warmed up when they were treated with congeniality and respect. This was more the case with the older folks; the younger ones frequently displaying a militancy born of their situation in life.

As Jed doubled back to the Mississippi River and followed it north, sometimes venturing west into Arkansas, he had another troubling experience.

A bend in the Arkansas River just upstream from where it joins the Mississippi proved to be an isolated and scenic spot to park for the night. Where Arkansas Highway 10 ended just west of the confluence, a gravel road trickled out on a narrow spit of land between the river and small Ozark Lake to the south. Several burned-out campfires evidenced that Jed was not the first to discover this secluded hideaway, but as the sun settled he was the only inhabitant.

After a tasty supper of fire-roasted Polish sausage and corn-on-the-cob, Jed brewed a cup of Taster's Choice and settled back in his canvass camp chair to read under the light of a Coleman lantern. As a few pesky mosquitos began their buzzing and Jed's eyes began their drooping, he heard a vehicle coming toward him down the gravel road. Rounding the last bend, a 1968 Chevy Impala station wagon with more rust than paint and in dire need of a new muffler stopped thirty yards away with blinding lights illuminating him. Four good ol' boys climbed out, rather, stumbled out, two holding half-empty pints of some wicked brew. The driver, whose ten-inch beard was matted with whiskey and unidentifiable foodstuffs, spoke first. "Well, well. Lookee what we got us here, boys. Some damn unlucky loner in one of them damn hippie-mobiles."

"Prolly ain't got nothin' worth shit," said one of the bleary-eyed cohorts.

"Hey," mumbled another of the fuzz-brained Clyde Barrow wannabees, "brand-damn-new lantern's good for me."

As the four, backlit by the headlights, approached Jed in a semblance of a semicircle, he knew what was coming and thought to himself: *Again? Why me*? One of the motley crew was brandishing a tire iron and another a hunting knife with a four inch blade. "Stand yer ass up," growled the driver-leader.

As he might have been wont to weigh the whole evolving affair on his theological/ethical scales, there wasn't a lot of time with the advancing horde now about twenty feet away. Besides, his USMC-trained predispositions were kicking into overdrive. Nevertheless, he thought he should try the rational approach. "Evening boys. You needing some kind of help?"

"Bet yer dumb ass we do," Tire Iron slurred. "Get yer clothes off and head fer the river, like, runnin', less you want to see what a gen-u-wine Arkansas skinnin' party's like."

Jed stood up and thought he'd try one more waste-of-breath tactic. "Fellas, why don't we just pretend we never met and you all head on back to the bar for another round. That way nobody'll get hurt."

"Only one doin' any gettin' hurt gonna be you," said Hunting Knife.

Jed assumed a defensive stance and said with steel in his voice, "You boys pile back in and drive out of here now or else you'll be waking up in the county hospital. Count on it."

"Har, har, har," guffawed the bearded driver. "Four against one. Yer nuttier 'n a fruitcake."

Jed said nothing more and remained in a semi-crouch, slightly swaying from side to side. "Well now, we got us a fancy-ass dancer," said the driver. "Go get 'em, boys."

Tire Iron stumbled toward Jed and when three feet away haphazardly raised the tool above his head. Before he could even begin his downswing, Jed's right foot crashed into his left temple. With his head struggling to stay connected to his body, the hapless lad crumpled, unconscious before he hit the ground, with blood streaming out of his nose.

Beard took a step or two backwards as Hunting Knife, on Jed's left, and the fourth guy rushed him simultaneously. Number four hesitated as he waited for his armed comrade to begin slicing their quarry into little pieces. As a novice in hand-to-hand combat, the knife-wielding drunk swung wildly for Jed's neck. Jed simply moved his upper body back far enough to watch the blade miss his throat by an inch or two. Then as his assailant's arm reached the end of its swing Jed grabbed the fellow's elbow with his left hand and his wrist his right hand, pulling up on the elbow while pushing down on the wrist. The blade went almost to the hilt into Hunting Knife's right thigh. At the same time Jed twisted to the left and with his right foot extended in an explosive kick caught the other attacker's right kneecap. Both went down screaming and holding their severely damaged legs.

As the initial three were disabled, Jed, in his peripheral vision, saw Beard lunge for the car. In sprinter mode, Jed was eight feet from the vehicle as Beard was straightening up with a double-barreled 12-gauge shotgun. Seeing the gun moving toward a firing position, Jed launched himself with right foot extended at his assailant. The barrel had not yet reached the horizontal when Beard pulled the trigger as a size eleven boot slammed into his trachea. The buckshot went underneath Jed and he landed lightly on his feet as the leader of the pack dropped to the ground gasping for air that had no way to get to his lungs.

While Knife-in-Leg and Crushed Patella writhed in vocalized pain, Jed packed his gear into the van, drove around the rust-bucket Impala, and headed north. He thought he better make tracks for Tennessee.

Chapter 24

August 1976 - On the Road to Madison, Wisconsin

Jed didn't think Arkansas authorities would be looking for him. Not only would it be unlikely that the four disabled rednecks could concoct a believable story – *we had guns, knives, and tire irons and one guy with no weapons beat the holy crap out of us* – but they would probably be sorely embarrassed if what really happened came to light.

Nevertheless, Jed was more than a little comforted when he crossed into Tennessee and turned north toward Kentucky.

With winter on the not-too-distant horizon, Jed thought it prudent to begin winding down his trekking escapades. In addition, some next-step decisions were beginning to form. He had alerted Pastor Darrell with an estimated time of arrival, noting that there were several more high spots he wanted to hit on his way back north.

Paris, Kentucky, was his next purposeful destination. Having read of Secretariat's wondrous racing career and after talking to some breeders at a track outside Atlanta, Jed was hoping for a viewing of the famous horse who, two years earlier, had been the first steed in twenty-five years to win the Triple Crown. He zigzagged north from Knoxville toward Lexington, following his pattern of using rural byways instead of the major vehicular arteries. This not only afforded him opportunities to savor the local cultures and people, it also provided much more interesting spots to park his van for the night than KOAs on interstate highways.

At Claiborne Farm he was pleased to learn that there were daily no-charge walking tours. Jed's congenial nature won an instant friend in the groom who guided his group. The horseman asked if Jed would like a close-up introduction to Secretariat at the end of the tour. Patting the neck of that magnificent animal was a thrilling experience, and Jed wondered later why all people couldn't be as amiable and cordial as his equine friend.

Indianapolis was next on his list. Jed had seen pictures of the famed Monument Circle and decided he wanted to walk around it himself. He did better than that. Splurging a bit, he treated himself to a night at The Columbia Club right on the Circle. After a splendid evening meal and a world-class night's sleep, Jed donned his running gear at five the next morning and took off for a ten mile run which ended with ten laps around the circle. The few people who were out and about at six a.m. found themselves transfixed by a handsome, tremendously muscled hulk circling the monument like he was warming up for the Indy 500.

As Jed conversed with the locals about what he should see before leaving the Circle City, several mentioned the Riviera Club on the north side of town. So on the last day before pointing toward Chicago he stopped at the pool tucked in between the White River and the Indiana Central Canal. Granted a guest pass, Jed surveyed the whole eye-popping complex before swimming laps for an hour and a half. Fully refreshed, he grabbed a couple of burgers and a frozen Milky Way at the pool snack bar on the way to his home on wheels. Exiting down the long divided driveway out to Illinois Street, he would have had no reason to notice the Torkelson family just driving in for an afternoon's recreation.

The great Midwestern city of what was originally called *shikaakwa*, a name derived from a French rendering of the Native American word translated as "wild onion," was next on Jed's itinerary. One hour in the Chicago megalopolis was enough. The crowds, the traffic, the confusing complex of roadways, and the divided highway cloverleafs moved him to forego the museums and inner city historic sites. New York had provided enough similar urban situations for his liking, so off he went into Wisconsin hoping to find a suitable spot in the northwoods to spend his last night before arriving at Pastor D's.

Their friendship had deepened and matured to the point where they both relished spending time together. Due to his sense of the relationship, Darrell asked Jed to drop the pastor moniker and use his first name. After all, he wasn't Jed's pastor anymore, and each viewed the other as a brother, both in the faith and as intimates who continually grew in their mutual affinity. Although their bonding was purely platonic, a contributing factor might have been that both were single and neither one seeking a female companion.

Late one afternoon they were sipping hard-to-find Anchor Steam beer in the book-crammed parsonage study. Jed had showered after completing a 13-mile run around Lake Monona, the second-largest of the chain of four lakes along the Yahara River and just southeast of the larger Mendota. Recounting a short version of his travel years, Jed focused on some of the highlights and most interesting people.

After a couple of hours of listening with some degree of envy, Darrell queried, "So did you find what you were seeking?"

Jed replied, "I might be able to answer that better if I knew what I was looking for."

"I mean in a general sense," Darrell went on. "Exploring in-depth the issues you've been struggling with, and what your conclusions might have to do with the rest of your life."

"I don't think I'd call them conclusions, Darrell, but in my travels both in Africa and here I sure saw a lot that gave me more to put on the scales. And as we've talked about in the past, the problem is figuring out how much each thing weighs and then what to do with it."

"Have your experiences been any help in dealing with your questions about violence?"

"I'm back in the yes-and-no territory with that question. For me it depends on the circumstances. And sometimes a given circumstance doesn't give a guy a lot of time to mull over details. For instance, you see a puppy about to get run over by a car and maybe you can run and scoop it up without getting hit yourself. There's no time to measure distances, speed, and calculate what your chances are. You also don't have time to have a philosophical discussion with yourself about the value of a puppy's life, the effect of the dog's possible death on the little boy who's watching, and the like. We can kick around the merits of the possible actions in that situation while we're sitting here in a comfortable study, but in real life things happen that you respond to, one way or the other, at the given moment."

"What's the puppy story have to do with violence?"

"That was just an example to illustrate the fact that we don't always have the luxury of time for contemplation when something happens that calls for an immediate decision."

"But," Darrell said, "doesn't our general nature, all the thinking we've done up to any given point in time, influence what action we take or don't take in any given situation?"

"In general, sure. But, as you've helped me see, there are exceptions to everything. I can think that stealing is wrong and go through life not stealing based on that belief. But if stealing something was a way to save your life, I'd do it in a heartbeat."

"That ambiguous gray area again."

"Maybe. But there's no gray involved for me if it's a choice between stealing and saving your life."

"Ya got me there."

"OK, what do you think about this?" Jed asked. And

he then described in some detail his encounter with the four Arkansawyers who were probably still licking their wounds.

They sat in silence for a time as Darrell processed the happening. "So what would have been the consequences," he asked, "if you would have done what they demanded and run off into the night?"

"I wouldn't be sitting here right now because I'd be hitchhiking buck naked down some road in northern Arkansas while my van and gear enriched the lives of those redneck bums."

"So?"

"So I don't think that's right. Don't I have the right to defend myself and my property?"

"Oh, indeed you do," Darrell answered. "The question is: should you claim that right?"

"I don't know. Again, maybe the circumstances determine that. If I'd have been jumped on the street somewhere and all they wanted was my wallet, maybe putting them in the hospital would have been a poor choice. But I was out in the middle of who-knows-where, and maybe in their drunken state they would have decided that just taking my things wasn't enough . . . that using that skinning knife would add to their night's fun. What would you have done?"

"That's easy to answer," said Darrell. "Not having even a fraction of your fighting skills, I would have been motoring through the bush in my birthday suit chanting St. Paul's words, "I did not run in vain."

"Well, there you go," Jed replied. "In that situation I was equipped to act in ways that you wouldn't have been. Maybe like I was trained and able to fight in Nam for many Americans who would have simply been physically unable to do so no matter how much they might have wanted to. Aren't we talking about situational ethics?"

"Nasty term," Darrell replied, "at least for lots of people."

"People who somehow convince themselves that life can be lived based on absolutes, yes?"

"Absolutely, if you'll pardon the word play. I'd like to segue to another question, Jed."

"Be my guest."

"You indicated in your letters and calls that Dorothy Day has influenced your thinking. And, by the way, I can't believe you actually got to meet her. I haven't read a whole lot of her writings, not nearly as much as you, but she seems to have a lot to say about violence."

"Yes, she does. A lot of her emphasis is on war, on not playing that game. But she writes about another kind of violence that I never thought of that way."

"Which is?" Darrell responded.

"The kind of violence we do to each other with purposefully designed societal structures. As you probably know, violence comes from the Latin verb *to violate*, and there's lots of ways to violate people. Dorothy rejects communism because of its inherent atheism. But she embraces the Maxist maxim, *from each according to their ability; to each according to their need.*" Draining the last of his Anchor Steam, Jed continued, "Just about every school kid knows that our Declaration of Independence says that life, liberty and the pursuit of happiness are the rights of all people, and yet we design systems that deny people exactly those things. The Catholic Worker Movement from day one has focused on the needs of the poor, those who the system has either created or doesn't seem designed to help. And not just offering charity, but rather, working to create societal structures for dealing with systemic poverty. Day certainly believes that short-term, band-aid help is needed, but she also strongly believes that forming a just society is eminently more important than just providing charity

"Wow, Jed. You've obviously given this a lot of thought."

"Yeah, Darrell, I have. And my reading of Day's writings as I wandered around was augmented by what I saw with my own eyes. On the one hand you've got Thomas Jefferson, author of those words about inalienable rights and president of the U.S., living in an 11,000 square foot mansion and owning over two hundred slaves, even bringing some of them with him into the White House. That tradition is alive and well today. I saw multi-thousand square foot mansions in every state I visited, and while the servants employed by the owners are technically free, many go home to living conditions that you and I wouldn't countenance for a minute. I spent time with lots of them. Saw kids dressed in rags going to schools that President Ford wouldn't send his children to for love or money. Over and over I kept thinking to myself, something's wrong with this picture."

It was obvious to Darrell that all this was leading Jed somewhere. But their conversation shifted to other more benign subjects as they headed for supper at their old favorite, the Brat und Brau. Over sirloin steak brochettes and breaded, deep-fried shrimp with homemade onion rings Darrell took the step of asking what he thought might be a risky question. "It's been a number of years now, Jed. Have you thought about the possibility of future relationships? You've never mentioned once any gals that have caught your fancy." He searched Jed's face for any sign of anxiety over the query.

Wiping butter off his chin from the last piece of delicious shrimp, Jed looked Darrell in the eye and said, "I think that's out of the picture, at least for now. I don't know how to explain it, but since learning of Angela's death I haven't had the slightest inclination for female companionship, at least not the romantic kind."

"Sometimes it works that way, Jed. Might last, might not. But judging from your past with Angela it's hard to think of you as celibate."

"People change. Maybe that's what happened. Even though the Catholic Church forces it on their priests, some I've talked to speak of genuine celibacy as a gift. Maybe that's where I'm at now. What about you, Darrell? I've never known you to be with a woman since we met."

"You noticed, eh? Well, it's not because I'm homosexual or that I don't appreciate women. I believe I've been given the gift you're talking about."

"And it doesn't bother you?"

"Why would I be bothered with a gift from God that makes me what I am? I'm sure some people might wonder, but that's their problem. Neither of us seem a fit the standard role. So what? If we feel good about who and what we are, who's to judge us?"

"Thanks for sharing that. I guess time will either bring changes or it won't, but I'm comfortable with the situation as it is. And, by the way, wasn't Jesus celibate?"

"Good point," Darrell said with a smile even while knowing that some biblical scholars question that presupposition.

They turned in early and Darrell's last thoughts as he drifted into sleep was Jed's announcement that he had made a decision which he'd share at breakfast the next morning.

Jed had completed his early morning ten mile run, showered and had coffee brewing and eggs frying when Darrell walked into the breakfast nook rubbing sleep from his eyes and whispering, "*Sine coffea nihil sum*! Coffee, coffee!"

"Here you go. Black and bubbling," Jed offered as he sipped his second mugful. "What's with the Latin?"

"Thanks. Just a little phrase about loving the stuff. You mind making the *easy* really easy on the eggs? Last time you tried these it felt like I was chewing on racquetballs."

Jed chuckled. Easy-going, poking-one-another-in-the-ribs banter had become par for the course in their relationship. "Sit down and put your bib on. In a couple of minutes you'll have eggs to die for."

"You've indicated that you're only going to grace me with your presence for a short time," Darrell said as they finished the meal and refilled their mugs with the last of the pot. "So what's this decision you mentioned last night?"

Jed's countenance took on seriousness and determination. "I'm going to become part of the Catholic Worker Movement."

"Part of, in what way?" Darrell replied.

"I want to become a volunteer. Hands on with the band-aid stuff while I grapple with the larger scope that we talked about last night."

"Have you worked out where? Doing what?"

"I've learned that St. James Cathedral has just opened a kitchen to provide free meals for the poor. I can cook, spoon mashed potatoes, and wipe tables, and I hear there're job openings in that department."

"And, might I ask, which St. James Cathedral, located where?"

Jed replied with a wink, "My old neighborhood. Seattle."

As they talked for the next hour about Jed's plan, Darrell felt better and better about the rightness of this decision at this point in his friend's maturing spiritual life. Jed said that he didn't know whether it would last six months or six years, but this is what he felt impelled to do right now. Darrell could be nothing but supportive and, in that regard, asked Jed another question. "I know I asked a few years back, but how are you fixed financially, Jed? Seems to me like you might have run through most of your savings by now."

Hesitating a moment or two, Jed finally said, "Since you asked, I'm getting pretty low. Maybe enough to get me to Seattle and pay the bills for six months or so."

It was obvious that even living simply, one needed some money to cover basic living and car expenses. So Darrell made Jed an offer. "You've probably heard about the proverbial old rich uncle who dies and leaves you a bundle. Well, for me it turned out to be a rich aunt. While my parents were middle or lower middle-class, Aunt Julia wasn't. She married an oil tycoon down in Texas and they never had any children. She and my mom were exceptionally close sisters, and Julia always kind of looked at me as a surrogate son. In fact, my parents had it in their will that if they died while I was still a minor, Aunt Julia would become my legal guardian. When I began seminary, my mother had died and my father was looking at the world with beer bottles for glasses, so my aunt gave me a lot of financial aid to help make it through those years."

"Sounds to me," Jed said, "like the kind of person the world needs more of."

"No question. And here's the kicker. While you were in Africa, Aunt Julia died. Her husband predeceased her and she left the bulk of her estate to me."

"Wow! No kidding? I didn't think Lutheran pastors were supposed to have lots of money," he jested.

"Well, this one does now," Darrell added. "And I'm talking off-the-charts big bucks. So here's my proposition. I don't need it, don't even really want it . . . but since it's there, I'd like to help support you getting started with this Cathedral Kitchen thing. If you want to think of it as a loan and repay it someday when you're able, so be it. But I'm happy to think of it as a gift. Let's say a gift to the ministry of the Catholic Worker Movement." Jed had kept his funds in a Seattle bank, so Darrell asked for the account number and said he'd transfer some funds into it.

Jed didn't know what to say except "thank you." He felt like he should consider it a loan and repay it someday, but for now it would give him the cushion he'd need to begin this next phase of his life. Wherever it might lead.

After five days of continued dialogue and a promise to stay in very regular touch, Jed found himself rolling west in his VW van on Wisconsin State Highway #14. He had not contacted the Cathedral Kitchen in advance to see if his services were needed. He was pretty confident they would be.

Chapter 25

November 1976 - on the road to Seattle, Washington

It was late November 1976 when Jed pointed his van toward Seattle. There was some risk in driving from Wisconsin to Washington this time of year, but he vowed to himself to check the weather forecasts daily for any storm warnings. The little Westfalia wasn't exactly what you'd call a storm buster, but with the engine in the rear he figured there was enough weight on the wheels to keep him mobile through light snow.

The plan was to take highway #14 to where it crossed the Mississippi just south of La Crosse and then jag north to join Interstate 90 at the southern end of Lake Onalaska. Jed pulled into a rest stop on the historic river's muddy banks and ate a deli sandwich watching aircraft take off and land at the La Crosse Regional Airport on French Island in the middle of the channel. He was momentarily startled as a low-flying National Guard helicopter came over a bluff behind him and descended rapidly to a picture-perfect landing on the island. Jed mused that it might be a long time before the sound of a chopper didn't bring up some memories that weren't that far behind him.

Once on I-90, it was interstate divided highway all the way to the Emerald City, also known as the coffee capital of the world. While not in any particular hurry, prudence dictated foregoing the scenic byways this time of year. Highway crews did a decent job of keeping the interstates open to traffic unless there was a show-stopping blizzard. At his mosey-along pace he figured he could be in Rapid City in two days and, if weather permitted, make the twenty-five mile jaunt south to see the famed Mount Rushmore. Which is exactly what he did, and then headed for Butte, Montana, and another experience out of Ripley's Believe-It-or-Not.

A few miles north of Butte was the turn off to Highway #1, a west-then-north loop of about seventy miles just off the Continental Divide that passed through some of Montana's most spectacular scenery and rejoined I-90 at Drummond. With nothing ominous in the weather forecast, Jed thought this would be a fun side excursion, promising himself that if road conditions were threatening he'd turn back to the interstate forthwith. He also liked the idea of visiting the mountain town of Anaconda, if for no other reason than its name. Snakes were not really his thing, but a town with the name of the largest constrictor on earth piqued his curiosity.

During his walkabout and lunch in Anaconda, Jed didn't see a single snake. It was a pleasant enough little burg, but by early afternoon he was ready to head for Georgetown Lake and environs. The highway itself was a scenic drawing card for travelers, but not at this time of year. While the surrounding hills were white, the snow was not deep and the road was clear save for the occasional powder dusting. He had passed by Philipsburg and calculated that it was about twenty miles back to I-90 where he hoped to find a room in Drummond.

He didn't make it.

Heading north into the Flint Creek Range, Jed was pleased both with his progress and the sense that he had the rugged mountains to himself. Seeing deer, elk, and even a pair of mountain goats added to the pleasure of his sojourn. Then the sickening sound of a blowout intruded on his peace as the right front tire collapsed and jerked the van sharply toward the ditch. Fortunately a drop-off to the creek was on his left and the veer to the right was into a fairly shallow depression with light brush on the other side. Stopped cold with the van listing sharply to starboard, Jed climbed out to survey the damage. Even if he could have changed the tire, it was questionable whether the rear tires could get enough traction to pull the vehicle back onto the road. But changing the tire wasn't an option because upon checking, Jed found that the spare was flat. Immediately to his mind came the Marine Corps 7-Ps: Proper Prior Planning Prevents Piss Poor Performance. Since he hadn't seen another vehicle for close to an hour and it was now late afternoon, Jed thought this just might be where he would be spending the night. He'd done worse. The temperature didn't worry him because he had warm clothes and a sleeping bag along with enough foodstuffs to stave off hunger pangs. Then he heard a vehicle chugging up behind him.

Sometimes it doesn't take much for hopeful opportunity to turn into a bummer. An early model Ford F350 four-wheel-drive crew cab pickup that looked like it hadn't had a bath for at least five years stopped twenty yards behind him. Three fellows got out that fit one's wildest imaginations of what mountain men might look like. Scruffy and with beards that looked like they were relatives of ZZ Top, they gave Jed the eagle eye for a moment or two and slowly approached. The guy in the lead was one of the largest human beings Jed had ever seen. He had to be pushing seven feet, and carried his four hundred pounds well. Of the two backing him up, one clutched a tire iron. *Not again! What am I doing wrong, Lord?* Jed thought. First Arkansas, now Montana. It occurred to him he should probably quit listening to John Denver's "Take Me Home Country Roads." While he generally liked to give people the benefit of the doubt, Jed's assessment of the giant's size and scowl started him edging toward his own tire iron. Until, that is, the giant's face broke into a smile as he said, "Needing some help there, fella?"

The three were indeed mountain men. They lived off the beaten track – *way* off the beaten track – down logging roads most people forgot existed. What appeared to be scowls and forlorn appearance were simply a product of their hardscrabble existence. But they were friendly. Very friendly, in fact. Looking over Jed's predicament, they came to his rescue in several ways. First, they had a portable compressor which they used to pump up Jed's spare and then used it to replace the totaled front tire. Second, since a light snow had begun falling, they invited Jed to their family home some ten miles up the next forestry road. Jed hesitated momentarily, but not for long. He sensed that these folks were genuinely hospitable and really did want to help a man in hot water. So after depositing his van on a side trail off of the forestry road and about a mile in from the highway, Jed climbed into the Ford for a bumpy ride through deepening forest and waning light. With just enough daylight left to see, they rounded a bend into a clearing that held a log home surrounded by chickens, a couple of pigs, four horses, and a milk cow. "Welcome to the Logan homestead," the giant said.

Huck, Bodean, and Harley Logan. The first two were brothers and Harley was a cousin. Big Mama Logan welcomed Jed with a slap on the back that took his breath away. She was called Big Mama for a reason, and it was easy to figure out from where Huck got his size. Mama towered over Jed by half a foot and looked like she'd win a bench pressing contest at the local gym. Big Daddy, assuming he'd have to have some size to handle his bride, was no longer with them. He had gone to the happy hunting grounds several years back when, chasing a trophy bull elk, he tripped and went over the edge of a sheer cliff, the bottom of which was called The Crater. The boys always made an annual pilgrimage to the site to pay their respects to his bones . . . down there somewhere.

Bodean's wife, Lucy, and Harley's wife, Bonnie, along with their two boys, Harlan and Clint, completed the clan, at least the part that lived on this site. The Logans had begun populating this area of the range since Great-Great-Great-Grandpappy Harvest Logan registered Philipsburg as an official town in 1867. After a half dozen years of smelting ore, Harvest was done with it. He headed with his family up the valley toward Black Pine Ridge to eke out an existence largely subsisting off the land supplemented with contract logging and government assistance. Over the decades the clan members became known for their honesty, hard work, and family solidarity. They were basically a courteous and friendly bunch, but messing with one of the family meant messing with the whole family.

Jed found all this out over the course of the next week. The morning after the blowout they woke up to an early December snow coming down like it wanted to drown the world. The knobby-tired F350 was covered with a foot of white, and the hollow around the first bend away from the homestead had drifted in with over four feet of snow. When Huck (Jed had to work at it to keep from calling him Hulk) asked if Jed was pressed to get somewhere, he said they could probably dig themselves out in half a day or so. Since they seemed to appreciate some company, and with the aroma of something heavenly floating out of the pot over the hearth fire, Jed said that his only object was to get to Seattle before Christmas. With smiles all around, they said the workshop, crude but with a pot-bellied stove and a cot, could be his for as long as it suited him.

During the week that it took for the weather to clear and the men to plow their way back to Highway #1, Jed simply fit into their daily routines. He chopped firewood, helped repair the starter on an old John Deere 4020, and even tried milking the cow one morning. The initial affinity grew into a quick friendship, and the Logans seemed to relish listening to his stories of Africa as much as he did their family history.

The day for leaving arrived and the three Logan mountain men drove Jed back to where his van was parked. The day before, Bodean had made a run into Butte to get a replacement tire put on Jed's rim along with another new one for a spare. He seemed happy enough that Jed paid for the round trip gasoline, and then some. As they prepared to part ways, Jed shook their hands and said, "Fellas, I can't say I've ever been treated more royally than by you folks."

Huck, a little flushed, said, "Jus' happy we's the ones happened along. Ya'll been a bless'n while's with us too."

"Blessings a good word for it, Huck. And it's worked both ways."

"I's worried at first," Harley added. "But bein' yer education and knowin' and doin' all that stuff, you's treatin' us like kin. Lotta folks high on their horses look down on us like worms or somethin'. Never felt you's doin' that."

"Well, I got to say that the Logans help restore my faith in humanity," Jed replied.

The three looked sideways at one another with a mixture of embarrassment and confusion. "We're not sure what you mean, Jed," Huck finally said.

"What I'm saying," Jed explained, "is that if there were more people that thought and acted like you folks, the world would be a whole lot better place."

Now more embarrassed than ever, they mumbled some things along the lines of "Aw shucks," and "Golly gee."

Something like that. They shook hands, Huck being careful not to crush all the bones in Jed's as he said he hoped they might cross paths somewhere down the line. Jedediah said, "I know where to find you guys."

Heading north to Drummond on his new tires, Jed felt even more reinforced in the decisions he had made for his life.

Standing in front of St. James Cathedral, Jed felt as small as a church mouse. Built in 1907, the massive structure was a major landmark in the First Hill neighborhood. While the one hundred and twenty-foot dome collapsed in 1916 and was never replaced, twin one hundred and seventy-foot spires lifted Jed's gaze as they pointed heavenward in symbolic profession of the faith which the church embodied. Based on his own experience Jed thought, *We Lutherans don't build things like this*.

It was three days before Christmas. Jed had taken his sweet time traversing the rest of Montana and then the Idaho panhandle and Washington State. Winter weather held him up here and there, and he alternated between sleeping in the van and opting now and then for a snug local-flavor motel with hot shower. He even tried downhill skiing outside of Coeur d'Alene and discovered in short order that running was much more his cup of tea. Entering the Evergreen State gave him something that approximated a homecoming tingle, but it was accompanied by what were still gut-wrenching memories of Angela. At any rate, Jed's globe-trotting exploits had brought him full circle – maybe half circle – to a point in time and a geographic place that seemed very right to him.

It took some investigation of the large cathedral

grounds with its maze of buildings, pathways, and doors to find the new outreach ministry called the Cathedral Kitchen. He had to wait until the noon meal clean-up was finished, and was then invited by the director, a rotund, jolly character named Thaddeus, to join him for a cup of brew. To Thaddeus, brew meant black, strong, and just below the boiling point.

After Jed shared a thimble-sized account of his life's journey, Thaddeus said, "So, you now want to become part of the Catholic Worker Movement, eh?"

"That's why I'm here," Jed replied. "This isn't a snap decision, and it's one I feel fully convinced about."

"Well, things are just getting off the ground here," Thaddeus continued. "and we can use all the help we can get. But I gotta tell you that the pay is outta this world."

"I thought it was all volunteer help," Jed quizzically said.

"Yep. That's what I mean. So you'll have to figure out how much you can help here depending on what you do to make a living."

"Right now," Jed went on, "I don't plan on getting any other job. I've got some resources stacked up that will allow me to work here full time if needed."

Thaddeus looked at him sideways, like one might look at a saint, and said, "Well Jed, there aren't many of your type around. And you tell me you're not even Catholic."

"Does that pose a problem?" Jed asked.

"Not in the least. Our only goal is solidarity with the poor. Seems to us that Christ didn't parcel out his love just to folks who met some preordained standard. So server or served, we don't require special identification badges."

And so it was that Jed found himself mashing potatoes and serving apple pie on Christmas Day in 1975.

As time went on he also found himself attending the community worship services and Bible studies, something which he had let lie fallow for quite some time. This became a period of growth and challenge in Jed's life, one which eventually led to something he never would have imagined. Jed had gone to his bank and had been astounded to find a balance of twenty thousand dollars. He knew it was Darrell's doing, and all he could do was reaffirm his gratitude for his friend's kindness. These funds enabled him to find low-income housing near the cathedral and begin the work for which he had come to Seattle.

It was not that Jed courted trouble, but it seemed to find him now and then. He had become a valued member of the Catholic Worker community due to his organizational skills, enthusiastic attitude, and commitment to the program. It was late one evening during his second year at the Kitchen where Jed had become one of the supper meal supervisors. The full-tummy crowd had melted back out into the mist of a typical Seattle February drizzle, and the clean-up crew of five was finishing the final wipe-down and stowing of industrial-sized pots and pans. Lights were off in the dining hall so at first nobody saw the dark figure that stood just outside the kitchen door.

Pietro, a Jesuit from Milan who had come to study at Seattle University and volunteered at the kitchen often, first saw the man and said with a lilting Italian accent, "Sorry, sir, but the meal is over. Can we help you with something?"

The figure stepped into the doorway and the light revealed a disheveled, slightly-built young man whose eyes darted back and forth as if electrified. "All of you, empty your pockets on the counter. Now! Then step back."

The man appeared unarmed to Jed, so he wasn't too worried about the danger factor. About ten feet from the man, Jed took a couple of steps toward him and said, "Hey, friend. We don't carry money on us when we work here, so let's just let these folks go about their business and you and I can go get some money. There's an automated teller just around the corner and I'm happy to help you out a bit." Jed was becoming more convinced of one of the main tenets of the Catholic Worker Movement, nonviolence. In earlier times he would simply have physically escorted the fellow back out to the street, but now words and deeds of kindness were his adopted modus operandi.

"You think I'm some kind of dumbshit, get me outside and beat the crap out of me," the disturbed man blurted after noticing Jed's musculature. "I'll show you my automated teller," he shouted as he pulled a snub-nose pistol from under his ragged jacket. Waving it around unsteadily, he looked back at Pietro and said, "You first, asshole. Move it *now*, unless you want some extra holes in your body." His speech was rather slurred, as if some chemical was inhibiting enunciation.

Jed was close enough that he was confident a leaping kick would have disabled the fellow before he had a chance to pull the trigger. But his newfound faith in nonviolence provoked another try at the gentle way. "No, I'm serious, man. You don't need that gun. I meant it when I said I'd help you."

Pietro, who had a large soup ladle in his hand, approached the man, saying, "Yes, yes. Indeed we wish to help you. If you would only . . ." But didn't get to finish the sentence. The intruder apparently took Pietro's advance with what he likely thought was a weapon in his hand as an attack. He fired four shots before the hammer hit on an empty chamber. Two missed, but one hit Pietro's right shoulder and another plowed directly into his heart. He was probably dead before he hit the floor.

As everyone froze, the man turned and ran out of the building. Jed let him go as he ran to his friend's aid while another bolted upstairs for the priest. As he cradled Pietro's lifeless body, Jed thought to himself: *So this is what nonviolence gets you.*

The whole Cathedral community was thrown into a state of shock and sadness. Some wondered if this might even derail the new Kitchen program, but the commitment of the servers kept uninterrupted meals on the table. After all, sad people were still hungry people. Extra priests were on hand to comfort and counsel the bereaved and confused, and some of the volunteers who had come to know him even sought out Jed's compassionate ear. While Jed mourned the loss of his full-of-life Italian friend, he also felt something else moving around down deep: anger. With the help of Father Samuel and the support of the co-workers, he was able to cool the lava that bubbled inside. At least he got the temperature to a manageable level.

By the spring of 1979, Jed had been a faithful participant in the Cathedral Kitchen organization for three and a half years. The attack on Pietro had affected him deeply, as it had the whole Catholic Worker community. Nothing like it happened again, but it contributed to Jed's thinking about his future. All the while he had worked at the Kitchen it had been constantly reaffirmed to Jed that this is what he should be doing at the moment, but ruminations about the longer term engendered a possible course of action that seemed to beckon repeatedly to him. This possibility was frequently reinforced by his growing felt need for more tools. Theological, philosophical, ethical tools. The Cathedral pastor, for whom he had developed respect and admiration, told him where he could go to acquire these tools: seminary. Hence his phone conversation with Darrell.

"You really think that's what I should do?" Jed asked.

"The question, Jed, is whether *you* really think that's what you should do. You know I'm not going to try to answer that for you."

"Yeah, I knew you'd say that. It's just that, well, how do you know for sure?"

"You don't," Darrell said. "If you feel moved in that direction, and I mean really moved, then you give it a try and see if it proves out. That's kind of the way it happened with me, and I'm still trying."

"So if I go this route, what's the next step? And which seminary is the best?" Jed asked.

"Can't go wrong with my alma mater in St. Paul. Why don't you give Luther a call and see what they have to say. Get an application and stare at it for a bit with a large stein of Leinenkugel's in hand. The spirit will guide . . . and I don't mean the brew. And, by the way – and I don't want any backtalk here – don't worry about the financial aspect. The growth of my investments has skyrocketed out of sight, so that's covered."

"Darrell, you've done . . . "

"Hush, lad! I said no backtalk. We'll think of it as part of my contribution to the ministry of the church."

So Jed, doing something he never had pictured for himself, took an intensive eight-week course in New Testament Greek at Seattle Pacific Seminary as a prerequisite for admission to Luther Seminary. In late August he bid a very fond farewell to the Catholic Worker community that had become his family in Seattle and pointed the still-chugging Westfalia van back east toward St. Paul, MN.

Chapter 26

May 1983 - St. Paul, Minnesota

As Jed, in regal cap and gown, walked up to get his Master of Divinity diploma, he thought to himself again how right this decision had been. Luther Theological Seminary was formed as a result of a 1917 merger of three small Norwegian Lutheran seminaries in Minnesota, the oldest one established in 1876. The first Norwegian Lutheran church built in the United States, an 1845 log structure from Wind Lake, Wisconsin called Old Muskego Church, had been dismantled and reassembled on the Luther campus in 1904 as a visible reminder of that august history. Even though he never knew his birth parents, the fact that they were from Norway, coupled with the Norwegian ethnicity of his U.S. guardians, the Hofstads, instilled in Jed a sense of those roots. Every now and then he would go into the historic Muskego Church and sit for a while thinking about his humble background in Rhodesia and how he might still be there if not for the love of Don and Ingrid Hofstad.

The four years had progressed more quickly than he ever would have thought possible, and now he stood poised to be addressed by that affectionate Lutheran term of relationship, *pastor*. He had kept his parents in the Matopos Hills apprised of his progress on a regular basis, and the few responses he received back, posted by the still-present Sommerfelds, communicated extreme pride with the promise of daily prayers for him.

The academic challenges of theological study were in no way burdensome to Jed. To the contrary, they were invigorating. Not only did he have the intellectual capacity and educational background that enabled a facile handling of the study load, but his zest for the substance of the courses made the whole experience by and large enjoyable. Be it Old and New Testament interpretation, constructive theology, church history, homiletics, biblical archeology, or pastoral care, Jed dove into it like a hungry man facing a feast. With his memory capabilities, the requirement to learn Greek in order to read the New Testament in its original language was a challenge easily conquered. By the end of his first year Jed could study the Greek New Testament as readily as if it was written in English. Courses in biblical exegesis, hermeneutics, epistemology, apocalyptic literature and the like opened a whole new world to him. Sometimes he just wandered around the small, oak and maple-filled campus thinking about and giving thanks for the mysteries of life that had brought him to this point.

Even though he found joy in the studies and regular affirmation that he was on the right track, Jed wasn't at all sure where this track might lead. The church's policy was that a seminary graduate should spend some years as a parish pastor before branching off into some other kind of specialized ministry. While Jed had no real objection to this, his heart was really for the poor and marginalized of society, and he hoped there would be opportunities for serving in that environment. Seminary readings of thinkers like Gutierrez, Moltmann, and Cone who championed what was called "liberation theology," augmented his Catholic Worker experiences to produce a determination to eventually find a ministry that focused on downtrodden and oppressed people. He could not have guessed what was in store for him.

Toward the end of Jed's second year, Ole Thorsdahl had fallen in alongside him on one of his campus walks. Thorsdahl was one of the senior professors and also one of the few scholars who made a specific point that working for societal justice was intrinsic to the Christian faith. Jed welcomed his company that day. "So, Jed, how are you feeling at the midway point?" Professor Ole asked.

"Good, Professor. I'm looking forward to internship to see how the parish pastor role fits."

"I'm sure you'll do very well, son. Fergus Falls is a pleasant little community."

On a shaded bench in front of Bockman Hall, they sat in silence for several minutes taking in the warmth and beauty of the spring day. Then Jed said, "I might change down the line, but right now I'm not thinking about lifetime ministry as a parish pastor. You've stimulated even more so my felt calling to the people who live on the edge in our society. I'm just not at all sure how to work that out."

Having stuffed and lit his omnipresent pipe, Thorsdahl puffed a time or two and replied, "The opportunities are manifold, Jed. Here or overseas. Get some basic pastoral ministry under your belt and you might be surprised what ends up presenting itself."

"I know you're right, Professor. And I'm content to play it out as it comes. I just can't help thinking about the future and what the long term might bring me," Jed responded. Then, "Do you have time for quick question?"

"Sure," said Ole. "My next class isn't for another hour."

"I realize," Jed went on, "that we don't have time for what could be a prolonged discussion, but I'm wondering about the question of violence and how it relates to the struggle for justice and liberation for people. I mean, can we ever justify resorting to force, armed force, if the nonviolent way just isn't working? On the one hand we've got Ghandi, a man absolutely committed to nonviolence who was assassinated for his convictions, and on the other hand Nelson Mandela who sits in prison for resorting to violence. You've had us read activists like Frantz Fanon and James Cone who seem to come pretty close to advocating violent revolution. And doesn't the church in Namibia support the armed liberation movement? How does one decide which path to pursue? When, if ever, can force be justified?"

"You weren't kidding, Jed, when you said this could be a prolonged discussion. I can't really give you a short answer that will satisfy. In fact, I'm not sure a long answer would satisfy either. But let me say this. The church has supported the use of armed force since the Constantinian era, and most of the time, I would posit, unjustifiably so. We've jumped the gun, so to speak, or jumped on the use-of-force bandwagon all too often as a way to respond, often even as our first response. I'd say that most of the time we've allowed, even blessed, the violent path either because we haven't thought it through properly or it's simply been the way to get what we want. That being said, I can't classify myself as a one hundred percent pacifist who, like Gandhi, would not resort to using force or violence ever. Would Jesus? Interesting question. Folks all the time hold up his cleansing of the temple as an excuse for resorting to violence, again, most of the time unjustifiably so. But whether Jesus would use physical force, whatever form that might take, to stop one man from killing a hundred . . . what do you think?"

"I think you're going to tell me that each one of us has to make that judgment for ourselves and then apply it to our own decision-making."

"Precisely. The church can, and should, dialogue on this subject till the cows come home, but in the end you and I have to come to our personal conclusions and act accordingly."

"Kind of thought that's what you were going to say. Although, unless I'm mistaken, I hear you suggesting that there are situations in which a Christian *can* justify resorting to violence."

"I might find a different word than justify," the professor said. "I guess what I'm saying is that I can imagine situations in which I would in fact resort to violence while saying 'God forgive me' as I do it. And I don't believe that's a cop-out. I simply believe that while we are called to be nonviolent peacemakers, taking the Gandhian route as an absolute is something we don't always have the luxury of adhering to."

After kicking around a few parting thoughts, Jed thanked the professor for his time and headed back to his dorm room. Although he really wasn't expecting a definitive reply from Thorsdahl, their discussion gave him more grist for the mill of his struggle to determine the relationship between Jesus' way and the Marine Corps way.

After two years of academic study on campus, the third year in the seminary plan was to work in a congregation as an intern. The goal was to acquire, under a supervising pastor, practical ministry skills from leading worship to making hospital calls and everything in between. Jed was assigned to Christ the Servant Lutheran Church in Fergus Falls, Minnesota. The year there was eventful and uneventful. Eventful in that Jed indeed experienced just about every aspect of parish ministry and acquired the tools needed for it. Uneventful in that the year proceeded smoothly with just about everything on a positive note. Things like learning liturgical ropes and church administration were necessary if not overly exciting, but Jed's true joy came from interaction with the people. Be it grieving with a family who just lost a loved one or simply having coffee with widower Munsen, Jed found that others yearned to realize God's presence in their lives . . . just like he did. And they had problems that called for healing balm, and questions that called for answers . . . just like he did. If he provided solace, comfort, and companionship to others on their faith journey, it felt like he was fulfilling his calling.

He had returned to St. Paul in August 1982 for his last year of academic study to find a great and welcome surprise. After having served his congregation in Madison for eleven years, Pastor Darrell had accepted a new call to a congregation in Minneapolis. This meant that for his final year at the seminary Jed would have his best friend in the world a few miles away.

When Jed went to visit Darrell in the modest home he had purchased overlooking Minnehaha Creek, he was shocked at his mentor's appearance. Darrell, who had always carried more weight than was healthy, had shed over fifty pounds. After hugs and backslaps, Jed said, "What the hey, man? You're not sick, are you?"

"Not that I know of," Darrell replied. "Just watching you do all that sweaty stuff for years finally got to me. That and reading up on how much my extra weight was stressing my aging body. So I joined a gym and took up cycling. Now, what you see is what you get."

"I like what I see, old man. And now I've got a running partner!"

"Whoa! Slow down there, boy. First off I said cycling, not running. Second, even if I did run all I'd do would be to slow you down. I think my best mile was clocked at, like, fifteen minutes."

“Okay, okay. But good for you! You’re looking great and I’ll bet feeling a whole lot better too.”

“That’s for sure,” Darrell said. “Don’t know why I didn’t do this years ago.”

Over dinner that night, even though he knew it wasn’t necessary, Jed tried to express his gratitude again for all the financial help over the years. Thanks to his benefactor, he really hadn’t paid a red cent of his own to go to seminary. Darrell reaffirmed not only his capacity for doing so, but the joy it gave him to assist his friend. He also made it crystal clear that he did not expect nor want Jed to attempt repayment of a single penny. God had gifted him with the resources and he was overjoyed at being able use them in this fashion.

The last year at seminary was designed to amalgamate the internship ministry experience with the years of academic course work. Several electives were built into this home stretch, and Jed always chose courses that dealt with social issues and practical pastoral care. Jed knew that the theological, homiletical, and interpretative studies were all necessary foundational matters, but his growing focus was on concerns such as the uneducated mother of three youngsters whose husband was just killed in an industrial accident. She didn’t need a sermon or theological lecture; her challenge was how to survive. Jed wanted to try to help her do that.

There was just one bump in the road during this final year. A bump not in the sense of totally upsetting the applecart, but one that added to Jed’s constant juggling of his ethical apples.

A common sight on the seminary campus and surrounding neighborhoods was Jed, scantily clad in the summer heat and bundled up in the winter cold, running like a demon possessed. Along with his studies, he continued a regular physical fitness routine, something that was simply a part of his being. Now and then as time allowed, Jed also worked out at a martial arts training center on North Snelling Avenue both as part of his overall fitness regimen and to keep his capoeira skills honed. While they may have heard of it, no one at the center had ever encountered someone practiced in this little known martial arts form.

Karate was Kyoshi Ben Yamaguchi's life. He was a Hachi-dan, or eight-degree black belt, who had not been beaten on or off the mat for over twenty years. He barely came up to Jed's chin and maybe tipped the scales at a hundred and fifty pounds dripping wet. But his lightning speed, perfectly toned considerable muscles, and expertise in karate combined to make *fearsome* a good description of his prowess. His one flaw was pride. Part and parcel of the practice of karate is humility and respect. But not all practitioners adhere to this philosophy, and Kyoshi Yamaguchi was one of them. Subduing his opponents was not enough. In a rare exception to the great majority of karate practitioners, Kyoshi Yamaguchi often bragged about his conquests and projected a self-centered arrogance. He intimated that he could not be beat, and when anyone dared to take up the challenge, the acknowledged master generally thrashed them with more damaging kicks and punches than that which was protocol for the sport.

When, in friendly matches of skill, Jed had bested every challenger in the center, Yamaguchi thought it time to teach the upstart what a true master could do. While each of the martial arts has its particularities of form and technique, a scoring system based on the number and placement of blows had been developed to determine winners in bouts involving mixed disciplines. The object was to amass the most points by landing kicks and punches that connected but were pulled so as to not cause injury. Bruises sometimes resulted from a participant inadvertently not pulling back with sufficient reserve, but in those cases a good referee would always give a warning and sometimes penalize the offender by taking away points.

It was standing room only for the match between Jed and Yamaguchi. For the former, it was a friendly match of skills. For the latter, it was a fanatical matter of honor. The bout was hard- fought on both sides, with Yamaguchi leading for most of it and coming dangerously close to being penalized for the use of overzealous power. But the karate champion was unaccustomed to and could not adequately adjust to the crouching and swaying machinations of capoeira. When the bell rang on the final round, Jed had won by two points. After the announced judgment and the obligatory final salute, or bow, to one another, Jed saw humiliation in Yamaguchi's demeanor and blood in his eyes. Jed didn't know it, but his opponent was determined to not let the matter end here.

It was about a month later and the week before Jed's graduation ceremony. He went for his last session at the martial arts center and to thank his workout buddies for their help and companionship over the past few years. They had a little surprise reception for him just before his leaving. Jed had not noticed Yamaguchi's absence throughout. After the final goodbye, Jed headed to the vacant used car lot two blocks away where center members often parked while working out. In the last light of the waning day he didn't see the group until they stepped out of the shadows from behind his van. The still-angry Japanese-American was accompanied by six sycophants who did the master's every bidding. Yamaguchi didn't waste time in stating his business. "It is time to teach you true humility, Mr. Bazo. We shall find out here and now who is the master."

"Look Kyoshi Yamaguchi," Jed said adjusting to the unexpected encounter. "We had our match and I got lucky. But I don't have the time or desire for a rematch, so please excuse me."

"There is no excusing," Yamaguchi responded. "This is necessary both for you and for me."

Sensing that talk wasn't going to accomplish anything, he moved toward the door of his vehicle hoping simply to ignore the man and leave the scene. But before his second step the six minions encircled him, each adopting a Zenkutsu-dachi stance. He realized that Yamaguchi had no intention of letting him get away without a fight. He felt a light tap on his shoulder and when he turned around the karate expert gave him a light shuto chop to the right side of his neck. It was not a disabling blow, but it was hard enough to let him know that Yamaguchi meant serious business. The circle widened to an acceptable radius as the 8th-degree black belt Hachi-dan moved to the middle and indicated Jed's position for the face-off.

Being pretty sure what the answer would be, Jed asked, "Shall we move this match back to the center where a qualified referee can judge?"

"The judge will be the one who is still standing in a few minutes. If you choose the coward's way you will receive the coward's reward. And it will not be pleasant."

So here Jed was again. With no desire to fight or inflict harm, he was backed into a corner where it seemed the only options were to take a severe, perhaps even debilitating, beating or to defend himself. He didn't even have time to think about what Jesus might do, because before the customary initial salute, Yamaguchi's right leg came at him with lightning speed. Jed had been instinctively anticipating something like that, and with the same speed he crouch-dodged the foot whose intention was a crippling blow to his head. What turned out to be an air-kick shocked the foot's owner because no one had escaped this maneuver for at least a decade. He whirled for his next move to find Jed performing the swaying dance motions peculiar to capoeira. He observed what appeared to be a pattern, so Yamaguchi intended his next blow to match Jed's body on the upswing. His goal was not to kill Jed, but a four-knuckle jab to the Adam's apple would put him on the pavement, leaving him gasping for breath and then speechless for at least a week.

Yamaguchi's mistake was that his eyes telegraphed his intent. As he stepped forward and aimed his punch at the anticipated contact point with Jed's throat, he got the surprise of his life. Before Yamaguchi's toes touched the ground on his forward step, Jed had halted his rising motion, swung around with his back to his adversary, then stood on his hands with his knees bent, and kicked back and upward with both of his heels into the forward-moving assailant's jaw. If Yamaguchi had ever contemplated what it might feel like to be kicked by a zebra, he didn't have to wonder any more. Except that in the second that it took all this to happen, he really didn't feel anything. Instant unconsciousness turned off all the lights. He would later mentally examine the occurrence over and over to try to understand what had happened. He also nursed a very sore neck for the better part of three weeks.

Jed had recovered into a fighting stance to face the other six warriors, all of whom stared in horror at their fallen idol and slowly backed away. Jed cautiously retrieved his gym bag, entered his van and headed out of the lot. On the way back to the seminary dormitory he thought again: *Is it just me, Lord? Is this a test? Can't You just give it a rest?*

Long after the graduation ceremonies, the two good friends sat on Darrell's patio after a late celebratory meal of grilled fillet mignon, twice-baked potatoes, and stir-fried veggies. Darrell toasted Jed, and with a clinking of glasses they sipped their favorite Malbec from the Mendoza region of Argentina. "So are you okay with going to South Dakota?" Darrell asked.

"Could be worse," Jed responded. "Might have been Louisiana."

"Seriously, you feel good about this next step?"

Jed had pondered that for the month or so since accepting the call to the local Lutheran church in Lemmon. "Yeah, I really do. A small rural community on the prairies will be a new experience for me, and I'm told that the folks out there will love me to death."

"And you're only eight hours away from the Twin Cities where you know you've got bed and board whenever you need a break. I'm glad you finally moved out of that van into something that'll do better in our winters out here."

Jed, with a considerable balance still in his bank account, had traded in the trusted Westfalia for a 1980 Chevy Suburban 4x4. He knew the gas mileage would be lousy with its big V8, but it would plow through most snowstorms and could carry a lot of gear. Another selling point was that with the rear seat folded down you could sleep in the back.

"Goes both ways, Darrell. I'm expecting to see you out my way now and then too. The president of the congregation told me that there's great pronghorn and mule deer hunting in the area, so you might finally let me teach you how to shoot."

"Just might do that," Darrell said. "Especially now that I'm fit to walk up and down those rolling hills." Then after a pause, "I'm really proud of you, Jed. Maybe proud isn't the right word, but what you've accomplished is doggone commendable. You might not know where this is all leading in the long run, but I'm betting the folks out there in South Dakota are going to be blessed in many ways by your presence."

They bantered back and forth for a while longer and then hit the sack. Jed's last thoughts as sleep overtook him were of the newness and the unknowns that awaited him in a little South Dakota town. In his middle-of-the-night dream, Jed was sitting on the roof of the church in Lemmon looking toward the western horizon. Lightning rent the sky, which was all black and red.

Chapter 27

May 1983 - Tam Ky, Republic of Vietnam

Spending one's formative years in a war zone is something no child should have to endure. Add to that a sadistic, psychopathic step-father and it's a recipe for disaster. Both situations describe Bo's young life.

The five years of Thao and Yuan's marriage could have been a chapter from Dante's *Inferno*. By late-70's Vietnamese standards, they had a rather secure existence as Thao's pig farm managed to squeeze out marginal profits. He was working for the government, of course, and that, along with being a Viet Cong veteran, assured a half-decent roof over their heads and three meals a day. But a combination of problems assured the disintegration of what could have been a reasonably stable life.

First, Yuan never kicked the drug habit acquired during the war years. This resulted in more than a little anger in Thao primarily because of the strain it put on their meager financial resources. There were also hours and days wasted while Yuan was in lotus-land, thereby neglecting, if not totally ignoring, the management of their household and of the scar-faced urchin she brought into the relationship. So then Thao would rant and rage, more often than not accompanied by merciless beatings of both Yuan and Bo. The odious and doleful nature of her situation generally resulted in Yuan's simply looking for more chemical escape from reality.

Second, Yuan produced no children to insure Thao's hoped-for security in old age. Neither of them knew that in her years of self-survival prostitution after Bo's birth, her reproductive organs had been irreparably damaged. Further pregnancies were impossible. As one barren year turned into another, Thao became more and more embittered toward his infertile wife and the one child she had borne. It did not help when the gang at the local watering hole started ribbing him about his lack of prowess between the sheets, chipping away at his already low self-esteem. That occasioned more than one fight, after which Thao usually came home drunk with bruised body and pride, and then lit again into both his miserable wife and her bastard son. As unpleasant as it was,

Bo came to perceive this recurring situation as normal.

Third, Bo seemed to Thao more and more of a millstone around his neck. He hated the boy enough for his simple presence and disfigured face, but as Bo began to grow in stature and defiance, Thao's response was beatings with a combination of sugarcane switches and fists. With his sociopathic psyche and his size advantage, the thrashings became more severe. Whenever Bo tried to hide or run, he was eventually caught and even occasionally pummeled into unconsciousness. At times he thought about escaping, but to where or to whom? When not stoned, Yuan protested weakly every now and then, but that simply resulted in Thao's transferring his fury to her. So little Bo was then forced to watch his mother being beaten bloody, and hope that the evil man would not turn on him again.

One day in 1980 Thao came in from the pig barn where he had been sweating all morning. It was labor-intensive work and the master's stomach was growling for the noon meal, which he had earlier indicated to Yuan better be ready on time. He hadn't noticed the lack of smoke from a cooking fire as he approached their humble three-room dwelling, so the shock of finding the house empty and no meal prepared froze him in his tracks. As he searched the home and the small property surrounding it and found no one, his anger grew. Stuffing down some raw vegetables and cold rice, his anger turned to rage. Throughout the afternoon's work back in the pig barn the rage turned into blinding fury. Returning to the house a little earlier than usual and finding it still empty and no evening meal being prepared, his fury became a homicidal frenzy. He sat down on a bench in front of the house with a bottle in one hand and a club in the other. And waited.

As the sun was sinking behind the verdant hills to the west, Yuan and Bo came up the path from the road to Tam Ky. Yuan was walking erratically, trying to stay on her feet in her drug-induced state. Bo trudged along a few steps behind, knowing that whatever Thao had in mind would be unpleasant in the extreme. He did not notice the club hanging alongside Thao's leg.

Several paces away, Yuan stopped and was trying to put together some words that might mitigate her husband's anger. She had dreamed up a story about having to help a neighboring farmer's wife who was sick, yet knew that whatever excuse she offered would not pacify her husband. As she opened her mouth to attempt a futile "I'm sorry," Thao swung the club with every ounce of his strength. It caught her on the left side of her head with the sound of smashing a squash. The force drove her whole body to her right and she crumpled to the ground without a sound. There was nothing left. Not a breath. Not a heartbeat. Just a lifeless carcass.

As Bo ran to his mother's side, Thao put both hands around his neck and lifted him off the ground. Holding Bo's face three inches from his own, Thao hissed through his rotting teeth, "Get a shovel from the barn and meet me in the field behind. Do it now if you want to stay alive."

Bo was forced to bury his mother in a grave that no one would ever see or visit. When he had finished digging, whipped from time to time by Thao who wanted it deeper, the murderer threw Yuan's frail, drug-ravaged body into the hole. He instructed the boy to fill it and blend it in with the appearance of the field, noting that if he did not do a good enough job he might just be digging another hole for himself when Thao returned. He then pivoted and headed into town for a meal and more alcohol.

Three years later Bo was still on the pig farm, although he took pains to cross paths with Thao as little as possible. The years following his mother's death carved scars on his soul to match the one on his face. Although his loathing had not diminished, Thao threatened to kill him if he ran away. After Yuan's death, Bo was charged with housekeeping and cooking duties which, if not up to Thao's standards, occasioned more beatings. And there was another reason his presence was required.

With Yuan out of the way, Thao had begun bringing women home for play. He didn't even have to pay them because most had the ulterior motive of snaring this single, relatively well-to-do farmer as a permanent meal ticket. Sometimes he would bring two or three at once, and Bo would be forced to watch the shenanigans. He actually thought watching the pigs was more interesting.

The big change had come when he was eleven years old and Thao brought two women and two men home for an evening orgy. The miscreant had turned his bedroom into a business where, for a few *dong*, the local currency, clients could design whatever sexual experiences they preferred. Added to Bo's miserable life was his now-required participation. Some, female or male, preferred young boys, and Thao had just the ticket right under his roof. It did not bring in huge cash gains, but profit was profit and a tryst with Bo could mean another bottle of rice wine for Thao.

As time went on, Bo's protestations were met with a withholding of food and the familiar beatings. But something else was changing. Due to his genetic makeup, by the time Bo was thirteen he was turning into a strapping young lad with height and bone structure significantly larger than other Vietnamese boys his age. In fact, he now stood a couple of inches taller than his step-father and outweighed him by twenty-five pounds . . . a fact that seemed to escape Thao. Then one day a revelation hit Bo as a lightning bolt: he did not have to take this anymore. It wasn't as if he consciously thought it out and developed a plan. But one evening as he saw Thao approach from the pig barn with his normal malevolent countenance, something snapped. Without any forethought for what might follow, all he knew in this instant was that he didn't have to take it anymore. He *wasn't* going to take it anymore. Looking around and seeing a short length of rope used occasionally for a clothesline, he coiled it in his left hand and held it behind him. Hanging by his side in his right hand was the club used for killing his mother.

Walking in and smelling the rice and pork which Bo had prepared, Thao growled, "Hey, bastard, that better be ready and better be how I like it. And clean up as soon as I'm done 'cause we've got company coming tonight." The two never ate together, the boy being allowed only whatever was left after Thao was done.

Bo didn't move.

"You hear me, boy? Get my food on the table now!"

Bo swung the club and hit Thao behind his left ear. It was a glancing blow, but hard enough to force Thao to his knees. Bo dropped the club and leaped behind him, wrapping the rope around his neck. The lad then fell onto his back, put both his feet against Thao's shoulder blades, and pulled with all his considerable strength. Thao's wiry physique and labor-hardened muscles notwithstanding, he was no match for a developed adolescent who outsized him and was infused with a passion verging on madness. Eight years of horror at this man's hands, including watching him murder his mother, went into the pull Bo exerted on the rope. The revolting excuse-for-a-human-being thrashed and twisted and kicked while trying to get his fingers underneath the rope that was slowly but surely choking the life out of him. There were no dying gasps since Thao's esophagus had been totally blocked, and as the body went limp, Bo pulled the rope tighter than ever until he sensed a complete cessation of heartbeats. He finally released his hold and stood up. He then spit in Thao's face, followed by urinating on him head to foot.

Not knowing what the future would hold except that it would not include the human wreck lying on the floor, Bo packed a few meager belongings in a sack, took the money he found on Thao and in the cracked, black flower pot, and walked out of the house. As he headed down the road toward Tam Ky he did not look back.

Chapter 28

August 1983 - Indianapolis, Indiana

In the nine years since the White River swim, Gunnar had matured considerably in body, mind, and spirit. He was pushing six feet tall and still climbing. At fifteen years old he was a superb athlete, excelling particularly in basketball and diving. His developed musculature, fair complexion, deep blue eyes and tousled straw-colored hair were complemented by a boyish smile that melted more than one female student's heart. An affable personality and genuine acceptance of others made for no lack of friends, and he was known for his ready helpfulness, be it assisting a teacher with a classroom project or tutoring another student who was struggling in a given subject. Many young gals seemed to develop academic problems that required his services.

Sonny and Linn had discovered long ago that a concern about Gunnar's grades was a non-issue. From elementary through junior high school every single parent-teacher conference was the same: nothing but commendation for Gunnar's work and positive projections about his future. At the end of his sophomore year at Broad Ripple High School he had straight A's. Every now and then a teacher would give him an A-minus on a paper or project, but generally only to instill a bit of humility. Not that Gunnar was boastful or arrogant. On the contrary, the lad was the picture of unpretentiousness and modesty, usually preferring to remain in the background.

As a second-year high school student, Gunnar was a starting guard on the team in a city that was basketball crazy. If his performances during that year were any indication, he was headed toward breaking many of the school point records. But that was not a goal that concerned "The Gun," as the local papers began calling him. In fact, when they won a game with Gunnar being the high scorer, in the post-game interview all he talked about was the team effort and how well some of his teammates had played. Repeatedly the all-American youngster proved that humility was not a lesson he needed to learn.

The Riviera Club continued to be a regular part of

Torkelson family life, especially since Gunnar began proving his ability on the diving boards. At eight years old he was doing flips and back dives off the one-meter spring board. By the next year he was doing one and a half somersaults off of the three-meter board. At ten years old he was on the junior diving team and the coach recognized a world-class potential. At twelve years old and after two years of intensive training, Gunnar was easily performing difficult dives such as a pike position forward two-and-a-half. At fifteen years old he had won the state three-meter springboard diving championship and placed in the nationals. His coach thought he actually might qualify for the national team at the upcoming 1984 Summer Olympics in Los Angeles . . . if he would just stop growing.

Although imagined careers are generally just hazy directions for high school sophomores, Gunnar's proclivities were distinct. He excelled in the extreme in all the sciences, primarily focusing on things mechanical and electric. His accomplishments allowed him to take courses for credit at Indiana University-Purdue University Indianapolis, the acronym IUPUI affectionately pronounced "Ooey-Pooey." In both systems theory and applied mathematics he outshone second year college students. None of this surprised his parents, who were well accustomed to his scholarly prowess. Mix Masters and hair dryers were hardly an intellectual challenge, and after he dismantled and fixed their broken portable air compressor when in eighth grade they figured he wasn't headed toward being a fashion designer.

Coinciding with Gunnar's excellence in both the academic and athletic worlds was an unquenchable desire for adventure. This quest often involved some degree of risk . . .

risk which never seemed to faze the young daredevil. In 1982 while the family had been staying at a resort on the Baja California coast, a warning was issued that several great white sharks had been spotted not far offshore. After discovering Gunnar's snorkeling gear gone, Sonny and Linn ran to the beach to observe their son paddling in the bay with a shark's fin some thirty yards away. Knowing that exhibiting their felt hysteria might cause Gunnar to thrash and flounder around, thus triggering an attack, they called to him with measured voices to swim slowly and gently back to shore. Balancing extreme relief with the desire to throttle his son's throat, Sonny asked, "What in the world were you thinking, Gunnar? You'd have hardly been a snack for one of those monsters."

"Oh, Dad," Gunnar countered. "We've studied great whites in school and it's perfectly safe to swim with them if you keep your cool. Besides, how many people in Indiana ever get a chance to see these beautiful creatures up close?"

"We don't know," Sonny said with his temperature rising, "because no one has lived to tell about it!"

"I'm sorry if it scared you," his son replied with downcast eyes and remorseful voice, and then with growing animation, "but it was wonderful, Dad. Exciting beyond belief. They're so cool. Wait'll you see the report I'll be able to make for biology this year."

When they talked about it later, Linn and Sonny acknowledged two things: that Gunnar's curiosity and risk-taking would not likely abate, and that, given his age, the opportunity for parental supervision of such was rapidly diminishing. But they agreed to ratchet up their vigilance to whatever degree was possible.

Diving continued to occupy a considerable amount of Gunnar's time and energy, but by the end of the summer of 1983 several things began to dampen his future as a world class competitor. The first was his size. Physicians and professional trainers projected that by the end of his high school years he would be somewhat over six feet tall. Due to the mechanical and aerodynamic particularities involved, it is much more difficult for very tall individuals to complete the moves involved in increasingly complex dives. The average height for Olympic medalist male divers was five foot seven. The second factor was Gunnar's newfound and growing love relationship with weightlifting. Divers are lithe and smooth-muscled rather than bulky and ripped. He had no illusions about winning the Mr. Olympia contest, but Gunnar enjoyed both the workouts themselves and the progressive change in his body. Put simply, he liked being and looking well-muscled. Who knows if someday it would be put to some good practical use?

Between pool and gym and his summer lawn-cutting business, Gunnar had little time to loiter. Which was fine with him since loitering produced, well, nothing. Not that he was obsessed with production, but, even at this young age, he wanted to use his time and energies wisely. His parents had instilled in him a sense of purpose and determination that he would carry throughout life. How he put this to use in the future would astound the unknowing and horrify the faint-hearted.

Chapter 29

November 1989 - Minneapolis, Minnesota

"From what I've seen, you're a doggone good parish pastor, Jed."

"Well, I hope so. I'm giving it everything I've got, but I think it's time for a change."

"Change in location or what you're doing?" Darrell asked.

“Still feel a call to parish ministry,” Jed responded, “and there’s things I really like about being pastor of a congregation. But I think moving on at this point would be good both for me and for the congregation. They’ve been great to me, but I’d like to get farther west, probably back to Washington if something opens up.”

Jed had been in Lemmon just shy of six years. He worked hard at faithfully carrying out his duties as parish pastor to this small rural congregation, and for the most part was well received and appreciated. If there was any rub, it came from the time he spent on the Standing Rock Indian Reservation about twenty miles to the east.

In the small Lemmon public library Jed had run across an old, worn copy of *My People, the Sioux* by Luther Standing Bear. That led him to search out and order additional writings by and about the Lakota and Dakota peoples, many of which lived not far away. Because the 1890 Wounded Knee Massacre and the 1973 American Indian Movement standoff on the Pine River Reservation had taken place barely three hundred miles due south, he also read extensively on that history. He even used some vacation time in 1987 to visit Wounded Knee, particularly seeking conversation with tribal elders on the reservation. All of which began to get on the nerves of some of the church elders since in their minds they were *not paying Pastor Bazo to spend time with Indians*. Of course, no one acknowledged any prejudice against Native Americans, but no Indians were members of the congregation so *why was their pastor so often with them instead of recruiting new souls for the Lemmon Lutheran church*?

The church council had had a conversation with

Pastor Jed to voice their concerns, but when little changed, council president Alex Nelson finally contacted the synodical bishop in Sioux Falls. In time, the bishop, on one of his cross-state visits, stopped in at Lemmon for a chat with the recalcitrant pastor. Jed, who had met him once, ushered the portly cleric into his office. Bishop Foxworthy was outfitted in a purple clergy shirt with white round-the-neck collar. Hanging just above his navel was an ornate silver pectoral cross with a multi-colored Ethiopian Welo opal in the center. It looked to Jed like wearing it would produce a neck ache by noon. The bishop's shined shoes would have made any Marine proud, and his fingernails had to have been manicured no more than forty-eight hours ago. After several minutes of chit-chat, Foxworthy said, "Jed, I received a call from Alex Nelson not too long ago requesting my assistance with your situation here."

Pretty sure he knew what the answer would be, Jed replied, "To what situation might you be referring, Bishop Fred?"

"The Native American situation, Jed. I believe the church council has discussed this with you previously."

"Yes, they have. But I thought we had come to a mutual understanding. Alex never indicated it was a problem that he thought required your attention."

"Well, apparently in his mind it is. Numerous church leaders here think that you have been neglecting your pastoral duties by spending an inordinate amount of time with the Indians."

"In town or on the reservation?" Jed asked.

"Both," the bishop responded.

"My own assessment," Jed offered, "is that I have in

no way been delinquent in my congregational responsibilities. I keep detailed records of my time and activities, and I'd be happy to share them with you if you feel it's necessary. No congregational needs or individual members have been shortchanged. Besides, I thought part of our mission was reaching out to the unchurched."

"Please tell me, Jed, how many of the Indians that you've reached out to have become members of the church?"

Jed began to feel a hot spot on the back of his neck. The Native American communities, both in town and on the reservation, were among the poorest and most neglected in the state. This reality was the result of their historical oppression and persecution by the white tribe that simply came west and confiscated their lands, oftentimes accompanied by purposeful genocide. And most of it happened with the blessing of clergy and church members, or at least with the tacit acceptance of such. "Are you suggesting, Bishop, that Jesus would ignore what has happened to these people and leave them off his visitation list?"

Beginning to fidget a bit, Foxworthy replied, "Of course not. But Jesus also knew how to arrange his priorities. I'm sure you remember in Matthew's Gospel that Jesus said to the Canaanite woman that he came only for the lost sheep of the house of Israel. And would you not agree that your chief priority is the congregation that called you to minister to them?"

"You also remember, I'm sure, that Jesus ended up healing the daughter of that woman. He was challenging her, but not in a way that made it an either/or. I would hope that the good people of our congregation would see that reaching out to the estranged Native American community is part and parcel of our mission."

They palavered back and forth for a time until both seemed to realize that all had been said and neither was ready to abdicate his position. As it became obvious that the bishop was ready to move on, he said, "I hear of much of the good work that you're doing here, Jed, and I pray blessings upon its continuance. But I must caution you to heed the wishes of your congregants. You are, after all, called to serve them, and in the ways they deem most needed."

Jed had no more to say. He wished the bishop well and thanked him for coming. But he also began to see the writing on the wall.

It didn't take long after Bishop Foxworthy's visit for Jed to conclude that it was time for someone else to serve the Lemmon congregation. Someone who didn't give a rat's ass about Native Americans. So after making his desires known to the bishop of western Washington, in February 1990 Jed accepted a call to Yakima, Washington, to be pastor of St. Timothy Lutheran Church. It was a bonus for him that the community was on the northeastern edge of the Yakima Indian Reservation. To his surprise and delight, the congregational leadership had no problems with reaching out to the native community. They actually saw it as part of their mission, and several Klickitat families had become members of the church. But a different problem here manifested itself that led to a major change in Jed's life.

It was good to be back in Washington. Life in Yakima was pleasant and the congregation was enthusiastically engaged in a variety of social ministries. Then in the summer of 1993 Lila moved to the area from Aberdeen, Washington, and joined the church. She had a single sister about twenty miles south in the small rural town of Zilla and they were both happy to be that close to each other. Lila McIntosh was a forty-six year old widow whose husband had drowned in a fishing boat accident two years earlier. Her period of mourning seemed to be over and she was hot to trot. She was also "hot" with respect to face and figure. When it turned out that a forty-seven year old bachelor, especially one with the looks and physique of Jed, was the pastor of the closest church, her sights were set.

Several seminary professors had cautioned students that sooner or later they might find themselves in a situation that invited them to compromise their values, indeed, their ordination vows. The reference was to the possibility of finding themselves in a situation where inappropriate sexual innuendos were made. Not only were such occasions embarrassing both for pastor and parishioner, but there had been cases where a spurned person turned such rejection into a vendetta. When the latter happened it was never easy. As Jed found out.

Pastors always wanted to make new members feel welcome, which included home visitations. Jed was sharp enough to intuit that placing himself alone in a home with a relatively new widow was simply not prudent. His first visit with Lila was at a local coffee shop where they began to get to know each other. For Jed, this was par for the course as a pastor who wished to know enough about parishioners to be able to minister to them effectively. Relationship-building was simply part of the equation. Except that Lila was trying to solve a different equation.

It wasn't that Lila was unlikable or unattractive. Jed

simply felt that a romantic relationship was not the hand he played anymore. Celibacy had become a matter of fact. Jed repeatedly had to find reasons to excuse himself from invitations to dinner at Lila's. But at congregational events she seemed to always be hanging on his arm, so much so that there was talk among parishioners about their budding relationship. More often than he would have liked, Lila would drop by the church asking if he had time for a quick cup of coffee. It got to the point that Jed would either make sure someone else was in the facility when Lila showed up or, if not, manufacture the need to be elsewhere immediately.

One day, making sure Jed's suburban was the only car in the parking lot, Lila came in and said she really needed to talk with him in private. It was against his better judgment, but he was caught unaware, and she had already barged into his office. He did say that he only had a minute, and made sure his office door was open to the public. The problem was that no public were around at the moment. When Lila took off her sweater, she revealed a considerable cleavage that left very little to the imagination. Before Jed had a chance to say or do anything, Lila announced that she was for the taking, either now or later. As Jed began to protest, she threw herself on him and buried her face in his neck, brushing her full and burnished lips against his collar and pulling his shirt part of the way out. Jed pushed her off, said that this was most inappropriate, and demanded that she leave the office at once.

As coincidence would have it, the church secretary pulled into the parking lot at the end of her lunch break just as Lila flew out the door crying crocodile tears and with her blouse partially ripped. Running erratically toward her car she called to the secretary, "Help me! Keep that monster away from me! I never expected this from a pastor!" She jumped into her foxy Mazda Miata and squealed the tires as she gunned it onto the street. Mrs. Maurer came into the office to find a flustered Jed tucking his shirt back in and lipstick very evident on his collar.

Two weeks later Jed was on the phone trying to keep his voice under control. "This is crap, Darrell. First class bull-crap!"

"Jed, I know you well enough to believe your version one hundred percent. But apparently the bishop doesn't."

"Oh, he says he believes me, kind of. But he also says his hands are tied. It's her word against mine. Plus, the secretary's account doesn't exactly support my version. And she's been a trusted stalwart here for over twenty years."

Darrell wasn't sure what direction to go with this. He knew Jed was squeaky clean, but in cases like this it didn't seem to make much difference. Once accused, it was generally guilty until proven innocent. "But there's no way to prove anything," Jed angrily said. "This Lila is now under a psychiatrist's care for post-traumatic stress and is making noise about suing both the church and me."

"I don't know what to tell you, buddy. If you fight it, the chances of winning are historically pretty low. What about the congregation? Won't they support you?"

"They seem to be pretty split on that," Jed replied. "Several key people say they really believe me, but when it comes to proof in court, all they can do is be good-character witnesses prior to sentencing."

"Do you really think this woman is going to take you to court over the matter?"

"I'd guess not. She doesn't need the money. My hunch is that she'd be happy enough if I just lost my job. You know what the old saying is, *Hell hath no fury like a woman scorned.*"

"What does the bishop advise?" Darrell asked.

"He's not advising anything. He said outright that for the good of the church I need to resign immediately."

"And what then?"

"Nothing. He says he cannot in good faith recommend me for call to another congregation with this on my record. So much for believing my version, huh?"

Darrell could tell from Jed's tenor and disposition even over the phone that he had come to a conclusion. "So . . . your thoughts?"

"My thoughts are history. So is the church. I'm leaving."

Not knowing exactly what he meant, Darrell asked, "Leaving what? The ministry?"

"That remains to be seen," said Jed. "But I'm fed up with church bureaucracy and the games people play. Bishops, two of them, council presidents, members who feel sorry for themselves, women who want to ruin you because you won't jump in their pants, colleagues who won't support you . . . this isn't what I got into the ministry for."

"I can understand how you feel that way. I really can. Unless you have something else in the works, why don't you store your stuff and come here to Minneapolis to try to sort out your thoughts. Go ahead and resign and hope that gal lets the legal thing die. You can just kick around here until you figure out your next move, and it'll give us some time together that we haven't had for a while. I might even run around a small lake with you this time."

"Thanks, Darrell. Let me think it over for a few days, but it's probably what I'll do. I'll get back to you shortly to let you know what's happening."

A week later Jed had resigned from the congregation, cleared out his office, put his meager belongings in a self-storage facility, and headed east to the Twin Cities. Given the circumstances, there was no going-away party for him. He simply thanked those who he felt really believed him, said goodbye, and rumbled out of Yakima. Fifteen hundred miles of solitary driving would give him time to think about how he might exercise his felt calling to be a pastor, but outside of the very unfair institutional church.

Chapter 30

September 1985 - West Lafayette, Indiana

By the time Gunnar walked across the stage to receive his graduation diploma, he owned three records at Broad Ripple High School. First, he had set individual records in basketball for both a single game and total career points. In 1983 he helped take the team to the semi-state finals, although they failed to make the championship game. Second, he was the only student in the history of the high school to make straight A's all four years. The latter opened up opportunities to attend almost any college of his choice, with most of them offering full-tuition academic scholarships plus additional living expenses. Yale, Harvard, Stanford, University of Michigan, and UCLA were all beating on his door, but there was never much question in Gunnar's mind. Purdue University won hands down.

It wasn't that Purdue was only an hour's drive from Indianapolis, although Gunnar's closeness to his parents gave that an added plus. It also had nothing to do with costs since the financial package offered to him meant about all he'd have to do was come with change for extra expenses like laundry and burgers. Purdue won because it had an engineering faculty second to none and offered a major in multidiscipline engineering. This major was for students who planned to practice engineering but whose specific career goals had not yet been defined. The program offered considerable flexibility designed for exposure to a broad range of diverse engineering specialties which, in turn, permitted students to develop an individual plan of study. Gunnar felt like it had been designed specifically for him.

The Purdue campus was not what you'd call Ivy League pretty, but had an air of Midwestern majesty about it. Some might substitute *massive* for *majestic*. Brick and concrete were everywhere, with a few fountains and spires thrown in for spice. One might not go so far as to describe the environs as *stoic*, but *serious* might be a good alternative. Everything was functional, practical, and . . . well, serious. Which suited Gunnar just fine. He wasn't there to party, but to get a serious education. He was affable, gregarious, and well-liked, but football games, fraternities, and weekend beer-bashes were all far secondary to his studies.

Deciduous trees in full fall color blessed the open ground between walkways, classrooms, and parking lots. As Gunnar walked from an advanced calculus class to one on quantum physics, he appreciated how manicured the small grassy areas and planted flora were kept. He thanked his concept of God, which was something like The Force in the Star Wars series, for the opportunities before him. His studies were eminently more challenging than in high school, and he drank it all in thirstily, impressing his professors with the ease with which he assimilated facts, figures, and concepts.

Athletics being a part of his life ever since he could remember, Gunnar took pains to fit regular workouts into his schedule. Even if it meant missing the odd meal or social gathering, he would run or swim instead. He also found a bit of time for female companionship. A bit. The heavy demands of his studies simply did not allow for the kind of time and attention most young women seemed to want or expect. With his all-American-boy good looks and lean, well-honed physique, he disappointed numerous young women who earnestly vied for his attention. The odd movie or a bit of kissing and hugging in the bushes was as far as Gunnar would take it. So eventually the gal would let him go in favor of some hunk who would lavish her with the attention she felt she obviously deserved.

Gunnar's loading or overloading his course schedule every year, which for him was twelve months a year, enabled him to graduate *summa cum laude* in three years. He then progressed immediately into a master's degree program in civil engineering, which he completed in two years under a teaching fellowship. By the spring of 1990, the young man was educated up to his eyeballs and ready for some hands-on engineering experience. He also hoped to find some employment that would include some of the adventure he craved. He had been such a earnest student for so long that he thought he needed to descend to the ocean's depths or ascend Mt. Everest to balance things out. His first job offer promised the opportunity to both begin practicing his trade and pursue some genuine excitement.

As Gunnar was finishing up his master's thesis and assisting with his last teaching assignment on thermal dynamics, one of his advisors informed him that Linden Technologies International was going to be recruiting on campus in the near future. Linden Tech was a world leader in water development and management, specializing in renovation or replacement of corrupted systems. Since Gunnar had narrowed his focus to this precise field of study, he was keenly interested in what Linden might have to offer. He thought that his thesis, "Impacts of Rapid Urban Residential Expansion on Drinking Water Quality: The Effects of Poorly Managed Development," might help gain him an interview. Which is exactly what it did.

Five weeks later he met on campus with representatives of the company and learned that they sought an Assistant Project Manager for an upcoming contract to assess, rehabilitate, and expand the water and sewer system for the city of Guadalajara, Mexico. A senior field engineer would head the project, but the company knew that a qualified new graduate could be acquired at a much lower cost than another engineer with years of experience. Besides, they were committed to fostering talent for this growing overseas market, talent which might be of long-term benefit to the company. The Guadalajara contract was projected to take three years to complete, after which time Linden would evaluate the performance of the new employee with respect to a possible ongoing relationship with the company.

Gunnar liked the company, the project, the location, and the two recruiters who interviewed him. They apparently liked him in return because two weeks later he was offered the position with the understanding that further association with the company upon project completion would be based on evaluated performance. The young engineer could find nothing wrong and everything right with the proposal, and felt eager to accept it. He called his father the night of the offer to talk it over.

Sonny was as proud as proud could be of his son. After listening to Gunnar's initial description and obvious enthusiasm, he said, "It sounds to me, Son, like just the sort of thing you were hoping for. You okay with being that far from home?"

"Dad, it's only a six-hour plane ride. And don't you think it's about time I started exploring something other than Indiana corn fields?"

"Hey, just checking, and you're absolutely right. Your mother and I've got to cut the apron strings sooner or later. In fact, we were just talking the other night about how fortunate we were to have had you so close during your college years. It could easily have been Stanford, you know."

"I've felt the same way, Pop. But now, at least for several years, you'll have a ready-made vacation spot waiting for you whenever you want."

"Never really thought about going to Mexico," Sonny responded, "but with you down there it'll be a given."

"Well, as far as Mexico goes, Guadalajara looks really cool. It's got this place they call Libertad which the brochures say is the largest market in the western hemisphere. It seems to be a pretty modern city, and if you like mariachi, they have a giant festival every September. There's also . . . "

"Whoa, slow down, Gun. Sounds like you've done your research and are planning to accept their offer. What outfit was that again?"

"The full corporate name is Linden Technologies International, but the recruiters said most people shorten it to LinTech. I checked out their profile and the company appears to be rock solid. They're financially way in the black every year and have a global reputation for doing good work. Their headquarters are in San Diego, so I imagine I'll spend some time there now and then."

"So I'd say go for it. By the way, if Guadalajara is so progressive, how come they need a multi-million dollar renovation of their water and sewer system?"

"Do a little reading on Mexican history, Dad. You'll find that Guadalajara is as old as dirt, and apparently a lot of that dirt is getting into their water system. Some of the newer areas are more or less up to date, but the old city needs a total revamp of the whole structure. And LinTech are world class experts at this sort of thing."

They chatted a while longer, and at the end Gunnar said that he was ninety-nine percent sure he was their man. The project was scheduled to begin in a month, so that gave him two weeks to pack up and take his belongings home for storage, and spend some quality time with his folks. Then he would undergo a two-week orientation period at the San Diego headquarters developing relationships with his co-workers and learning the project details. By early July he'd be practicing Spanish phrases on a flight south to his new home.

Gunnar had been so busy that he couldn't believe it when he got a card from home congratulating him on successfully completing his first year in Guadalajara. The beautiful city had a myriad of fun and interesting things to do, yet they were largely put on hold due to the demands of the job. His extracurricular activities were running and weightlifting, and learning to use firearms at a local shooting range. He thought about buying a handgun, but thought he'd first better become familiar with operation, safety, and marksmanship skills. Mexico also had severe restrictions on owning firearms. He didn't mind his work schedule because he loved the job and was gaining important practical knowledge and skills day by day. The senior supervisor, Jason Greene, had been with LinTech for twenty-four years and took an instant liking to Gunnar. Jason had a well-tended pot belly, wore his hard hat a bit askew, and was usually chewing on an unlit cigar. And the man was good at his trade. Excellent, even. At the end of that first year he had increased the profit margin by being a month ahead of schedule, performance that any company appreciated and rewarded. Greene made it clear to the company brass that part of their success was due to his sharp and hardworking assistant manager.

When Sonny and Linn visited, Gunnar took a week off and did a few sightseeing excursions with them. Linn went a little nuts in the Libertad Market with the astounding amount of wares at astoundingly low prices. Sonny had more fun in the nearby village of Tequila, the town where the famed drink originated and for which it was named. The Torkelsons enjoyed their time so much that as they boarded the plane for the flight home they covenanted to return soon.

Toward the end of Gunnar's second year, the project was going so well that he took ten days off to do some of that adventuresome exploring that was in his bones. It was no small advantage that by this time he had picked up the Spanish language, easily carrying on conversations with the local populace.

Rock-climbing was something Gunnar knew existed. He had seen videos and picked up a couple of climbing magazines, hoping that someday he might be able to try it. It wasn't long before he learned about El Diente, a rock-climbing haven a half hour south of the city that had over two hundred routes up scores of rock faces. One could only learn bare rudiments in such a short time, but he hired a climbing guide to show him the ropes, and by the end of the week he was handling slopes rated 5.8 with the intent to improve to 5.10 on his next trip down. He finished off his time away with a scheduled two-night stay at a resort on Largo de Chapala, a popular lake recreation area. *Who knows*, he thought, *one might even meet a pretty señorita who could enliven the end of his vacation*. Little did he expect the offer that came his way the first evening.

He was sitting at the bar in the resort's comfortable lounge with a Corona in hand while watching a Mexican soccer match on the wall-mounted TV. A man sat down on the stool next to him. He wore an open-collar crimson silk shirt under a while linen suit. His primped hair, trimmed mustache, and manicured nails bespoke genteelness if not financial well-being. "I have not seen you here before, *amigo*," the Mexican said in flawless English.

"Hello. This is my first time to Chapala. Do you live here?" Gunnar assumed he was simply a local either lonely or just being welcoming. Might as well make small talk.

"Yes, *amigo*. This has always been my home. Are you visiting from *Los Estades Unidos*? Pardon me, I tend to mix my English and Spanish. Do you speak Spanish?"

"Very elementary. I've only been down here a couple of years and have been so busy working that I haven't had time to become more proficient with your beautiful language."

"Ah, you live here, yes? May I respectfully ask what brought you to Mexico?"

"Sure. I'm with a company working on a water and sewer project in Guadalajara. We've probably got around another year to go to completion."

With his eyes narrowing slightly and the beginning of a smile, the man said, "And you left your wife back in the States, no?"

Gunnar was beginning to get a little uneasy with the questions. So offering his hand he said, "My name's Gunnar. And yours?"

"José Vega at your service, sir," he said as they shook hands.

"Well, nice to meet you, Mr. Vega, but I don't really need any servicing this evening." Gunnar's unease was warming up and he was ready to terminate the conversation.

"Ah, Gunnar, a young man like you is always ready for some fun, si? And I can direct you to some *señoritas* who can make this a night you will not easily forget."

"Thanks for the offer," he replied, "but that's really not my style." Gunnar certainly wasn't anti-women, but patronizing prostitutes was far off his radar.

"I understand, *Señor*, but I have something in mind that perhaps you have never tried but you might find fitting your style."

Gunnar was reaching the limits of his patience, but curiosity engendered one more question. "And just what is it that you think I might have never tried?"

"Perhaps you have had a virgin, yes? But not one so tender and tight as my young friends who are so willing to please."

Under the bar, Gunnar's hands began to ball into fists as he asked, "And just how young might they be, my friend?"

Now with a twinkle in his eye, José said, "What is your pleasure? I have a lovely young maiden no older than ten who would be anxious to experience the machismo of a handsome man like you. And since this is your first visit to Chapala I will arrange this for a special price."

Gunnar couldn't believe his ears. He had read that things like this existed, somewhere. But to sit face to face with a pimp offering him a ten year old girl was like something out of a dream. A nightmare. While he had never hit anyone in the face with his fist, he was a matter of seconds from doing so. Probably the only thing that stopped him was not wanting to call Jason to come bail him out of a Mexican prison, not to mention what it might do regarding his standing in the company. With eyes shooting daggers and teeth clenched in rage, Gunnar quietly hissed, "Get out of my sight, you bastard."

Jose, for whom this wasn't a first time experience, said, "Okay, Yankee. You want to miss the time of your life, that's up to you. *Adios.*" And he sauntered out of the lounge.

Later while lying in bed trying to sleep, Gunnar mulled over the episode. What kind of human being would pimp a ten year old girl? Is that even human? Would anyone care if a walking suit full of fecal matter like that was wiped off the planet? While he was also a mite stunned at the amplitude of his abhorrence and anger, it occurred to him that if he had the opportunity, he just might actually pull the trigger on such a repulsive piece of scum like José.

Jason and Gunnar shepherded the project to completion five weeks earlier than projected and seven percent under estimated production cost. Since the contract was for a set price, the savings meant an even greater profit margin for what was already a fruitful undertaking. Not only did Gunnar receive a healthy bonus out of the deal, but the evaluation of his work combined with a series of high-level management interviews led to the offer of permanent employment. His intelligence, knowledge, and work ethic were recognized as far above average, and LinTech did not want this outstanding employee lured away by the headhunters who were always looking for talent such as his.

"Hi Mom, Dad," Gunnar said to his parents who were both on the phone. "We've finished up things here in San Diego and I'll be home for a couple of weeks before my new assignment."

The Torkelsons knew that their son had accepted the company's offer of a long-term relationship, but they had been waiting to learn where the next project would take him.

"That's wonderful, dear," Linn beamed. "These last years have been so demanding, we can't wait for you to just come home and relax for a while."

"So," Sonny chimed in, "are you going to keep us in suspense? Where to now, Champ?"

"Okay. Are you ready for this? I'm going to Vietnam."

When Gunnar walked off the plane onto the tarmac it was one hundred and three degrees Fahrenheit with eighty-eight percent humidity. The world was a sauna. As he looked toward the glow of what appeared to be the center of the city he said quietly to himself, "Da Nang, get ready to meet Gunnar Torkelson."

Chapter 31

July 1993 - Da Nang, Republic of Vietnam

Bo had changed his name. Not much of a change. He simply added an "a," making it Boa. Boa liked snakes, constrictors in particular. Never mind that Vietnam only had Burmese pythons and not boa constrictors. They both operated with the same modus operandi: they killed by squeezing, squashing, crushing. Boa liked that. He had no affection for his given name, especially since he had heard it primarily as a cuss word on the lips of his degenerate, now-dead excuse-for-a-father. So adopting this particular reptilian moniker not only helped him psychologically distance himself from his past, it provided an identification that, particularly in later years, instilled terror in the hearts of adversaries.

Significant things had happened in the ten years since Boa constricted the life out of Thao. Given the historical situation, it was not uncommon for a thirteen-year-old to have to make his own way in life. Even though in 1983 the war had been eight years past and a peace of sorts tried to exert itself over the ravaged land, reconstruction was still in the early stages. Amidst the Communist regime's ongoing attempt to sort out who had been for or against them, the land-scape abounded with war bastards and orphans. Who survived, and how well, depended on one's wits, ingenuity, connivery, and viciousness. Boa scored well in all categories, with the last being a specialty. Anyone who crossed him, and sometimes all one needed was to literally cross his path, experienced the consequence of his heinous nature.

During his final teenage years he lived from hand to mouth. His hands were used primarily for killing and his mouth savored the proceeds. Upon leaving Tam Ky he had made his way to Da Nang, a city pushing three quarters of a million people where he could much more easily fade in and out of the woodwork, and in which the pickings seemed endless. His initial victims were shopkeepers or lone stragglers on some dark street. If someone had a watch or wad of cash, they would end up as one of his targets. His dispatching tool was a piece of hemp rope with two knots close together that would nicely compress the trachea when tightly cinched, and knotted loops at each end which fitted around Boa's wrists. The garrote's length was such that when he fitted it around someone's throat it placed his hands in perfect position to exert maximum pulling pressure while at the same time severely limiting the victim's ability to turn his body in order to retaliate. By his seventeenth year he had killed no fewer than thirty individuals, in part for the material gain but almost as much for practicing the technique. Besides, it gave him some unexplainable pleasure to choke the life out of someone. As his proficiency grew, he began picking what looked like more lucrative targets. Or, just for fun, stumbling drunks that reminded him of Thao.

Traumatic as his childhood might have been, Boa was no dummy. Three attributes contributed to developing his future vocation: an above-average-Vietnamese size inherited from his American birth father, his scarred face that tended to scare the ever-living crap out of anyone on whom he directed his intense gaze, and enough of a working knowledge of English to enable rudimentary conversation in that language. He had acquired the latter in his late teens by doing piecemeal day jobs for U.S. contractors who were paradoxically now being used in the reconstruction effort. He garnered as much from listening as he could, and received the odd tutoring session from friendly U.S. employees. With what seemed to be an inborn foresight, Boa looked to the future with a fuzzy basis of a plan for which a working knowledge of English would be a great asset.

Boa's plan revolved around sex. He was personally asexual, undoubtedly a result of childhood exposure to both his mother's and Thao's perversions and the abuse he had endured. If there was anything that aroused a sensation akin to sexual excitement it was when he stalked and strangled some unfortunate prey. He was a constrictor of the first order, the name Boa describing it perfectly. By the time he was twenty-one, the mention the nickname by which he became known, *con ran*, the snake, could cause the hearers uncontrollable tremors and people would start looking over their shoulders. This was a given in the small province of Da Nang, but was also spreading to the larger ones of Hua Thien Hue to the north and Quang Nam to the south. Boa, The Snake, was becoming synonymous with death, and one particular incident accelerated his infamy.

The city of Hue had been decimated by the war, particularly during the Tet offensive of 1968, the year before Boa was born. Although in 1990 the reconstruction effort still left much to be accomplished, as everywhere in the world, there were pockets of wealth. Some people always found a way to suppress their consciences, assuming they had one, and manipulate others, generally the poor and downtrodden, to their own advantage. Boa enjoyed taking advantage of these unscrupulous manipulators for his own pleasure and enrichment.

Boa had recruited three accomplices for the beginning of what was to become a very successful gang. He made sure of two things: that they were not nearly as smart as he, and that he had their undying loyalty. In fact, once they joined his efforts, he made it clear to them that disloyalty would result in death. Duc, an inveterate weightlifter whose muscles were testament to such, was imposingly large. One quickly learned that if he was mad, it was best to be nowhere near his orbit. Trang was small, wiry, and quick, and possessed an affable nature which confounded Boa. Lanh was street-smart like his boss, and simmered with a rage that was, if possible, stronger than Boa's. Each one had been necklaced by Boa's garrote to within an inch of his life, and each one had seen Boa strangle more than one victim with ease. No one knew where Boa lived, only that he would show up like a ghost whenever he wished and often when least expected. In short, Boa ruled by fear and cunning, and he trained his henchmen to do the same. Providing for their sustenance also kept them on a string.

It was a cool evening during the rainy season, and the four sides of the bordello were being watched by Boa and his crew. Prostitution was officially frowned upon by the righteous Communist government of unified Vietnam, but eyes were turned away especially when it came to Party and community leaders' needs. After all, men would be men, ideology notwithstanding. This particular whorehouse in Hue appeared to be a family restaurant which had private "dining rooms" on the second floor. Boa knew it housed a half-dozen high-end harlots who catered to the Hue aristocracy. As Boa anticipated, there were ill-equipped and lazy security guards at the front and rear doors. The establishment had been operating profitably for several years without incident and there was no reason to suspect it would be the target for anything other than someone desiring discreet, good-quality sex. Madame Ngoc Bich ran an orderly ship and as long as she provided what they wanted, the authorities were happy to let the "family restaurant" continue to serve delicious meals.

The guards were bundled against the night's chill with thrown-over ponchos providing some semblance of dryness. The coated nylon raincovers also provided an impediment to employing a weapon with any speed. Not that Boa worried about that in light of the guards' inattentiveness and lack of training. Duc was told to keep his eye on the back door sentry while Trang, who was dressed in a stolen suit and tie, approached the front door. It was the guard's task to check the credentials of each client to insure he had called ahead for a reservation and was approved by the Madame. Trang engaged the man and made a show of fumbling under his raincoat for his identification, making sure the guard's back was to the alley. Boa quietly crept around the corner and up to the guard, slipping the trademark garrote over his head. Unable to utter a sound, the guard became unconscious within ninety seconds as the two intruders pulled him into the alley. Trang then proceeded to where the alley opened to the back of the building and stumbled out limping and gasping for breath. As the backdoor guard turned toward this diversion, the hulking Duc rushed from his hiding place in the recessed doorway of a warehouse directly behind the target building. Travelling at full speed he plowed his shoulder into the fellow, sprawling him breathless onto the pavement. He had specific instructions not to kill him. This was to be saved for Boa, who immediately came around the corner to ply The Snake's specialty. There was little fight in the barely conscious guard, so it wasn't as much fun as a desperate, wriggling opponent. But it added its own little bit of enjoyment to the evening.

Trang went to the corner and waved to Lanh who then proceeded to the front door. The other three came in the back. Again, the three accomplices were under orders to hold all others at bay until Boa could dispatch each personally. The first floor contained a receptionist, a bartender, a short order cook, and three men with sluts in the lounge. Duc held them there with his refurbished AK-47. On the second floor, three out of the four bedrooms contained a trysting pair, all of which were herded downstairs to the lounge. All valuables and cash were collected and they were told that Boa wished to interview each of them individually. The fifteen were held in the lounge area with no arguments since three fully automatic assault rifles were pointed in their direction. Thirteen were sent one at a time to the storeroom behind the kitchen. Thirteen in turn were strangled to death by Boa who would pounce on them from behind as they came through the door. Fun turned to increasing joy with each new corpse, and as he imagined the looks on the faces of the authorities when they arrived at the scene.

The bartender and short order cook were made to carry the thirteen bodies back to the lounge and then haul in the two dead guards. They were laid side by side as Duc went to the van parked a block away to retrieve a canvass bag holding special cargo. Back in the lounge, Trang and Lanh helped him string out a dead fourteen-foot python across the fifteen lifeless bodies, and Boa wrapped a garrote around the snake just behind the head. The two survivors, who Boa wanted alive to tell the tale, were released and sprinted out of the building as if trying out for a new world sprint record. As a last-minute inspiration, it occurred to Boa that an additional special effect would enhance his reputation. So he had his three cohorts shoot each of the corpses in the groin. By the time they were done, the scene was sufficiently infused with a sanguine, blood-red pool. Satisfied with the best night yet of his blossoming career, Boa sent the three on their way to assess their profits as he simply faded into the night. They would meet back in Da Nang in a few days.

Fortunately for Boa, the two witnesses informed the press as well as the police. The latter were as frustrated as ever in their attempt to apprehend this growing menace. But the press seemed to take great delight in publishing the pictures and attendant stories that produced a rising fear of "The Snake." There was a madman loose in their midst, and people across the provinces began felt the need to heighten their vigilance evermore.

Poor demented soul that he was, Boa knew what he was doing. Intrinsic to his design for the future was the breeding of fear . . . knee-knocking fear at the very thought of Boa, The Snake. Strangled people had been popping up with some regularity for some time around Da Nang and the north and south bordering provinces. But the massacre in Hue, unmistakably The Snake's handiwork, induced a subtle and rising panic in the populace in general. From Boa's perspective, it simply added weighty prestige to his reputation within the underworld of crime and depravity. And the more weight the better as he set his sights on the goal that would make him rich, dreaded, and happy.

Police forces throughout the area were consistently confounded in their attempts to capture this formidable predator. In fact, no one was even sure what he looked like. There were reports of a hideous scar crossing his face, but only a few had had a brief glance at his visage, and most who viewed it clearly never lived to describe it. He moved from location to location, seldom sleeping the same place two nights in a row. Anyone who did have a clue as to his whereabouts kept it to themselves if they wanted to keep breathing. Due to his elusiveness, he gradually became referred to as the Ghost Snake, and Boa thought it was cute. The authorities looking for him did not.

His three comrades in crime would form the foundation of what was to become one of the most formidable and profitable gangs to surface in unified Vietnam. Boa knew he must plan and step carefully, but he was confident that before too long all he would have to do is hiss and virtually anyone would do his bidding.

Chapter 32

August 1993 – Minneapolis, Minnesota

Late in the afternoon in the last week of August 1993, Jed pulled up to Darrell's after a leisurely, meditative pace across half the continent. He was in no big hurry because he had nowhere in particular to go. To be sure, he was headed to his friend's home in Minneapolis, but that was simply a stop-over on the way to who-knew-where. His seminary education followed by six years of parish ministry was supposed to set the course for his professional life. But after being shafted, at least by his reckoning, by the church, he felt vocationally adrift. His personal faith had not been shaken in the least; now he just wasn't sure what to do with it.

It was one of those hot, muggy Minnesota days when hopping in a sauna would have seemed like relief. He knew that due to an evening meeting Darrell wouldn't be home until later, so he found the hidden key as instructed and let himself in. There was a note on the kitchen table: *Welcome to Leinenkugel Land. They're in the fridge.* After a shower and a brief snooze, Jed grabbed a cool one and headed for the bench down by the creek. The temperature and humidity had dropped enough that it didn't feel quite like hell – just at the gates – and he had sprayed himself with something that was 90% Deet to ward off the kamikaze bloodsuckers. Mosquitos and heat stroke notwithstanding, Jed preferred the outdoors to air-conditioned confines.

When Darrell finally arrived, they went through their man-it's-good-to-see-you ritual and then moved to his comfortable den, each with a Leinie in hand. Jed felt at home with the oak bookcases filled with biblical commentaries and reference works. He had continued to pursue his own theological development while in the parish as it provided more and more of a foundation for his vision of ministry, at least the kind of ministry to which he felt called. He intended to use his training and skills somehow, somewhere in the future, but at the moment all Jed was interested in was respite. He had enough inner strength and courage of conviction that his commitment to ministry had not been obliterated by the two unfavorable experiences with local congregations and the church hierarchy. Only time would tell if his developing idea of working with down-and-outers could mesh with the formal, institutional church.

After chatting a bit about how the country was doing after the first half year of Clinton's presidency, the 54-72 won/loss Twins record placing them one away from the basement of the American League West, and a few other things that could change planetary orbits, Darrell asked: "So, did you come up with any grand plan on your way here?"

Jed lifted his bottle with a smile and said, "Yeah, to drink Leinenkugels with you."

"Cheers," Darrell replied as they clinked bottles. "But, seriously, have your experiences given you second thoughts about sticking with ministry?"

"Let me put it this way," Jed responded. "One of my former commanding officers once told me, 'We are going to Marine. When we can't Marine anymore, it's time to retire and go sit on the porch.' I'm not ready for porch-sitting yet."

Darrell let a pleasant silence hang in the air while he drained the last of his brew before saying, "Thought you'd say something like that. But from what you've told me, working within the church structure could be problematic for you."

Drawing again from his quote-collecting hobby, Jed replied, "Well, Groucho Marx speaks to that. He once said that he refused to join any club that would have him as a member. I'm coming to the basic conclusion that my membership in the club you're talking about is kind of like trying to mix oil and water. I don't want to disparage the church and all the good things it's doing, but trying to put a round peg in a square hole seems to apply to my situation. The bureaucracy did what it figured it had to do, but I'm not willing to live with the poor results of their good intentions, if that's what they were."

"I can see how you feel that way, Jed. The question becomes what game plan might enable you to serve the way you want to. Any ideas?"

"Pretty hazy at this point. I need some time to try to put meat on the bones 'cause right now all I've got is a skeleton of an idea."

"Care to pull it out of the closet for me?" Darrell asked.

Which Jed did. At least in bare bones form. Darrell affirmed the concept in general, and agreed that some serious thinking was needed to flesh it out. As before, he offered his domicile to Jed for as long as it took. The two confirmed bachelors enjoyed each other's company as much as ever, and Jed really didn't have any other place to go. In addition, the seminary in St. Paul was close by so he could use the library as well as touch base with some of his valued past professors. Maybe one of them could help him sort out what to do with what the church had done to him. As it turned out, time didn't allow for much of that to happen.

Arriving back at the house around suppertime one day after a fifteen mile run around both Lakes Harriet and Calhoun and environs, Jed found Darrell holding a telegram. It was from The Rev. Xolani Jabula of the Evangelical Lutheran Church in Zimbabwe. Rhodesia had become Zimbabwe in 1980, and the Lutheran mission had become an independent, autonomous and indigenous church long ago. The Rev. Jabula, working out of Gwanda, was pastor to the Bazo clan, and had sent a telegram to Jed in Yakima which had returned marked undeliverable. Jed's mother, Naomi, suggested trying the address of his long-time friend in Minneapolis. The message was terse: *Your father, Jacob, is very ill and has asked for you. Please come if possible.*

After a long, involved effort, Jed finally reached Pastor Jabula in Gwanda by telephone. The connection was better than he expected, and Jed informed the pastor that he would be on his way within twenty-four hours. Jabula encouraged Jed to hurry. As Jed was about to arrange for the flight, Darrell asked him if he'd like company. Darrell had a good month of vacation due him which he was scheduled to take, and had never been to Africa, so what did Jed think?

So it was that Jed and Darrell debarked at Harare thirty-six hours later into a sunny and cool Zimbabwean spring day. They rented a Land Rover at the airport and headed for the Matopos Hills.

Holding Jacob's limp, hot hand, and speaking in isiNdebele, Jedediah said to him, "My father, you have blessed me beyond words with your life. So much of what I am I owe to you."

Suffering from the same meningitis that had taken the life of Jed's birth parents, Jacob replied with an almost inaudible whisper, "God's love and my love will always be with you, Jedediah, my son. We shall meet again and dance together with the angels."

Caring not at all that tears were streaming down his cheeks, Jedediah leaned close to his father's ear and spoke the benediction upon which both had built their lives, "The Lord bless you and keep you; the Lord make His face shine upon you and be gracious unto you; the Lord lift up His countenance upon you, and give you peace. In the name of the Father, and of the Son, and of the Holy Spirit. Amen."

As Naomi held Jacob's hand, and Jedediah and his siblings knelt together at their father's bedside humming Ndebele hymns, Jacob slipped peacefully into life on the other side. After a time Jed went out of the family dwelling with his eldest brother, Mandlenkosi, who announced the patriarch's passing. The women of the assembled clan immediately broke into the high-pitched keening that vocalized the grief of the whole community. The following day Pastor Jabula conducted the Christian funeral service, and Jacob was interred in the cemetery next to the humble church structure.

Jedediah stayed with his mother and siblings for two weeks. Not only was this part of the family grieving process, but Jedediah was not at all sure when, if ever, he might get back to see Naomi. During this period he also gave Darrell a tour the Matopos Hills in which he had grown up. They visited other villages, hiked the bushveld, and climbed some of the larger kopjes upon which they sat as Jed related memories of childhood in rural Zimbabwe. When it came time for Darrell and him to leave, the Bazo family asked Pastor Jabula to come and hold a special service of thanksgiving. It was followed by an Ndebele community feast during which each member of the clan touched Jedidiah with a blessing. Darrell watched this amazing display of clan and community closeness with awe, knowing he would have many stories to tell back in his Minneapolis congregation.

Darrell had another week before needing to return home, so they headed toward something Jed told him he could not miss while in Zimbabwe: Victoria Falls. They headed northwest out of Bulawayo along Highway #8 making sure to take the loop road through Hwange National Park. Darrell ran out of superlative exclamations as he clicked his new digital camera non-stop. He had been in zoos, of course, but to see lions, cheetahs, elephants, giraffes, zebras, and a wide variety of antelopes all running around with no fences was a breathtaking sensory bombardment. He was particularly taken with the white-socked gemsbok, majestically eyeing them with their Lone-Ranger-faces and three-foot spiked antlers. When they came upon a leopard with a freshly killed impala calf on a dusty road to one of the watering holes, Darrell was thankful for the security of their tank-like Land Rover. Jed was excited to sight an African fish eagle which caused his hand to press the ever-present medallion against his chest.

Victoria Falls, as Jed knew it would, stunned Darrell speechless. With its five thousand six hundred-foot width and three hundred and fifty-foot drop, it is the world's largest sheet of falling water. Along with being overwhelmed by the scope and majesty of the falls, Darrell's dominant thought was that no human power manufactured this magnificent spectacle. They splurged on two nights at the Imbabala Zambezi Safari Lodge on the banks of the Zambezi River before heading to Harare and Darrell's flight home.

At the airport coffee shop while waiting for his flight to be called, Darrell said, "You're sure you don't want to head back with me?"

"Yeah, Darrell, I'm sure. I need some more time alone

to try to figure out what to do with the water that's gone over the falls, and I seem to do some of my best thinking in this part of the world."

"I can buy that," Darrell said, and then continued, "but don't take too long, ol' buddy. I just might be able to help with that hazy plan of yours, and the sooner you get those thoughts in order the sooner we can work on turning 'em into something concrete. And, by the way, how's the bank account holding up?"

"No problems there. My living expenses while in the parish have been minimal so I've been able to bankroll a good share of my income. Besides, there was still a fair chunk of change left from your generous support over the years which I've got tucked away in a savings account that I can get my hands on if needed."

"Well," Darrell added, "you know you can tap me on the shoulder if worse comes to worse. If I've got beer and a hunk of Colby cheese in the fridge I'm a happy camper, so most of my fortune has just been sitting there growing on its own."

"As always, Darrell, I appreciate your generosity. When I get back to your place, whenever, we can talk about what financial resources might be needed for my next step."

They chatted on until Darrell's flight was called and parted at the gate with a manly hug. Jed told him that he didn't know where or how long his wanderings would take, but promised to stay in touch when possible.

Some months later Jed was in a lounge chair on the balcony of his B&B room on the far north edge of Swakopmund, Namibia. The view westward was stunning as he watched the mellowing red-orange sun slowly sink into the contrasting aquamarine ocean. Thoughts came to him similar to those Darrell had while staring at Victoria Falls: *Let's see human beings make something like this*. With the city of forty thousand some miles to the south and nothing to the north but sand dunes, the sound of gently breaking waves and plaintive sea gull cries lulled him into a peaceful reverie. At the point where he was having trouble keeping his eyes open, Jed suddenly leaped to his feet. No more than a hundred yards offshore, a southern right whale breached the surface in a stunning display, more than half of its fifty-foot, fifty-ton body shooting out of the water before crashing back and waving goodbye with its notched fluke. Not having grown up nor spent any appreciable time on the water or ocean beaches, Jed watched with fascination as the whale performed the aquatic acrobatic maneuver a half dozen times before disappearing to do whatever right whales do. Jed marveled again at the amazing and stunning variety of life on our planet, and was glad he came to experience this portion of it.

The day after Darrell's departure from Harare, Jed had booked a ticket to Windhoek with a connecting flight to Swakopmund. It had been some twenty years since his sojourn in the northern part of Namibia, and a profound change had taken place. In 1990, after years of political and armed struggle with the occupying South Africans, the country gained its independence. Having been invaded by the Germans in 1884, it was still struggling with the effects of over a hundred years of colonization. But the national joy of the native Namibians was immense over finally re-acquiring the right of self-determination.

Twenty miles north of Walvis Bay, one of the country's two ports, Swakopmund is primarily a beach resort. German colonial architecture dominates the landscape of the seventy-five square mile city carved out of the desert, and a preponderance of the population is still German-speaking. Jed chose this destination because of his long-held desire to experience the Namib Desert. The Namib stretches over one thousand miles from southern Angola to western South Africa. The most arid regions along the coast get eight one-hundredths of an inch of rain annually, and the sand seas contain some of the earth's most spectacular dunes . Its formation estimated to be seventy-five million years ago, the Namib may be the oldest desert in the world. The coastal regions can experience more than one hundred and eighty days of thick fog a year, proving a major hazard to ships, and occasioning the term Skeleton Coast from over a thousand wrecks that litter the offshore waters.

Not only did Jed want to experience this natural wonder, but he reckoned that it might be a good place to come to grips with his future. At seminary he had read about the ancient desert fathers such as Anthony and Moses the Black who were hermits in the Egyptian sands and blessed the church with much of their wisdom gained there. He had also remembered an old Islamic adage which said: "Allah will hear you as well if you pray in a mosque with a full belly or in the desert with an empty belly. But if you want to hear Allah, go hungry to the desert." He thought maybe he'd try the latter.

After renting a reliable-looking 1990 Toyota Land Cruiser, Jed headed north of Swakopmund on Highway C34, the one and only road along the famed Skeleton Coast. It was roughly two hundred miles to the last outpost at Terrace Bay, and he intended to stop, explore, rest, and meditate at his pleasure along the way. The plan was to spend the night somewhere along the Ugab River, about halfway to the north end. The Ugab is an ephemeral river with a flow above the surface of its sandy bed only a few days each year. But its subterranean water surfaces here and there as pools to provide life for species such as the mountain zebra, the rare desert elephant, and the largest population of free roaming black rhinoceroses in the world.

Driving non-stop from Swakopmund to the Ugab would normally take about two and a half hours. It took Jed eight. He started out with a full gas tank plus three five-gallon jerry cans which he figured should get him to his northern terminus and back. The 4x4 vehicle handled the hard-packed salt and sand road with ease, and Jed religiously followed the instructions to keep the vehicle on the highway to preserve the fragile off-road desert ecosystem. Jed's extended time resulted from his stopping often to explore whale, seal, and shipwreck skeletons along the coast named for them, or simply to luxuriate in the pleasant solitude. The fog that frequented the shoreline with its attendant cool temperatures lifted by late morning and provided Jed with longer range views of the alternating sand dunes and ancient rock formations. He cut northeast on D2303 to the primitive Ugab River Rhino Camp where he parked the Land Cruiser while he headed upriver on foot for the night. His backpack contained a one-man tent and enough food to get him through a couple of days. There were signs noting the presence of elephants, rhinos, and lions in the area, but Jed's familiarity with the African bush and its fauna gave him a confidence of which the average tourist could only dream.

Jed spent two days exploring the geologic folds of the cliffs bordering the river further inland, which included more dense vegetation owing to the underground water table. Some distance from the coastline it was considerably warmer during the day, but he was glad to have his newly-purchased sleeping bag for the chill nights. He had seen a variety of wildlife including gemsbok, zebra, one solitary lion, and two rhinos, but not any desert elephants known to frequent this valley. Jed calculated that it would be an easy several-hour walk back to his vehicle in the morning. Little did he suspect the hike would begin somewhat later than anticipated.

His bed was within a circle he had constructed of camel thorn branches and lying close to the embers of his campfire. He also had put his resting place some one hundred yards from the small, shallow pool that formed part of the riverbed here. The fence and fire, and a pile of fuel placed within hand's reach, would keep night predators at bay, and Jed drifted off to a peaceful, if not too deep, slumber. Several times during the night he awoke to hear animals skirting around his protected lair, after which he would add several wrist-thick branches to the fire and go back to sleep. What woke him in the morning was the ground shaking.

Peering through his thicket-fence Jed saw what was causing the tremors. A family of desert elephants basically surrounded his encampment. He counted four adult cows, two with new calves, three adolescent youngsters, and two bulls. None seemed bothered by his presence, especially the two bulls who were engaged in a serious pushing-and-shoving match. Jed couldn't determine if they were in musth or if the younger one was simply challenging the dominant older one. But it didn't really make any difference as, seemingly completely unaware of him, they edged closer and closer to where he was peeking out of his sleeping bag. His little picket fence gave him about as much protection as a pair of socks would against a puff adder, and the dust from their scuffle was now a cloud around his head. Getting up and making a run for it would surely trigger an attack, if not by the bulls, at least by the cows protecting their young ones. The only viable option was to slink back into the bag and hope for the best.

He couldn't help but peer at the nearby fascinating battle, nearby meaning about fifty feet now, since being this close to two six-ton fighting behemoths wasn't something one was likely to experience. He did close his eyes when the smaller of the two, which meant probably only five and a half instead of six tons, backed right up and stepped on his four-foot-high thicket. The bull's left rear foot landed five feet from Jed's head before it gained some purchase and drove the larger bull backwards a bit. The fight lasted about five minutes, which seemed to Jed more like five hours, and then the young bull gave way and scurried east into the river scrub. Jed lay motionless and tried his best to smell like elephant dung, which wasn't all that difficult since some had been slung around the area. The herd milled about for another half an hour or so and, after all had drunk their fill from the pool, ambled leisurely upriver. When Jed finally exited his sleeping bag, he was somewhat proud that it did not smell of urine.

He was happily back at his vehicle by mid-afternoon, happy to be alive, and happy to replenish his water and food supply. The drive to Terrace Bay took the remainder of the day, and he found that the camp there fortunately had a room vacancy which he booked for five days. He spent those days hiking the beach, participating in a guided sand dune tour inland, and thinking. Thinking about his future, which was taking more formative shape in his mind. But he had one more place to visit before heading back to the States.

While there are many claims regarding the origins of capoeira, there is general agreement that in Brazil it is directly connected to the importation of Angolan slaves by the Portuguese. One old letter claims that its roots are an ancient native acrobatic zebra dance known as *N'golo*. Its development and practice was refined by slaves in Brazil from the 17th century on, but as they and their descendants were freed and returned to Angola, they brought capoeira with them. Over time it became embedded in Angolan culture, with schools and contests existing throughout the country. Having practiced this martial arts dance virtually all his life, Jed wanted to visit the place of its birth and perhaps visit with some of the current masters. Back in Walvis Bay he turned in his Land Cruiser and booked a flight for Luanda, Angola.

It didn't take long in Luanda to be directed to a capoeira master. Jed found him at a neighborhood martial arts center and was granted an audience. Mestre Joâo Kasanje eyed Jed with appreciation and asked, "So how long have you practiced capoeira, my friend?" His tone was gentle and respectful.

"All my life, Mestre," Jed answered. He went on to share an abbreviated history of his journey, indicating that for many years he had not been in a position to actively practice the art within a community even though being very self-disciplined about his own exercises. "I must return to America soon, but I was hoping to first learn from some of the masters in the country of its origin."

"We are happy to teach, Bazo. But I hope you know that a true disciple of capoeira embraces its philosophical foundation. That is the only basis for learning and advancement."

Jed had long known that sincerity, justice, and loyalty were the underpinnings of the discipline, and they fit well with his biblically-based complementary values. "To deepen my embrace of capoeira in its totality is my goal, Mestre Kasanje. Is there anyone who might be my mentor?" he asked.

"I have someone in mind. Please come back tomorrow after I have had an opportunity to discuss the prospect with him."

And so it was that two days later Jed was driving another rental on the coastal highway to Benguela, three hundred miles to the south. There he met with Mestre Enyama and they mapped out a plan of intensive, advanced capoeira immersion for two months. Jed secured a modest beachfront hut not far from the community center where for up to four hours a day he was tutored in the discipline of advanced capoeira. It was also convenient for his alternate-day ocean-front runs of ten and twenty miles. The two months turned into three by the time he headed back to Luanda to book flights west across the Atlantic.

At forty-eight years old, Jed was in as good a shape as he had ever been, and was a world-class expert in capoeira. Listening to the jet engines purr at a cruising altitude of thirty-nine thousand feet, Jed wondered how he might combine those traits with his felt call to ministry. How it actually worked out in the coming years was certainly something that would never be found in any seminary curriculum.

Chapter 33

January 1995 - Minneapolis, Minnesota

After the long, long series of flights from Luanda to London to New York City to Minneapolis, Jed was more than ready for a cab ride to Darrell's followed by some quality sleep on a genuine Sealy Posturepedic mattress. After paying the cabbie and heading for the house up a sidewalk bordered by a foot of snow on each side, he was glad that he'd stashed some winter clothing in his Suburban which had been resting in Darrell's two-car garage. Darrell knew his flight plans and told him to just let himself in and hit the hay until he smelled breakfast coffee. Although it was pitch dark, Jed found the key still in its regular hidey-hole, but was shocked when he reached the front door to find it barred with crime scene tape. Without caring if it was a violation, he unlocked the door, ducked under the tape, entered and flipped on the hall light. Spilling into the hallway from both the living room and the study were books, papers, and broken glass. Turning on lights in both rooms revealed a scene reminiscent of a tornado's aftermath.

Jed's tension level rose measurably when he proceeded to the kitchen and found, in addition to an unholy mess of emptied drawers and broken dishes, a substantial splattering of blood on the walls, cabinets, and pooling on the floor. At this point Jed began to wonder about his friend's bodily well-being. While pretty confident he wouldn't find Darrell upstairs, Jed raced to the second floor. Darrell was, in fact, not there, but all three bedrooms looked like the Gestapo, the KGB, and the FBI had taken turns looking for some evidential prize. Everything was upside down, inside out, and thrown about.

Even though it was past midnight, Jed went next door to see if he could obtain any information. Retirees Ken and Martha Songster knew Jed from his previous stays with Darrell, and Jed knew he wouldn't sleep a wink without some answers. He woke up the Songsters and they were insistent that he come in while Martha made coffee.

"It happened the night before last," Ken began. Jed noted that this would have been shortly after his last call informing Darrell of his flight schedule. "There have been a series of burglaries all over the south side of the city, most of them happening when people were away, although one homeowner over near Lake Harriet surprised them with a shotgun and chased them off. The police think it's the same guys, but this is the first time they've used this kind of violence."

With a calm voice that did not betray the knot in his stomach, Jed replied, "Please tell me about Darrell."

Jed heard Martha sniffling as he poured the coffee and Ken's wrinkled brow furrowed even more deeply as he answered. "The officer who came to talk to us said he couldn't give us a lot of details, but apparently Darrell put up some resistance to the intruders. All we know is that knives came into play at some point and Darrell got the worst of it. It looked like they left him unconscious on the kitchen floor while they ransacked the whole place. He'd probably be dead now if the Westons across the street hadn't come home late and noticed unusual movement in the house. They called the police but by the time they got there the burglars were gone. One of the two officers put a tourniquet on to stop the blood flow, and the ambulance got him to the hospital in time."

"In time?" Jed responded. "You mean he's okay?"

"He's alive, Jed, but not what you'd call okay. They wouldn't let us see him since he's in ICU, and all they'd tell us is that he lost a lot of blood but is hanging on. Apparently his father is on the way from San Diego, if he's not already here."

"What hospital is he at?" Jed asked.

"U of M Med center," Ken replied, "but as of yesterday he was still in ICU. And if you were thinking about heading over there now, I'd encourage you to wait until morning. I can almost guarantee you that you wouldn't get past the front desk at this time of night, and in the morning everybody will have a better idea of how he's doing. Besides, you look absolutely beat yourself. Why don't you use our guest bedroom and we'll see what the morning brings."

"That's very gracious of you, Ken, and makes a lot of sense. I left my duffle on the front porch, plus I need to grab some cold weather stuff from my vehicle. I'll be back in a minute."

Meeting the Sandman face-to-face didn't come as easily as Jed anticipated. Basically he just wanted a few hours of battery recharging before going to the hospital. But when sleep finally fell on him like a brick, it came deeply. He thought he was dreaming about bacon, eggs, toast, and steaming coffee when he realized that it was actually their marvelous aroma drifting in from the kitchen. After showering and a delicious but quick breakfast, Jed headed for the University of Minnesota with a promise to call Ken with a progress report.

In the ICU lounge area a stout but well-proportioned man with a full head of hair, the color of which reminded Jed of a silverback gorilla, and a salt-and-pepper handlebar mustache stuck out his hand. "Glad to meet you, Jed. I'm Darrell's father, Percy." Jed knew of Percy's existence although he had never had an occasion to meet him. Darrell's mother had died of cancer when he was a freshman in college, and in the years since, Darrell and his dad had more or less drifted apart. Darrell never really talked about it at any length and Jed wasn't sure who was more responsible for the rift. Nevertheless, Dad was here now and Jed hoped he would be forthcoming with information of his son's condition.

"Pleased to meet you, Percy, but I'm sure sorry for the circumstances."

"That's a fact. You know crap like this happens every day, but you don't picture it happening to your kid."

Anxious to learn some particulars, Jed replied, "Well, this has certainly been a shock, and I'll bet you're having as hard a time as I am believing it. Can you fill me in on Darrell's condition?"

"Well, there's good news and bad news. The good news is that he's off the critical list and they're moving him outta ICU later today. The bad news is that he got cut up pretty bad and it's going to take a fair bit of time to heal. He'll also have some nasty scars, but being able to see 'em in the mirror is better'n not being there to look. He lost a pile of blood too, and I guess it takes a while to come back, even with the transfusions. Plus, we both know he's no spring chicken."

"Did they cut his face?"

"No, but damn close. Big slice out of the left side of his neck, but they missed the carotid by a hair. His arms and torso took quite a beating too, but most of the blood came from that big artery in the leg, the . . . the . . ."

"Femoral artery?" Jed proffered.

"Yeah, that's the one. The doc said that if the cop had been five minutes later with the tourniquet he might not have made it."

The thought made Jed shudder. He then asked, "Have you been able to talk to him?"

"They let me in for a few minutes when I arrived early

this morning. Any talking was done by me though, since he was pretty drugged up."

"Did he recognize you?"

"Yup. Squeezed out a bit of a smile and patted my hand. Had to go adjust the blinds so he didn't see this ol' coot dripping saltwater in his beer."

Jed sensed that the eighty-one year old dad was experiencing some melancholy mixed with regret over the estrangement from his son. He didn't want to push too hard, but he was starving for information. "I understand. Percy. Have you been able to learn anything from the police about just what happened?"

"Not much," Percy said. "All they could tell me was that whoever broke into the house ran into Darrell and carved the almighty crap out of him. They haven't been able to have a decent conversation with him yet, but I imagine they'll be here before long once he's out of ICU. Before passing out he did manage to tell them that he sliced one of the attacker's arms with a butcher knife. Last I looked he was sleeping like a baby. 'Course that juice comin' in through the IV helps."

Thinking it might help both of them to do something other than pace around the lounge area, Jed said, "How about we grab a coffee in the cafeteria downstairs? Unless, that is, you want to stay nearby."

"No, that's fine. I mean, okay, good idea. He's going to be down for the count for a while and I'll let the duty nurse know where we'll be. In one of our infrequent phone calls Darrell mentioned you as a very good friend. I'd like to get to know you . . . and maybe you can help me get to know my son again."

Percy and Jed spent the next hour and a half slurping not-that-bad-for-a-cafeteria jet-black coffee and sharing a bit about each other's lives. Although Percy said he wouldn't really call himself a man of faith, he respected the path his son had taken. He thought that, along with the distance, perhaps their differing outlooks on life had contributed to their gradual detachment from each other. His story included the fact that although he'd been sober for years, after his wife's death he swam the rum river for a couple of decades. When it became evident that drowning was likely around the next bend and he got his feet back on the sober shore, Darrell was somewhere else in a different world. There had been some perfunctory contact now and then, but the distance between them, physically and psychologically, had not enabled a rejuvenation of a close father-son relationship.

"Well, your showing up in this crisis is a good start," Jed said. "Do you think Darrell is open to some healing and reconciliation?"

"He patted my hand," Percy whispered as he turned his head to wipe the corner of his eye. "I'm going to stick around as long as I can be of help . . . if he'll have me."

"I don't think that'll be a problem," Jed replied. "He'll be taking some time off, and it's a proven fact that a minimum of two pots of coffee a day can bring together even Republicans and Democrats."

With hope in his eyes Percy said, "Hey, in my hitch-hiking days I used to carry a sign that said 'I don't talk religion or politics.' Got me a lot of rides, so maybe that'd be a good policy with him."

"I don't expect that your son will be trying to convert you, Percy, but simply being in each other's presence and sharing a bit of life together again can work wonders."

"You talk sense, Jed. You're a padre too, aren't you?"

"Well, I was . . . still am, I guess. But I haven't been working actively with the church for a while. Not that it's bad, but I'm pretty sure I'm not cut out for the structured, institutional church. One of the things I came here to talk to Darrell about was what I might do next. I've got some fuzzy ideas that he might be able to help me get into focus."

"Jed, if you stick around for a while, maybe you can be sort of like a go-between, a medi . . . medi. . ."

"Mediator?"

"Yeah, that's it. Help me and Darrell through some first steps, if he's open to it."

"Sure willing to try, Percy. And knowing your son, I have no doubt that he'll be willing to give it a go. I think both of you feel that it's long overdue."

"Amen to that! Is that the right word? Is it okay for an old infidel to say amen?"

"Absolutely," Jed said with enthusiasm. "But the first order of business is to help him along with the healing of his injuries. Even though he's getting on in years, he's gotten himself in pretty good shape and that'll help the process."

"Speaking of good shape," Percy responded, "you look to me like I want you on my side if trouble's brewing. Wish I'd have been half that fit when I was, what . . . in your late thirties?"

"Thanks, Percy. My next birthday I'll be forty-nine."

"Hot damn! Could've fooled me. What's the secret?"

Jed answered, "No big secret. Combination of good genetics and a lot of hard work."

"Amen to that!" Percy chuckled, kind of taking a liking

to his new word.

“Listen, let’s figure out what’s next. Where are you staying?”

“Little flea bag hotel about six blocks from here. It’s all I can afford and it’s close.”

“How about this. You head back up to ICU and I’ll check to see if the police are done at the house and then arrange for it to be put back in order. I’ll meet you back here no later than mid-afternoon when Darrell might be on a regular ward. We can talk then about moving you over to the house.”

“Whoa. That might not be such a good idea. I mean, Darrell might not be ready for that yet.”

“Well, ask him. Or if you’re hesitant to do so, I’ll be happy to do that mediator thing.”

They parted company for the present and Jed went to the local police station to see if the house was still a hands-off crime scene or whether it could be reassembled. After being informed by the desk sergeant that the forensics team was done and had given a go-ahead to repossess the property, he contacted Darrell’s every-other-week house cleaner to come help him straighten and clean up the giant mess. Fortunately she was available immediately and came with another helper to spend the rest of the day restoring order. By the time Jed arrived back at the hospital, Darrell was dozing in a private room on a regular ward. Percy was fast asleep on a recliner chair in the corner. It was an hour before a nurse arrived to take Darrell’s blood pressure and temperature. When he opened his eyes and saw both Jed and his father keeping vigil, he smiled with both his mouth and his eyes.

After the nurse completed her duties, Jed walked to the bedside and said with an ersatz frown, “Didn’t anybody ever tell you not to play with knives?"

"Hey, Jed," Darrell said with a soft but firm voice. "I wish you'd have been there for the party."

"Me too, my friend. Maybe we could have had a theological discussion with the bastards about the ethics of knife-fighting. After, that is, I relieved them of their blades and turned them into duct-tape men."

"Yeah, yeah, I know where you're going with that. But let's save it and just be glad we're here yapping at each other."

"Amen to that! To quote someone else I know . . . who seems to be waking up as we speak."

Percy struggled back into the conscious world and came over to stand next to Jed. "Hi, Son. How are you feeling?"

"Must say I've felt better, Dad. But as long as I don't move too much the pain is bearable. I'm glad you're here."

That seemed to fluster the old man a bit. He shuffled from foot to foot and said, "I wish I'd have been here a couple of nights ago along with my two friends, Smith and Wesson. Somebody besides you would be in the hospital."

They bantered back and forth a bit before Percy excused himself to answer nature's call. Jed didn't want to elicit a long conversation, but asked, "What's this about you cutting one of the intruders? Since when did you take up knife fighting?"

"Long story, Jed . . . for later. But I did put a pretty good slice in one of the guy's arms. I think that pissed him off severely. Maybe I wouldn't have it so bad if I hadn't done that."

"Save the details for later. There's an important issue

that . . ." and before he could finish, Percy was back at his side.

"Darrell, they did a number on the house but it's now more or less put back together. I think your dad has a question for you."

Percy got a worried look on his face, but decided to go for it. "Son, I can stay around for as long as I can be of help. Jed was wondering . . . or, I was wondering . . . well, that , maybe . . . I mean, it might make sense . . . no, what we were thinking . . . that is . . . "

"Dad, please just say what you mean." Darrell said with gentleness.

Percy looked to Jed, who simply nodded. "Well, if it would help, I mean, if you'd be okay with . . . like . . . I mean . . . oh hell, can I say at your place and play nursemaid?"

Darrell had a difficult time suppressing a smile. "Dad, of course. I'll probably be in here a couple more days while they make sure the cuts are knitting properly, but go ahead and get yourself over there. You take the guest bedroom and Jed can have the very comfortable couch in the study. Okay with you, Jed?"

"Hey, you know me. Sleep like a baby on the dining room table if that's what I've got. I don't know how long I'll be around, but you and I have some business to attend to once you're back on your feet. Besides, it often takes two nursemaids to handle difficult patients."

And so the conversation went, and Jed noticed a sense of relief on Percy's face. After a while they noticed Darrell's drowsiness kicking in, so they left him with a promise to be back in the morning.

Five days later, after the doc felt sure that no infection had set in, Darrell was released from the hospital with instructions to keep physical activity to an absolute minimum for the next couple of weeks and to take his antibiotics faithfully. Jed had the house back to a semblance of its former self, and he and Percy had a good start on what appeared to be a mutually appreciated relationship. Matter of fact, Jed was growing to really like the old codger. Shuffling around in his baggy khakis and faded-letter San Diego Chargers sweatshirt, Percy tried to help as much as he could. One thing Jed definitely liked was his culinary abilities. The Navy initially had trained him as a cook, and after being discharged he stuck with it and was on his way to being a quality chef when Darrell's mother died. That all more or less went down the drain along with the rum going down his throat, but once permanently sober he picked it up again. Working in a series of restaurants in southern California until retirement, he carried on with the pots and pans in his own home. His poker buddies were always pushing to meet at his place because they knew they'd get world-class munchies instead of the Fritos and donuts that defined their own abilities in the kitchen.

"Percy, I haven't had cordon bleu for a long time, but I guarantee you I've never had any as delicious as this," Jed mumbled as he savored the most tender chicken and ham combo he had ever tasted. "What spices did you use for the breading? It's marvelous."

"Sorry Jed. Trade secret," Percy replied with a quick wink. "Long as you like it, that makes my day."

"Well, you keep feeding Darrell like this, he'll be good as new in no time." Then addressing the patient, "But ol' buddy, you're going to have to watch your waistline if Dad keeps this up."

While it was still on a pretty elementary level, Jed could tell that both father and son were making efforts to recover a relationship they both seemed to desire. He knew it would take some purposeful, determined work by both of them to make progress and make it stick. If he could help the process in any way, he was willing to try. After all, he was presently under no pressure to be anywhere else, and he sure-as-shooting wasn't leaving until he knew Darrell was well down the recovery road.

Jed had stopped by the precinct the day before Darrell's return home to see if there were any developments leading toward an arrest. Their interview with Darrell hadn't given them much to go on since he reported that it was dark and all happened in such a blur that he couldn't even give a reasonable description of the attackers. The fact that there were two of them fit with the reports by several other victims who had caught a glimpse of the fleeing burglars. Jed was able to learn that in at least four cases in different south side locations neighbors reported seeing an older white or tan Ford pickup with a black topper over the box around the time of the robberies. No one had a plate number, but it was at least a common denominator upon which the cops could focus.

As the days continued, Darrell exhibited a bit of uncharacteristic nervousness. Jed knew this was natural when one has been violated, especially in the supposed sanctity of his own home. When Darrell queried him about the advisability of getting a handgun, Jed told him he didn't think that was a very good idea. He told him that it takes a tremendous amount of training to not only handle a pistol properly, but also to actually pull the trigger on a human being. He'd seen more than one person go to pieces when under fire. Besides, Jed told him, burglars didn't come back to hit the same house again, like lightning not striking the same place twice. Darrell acquiesced, but expressed the hope that the bad guys would be tracked down and caught sooner rather than later.

Jed hoped the same thing. He also contemplated what he might have done if he had come across the thieves carving up his closest friend.

Chapter 34

March 1995 - Minneapolis, Minnesota

Another week passed and Darrell was healing and gaining strength day by day. He was feeling so much better that he told the pastor who was filling in for him that he'd probably be able to resume his position in two or three weeks. Jed and Percy cast glances at each other and announced almost simultaneously that it depended on the doctor's okay. Darrell mumbled something about carrying this nursemaid thing too far, but knew they were making sense.

The reestablishing of a father-son camaraderie was going better than Jed expected, and most likely better than Darrell and Percy anticipated as well. After a few guided sessions that included a mutual sharing of shortcomings, regrets, and apologies, they both seemed content to let the past be the past, and concentrate on the present and the future. Jed knew it would take someone more practiced than he to enable a constructive probing of the deeper psychological ramifications of their decades-long disassociation, and whether both wanted that to happen would remain to be seen. For now they seemed to appreciate the hopeful baby steps they were taking to build a consanguinity for which both had longed for quite a while.

Jed felt rested and restive at the same time. He had come to a sense of peace with regard to leaving behind the bureaucratic entanglements of the institutionalized church. His experience was that, although most of its members were good, well-meaning souls, all too often their primary concern seemed to be worshipping Jesus instead of following him. Add to that the minority who acted as if they missed the point altogether but incongruously wormed their way into leadership positons, and Jed was pushed over the line. He was also tired of people who he termed practical atheists. These were folks who, in Jed's experience, would never *say* there is no God, but *acted* as if there wasn't one. By his lights, too many people with crosses around their necks were living as if what Jesus modeled and taught wasn't worth the ink and paper that recorded it. The conundrum, of course, was to figure out the nuts and bolts of how to put one's faith into practice in any given situation. For years Jed had been stirring the ethical and theological embers waiting for the burst of luminosity that he could use as his guiding light. He figured it lay somewhere between a set of absolutes, and principles applied situationally. The former was simply untenable while the latter still begged for something other than one's subjectivity. What happened to Darrell added fuel to the fire.

What should society do with people who did things like the thugs did to Darrell? It was one thing to read about such things in the paper, but when it happened to a person with whom one has a deep personal relationship it set emotions swirling that the nightly news didn't evoke. Then there was the fact that, like the southside burglars, the cops often didn't catch them, or, if they did, the so-called justice system couldn't seem to hold them. Jed certainly didn't see himself as a vigilante, but he knew himself well enough to know that if he would have caught the perpetrators in the act, it would have been likely that Darrell wouldn't have been the only one bleeding.

One night he was kicking around such thoughts after he woke up around two a.m. and couldn't get back to sleep. A warm front, meaning about twenty-five degrees, had come in from the southwest so he decided to go for a drive to clear his head. He slowly wound his way east on Minnehaha Parkway with the window down, enjoying the brisk night air. Tuning north on South 28th Avenue he eased past his old home overlooking Lake Hiawatha and enjoyed a flood of pleasant memories of his years with the Hofstads. Continuing north he came to his alma mater, Roosevelt High School, the first sight being the football field on which he had played so many years ago. Lots of good memories again, and he recalled a few of his friends' names and wondered what they might be doing in life now. After circling the campus, he browsed aimlessly through the streets of his high school years and ended up on East 43rd Street. Passing Northrop Elementary School something caught his eye. The school was dark and the parking lot on 43rd held one vehicle. While it might not be unusual for someone to leave his vehicle there overnight due to mechanical problems or whatever, a second look at this vehicle set off a lightning bolt in Jed's head. It was an early model light-colored Ford pickup with a black topper over the box.

Jed passed the school and pulled into the far-side parking lot of St. Helena Catholic Church directly to the east. He turned off his motor and with the window down sat quietly and listened. After ten minutes or so he disabled the dome light in his Suburban and gently eased out into the dark. Still surrounded by the night's silence, he decided to walk back west across the front of the church and across 32nd Avenue back to the school parking lot. He thought that maybe he could find tracks in the new inch of snow leading away from the Ford and to whatever home the perps were now burglarizing. Jed thought about seeing if the church was open and calling the police, but thinking about what happened to Darrell prompted a felt need for quick action before anyone else fell victim to the robbers' viciousness.

Visible footprints of two individuals in the snow led away from the truck and toward the rear of the church where the rectory was located. The prints led directly to the west side door of the residence where there was a buzzer, presumably for priests who are on duty 24/7. The door, the frame for which was a bit off square, was slightly ajar. Jed pulled it open enough to peer down a dimly lit hallway, and to hear someone moaning quietly. Slipping inside and pulling off his Sorel snow boots for quietness, he slowly crept toward a door open to the hallway from which the moaning came. Cautiously peeking around the corner he saw a man lying on his back, semi-conscious and holding his head from which blood was leaking onto the floor in a widening pool. Jed overcame the desire to leap instantly to his aid by recognizing that the hoodlums could materialize anytime from anywhere, so he proceeded to follow the markings from the feet of whoever had stepped in the priest's blood.

Knowing the Roman Catholic Church's penchant for valuable religious paraphernalia and sacramental vessels that were often gold-gilded, if not solid gold or jewel-encrusted, Jed figured that this was probably the perpetrators' object in attacking a church. Also, given what happened to Darrell and now this priest, these criminals had progressed from burglary to armed robbery. The sacristy was where at least some of the valuables would be kept, so Jed began looking for a door to the area of the church behind the altar where that room would generally be found. The rectory hallway ran parallel to the nave, and after passing several other locked doors Jed came to a short branch that turned toward the church proper. He saw light at the bottom of a door at the end of the offshoot. Jed pushed the unlocked and thankfully well-lubricated door ever so slowly and cautiously to find another hallway. He heard a muffled clicking sound coming from behind another door at the end of the hallway to his right. A few light blood spots marked the path of whoever was in there, while wet footprints disappeared down the hallway to his left. Jed silently crept up to the door, which was marked "Sacristy" and had not been closed completely, and put his eye to a quarter-inch space.

Narrow glimpses were caught of a figure standing sideways to Jed and trying to stuff what looked like a pair of gold candlesticks into a canvass bag already heavy with loot. Locked storage cupboards on the far side of the room had been crowbarred open and worship trappings were strewn about the countertops and floor. This worship preparation area consisted of open space with cupboards and countertops on three sides. There being no conversation or other movement, Jed judged that the visible thief was the only person in the room. Not knowing where the partner might be, he decided to disable the first burglar before looking for his accomplice. All in one motion he yanked the door toward himself, dove across the room, and crashed into the man. The startled outlaw was a wisp of a man, about five foot seven and maybe a hundred and thirty pounds if he'd just eaten dinner, and he let out a loud yelp just as Jed applied a half nelson choke hold. Jed could have put him out of commission with one arm behind his back, and as the little twerp began to lose consciousness Jed backed off on the pressure just a tad so he could ask about the presence of the other. Before he could verbalize the question, the door to the sanctuary, which was behind Jed and which he hadn't noticed, burst inward and Jed felt the muzzle of a pistol pressed into the middle of his back along with the words, "You move, dickhead, and you die. Let go of my asshole buddy there nice and slow. You try anything funny and a quarter pound of pressure on this here trigger will blow your spine in two." Even in the heat of the moment, the thing that impressed Jed most was that he couldn't remember ever smelling such a foul stench coming out of someone's mouth. He thought maybe the fellow hadn't been clued in on the advent of the toothbrush.

Jed did as he was told. The man he let go stumbled forward holding his neck, cleared his throat a couple of times and then turned around to face Jed. Smiling, the fellow drew a shining Buck skinning knife out of a sheath underneath his ragged, dirty down jacket. Halitosis hissed in his ear, "You done it now, big guy. My little friend here just loves knives and I'd bet one of them there candlesticks yer gonna get a demonstration." Buck-Knife-Guy's smile widened.

Fortunately, Jed thought, the dumbass with the gun in his back had the IQ of a rock, although a rock had better breath. If he had been standing, say, four feet away from Jed, the former Marine would have been screwed. But what the crook obviously didn't know was that by snapping his right arm backward and laterally Jed could knock away the gunman's arm faster than the latter could pull the trigger. Which is exactly what he did, and four things happened. First, the gun fired but with the bullet passing some six inches to the left of Jed's torso. Second, as Jed's forearm connected with his adversary's, the latter's ulna was shattered. Third, as Jed's body spun around, he carried through with his left fist to the assailant's right temple. Fourth, Halitosis crumpled to the floor where he twitched convulsively several times and then lay still.

In the one point eight seconds it took for all this to happen Jed completed his three-sixty to face the other fellow. It took a couple more seconds for Buck-Knife-Guy to psychologically acknowledge what had just happened to his partner in crime, and then he launched himself at Jed with a banshee yell and spittle flying. Jed sidestepped him so easily it was almost comical, grabbing the knife hand by the wrist in a vise-like grip and twisting the arm while picturing Darrell bleeding to death on his kitchen floor. The man's shoulder was dislocated, his wrist broken, and he crashed headfirst into one of the lower cupboard doors which left him dazed, bleeding, and screaming in pain. From the time Jed entered the room to the floor being littered with two very disabled burglars was somewhere in the neighborhood of thirty seconds.

The old .45 caliber Colt M1911 lying on the floor would have blown a baseball-size hole in his back. He picked up the pistol and the knife with a towel and went to the wall phone to call 911. Six minutes later cops came running in from the parking lot while Jed was checking on the fallen priest. "You'd better call at least two ambulances," he said to the first of Minneapolis' finest on the scene. "There are two other casualties that are going to need medical attention."

An hour later Jed's statement was being taken at the 5th Precinct station on Nicollet Avenue. There were some initial questions at the church about what he was doing out roaming around at two in the morning, but when they got to the station the desk sergeant recognized him from Darrell's case and vouched for his credibility. It also helped that they found numerous recently- stolen items in the back of the perps' pickup truck, and Buck-Knife-Guy had a serious laceration on his left forearm consistent with Darrell's report of getting in at least one lick. Since Jed's version of events seemed to jibe with the initial perusal of the crime scene, he was released after he read and signed the statement, with instructions to stay in the area until the investigation was complete.

When Jed returned to the house, he found Darrell huddled over a fresh pot of coffee in the breakfast nook. Although far from complete, his wounds were healing as expected and thankfully with no sign of infection. But such things always take longer for a sixty-year-old than a twenty-year-old, and the shock to Darrell's system was still evident in his lowered energy level. This not being the first of Jed's night wanderings, he exclaimed, "Well, if it isn't the roaming night stalker," as Jed grabbed a mug and headed for the table. Then, glancing at Jed's flannel-lined khakis and with a seriously furrowed brow, he asked, "Hold on there! Are those blood stains on your pants?"

"Pretty sharp eyes for an old fart." And easing into a chair he said, "You're not going to believe what happened."

That Jed could so handily disable the hoodlums was no surprise to Darrell. What was near the realm of unbelievable was the fact that it was Jed who stumbled onto the pair that nearly did him in. Darrell pressed him for every little detail and was thankful both that the perps were behind bars and that Jed came out unscathed.

"Well, they're not exactly behind bars yet," Jed added. "Both are in the hospital, and from what the med techs said, one of them might be there for a while."

"As long as they're off the streets it's a start. You must have busted them up pretty good."

"I did what needed to be done. Fortunately, Father

Donovan isn't as bad as he looked at first. Just as I was leaving the precinct, one of the arresting officers came in from the hospital and said that a cut on his scalp and a mild concussion was the extent of the damage. They're keeping him overnight for observation."

They both stared pensively at their mugs for a time and then Darrell said, "You going to be able to get some sleep now?"

"Yeah, I'm ready. My juice level should be about back to normal and I'm beat."

"So go hit the hay. Percy's hotcakes and bacon should wake you up later this morning and we can rehash things if you want."

It was less than sixty seconds after hitting the pillow that Jed was on the way toward the bottom of his sleep cycle. His last thought before totally losing consciousness was, *Score one for the good guys*.

The heavenly aroma of breakfast snapped Jed's synapses to attention after four hours of quality rest. Back in his Marine Corps days he had learned that sleep could be an important part of one's personal arsenal. An hour or even fifteen minutes here and there would provide at least a partial recharging that could contribute to one's alertness and stamina. A shave and steaming hot shower added to his feeling of well-being, after which he followed the scent of coffee and pancakes like a grizzly heading for a beehive.

"Well, lookee here." Percy said with a grin. "Another fifteen minutes and I'd a-been shutting down the grill. You're looking like a serious need for coffee, yes?"

"Coffee first, followed by a whole side of bacon and

a six-inch stack of cakes," Jed replied, trying to keep from drooling.

As Percy carried over a mug his squinted eyes foretold the coming question. "Hear you's out doing some night-stalkin' early this morning. Darrell said you'd fill me in."

"How's our boy doing this morning?" Jed asked.

"None too worse for your keeping him up at all hours. So fill me in, eh."

Even though Percy interrupted occasionally hoping for more juicy details, Jed gave him the short version. He wasn't one to brag about his abilities, so his emphasis was on the fact that the culprits were now off the streets. After finishing the story Jed asked, "Is Darrell up and about yet?"

"Yeah, phone woke him up. He's answering the call of nature right now, but I think he's got a message for you."

As if on cue, Darrell shuffled in still wearing his lavender pajamas and deep merlot bathrobe. Heading for the coffee pot for a refill he said, "Morning Jed. I didn't expect you to wake up 'til noon."

"Hi, Darrell. Old habits die hard. Just can't seem to sleep once the roosters start crowing."

"Roosters?" Percy said. "I didn't hear nothin'."

"Figure of speech, Dad." Darrell said. "But it's just as well, Jed, because they want you back down at the police station."

Raising his eyebrows, Jed asked, "Did they say why?"

"Something about a few additional questions. Some lieutenant named Jospers who apparently just came in this morning. He said the sooner the better."

"I'll head down as soon as I pass judgment on Percy's pancakes. If they're as good as mine we just might put him on the permanent payroll."

"Might as well start writing the checks, young man. Slather some of that Vermont maple syrup on 'em and you'll think yer standing at the Pearly Gates."

Which was just about right. Being fully satiated and with a travel mug of steaming Costa Rican Dark Roast, Jed headed his Suburban toward Precinct Five headquarters.

Lieutenant Jospers, a twenty-two year veteran of the Minneapolis Police Department with starched shirt and immaculately pressed uniform on a trim and athletically honed body, reminded Jed of how a Marine carried himself. His obvious professionalism was complemented by a congenial disposition and the same respect for others that he expected from them. Part of his reason for wanting to interview Jed, which also added a layer to his respect, was to meet a fellow who, with his bare hands, could disarm two perps with guns and knives.

The conversation was affable even though Jed didn't think he was adding anything new to the statement he had given earlier in the day. He figured it was just part of all police departments' tendencies to check and re-check witnesses in the hope of maybe turning up something heretofore left out. The Lieutenant told Jed that the arresting officers were writing up his part in the incident as self-defense, pure and simple, even though they were still amazed at what he did. Jed said he regretted having to react so violently, but felt that there wasn't much choice if he didn't want to end up like Darrell . . . or worse.

"Have you received any reports on the extent of their injuries?" Jed asked.

“Matter of fact we have,” Jospers responded. “One of our officers went to the hospital this morning to find out when they would be released to our custody. Turns out we might get only one of ’em.”

“What do you mean?” Jed asked with some anxiety.

“When you hit the gunman in the side of the head, the vertebra at the top, C1 I believe it’s called, fractured and ruptured his spinal cord. His cognitive functions are OK, even if a bit fuzzy at this point, but he’s probably lost the use of his arms and legs for good. A few folks recover from that type of trauma, but not many.”

Jed stared at his feet for a while wondering how he should feel about this. He would not have intentionally caused this kind of injury, but in a fight for life one doesn’t generally have the liberty to measure all the possible consequences of a given action. With a triggerman’s finger is only two and a half pounds of pressure away from sending you to the morgue, one does whatever it takes to stay alive. Of course Jed felt bad that any human being would end up a quadriplegic, but he knew that given the same situation he’d repeat his actions.

“How about the other guy?”

“He won’t be using his right arm to carve on anything for quite some time. Probably has a concussion, but not as serious as the one they gave Father Donovan. Should have him in our lockup in a couple of days,” Jospers replied. “I understand that you’re just visiting Pastor Lee. How long were you planning on being in the area?”

“That’s somewhat up in the air,” Jed said. “But I’m guessing you’ll want me available.”

“At least until we complete the investigation. There’s

no question that charges will be laid, but it could be some time before it actually goes to trial. When it does, you're going to have to be available as a witness. Will that be a problem?"

"No. Not that I can see. I might be on the west coast depending on the time factor, but planes make it easy to get around these days."

After a few more pleasantries, Jed took his leave. He went back to Darrell's to fill him in on his meeting with Lieutenant Jospers. Then he excused himself to take a long walk along the Minnehaha Creek trail. He needed some time alone to sort out a thunderstorm of conflicting thoughts.

Although there was still a foot and a half of snow blanketing the area, the creek trail had had enough foot traffic that Jed could trek along the packed center. Light glistened off the white crystals with the blinding intensity of millions of diamonds reflecting late morning sun. Passing north of Pearl Park and heading east toward Lake Nokomis, he was alone with his thoughts. These decades later he still had mental pictures of Angela walking alongside him, but then forced himself to wrestle with the events of the last thirty-three hours.

Did I do the right thing? That was the question burning in Jed's mind as he meandered along the creek. He reasoned that he could have found a phone and called the police when he first saw the truck, but the perps could have been doing something to someone else similar to what Darrell had experienced. Or maybe by the time the cops arrived they would have been long gone. Jed believed in the concept of law and order, but he also knew that too often those who were supposed to implement it didn't get the job done. The job in this case being apprehension of the bad guys. While most people would not be remotely competent to take on individuals with knives and guns, Jed was aware of his own capabilities and reasoned that his actions could have prevented a wrong greater than taking the law into his own hands. He was comforted somewhat by the fact that the authorities seemed to view it in the same light since no charges were being laid against him.

Gray. Of the myriad of decisions facing one in life, most of them seemed to be in that proverbial gray area for which subjective judgment was called. *Why can't it be black and white more often? Why isn't most of life simply a matter of right or wrong? And when muddled down in a gray fog of choices, what factors or forces guide the proper decision?* Jed could conjure up numerous hypothetical cases where it would appear that *proper* was not a concept to apply to any available action. It surely wasn't proper for him to turn a fellow, no matter how evil, into a paraplegic. But then, that wasn't his intention either. It was simply an unforeseen consequence of defending himself when attacked. *Why is life so complicated? It would be so much easier if it was, well . . . easy.*

It seemed to him that the only folks to escape the agonizing complexities of life that force one to make decisions affecting others were hermits. Recluses like Godric of Finchale or Pachomius the Great must have had it easy. All they had to do in their own little private worlds was be concerned about themselves. Yet that, in itself, was a problem. Jed's reading of the Gospels revealed a Man whose life was spent living for others. A Man Jed felt committed to follow.

Which meant dealing with the complexities inherent in being involved in this gray, oftentimes very, very dark gray, world.

It was time to get serious with Darrell about where Jed felt himself being pulled. He would need his friend's assistance to proceed with his plan, although he had no idea to where it would lead. In the coming years Jed would find the grayness of the past child's play compared to the fog of war in which hard, hard decisions would be made. Like most things along one's journey, it was best he couldn't see the churning rapids that lay around the bends on the river of his life.

Chapter 35

April 1995 - Minneapolis, Minnesota

Darrell's wounds were healing nicely, and he and his father seemed to rejoice in their newfound relationship. Perhaps making up for lost years, they spent hours together watching movies, visiting museums, cruising the Twin Cities, and sharing thoughts about everything under the sun. Percy had totally lost contact with his wife's sister, Julia, so when

Darrell told him about his financial windfall from her it was news to him. When Darrell apprehensively probed his dad's possible need for assistance, Percy said, "Not to worry, Son. I got enough with the bit I laid away plus a small veteran's disability pension, so I'm doing fine. My needs are pretty simple, too."

Darrell responded, "Well, I want you to know, Dad, if you ever find yourself in a tight spot that I'm in a position to help."

"Appreciate that. But you use it where it's needed more. I ain't planning to have to stand in no soup kitchen line."

Darrell had returned to work toward the end of February, and Percy indicated that he'd better be getting back to San Diego before too long. Darrell could also sense that Jed was getting a little antsy, and figured it was time to have that planning session about his future. Early one morning while Percy was still sawing logs and the March sun was promising to melt the receding snowpack even more, the two friends huddled over toast and coffee in the solarium Darrell had built on the back of the house.

Jed explicated the concept as his thinking had evolved, and was formulating an outline of his basic needs. His goal was to embark on a street ministry in Seattle, reaching out to the down-and-outers, the homeless, hookers, addicts, and runaways. He didn't know exactly how it would play out practically, but those who were rejected by most of society needed someone to care for them, assist them, give them hope. He envisioned more of a hand-up rather than a handout, helping them to help themselves in whatever ways he could find. A lot of it was going to be trial-and-error.

“So how specific can you be about the needs for this new ministry?” Darrell asked.

“We’re not talking about a lot,” Jed replied. “An office of some sort, ideally with a kind of reception center or large room that would accommodate some tables and chairs and a coffee pot. And it should be in one of the poorer neighborhoods where the action’ll take place. I’ll also need some basic equipment: computer, phones, printer, etc.”

“We’re not talking big bucks here for the startup. But you’ll also need funds for monthly living expenses, yes?”

“Not at first, Darrell. I’ve still got a modest amount tucked away that should carry me for a year or more. If I can find a converted garage space, or something like that, to rent, that’ll do the trick. I’m not looking to move into Bill Gates’ neighborhood.”

“Well, when you get there and determine an actual figure, let me know if your account needs a boost. I think you told me that the last time you checked, it was still around fifty grand, but if that’s not enough, give me a shout. I take it you’re not going to be asking the church to throw in any bucks.”

“Not hardly. As soon as there are money strings, there’s generally a control factor. And I’ve had enough of their control that I want to do this on my own.”

“Point well taken. This could really be interesting.”

“Darrell, you’ve helped me out above and beyond the call of duty over the years. I thank you again and hope that together we can make this a ministry that really helps people in need.”

“I’m sure it will, Jed. Knowing you, I’m sure it will.”

Both Jed and Darrell went with Percy to the airport to see him off for his return to San Diego. Father and son were both wiping the corners of their eyes as they promised to stay in regular touch by phone and to book frequent visits both ways. Having made a good friend for life, Jed gave the old man a Marine Corps bear hug and said he'd likely get down California way one of these days.

"Miss my cooking, will you, young fella?" Percy smiled.

"Absolutely! And more than that. I look forward to deepening our relationship, Percy. Thanks for coming when Darrell needed you."

Another cough that was really an attempt to mask what could have been a manly sob, and Percy waved so-long as he disappeared down the ramp to his plane.

Three days later Jed packed the Suburban with his meager belongings, gave Darrell the same bear hug, and pointed the hood ornament west on Interstate 94. With lots of unknowns ahead, he was filled with excitement and anticipation. Given what was to come, if it was the Almighty's modus operandi to direct traffic for individuals, God just might have had Jed headed for Cincinnati instead of Seattle. Then again, maybe not.

Chapter 36

July 1995 - Da Nang, Republic of Vietnam

Gunnar had arrived at the conclusion that in coming to Vietnam, he was like that merchant in Matthew's Gospel who found a pearl of such great value that he sold everything but his underwear to get enough funds to purchase it. Except for one difference: Gun would have sold his underwear as well. Four factors contributed to his feeling this way.

For a civil engineer specializing in water systems development and management, the post-war reconstruction effort in Vietnam provided exciting challenges and almost unlimited opportunities for professional growth. Linden Technologies International appeared headed for decades of contracts in the country, and they compensated their employees with virtually unmatched salaries and benefits in the industry. Relationships with managerial colleagues, who had taken to calling him Gun, were as good or better than what he had experienced in Mexico, and his expertise, fairness, and encouragement produced a fraternal loyalty among those under his supervision. In short, he loved both what he was doing and with whom he was doing it.

In addition, he quickly developed a fondness for the country. The climate seemed to agree with him, and within the first half-year his system had acclimated so that one hundred degrees Fahrenheit seemed like just a good start. He worked in the coastal lowlands, but on days off he generally headed up into the highlands which he thought were as beautiful as any place he'd ever seen. The terraced rice paddies, the stunning beaches with green-shrouded rock mountains rising out of the offshore waters, the high country jungle rainforests, the Tulan cave system that traversed under two mountains, and on and on. As beautiful as parts of Indiana might be, it all seemed pretty tame compared to this fascinating country.

The third factor was the people. While some ethnic groups seem to cultivate incivility, and every society has its share of downright boorish and graceless folk, the Vietnamese in general came across to Gunnar as loving, caring, and respectful. He especially appreciated the adulatory, almost reverential treatment of their elders. And given the history of not too long ago, he was, as an American, surprised and gratified to be welcomed with apparent sincerity and approbation. Aiding his assimilation into Vietnamese society was the fact that, similar to his experience in Mexico, he was quickly learning to speak their language.

The factor that put the icing on the cake, if not the cake itself, was Thanh. It was February 1994 at a benefit supper to raise funds for a neighborhood community center, and the room seemed to brighten when she walked in. Thanh, the name meaning bright or sunny, was the most beautiful woman Gunnar had ever seen. Her classic Vietnamese features – a slender and lithe frame, flawless and darker than usual butternut skin, black silken hair that fell to her waist, and large hazel eyes that could melt an iceberg – were complimented by a smile that would make the Koh-i-Noor diamond look lackluster. Gunnar had never been in more than a casual and fleeting relationship with a woman, and at times wondered if real love was ever going to be part of his life. Meeting Thanh changed that for him in the first ten minutes. Any man trying to thwart his plan to pursue this twenty-five-year-old treasure would have had a fight on his hands.

Thanh Luu was part of a long-standing Da Nang family that would be considered middle class by Vietnamese standards. She, like Gunnar, was an only child, and her parents were firm believers in some of the old ways, namely, courting a woman with time, care, and respect. If they had any qualms about their daughter developing a relationship with an American, those were quickly put to rest as they got to know this responsible, upstanding young American. It also impressed them measurably that Gunnar spoke quite good

Vietnamese. Passionate love between the two vibrant young people grew quickly, and both were overjoyed that Chú and Cô Luu seemed happy with the situation. In Gunnar's mind, Thanh was the apotheosis of what a human being could become.

Gunnar also talked things over with his folks back in Indiana. With both his parents on the phone he said, "Mom, Dad, I'm hopelessly in love . . . and Thanh feels the same way. We both know that we can't live without each other, or at least we don't want to."

"Now, dear," Linn said, "how can you be so sure in such a short amount of time?"

"Don't forget, honey," Sonny cut in, "we got engaged seven months after we met."

"And Mom, I don't care whether it's been two months or two decades. This is the most wonderful woman I've ever met and I want to spend the rest of my life with her. Just wait till you meet her. It'll take about fifteen seconds for you to know this is right for both of us."

"Oh, Gunnar," Linn responded, "we certainly trust your judgment, and all we really want is your happiness. If you're sure, we're sure."

Sonny popped the big question. "Son, are you talking about doing the marriage thing in the near future?"

"If you consider next month the near future, then yeah," Gunnar teased. "Seriously, I'm going to ask her later tonight and my guess is that her parents can arrange things in about six weeks. So I'm hoping you both can take some time off to use the tickets I'm ready to book for you."

"No need for that, Son, because . . . "

Cutting him off, Gunnar said, "Dad, I'm in great shape

financially and I want to do this as a gift for you two. I can't imagine getting married without you both being there, so I'll give you another call with the arrangements as soon as things are finalized."

The call ended with everybody seeming to feel pretty good about what was happening. Both Sonny and Linn were excited beyond words to meet the woman who captured their son's heart.

It was after the evening meal and they were in the garden behind the Luu family home. Gunnar seated Thanh on a bench next to the three foot waterfall cascading into the goldfish pond. He dropped into the traditional one-knee position and took her hands in his. Looking into those hazel eyes that saw into his soul and reflected back the love he felt, Gunnar recited to her a poem he had composed for this moment. "In the woods I found a heart / I planted it in myself / And it took root so deep / That now / It is as my own." And after a deep breath to keep from choking, "Thanh, my love and my life, will you be my wife?"

She answered him with a passionate kiss that said exactly what he wanted to hear.

The event took place in September. Sonny and Linn had come over a week earlier, both for Gunnar to show them a bit of his new country and to spend some time with the Luu family. Since neither the Torkelsons nor the Luus knew each other's language, Gunnar acted as interpreter to facilitate some basic communication. A lot of bowing, hand-shaking and nervous laughter took place, but at least there was a sense of camaraderie and being comfortable in each other's presence. Gunnar's parents were happy that Thanh had a primitive proficiency with English, a result of Gunnar's intense tutoring, so that some conversation could take place. They became, as Gunnar knew they would, enraptured with his bride and conveyed to her that they felt very blessed to think of her as their daughter. Hearing this, tears of joy ran down Thanh's cheeks.

The wedding was a glorious traditional Vietnamese affair, the ceremony taking place at the Buddhist temple on top of Marble Mountain and the reception at the prestigious Ngoc Quý Club on the banks of the Hàn River. Festivities continued the second day at the Luu residence with many a young man present wishing he was standing in Gunnar's shoes.

The next day and just before he and Thanh began a short honeymoon up the coast, Gunnar took his parents to the airport. While waiting for the flight to be called, Sonny, with some solicitude, posed an obvious question. "Any idea, Son, when, or if, you might be returning to the States?"

Gunnar, who had been waiting for this question, replied, "At this point I really can't say, Dad. One never knows what the future will bring in terms of opportunity, but for now I'm planted here. LinTech has at least a decade of contracts to complete around the country, and how long I might stay for those or whether they make me an offer I can't refuse somewhere else remains to be seen."

"San Diego is a wonderful place to live," Linn chimed in, "and your father and I are starting to think about whether we want to spend our retirement somewhere with a more amenable climate."

"We'll just have to see, Mom. We all know how quickly things can change. And in the short run you can count on seeing us in Indiana at least once a year, and I'm in fine shape to help get you over here whenever you want."

They hemmed and hawed back and forth a bit more on the subject before their flight number was called. As the Torkelsons boarded, they felt that common mixture of emotions: joy over their son's happiness combined with sadness at not being able to physically participate in it with any semblance of frequency.

Three months after the wedding, Thanh confirmed that for which they both hoped: she was pregnant and due in seven months. On July 31, 1995, she gave birth to a healthy baby girl. The baby seemed to both of them like an angel from heaven, so that's the name they gave to her, Tuyen. Tuyen – "angel" – a precious gift from the love they shared.

Chapter 37

January 1996 - Da Nang, Republic of Vietnam

Two of the biggest words for Boa were fear and power. By his reckoning, the former led to the latter . . . and power was to him what gasoline is to an engine. Although the Ghost Snake had no conscious recognition of such, any college psych major could tell you that the underlying cause had to do with his childhood. From his first conscious memory until the day he walked away from choking the life out of Thao, he had felt like a prisoner. There had been no escape, no options, no power. The horrors of his early years had gripped and squeezed and crushed his soul into something inhuman, and it was permanent. If any hint of goodness, conscience, or heart remained, it would take a team of cardiac surgeons and shrinks to find it. Boa did not want anyone to have any power over him, and the more power he had to suffocate asshole humanity, the better.

The python caper in Hue a couple of years back had substantially increased his reputation in spite of the fact that no one knew who he was. The conventional wisdom in the three-province area of his main operations was that you really didn't want to know the identity of the Ghost Snake, and that contact with him was to be avoided at all costs. The stranglings continued with some frequency as a result of Boa's need for cash, the desired reinforcement of the terror his nickname struck in the hearts of most citizens, and the momentary quenching of the lust for blood that dominated his life. And there was another reason.

Because of the strict nature of law enforcement, gangs in the unified Vietnam were not as flourishing as MS-13 in El Salvador or the various cartels in Mexico. Commit a crime and get caught, you went to jail. Pure, simple, fast. The only gun a citizen could possess was a licensed shotgun for hunting, and being caught with any other firearm, handgun or rifle of any kind, meant watching the world through bars for a considerable time. The Communist regime worked hard to control crime and came down on it with a sledgehammer. Nevertheless, illegal activities such as selling drugs, smuggling, and prostitution still operated under the radar to some degree. One illicit industry in particular attracted Boa's attention because of the profit margin and the nature of the product. Kidnapping and exporting young women for the sex trade produced maximum profit with minimum risk, and it facilitated his revenge on the most despicable portion of the human race: women. One might think that due to Thao's malevolence, Boa's primary choler would have been directed at males. But virtually every female brought to Boa's mind, consciously or subconsciously, his loathsome mother and the myriad of callous, unscrupulous, and heartless women who had used him as a sex toy.

Ho Chí Minh City was too far away to be a concern. The racketeers there controlled human trafficking basically south of a line from Da Lat to Cam Ranh, and left the less populated reaches north of that to whoever had the gumption. Leaving the far north to the longer-standing powerful gangs there, Boa determined to control the territory between the coast and the western border from Quang Tri to Quy Nhon. The large area was primarily rural, which meant it was more difficult for police to administer, and there were easier pickings for the desired product. Only two gangs dabbled in human trafficking, the weaker one being, *Bàn Tay Sat* or Iron Fist. The stronger one was *Khung Bo*, a name which made Boa smile. Eliminating *Bàn Tay Sat* and then becoming the supreme leader of *Khung Bo* would provide him with an impenetrable empire of power. This vision gave him wet dreams in the middle of the night.

Duc and Lanh were still with him. Trang had taken a liking to heroin, and a year earlier a dirty bag of the stuff had led to his early demise. Duc was larger and meaner than ever, and Lanh had cultivated a growing expertise with blades of all kinds. He liked to slit throats as much as his boss liked to strangle them, and Boa sometimes gave him the honor if his appetite to choke had been satiated.

The Iron Fist went down like a limp-fish handshake. It took some doing, including several elongated necks, to learn the location of the gang's headquarters on the outskirts of Hoi An. The small, loose gang was led by three individuals, one of whom was mentally unbalanced and another mentally handicapped. A paid informant had notified Lanh that on a certain night all three would be in a planning meeting in their abandoned shop on the edge of the old port area. A nearby leased warehouse was where they often kept their human cargo in oceanic shipping containers until a vessel was available to transport the women to another country. Boa was certain that if the gang's head was cut off, the leaderless body would wither and die.

With Lanh guarding the back door, Duc easily smashed in the front door with his massive shoulder, and he and Boa raced into the small space to face the three totally surprised leaders of *Bàn Tay Sat*. Lanh crowbarred the rear entrance and joined them. Boa promised them life and freedom if they handed over all their cash, a substantial amount of which they had hidden under the floor, transferred to him their current human stock awaiting shipment, and pledged to disband the gang and disappear. The leader, a ragged squirt with beady little eyes, knew a good deal when he saw one, so he gave them the money plus the keys to the warehouse and shipping containers. He said they had only nine women at present, but they were prime flesh that promised to bring a good price. After receiving all with a polite thank you, Boa jumped the leader with his garrote, Lanh sliced through the mentally disabled one's neck, and Duc nearly took the third's head off with a full-strength swing of a piece of three-inch lead pipe. With the leadership gone, so was the Iron Fist.

Khung Bo was a different matter. What Boa needed to do here was, again, eliminate the leadership, but then keep the gang together with himself as its new head. This would need to be done with some finesse so as to command the loyalty of the remaining members. Although loyalty was a euphemism for adherence due to greed and fear. Boa's small group was not large enough for the larger-scale plans he had in mind, but commanding an organization of a couple score of trained operatives would do the trick. But first he had to take care of Chien Chu.

The honcho of *Khung Bo*, which means terror, was the second generation head, his father having formed the gang fifteen years earlier. Chien ruled, as his father had, with merciless ruthlessness. At nineteen years old he had made his first kill, in fact three on the same day, as his dad systematically assassinated any possible opposition to his corner on the market. Eight years later an informant tipped off the local authorities to the Chu hideout, and the elder was cut down in a hail of gunfire. The informant was inevitably found, and Chien personally strung him upside down in the town square one midnight and gutted him alive. Diligent research revealed the identities of the eight policemen who had participated in the raid resulting in his father's death, and within two months all eight were dead, along with their wives and children. The son took the father's place without objection.

Boa's plan was simple. Enable Chien's disappearance,

and then offer his assistants either a continued position of authority in the gang now headed by Boa or a quick demise. The finesse part had to do with Chien's cunning and paranoid watchfulness. But Boa discovered a critical weakness in *Khung Bo*'s leader: a fondness for young boys. He intended to exploit it.

Careful, secretive observation revealed Chien's perverse addiction. And then fortune smiled when one of his underlings approached one of Boa's new recruits for assistance in borrowing a youngster who had caught his master's fancy. The recruit relayed the request to Boa and a plan began to form. It involved a thirty-eight foot luxury yacht which Boa had leased through an intermediary to entertain his foreign buyers.

"What makes you think he'll get on board without some of his assistants?" Duc asked.

"First," Boa said, "our guy, who Chien thinks is his guy, will tell him that the owner of the boat has his own onboard guards and will only allow one customer at a time. We'll make him think the owner is paranoid about somebody making off with his boat. Second, he'll be told that he can station as many of his men as he likes all around the wharf and the ship's particular slip. Third, the boy will be smiling and waving to him at the top of the gangplank. Chien may be smart, but too often he thinks with the wrong head."

"And if he doesn't take the bait?" Duc posed.

"He runs and we run. There's always another day and something else that'll work."

Getting their hands on the ten-year-old was a cake walk. His uncle was in dire financial straits and for a generous fee agreed to facilitate the boy's availability. He told his brother that a photographer friend of his needed several young boys to model for some magazine ads, ostensibly for a photo shoot. Lanh picked the boy up on the appointed day after the evening meal and promised to return him before nine o'clock. However, at eleven o'clock, when Da Nang was essentially shut down, the boy stood at the top of the gangplank. He had been told to smile and wave or his parents would die. It was a weak smile and a feeble wave, but Chien was too far away to notice and he was primed for an exciting encounter. He stationed four men with AK-47s at the bottom of the gangplank in addition to six more strategically placed within the wharf area. The ship's "captain," Lanh dressed in the appropriate uniform, stood smiling behind the boy with a perfectly honed stiletto poking gently in the middle of the boy's back.

Crossing the gunwale onto the ship itself, Chien took the little boy's hand as Lanh, knife concealed, led the way to the main stateroom. Chatting cordially about the balmy evening, Lanh opened the door and as he bowed and stepped backward while Chien entered first, he forcibly yanked the boy backwards while kicking the warlord into the room. The door slammed shut and as Chien was about to rise from the hands-and-knees position into which he had fallen, Boa leaped forward and slipped a noose around his neck. Frisking Chien beforehand had not been an option, so the hope was that Boa could work his deadly magic before there was any chance for retaliation with a weapon. But Boa was not quick enough. Chien pulled a dagger with a five-inch blade from beneath his shirt and swung backwards into Boa's right side. A crimson fountain gushed out along with an involuntary scream of pain. Boa released the garrote and fell back holding his wounded side.

Seeing the scar across Boa's face and knowing the rumors, Chien said, "Ah, Ghost Snake. You think you can defeat *Khung Bo* so easily? I'm afraid you have chosen your last victim, and I shall take pleasure in being recognized as the one to end your serpentine reign."

He was two steps from plunging the dagger into Boa's evil heart. After the first step, the door to the stateroom exploded inward and an arm's length away was two hundred and eighty pounds of muscle holding a twenty-four-inch length of three-inch lead pipe. A second later he saw the pipe coming toward his head and he ducked while at the same time aiming the knife at Boa's left breast. The pipe missed his head but connected with his right shoulder, shattering it into at least a dozen pieces and rendering the knife hand useless. In spite of his pain, Boa rolled adroitly to the side as Chien crumbled on the spot where he had lain a moment before. Kicking the knife aside, Duc smiled. Chien did not.

Tying Chien's hands behind him in spite of his shrieking from shoulder pain, Duc and Lanh then staunched Boa's blood flow and bandaged the cut. It was fairly deep and would require stiches, but that could be attended to later. They knew a veterinarian who would do the job for a bottle of wine and a few *dong*. All this happened within ten minutes and with none of the commotion observed or heard by Chien's guards. As preplanned, special mooring ropes had been slackened and rigged to be cast off from the boat. With Duc at the bow and Lanh at the stern, the boat's real captain started the engine and gunned it as both lines were dropped in the water. When the powerful yacht leapt away from the dock, the gangplank fell into the water and Chien's guards watched helplessly as their meal ticket disappeared to the east. A couple of them fired aimlessly at the boat's wake so that in case Chien survived he would know they at least tried something.

It took a little over a half an hour to skirt Da Nang Bay and reach the north side of Son Trà Peninsula. This was an area known for the several species of sharks often cruising there, and Boa thought it was as good a place as any for their adversary to disappear. Chien stoically said nothing but winced with pain as they wrestled him into a life jacket. They wanted him floating so that they could watch as the bull and white sharks came for a midnight snack. Lanh did some mischief with his blades beforehand to make sure there was blood to draw their finny friends. It didn't take long before the only sound they heard was that of thrashing bodies vying for part of the action.

The ship's captain knew that if he wanted to live, he would keep his mouth shut. Besides, he earned a nice bonus for the night's venture. When all that was left was a bit of flotsam and a couple of dorsal fins, they completed the evening by getting rid of the one other witness. They threw the little boy overboard and headed for a night at anchor off Hon San Tra Peninsula.

Boa's wound wasn't as serious as it first appeared. No vital organs were damaged, but the messy flesh wound required twenty stitches and a bag full of pain killers meant for swine. The irony of the medication did not cross Boa's mind. After a week of rest aided by the pills and rice wine, he had Duc arrange a meeting with the remaining leadership of *Khung Bo*. Leadership was a loose term for an even looser organization. Figuring out who was in charge, now that

Chien was history, was like trying to identify the commander of a group of piranha. After the report by the henchmen supposedly guarding Chien's life and his subsequent non-appearance, anybody with ten brain cells knew he would never been seen again. The confabulation was to take place on a dirt road offshoot of the Hai Vân highway north of Da Nang and within the eastern extreme of Bach Ma National Park. The agreement was for the participation of no more than three individuals from each party with no firearms allowed.

Boa, Duc, and Lanh entered the dirt track for the half mile walk, and eventually arrived at a small clearing in a valley surrounded by forested hills with a narrow but loud waterfall which would mask any sounds from reaching the highway. It was a peaceful and beautiful mountain setting, unlike what was to come. The *Khung Bo* contingent had concealed a group of ten armed men in the roadside bush a mile south of the dirt road junction who could be called into action if they heard gunfire to the north. Due to the precipitous and isolated terrain, the meeting was also being held in the late afternoon while there was still enough light to find their way out. It was risky, but dramatic times called for such.

The *Khung Bo* henchman who had been Chien's more-or-less second in command was a street-toughened and savvy thirty-two year old who had saved his boss's skin more than once, and had survived at least a dozen attempts on his own life. His name, Quy, in one of those ironic coincidences of life, had the same meaning in Vietnamese as Boa's given name meant in Chinese: precious. He figured that his hand-fighting skills and quickness could best the hulking Duc if need be, while the other two had three-inch blades sheathed in thin leather gently pushed up their rectums with which they figured they could handle Lanh and Boa.

The Montagnards, roughly translated from French as "people of the mountain," were composed of some thirty tribes that lived in the mountainous central highlands. They were considered savages by most lowland Vietnamese, and they were loyal U.S. allies in the fight against the Viet Cong and NVA. One of their primary weapons prior to being equipped with modern firepower had been the crossbow. A Montagnard, one of the dozen comrades that Boa had much earlier secreted in the undergrowth on both sides of the clearing, had one.

Gang members from both sides reached the clearing and faced off, Boa making sure the *Khung Bo* three had their backs to the west. Quy had a difficult time looking directly at Boa since the jagged cross-face scar and his sneering, scowling countenance tended to inspire a constricted anal sphincter in most men. Nevertheless, he began with, "Okay, what's this all about? We both know that Chien is . . . " and before he could finish the sentence a three-blade arrowhead had pierced his right lung and its shaft protruded eight inches out of his chest. As he sagged to his knees and then fell to his side, Boa's men, each with either an assault rifle or a semiautomatic handgun, stepped into the clearing.

Boa hissed, "Throw down your blades. You will die if we strip search you and find any." The two gangsters slowly reach down the back of their pants and deftly extracted the blades and did as they were told.

"Good," said Boa. "Now you have one more choice. We either return to Da Nang and you proclaim my leadership of *Khung Bo*, or you die. And you will not like the manner of death." Seeing in their peripheral vision Lanh licking a razor sharp machete as he stood over Quy's body, they immediately proclaimed loyalty to Boa as the new supreme leader. They might have been stupid, but they weren't crazy. Boa needed these two to return to Da Nang and spread the word among the leaderless and largely incompetent *Khung Bo* rank and file. They would be most happy to have someone provide the planning and protection that would enable the gang's continuance. They wouldn't get rich like Chien or Boa, but they would likely have enough of a sustaining income to pay for bread, booze, and broads.

And so it was that Boa became king boss of the *Khung Bo*, "The Terror." If the gang had lived up to the meaning of its name under Chien, Boa brought it to new heights. Police were either bought off or killed, and any of the populace with a lick of sense in the three province area wouldn't oppose the gang if their lives depended on it . . . because they did.

The gang profited from extortion, gambling, prostitution, drugs, and robbery. But Boa cultivated a specialty that brought in bigger money and fed his warped psyche. More and more young Vietnamese girls began disappearing. One in particular would bring consequences he never could have imagined.

Chapter 38

July 2001 - Da Nang, Republic of Vietnam

Tuyen's name could not have been more appropriate. At six years old she was a beautiful Amerasian angel who embodied both the strong Anglo-American features of her father and the delicate lineaments of her Vietnamese mother. She was being raised with gentleness and love, and imbued with the values of her hard-working and responsible parents. She enjoyed helping her mother with cooking and housework, and, with home tutoring, was far ahead of her first grade classmates in basic reading-writing-arithmetic. With both languages being used at home, she was already bilingual in Vietnamese and English. In short, she brought immense joy in every respect to her devoted parents, Gunnar and Thanh.

As far as Gunnar was concerned, Vietnam was his home. He was now the administrative assistant to the CEO of Linden Technologies' Vietnamese operations, and was in line to succeed his boss when he returned to the United States. Gunnar was involved in overseeing development projects from Hanoi to Ho Chí Minh City, and had developed Vietnamese language fluency to the point where people on the phone did not know they were talking to an expatriate from the U.S. His parents had visited three times since the wedding, and he had taken Thanh and Tuyen to Indianapolis twice. The Torkelsons were proud of their son and happy for the joy he found in both his work and his family in Vietnam. They knew he was very hesitant to move Thanh away from her family, so they simply resigned themselves to the long plane ride for visits once or twice a year.

Thanh was also blessed with outstanding intelligence and the Vietnamese determination to succeed. As in the rest of the world, computers had become the working tool for business and industry in Vietnam. So with the assistance of her tech-savvy brother, Thanh learned the tricks of the trade on the best equipment that Gunnar's money could buy. She continued her self-education with online courses that increased her skills to a point where she could do complex programming and utilize existing applications with ease. She was not only able to help Gunnar with intricacies of the company's techno-management, she began an out-of-home business that provided computer setup and maintenance for other commercial ventures. In the decades since the war's end, Vietnam had progressed to a socialist-oriented market economy where SMEs, small and medium enterprises, were not only allowed but encouraged. Most of the entrepreneurs had only rudimentary computer skills, which resulted in a rich environment for someone with Thanh's talents. It wasn't a full-time or high-pressure job, but it enabled her to work at home for some unnecessary but decent personal income, and for an opportunity to contribute to her country's growing economy.

The family lived in *Vuon Hòa Bình*, or Peace Garden, a gated, up-scale area of Da Nang patrolled by private security guards. Their home was comfortable but not pretentious, and they slept well at nights after activating the best alarm system money could buy in Vietnam. Central air conditioning, used sparingly, brought a level of comfort in the hot season that few others had the means to enjoy. Compensated handsomely by the Vietnamese government, Gunnar's company was valued for its contributions to the ongoing development that was still needed two and a half decades after the cessation of hostilities. And due to his congenial disposition and excellent fluency in the Vietnamese language, Gunnar was ever more appreciated by his indigenous business associates as well as the neighborhood community.

After reading one of Tuyen's favorite books and putting her to bed, Gun and Thanh sat on their deck overlooking the Han River sharing an evening glass of their favorite Australian wine, Rosemount Estate Cabernet-Merlot. It was in the pleasant low 80's with a forecast of close to seventy-five for a cool night's sleep. Thanh was still so dazzlingly gorgeous in Gunnar's eyes that he found it difficult to believe this supernova among women was actually his wife. But much more than that was the depth of her character, her quintessential embodiment of all that is pure and excellent and commendable in a human being. Catching his adoring gaze at her, Thanh asked, "Is everything all right?"

"More than all right, my precious wife. There are times, like right now, that I'm just a bit overcome with my love for you, and the fact that you love me," Gunnar replied.

Blushing at his American forthrightness, she bowed slightly and said, "The good fortune is mine, Gunnar." Still not used to being put on such a pedestal, she sought to re-direct the conversation. "And we are both blessed beyond anything I could have dreamed with little Tuyen. Can you imagine life without her?"

"Indeed not. I don't even want to imagine it. And we have many wonderful years yet to watch her grow into a beautiful woman like her mother."

Another flush of color to her cheeks, Thanh tacked to a new subject. "I got a new account today, dear, that looks very promising."

"Oh? What's the nature of this one?"

"It's called *Khá Đep* Trading Company, a small but apparently stable export business that specializes in traditional Vietnamese textiles. They are seeking to expand and apparently there is a growing market for their products on the west coast of America."

"I hope this won't be putting too much more pressure on your practice. You've been talking about how you don't want to devote much more time than your current accounts already demand."

"I don't believe this will be a problem," Thanh continued. "They've just acquired a new system and need help setting up their network and software installation."

"Well, good for you. Not only do I have a beautiful wife, but soon I'll have a rich one," Gunnar teased.

Changing the subject again, Thanh asked, "By the way, have you seen on the news lately about all these young women disappearing in our part of the country?"

"Yeah, I have, but I haven't been paying much attention to the details. Are the police linking them together and do they have any clues about what's happening to them?"

"At this point it seems to be pretty much a guessing game since they haven't caught anybody, but there are rumors that it might have something to do with trafficking these women for slave labor or sex," Thanh replied. "A lot of the missing women are from the poor areas where they don't have money for adequate security and the police don't seem to care much."

"Still, my dear, please take extra care when you're out and about. Until they catch whoever is causing the problem I don't believe we can be over-cautious."

"Do not worry, Gunnar," Thanh replied. "You know I never go out alone at night, and my daytime visits are always in busy commercial districts. But I will still be cautious as a tiger," she said and then purred throatily like one of the big cats on the prowl.

"Ooooh, that would scare me," Gunnar feigned as he put down his glass and slid his hand behind her neck. "But I know a place where you can purr all you like, and scratch my back with your beautiful claws."

Thanh fluttered her eyelids and took his hand as she said, “Come into my lair and you just might be sorry . . . or then again, maybe you won’t be.” So, after a final check on Tuyen, Gunnar very willingly went to look into the eye of the tiger.

Chapter 39

July 2001 - Seattle, Washington

Six years after leaving Minneapolis, Jed felt like he was living in a different world. A whole different world from the Matopos Hills of Zimbabwe, the Hmong village of Nhon Phat, the rolling prairies of Lemmon, South Dakota, or the peaceful shores of Lake Hiawatha in Minneapolis. And even though he was back in Seattle, his environs, lifestyle, and vocational pursuits contrasted markedly from his university days or even his time with the Cathedral Kitchen. Late one evening as he plodded toward his garage-apartment, he reflected on what had transpired since rolling back into town in the early spring of 1995. His dominant awareness was the rectitude of the course he charted for himself. If there had been any doubts about the direction his life had taken at the ripe old age of forty-nine, they had been dispelled early on by the reactions of the people with whom he formed relationships and the concrete, positive ways his actions appeared to affect their lives.

Passing by Waterfall Garden Park as he headed west on Main Street back to his office in Pioneer Square , Jed remembered where his *impertinent* ministry began. He thought of it in those terms because that was what was more or less communicated to him by the ecclesiastical authorities governing the church body into which he had been ordained. He was still on the clergy roster of the Lutheran church, but only because he had done nothing that qualified him for defrocking. Yet.

Jed operated on his own, at least with no strings, financial or imperial, attached to the corporate church's structure or strictures. He didn't know if he was an embarrassment to the ecclesiastical hierarchy or not, although his guess was that they were content to ignore him while rejoicing that he wasn't asking for any money. The church officials were somewhere between perplexed and miffed because Jed was doing the kind of ministry that, well, Jesus would be doing, but he wasn't under their administrative control. While he identified himself as a Lutheran pastor, Jed felt no allegiance to the established, formal church, matching their demonstrated indifference to him with his own. In the accredited, hallowed halls, terms like renegade or radical or rebel were used for him, even though some who would never set foot in the neighborhoods Jed prowled appreciated what he was doing. The arrangement, or lack of one, suited Jed just fine. He was finally exercising the vocation to which many years of varied experiences had led him, and whether anyone else approved or not was of no concern.

In a nutshell, Jed wanted to try to assist the down-and-outers in whatever ways his imagination and wits might lead. Time and again he had seen the dead ends to which so many had come in their lives and how they were by-and-large abandoned by affluent America. The uber-rich didn't seem to care about anything but adding another hundred thousand dollar vehicle to their current fleet of a dozen, and protecting the lavish lifestyles to which they somehow felt they had a right. The middle class was largely tied up with making the house and car payments and trying to figure out if they'd have enough to live on in retirement. The poor . . . well, they were simply trying to exist, trying to keep from becoming homeless beggars with kids in tow. And an unhealthy share of all Americans simply buzzed through life without any consciousness of what it was like to be a bipolar homeless person or a castaway child turning tricks to get money for a fajita or a fix. Or how many people actually lived in such manner. Ignorance-is-bliss characterizes the bulk of a society whose only brush with any of this is to watch a forty-five second news spot some evening while waiting for the baseball game to start.

After arriving in Seattle in 1995, Jed had rented a downtown garage tolerably reconditioned into living quarters for a person with a discerning eye for low-end shed décor and no fear of cockroaches or spiders. His basic plan was to have no basic plan. Meaning, what he intended to do was walk the streets and visit the haunts to where the marginalized were relegated. He would meet people, hopefully form something that resembled trust relationships, evaluate their needs and personal resources, and connect them with agencies with which they might qualify for assistance. It was not Jed's intent to be in the welfare business. Rather, he wanted to help others take steps toward a greater state of well-being. If nothing else, he could be a friend, a listening ear, a shoulder upon which to lean or cry.

From the beginning he always wore a shirt with a clerical collar because he wanted that visual connection with the One who motivated his actions. He also wanted to demonstrate that clergymen didn't all fit the movie stereotype of a silver-haired, stooped-shouldered, stay-in-the-background figure who basically offered platitudes and trite banalities. In addition, a clerical collar often engendered respect and could even get one into places such as restricted hospital areas.

Jed didn't see himself as a savior, but if he could contribute to anyone's salvation in any little way, it would accomplish that for which he was there. Whenever he passed under the Union Gospel Mission neon sign that proclaimed "Jesus Saves," he would wince at what that meant to most people. While the Mission indeed helped folks with material needs, to the providers – indeed, to most people who wore crosses around their necks – being saved meant going to heaven and not to hell. Jed's study of the Bible had convinced him that there was no such thing as hell, and that any concern God has with saving folks has to do with things like adequate food, shelter, medical care, education, and the like. Whether it was in the shanty towns outside Harare or the slums of Chicago, salvation to the folks who lived there began with being able to live in peace and without hunger pangs ripping their midsections when they hit the hay each night. Different things inspire people to recognize the value of every human life and motivate them to work for all people to have enough. For Jed it was his faith. Hence, he wore the collar as an observable symbol of such.

He could not remember just when it began, but the Roman Catholic tendency to see a man wearing a clerical collar and to address him as Father stuck as his street name. "Here comes Father Jed" or "Go see Father Jed" or "Father Jed'll know what to do" became the stock phrases. At first he attempted to put a lid on the practice, but it caught on and flourished to the point where he finally gave up. If thinking of and addressing him as Father Jed opened doors to relationships, so be it. Over the years he simply got used to it, inwardly chuckling that he was likely the only Lutheran pastor in the U.S. who was called Father by those he served.

Since he couldn't imagine life without regular, strenuous exercise, Jed also kept up his physical fitness routine. For him it was simply part of being alive. In the area from the south end of Lake Union to West Seattle to Lake Washington, people became accustomed to seeing him cruise the neighborhoods at a seemingly effortless pace. He liked to run ten miles at least four times a week, but every other week or so he'd punch out twenty miles for old time's sake. He was starting to feel age and city streets in his knee joints, but his leg workouts in the gym kept the surrounding muscles so toned that they held things together and took the lion's share of the beating. Jed's one splurge was a gym membership that he felt he needed for a total body workout. He located a hard-core basement gym in the older section of West Seattle where he could exercise in anonymity. And he didn't wear his collar when either running or at the gym.

One other change in his life was to jettison his trusty Suburban. Its gas-guzzling size didn't fit with his new location and lifestyle, so he traded it in on a 1990 Honda Civic that barely fit into the parking space that came with his rented garage suite. Jed also barely fit his bulk into the driver's seat, but in spite of the rust and dents, it ran well and was economical. It also made a statement about what was, or wasn't, of value to him.

It had been slow going at first. A lot of street people had a distrust of churchy folks bred into them by the latter's too-often tendency to try to save their souls. Some of the so-called gospel missions would even require religious service attendance before a walk-in was given a meal or a bed. Also, the scroungers, panhandlers, guttersnipes and such had eyes and access to televisions, and there was no love lost for televangelists arriving in Cadillacs who then browbeat the forlorn crowds for cash before checking into their two-thousand-dollar-a-night hotel rooms. So when this middle-aged, good looking, athletically-honed hunk with a clerical collar began roaming the neighborhoods with no apparent agenda, they didn't know what to make of it.

When asked what he was doing there, Jed's stock answer was that he was just living from day to day like they were and looking to make the world a better place in his own little way. That puzzled most of them initially. But when he didn't go away and caused no harm, they began to recognize and accept him as part of the community. Two incidents helped secure his favorable standing, not to mention a formidable reputation.

One fall evening about a half a year after his arrival on the scene, Jed was walking north of Jackson Street underneath the Alaskan Way Viaduct as he headed toward the Hole in the Wall BBQ in Pioneer Park. He had been losing against Three Fingers Jack on the north side of the Seahawks Stadium. Jack, who had lost two digits on his left hand when he had fallen off a freight train in Oregon in his younger days, was known as the neighborhood chess shark who supplemented his GI disability pension with low-stakes games in Seattle's back alleys. Jed had played now and then over the years, and had virtually committed to memory several books on winning strategies and tactics. In addition, he could visualize and remember at least ten moves ahead and at least three possible responses to each by his opponent. But Three Fingers was winning because Jed was holding back, yet in a fashion that did not prompt Jack's suspicions. Jed had come to recognize that to beat Jack on the board too often resulted in the latter's loss of face and diminished his standing in the street community. So licking his wounds from Jack's latest checkmate, he was looking forward to licking his fingers with one of Hole in the Wall's mouthwatering barbequed pulled pork sandwiches. Then he heard a muffled scream.

Peering in the direction of the sound, Jed saw movement about thirty yards away in the deepening shadows underneath the viaduct. As he edged toward what appeared to be a scuffle, he heard another higher-pitched scream followed by what was obviously a forceful slap of skin on skin. As he moved around a pillar to within ten yards of the activity, he came upon a woman on the pavement whose legs were straddled by one man while another held her arms down. He recognized the woman, who went by Lovelace, as one of the neighborhood ladies-of-the-night, but he had never seen either of the men. "Hey, what's going on?" Jed said with force.

The one holding the woman's arms stood up and sneered, "None of yer damn business. Get the hell out now less'n you want yer night spoilt." He was maybe two inches taller than Jed but at least thirty pounds lighter. Grime covered his skin and clothes, and one would need a magnifying glass to find any white on his nicotine-stained teeth.

"We don't want to spoil anything for anybody, do we? Just let the lady up and go on your way and we'll all call it a night."

The man on top of Lovelace was a foot shorter and fifty pounds heavier than his companion, and just as grubby. In the poor light he didn't see it at first, but then registered Jed's clerical collar. "Well I'll be damned, Slick. It's a freak'n padre trying to do his good deed for the day. Think it's time we got religion?" he said with a grin.

Jed stepped to within five feet of the standing Slick and said, "Look, fellas, nobody wants to get hurt here and I'm now a witness, so just admit this was a mistake and clear out. I'm not fooling with you. I mean now!"

"Ha!" Slick spat, along with a wad of phlegm. "Churchman here's gonna teach us a lesson. Well let's just see who does the hurt'n."

The dim light and Jed's windbreaker must have obscured his size and muscular physique. Either that or the would-be rapists figured two against one was no contest. Two things happened almost simultaneously. As Fat Man rose to a half standing position, Lovelace put every ounce of energy she had into her right leg as she brought her knee to her chest and then straightened it directly between the fellow's thighs. The whoosh that came out of his mouth sounded like the releasing an inflated balloon, and he fell backwards clutching his crotch like someone was about to steal the family jewels. At the same time Slick reached behind and grabbed the .38 special he had tucked in the small of his back. As he worked his finger toward the trigger while his arm swung around, Jed timed it perfectly so that his capoeira kick hit the gunman's wrist with devastating force. The gun flew through the air and the man held his broken wrist while shouting obscenities. Jed took a menacing step toward Slick and growled, "Shut your mouth and sit down by your jackass friend there. Lovelace, there's a payphone up the street just this side of the ferry terminal. Go dial 911 and get the police here while I watch these guys."

Disheveled but unhurt, she replied, "No, Father Jed. Let 'em go. I think they've learned their lesson and I don't need no more cops in my life."

"You sure about that, Love?" Jed asked. "We don't want these guys thinking they can get away with this again."

"They didn't get away with nothing. Look at 'em. They gonna think twice 'fore trying this 'round here agin, 'specially when news gits 'round 'bout what happened. Besides, gonna be a while 'fore Fat Joe can get it up," she smirked.

"Look," Jed replied, "I'll go with your judgment, but I'd rather you keep this little encounter to yourself."

Which she didn't. Within forty-eight hours, anywhere

Jed went in Pioneer Square or surrounding areas people were slapping him on the back and expressing their gratitude.

The second incident had happened in February 1996, about four months later. It was approaching a year since Jed's arrival back in Seattle and he felt more and more like this was where he belonged. He was learning the intricacies of both the state and federal social agencies. He also established relationships with non-governmental organizations, both secular and religious, that focused efforts on those most in need. Even more important in Jed's eyes was the growing acceptance of him within the local scene. Folks were becoming convinced that he had no ulterior motives, but that he simply wanted to be a part of the community and to be a friend. Since he was unemployed yet apparently financially solvent, he was seen to be an odd sort of duck to choose this location and lifestyle. But his congeniality, sincerity, and obvious care and concern for his neighbors gradually overrode the initial qualms. After all, someone who would listen to you babble on about your problems for hours or spend half a day helping you move furniture from one tenement to another with no expectation of recompense was a person you could begin to trust.

So it was on a typical Northwest Pacific rainy winter day that Joma came to Jed's rented storefront office with concern on her face. Joma (street names instead of given ones were the norm) was somewhere between thirty and fifty, and had been living on and off the street for a good decade and a half. While the weather was still nasty, she was currently couch surfing with a friend who could afford a two room bachelor suite in Yesler Terrace, but spent most of her days lurking in the Pioneer Square environs. Her first encounter with Jed had been when he found her collapsed one evening at the end of Pier 54 on the waterfront. Gasping for breath, she didn't have the wherewithal to get up and throw herself into the water, which had been her intent. Jed cradled her head after summoning a passerby to call for an ambulance, and then followed it to Harborview Medical Center where it was determined that the primary cause of her distress was emphysema. Smoking a pack or more a day wasn't helping her situation. Jed assured the hospital personnel that he would be back in the morning to help guide her through the welfare process for obtaining assistance with health care costs. He also told the financial officer that, if needed, he would cover a night or two until she was released. Joma was now his friend for life, and she came by his office for coffee and a pep talk now and then when depression began to edge in.

Huffing and puffing, she said, "Father Jed, they's some folks in dire trouble and nobody's 'round to help any."

"Slow down, Joma," Jed responded. "Who's in what kind of trouble?"

"I don't know 'em, but a couple wit' two little kids sitting in the rain wit' nowhere to go."

"Where are they, Joma? Did you talk to them?"

"Yeah, Father Jed. They be in front of that ol' apartment on Dearborn. Throwed out cause they got no money. They say they ain't no place to go but sitt'n there in the rain with them little kids."

"You come with me, Joma, so that a big, strange guy doesn't scare them. Let's see what we can do."

When they pulled up in Jed's Civic he saw the family of four huddling under some trees on the boulevard with one umbrella doing a poor job of keeping everybody dry. The mother was holding a baby and the father had pulled a blanket around all of them. A toddler of about three was shivering. Jed was surprised enough when he recognized who, or rather what, they were, but the mother and father were genuinely shocked when Jed said, "*Nyob zoo, kuv lub npe yog Jed. Kuv cia siab kuv yuav pab tau*" in fluent Hmong. Nothing could have been more welcome than to have someone introduce himself and offer help in their own language. When Jed recognized them as Hmong, his rudimentary but adequate facility with their mother tongue came back from twenty-seven years ago. Riam Cha, once over his initial astonishment, explained their predicament. Between his partial ability with English and Jed's working knowledge of Hmong, they managed to communicate the essentials.

In short, Riam had legally immigrated to America with his wife and baby two years ago. He had some skills as a mechanic and had procured work at a southside auto repair shop that provided barely enough for rent and groceries. His wife, Nkauj, experienced complications with the birth of their six-month-old and had been unable to return to her part-time job at a Hmong flower stand in Pike Place Market. Two months before, the chain holding up a big V-8 from a Ford 350 pickup snapped and the engine plowed into Riam, cracking a vertebra. He was still in the recuperative stage, and had been out of work with no paychecks for two months. He also had no health care coverage. The Chas didn't know anyone in the Hmong community well enough to ask for financial assistance, but assured the apartment owner that they would make up for missed rent payments. When they didn't have funds for the second month in a row, the owner threw them out on the street with what they could carry on their backs, telling them they could come back for the rest of their possessions when they had money for the two months they had lived there without paying.

The apartment owner had conveniently ignored the regulation that the removal of a tenant from a rental property cannot be done by the landlord without a court order which must be served by a county sheriff. People who are illegally removed from a property can call upon the police for assistance, which is exactly what Jed did. A couple of Seattle's finest arrived and informed the owner of the tenant's rights, and ordered him to return the keys to the apartment to Riam. When his protestations edged toward belligerence, one of the cops threatened arrest, and the keys were handed over to Riam, albeit unhappily. Jed helped carry the family's meager belongings back into their living quarters and promised to check in with them in a day or two after he researched the legal aid and living allowance for which they might qualify.

"Father Jed, how you know to talk to them that way?" Joma asked.

"Oh, I spent some time in their country a long time ago. Kinda came in handy tonight."

Again, word about what happened spread via the grapevine. Along with his reputation garnering more respect and admiration than ever, the Hmong Association of Washington invited Jed to attend one of their council meetings in order to formally express their gratitude.

With these memories rambling around in his head, Jed looked forward to getting home because his good friend Darrell was waiting there for him. Darrell had flown in late that afternoon and, due to a community supper meeting Jed had promised to attend, this would be their first opportunity to lie back and tackle the world's problems. Pulling a couple of Anchor Steam beers from the mini-fridge, Jed settled into his Goodwill-procured rocking chair and Darrell into the worn recliner that had come with the furnished digs.

"So," Darrell said after some initial sharing about how his life and work were proceeding in Minneapolis, "you still feel this is what you should be doing?"

"Absolutely!" Jed replied. "You remember how it took a lot of patience that first year or so, but now folks in the community seem to be as comfortable with me as I am with them. Well, most of them anyway."

"Who isn't?"

"Some of the pimps aren't too happy that I've helped a few of their gals get out of the business, and a couple of the slum landlords think I'm the devil incarnate. But at least the cops and the social agencies seem to see me as a partner of sorts. They balked at first, but I've made a point of working with their policies and structures, which they respect. Their questions revolve around why I'm doing what I'm doing and how it's financed. Even though I'm living low on the totem pole, they know I've got resources tucked away somewhere. A big challenge for me is to keep my finances under wraps and not be seen by the locals as the guy to come to for cash."

"Speaking of which," Darrell added, "how are you holding out financially? You know I've got a stake in this that I want to continue."

"Glad you asked 'cause I couldn't wait to tell you. I took a good chunk out of the account you've kept up for me and bought a fixer-upper over in Rainier Valley. A couple of my friends in the Hmong community do renovations so I paid them to totally update and refit the place, and they did a beautiful job. Gave them some decent income for a couple of months and then I sold it for triple what I paid. So to answer your question, we're doing fine."

"You never cease to amaze me, Jed. Yet you're still content living here?"

"I need to be where the people are, and you know that my own needs are pretty minimal. My landlord here is making some noise about maybe selling out, so I don't know how long I might have this setup. But there are lots of places available if I have to move. My first goal is to find a larger space for an office and reception center, or lounge. And then I need to get an updated computer setup. Seems just about everything is done online these days."

"Know what you mean," Darrell replied. "But the beauty is that what you have at your fingertips would have taken weeks to track down even ten years ago. In fact, it's hard for me to think of doing parish ministry anymore without access to the web."

"Maybe tomorrow you can help me figure out what would be good for my needs. Then I'll take you around and introduce you to some really neat people . . . different from your Minneapolis crowd, but really neat."

"Looking forward to it. But now I think I'd better hit the hay. Us older folks don't have quite the stamina we used to, you know."

After insisting that Darrell use his bed, Jed lay on the

couch drifting off with thoughts of gratitude for his friend and for the position in life which he had carved out for himself. But it wouldn't be too many years before an aspect of his street ministry would change dramatically. Bazo, the Axe, would have to do some serious sharpening of the edge.

Chapter 40

August 2003 - Da Nang, Republic of Vietnam

Late at night they were in a room in the corner of a dilapidated warehouse in a little-used section of the Da Nang port area. Although Boa was incapable of feeling joy, something akin to the sensation of great pleasure filled his warped mind as he watched Duc and Lanh ravish the twelve year old Vietnamese girl. Boa himself had no interest in personal sexual activity, but it created genital responses to watch others. The louder the wailing and screaming of the victim, the greater the excitement for Boa. The two henchmen had learned that they better perform well for their boss lest the Ghost Snake find them in the middle of the night. Besides, he was the bread and butter they were not anxious to lose.

When the little girl was exhausted, bleeding, semi-conscious, and unable to utter anything other than a whimper, Boa took over. Using the woven leather lariat that had become his garrote of choice, his goal was to manipulate the stranglehold in order to draw out the death process as long as possible. His last victim three weeks ago lasted almost five minutes before dying as he alternately tightened and loosened the noose. Maybe he could set a new record today.

The gang kidnapped aesthetically pleasing little girls for shipment overseas. Most perverts would take what they could get, but a pretty one always brought a higher price. Yet every now and then the *Khung Bo* leader felt the urgency to satiate his depraved need for voyeurism and strangulation, and for this his minions would provide an ugly little bitch. Who would miss her anyway? Boa thought the family would probably thank him for relieving them of an unwanted mouth to feed.

Mai, meaning Golden Flower in Vietnamese, frustrated Boa because she expired too soon. Just over four minutes. Way too soon. This put him in even more of a foul mood than that which generally characterized his disposition, so Duc and Lanh were anxious to absent themselves once their duties had been accomplished. They knew the expectation was for them to use the small, dead carcass as shark food, so they quickly left with her after receiving instructions for the coming day.

The name Boa, the Ghost Snake, brought terror to those in the three-province area of Hua Thien, Da Nang, and Quang Nam, particularly in the hearts of those with young female children. During the past half dozen years the *Khung Bo* gang had become the no-contest controller of the criminal enterprises in Da Nang and surrounding areas. True to the meaning of its name, it ruled by terror and intimidation. Politicians and law enforcement authorities were compensated financially for their blind eyes, or treated to torture and death for any significant opposition. For the few who would not be compromised or intimidated, The Ghost remained just that. In addition to being protected by the corrupted, he also moved constantly, his sleeping quarters on any given night being anybody's guess. Only his most trusted, to whatever extent that concept had meaning for them, sycophants knew where he was or how to contact him. He seemed to move like a wisp of fog in the night, appearing out of nowhere to envelop opposition with suffocating destruction. The gang's handiwork was always evidenced by the signature ligature marks on the neck, and Lanh's bloody handiwork with one of his many knives. When anyone was struck by *Khung Bo*, Boa wanted people to know who did the striking.

As was the case for much of the world's illicit goods, the U.S. was a market waiting to be exploited. The taste for young flesh was a prime commodity, and Boa saw the west coast as a potential source of new and bigger profits. He had made contact with a Vietnamese expat to America who had done some work with his gang before heading for the promised land. After some surreptitious research, the man communicated back to Boa that one of the leading prostitution rings on the coast was looking to expand upward, or rather downward if age was the benchmark. He offered to make some inquiries to see if they were interested in and had the resources to import young Asians, and Boa gave him the go ahead. The result was that within nine months a tentative agreement had been reached regarding commodity amounts and a pricing structure. An intermediary set up the system with a guy from Washington State known only as BJ. While Boa found the numbers satisfactory, he would conclude no deal without a face-to-face with BJ. This could be accomplished due to Boa's working facility with English acquired during the U.S. occupation in his childhood, and some tutoring in later years with a Brit expat living in Hoi An.

As the details were worked out for a prospective meeting, Boa devised a plan for transporting little girls across the Pacific: he bought a ship. It was a small 4000-ton container vessel called a feeder that was rated to transport up to five hundred standard ISO Twenty-Foot Equivalent Units (TEUs). This meant five hundred twenty-foot long or two hundred and fifty forty-foot long shipping containers. Registered in Indonesia, it was an old workhorse named the *Keindahan* which, aesthetically, had seen better days but checked out as trustworthy on the high seas. *Khung Bo* needed a legal business to act as a front through which to funnel the large amounts of cash accumulated by his criminal enterprises. An import/export company seemed the perfect setup for bringing in legitimate profits, at the same time laundering his ill-gotten gains. While picking up and conveying genuine cargo from all the ports along the Vietnamese coast, often stopping off at Hong Kong to feed larger vessels heading for destinations around the globe, the *Keindahan* could also be used to transport the kidnapped little ones to the U.S. and other potential markets.

Since indications were that BJ could only handle a small number of girls at a time, a special compartment was built on the ship to accommodate several girls and their "mother." The plan was to have a mamasan on board to guard the young ones. She would have papers proving her marriage to one of the crewman along with the girls being her documented daughters. She would nominally be an assistant cook on the ship while in actuality her job was to watch over the girls and provide whatever comforting presence was possible.

Boa didn't want to coddle the kids, but he had to keep them healthy and looking relatively good for introduction into the American market. They were told that they were going to a new country and a new, much better, life and that after several years of earning their keep they could either return to Vietnam or bring their families to America to enjoy the wealth they were bound to accumulate. The trip would take about three weeks, but they would be well cared for and over-joyed with what awaited them. The mamasan kept reminding them that this was all for their good and the good of their families.

What was initially a state of confusion and fear was significantly mitigated by the colorless, odorless, tasteless powder that was mixed with the drinking water provided for the captives. Scopolamine was the new wonder drug that rendered a person docile, drowsy, and incapable of exercising free-will. It also helped relieve seasickness. A couple of days before journey's end, the dosage was lessened so that the girls exhibited a partially revived sense of alertness for the transfer to BJ's organization.

Boa and BJ had met in Shanghai in September 2000 to formalize and detail the arrangement between their two gangs. Boa was then thirty-one years old, rich, and self-confident. BJ was suitably impressed by the hardened face with diagonal scar that was matched by the menacing tone of his gravelly-voiced, heavily accented English. It was evident to BJ, who was no slouch in his own environment, that the head of *Khung Bo* was not a man with whom to trifle. He had no doubt that Boa's tentacles could reach across the seas, so he'd better stick to whatever plan was concocted together. Boa was pleased to learn how much BJ was willing to pay for a beautiful young virgin, a figure that would nicely augment the profit from legitimate cargo. The meeting was short – Boa was not long on words – and they set in motion the machinations for the first trial run. If all went well, it could become a regular business deal that would enrich both measurably.

The *Keindahan* was outfitted for the first voyage and a small entourage of kidnapped Vietnamese virgins was assembled. Legit cargo had been contracted and loaded. The name of the corporation that owned the ship was the *Khá Đep* Trading Company.

Chapter 41

September 2003 - Seattle, Washington

The shrinks could debate ad nauseam whether Benny Jepson was a psychopath or sociopath. Having been diagnosed with ASPD, Antisocial Personality Disorder, at age fourteen, Benny spent the next two decades perfecting the symptoms. He was the walking embodiment of the traits shared by both maladies: a disregard for laws and social mores; a disregard for the rights of others; a failure to feel remorse or guilt; and a tendency to display violent behavior. His occasional spontaneous fits of rage would indicate a socio, but the majority of the time he exhibited psychopathic traits by his inability to form emotional attachments or to feel real empathy with others. In spite of not feeling them, he learned to mimic emotions and gained people's trust with his pleasing personality and manipulative skills. If there was any actual emotion he experienced, it was schadenfreude.

Moral turpitude was an unknown concept to Benny because right and wrong or shame and guilt were concepts simply not a part of his thought processes. Not all psychopaths are serial killers; they come in violent and nonviolent models. Benny was unquestionably of the violent type. And he was good at not getting caught.

Geraldine Spatsky was a widow with a kind heart. Her own children and their families lived half a continent away, so she exercised her grandmotherly instincts with the neighborhood kids. The shed in back of her house in Renton, the town where Benny grew up, had been her deceased husband's workshop. She sold off all his tools and fixed it up as sort of a playroom for Benny and his pals. An old microwave was one of the items she had left in the shed, and in his late elementary school years Benny amused himself by experimenting with how long various animals could last with the power on high. Watching a cat do a death dance inside the box aroused no emotion in him other than curiosity, although his mental file would include how the device might be used profitably for some purpose or other in the future.

By the time he was seventeen he demanded that everyone call him BJ. He didn't consciously connect that with any sexual act; to him Benjamin was too formal and Benny was too infantile. In the middle of his senior year in high school he was expelled for pouring sulfuric acid on a girl's hand in chemistry lab to see what it did to human skin. Two months later, after he had discovered and stolen his mother's secret stash of eight hundred dollars, his folks had had it and kicked him out. Which was fine with BJ, and he headed for the streets of Seattle.

BJ didn't look much like the typical teenager living from hand-to-mouth on the street. To begin with, he was good looking. He wasn't exactly a Robert Redford, but close enough that he turned most women's heads when he walked into a room. As a matter of fact, he had watched Butch Cassidy and the Sundance Kid three times, and then practiced both Redford's swagger and his world-class smile. His six-foot frame carried no excess fat, and his curly jet-black hair tumbled down around his ears to his neckline, framing a square head with deep amber eyes and a full mouth. In a word, his looks were captivating, masking his felonious nature.

In addition, he was a coxcomb who prided himself on his appearance. BJ's first order of business was to look good. And looking good meant dressing to the nines. Some of his first burglaries were of men's clothing stores. He learned early on how to disable all but the most sophisticated alarm systems, so after jimmying his way into a medium-to-high-end men's store, generally in the outlying areas, he might spend an hour or two sampling the wares before walking away with a couple of new outfits and a three-hundred-dollar pair of shoes.

Sleeping in the alleys was also not his style. There

were always single gals in bars who felt blessed that BJ selected them for a relationship. Which could last six days or six weeks. So he shuffled around from gal to gal, bed to bed, until he accumulated enough money to rent his own place, often leaving a broken heart in his wake.

In the years since being ejected from his family, Benny had come a long way. Progressing from petty crime such as B&E and muggings to drug dealing and arms trafficking, his primary enterprise became prostitution. After years of striving, he attained the position of pimp of pimps in the greater Seattle area, dispatching competition with lethal drugs. Since the toxicology report on a dumped body would reveal simply a prescription drug overdose, there was nothing to indicate a homicide. BJ's drug of choice was the "Houston Cocktail," also known as the Holy Trinity, which consisted of three drugs: the narcotic Vicodin, the anti-anxiety drug Xanax, and the muscle relaxant Soma. It was not an altogether unpleasant way drift into oblivion, one which was the obvious choice given the alternative. BJ would offer them either the cocktail or being skinned alive by himself and an assistant using an Italian-made Viper hunting knife with four inch blade. A couple of years back three Salvadoran *chulos* had been presented with the choice. When one sneered that he didn't believe BJ had the balls to do the skinning, the other two watched as it took fifteen minutes for their mistaken amigo to pass out and bleed to death. The second one eagerly drank the cocktail and BJ let the third one go to spread the word. He didn't really care one way or the other which choice was made. The removal of rival parties was all that really mattered.

Shortly before meeting with Boa in Shanghai back in 2000, BJ had met with the number two in his organization. "What'd think, Hack? Can we make the numbers work?"

Hack, who served as the Chief Financial Officer for BJ's enterprises, said, "Looks good to me, Boss. I just got back from talking with Bambi Scalerzi in Jersey and he says they ain't a bit sorry. Get'n better returns on the buck with little bitches."

"But, hey, we're talking little bittie bitches. Your east coast buddies going that low?"

"Bambi says the teen runaways have been bread and butter for years. But there's definitely a market for the little ones. They got no steady supply source, but when they can get 'em they make fifteen to twenty percent more," Hack responded.

"If that's the case, then I say we see what kind of a deal we can make with this Boa. My inclination is to go for a trial load and if we do okay then make it a regular thing."

"They likely gonna want some cash up front to do that."

"No question. So make sure our Hong Kong account has enough for me to play with and I'll see what kind of figures he throws around. This guy will understand that this won't be workable if there's no profit in it."

"What about distribution?" Hack asked. "We got pimps with customers standing by?"

"First load, no problem. I've got orders for half a dozen in hand, and the research points toward a growing market all up and down the coast. If we get a monopoly on the pipeline, we should be able to expand south all the way to L.A."

"The Mexican trade could be a problem. I hear they're

bring'n 'em up younger all the time."

"They are. But the border crossing is more of a problem. And they can't begin to match the numbers Boa's talking about. Besides, a few Houston Cocktail parties will also let the spics know who's gonna control this market."

So BJ went to Shanghai and the wheels were set in motion. Getting the girls to the American side of the Pacific was accomplished by the *Keindahan*, but getting them into the country was another issue. As human trafficking had became more profitable and more prevalent, both the U.S. Coast Guard and the U.S. Navy had dramatically increased their surveillance of incoming foreign vessels. Young Vietnamese beauties posing as family members of a crewman would likely wash on the high seas or in the ports of other countries, but it would be touch-and-go with American authorities, especially if it was noted that the *Keindahan* arrived repeatedly with different sets of girls. Computers were a great aid to criminals in many respects, but also worked against them in cases such as tracking all foreigners who came ashore from visiting ships. BJ had to come up with a safer way to smuggle the little lovelies into the country. A method of undetectable transfer from ship to shore had to be devised.

The answer was another boat. BJ loved the water and had his own seventy foot Viking yacht with enclosed bridge and added skybridge, a luxury boat built for the high seas. The boat's registered name was My Girl with her home port being La Conner, a lesser known recreational marina off Skagit Bay about seventy miles north of Seattle.

My Girl would rendezvous with *Keindahan* in the

dead of night thirty miles or so west of Haida Gwaii, B.C., commonly called the Queen Charlotte Islands by non-First Nations people. The girls would be transferred, and then My Girl would head southeast to the Strait of Georgia. While there was understandable confusion about what was happening to them, the luxury of the yacht and the warm welcome by the bimbos BJ brought along for that purpose would hopefully provide some semblance of comfort and security for the girls. Slipping by Port Hardy and Campbell River, B.C, BJ would off-load his cargo near the sleepy little coastal town of Powell River in the wee hours of the morning. Some ten miles up the Sunshine Coast Highway from the town itself, a little-used road branched off to an unpopulated section of beach. My Girl's Zodiac ferried the youngsters to BJ's waiting cohorts who then loaded them into a vehicle for the overland trip south. A middle-aged, homeless Vietnamese woman had miraculously been found who was well-compensated to come along and act as the new American mamasan. Freshened up and tutored for the task, she provided a small hint of comfort and security which was bolstered by the scopolamine-laced soda pop the girls eagerly drank.

Generally three to five youngsters was the maximum number transported in one shipment. This was due to both the limits of BJ's distribution capacity and the danger of moving more than that many individuals in one group. But the high prices these excitingly exotic little creatures commanded made the effort worthwhile. If the right buyers could be found, one shipment could bring in close to a half million bucks. For Boa, it was a tidy add-on to the shipping container profits from his import/export company. For BJ, it was a big boost to his income since the sale or management of a pre-pubescent virgin brought in many times over what a used-up street whore could produce. A regular stream of the little ones was also needed since, after a year or a year and a half at most, a twelve or thirteen year old could no longer pose as a virgin. If not decimated by drugs, a sexually transmitted disease, or physiological damage, a young one might graduate to the less prestigious position of a street walker. The income became considerably less, but, hey, something was better than nothing. And a seasoned veteran could still bring in hundreds of bucks a day at fifty dollars a crack.

A 4WD Chevy Suburban with darkened windows would be waiting for the precious cargo, into which they were loaded to wind their way down the beautiful Sunshine Coast Highway to the Langdale ferry terminal just north of Gibsons, B.C. The trip would be made in the dark, arriving in time for the 6:20 a.m. ferry to Horseshoe Bay where they picked up the Trans-Canada Highway. This would be a leisurely journey since darkness was needed again for the crossing into the United States.

At a bit over five thousand five hundred miles, the U.S.-Canada border is the longest international border in the world. It is commonly referred to as an undefended border, and the large distances between U.S. Customs official border crossings are left to local law enforcement to patrol. The huge area involved, much of it in wilderness or sparsely populated environs, make detection of illegal crossings spotty in the best of times. While residents on both sides are required to report to their respective governments construction of any physical barriers at border crossings on their land, sometimes this happens, sometimes it does not. The U.S. also places hidden sensors on various roads, trails, and railways, but local folk know which entry points are covered and can circumvent them with ease. With inadequate border personnel on either side, all of this is largely ineffective in stopping concerted and coordinated incursions.

BJ's minions had done their homework, and over the years had paid good money to be guided to remote border crossings over which to bring the girls. There was danger of detection, to be sure, but the risk was minimal and not a single shipment had yet been interdicted. In case they were ever stopped, the driver and guard carried large amounts of cash to tempt a poorly paid cop to look the other way. In case that didn't work, payment would be made with lead.

An ingress that worked like a charm for them was midway between the Lynden and Sumas crossings on the B.C-Washington border. Immediately to the west of Judson Lake was a little-used dirt track in the midst of fertile farm country. Around three a.m., with the farmers at the bottom of their diurnal cycle, the Suburban would cross through a locked gate, a key for which they had paid the landowner handsomely, and wind its way through Lynden south and west toward Interstate 5. It would then be a straight shoot down to Seattle where the girls would either be ensconced or moved to other locations.

Three years later the system was working like a charm. BJ's gang had received and placed some twenty girls from ages ten to twelve and profited handsomely in the process. Since a little "virgin" cost a john significantly more than what an older, used whore would be, BJ usually kept one or more of the little ones under the auspices of his own pimps. The rest he sold to individuals or gangs for a two to three hundred percent profit over his cost.

BJ had sex with some of the older runaways recruited from the streets, not because he got any emotional charge, but simply as a way to relieve some pressure. The little ones did not interest him in the least, but they needed some bit of training before being offered to a client. American prostitutes who were hooked on drugs and dependent on BJ for their supply were used as mentors. The children found out in quick order that their old lives in Vietnam were far superior to the promised new life in America. They were schooled in fellatio, cunnilingus, group sex, sexual role play, and basic intercourse positions. Scopolamine kept them reasonably pliable and they had no way to resist anything that was happening to them. If some behavior began to approach belligerency, the offender would receive non-disfiguring beatings until appropriately submissive again. It was all confusing and terrifying to the girls, but what could an eleven-year-old do against adults in a strange country where they didn't even speak the language? If there was a hell, they had entered it.

By the fall, BJ had girls placed within a network that extended from Bellingham, Washington, to the Bay Area in California. He saw only good fortune and profit growth in his future. What he didn't see was the two-edged sword coming his way.

Chapter 42

June 2004 - Seattle, Washington

The American dream in an Armani Giorgio grey cross-hatch wool suit, fifty-two-year-old Fitz Holbrooke walked out of the corporate headquarters like he owned the world. And he did, at least a significant part of it. If success was living in a two mil waterfront mansion on Mercer Island, sporting a quarter of a million dollar Meteorite Diamond Pearlmaster

Rolex watch, driving a new-every-year Porsche 911 Turbo S Cabriolet, and having a movie star mistress in Vancouver, B.C., in addition to his twenty-six year old trophy wife, he was it. Fitz, a genius with doctorates in both business administration and computer science, had worked his way to the position of Executive Assistant to the CEO of one of America's leading software companies. His talents and contributions were recognized both financially and professionally as expert in a field that would only keep growing. But he had one little problem.

Well, it wasn't so little. He was a sex addict who had tried everything under the sun from every form of heterosexual activity known, to homosexual liaisons, to group bisexual encounters to sadomasochism. He had even dabbled into a little bestiality. The side ventures were just that – dilly-dallying around for sport – but deep down he was unabashedly a man-on-woman kind of guy. The sum of Fitz' theology was that god (which he wouldn't spell with a capital G) made men to run the world and women to make men happy. So why wasn't he happy . . . at least as happy as he thought he should be? On the odd occasion when he asked himself that question, the answer always came down to sex. In spite of his many and varied lascivious activities, he still felt that there was something missing, something that might actually result in a sense of satisfaction if not fulfilment.

When he read an article in the Seattle Post-Intelligencer about a growing problem, it struck him that this might be the answer to his dilemma. The brief piece attempted to elucidate what was happening, and the difficulties authorities were having stemming the rising tide. The oncoming wave being reported on was the increase in child sex trafficking. Some were genuine born-in-the-USA youngsters, but importation of so-called exotic little girls appeared to be gaining strength. A myriad of obstacles hamstrung the effectiveness of law enforcement's fight against this scourge: the secretive nature of the trade (eleven-year-olds were not parading their stuff on street corners), the ease with which the girls could be disguised and moved, and the absolute helplessness of the little ones in the grip of their handlers. As the upstanding Mr. Holbrooke read the article, a smile formed at the corners of his mouth and he experienced a very pleasant sensation between his legs. In the days that followed he knew that pursuing this course of action would take special caution, but he also realized that this was something he was going to have to try in spite of the risk to his reputation, or perhaps even to his freedom.

Fitz used an untraceable disposable phone to set up encounters. It wouldn't do his impeccable community image any favors if illicit sexual liaisons were traced to phone lines associated with him. Rūpee Singh was his personal procurer, not a pimp per se, but with connections to others who could provide whatever one's erotic little heart desired. Rūp had previously provided teenagers galore, but Fitz had never asked him for something this . . . this . . . forbidden. And Mr. Singh wondered if the man could, or would, stoop so low.

Mr. Holbrooke did in fact recognize the lowness of this stoop. He was neither stupid nor without a conscience. In fact, he prided himself on being up-front and fair in all his business dealings. But in the secret world of satisfying one's deepest needs, desire overcame morality. At least that's the house of cards in which Fitz lived, and he subconsciously justified what he did as if there were no significant contradictions between his right thoughts and his wrong actions. So one evening, enjoying the sinking sun while sitting at water's edge in his Cape Cod Company Nauset Recliner facing Seward Park and sipping a Pimm's Cup #1, he dialed Rūp.

"You know who this is. Remember, no names."

"Ah, not to worry, my friend. I well know the routine by now. How may I serve you?"

"I don't know any way to put this delicately, but I am interested in exploring, shall we say, someone younger, inexperienced."

"And how young, may I ask, is younger?" Rūp replied.

"You remember my last adventure, the one in Ballard?"

"Indeed. And I thank you for your generous tip on that occasion."

"I'm thinking maybe two or three years younger."

"Ah, that is possible, but for purity, which I assume is your interest, the price will be considerably more."

"You ought to know by now," Fitz said irritably, "that cost is no issue. And an additional requirement is that she is not American. I would lean toward Asian in particular."

"Would a beautiful Vietnamese virgin be acceptable?"

"That would be very acceptable. How soon might you set this up?"

"Let me contact my source and see if what you seek is available. I believe a shipment came in last week, but I'll have to ascertain their status and location. Call me back at this same time in forty-eight hours and hopefully I'll have good news for you."

"Right," Fitz shot back brusquely and then disconnected the call.

The more he thought about it, the more anxious he was for this new experience. As he walked up toward his mansion a thought struck him: *The damn VC screwed us for all those years. Time we screwed some back.*

So it was that six days later, while his golddigger-wife was on a shopping spree in San Francisco, Fitz walked toward the Falls View Motel in Snoqualmie at half past midnight. Under guard and waiting for him in room #117 was a small girl whose Vietnamese name was Lan but who was now called Little Flower. Fitz was going to have fun de-flowering her, and assumed that she would enjoy it as well as he. Lan was eleven years old.

Chapter 43

March 2005 - Seattle, Washington

People who did most of their living on the Seattle streets rarely used their given names in daily traffic with one another. One's nickname, or *nom de guerre* as one joker self-named Che Latte liked to put it, was generally all anyone else knew. It also kept the cops guessing. Juke Box didn't worry so much about the cops since he had his hands full guessing about himself.

Sergeant Green was a twenty-year veteran of the Seattle police force. His uniform always looked as clean and pressed as the day he took the oath of honor, and his years of experience had honed a no-nonsense attitude that combined a commitment to the community's well-being with I-take-no-bullshit. He had just booked Juke Box for vagrancy – again – and Jed came in to the King County Jail to see what he might be able to do to help.

"Look, Father Jed, it's not that I don't have any compassion for folks like Juke, but there are limits to what we can tolerate and he just doesn't seem to get it."

Juke, as most associates shortened it – to Juke Box's consternation – was a panhandler with a an IQ around seventy-five who lived by his wits, which meant living pretty low. Most casual observers readily wrote him off as an obnoxious practitioner of nutbaggery. He moved around Seattle's inner city begging for a living, which included working the crowds attending Mariners games in the spring and summer, and Seahawks games in the fall and winter. The city council finally yielded to pressure from law-abiding, hard-working, upstanding citizens to pass bylaws limiting if and when the professional mendicants could besiege others for alms. These regulations meant nothing to Juke.

"We both know, Sergeant, that Juke doesn't have the mental capacity to understand a lot of things. Keeping him in the slammer isn't going to change that."

"I realize that, sir, but what would you have us do? Do you not think that the tax-paying citizens of our city have the right to walk the streets without being accosted by hordes of beggars?"

"I understand the concern, and your point is well-taken," Jed replied, "but at the same time it does no good to treat a harmless, mentally-challenged person like Juke as a criminal and lock him up with folks who could do him serious harm."

"And I understand what you're saying," Green responded. "But my responsibility is to enforce the laws regardless of one's understanding of them. I ask again, what would you have us do?"

"Would you be willing to try this? I'll pay whatever fine he owes this time, and then you release him into my care. I know we've been down this road before, but let me give it another shot. With my network of connections, I've got some new options to try that might help impress on Juke what is truly unacceptable."

Green scratched his head momentarily, wondering why this man was willing to keep going these extra miles with the likes of Juke Box, but also glad for him to take the vagrant off his hands. "Well, if you're up to handling the fine, that'll satisfy the legal part. I'll turn him over to you, but I've got to let you know that if we find him parked at the entrance to Nordstrom again he's going to end up right back here."

As the paperwork was being prepared, the policeman asked Jed, "Why do you do it, man? What's in this for you?"

"I'm not in it for me," said Jed.

"Well, I'll have to take your word on that. But I still don't get just what you're trying to do."

"I'm trying to help folks in need, especially those nobody else seems to care much about."

"But Father Jed," Green responded, "you're just one man, and this city's got thousands who might benefit from whatever help you might provide. Then you add the millions more just up and down the west coast. What possible difference can you make?"

Jed looked him straight in the eye and said, "Sergeant Green, it makes a difference to Juke."

After Jed had completed the necessary formalities for him, Juke came into the reception area with greasy shoulder-length hair, dumpster-salvaged clothes, and a big smile on his face. Of all the people in the world who didn't give a rat's ass about him, he knew Father Jed wasn't one of them. Clergy-collared priest and stinking vagabond rode to a Gospel Mission flophouse where Jed had made arrangements for a bed. Depositing Juke, Jed told him to sleep tight and wait for him in the morning when he would come by to pick him up. A coalition of churches in West Seattle had recently opened up a group home for the likes of Juke Box, and Jed was going to see if they might have a place for him.

The years rolled by with unnoticed alacrity for Jed as he became more deeply entrenched in Seattle's street community. Starting the day with buying a sidewalk sleeper some coffee and oatmeal, or attending to the likes of Juke Box, was as normal to him as were the jobs to the masses that populated the offices and shops of the bustling city. For ten years he had been operating a self-sustaining outreach to Seattle's downtrodden. Sometimes they trod on themselves; sometimes they were trod upon by others. One usually led to the other. To Jed it made no difference. If he could help foster their well-being in any way, to him it was worth the effort. If a person wanted to dialogue on the nitty-gritty of what led to living this kind of life, he was willing to engage. But he didn't push his faith or his values on anybody. If a man was drowning, Jed was simply glad that he was there to throw the fellow a life preserver, if possible.

Jed noted that one of the maladies seeming to afflict too many people as they went about their daily tasks, be it banking or homemaking, was ennui. That was simply not in his catalog of emotions. If variety is the spice of life, Jed's was, metaphorically speaking, characterized by culinary gusto. He never knew what any given day would bring, and most included a combination of stimulating challenges and laid-back living with people who needed a listening ear and a pat on the back. Late one evening when Darrell was visiting, he asked Jed what kinds of activities characterized his days. Jed ran through a sampling of his activities.

Loosie wanted out of the business. She was tired of being a screw-machine for filthy-mouthed johns who in some perverted way felt that paying for sex made up for the other forty-nine inadequacies in their lives. But she was tied to her chemical addiction and the pimp who used it to keep her on a leash. Father Jed hooked her up with a foundation that paid for six weeks in a treatment center and then provided help finding a legit job. But her pimp, a hundred-pound-overweight mulatto who liked a rawhide lash dangling from his belt and went by Cool Whip, got rough with Loosie when she told him she was leaving. After she came to Jed with one eye swollen shut and a busted rib, he went to have a talk with Mr. Cool. He took his KA-Bar. When Jed walked out of the five-minute encounter he left behind two of the pimp's supposed-to-be bodyguards out cold, Cool's whip chopped into a dozen pieces, and the man himself with his pants cut off and a warning scratch on the end of his phallus. He was sure the fellow got the point, but as he headed back to his office to pick up Loosie and take her to the treatment center, he pondered losing his cool.

Either he didn't know his name or simply refused to give it. The little guy looked to be somewhere in the neighborhood of eight years old. He was four feet tall and maybe fifty pounds on a good day, and after the street urchin had been seen scrounging the dumpster behind Zeke's Cafe for several days, the owner reported it to Father Jed. The boy wasn't hard to spot as he roamed Pike Place Market looking to steal or to be given scraps. Having first speed-dialed Child Protective Services on his cell phone, Jed was sharing a giant banana split with the youngster at the nearby ice cream parlor when, as pre-arranged, authorities showed up. The care and recognized compassion of the social workers won over the boy in a matter of minutes and he willingly went with them in the hope of finding a life with more security than that of an abandoned waif.

The eleven-hundred-acre American Lake southwest of Tacoma and a couple of as-the-crow-flies miles from the south end of Puget Sound is home to perch, rainbow trout, largemouth bass, and kokanee. Fort Nisqually was the first military installation on its shores, established by the British in 1833 before the U.S.-Canada border was fixed. Today a Veterans Administration hospital, part of the VA Puget Sound Health Care System, sits on the site. Psychiatric care is one of its busiest sections, and that's where Jed was headed. Sitting next to him in his trusty Civic was the reason.

Forty years after Nam, Alistair "Tank" Windhammer was still having trouble shaking demons in conical hats carrying AK-47s. Never having served in tanks, he didn't get his nickname from them. It was because he looked like one. Five foot seven, he would have qualified for the heavyweight division and his fists looked as big as boxing gloves. In the good ol' USMC days, his considerable bulk was maybe nine percent body fat. Even though he now carried twenty-five unneeded pounds and his fat percentage was more like twenty-two, he was still a formidable presence that encouraged one to hit the road fast if something pushed his anger button.

As a Marine grunt, Tank had served two full tours of duty in I Corps, most of it in the jungle environs just south of the DMZ, and had been with the 1st Marine Division in the Hue area when the '68 Tet offensive blew things all to hell. He had seen and done things no person should see and do, and it left him with nightmares, flashbacks, and a startle-syndrome that put more than one unsuspecting victim in the hospital. He was a PTSD poster boy who needed both meds and psychotherapy regularly, and whose episodes had cost him his wife, his job, and most of his self-esteem. Jed was taking him to his counselor at American Lake after bailing him out of jail for causing roughly thirty thousand dollars damage to the AWOL Bar and Grill in West Seattle. Father Jed's collar didn't mean much to Tank, but their shared Vietnam past was the link. This wasn't the first time they'd made this trip together. Jed hoped it would be the last.

A little after midnight five men wrapped with rotting tarps to ward off the light mist for which Seattle is famous sat on scrounged, falling-apart lawn chairs around a fifty-five gallon half-drum "campfire." Father Jed was one of them. The other four would have been called hobos in the 1930s but were now simply termed homeless, and considered by most people with homes to be a nuisance. Two of them, both in their sixties, had been partnering on and off the streets for some twenty years. Another was a thirty-something Iraq war vet with only one arm and a proven inability to hold a job. The fourth was a forty-two-year-old schizophrenic whose paranoia kept him rotating between half a dozen various disguises. They were passing around a bottle of André Cold Duck and puffing Montecristo Platinums pilfered from the back seat of a Chrysler Sebring someone was stupid enough not to lock. Father Jed respectfully declined both the wine and the cigars, but offered leftover sandwiches from the Cathedral Kitchen which the staff was happy to see put to good use. And the four fellows put them to good use since nary a one had had a full meal yet that day. Jed also provided bags of chips, a chocolate cake from the corner store that was past the best-used-by date, and friendship.

They wanted to hear some war stories, so Jed made some up. Then they made up some of their own, maybe even believing them to be real. After the bellies were full and the last inch of the cigars were cast into the dying embers of their urban encampment, they wandered away to the various cubbyholes each had fashioned as a sleeping nook. Jed gave each one a now-expected hug before they trudged off, that being the only tactile affection any one of them had experienced for many years.

Kleptomania is a disease. Saddles had it. His street name came from his inclination to wear saddle shoes, brown and white being his preference. He might be wearing torn jeans and a grungy T-shirt, but the shoes were always unscuffed and almost polished. The twenty-year-old had been disowned by his family after flunking out of two area colleges and being charged with stealing more times than mom and dad could remember. The folks were out of money, patience, and whatever passed for love in their minds. That put Saddles on the streets, working odd day jobs now and then for survival money and to pay misdemeanor fines. He didn't steal big. A candy bar would suffice some days; other days it might be a pair of gloves or a set of earrings. It just made him feel good . . . or at least alleviated the bad feelings that plagued him. He was a nice kid, a good kid really, pleasant to be around. He just had this problem and it kept landing him in front of a judge.

The court-appointed lawyer did her duty and the guilty plea had been accepted. Again. Judge Samuel Jeter asked, "Mr. Smithson, how many times have you stood before me in this court?"

With sagging shoulders and not wanting to look up, Saddles said, "I don't know, sir. I've lost count."

"Well, we haven't," the judge replied. "This is the sixth time in the past four months. How can we put a stop to this?"

"I really want to try, sir. Father Jed says there is something that might work."

"Ah, good. Hope springs eternal . . . most days. Father Jed, may we hear the details of this something?" Jeter asked.

Jed approached the bench and proceeded to explain that through his research he had found that Good Samaritan Behavioral Health Center in Portland, OR, had a staff person who specialized in treating kleptomania and had a high success rate. He had contacted this mental health worker and ascertained that there was an opening for a two-week therapy course which began in three days. Jed offered to help the young man apply for state financial assistance for this purpose, and then to arrange for his transportation to the center.

"Mr. Smithson, would this be acceptable to you?" the judge queried.

"Yes sir. No one wants to get better more than me," Saddles replied.

So after a fine for his latest theft, a teddy bear from the Dollar Store, the judge released him into Jed's custody with the requirement that a progress report be made to the court no later than a month from this date.

"Young man, I never want to see you in my court again," Jeter said.

"You won't, sir," Saddles responded. "I'm going to get this all straightened out. Father Jed is going to help me."

Craig and Alfie Hubbard weren't homeless. But the cupboards in their southside tenement flat were essentially bare. Their six-year-old daughter, Evangeline, and their three-year-old son, Tyson, were hungry, and the shelves contained fourteen stale Saltine crackers and a jar of jalepeño peppers. Period. With Craig being an out-of-work carpenter and Alfie's fibromyalgia prohibiting employment, the social assistance they received barely covered the rent and utilities. Their car had been repossessed and Evangeline's only footwear was a pair of Goodwill flip-flops.

Jed had met them at the emergency room one afternoon when he brought Snooks there. She was a transgender female who had contracted a serious case of genital herpes now augmented by shingles and needed immediate attention. The Hubbards were there because of someone's careless use of a Sawzall that resulted in a deep six-inch gash on Craig's left shoulder. Alfie had been brought up as a faithful Roman Catholic, and she automatically looked to the man in the clerical collar for some comfort. They struck up a conversation in the buzzing waiting room which eventually progressed to the beginning of a relationship. Over time they became friends, and Father Jed would sometimes bring them leftovers from Cathedral Kitchen.

On this particular day the street priest was standing in line under an umbrella with Craig at the downtown Seattle food bank. Not only could Jed vouch for their need, but he had a vehicle in which to transport the man and several boxes of food back to the apartment. He also had in the trunk several cases of staples such as canned milk, baked beans, and soup which he picked up for a song at the local discount food outlet.

After helping to carry the boxes into their sparse living quarters, Jed said, "I'll be back around six-thirty. The bakery over on Western closes at six and always dumps the day-old stuff that didn't sell. Should be able to scrounge several loaves, maybe some muffins."

"Father Jed," Alfie said, "I don't know what we'd do without you . . . or how to thank you."

"Seeing that you have something to eat is thanks enough, and I appreciate your sentiments. But we've got to keep working on getting your feet on some solid ground so this doesn't become a way of life."

"I've got an interview with a construction company on Wednesday," Craig said. "I've heard they've got lots of projects and are looking for guys good with a hammer who'll show up for work on a regular basis. I've got some good references so I'm very hopeful."

"Good deal, Craig. If you need a personal reference don't hesitate to give them my name. Here's a card with my office address and phone."

After a warm hug from both children, he left with as much hope as Craig had.

Bennie's Best Donut Shop was a favorite cop hangout. Contrary to the TV-induced image, most of the police officers were in pretty decent shape. But they still liked their donuts and made up for them with time in the gym and miles jogged. About every other week after his morning ten mile run, Jed would stop by for some chit-chat with whatever group of Seattle's finest were helping support Bennie that day. He had become a well-known figure to the inner-city law enforcement officers. The purity of Father Jed's intentions became evident early on, and he had assisted them often in helping the helpless through difficult times. One activity for which they quite often sought his support was death notification to the next of kin. While this was technically part of the cops' job, most had no training for this task and were very happy to have someone like Father Jed accompany them and do the lion's share of the talking. Over time they came to see him more or less as a co-worker, or at least one whose activities and purposes dovetailed with their own.

"Father Jed, what's up these days?" greeted a prematurely gray forty-year-old veteran whose given name was Stu Oxley but who was expectedly called Ox.

"Hey, Ox," Jed replied. Then with his infectious smile,

“Just the usual . . . hob-knobbing with the mayor, entertaining President Bush and such.”

“Yeah, you sitting down with Bush will happen about the same time I have lunch with Gary Ridgway,” chuckled a vibrant redhead named Tess Ford who was in her third year on the beat.

Tess’s patrol partner, Cal Muntz, a beefy but well-proportioned middle-ager who was battle-hardened by years on the streets, said, “Pull up a chair, Padre. We’d like a few more details about how you stopped that 1st Avenue liquor store holdup last week.”

Jed grabbed a cup of Bennie’s Best dark roast and joined the crowd. “Not much to tell, Cal. The perp just happened to be backing out as I was walking by and accidently tripped over my foot and hit his head on the sidewalk.”

“Yeah, yeah,” Ox said. “That’s not the story the night clerk is telling. He said he thought he was watching a cross between Chuck Norris and Jackie Chan.”

“Can’t believe everything you hear, Ox. It was dark and the fella’d likely been watching too much TV. But to change the subject, anything new happening around town?”

Tess was the first to respond. “Mostly same-old-same-old. Only new blip on the screen has to do with the hookers seeming to get younger and younger.”

“How young we talking about?” Jed asked.

“Caught a john last week with a 13-year-old. She was some kind of exotic Mexican-Asian mix. You could tell she used to be cute as a button, but drugs and abuse had ruined most of it.”

“She lead you to her pimp?”

“She flat refused. Said the bastard would kill her if she

didn't keep her mouth shut."

"And the john?" Jed asked.

"Charges dropped. Seems he has friends in high places looking out for him."

"And, of course, they can't be charged with anything."

"'Course not," Ox chimed in. "Ain't love that makes the world go round. Money and politics are trump cards any day of the week."

"That must get you down now and then, being commissioned to do a job that they won't let you do," Jed said.

"Tell me 'bout it, Father Jed," Cal chipped in. "Doesn't mean we stop trying, but a bunch of the time we feel like the system is designed more for the perps than the vics."

And so the conversation went, moving on to a few of Jed's latest escapades interspersed with a few new cop jokes. By the time the party broke up and they headed for their respective duties, Jed's appreciation for the Seattle police force had received another boost.

"There you are, Darrell," Jed said. "Take your pick."

Darrell was now retired from parish ministry and came out to visit Jed at least a couple times a year. "That's some catalog, Jed. I don't know anyone else who could handle all those situations on a daily basis, or would even want to try. This really has turned out more or less like you'd hoped, yes?"

"Pretty much. Even though I'm not in the official system, most of the local pastors have gotten used to me and are largely supportive of what I'm doing. A few even funnel in support from their congregations now and then."

"You talking greenbacks?"

"They know I'm pretty self-sustaining that way, but some like to kick in a few occasionally to feel like they're helping at least a little bit. Other times they actually send me the odd volunteer."

"How do you involve these folks?" Darrell asked.

"Mostly handing out coffee and snacks here in the center. I give 'em a bit of training; tell 'em just to be themselves and be open to relationships. For most of them it comes as a surprise that there's nothing to fear and that the street people are looking for friendship just like anybody else."

"Have there been any problems?"

"Nothing to speak of. A couple of volunteers wanted to get drawn deeper into the personal lives and needs of the visitors, but I've asked them to leave that part to me. Yet it has been helpful when they bring specific needs to my attention."

"And can you generally find a way to get those needs met?"

"Sometimes yes. Too often no. Most of the time it's just encouraging and teaching them to take baby steps that will eventually lead to increased well-being. Some take them; some don't. Lots of them still die on the streets, but if I'm there at least they don't die alone. I have the feeling that a good share of them simply appreciate that anyone at all seems to care about them."

"There are days," Darrell said, "that I'm tempted to move out here and partner with you. But at my age I don't think that's going to happen. The least I can do is help keep the work alive financially."

"And, Darrell, that's more appreciated than you'll ever know. By me, of course, by also by the folks in the street community who don't even know where it's coming from. Between your generosity and the profitable investments I've made, the kind of thing we're doing shouldn't have any funding problems for as long as I can last."

As Darrell was about to respond, Tracks burst through the door panting, and exclaimed, "Father Jed, you'd better come right now."

Tracks was a graduate school dropout. He had an undergraduate degree in psychology from the University of Montana but dropped out of The Evergreen State College MPA program when his bipolar disorder got away from him. Not taking his meds regularly led to mood variations from extreme depression to grandiose delusions. Although he never harmed himself or anyone else, the weird behavior kept both professors and colleagues on edge. The capstone was when the executive secretary to the university president came in one morning to find Tracks, known to them as Ernest Sprinter, sitting behind the desk in the president's chair claiming that the Board of Regents had deposed Dr. Longacre and replaced him with yours truly. Under forced psychiatric care and back on his meds, Tracks saw the light, dim as it might have been, and voluntarily withdrew from the program.

Tracks rotated from homeless shelter to flophouse to homeless shelter, but always wore a button-down white shirt and tie. Jed had known him for about two years, sometimes sitting on park benches listening to him rant about one thing or another at three in the morning. Noting the look of consternation on his face, Jed asked, "What's up, Tracks?"

"It's Isis," he said while trying to catch his breath. "She's got a gun and heading for Breaker's place."

Chapter 44

March 2005 - Da Nang, Vietnam

Life was good for Gunnar and Thanh. In fact, very good. Gun's work with Linden Technologies International was nothing short of stellar, and early in 2005 the company grapevine included the likelihood that he was going to be offered the position of CEO of LinTech's Southeast Asian Region. He knew that if this came to pass he would be required to spend a couple of years at the corporate headquarters in San Diego to become intimately enlightened on the structure, administration, and policies of the company. Should it come to pass, Gun saw this as an opportunity for Thanh and Tuyen to connect with his American roots. While mother and daughter both had a working facility with English, actually living in America for a time would beneficially add to their knowledge of and fluency with the language. It would also provide an opportunity for Sonny and Linn to come west, even if just temporarily, for some extended quality time with their son and family. Gunnar relished the thought of his daughter being able to develop a deeper relationship with her paternal grandparents than being on the other side of the globe allowed.

Thanh's reputation in the business community had also blossomed. In helping companies start up and maintain their computer systems, her enterprise had grown to the point where she now contracted specialists for the actual installing of hardware. She networked with her clients out of her home to meet their programming needs and troubleshoot whatever problems arose from time to time. There was an occasional requirement to meet with the contracting company's officers or techies for one-on-one training or to discuss contractual arrangements, but the lion's share of the time she had the good fortune to provide her services from within the secure and comfortable environs of their *Vuon Hòa Bình* neighborhood dwelling. The daytime parenting load had lightened ever since Tuyen began full-day school at age seven. This freed up Thanh to marginally expand her business, although she still kept it at a level that enabled giving full attention to mothering outside of school hours.

Gunnar and Thanh had procreated a child who, put mildly, was exceptional. In fact, exceptional was an extreme understatement. From time to time individuals are born that are so gifted as to be almost superhuman, *wunderkinds*. Norbert Wiener, American mathematician, graduated from high school at age eleven, received a BA from Tufts College at age 14, and awarded a PhD. at age eighteen. Indian-American Balamurali Ambati graduated from New York University at age thirteen and Mount Sinai School of Medicine at age seventeen, becoming the world's youngest doctor. Tuyen was in that category.

Her parents could afford the best private school in Da Nang which they augmented with experienced tutors bilingual in English and Vietnamese. By age seven, Tuyen had read both the Vietnamese classic *Kim-Vân-Kieu* by Nguyen-Du and Mark Twain's *Adventures of Huckleberry Finn,* and could recount the entire story line of each if queried. By her eighth birthday she could explain the Fibonacci sequence and describe the difference between theoretical and applied mathematics. An aid to her unbounded capacity for learning was Tuyen's eidetic memory. While this phenomenon generally involved recalling images in great detail for a few minutes after seeing them, she had the rare ability to permanently store this information for recall. For instance, in her third year of elementary school she memorized the Periodic Table of Elements in fifteen minutes. A year later if asked about tungsten she could instantly tell you its chemical symbol, "W," and its atomic number, seventy-four.

The depth of her acumen and discernment of complex concepts was so far above the norm that being challenged in a classroom with her peers became problematic. Gunnar foresaw that a big advantage to spending several years in southern California would be the opportunity for Tuyen to access advanced learning environments.

Another notable feature of Tuyen's was her appearance. If Thanh was extremely beautiful, her daughter was beyond-description gorgeous. While embodying most of her mother's classic Vietnamese configuration, the genetic heritage from her six-three American father provided the height of a youngster several years older. Like her mother, she had a congenial personality and a sunburst smile that would light up any room into which she walked. Her social skills being developed far beyond her years, she was as comfortable having tea with one of her father's business associates as playing dolls with other girls. When Tuyen reached five years, her parents began getting requests to use her as a child model, all of which they turned down.

Put simply, with Thanh and Tuyen by his side, Gunnar felt like he was the most blessed man on planet Earth. Although he loved his work and approached it with consummate conscientiousness and professionalism, it was far secondary to the love for his wife and daughter. He was a strong man with commendable values and something akin to faith, but he could not imagine what he would do if anything happened to either one of them.

After Thanh had helped set up or revamp their computer systems, many companies would contract her to perform periodic maintenance and troubleshoot problems that arose from time to time. Such was the case with the *Khá Đep* Trading Company. While this import/export business seemed to be operated by personnel with a keen sense of accounting and financial management, their information-tech and computer skills were primitive, and they preferred a contract arrangement for those needs rather than hire another employee.

The trading company was experiencing an increasing number of error messages on a daily basis. Sometimes they weren't able to do something as simple as saving a document, and keeping internet connectivity became almost an hourly issue. Thanh guessed that it was a problem with the DLL (dynamic-link library) files which house information for an operating system on how to perform various functions. If files are damaged or lost, then the computer doesn't know how to respond in certain situations. The problem is generally solved by down-loading the subject files back on to the computer. But every time Thanh tried to do this from home, the network connection would cut out and terminate the process. The easy solution was to stop by *Khá Đ*ep's office and re-install the files from a hand-carried disc. Since she passed within two blocks of their office on her way home from picking up Tuyen from ballet lessons, she stopped in to take care of what would be no more than a fifteen-minute process.

The unpretentious but functional office was staffed up front by a receptionist/secretary, an accountant, and a salesman. The receptionist was a heavyset and cheery young woman named Nhu who was happy to entertain Tuyen and be entertained by her while Thanh worked her magic on the computers. Both the accountant and salesman bowed politely to her and remarked on what a beautiful child with which she had been blessed. The salesman showed Thanh a picture of his own twelve-year-old child and expressed surprise when learning that Tuyen was a few months short of being ten. Perhaps, he said, they might play together some day.

The DLL files were downloaded in exactly sixteen minutes, and Thanh told the secretary that she would do a thorough test of the entire system from home to make sure all was working properly. It never occurred to her that surveillance cameras recorded her entire visit, including purposefully zoomed-in footage of mother and child. If it had been a screen test by Metro-Goldwyn-Mayer, Thanh and Tuyen would have both passed with flying colors.

Ten days later Boa was reviewing a video with Lanh. The receptionist, who earned at least quadruple what she would have with any other company and who had spent several minutes with Tuyen, had alerted her boss that he might like to take a look at the film clip of the little beauty that had wandered into the office with her mother. Due to his necessary anonymity, Boa never used the trading company premises as a working base for himself. The DVR data had been transferred to a flash drive and Lanh brought it to one of Boa's subterraneous hideouts in the *Nai Hiên Đông* district. Boa had his scouts always on the lookout for prospective candidates for shipment with instructions to focus on physical beauty, which always brought top dollar.

"Hey boss, got something special for you," Lahn said. "I'll give up a month's pay if you don't like this one."

Boa subconsciously massaged the scar on the left side of his face and said, "She better be good, *lo đít*. The last two you brought me were dogs."

To whatever minimal degree Boa's face could light up, it did so when he watched Tuyen on camera. He wasn't much for words to begin with, but the beauty of the child left him speechless. This was far, far above the norm, and the *Khung Bo* malefactor could see thousands of *dong* dancing in his mind's eye.

"We must have her." The words came out as a guttural hiss, and when Lanh heard that tone he knew his master's bidding must be done. He had seen the consequences when it was not.

Obtaining the Torkelson home address was child's play. Boa also paid big dollars to an indigenous LinTech employee for Gunnar's work schedule and learned that he had an upcoming two day business trip to Saigon within the week.

Boa, Lanh, Duc, and two more of *Khung Bo*'s best men positioned themselves a block away from the guarded gate to *Vuon Hòa Bình*. Boa did not personally participate in many kidnappings any more, rather leaving them to his henchmen. Occasionally he did so when his bloodlust peaked and the passion to joyfully extinguish another's life became unbearable. In addition, he was along for this operation to make absolutely sure it was not botched.

Intelligence-gathering forays earlier in the week revealed that in addition to the gate guard there was only one patrol vehicle manned by two individuals. The car would roam the compound for fifty minutes and then stop for a ten minute break at the guard shack. Duc's research found that Good Fortune Security provided the personnel, which meant that they had minimal training. The boring nature of their night-after-night patrols would also have minimized their alertness and the anticipation of any perceived threat. Attempting an abduction of a rich bitch in one of the elite neighborhoods of the city was not Boa's normal modus operandi, but the little girl in the video drew him into this anomaly.

It was three o'clock in the morning, generally the hour of deepest sleep and a time when the security guards would likely be at their lowest level of alertness. Both the gate guard and the roving patrol had been on duty for seven hours, and things were, as always, as quiet as the calm before a storm on the South China Sea. Only a sliver of the waning moon dimly lit the night. With the others out of sight and ten minutes before the patrol's next scheduled rest, Lanh approached the gate stumbling, mumbling, and with a half-empty bottle of rice wine in his hand. As he came abreast of the guard shack he muttered something incoherently, dropped the bottle, and clutched his chest as he fell to the roadway. Rolling on the ground he cried weakly for help, "*Giúp tôi. Giúp tôi.*" After stepping through the doorway and cautiously looking both ways down the street, the guard came out and knelt down over Lanh. Just as he was about to ask the gasping figure what the problem was, an eight-inch stiletto pierced his Adam's apple and came out the back of his neck, severing his spinal cord. After enjoying the sensation of warm blood dripping on his face, Lanh dragged the corpse into the shack and keyed his walkie-talkie to signal the others to proceed.

All hid inside the cramped guardhouse waiting for the patrol car to arrive, except for Duc who positioned himself behind some flowering pyracantha next to the shack. Lanh was using some tea from a pot sitting on a warming plate to clean his knife when he spotted the approaching vehicle. It was actually a couple of minutes early since the patrol's radio check with the gate guard had not been answered. The rovers figured he had fallen sleep, as he was wont to do. Lanh issued a soft whistle to alert Duc. The man riding shotgun got out, stretched, and walked into the little structure to awaken his lethargic co-worker. As he came through the door, Boa stepped from behind it and slipped his woven leather garrote around the man's neck, instantly cutting off both air and the capacity to make any sound. Within forty-five seconds he was unconscious, and Lanh finished him off by inserting his stiletto into the man's brain through his right eye socket. After several more minutes without his partner appearing, the driver came out and approached the door. A shot from Duc's suppressed CZ52 Czechoslovakian-made semiautomatic pistol sounded to him like his grandfather's cough. The 7.62×25mm Tokarev cartridge hit just below his left nipple and exploded his heart. Duc threw him into the flowering bushes.

Boa commanded one of the extra gang members to stay with Duc at the guardhouse just in case anyone from either the security company or the local police came by to check. With him he took Lanh and Trung, the latter being the duty expert on alarm systems. Trung had disabled the master panel in the guard shack, but wanted to check out the house to make sure any possible backup system was also sabotaged.

The Torkelson residence was the second house on the left, the third street in from the gate. Except for the solar lanterns lining the driveway and the soft lights submerged in the reflecting pool, the house was dark. As Boa crept along the inner side of the perimeter wall, his emotions roiled as the contrasting, always-close-at-hand images from his childhood surfaced. Although he would never have to live in poverty again, when in the midst of aristocracy and intelligentsia his ingrained hatred of those brought bile to his throat and blood to his eyes. Watching the video of beautiful Thanh conjured memories of his pitiful mother's features disappearing as he shoveled dirt on her face, and he was incapable of trying to understand the searing anger in his gut as he approached the house. All he knew was that he was going to relieve the planet of one more lady-of-the-night and acquire a crown jewel for his flesh trade.

Lanh stayed in the shadows and watched the front in case something unexpected happened either from the interior or exterior of the house. In addition to his stiletto and skinning knife he carried a pilfered K-54 Chicom semiautomatic pistol with three eight-round magazines. Chambered for the same 7.62 as Duc's CZ52 made for easy sharing of ammo. There was no silencer on Lanh's gun, but it didn't make any difference because if the police showed up in force, the slugs would be flying all over the neighborhood as stealth went out the window.

Boa and Trung crept to the back of the dwelling where it didn't take long to locate the junction box for the backup alarm system. Mini bolt cutters made short work of the padlock and Trung then slowly and carefully identified and disconnected the wires to disable the device. Picking the back door lock took longer than expected, which heightened both Boa's natural anxiety and his blood pressure. By the time they were tiptoeing on soft-soled shoes toward the stairs leading up to the bedrooms, his adrenaline level was spiking and drool slid down from the side of his mouth unheeded.

After locating the girl's room, Boa left Trung at her door while he proceeded to the master bedroom. He glided silently to the bedside where Thanh reposed fast asleep in a lacy negligee, covered to her waist by a light sheet. To a normal person she would have been an enviable picture of elegance and grace embodied in perfect human form. To Boa she was the most beautiful creature he would ever have the pleasure of extirpating.

Nightmares can be good in the sense that one wakes up to discover they were nothing but dreams. A joyful dream can cause disappointment when one wakes up to find that it isn't really happening. The reality into which Thanh awoke was a real-life, terrifying nightmare.

A hideous face on top of a foul-smelling body hovered over her with a grimy hand clamped over her mouth and nose. An instinctive scream was quelled by the fleshy paw pressing upon her, but in desperation she bit as hard as she could into the thenar muscle at the base of her assailant's thumb. Boa ripped his bleeding hand away and, balling it into a fist, smacked Thanh's temple, knocking her unconscious. The anger which simmered constantly in his subconscious boiled to an uncontrollable fury. Wanting the woman to be aware of what was to come, Boa brought two glasses of water from the king size bathroom and doused Thanh with them while gently slapping her cheeks. As she gradually regained consciousness, Boa turned on the nightstand light, pulled her into a sitting position, and crawled onto the silk sheets behind her. Fortunately, from the murderer's perspective, a large mirror on the wall opposite the foot end of the bed gave him a frontal view of Thanh's terror-stricken face. Placing his leather garrote over her neck and holding her legs down with his own, he was able to see her veins expanding and eyeballs extending outward as he steadily applied pressure. After realizing the futility of trying to wrest the loop from her windpipe, Thanh began reaching back for her attacker's face. Though her strength was ebbing quickly and her grabs were losing force second by second, she managed with her long, manicured fingernails to rake both of Boa's cheeks. Tasting the dripping blood as it mixed with his drooling saliva provided Boa with the closest he would ever come to experiencing sexual excitement. Putting to affect his tighten-and-loosen technique for prolonging the ecstasy of the kill, he accomplished a new personal best by manipulating the dying process to just beyond six and a half minutes.

While Boa had his fun, Tuyen was bound and gagged with duct tape as instructed. Boa now radioed Duc to go get their vehicle while he and Trung carried the child to the front door. Even in the dim light Boa saw that he had captured the prize of prizes, striking a blow to one of the nouveau riche in the process. A grin that looked more like a grimace passed across Boa's visage when he thought of Gunnar's reaction when he arrived home. As they waited for Duc, Lanh was given permission for a quick foray to the master bedroom for some enjoyment with his knives. By the time they were heading for the industrial area with Tuyen in the trunk, Thanh was hardly recognizable as a human being. As he was leaving the bedroom, Lanh noticed a black silk scarf embroidered with gold and silver thread. He impulsively grabbed it for a trophy or possible gift.

The hoodlums drove away without anyone having a clue that a neighborhood family's life had just been destroyed.

Chapter 45

March 2005 - Seattle, Washington

Jed told Tracks he'd meet him at his car in ten minutes . . . and to try to find Tats to come along. He said that at this time of the day he could likely be found on a stool at Flo's Alehouse.

A couple of years before, Tats had been fed up with his

wife, his old biker gang, and the Chicago cops. In fact, he had had it, period, with the whole Chicago scene. He didn't like the thoroughly unsatisfactory way his life was turning out, and figured an escape to the west coast could provide a fresh start. The newness of a geographical switch was accompanied by an attitudinal change engendered by a prison chaplain who seemed to take a genuine interest in his welfare. The Reverend Mike O'Neil spent a considerable amount of time with Tats, both in and out of the lockup, doing more listening than talking. Tats appreciated that, since in his general experience all most people were prone to do was flap their gums at him, usually with the volume on high and slinging deprecatory remarks designed to injure. But The Rev, as Tats called him, said one thing that stuck with him. *We live as we think*. Which Tats appropriately deduced to mean that if one's living was screwed up it was likely due to one's thinking being screwed up. He thought about that all the way to Seattle while listening over and over to Bob Dylan's classic song, "Gonna Change My Way of Thinking." That was the goal. Tats was tired of being influenced by fools.

The tattooist who branded in the last one, a rendering of knife wound scars spelling the phrase *So It Goes*, estimated that roughly forty-three percent of Tat's skin remained un-tattooed. Hence his street name. His large, square-jawed head was unmarked, and navy blue eyes squinted beneath a peroxide blonde buzz cut. But it wasn't the tattoos that intimidated people. Tats was a gym rat who averaged three hours a day pushing heavy iron, accompanied by roughly 3,500 daily quality calories and a host of nutritional supplements, some of them legal. The result was two hundred and eighty pounds on a six-foot-five frame, most of it muscle that stretched tight his artist's canvass skin and produced eye-popping, mean-looking veins that communicated don't-mess-with-me. And basically nobody did . . . save the fools who tried and ended up in the hospital.

Since he had arrived penniless, living on the streets, or couch-surfing when he could, was his domain. He did odd day jobs for small amounts of cash, some of which was needed since his new way of thinking meant stealing was out the window. The big man reasoned that he ought to lower his consumption levels considerably, but that didn't mean cutting out a couple of his favorite daily brews. Shortly after arriving in the Emerald City, Tats was blown away to see a fellow wearing a clerical collar sipping suds at Flo's Alehouse and, with memories of The Rev fresh in his mind, meandered over to introduce himself. Even with his best intentions, Tats thought it made good sense to keep a level-headed friend close at hand, sort of like a safety valve, and the beer drinking padre seemed a likely candidate.

Thus began a good and growing relationship between the two. And it turned out to be rather symbiotic in that Jed needed some backup on occasion and Tats turned out to be the perfect accomplice. From time to time Jed would be called to attend to someone's needs late at night in one of the more dangerous quarters of the city, and he would take Tats along. The latter's mere physical presence proved a deterrent to almost anyone who approached with dark motives. Tats was big and an experienced street fighter, but Jed ascertained that tutoring in some of the finer points of hand-to-hand combat would add to his effectiveness if needed. Jed's goal wasn't to cause mayhem and destruction, but he was also a realist and believed that if backed up against a wall, a fellow needed to be able to defend himself and others. Affirming and striving to live a righteous, peaceful life was well and good, but Jed had come to acknowledge that it didn't always work with others who played with a different set of rules, rules that often included knives and guns.

One day several months into their relationship, Jed met Tats at the gym and took him to the bounce-and-jiggle exercise room which had a dense foam mat covering the floor. "You pretty good on your feet, Tats?" Jed asked.

"You talking about fight'n, Father Jed?"

"Precisely. You figure you're pretty good?"

With a somewhat smug smile Tats replied, "Ain't never been beat since I was ten years old."

"So show me what you've got."

"What d'ya mean?" Tats asked with furrowed brow.

"I mean, let's have at it. Pretend I've got you cornered and want to do you serious harm. Show me what you'd do."

"Father Jed, with all due respect to a man your age, it wouldn't even be a contest. And the last thing I want to do is hurt you."

"And neither would I want to hurt you. Let's pull our blows so they won't do any harm. Kind of like the Plains Indians' practice of counting coup."

"Count'n what? Never heard of that."

"Never mind. I'll explain later. The goal is to hit me with a blow whose full force would do serious damage, but letting up just as contact is made so that no harm is actually done. You game to try?"

Tats scratched the three-day stubble on his chin and said, "Well, I'll try. But I'll have to be damn careful. And I don't really want to embarrass you."

“Hey, I can take it like a man. Let’s give it a whirl and see what happens. I’ll start things off.” And Jed cuffed him gently on the left ear and leaped five feet backwards before Tats could even get his hands up.”

“OK, that was a bit of a sucker punch. That ain’t gonna happen again.”

Just as Tats was about to charge headlong into the fray, Jed began the classic capoeira dipping and swaying motions that provided no stationary target to an assailant. Surprised and confused, Tats stopped short to figure out what to do next. Just as he was about to plunge forward and tackle the dancing figure before him, Tats’ jaw dropped when he saw Jed do a one-hand handstand facing him. Since nothing could be easier than pushing over someone so precariously balanced, Tats stepped forward to give Jed’s feet a shove, after which he’d be on him like a grizzly bear. But as he reached out for the shove, Jed moved so fast that Tats couldn’t register what happened. As Jed collapsed the arm holding himself up, he twisted his body to the left and threw his weight forward. Passing through the arc, his right foot connected shin-high with the left side of Tats’ legs, sweeping him off his feet and crashing to the mat. When the fallen warrior looked up, he saw Jed standing upright, smiling and with his arms crossed.

“How’d you do that?” Tats asked incredulously while rubbing his left calf.

“Something I’ve been practicing for many years. I hope I pulled back enough that I didn’t cause anything more than a slight bruise. But you’re a big guy and I wanted to make sure you ended up on the mat.”

“I sure did that. Shocked the hell out of me, yer doing

that one-handed thing. How'd you get down to ground level so fast? I never even seen that happen."

"Like I said, Tats, lots of practice. You should know that if I had used full force you wouldn't be walking out of here. I'd have broken your fibula."

"My fib-what?" Tats asked.

"Later maybe. What I wanted to demonstrate is that big and strong doesn't always win. There are some principles involved that might save your life, or somebody else's, someday. For instance, if you want to disable an attacker, where would you aim your blow?"

"I always go for the head," Tats said. "A solid punch there always puts a guy out of his misery."

"And sometimes that works. Maybe even most of the time. But a head punch is always the easiest to duck for a good fighter. Plus, if you don't hit 'em just right, maybe all you'll do is break a jaw or nose but they'll keep fighting. And there's always the chance of serious hand damage when you put bone on bone, and the head is one of the hardest bones in the body."

"Yeah, I know about that," Tats responded. "I've broken three different fingers on people's noggins over the years."

"So we need to work on not always doing the bull-in-a-china-shop approach every time. There are better ways to put an adversary out of commission and at the same time protect your own body."

"Where'd you learn this stuff, Father Jed? You're a good size and look pretty fit for an old . . . I mean, for someone your . . . oh hell, I mean for someone who's been around as long as you have. And I think it's safe to say that preacher types don't get trained in this hand-to-hand stuff."

Jed chuckled at Tats' discomfort and replied, "Africa, the Marine Corps, and decades of hard work. We're not in the fighting business, Tats, but a man still has to be able to confront evil when it confronts him. You willing to take a little instruction from an old man?"

"Hey, you ain't old in my book. And if you can teach me something, I'm up for trying."

And so they embarked on an every-other-week training schedule. Jed wasn't going to try to teach him capoeira per se, but schooled him in some of the basic principles while throwing in some tidbits from his Marine Corps days. While it took months getting it to sink in, Tats finally realized that there were three weak spots where a good connect could disable an opponent: the larynx, the genitals, and the tibia, the large frontal bone in the lower leg. One had to be careful with a blow to the larynx. A blow of medium force would leave a man grasping his throat and gasping for breath, but too much force could crush the voicebox and even cause death. The effect of a square hit on the genitals is something every male knows, but, surprisingly, many brawlers never think that low while often presenting their own as an open target. An attack on the tibia is for simply taking a person off his feet. A tibia smashed to smithereens with a tire iron will cause unbelievable pain and render the leg useless. Breaking both tibiae means the other fellow is relegated to a wheelchair or crutches. Obviously, the lower leg attack is for opponents who aren't equipped with firearms or throwing knives.

Tats was a good student, and they always finished their workouts with a meal at a local café where Jed regularly picked up the tab. In addition to the food, those repasts always included discussion on the changes in Tat's ways of thinking on which he wanted to continue working. He was duly impressed with Jed's appreciation of and respect for all kinds of people, even those who made choices at odds with his own values. They also reflected together on the dark forces that brought people down and kept them there, and how they might be combated. Their relationship grew, and Tats began to think of Jed as a father figure for whom he'd give his life if need be.

With Tats in tow, Tracks arrived at Jed's Civic in twenty minutes instead of ten. Turned out that Tats had left Flo's five minutes too soon, so Tracks had to scurry to Occidental Park where the big man had gone to play in an evening cribbage tournament. For Tats, when it came to Father Jed, cribbage could wait.

"So what's happening? You know anything more?" Jed asked Tracks.

Catching his breath from the short jog, Tracks said, "You know Isis has a kid, don't you?"

"Yeah, a little girl about, what, ten years old? I think her name is Marissa."

"That's it. A sweet little thing who apparently Breakers kidnapped."

"Kidnapped! Why the heck would he do that? I know he's ticked off about Isis leaving, but what would kidnapping her daughter accomplish?" Jed exclaimed.

"Hey, I don't know Breakers well," Tats chimed in, "but I get the feeling logical thinking ain't one of his strong suits."

Tracks added, "And, Father Jed, you've probably never been around him when he kicks into overdrive. Breaking heads is his idea of having fun, and when he loses his cool, which is about every other day, most smart people find some other place to be."

"So," Jed went on, "do you know where Isis is going to look for him?"

"Well, he's not going to have little Marissa at The Den, so she's probably heading for his pad over on Yesler. He squats in an old abandoned house just this side of 23rd."

"He won't likely be alone, will he?"

"No way. You won't find Breakers anywhere without his two goons nearby. One of 'em's a huge retard who goes by Jocko. I'm guessing six-ten and maybe three-fifty. He looks intimidating but is slow of both foot and brain. The other is a wiry little Spic, La Bamba, who supposedly was some kind of hot stuff on the MMA circuit. You can bet both are packing."

"Okay," Jed said, "pile in, guys, and we'll head for Breakers' place on Yesler. Best case is that we find Isis and cool her down without having to confront the boys."

"You think we should call the cops?"

"Let's find out what's happening first, Tracks. I don't doubt your word, but maybe Isis changed her mind, or found out that Marissa was really somewhere else. Besides, Isis doesn't exactly have a good relationship with Seattle's finest. Looks like she may have really turned an important corner, and if the cops pounce on her it could set things back measurably. We find out that Breakers really has the girl, I'll be the first one to call it in."

Breakers was an independent pimp who ran four

street walkers, Isis being one of them. He kept them on a short rein and got nastily physical if they didn't measure up to his expected income level, which was a minimum of four hundred bucks every twenty-four hours, seven days a week with one day off every other week. With four hookers doing their jobs, which meant servicing anywhere from four to eight johns a day, the weekly take was eleven thousand dollars and change. For their part, the women got a hundred and fifty bucks a week and minimal drug needs.

Isis had been doing her job, but began siphoning off a bit of her earnings to take care of Marissa, a child from a relationship several years before she got into the street life. Breakers eventually suspected that she wasn't turning over all the proceeds from her tricks, and had a tune-up session for her in the basement of his squatter-home. Bruised kidneys and broken fingers taught a lesson but didn't leave any visible mars that might turn customers away. Feeling used up, mad as hell at the whole world, and wanting to become a respectable mother who could actually care for her child, Isis was looking for a way out. Meeting Father Jed made it look like an actual possibility.

As their relationship flourished, Isis actually felt respected and valued. No man, including her abusive father, had ever made her feel that way, and she began to think that there might really be some other kind of life worth living. Father Jed was nonjudgmental, caring, and genuinely sincere. A casual observer might think it odd to see a man in a clerical collar having intimate conversation with a known prostitute in a neighborhood café. But the local cops, the social workers, and the street community in general knew his motives were pure and his friendship unencumbered by self-interest.

He guided Isis to a drug rehab program, the cost for which was covered by an anonymous donor, and a job training center geared for people on the rebound. With all the hope that she could muster, Isis had gone to Breakers at his bar of choice, The Den, and told him she was quitting. That's when the proverbial shit hit the fan.

When the pimp told her that was not an option, Isis told him he didn't own her anymore and she was outta here whether he liked it or not. He slapped her so hard across the table that her chair fell over backward, her head smacking the floor with such force that she blacked out. When she came to, likely with a mild concussion, she staggered toward the door of The Den, picked up a chair, and threw it at Breakers accompanied by a healthy wad of phlegm. Before he could grab her, she rushed out into the busy street and collapsed in front of a bus stop bench occupied by two middle-management executives in pinstripe suits. They called an ambulance.

"So how'd we get to this current crisis?" Jed asked.

"The story is," Tracks continued, "that Breakers went stark raving mad. Busted up everything he could lay his hands on in The Den and skiddooed before the cops got there. Long story short, he knows Marissa lives with an aging aunt, and where it is, so he nabbed the girl and put the word out that Isis better be on the street tonight or she'd never see her little girl again. Claims he can get big money for a cute little bitch like her."

"Didn't Mac at The Den send the cops after him at his house?" Jed asked.

"No one seems to know where Breakers calls home.

Only reason I know is that I ran into Isis on the street with blood in her eyes and she told me where she was going. I saw the outline of the gun in her jacket pocket, and seems like she's not thinking too level-headed. So I came to you."

"This is not good," Jed said. "But let's check out the house and see if we can intercept Isis before she does something crazy."

Dusk had just turned to dark and, after a drive-by, Jed pulled into the parking lot behind an apartment building a block away on the north side of Yesler. He gave walkie-talkies to both Tracks and Tats and said, "These are on the same channel as mine. Keep the volume low and don't talk unless you have to."

"What's the plan?" Tats queried.

"You two head through the trees to Washington and take it over to 22nd. Tracks, you come north on 22nd and Tats, you snoop-and-poop up the tree line between the house and the tenements to the east. Stay as quiet and invisible as you can. I'll be in the bushes across the street from the front of the house. What we're looking for first is Isis. If you see her anywhere, key the talkie twice. And remember, keep the volume so low you can barely hear it."

"What if we bump into Isis?" Tracks asked.

"Don't confront her. Try to keep her in sight and just key the mic. Stay as far from her as possible and I'll contact you for info on what she's doing. Okay, let's go."

Jed could tell that Tats was pumped up, so he added, "Don't forget, Tats, snoop-and-poop. I'd appreciate an appraisal before we take any action. If you see nothing by the time you circle the house, both of you join me in the bushes."

"You got it, Father Jed," Tats responded. In the dark, Jed had not seen the two-foot section of three-quarter-inch rebar that Tats held alongside his leg.

The first hint that something was amiss was when Tracks showed up by Jed but Tats didn't. Jed was hesitant to key his mic lest the static alert someone close to the big fellow. After several minutes Jed was just about to move around the east side looking for Tats when his walkie-talkie emitted two short static bursts indicating that Tats had seen something. Then a whisper-quiet voice came through, "Stay put. I'm on my way."

Within three minutes Jed saw Tats, moving amazingly quietly for his size, coming through the tree line to his left on the north side of Yesler. "What's happening?" Jed anxiously asked.

"Bad news, I'm afraid," Tats said. "I saw light and shadows coming from one of them low basement windows around back. Made it there and saw Isis inside with Breakers' two goons. Didn't spot Breakers or the little girl, but Isis is in bad shape."

"What kind of bad shape?" Jed inquired.

"Hard to tell what all's happened. But she's strapped to a chair naked. Duct tape over her mouth and part of her nose. I could tell she's having a damn hard time breathing. Something's also wrong with one leg and there's a fair amount of blood on the floor."

"Let's call the cops now," Tracks said.

"Don't think we can wait for 'em to get here," Tats said. "I think she's missing at least one finger and the little squirt was standing over her with a meat cleaver."

Jed knew this was bad news that called for something to happen right now. He'd usually like a lot more info before jumping into action, but from what Tats reported, he felt that an immediate response was necessary. Since he also knew that Tracks wasn't into the hand-to-hand thing, he instructed him to stay put and watch for anyone coming out the front door, Breakers with Marissa in particular. If that happened, he was to radio Jed immediately. Jed also gave him his cell phone and told him to dial 911 for the cops as soon as he and Tats moved out.

Tats reported that on the east side there were six steps down to a door into the raised basement which he found amazingly unlocked. It opened to a room on the other side of which was another door into the room where Isis was being held. He didn't know if that door was locked or not, but noted that it opened inward into the farther room.

"Okay, here's what we'll do," Jed said to Tats. "We'll enter the first room quiet like mice. If the other door isn't locked we'll simply open it and charge in. If it's locked, you put your shoulder to it and I'll follow you in. Did you see any firearms?"

"The spic has what looks like a .38 in a belt holster in the middle of his back. Didn't see anything on Jocko, and he was just standing there with his hands in his pockets grinning."

"Any idea how far from the door to the chair Isis is in?"

"It's not a big room. Maybe eighteen feet across, so probably nine or ten feet to the chair. On the far side of the room is a stairs heading up to the first floor."

"Here's the deal. You go in first and go for the big

guy. Put him out of commission but we need him conscious. I saw the piece of rebar you're carrying. Keep it away from his head. I'll take Mr. Meat Cleaver. We don't know where Breakers is, but I'll have La Bamba's .38 just in case he comes barreling down the stairs."

As they headed for the basement door, Tracks dialed 911. Jed figured they might show up in somewhere between five and ten minutes. Three, if a patrol car just happened to be in the neighborhood.

In two and a half minutes, Jed and Tats were inside the basement and in front of the door to the room holding Isis. They heard a muffled scream accompanied by sinister chuckles. The door was in fact locked, so Tats backed up five feet and looked at the door with the anticipation of a kindergartener on Halloween night. His shoulder hit the door with the force of an artillery shell and it exploded off its hinges, falling inward flat on the floor. Although shocked, the two sadists acted surprisingly fast. But not fast enough.

Jocko, who was sitting on a chair against the far wall, jumped up and lunged toward the hulking figure of Tats heading straight for him. He could subdue just about anybody with a bone-crushing bear hug, and that was his instinctive reaction. When, with arms outstretched, he was a step away from Tats, the latter dropped into a slide-into-second-base slither and brought the rebar full force into contact with Jocko at a point on his right leg midway between his knee and ankle. A very audible crack sounded, followed by something between a scream and a bellow as the huge goon crumpled to the concrete floor. He fell face-first, breaking his nose, and Tats was on top of him instantly pulling both arms behind him and pinning them there with his weight.

Jocko was big, but he couldn't shake off almost three hundred pounds of muscle pulling his arms up behind him. Tats growled in his ear, "Quit wiggling, dumbo, or I'll pull both your shoulders out of their sockets." Jocko quit wiggling.

At the same time, Jed approached La Bamba as he lifted the meat cleaver with his left hand and reached behind his back for the revolver with his right. Anticipating both, Jed left the ground after his first step into the room. His body parallel to the floor and propelled by his forward motion, Jed's left foot connected with the center of the little man's forehead. He wasn't trying to kill him, just render him inert. But if he did clock out, Jed would deal with his feelings about it later. La Bamba's head snapped back looking like it stretched his neck an inch or so. He went down like a rock, but as he did so, the falling meat cleaver grazed Jed's leg, slicing through pants and skin.

Isis' chair had toppled in the melee. Jed could see that she was in severe pain, so with the Buck 110 he carried almost everywhere, he began cutting off the duct tape, first over her mouth and then the strips holding her arms and legs to the chair. Being semi-conscious and delirious, she couldn't answer any of Jed's questions. The tip of a bone was protruding from her left thigh, awfully close the femoral artery, Jed thought. She was missing the thumb and middle finger on her left hand, and the middle finger on her right. Both eyes were swollen shut and her left nipple had been sliced off. Jed wondered what kind of monsters would do this to another human being.

Even though Jed had confiscated La Bamba's .38, Breakers hadn't appeared on the scene, so Jed turned to Jocko, still lying facedown with Tats on top of him and leaking a steady flow of blood from his flattened nose. The whole affair had taken less than fifteen seconds, and no sirens were yet to be heard. Jed leaned down and said, "Jocko, where's Breakers?"

"Kiss my ass," was his reply.

"We don't have time for this," Tats said. "Do me and yourself a favor and go out to Tracks and call an ambulance for Isis. The sooner one can get here for her the better. We can't wait on the cops. I'll get the info out of our big buddy here."

Jed didn't question how Tats was going to get the information. He just knew that if Isis' little girl was to be found, they needed to know where to look immediately. After what had happened to Isis, there was no telling what a sicko like Breakers would do to a bastard child for whom he cared nothing. So he sprinted for his cell phone, leaving Tats to gather the needed intelligence.

After Jed left, Tats took the roll of duct tape Jed had handed him and secured Jocko's arms behind him. He rolled the giant on his back and then pulled a six-inch stiletto from his pocket. "You and me gonna have a talk, big guy."

The police arrived within minutes of Jed rejoining Tracks on the street. An ambulance showed up another few minutes after that, loaded Isis and headed for the emergency ward at Harborview Medical Center. Fortunately, the lead patrol car included Officer Stu Oxley, who knew Jed well. The first thing they did was ascertain that Breakers wasn't on the premises, and when Jed took him into the basement they found both thugs with their hands duct-taped. La Bamba was barely conscious and Jocko, a stream of blood still oozing out of his nose and crying like a baby, had a cut under his left eyebrow with the eyeball leaning a bit too far forward in its socket. Jed described in brief detail what had led them there and what had happened, and promised to come with his friends to the precinct station immediately to give full statements. Officer Ox told Jed that they'd been trying to get something solid on Breakers for quite a while, and maybe this would be the ticket.

"By the way, Father Jed," Ox said, "how bad is that cut on your leg?"

"Superficial slice," Jed replied. "I've got a first aid kit in my car with stuff that'll hold it together until we're done. I'll get it checked out after we're through with you folks."

On the way to the police station Jed asked Tats, "So did Jocko tell you anything useful?"

"I got some info. It's not good, but it's at least a place to start."

"He tell you where Marissa is?"

"Not where, but who."

"We know the who. It's Breakers."

"Not anymore," Tats said. "He might have lost Isis as a money maker, but apparently he can make up a good part of it by selling the little girl."

"Selling?" Jed said incredulously.

"Yeah. Seems to be a growing market for virgins. And the younger the better for some whackos."

This was hard for Jed to believe. *I mean, come on, this is the twenty-first century.* "And Jocko probably didn't know who he might be selling her to."

"Yes, matter of fact he did."

"You want to tell me how you pried this info out of the

man?"

"Father Jed, you don't want to know."

"At least tell me where we can start looking."

"The where will take some serious investigating. But at least we know the who."

"Come on, man. Who are we talking about?"

"Don't know his full name. But he goes by BJ."

Chapter 46

March 2005 - Da Nang, Republic of Vietnam

Gunnar was in a semi-catatonic state. He sat in an interview room at the *Hoà Khê* ward police station. A kindly, older officer had brought him there from the morgue where he had collapsed after having to identify Thanh. He couldn't speak, couldn't even pick up the cup of tea placed in front of him, and stared glassy-eyed at the wall straight ahead. While the police needed some sort of official statement from him, they were sensitive enough to not press the issue until he had recovered enough composure to talk.

The police had been called when the first neighbor leaving for work had come to the *Vuon Hòa Bình* security gate. Pale yellow-streaked spiderhunters flitted about the palm trees calling to each other with their metallic chirping while vying for the sweet nectar of the red hibiscus blossoms. With the sun peeking over the horizon promising temperatures no higher than the low eighties, the driver felt refreshed after a good night's sleep and could not have imagined what was about to ruin his day. The gate wasn't open and the always-cheery early morning gatekeeper, Minh Ngô, was nowhere to be seen. A little peeved, the software company executive exited his metallic pearl Toyota Solera and approached the gatehouse to ascertain what was holding him up. He knew Minh had been on since midnight and had another hour to go, but that was no excuse for falling asleep at his post. Upon entering the hut he was greeted with the sight of the night's carnage and barely made it back to the cell phone in his car.

The police arrived in force and began going door-to-door to investigate what other mayhem the night's intruders might have caused. The officer who came to the Torkelson home first found the gate in their security wall open, followed by no answer to his repeated ringing of the door-bell. He then noticed a faint bloody footprint on the stoop, after which he tried the front door and found it unlocked. At that point he radioed his superior, and a team of three others joined him before entering the house. Finding Thanh in the upstairs bedroom, it was all they could do to keep from gagging. Blood was everywhere and each officer had the same reaction, namely, that only a horrendously sick monster could do something like this. While Thanh's body had been blade-ravaged, one area had not been touched with the knife: her neck. But that neck had clearly visible marks of a ligature which they all knew to be the signature trademark of the Ghost Snake. As usual, Boa wanted his handiwork recognized.

Canvassing the closest neighbors for additional information about the family, they learned that Gunnar was on a short business trip and that they had a daughter, Tuyen, who was about ten years old. There was no sign of the little girl.

Gunnar's flight from Saigon landed in Da Nang mid-morning and he took a cab home, planning on taking the day off after two ten-hour work days in the south. He arrived at *Vuon Hòa Bình* to find the gatehouse cordoned off with crime scene tape and local police milling around with the fresh commercial security detail. When he identified himself, the patrolman radioed the chief investigating officer who was still at the Torkelson residence. By now every nerve in Gunnar's body was on red alert as he was forced to wait for the officer on his way down from the house. Detective Văn Khúc, an old school cop who had seen most of what there was to see in his decades with the department, asked Gunnar to sit with him in his government-issue sedan and told him as compassionately as he could what they had found. In the space of thirty seconds Gunnar's world was shattered.

The horrific sense of the loss of Thanh, even though the extent of what happened to her was prudently not shared with him, was like a bomb exploding in Gunnar's head. If that was not enough, the disappearance of Tuyen escalated the bomb to a nuclear level. He leapt from the car and ran screaming toward his residence three blocks away. He made it to the crime scene tape surrounding his property before finally being tackled by two policemen on guard. Detective Khúc pulled up in his car and helped the other officers guide the subdued Gunnar into the back seat. Neighbors stood nervously on their porches or peeked out of windows wondering how this could happen in their quiet little community. Gunnar was well-liked by virtually all the other residents, and details of the tragedy were spreading quickly from house to house.

Unlike the host of normal daily experiences, traumatic events are often unable to be processed by the mind and body due to their overwhelming and shocking nature. They are not integrated or digested as the trauma takes on a life of its own. A physical and emotional numbness often includes feeling robotic or disconnected from the world around one. Detachment, hopelessness, estrangement and withdrawal could be described as emotional anesthesia. In Gunnar's case, the emotional mix included guilt and anxiety. Guilt that he had not been there to protect his family and anxiety over finding Tuyen, alive or dead.

By the time he had identified Thanh's body at the morgue and been transported to the police station, he sat immobilized with tens of thousands of synapses firing through his brain at warp speed. He didn't know what to think, do, or say, so he did none of the above. As the news spread to LinTech, one of the workers there named Ted Vyverberg, an expat from Colorado with whom he had worked closely for a couple of years, came to the police station. They let him sit with Gunnar. It took several hours, but Ted eventually coaxed his friend out of his stupor and got him to drink a bit of tea.

Having been watching the room through a one-way mirror, Khúc came back in and asked if Gun was able to answer a few questions. He nodded faintly and responded to the policeman's inquiries mostly in monosyllables.

"Do you have any idea who might do something like this?"

"No."

"Do you have any enemies that you know of?"

"No."

"Does your wife or her family have any enemies that you know of?"

"No."

"Can you verify your whereabouts for the last twenty-four hours?"

Gunnar's eyes hardened and narrowed to slits of rage. "Yes."

Khúc realized that not much more was going to be forthcoming at the moment, so he told Gunnar that he would get a more complete statement the next day. He also told him that he would not be allowed in his home for several days until the crime scene had been thoroughly processed and a cleaning service engaged. The cop was savvy enough to know that it would do Gunnar no good to see the results of what had happened in their bedroom.

Before leaving, Gunnar found his voice to ask, "Was my home checked thoroughly for my daughter?"

"Every square inch," Khúc replied. "There is no possibility that she was hiding anywhere on the premises."

"And how do we go about finding her?" said Gunnar.

"We have search teams combing *Vuon Hòa Bình* and we're distributing pictures of her to every police station in the city. Odds are good that she will turn up."

"Please contact me immediately with any sightings or leads you have. I will be staying at the HAGL Plaza Hotel until I am allowed to return home." Even as he said it, Gunnar had his doubts about whether he would ever set foot in that house again.

Ted took him to the hotel, saw him up to his room and said he would be back in a couple of hours to spend the evening, or even the night if need be, with him.

"I'm sincerely grateful, Ted. But you don't need to do that."

"Yes, I do," Ted replied. "You might not realize it, but now is not a time for you to be alone. I can't imagine what you're experiencing, but I want to be there as a sounding board, a shoulder, hell, just to be there with you so you're not alone.

Tears leaking out of the corner of his eyes, Gunnar just nodded.

"You call your folks, Gun. I'll be back with something good to eat shortly. Here's a card with both my home and cell number on it. If you need something, anything, before I get back, call me." Then putting his hands on both of Gunnar's shoulders and looking him straight in his teary eyes, Ted said, "Call me."

Something snapped.

Neurologists might be able to chart brain wave activity and pinpoint the prefrontal cortex as the locus of identifiable changes, but then turn over analysis of the effects of these modifications to psychologists and psychiatrists. While behavioral scientists find examination of neural functions and physiological changes useful, linking this hard data in a cause-and-effect fashion to specific cognitive and personality changes is a best-guess situation. To be sure, the traumatic events in Gunnar's life were bound to produce anger, confusion, depression, fear, and a host of other emotional reactions. But deep down where no one with three doctorates in psychology could see, something had snapped. A radical transformation that would produce, in effect, a different human being.

How it would play out in time was yet to be seen. But Gunnar – the all-American boy with the values and ethics that led to stellar success; the personable, responsible, loving man who anyone would appreciate having as a neighbor – experienced a defining vicissitude that was real and dramatic. Seeing his beloved wife who he would never hold again, and not seeing his precious angel of a daughter, who he might never hold again, produced a core hardness that neither Gun nor anyone else would have ever thought possible.

Sitting in the hotel room staring at a blank television screen, two objectives gripped his soul. Objectives which he swore on everything that was sacred he would accomplish. He would find and rescue Tuyen, and he would exact payback on whoever had destroyed his life.

Two days later Gunnar was still not allowed on his property. Not that he wanted to go there himself, but he needed some clothes and other personal effects. The police told him it might be another day or two, after which he thought he'd send Ted there with a list of items to pick up. LinTech had, of course, told him to take as much time off as needed, and Ted simply told the firm he was going to stay with Gun at least until his parents arrived.

Sonny and Linn had been, as expected, shocked to the core. They booked the first flight they could get out of Indianapolis to Da Nang via Los Angeles, and were due to arrive that evening. Ted had arranged a short-term rental of a two-bedroom suite in the hotel where Gunnar was staying.

Gunnar was a nominal Christian, and Thanh part of the eighty percent of Vietnamese who identify themselves as "no religion." But, as often is the case when death strikes, individuals look to religious professionals who have experience with end-of-life situations. So Gun called an old college chum, Chuck Leeds, who had become a Presbyterian minister and was serving a congregation in Escondido, California. They had maintained contact over the years and even got together for a beer every so often when Gunnar was at LinTech headquarters in San Diego. Chuck wouldn't have thought about turning down the request, and hopped a plane for Da Nang immediately.

The short service, rather generic and reliious-non-specific by Gunnar's request, was held in a local rented meeting hall. The Luu family was there in force, and at the graveside ceremony Thanh's father, Chú, at his request placed a beautifully crafted wreath of lotus flowers, the lotus being a symbol of purity in the Buddhist tradition, on the casket. It was a moderately attended service with colleagues from LinTech adding a few numbers to the Torkelson and Luu families. A reception afterwards was hosted at the Luu residence, the whole day overcast by the nature of Thanh's death and Tuyen still being missing. While the loss of Thanh was an oppressive pall that dominated the day, the concern for Gunnar that bubbled like a cauldron of hot oil just below the surface was Tuyen. Thanh had been laid to rest and was no longer a part of his life except in his memories. At the end of the day as people drifted back to their normal, un-traumatized lives, Gunnar felt like a bow with arrow at its maximum pull back. His whole being would now be focused on the two objectives, the first of which would be finding Tuyen. Whoever had taken her would feel the broadhead explode his heart.

"Son, there just aren't any right words," Sonny said with a husky voice, still choking back tears. "You probably know that. All I know to say is that I'm so, so sorry."

It was four days after the funeral and they sat in the living room area of Gunnar's suite at the HAGL Plaza. The police had cleared his house as a crime scene, but Gun couldn't bring himself to go there. Ted and Sonny went with a list of things to procure which included several specific pictures of Thanh and Tuyen. A month's deposit had been placed on the suite, a suitable time period, Gunnar thought, for figuring out what to do next.

The controlling concern, of course, was finding Tuyen. Gunnar was either at the police station or calling Detective Khúc a half dozen times a day. But the result of a city and three-province-wide search was . . . zero. The little girl had simply disappeared without a trace.

Sonny and Linn had booked an open-ended ticket because they didn't know how long they might be in Vietnam. "It will be no problem to stay as long as you'd like us to, but I feel so helpless," Linn said.

"Mom, I don't know what I would have done without both of you here." Gun spoke in quiet tones, which was all he had done since the day after arriving back in Da Nang. This did a surface job of masking the rage burning inside of him. "Why don't you schedule a flight home early next week. If the police still have nothing by then I'm going to have to make a trip to San Diego to meet with the LinTech brass about my future . . . at least my short term future. I'm not at all sure what part I can play in finding Tuyen, but I've got to try. Until I have her back, dead or alive, I won't have any peace. What I'm saying is, I could be on the move all over who-knows-where until she's found."

"But," Sonny asked, "what if she isn't found?"

"Do not say that, Dad. I will find her."

"OK. Right. I'm sure we will. But can you leave your job for an indeterminate period of time?"

"Right now I'm not concerned about the time factor, my career, or the job." Then with eyes perceptibly squinting and his voice sounding like how one might imagine the devil's, he said, "I – will – find – Tuyen."

Gun's parents were taken aback at his tone and demeanor. They had never experienced their son like this. Then again, nothing like this had ever happened to any of them before. They later conferred in private and decided that it would probably be best if they stayed another four or five days and then head back to Indianapolis, giving their son some space to deal with the current situation without them seeming to hover over him too much. As close as they were as a family, Gunnar had always had an independent streak and they wanted to respect that. They knew he would be in touch regularly, and they could be back in Da Nang within forty-eight hours if need be. Secretly, they wondered together how much of his life remained to be lived out in Vietnam.

The family embraced warmly at the airport, although both parents could sense a deep-seated alteration in their son's comportment. They acknowledged this as normal, given the circumstances, and knew it would take considerable time to work out whatever the new normal might be. Gunnar said he'd call them from San Diego in a couple of days to let them know the result of his meeting with company officials.

As he watched the Korean Air Boeing 777 lumber into the sky and eventually disappear, Gunnar wondered how long it would be before he saw his parents again. For Sonny and Linn it would be way, way too long.

Chapter 47

April 2005 - Seattle, Washington

Ten days had passed since the Yesler Street incident. Isis was still in the hospital since she had contracted pneumonia as well as an infection around the compound fracture in her leg. Father Jed stopped in to see her at least once every day, most of the time just holding her hand as she drifted in and out of consciousness. When she did mumble something mostly incomprehensible, it sounded like questions about her child. Jed would try to calm her by saying that she was just fine, or try to change the subject. He was thankful that pain and drugs kept her from thinking too clearly about it.

Both Breakers and Marissa had disappeared. A county-wide APB had been put out on the pimp, and state, county, and local police forces were all looking for the little girl. The FBI wasn't in on the search yet because a bona fide kidnapping had not been established. Jed was plumbing the street grapevine and privately offering a modest reward for any reliable information that would lead to Isis' daughter. Tats came up with the first substantial tip just as the sun was rising and Jed was stoking the coffee pot in his office.

"Where was this sighting?" Jed asked.

"You know that crappy motel on Alaska in West Seattle called Log-something-or-other?" Tats replied. "Got a sleaze bar attached where a guy can pick up a gal and a case of the clap."

"Sawing Logs," said Jed. "I've been by it but never in it. Who saw what?"

"Neck, one of my lifting partners, was helping close the place down with some drinking buddies around one this morning. He knows who we're all looking for, and he sees this big black bro bring a little mulatto girl out of a back room and hand her over to some white dude dressed up like a golf pro. Something passed hands under the table and the white guy dragged the scared-looking little one out the front door. Neck figures it had to be Marissa."

"Did Neck try to follow or get a plate number?"

"Said by the time he got out the front door the car with the two of them was too far away in the dark to see the plate, but it was some kind of light-colored little SUV. Back inside, the brother was also gone. He came by my pad about half hour ago and told me."

"Thanks for passing this on, Tats. You mind staking out the bar this evening on the odd chance that someone brings her back there? Beers are on me."

"No problem. I've got your cell on my speed dial. She shows up and you'll be the first to know."

"Thanks. In the meantime I'm going to pass on this sighting to the Seattle cops. She could be anywhere by now, but at least they'll know to be on the lookout for a white man with a small, light-skinned African-American girl."

"I'll keep working our street contacts during the day, and hit the Logs joint once it gets dark. By the way, one beer will be enough, but you can keep the burgers and fries coming," Tats said with a grin.

Tats' stakeout that night proved fruitless. The next day brought two discoveries that provoked a significant turning point in Jed's life.

The first discovery was Marissa's crumpled little body behind a grocery store on south Second. A seasoned dumpster raider called G&T started to climb in to look for breakfast and saw the girl face down in a pile of rotting produce. Her screams brought out the store personnel who promptly called 911. Officer Stu Oxley stopped by Jed's office mid-morning to give him the news.

Jed had seen enough evil in his life that nothing much surprised him or precipitated the blues. But the news of Marissa's demise triggered something deep down with which he was unfamiliar and pretty uncomfortable. The more he heard, the more it grew.

"What do they know, Stu?" Jed inquired.

Before he could say anything, the policeman took a deep breath and gulped down what might have been a muffled sob. "Just a dead little girl, Father Jed. A precious little one thrown away like an unwanted rag doll."

"Do we know what happened?" Jed pressed.

"I don't think you want to know. I just hope it happened quickly."

"Stu, I need to know this. There's going to be all kinds of rumors on the streets and I'm going to have to break this somehow to Isis. I want to know what this evil is that's infecting our community if I'm going to be of any help to the victims."

Steeling himself, Oxley spoke with as grim a countenance as Jed had ever seen on a Seattle policeman. "Short story: she was physically abused, raped, and her neck broken. There were contusions all over her body and semen in both her mouth and vagina. That enough?"

Jed stood stock-still and felt something like molten lava roiling inside as he tried to force out of the back of his mind the picture of a grown man doing this to a little girl. He couldn't envision just what an eruption of his emotions of the moment might look like, but he was sure that the perpetrator of this evil wouldn't have wanted to experience it had he been in the room. He finally spoke in a purposefully controlled tone. "What are the chances of finding out who did this?"

"I hate to say it, but not good," Ox replied. "You can't get fingerprints off of a naked body, and the CSI team found next to nothing useful at the scene. It was so polluted that it would be impossible to match any clues to specific individuals. They're working on it, but don't bet the farm."

After rubbing his face with his hands, almost like trying to wipe off dirty news, Jed asked, "You got a couple more minutes to give me, Stu?"

"Sure, Jed. I'd be obliged for a cup of your java over there."

Pouring mugs for both of them, Jed motioned for Stu to grab a seat in his makeshift lounge area. After a few sips in silence, Jed asked, "Is this an isolated incident, Stu, or is there something happening, a pattern of sorts, that this might fit into?"

"This is the first homicide, but it seems to fit a phenomenon that's been growing for the past couple of years."

"Which is?"

"Little girls. The hookers have always been here, and the average age seems to be getting lower and lower. But several real young ones have been rescued. We're talking eleven, twelve years old. And the undercover guys keep hearing rumors of the availability of little virgins. Believe it or not, there seem to be more and more johns looking for pre-pubescent youngsters. Makes me sick to my stomach and my blood boil."

"I wonder about any man who doesn't have that reaction."

"God help me, Father Jed, but if I find the guy who did this I don't think he'll make it to the station."

They sat with those thoughts for a few moments and then Jed continued. "The initials BJ mean anything to you?"

"Where'd you hear that?" Oxley said with surprise.

"One of the goons told Tats that Breakers was going to sell Marissa to him. Anybody with that handle on your radar?"

"We know there's somebody called BJ floating around connected to the sex trade, but so far all we've got is street talk. Nobody seems to know who he is, what he looks like, or where he is. Anytime we push harder with the questions, all we get is a look of fear and closed lips."

"How about Breakers?"

"Gone with the wind. We've had his compadres in the lockup, so they know nothing. So far it's a dead end."

Jed rubbed his temples in an attempt to ward off the hint of a headache. "How can I help?"

"Eyes and ears. You get us some reliable intel and we'll take it from there. As capable as you are, Jed, you know to leave the action to us, right?"

"Of course. But we both know that I have lines to info about stuff going on that you guys might have trouble accessing. So, yeah, I'll keep working my end of the system to see if anything turns up that could be useful. I know where to get a hold of you."

"Thanks, Jed. Appreciate it."

"One more thing. Anyone I can connect with in Vice that might give me some additional background and tips on where to focus my energies?"

Thinking for a minute, Oxley answered, "Try a gal name Mercy. She's been with the squad a number of years and would probably be willing to sit down with you for a while."

"Mercy! Interesting name for a cop."

"Not what you think. Basically, may God have mercy on any perp who crosses her path."

The second discovery was another body. Isis.

Along with the normal crowd of gawkers, one of Isis' street cronies came upon the grocery store scene on Second and saw Marissa's body being lifted out of the dumpster. Without thinking through the possible effects, she immediately made her way to the hospital and broke the news to Isis. An hour after learning of her daughter's death, Isis pulled out her IV, limped to the bathroom, smashed the wall mirror with her fist, and slit her wrists with a piece of the broken glass. By the time one of the overworked nurses found her it was too late to attempt any kind of revival.

Officer Oxley phoned Jed with the news just as he was heading out the door to go see her. While he wasn't particularly close to Isis, her death felt like a mule kick to his midsection. After picking up the coffee carafe and throwing it against the wall he sat down at his desk and gripped the arms of his chair. He thought about a beautiful baby girl cradled in the arms of a loving mother, followed by pictures of her ravaged little body ten years later and the mother with missing fingers and a broken leg bled out on a sterile hospital bathroom floor.

The growing pressure forced the lava closer to the surface as heat began to dominate Jed's psyche. At the moment, he felt incapacitated to logically analyze what was happening in his gut. The swirl of emotions and confusion about what, if anything, to do clouded rational thinking. But he needed to do something for release. So he ran twenty miles.

At about mile sixteen he came to a resolve that would effect a major change in his life. It would also lead to major life changes for a number of other people.

Chapter 48

April 2005 - Da Nang, Vietnam

"I have to do something, Ted. I have to try."

The day after Gunnar's parents left for the U.S. the two men sat with morning coffee on the balcony of Ted's suite overlooking the Han River. At the lowest ebb in the cycle of monsoon seasons, the sky held puffy clouds upon which angels might have chosen to rest and the temperature was a balmy seventy-two degrees. The day might have seemed glorious under different circumstances, but the rather mournful, fluty song of the nearby black-throated laughingthrush matched Gunnar's mood.

Ted sensed a change in Gunnar that he was having difficulty identifying. It was more than the grief and confusion that one would expect. Dramatic anger would also be normal, but what Ted saw might be described as a cold hardness, like ice a hundred feet under the polar cap. The body language, the eyes, the measured voice all telegraphed determination and danger. Ted didn't know whether to be alarmed, bewildered, or sanguine.

"What *can* you do? This is a job for the police," Ted responded.

"The police!" Gunnar spat. "If I wait for them to find Tuyen I might as well start shopping for a casket. I don't doubt Khúc's sincerity or intentions, but if the percentage of solved murders is any indication, we'll be sitting here having this discussion a year from now."

"Yeah, we know their track record. But what can you do that they can't?"

"That's precisely the point. They're bound by their protocols and enormous caseloads. I'm not. I've got one focus and only one, and there aren't any laws that'll stop me from doing whatever it takes to find and get Tuyen back."

"Gunnar, you're making me nervous. If I'm reading you right, any misstep could end up with you in a world of hurt."

"I don't give a damn. Half my life is gone with Thanh and the other half is hanging in the balance." Then with his eyes boring into Ted like red hot lasers, Gunnar said, "If she is alive, I will find Tuyen. If she is dead, those responsible will find out what hell is like."

Ted was divorced and his ex-wife had custody of their eight-year-old son in Colorado. He sat quietly for a few moments and thought about how he would feel and what he might be willing to do if someone had kidnapped Danny. He also knew, as did his friend, that little girls like Tuyen were increasingly being kidnapped for the growing child sex-trafficking business. "Gunnar, how can I help?"

Gunnar nodded gratefully and said with a voice like Solingen steel, "I can't believe that choosing our house was a random act. Tuyen was selected and Thanh was simply in the way. So the question is, when and where did they see and mark her as a target? If we can figure that out then we'll have some targets of our own to question."

"So how do we go about figuring that out?" Ted asked. "Anyone could have seen her anywhere."

"Not really, Ted. Tuyen's world was fairly limited to her private school, ballet lessons, and our neighborhood. Even her violin lessons were at home. Thanh kept a pretty tight rein on her, especially given the rumors of increasingly more young Vietnamese girls going missing. No, it has to be someone who saw Tuyen and knew exactly where to find her."

"So where do we start?"

"All of Thanh's business accounts are on her computer, and her daily appointment book chronicles all her activities in vivid detail. She never allowed any of her clients to come to the house, but I'll start by checking which ones she visited on site within the past six months."

"What would that tell you?"

"When I cross check that list with her daily journal, I might find one where Tuyen was with her when she stopped in."

"Did she ever take Tuyen with her on business calls?"

"Not that I know of. In fact, she was persistent in not doing so. But even if it's a longshot, it's a place to start. I'm also going to interview her school principal and the ballet headmistress. Someone might have seen something suspicious, like an unfamiliar person taking undue interest in Tuyen. Another longshot, but I've got to check out everything I can."

"So what can I do?" Ted asked again.

"I'll get Thanh's laptop to you along with her passwords. See if you can pull a list of current accounts and addresses. Make me a printout and I'll check it against her appointment book for recent visits."

"Done. How soon do you want it?"

With his becoming-normal knife-edge voice, Gunnar said, "Yesterday."

It wasn't yesterday, but at eight that same evening they met in Gunnar's hotel room. Before taking a sip, Ted held up his Huda Gold beer to the table lamp and appreciated its golden amber color. Gun was nursing a ginger ale after covenanting total abstinence with himself because he wanted his brain to function without any encumbrances. A light, cool breeze fluttered the curtains but did nothing to lighten or cool the resolve infusing every cell in Gunnar's body. They had just finished cross-checking Thanh's schedule.

"Thanh recorded five visits to clientele offices within the past six months. Two of them bear investigation because it's possible she had Tuyen with her," Gun related. "In mid-January she stopped by May Man, a wholesale grocery distributer, after picking up Tuyen from her parents' home. Then just several weeks ago she picked up Tuyen from ballet class and paid a visit to *Khá Đep* Trading, an import/export company, on her way home. Those are the only two where it appears Tuyen might have accompanied her on professional visits."

"I don't know, Gun. Doesn't this seem like a shot in the dark to you?" Ted remarked. "I mean, really, anyone could have seen her in dozens of other places."

"I don't think it's dozens. But, like I said, at least it's a place to start. I'm still convinced that whoever did this was someone who saw them together and had access to information about where we live. Besides, from what I've learned, the way this was carried out smacks of someone who knew what they were doing, who's done this before. This wasn't just an amateur job pulled off by some bozo who saw her on the playground."

"Gotta admit, that makes sense. So what's next?"

"I'm going to visit these two businesses just to look around and ask some innocuous questions. My excuse will be to let 'em know that they need to find another computer consultant. Maybe I'll see or intuit something that warrants further scrutiny."

"I wouldn't think that will raise any suspicions."

"What I'd like you to do, Ted, is research both outfits to see if any red flags pop up. I'm talking in-depth examination of their finances, operations, personnel . . . any and everything."

"You know Mike, our IT techie?" Ted asked.

"Not well, but yeah."

"The guy is a super computer whiz. Can hack into NASA if he wants. I'll get him to dig into their records. If there are any irregularities, he'll find them."

"The sooner the better, Ted. I'm going to make those visits tomorrow morning after checking with Detective Khúc. If you can get off work by mid-afternoon I'll meet you at your condo and we'll compare notes."

"Gotcha. And, Gun . . . watch yourself!"

At the May Man wholesale grocery distributer company, Gun didn't notice anything out of the ordinary or anything that jigged his hypersensitive observation antennas. The manager was polite, remembered Gun's charming daughter, and expressed profound sympathies over the death of his wife.

At *Khá Đẹp* Trading Company Gunnar had an internal reaction that threatened to result in an external explosion. Upon entering, he didn't say who he was or why he was there. The only one in the office was a young clerk, and Gun politely asked if he could speak to the manager. The clerk said that the manager was away at the moment but that he would get the secretary-receptionist who was in the back storage warehouse and could perhaps answer whatever questions he might have. A few minutes later Nhu emerged from the warehouse and cheerfully asked how she might be of assistance.

For a moment or two Gunnar didn't notice it. Something blipped on his mental radar scope during the initial greeting, but a conscious identification didn't register immediately. Just as he was about to identify himself and relate his wife's death, his eyes focused on Nhu's neck. Wrapped around it in a graceful fashion was Thanh's embroidered black scarf. He knew it was hers because he had purchased it from a silk artisan who produced only one-of-a-kind creations.

Nhu would not have guessed that there was any recognition or emotional reaction. The molten ice that flowed through Gun's circulatory system enabled a purposeful control that he knew beforehand he would need. Yet the stunning discovery challenged his vocal abilities, at least any confidence he had at the moment that he could steady his voice. So he faked a violent coughing spell. Nhu ran to get a glass of water, and after downing some of it between raucous coughs he sputtered apologies and said he would come back later. Still coughing, he hurried out the door and made haste for his car.

Gunnar met with Ted late that afternoon. Mike had done a thorough check on both companies, much of it canvassing data that even some accomplished hackers would have had problems accessing. On the surface nothing came up that seemed unusual or out of order for either one. Both appeared to be legitimate enterprises that operated within the boundaries set for private enterprise in the new united Vietnam. Gun expressed his appreciation, relating that nothing struck him as unusual or out of order at either establishment. He said nothing about his discovery at *Khá Đep*, for his next step would be an unpublicized and solo one.

Since he did not trust the police either to acquire the information he sought or to pass it on to him if they did, Gunnar also mentioned nothing to Detective Khúc. What he was about to do was well outside the bounds of the law, but he was well beyond the point of caring. The one and only thing that mattered was finding Tuyen. If he or anyone else died in the process, so be it.

Gunnar did not have any military training, but he had kept himself in excellent physical shape. His familiarity with weapons was limited to his handgun training in Mexico back in the early '90s, and to the small knife collection he had acquired over the years. His focus had been on distinctive and unusual knives, and the one he carried now at three a.m. in back of the *Khá Đẹp* warehouse was a Gurkha Kukri knife which a friend of his had purchased from a Nepalese soldier when visiting Katmandu a few years back. It had a fourteen inch curved blade and enough weight to chop down a fair-sized sapling. He wasn't sure exactly what to look for or what he might find, but he knew without question that the trail to Tuyen began where he was standing.

To the right of the one small door in the back of the building there was a window out of which a faint light emanated. He also heard some kind of machine running inside. Gun found a sturdy, empty crate nearby and quietly carried it to the window, crept upon it and looked in. He saw a slightly-built man under one dim lightbulb with his back roughly ten feet from the door working on a grinder, with a pile of various knives lying on a bench next to him. He had on protective goggles and the sparks were flying. Gun carefully climbed down from the crate and moved to the door, ever so slowly trying the knob. He was shocked but gratified that it was not locked. Not thoroughly thinking through where it might lead, he made his move.

Lanh had the shock of his life when Gunnar's hurtling

mass hit him in the center of his back. His right hand holding the handle of the knife he was sharpening was pushed into the grinder. As the turning stone ground three knuckles to the bone, the knife jerked hard to the left and put a deep three-inch gash across his left palm. His yelp from the pain was barely audible since Gun wrapped his right forearm around the man's neck in a rear naked choke. He could have snapped Lanh's neck with ease, but he needed some information, so he applied enough pressure to induce unconsciousness within a minute. Blood was squirting from the damaged hands, the red matching the intensity of Gunnar's passion.

When Lanh regained consciousness, his bloody hands were bound behind him with heavy electrical wire taken from a nearby coil. His feet were similarly bound with knees bent, and another length surrounded his neck and connected down his back to his ankles. Any attempt to straighten his legs would tighten the slip knot against his throat. Gun left just enough slack so that the man could croak out answers to his questions.

"You will answer my questions or experience pain like you never thought possible," Gunnar began in Vietnamese.

"Eat my shit, asshole. I don't know who you are, but you're dead meat."

Gunnar didn't respond verbally, and Lanh felt the first stirrings of genuine anxiety when he saw the look in his assailant's eyes. Gun found a roll of duct tape and put a double strip over Lanh's mouth to quiet the coming sounds. Then using his Gurkha knife he cut off Lanh's light cotton pants, put a tight tourniquet on the scrotum end of his penis, and then sliced off the glans, or head. It did not bleed much due to the tourniquet, but Lanh's wide eyes and muffled screams indicated the desired effect. He couldn't move much lest he choke himself to death, and Gun sat and watched him until there was minimal movement and sound.

He put the tip of his knife at the corner of Lanh's left eye and said, "I am going to remove the duct tape. Make any loud noises and I will pop your eyeball out. If you think I'm bluffing, try me."

After eliciting a nod of compliance, Gun removed the tape from his mouth and said, "Where is my daughter, Tuyen?" As he said this he pressed the knife point in so that it was touching the eyeball.

All the manufactured bravado of Lanh's miserable life evaporated. He had always thought of himself as courageous, but facing a maniac who obviously had no qualms about inflicting pain and death converted his supposed fearlessness to abject terror. He had lost blood, flesh, and body parts, and faced possible blindness. So he told Gunnar what he wanted to know. He knew that Boa would without question kill him if he found out his betrayal, but if he provided the information and was released, he could grab his stash and head west into Laos, maybe start his own gang.

Writhing in pain and gasping for breath, Lanh said, "Okay. I give what you want. Boa is the cause of all of this. You let me go now, yes?"

In response, Gunnar shortened the length of wire between his neck and ankles. He knew that Lanh could hold his legs in the bent position only so long before the muscles gave out and the wire sliced ever deeper into his throat. He then headed for the door.

Realizing that there was no release, no escape, and that death was very near, in a last-ditch attempt to be the tough guy he thought he was, Lanh croaked, “I had much fun cutting up your bitch wife.”

Gunnar went berserk.

Chapter 49

April 2005 - Seattle, Washington

Mercedes Gutierrez had grown up the daughter of a career Marine, her dad serving the bulk of his time in Forces Reconnaissance. She had unexpectedly come along in 1963 after a ten year hiatus in her mother's child-bearing. Her ten-year-older brother, Pedro, enlisted in the Corps at age eighteen and was killed the next year in the battle for An

Loc as part of the North Vietnamese 1972 Easter Offensive. Mercedes had adored her brother and, at nine years old, was crushed when Pedro died. Master Gunnery Sergeant Mateo Gutierrez, also devastated by his son's death, focused his fatherly attentions on Mercedes with fervor, treating and training her no differently from how he would have brought up a son.

At thirteen years old Mercedes could run a six-minute mile, do eighty pushups, and strip down and reassemble an M-16 assault rifle blindfolded. At seventeen she set a new California state high school record in the mile and was hitting the weight room regularly and hard. By the time she graduated from high school she was five foot ten, heavily muscled, a lean hundred and fifty-five pounds, knockout beautiful, and her entire persona characterized by brio. Her attractiveness was problematic because it was offset by the fact that she intimidated just about every male her age. During her senior year, a hefty tackle on the football squad tried to put the make on her. She resisted and he persisted. The evening ended with the tackle in the emergency ward getting treatment for three broken fingers on his right hand. This enhanced Mercedes' reputation.

Toward the end of her first year at UCLA, Mercedes felt drawn to the field of criminal justice. She transferred to the Boise, Idaho campus of Broadview University and in two years completed the program of Associate of Applied Science Criminal Justice. She spent three years working with the Idaho Department of Correction at the Pocatello Women's Correctional Center, and then moved to the California system where she spent the next three years at the California Institution for Women outside Chino. These six years were enough to convince her that she did not want to spend her career behind bars. Rather, she thought her talents might be put to better use by putting others there. Being a west coast gal but wanting to get out of crowded California, she applied to the police departments in Portland, Oregon and Seattle, Washington. She scored off the charts in both the aptitude tests and the civil service exam, and in the physical ability evaluation the instructors couldn't believe what they were seeing. During her interview with the Seattle Police Department Oral Board they both knew they had a match.

She became a Student Officer in the Basic Law Enforcement Academy in May 1991, followed by a month at the SPD Advanced Training Unit. She then entered the Field Training Program with an experienced officer who tutored her well. Following a very successful completion of all this, she was assigned to the Patrol Division for her probationary year, after which she became a permanent member of the SPD. The regs said one must serve three to five years working Patrol before applying for a different assignment. The day after completion of her third year, Mercedes applied for the Vice Squad.

In 1997, her sixth year with the SPD, she picked up the nickname Mercy. The initiating incident happened in Gas Works Park, a rounded twenty-acre peninsula that juts into the north end of Lake Union. Based on a tip, she and her partner, Justin Latrel, were shadowing a known sex offender who was out on parole. It was sometime after nine p.m. and they had followed him through the university district where he picked up a ratty-looking partner and began cruising the sorority house area north of the campus. Drawing a blank there, the dirty duo wound their way west underneath Interstate Five and headed for the park. The officers were not in uniform, and there was enough traffic on a pleasant spring evening that Mercedes and Justin could slip unnoticed into the half-full parking lot on Northlake Way. The two rakes being tailed had disappeared into the trees, and anyone with two cents worth of gray matter knew their agenda was not a late-night picnic. The plan was for Mercedes to take the western flank and zigzag in a half-circle pattern while Justin did the same on the east. They would meet at the old gas works at the south end unless one called for assistance on the way.

Two lines of trees separated the parking lot from the open bulk of the park. As Mercedes slid quietly through the first line, she thought she heard scuffling and muffled cries in the second group of trees to her right front. She sprinted toward the noise and came across the two perps with a young woman pinned to the ground on her back. "Police! Freeze!" she yelled but had not yet reached for the Ruger GP-161 .357 magnum in the belt holster on her hip. The parolee, a five-foot-nine, hundred-and-thirty-pound meth addict with the inappropriate name of Christian, looked up and laughed. His partner, shorter but heavier, chuckled as well.

"Ain't you a purty one, sweetheart. Jest in time for the party." And both left their first victim, whose legs were entangled in her downed jeans and panties, and lunged toward Mercedes.

When it was all over, Mercedes radioed Justin. He arrived at the scene to find both perps in handcuffs, Christian with a broken nose and a rapidly swelling left eye and his friend squirming on his back mumbling something about probably never being able to father a child. Justin didn't see the actual happening, but gave it good press, generally enhancing the story with vivid, imaginative details. That was the first of numerous incidents revealing that when called to task, Mercedes showed no mercy. Hence, Mercy.

Jed and Mercy sat at the back of the Red Starfish in Pioneer Square. A banner hung on the wall over the coffee bar that said, "Make Java, Not War." Jed thought the White House would do well to adopt that slogan. With the aqua-blue walls covered with starfish of every size and color, it wasn't hard to imagine one sipping a latte two fathoms under. Antiquated New Age tunes interspersed with gentle surf sounds softly permeated the atmosphere. It was mid-afternoon and only two other parties occupied the coffee house, both out of hearing range.

Oxley had set up the meeting. Jed arrived early and when he saw Mercy walking toward him his first reaction was that if he was in the market for a woman he'd probably look like a bird dog on point. His second thought: *I really don't want her angry with me.* After perfunctory introductions and ordering the darkest black coffee on tap for both of them, Mercy took the lead.

"I've heard of you, Father Jed. Hoped to meet you someday. Is that what I should call you, Father Jed?"

"Use whatever you're comfortable with, but I'm not a father, figuratively or literally. It's more or less a street name that identifies what I do. But Jed's fine with me too."

"I was raised a Roman Catholic," Mercy said, "so I resonate with the Father thing. The priest for most of my upbringing was an okay guy, laid-back and not tied to the rigid structures of the hierarchy. I haven't done much of the church thing for some time, but it kind of seems embedded in my cells. At least the deeper meanings."

"And what meanings would you be referring to?" Jed queried.

"Hey, how much time you got?" she replied with a hint of a smile. "Let's save that for another day and talk about why you want to grill a vice squad cop."

Jed liked her spunk and made a mental note to try and have that "another day" conversation somewhere down the line. "I'm looking for some background on the sex trafficking situation in the Seattle area. It hit home to an acquaintance of mine and I'm wondering just how pervasive the problem is in our community. My goal is simply to be a supportive friend to folks living on the edge. If I'd have been more informed before, maybe I could have done something to help Isis and her little girl before it all went south."

"Yeah, we all heard about that. Sorry for the loss of your friend. I also heard that you and Tats took good care of the two assholes who were screwing her over."

"Small fry, I'm told. My understanding is that even Breakers is just a minor cog in the machine. Sounds like you folks need to get the guys more toward the top. Like BJ."

"What do you know about BJ?" Mercy said with sparked interest.

"Basically only that he exists. The goon they call Jocko said Breakers was selling Marissa to a guy called BJ. That's all he knew . . . and if he had known more he would have told Tats."

"This Tats fella, I like his style. You don't have a problem with his techniques?"

Jed took a deep breath and rubbed the back of his neck. "Just between you and me, Mercy, I really get caught betwixt and between. There's something inherently wrong with prying info out of a bad guy with a piece of rebar up his rectum, but maybe it's even more wrong to let someone sell a little girl as a sex toy if you can do something about it. How to balance those two concepts is something I've been wrestling with all my life."

Mercy replied, "I don't suppose I struggle with it on as deep a level as you do, but I know what you mean. A big difference between you and me, or Tats and me, is that I live under severe restrictions in a glass bubble. They know I push the envelope sometimes, and I get the job done. Nevertheless, there are limits."

"And are those limits part of why dirtbags and johns with the consciences of slugs can continue to market little girls and destroy their lives?"

"Part of it, yeah. Listen, Father Jed, we do what we can. We save the odd one and that makes it all worth it for me. But I'm tied to the system and can only push it so far. There are days when I want to pitch the badge and just charge into the fray with guns blasting. But while that might feel good for the moment, the end result would be me in the blackbar hotel alongside the perps. So, like I said, I do what I can."

Hoping he hadn't touched too delicate a nerve, Jed went on. "You have any idea how pervasive this is, and what percent of the traffic you actually stop?"

Something between sadness and anger flashed across her face as Mercy replied. "If you mean the whole west coast, we're talking about a multi-million, maybe billion, dollar industry. Most of the time we feel like the little Dutch boy with his finger in a hole in the dike. I have no illusions about eliminating the problem, but one life saved is one life saved."

"I can hardly imagine the frustration," Jed answered.

"Let me tell you one quick story to illustrate. A couple of years ago we busted a handler in his shithole apartment with two gals, fourteen and fifteen. Caught him dead to rights. We funneled the gals into the recovery system and hauled the jerk's pimply ass into court. Solid case, no brainer . . . we thought. The judge threw out the charges because the warrant had the wrong address on it, castigating our squad for not having the i's dotted and t's crossed properly. Damn procedure trumped caring for the vics. A week later the fifteen-year-old was back with the pimp and the fourteen-year-old hung herself."

"I take it this isn't out of the ordinary."

"You take it right. And it gets to be a bummer."

"Mercy . . . okay if I call you that?"

"Everybody else does. Kinda has a nice ring to it, don't you think?" she said with a winning smile.

"Mercy, I applaud what you do and all I want is to be helpful in whatever way I can, both to you folks and to the vics roaming the streets. Stu also recognizes that I sometimes have access to information that you all could use. But the more I know about what's happening, the better job I can do at getting you intel that might be of some value." Jed was choosing his words carefully, hoping to not tip off his other ulterior motives.

"Appreciate that. From what I've heard, you're pretty embedded in the street community. If you can get the network working, maybe something useful will turn up."

"We talking about nailing BJ?"

"BJ and anyone else screwing over these little ones.

And not just the little ones either."

"Can you share anything with me about this guy?"

"I'm afraid it's very little. We heard that his first name is Benny but no one's ever come up with a surname. He seems to have a network that goes down the coast a ways, but his working base appears to be the Seattle metro area. Like many of the top pimps, he has no permanent location. Word is he has a fairly large boat of some kind, but it would surely be registered under some alias. If that's his primary residence, it makes it almost impossible to pin him down. He can dock at hundreds of marinas up and down the coast, not to mention anchoring offshore."

"What about finding and putting the squeeze on some of his toadies? They've got to know where to find him."

Looking somewhat skeptical, Mercy replied, "If you can find me one, I'll buy you dinner."

"Not much to go on, but I'll see what's out there on the streets. By the way, you must have undercover guys working on this don't you?"

"We do. And, by the way yourself, gals too."

"Sorry. Didn't mean to leave anyone out. I'm usually more careful." Jed said a bit sheepishly.

"Not to worry. Just a hang up of mine," Mercy said in a more relaxed tone. "We're obviously not talking 'bout an army here, and the few that are working the gutters haven't been able to turn up any solid leads. We thought we had one local pimp primed to rat on him, but on the designated night we found him in pieces in the alley where we were supposed to meet him."

"Apparently this BJ doesn't mess around."

"In that sense, no. But he messes around big time

with women's and young girls' lives. I've seen enough of the effects that I'd just love to meet up with him one-on-one. He's probably so into his macho self that he couldn't imagine being bested by a woman, but I'll give you thousand-to-one odds on who'd walk out of the room alive."

Mercy's intensity sent a little shiver up Jed's spine. He had no doubt about what she said, and watching her forearm muscles bunch up as she clenched her fists made him think again that he was glad they were both on the same side.

"Here's my card, Father Jed. Department number is on the front and I've put my personal cell on the back. Call me anytime. And I mean anytime."

Jed saw a look in her eye that might have meant calling even if not for business. As she got up to go she touched his hand and said, "Thanks for caring." It was a kind of caress that was outside the professional realm and Jed appreciated it, even if he was seventeen years her senior.

"If I come up with anything," Jed added, "you'll be the first to know."

As Mercy walked across the floor and out the door, Jed's eyes followed her all the way. He thought to himself, *We just might make a team.*

Chapter 50

May 2005 - North Bend, Washington

King County Deputy Sheriff Toby Rasmussen arrived at the Taskins' home about twenty minutes after Judy called. The nearest sheriff's station was in Sammamish and was unmanned at this time of night, but fortunately Rasmussen was at the Swedish/Issaquah emergency ward taking statements from people involved in a multi-vehicle accident just west of

Exit 18 on I-90. Following Judy's description, an ambulance was right behind him and EMT's rushed into the living room. They found a small Asian girl of undetermined national origin and age who was covered with cuts, bruises, and burns, and wearing nothing but soiled panties.

On the way to the Taskins' the deputy passed a smoldering panel van on the east side of the Middle Fork Snoqualmie bridge. Tire marks and scrapes indicated that it had sideswiped the east end of the bride superstructure and then careened off the road on the north side, ending wheels-up in a scrub area just west of 434th Avenue. He radioed for any other county or state law enforcement units in the area along with another ambulance from Issaquah.

It took days to unravel what authorities knew to be rough elements of a much longer story. As best as they could piece it together, the little girl was Vietnamese and had been riding in the destroyed van. She had no idea where she was or where she was being taken. All an interpreter could decipher was that she had been kidnapped from her home in Tam Ky and had taken a long trip on a ship. Her injuries resulted from being in the panel van when it crashed, in which the police found two adult Caucasians and two other young Asian girls, all dead. The girl, who indicated that her name was Chau, remembered climbing out the open back doors of the van and crawling away just before it burst into flames. Dazed and confused, she began running down the nearest road, which was 434th Avenue. The first two homes where she sought help were unoccupied. Farther down the road she saw a light in a window, but as she approached screaming for help, a shotgun blast from the front door sent her streaking farther up the darkened byway. She just ran for her life, becoming genuinely delirious by the time she reached the end of the road, and the Taskins.

The van was stolen and the IDs of the dead men provided vacant lot addresses in Seattle. Within one of the wallets a piece of paper was found with the initials BJ and a phone number. The number turned out to belong to a throw-away phone that was no longer in service. With the sketchy information at hand, it was deduced that Chau was a victim of a child sex trafficking operation that was known to exist on the west coast. For information's sake, a report was passed on to all major law enforcement vice squads from Bellingham to San Diego. If nothing else, it might inspire ever-more-determined efforts to put a serious crimp in, if not obliterate, this horrible scourge.

Chapter 51

May 2005 - Da Nang, Republic of Vietnam

Nhu arrived at the *Khá Đep* Trading Company office not long after first light. She liked the quiet of an hour or so to focus on filing and correspondence before they opened for business and interruptions would plague most of her day. She primed the coffee machine for those who masochistically preferred that bitter devil's liquid, and then brewed herself a soothing cup of Tai Chi green tea. The volume of their import/export business was growing, which provided a semblance of job security in the sluggish economy. It also kept the *Keindahan* on the move between Vietnam and the U.S., which meant an ongoing viable transport link for the human cargo for which the Americans eagerly waited.

Being neither a religious nor an especially moral person, Nhu did not lose sleep at night over the company's subsidiary human trafficking business, especially since she got a small bonus after payment was received for newly delivered flesh. Life was hard and one had to make one's own way. Which Nhu felt she had done. Abandoned by her profligate father after her mother died of an overdose when she was eight years old, she had fought her way up through alleys, literal and figurative, to her present position. Knowing that women were deemed subservient to men in general, she played the sycophantic role in the office, but never wanted the domination of a man in her home. After work hours she could eat, sleep, and fornicate as she pleased.

The one thing that induced pure terror in her was the sight of the scar-faced Ghost Snake. He appeared at *Khá Đep* very seldom, but when he did, Nhu did her best to be invisible. An incident that had confirmed his reputation happened during her third month on the job. Boa came into the office with Lanh, locked the front door and pulled the shades. After ordering Nhu and two other office clerks to sit on the floor, he motioned for the firm's accountant to sit in his chair facing his computer panel. The accountant had been diverting small amounts of the profits into his own account, confident that with the company's dollar volume no one would notice.

He hadn't counted on Boa's paying an outside forensic accountant to check the firm's records.

Glaring at the floor sitters, Lanh's right hand held a highly polished French Coup Coup machete and his left held a finger to his lips indicating silence. Boa slipped his garrote around the accountant's neck with such speed and force that not even a gurgle escaped his mouth. What put the fear of the devil in Nhu was the rapturous grin on Boa's face as he constricted the life out of the kicking, thrashing young man. After letting the accountant's body drop, Boa turned to the other three and said, "You want to live, you not steal from me," and walked out.

With another quarter hour or so until the other employees showed up, and after enjoying her first cup of tea and making good a good start on her deskwork, Nhu had to relieve herself. The washroom was in the warehouse, into which she entered through a door in the back of the office. With only a little light coming in the one small window back by the packaging machinery, Nhu hit the switch to illumine the whole interior. The sight that greeted her was what used to be Lanh, lying in a large red pool. One of her reactions was that she wouldn't have thought one body contained so much blood. The shock suppressed any vocalizations, but it shortly turned to fear over how this would affect Boa. She was confused about where to call, who to tell, what to do.

As she stood indecisively motionless, shuffling sounds came from the office area. Knowing this would be her co-workers, Nhu went to inform and confer with them. The only known way to get a message to Boa was through Duc, the latter being contacted by leaving a message at the *Uong*

Lon Bar. Nhu wrote a short note emphasizing the urgent nature of the situation and gave it to the trembling hands of one of the clerks to deliver.

No one went back into the warehouse. When a delivery truck arrived mid-morning, they instructed the driver to offload his cargo onto the loading dock saying that they were having problems with the mechanical door. A very unpleasant odor was beginning to seep into the office when Duc arrived late in the morning. When he asked what was so damn urgent, Nhu simply pointed to the door to the warehouse. After Duc went in and saw the carnage he asked if anyone had any idea what happened or who was involved. Pleading absolute ignorance and innocence, the three office employees, plus two warehouse workers who had shown up, were told to stay put as Duc stormed out.

Forty minutes later Duc returned with Boa. They passed through the office into the warehouse, closing the door behind them. Boa went over to look at what was left of his fellow thug. It would be inaccurate to say he felt any sadness, since that emotion had long been excised from his psyche. But a lifetime of living on the edge of volcanic anger erupted. In fact, he went ballistic.

From a concealed storage locker he yanked out an AK-47 with a hundred round drum. Duc dove behind a mini steel cargo container as Boa started firing. Full metal jacket 7.62x39mm bullets whipped around the warehouse like angry hornets. With no regard for the cargo or the facility, Boa spent the first drum blazing away in an uncontrolled frenzy. Walls, windows, machinery, cargo, everything was riddled, shredded, blasted. He grabbed a second drum and continued to spray wall-to-wall, floor-to-ceiling until the breach overheated and jammed.

He called for Duc, who cautiously crept out from behind the steel container which had saved his life. Boa, under some modicum of self-restraint, told him to stuff Lanh into one of the empty fifty-five gallon drums, seal it, and take it to their assigned wharf in the harbor where Boa would meet him at midnight. He then stalked into the office to question the staff only to find that they had run for their lives.

"Duc, we will find the one who did this," Boa rasped. "And he will wish he had never been born."

Chapter 52

May 2005 - Tacoma, Washington

Gunnar looked toward the lights on the double-span Tacoma Narrows Bridge and swished some Old Fitzgerald bourbon around in his mouth. He was nestled in the treeline along the railroad tracks on the north side of Titlow Park. While waiting for his contact, he thought back over the past two months.

His rage had not mellowed. To the contrary, it had intensified to a level where it dominated his every waking moment and a hefty percent of his sleeping ones. He recognized and acknowledged this, and controlled it with the self-discipline of a man for whom failure was not a conceivable option. That discipline included a daily physical fitness regimen that had hardened his body to match his steeled heart and obdurate mindset. Crash courses in the use of firearms and knives provided him with adequate, if not expert, skills for the task at hand. The role Gunnar had assumed would require not just a convincing persona, but a willingness to commit heinous acts that four months previously he would not have thought himself capable. But at this point he would rip out anyone's heart with his bare hands who stood in the way of his finding Tuyen.

After learning from Lanh that his daughter was on the way to Washington State on board the container ship *Keindahan*, Gunnar's research into its sailing schedule revealed that it had already offloaded at Tacoma and departed for the trip back to Da Nang. Tuyen could have been farmed out, sold, or put to work anywhere, but he had a place to start looking. Or at least a set of initials: BJ. He was convinced that this was all Lanh knew, but also that BJ was a real human being who apparently directed much of the child sex traffic on the U.S. west coast.

Gunnar requested and received a year's leave of absence with LinTech. He then wrote his parents a letter stating that he was on the search for Tuyen but would necessarily be out of touch for an indeterminate period of time. He was purposefully cryptic about his plans, only communicating his determination to succeed and his love for them. He encouraged them not to worry and stated he would check in with them when possible.

Gunnar then began making plans to pimp little girls for the pleasure of demented degenerates.

His plan was both audacious and, by his lights, the only realistic avenue leading to the rescue of his daughter, should she still be alive. It would hopefully also include an avenue to punish those who had wreaked this havoc on his family. He had been around the block long enough to realize that law enforcement authorities, well intentioned as they might be, were not the solution. Understaffed and overworked, they were burdened with a caseload that precluded the kind of effort Gunnar knew was needed to find Tuyen. Added to that were the restrictions of the system that set limits on what they could do to elicit information and exact retribution. All too often the famed system seemed designed to protect the villains and hamper any serious quest for justice. Any casual observer saw how often the bad guys skipped out of court with a smirk and flipped the bird to the DA, and any jail time was generally a mild slap on the wrist for crimes that destroyed others' lives. Given these obvious realities, and the fact that one lost Vietnamese-American little girl wasn't about to get police departments all hot and bothered who were investigating serial killers and such, Gunnar knew that his best chance was to work from the inside as part of the sex trafficking network. Running with the hare and hunting with the hounds would be a dangerous and daunting proposition, to be sure. But for a man possessed it was the necessary step.

Portland was picked as the starting point since he

knew BJ's base of operations was somewhere in the Seattle area, and he needed to appear as an outsider coming out of nowhere. Some quiet inquiries greased with hundred-dollar bills led him to an expert in forging documents. It cost a bundle, not that money was an issue, and within a couple of weeks Gunnar had a driver's license, Social Security card, and passport all issued with the name of a real but deceased person only two years younger with the name Gaar Houtman. The address, should anybody check, was formerly a house that had been torn down and replaced with a Starbuck's shop. Sunglasses and a Navy watch cap were to be his trademark attire. Gunnar wasn't worried about anybody recognizing him since he had been out of the country for such a long time and had never lived or done business in the Pacific Northwest. As for his *nom de guerre* or street name, he chose Bolo. To anyone who asked him where that came from he would reply, "You don't want to know."

It took a bit of research to determine how he might get into the business, but the initial clues were readily available on the internet. He purchased a Voodoo Envy 171 laptop, a MCD-4800 Portable Satellite Internet Hotspot, and the HughesNet Gen4 satellite internet service, a combination which would enable instant connection anywhere on the planet. The only person whom he trusted and with whom he kept in contact was Ted back in Da Nang. While Ted didn't know exactly what Gunnar was doing, he completely supported his efforts to locate Tuyen and said he would assist in any way possible while keeping everything on the QT. A lifelong friend and confidant of Ted's was the IT director for LinTech in San Diego. He could hack into any computer system on planet Earth and, sworn to secrecy, communicated that he would put his skills to use in any way needed to help locate Gunnar's daughter.

While he couldn't exactly rush things, Gunnar knew that time was of the essence. As the days and weeks moved on, the likelihood increased of Tuyen's moving further into the netherworld of human trafficking. Researching news articles in depth, and FBI bulletins provided by Ted's friend, a plan began to take shape. It appeared that there were two major child sex rings operating on the west coast: BJ's and another mistily-known organization run out of the Bay area in California by an ex-con named Billy Dee. While the rings ran the traffic in their respective north and south regions, there were some contested overlapping areas in between, often with blood shed. Gunnar figured both BJ and Billy would love to control the whole west coast market . . . which provided him with a plan.

First Gunnar had to find Billy Dee. To accomplish this he found an escort service on the internet that offered "young and inexperienced" female companionship. He booked a late-night engagement and showed up for the appointment at a condo overlooking the Siuslaw River in Florence, Oregon. The beefy Eastern European with a huge handlebar mustache who delivered the submissive young Salvadoran girl and then waited in his Cadillac Escalade told the man named Gaar he had one hour max and that any damaged goods would result in the loss of his pecker. Gunnar went into the condo and spent forty-five minutes teaching the girl Gin Rummy. Then he duct-taped her hands and feet and told her to remain quiet and someone would rescue her shortly.

He went down to the SUV and told Mr. Beef that he would pay handsomely, meaning in the thousands, for some useful information. Knowing the girl would stay in the room until he retrieved her, the fellow invited Gun into the vehicle in order to explore the proposition, all the while keeping his hand on the .38 special in a shoulder holster. As Gunnar slid into the passenger seat, in one fluid motion he drew the door closed and swung his right hand to the driver's neck and zapped him with a Vipertek VTX-989 stun gun, holding it there while counting to five. The electric shock scrambles communication between the brain and muscles. Regular neurological impulses are compromised and, along with lactic acid build up, normal muscular functions are instantly disabled. Knowing that the duration of the effects varies greatly individual to individual, Gun quickly went around to the driver's side and dragged the incapacitated man onto the pavement. After taping his hands, feet, and mouth, he dragged him through the bordering trees to a narrow sandy beach on the river. After allowing some time for quasi-recovery, Gun told the man that all he wanted to know was who his boss was and where he could be found, and that failure to provide the information would result in a swim in the river, duct tape included. The tough guy tried to manage a sneer behind the duct tape, followed by several somewhat incoherent profanities. Gun simply dragged him over to the river's edge and held his head underwater with his foot while counting to twenty before pulling him out. That, plus a stiletto poked a quarter of an inch into the side of his neck, prompted a nodding of the head now devoid of bravado.

After getting the needed information, he roped a nearby cinder block to Beef's midsection and kicked him into the current. On the way to his next appointment he called 911 with his burner cell phone and told them where to find the girl.

Jord Samson, the name given to Gunnar, was apparently one of Billy Dee's chief lieutenants who controlled the traffic along the Oregon coast. After an hour and a half's drive over wooded, curvy roads, Gunnar arrived at the Eugene address provided by the now thoroughly waterlogged former escort of escorts, whose driver's license listed him as Misha Lejczak. It proved to be an old stand-alone farmhouse off Royal Avenue on the west side. Two vehicles were parked next to the house and no others were visible inside the barn, whose door was wide open. As the sun began to creep up in the east, Gun approached the front door and knocked gently. His stiletto was up his left sleeve and a silenced 9mm Ruger was tucked on the left side into his belt under his coat. The latter was purchased under the table from a drunk gun dealer in Portland.

A sleepy-eyed scarecrow who looked to be in his mid-20s and dressed only in filthy underwear opened the door and pointed an old Army-issue Colt .45 at the intruder. "What the hell you want, mister?"

With feigned nervousness Gunnar replied, "I need to speak to Jord right away. It's an emergency message from Misha."

Scarecrow squinted his eyes and tried to process how anyone might know how to find this place. After all, the fellow was standing there, and far be it for him to prevent a message from Misha getting to his boss. "Wait right there, Jack. This better be something good." As the fellow removed the pistol barrel from the opening and began to close the door, Gun hit it with the full force of his substantial frame.

The door crashed into the fellow's forehead and he crumpled to the floor semi-conscious. Gun edged in, pulled his Ruger and swung the butt with full force into the man's temple. He knew the man was either dead or out for a considerable period of time. He didn't care which.

Entering the hallway off the living room he heard shuffling noises in the far bedroom with a scratchy voice eventually emanating, "Pinky, what the hell's going on out there?"

Gun entered the bedroom to find two naked men entwined in spoon position. "I'm the hell what's going on. Which one of you is Jord?"

The larger of the two, with full beard and hair falling down to his shoulders, sat up and said, "I'm Jord and I believe you've just signed your death warrant."

Pointing his Ruger at the pair, Gunnar said, "If you're Jord, you better be the one worrying about dying." Then to the other man who was trembling and looking like he wanted to dive under the blankets, "Is that really Jord, or would that be you?"

"No. No. No!" he blurted. "That's Jord. I'm not him."

Gunnar answered with a bullet to his forehead, splattering blood all over his bedmate. "What the hell! Are you plumb out of your head?" Jord bellowed. "I don't know what you want, mister, but you just bought the farm."

Gun slowly walked over to the blood-flaked Jord and calmly swung the barrel of his pistol against the side of his head. When Jord woke up he was sitting in a high back wooden armchair in the living room with his arms and legs bound to it with duct tape. Gunnar liked duct tape with its many and various uses. Jord's head was bound to the chair's back, but his mouth was not taped.

"Only one question," Gunnar growled, "and answering it is the only chance you have of living."

Jord let go a great wad of spittle, missing Gun's face but hitting his throat. "Your choice, asshole," Gun said as he kicked him in the chest, knocking him backwards so that the back of the chair was now flat on the floor. Wedging him between the couch and coffee table so that he couldn't flip over on his side, Gun went into the kitchen and returned with a rag and bucket of water. Stuffing the rag into Jord's mouth with part of it covering his nose, he began pouring water onto it until it was thoroughly soaked. This produced the sensation of drowning, which would be the actual result if the process continued unabated. The pimp tried the tough guy act until realizing that his tormentor was actually going to let him suffocate. Since pressure from the barrel of Gun's Ruger held the rag firmly in place, Jord couldn't force the soaked rag out with his tongue or by coughing. So he began screaming as best he could, which sounded like someone playing a bassoon underwater. Gunnar tore the rag out and dispassionately watched as Jord fought to expel water and gasp for air.

When Jord had regained some semblance of normal breathing, Gun blew a hole through his right foot. After the screaming stopped, he said, "That was your first chance, Samson ol' buddy. I only give one more, so here's the question: Where is Billy Dee and exactly how do I find him? If I don't get an answer in thirty seconds I will shoot your other foot and both knees, and watch you bleed for a couple of minutes before playing the rag-in-mouth game for the grand finale. The count begins right now." He then pointed his gun at Jord's good foot while staring at the second hand on his wristwatch.

At the ten second mark Jord started babbling. It was a calculated gamble, but Gun was confident that the information given him was genuine. Not many men can put up a front when seeing the Grim Reaper twelve inches away, and Jord was not one of them. Stuffing the soaked rag back in the human wreck's mouth, Gun then shot him in the left foot and both knees, left an ace of spades playing card duct-taped to his forehead, and walked out. As he strode down Oak Hill Cemetery Road toward his rental car hidden in an off-road copse, it occurred to him that he forgot to say thank you.

Winding his way back to Oregon Highway 126, he followed it to Interstate 5 and turned north toward Tacoma.

Gunnar found that getting in touch with BJ was no easy matter. He didn't want to show up in the Emerald City yet, so he did his inquiring in the communities south of it. Even mentioning the initials in western Washington dives resulted in frightened looks and zipped lips. A couple of times he was asked if he had a death wish. Word, of course, filtered back to BJ and piqued his interest.

Within a week, one of BJ's minions caught Gunnar coming out of a Tacoma waterfront bar late one night, stuck a 9mm Hi-Point C-9 in his back and moved him into a side alley.

"Why you askin' for BJ, dude? You tired of them little balls swinging 'tween your legs?"

"Stay cool, man," Gunnar said. "Just want to get a message to him that I think he'll appreciate."

"How I know you're not a copper? Maybe I should just

take out one of your kidneys," he sneered and followed with a low chuckle.

With a voice that communicated cool authority, Gunnar replied, "BJ finds out what you made him miss and you'll be looking for your own balls, my friend."

Something in the tone of Gunnar's voice and his relaxed composure caused the assailant to take him seriously. "So what's the message, dude?"

"Uh, uh," Gun said. "You just tell him that Bolo's got some good news that he'll want to hear. If he's looking for credentials, tell him to check out what happened to Samson down in Eugene. He'll have heard. Ask him if he knows what was taped to his forehead. If he doesn't, I can tell him. Reach into my right jacket pocket and you'll find a piece of paper with a phone number on it. That's how BJ can get ahold of me. In Tacoma." The number was for another burner cell phone which Gun would monitor twenty-four hours a day.

Then Gunnar simply walked out of the alley confident that no bullet would slam into his back.

He waited in the dark. Gun hated bourbon, but he swished it around in his mouth and spilled some on his jacket to give credibility to his persona. He also lit a cigarillo which he thought gave him a bit of a Clint Eastwoodian aura. He had received a brief call telling him when and where to be. BJ was intrigued after investigating Jord's demise and learning of the ace of spades. If this character perpetrated that joyful happening, he might be worth listening to. BJ trusted no one. No one. And he wasn't about to walk into what could be some kind of intricately planned ambush. So he sent Big Joey, his ex-NFLer sidekick, to see what Bolo had up his sleeve. Loaded for bear, Big Joey was prepared to blow this guy's ass to kingdom come if there was any kind of warning sign.

Knowing roughly where to look, Joey found Gunnar by the whiskey smell and the glow of the cigarillo. He approached him cautiously and commanded him to brace against a big Douglas fir. Frisking him and finding nothing – no weapons, no wire, no ID – Joey simply asked what the life-changing message for BJ might be.

Bolo was all the identification he would give, and said he had a twofold message for BJ. First, that he had taped an ace of spades to poor Jord's forehead. Second, that he knew how to get to Billy Dee and could take him out. If BJ was interested, a personal meeting would be necessary to discuss the whys and wherefores. He gave Big Joey a piece of paper with a different cell phone number and said that if they were going to do business together it would have to be sooner rather than later.

Four days later Bolo got the call.

Chapter 53

May 2005 - Newport Beach, California

Two months shy of her tenth birthday, Tuyen sat in her spacious bedroom on a hilltop looking at the Pacific Ocean spreading like an endless aquamarine carpet to the horizon. The eighteen-thousand-square-foot, twenty-six-room palace sat at the pinnacle of the Pelican Crest community of homes that listed for no less than eight figures. On her bay window perch she was surrounded by Steiff stuffed animals, her favorite being a diamond eyes teddy bear her caretaker had picked up at the bargain price of $79,000. Her closet was filled with apparel from the world's most prestigious children's clothing boutiques, and at the moment she was wearing the Destiny Gown, a vintage-inspired pewter dupioni silk evening gown marketed by Posh Tots.

Juan Pablo Fernández de Aguiniga y García-Iglesias entered the room and said, "Ah, *mi preciosa* Angelita, please come join *Papacito* for lunch. What would you like to eat on this fine day?"

Tuyen slowly turned to look at him with an expressionless face. She said nothing.

Exquisite words could be used to describe the terror a nine-year-old felt when awakened from a deep early morning sleep, gagged, bound, and carried out of her house. She somewhat successfully mentally blocked the experience most of the time, but when the nightmare returned, the first vivid image was of a dirty, scar-faced visage with ragged teeth, and breath that brought to mind rotten garbage. After being hustled inside a waiting car, she was blindfolded and told that if she made any sound she would experience great pain. To drive home the point, Trung gave the inside of her thigh a nasty pinch and said to be quiet or there would be much worse.

After a short drive, the car came to a stop and Tuyen could hear water gently lapping against something along with the sound of heavy machinery. She was yanked from the vehicle and felt herself being carried uphill. This was followed by her being thrown over the shoulder of one of the captors who then ascended up two flights of very steep stairs. A door opened, she was set on her feet, and whoever had carried her left the room without a word. A soothing female voice told her to stand still while she removed the blindfold, gag, and duct tape. Tuyen remembered the duct tape hurting her wrists when the woman removed it. As her eyes adjusted to the dim light, the Vietnamese woman, who said to call her Mamasan, led her to a cot and told her to try to get some sleep because they were going on a long journey.

In barely a whisper, Tuyen said, "Where are my mommy and daddy?"

"They do not want you anymore," said Mamasan. "They have sold you to a man who will be your new daddy and give you a wonderful life. You must forget about your parents and be a good little girl."

Tuyen did not believe for a second what the woman said. But she also realized the direness of her situation and that she must act compliant until her daddy rescued her. Which he surely would. With barely a whimper, she lay down on the cot and let the woman draw a cotton blanket over her. As she turned toward the wall and closed her eyes she felt the sharp prick of something in her left shoulder and within several minutes she could not maintain consciousness.

The trip on the *Keindahan* took twenty days, during which time Tuyen was confined to the stateroom. Shortly before it left the Da Nang docks, two more girls were deposited in the room, a twelve-year-old Vietnamese named Kim-Ly and an eleven-year-old of Chinese descent named Meifeng. The girls were allowed to talk to each other. When Mamasan left the room, the heavy metal door was always locked.

Tuyen, who slipped naturally into the leadership position, told the other two that they must be *good girls*, and must act docile and obedient in order to avoid punishment. They were aided in this task by the scopolamine unknowingly administered to them in their drinking water. While the drug blunted cognitive capacity, the endless swaying motion and the incessant sound of the big diesel engines made Tuyen aware that she was on a large ship. Her school class had taken a tour of the docks once, watching container ships come and go, and she could see in her mind's eye one of the behemoths in which she was imprisoned.

The overseas journey had included one two-day stop in some port, but the girls were not permitted to leave their quarters. The room did have a commode and small shower stall at one end so that some measure of hygiene could be maintained, and the food brought to them was adequate if not excellent.

Then, in the dark hours one night, the three little ones were awakened and brought above deck and Tuyen noted that they were dead in the water. They were given light wool blankets to ward off the chilling early spring breeze, then found themselves guided down an overside gangway onto a much smaller vessel bobbing alongside the *Keindahan* in small chop. Except for the ship's lighting, the world was as dark as sin. They were ushered into a below-deck compartment that was luxuriously appointed but with the portholes shuttered. Their mamasan for the ocean voyage did not accompany them, but two young and beautiful women greeted them with hugs and hot cocoa. Tuyen was the only one who understood their English, but all three girls snuggled under down comforters on plush mattresses.

After a bouncy hour-long ride, the smaller craft in which they were riding came to a halt. The sea was measurably calmer, and the girls were again transferred to a twenty-two-foot Zodiac Hurricane 650 inflatable which ferried them to an isolated stretch of beach. Tuyen did notice in the glow of the stern lights that the name My Girl was emblazoned on the transom of the boat from which they had just alighted. Since no adults spoke Vietnamese, Tuyen was instructed to tell the other two that after reaching land absolute silence was required before they headed down a winding, wooded path. They were also told that some wonderful surprises awaited them after an overland ride. A detached observer who knew what awaited them would have deduced that being raped by a host of men each day would not seem very wonderful to the youngsters.

Prone in the back of a large vehicle with darkened windows, Tuyen, Kim-Ly, and Meifeng sensed the arrival of the morning sun as they wound down a curvy road. Then their vehicle drove onto another boat for a short ride, after which they felt themselves again being driven overland. They were let out at one point to relieve themselves at a wooded pullover, and given fruit, energy bars, and drug-laced bottled water. Night gradually fell, and the driver pulled into an isolated copse to wait for the early morning crossing from Canada into the U.S. The final leg of the journey took them to a house at the end of a long wooded driveway off the south end of Lake Ki, west of Smokey Point, Washington.

Two used-up street walkers awaited the three. They were being paid to mentor the girls in the fine points of customer sexual satisfaction. But they were to delay the beginning of training until BJ arrived to evaluate the new cargo and to assess their market value. The latter would determine whether he would control them within his own trafficking network or put them up for sale to uber-wealthy clients. In the two and a half years that he had been doing business with Boa, profits had well established the value of the little girl sex trade. One particularly lovely Vietnamese-Chinese mix had sold to a Saudi oil magnate for half a million bucks. BJ was hoping for another candidate in this latest shipment to provide similar potential. When he saw Tuyen he couldn't believe his eyes.

If he had believed in angels, BJ would have thought he was looking at one. Beauty was beauty, but Tuyen was off the charts. He had never seen such a gorgeous child, and her delicate elegance was augmented by advanced size at her age, which would enable marketing her as an eleven or twelve-year old instead of the nine-year-old that she was. BJ was told she had some facility with English – Tuyen had spoken as little as possible to her captors – but was astounded when she spoke it perfectly and with a vocabulary that surpassed his. Dollar signs danced in his head, and he knew who was the perfect prospect.

Juan Pablo García-Iglesias had the kind of wealth around which most people cannot begin to wrap their minds. He lived in a thirty-million-dollar mansion in Newport Beach, one of the most prestigious communities on the California coast. He was a Columbian drug cartel kingpin who had fought his way to the top, spilling enough *sangre* along the way to fill a Red Cross blood bank. It was a contest whether his rapaciousness or ruthlessness took top honors. When his assets totaled in the billions, he slipped out of the trade and invested in hedge funds and stocks, the latter almost always with insider information, which kept increasing his net worth exponentially. He named his hilltop estate *Gloria de Dios*, a blasphemous oxymoron if there ever was one. But one tragedy blighted his life.

In addition to having a myriad of mistresses around the world, Juan Pablo had wed a beauty from his home country, one Adoria Marmolejo, a recent Miss Columbia and second runner up in the Miss Universe contest. A nod to respectability occasioned the marriage, along with his desire to be a family man. Contrary to the dominant Columbian man's desire for male descendants, Juan Pablo was crazy to have a little girl. Adoria accommodated him by bearing a beautiful baby girl who became the light of his life. Juan Pablo doted on her as one would a goddess, feeling blessed by whatever gods were up there. When Iñes died at nine years old after falling off a swing and breaking her neck, Juan Pablo was inconsolable. The nanny who was supposed to be watching over Iñes was put to death, and in short order Juan went to work to produce a replacement offspring. Unfortunately, within two months Adoria developed endometrial cancer which resulted in a total hysterectomy. During the healing process after the operation, Juan Pablo informed his wife that he was going to look for a child to adopt so that she could be a mother again. One of his minions who had a penchant for sex with young virgins suggested to his boss that he contact a fellow up the coast called BJ.

When BJ faxed Juan Pablo a picture of Tuyen, he fell in love instantly. Viewing the soft hazel eyes that gazed at him via the photograph, he thought he was looking at Iñes. Through intermediaries, the forlorn and avaricious oligarch basically said name your price. When BJ came back with the figure of a million dollars, Juan Pablo chuckled at the paltry amount and concluded the deal.

Tuyen had been in her new home at Pelican Crest for ten months. Juan Pablo, not knowing or caring what her Vietnamese name was, ironically gave her the sobriquet Angelita, little angel. Even if he had been informed that she was called Tuyen, he would not have had a clue what it meant. The Torkelson genes and training proved operative. Tuyen resolved that either she would escape and find her way back home, or her daddy would find and rescue her. In the meantime, aside from the anguish of separation from her parents, life was not unpleasant. Although just shy of her tenth birthday, she was shrewd enough to play the game of being a dutiful and loving daughter. She knew her day was coming.

A complicating factor was Adoria. A combination of distress, depression, and anger at losing her own child and the inability to conceive another resulted in a mean-spirited attitude toward Angelita. It didn't help that Juan fawned over the little girl incessantly, often to the neglect of his wife. Not that she ever felt genuinely appreciated for anything other than her trophy-wife looks and the ability to bear children, but now that the latter was out of the picture, she was shunted aside both physically and emotionally most of the time. The jealously and emotional pain not only made for an unpleasant relationship between her and the little girl, it also produced her deepening sense of alienation from her husband. In the past she was resigned to living as an expensive toy, but seeing Juan transfer virtually all his affection to this little foreigner produced a growing fury.

As Juan Pablo took her hand and gently squeezed it on the way downstairs to lunch with bone china and sterling silver cutlery, Tuyen looked up and gave him a warm smile. Little did he suspect that she would have liked to have a dagger to thrust into his evil heart.

Chapter 54

May 2005 - Seattle, Washington

At fifty-nine years old, Jedediah Bazo was in better shape than most men twenty years his junior. Genetics, lifestyle, and years of experience in both self-discipline and martial arts resulted in a man who you didn't want to make mad. And he was mad.

Jed was also a man of high principles and matching

moral standards. Committed to the faith that had guided him his whole life, he continued to feel caught in that age-old quandary over if and when violence could ever be justified. Given recent events, it was fortuitous that Darrell called to ask if a visit for a couple of weeks would be in order. Jed's answer had been an enthusiastic yes, and they now sat in his small garage apartment late one evening.

"I really can't answer that question for you," Darrell said. "I mean, I could, but the answer that works for me might not be the one that works for you."

"Darrell, I know there is no absolute, no equation that works universally. But how then does one come to a conclusion in any given situation? Are there not some critical factors or principles that one can put on the scale?"

After taking a sip of the excellent Malbec Jed had offered, Darrell replied, "This is familiar ground we've covered a number of times over the years, Jed, and we both know there's not a definitive answer. Be just great if there was a divine rule book with instructions for what to do in each and every circumstance in life. But no matter how loudly we cry, 'Say it ain't so, Joe,' we get the same answer Mr. Jackson gave the kid in the parking lot: it is what it is. We put what comes from our intellect, our experience, our faith, and our gut on the scale, and one side or the other is going to go down."

"What if I don't like the side that goes down?"

"Jed, you ought to know by now that all too often we're not going to like whichever side goes down. But we either make decisions and act on them or sit in a catatonic trance."

Musing as he drained his wineglass, Jed finally replied, “Doesn’t that make it easy to justify almost anything?”

“I guess some people might see it that way. But we’re talking about genuinely struggling to do the right thing, or at least what we feel is necessary in the given situation. The key question so often is: What’s going to result in the least amount of damage? Hypothetically, if two options both seem wrong but you have to choose one or the other, I think a fella’s got to decide which one is more wrong than the other.”

“How ’bout just sitting on the fence?”

“Of course that’s an option,” Darrell proffered. “But you know as well as I do that generally that decision simply means supporting the status quo.”

“OK, I’m being the devil’s advocate here, but what about the old saying that two wrongs don’t make a right?” Jed countered.

“Again, there’s wrong and there’s wrong, at least with respect to the consequences. If it takes killing one person to keep him from killing fifty . . . see what I mean? Look, Jed, we can kick this around six ways from Tuesday and not come up with a definitive answer. At least if you’re looking for a proverbial textbook solution to all of life’s problems.”

“So are you saying it boils down to my subjective judgment?” Jed inquired.

“In one sense, yes. One generally has a number of objective facts to put on the scale, but determining how much each one weighs and which side gravity pulls down is an individual decision. I might, for instance, come to an opposite conclusion on any given issue than you do, even though we’ve got the same information. But unless one of us convinces the other to see it differently, you’d have to go with your judgment and I'd have to go with mine. And it goes without saying that issues vary in importance. Example: there's a significant difference between a vote in a state referendum on whether or not to condone capital punishment or whether or not to ban billboards on state highways."

"Point well taken. So, the devil probing again here, one might justifiably support Robin Hood's taking from the oppressive Norman lords and giving to the poor?

"Of course you can justify it. And someone else might justifiably, at least in his mind, condemn it. One's value system and moral compass will determine which."

Jed didn't say anything for a bit as he poured another two fingers of wine in each of their glasses. He sat down in his ratty old overstuffed armchair and appeared to be looking at something deep inside. Finally Darrell said, "This discussion is like a merry-go-round, Jed. Push too fast and too long and all we'll do is both get dizzy. And a fella's who's too dizzy can't even stand up."

"I gotta stand up, Darrell. I'm not going to take what's happening sitting down."

Darrell knew the situation at hand, so he thought he'd do a little devil-advocating himself. "You think you can do more than the police?"

"In some ways, yeah. Mercy gets frustrated beyond words with how her hands are tied by the system. That, and how even when they do catch 'em dead to rights they often get off with a slap or nothing. I'm not constrained in the same way, and sometimes I have access to more info on the streets than they can get."

"Jed, I think you know my sympathies lie alongside yours, and I trust you to do what you honestly believe is the right thing. But you gotta be damn careful about taking the law into your own hands. Good intentions often end up with bad results."

"My concern isn't upholding the law. There are little girls out there being abused, raped, mutilated as we speak, and if I can put a stop to even some of it when the system continues to fail them miserably, so be it."

Darrell wasn't too sure he wanted to know the specifics of what Jed had in mind, so the discussion wore down and they parted to their respective beds. Early morning brought a bright May day, and the two old friends headed for a church in the Cathedral area that gave out free breakfast coffee and donuts. But the two pastors donated fifty bucks each for their java and sweets, and went to a table occupied by three homeless men, one of whom was a fairly new transsexual, and a lesbian couple who were both trying desperately to shake a meth habit.

"Father Jed," one of the fellows exclaimed, "damn – excuse me – darn good to see you. Where ya'll been?"

"You know, Beany. Here and there. Let me introduce you all to one of the premier human beings on the planet."

Looking like one of the bushes, Jed huddled in camo raingear beneath the mature second-growth forest and scoped the cabin some hundred yards away with his Bushnell waterproof binoculars. He was at the terminus of a road which dead-ended on the southern boundary of Cougar Mountain Regional Wildland Park. This thirty-one-hundred-acre patch of wilderness was bounded by the southern portion of Lake Washington to the west, I-90 to the north-northeast, and Squak Mountain State Park to the east-southeast.

Numerous homes dotted the eastern extension of the city of Renton as it poked here and there into the hilly, wooded areas that pushed up against the southern border of the preserve. A few ramshackle cabins built by pioneers or hippies in the days before Seattle's population boom were doing their best to resist nature's destruction, a few of them occupied off and on by squatters or fugitives. It was one of these cabins upon which Jed focused his attention.

It didn't take rocket science to discern that one avenue to the elusive BJ was through Breakers. The latter obviously knew the former and how to contact him, so Mercy focused on locating Breakers and perhaps making him an offer he couldn't refuse. Mercy had acquired a new partner a few months back, a guy three years in Vice named Vern Bostitch, appropriately nicknamed Staples. Nice enough gent, competent even, but a straight-arrow-by-the-book-fellow who Mercy learned wouldn't push past Standard Operating Procedures. They had been tipped by an informant that Breakers was moving around the east-Renton/Cougar Mountain area, and they had been doing some limited cruising there with the hope that they might miraculously stumble upon him. A term Mercy preferred for pimps in general and child traffickers in particular was *predator*. But she was one too, except that she preyed on moral misfits instead of on hapless women and little children.

Although the search area was under the jurisdiction of the King County Sheriff, Mercy could justifiably operate there since she was a part of the WashACT team. The Washington Advisory Committee on Trafficking was a multi-disciplinary taskforce convened by the U.S. Attorney's Office for the western Washington district. The Committee's mission was to aid victims of trafficking and to identify, investigate, and prosecute exploiters (another of Mercy's favorite terms . . . well, behind *assholes* and *human garbage*). She was the rep to the Committee from SPD's Vice High Risk Victims Unit. The sheriff's office in Newcastle and the Renton Police had been notified of the sightings, and been asked to keep their eyes open. Because they were all busy bees and since Mercy herself had numerous other important irons in the fire, she thought cluing Jed in, under the table, of course, might add some manpower to their stretched surveillance capabilities. She also was looking for an excuse to simply spend some time with him again.

Seeing the light on in his storefront office late one evening, she ascertained that no one was with him and popped in. "Hey, Father Jed. How's my favorite priest doing?"

Always enjoying her self-confidence and winning smile, Jed replied, "Hey to you too, Mercy. Coffee?"

"Always," Mercy said.

As he brought two mugs over to the sitting area, he expressed something that had occurred to him more than once. "Mercy, why don't you drop the Father and just call me Jed."

"It bother you?" Mercy replied with a bit of a puzzled look.

"Not that exactly. It's just that I'm not really a father, either in the religious world or as a literal fact. And you and I don't have what one might consider a pastor-client relationship. So as friend-to-friend, Jed seems like the appropriate term."

"Do you mind it when other people use Father?"

"Most of the time, no. Not really. It's kinda like my

street name, and to lots of others it identifies what I do . . . what I'm here for."

"Gotcha," Mercy said. "I've been using it just sort of out of habit. Besides, I'd like to think we're closer than that anyway."

Jed got another hint of what he sensed as they had grown together over the past months. He really appreciated Mercy and greatly valued their relationship, but he was beginning to think that maybe for her it was turning into something a bit more than platonic. Wondering if she stopped by because of her hope for taking their friendship to deeper levels, maybe now was the time to address the issue.

"Mercy, I like you. I like you a lot. But there's something you need to know about me."

Mercy wasn't sure what was coming, but she didn't like his use of the proverbial *but*. "Fire away. I'm all ears."

"Mercy, I'm celibate."

Miss Self-Control couldn't keep her face from flushing. She hoped the office lighting was dim enough so that Jed didn't notice. "Well, that's uhhh . . . that's news that uhhh . . . well, why are you telling me this?"

"I might be celibate, but that doesn't mean I can't read signs. And unless the signs I'm reading are upside down and backwards, you're open to our friendship perhaps moving into something deeper . . . and of a different nature."

"Jed, I don't know how in the world you got . . . "

Cutting her off, Jed said, "Mercy, if our friendship is to prosper and last, we've got to be honest with each other. If I'm truly off base, then please help me wash the egg off my face. But if I'm anywhere near the target, we've got to deal with it."

While for her it was still in the infatuation-with-possibilities stage, Mercy had to admit that Jed's perceptions were right. And if he was truly and for-real celibate, then they had better face it sooner than later. "You got me, Jed. Not many men I've ever had these inklings for, and I don't give a damn about our age difference. But I'm fully aware that it takes two to tango."

"I guess the reason I felt the need to bring this up now is that maybe I've been sending some wrong signals. I couldn't be more happy that our paths have crossed, and I hope they don't ever get uncrossed. But celibacy isn't something one chooses, any more than anyone chooses their sexual orientation. It took me a while to recognize and accept it, but once it's there, it's there."

"Have you always felt this way, or did something happen?"

"Long, long story, Mercy. Maybe someday I'll be able to share it with you. But I'm simply asking you to understand, and to affirm our relationship in spite of it."

"Well, I'm sure glad you told me this before we jumped under the covers and you couldn't get it up." She said this with a grin and they both laughed. "Seriously, I do understand . . . and I sense that in a funny kind of way, being honest with each other deepens our friendship. We can get on with things without any pretenses or false hopes."

"I hope you're not just saying that to make me feel good."

"I'm a big girl, Jed. I can handle it. I'm very grateful for your honesty."

Jed leaned forward and took her hands in his. Looking into her eyes, he said, "You are a wonderful person and a wonderful friend, Mercy. I hope we can always be there for each other in the right ways. We really are a team. And I don't want our friendship to stop growing."

Mercedes swallowed hard. A teeny-tiny voice in the back of her head said, *Jedediah, you might not be as celibate as you think.* But she could live with the situation for now. So she said, "It won't, Jed. And speaking of team, that's the other reason I stopped in."

Mercy then proceeded to tell him about the Breakers sightings, and how a bit of nosing around on his part might turn something up. If he had time. Besides, she told him, if he and/or Tats could *persuade* Breakers to share information that he might not tell law enforcement authorities, so much the better. She knew that he knew she could keep her mouth shut.

Jed had cruised the dead-end roads along the southern and southwestern edges of Cougar Mountain Park for a couple of weeks looking for dwellings that seemed unused or abandoned. He found three, and surreptitious inspections revealed that two of them had no sign of any human habitation for a long time while the third had recent tire and boot tracks leading in and out. It was that one on which he was now focused.

A rusty and mud-caked early model Jeep Wrangler sat in front of a sagging porch, and wisps of smoke curled out of a crumbling chimney. Early in the evening he had parked a little over a mile away on an old logging road and had navigated his way through the forest to his current position in the bushes. He had seen movement in the cabin over the past hour, but no one had come in or gone out. Just as he was about to edge his way up to the cabin itself, the door banged open and two men stepped onto the porch. One of the fellows fit the description of Breakers given by Tats, and the other was a smallish man who looked like someone dug him up from the local garbage landfill. Breakers was gesticulating emphatically and yelling something about beer and cigarettes. Landfill got in the jeep and barreled down the access road with churning tires flinging mud to kingdom come. Breakers went back in the excuse-for-a-cabin and slammed the door.

Twenty quiet minutes later Jed stood at the front door. He had circled the cabin, looking in each window and confirming that Breakers was now alone. The bad guy was, in fact, splayed out on a dirty rug in front of struggling fireplace embers. A brand-new Model 327 Smith and Wesson .357 Magnum lay on the coffee table along with a box of Winchester Silvertip cartridges, and a beat-up Mossberg Maverick 88 pump action shotgun stood in the corner to the right of the fireplace. The place was littered with empty beer cans, cigarette butts, soiled frozen dinner containers, and a variety of newspapers and magazines.

Jed gently tried the door knob and found it unlocked. He knew if he tried slipping in quietly that the gummed up old hinges would scream bloody murder, so he charged in at full steam, grabbing the revolver off the coffee table before the slumbering pimp's eyes even opened. When they did, they saw the barrel of the .357 magnum two feet away from the center of his forehead while a combat boot was exerting an uncomfortable amount of pressure on his manhood.

"Don't think we've met," Jed said.

Breakers squinted as his fuzzed brain tried to figure

out who this guy was and how he had found his way here. He didn't think Jed was a cop, so maybe it was some Grizzly Adams type out-of-season hunter on whose property he was trespassing.

"Hey, buddy, keep it cool, huh. If this is your place, I'm sorry. We'll clean it up and pay for the use. No reason to get all ballistic here."

Breakers was about as big as Jed, but was in a very compromised position. A fireplace iron was about twelve inches away, but, hand-quicker-than-the-eye notwithstanding, he rightly figured that the speed of one of the Winchester Silvertips would beat his hand and arm movement by a long shot. Jed took a step backwards and told him to stand up.

"Listen very closely, Breakers. You got once chance to do this. You hearing me? One chance. One. I don't get what I need and you're going to spend the rest of your life in some kind of assisted living facility. So here we go. You listening? Where do I find BJ?"

"Mister, I don't know who you think . . ." BOOM! All Breakers got out were those seven words before most of his right auricle was blown off by one of the Silvertips. He screamed and shot his hand up to try to staunch the blood spurting from his mangled ear. "You mother. . ." BOOM! Another shot creased his right triceps, a calculated addition of pain and blood.

Tears were now coming to Breakers' eyes as he realized the hopelessness of his situation. With a calmness that communicated confidence and purpose, and which sounded like cast iron to Breakers, Jed said, "Your one chance has about three tenths of a second left, you piece of crap." Dropping his aim to the man's crotch, he added, "I get an answer now or the next one's gonna make you a eunuch."

"Wait, wait, wait, wait!" Breakers yelled. "WAIT, dammit! I'll tell you what I know."

"It better be good. You are one sorry excuse for a human being, and if you try leading me on so you can get out of this alive, I'll find you. Guaranteed."

"OK, man, OK. You gonna let me go then?"

"You tell me where BJ is . . . NOW!" Jed bellowed and Breakers wet his pants, "and I won't kill you." The .357's line of sight again went to the middle of Breakers' forehead.

Breakers started rattling off like he had to get out of a house on fire. "My Girl! That's all I know. The name of his boat is My Girl. I don't know where it is. He's always moving around. He checks in with me 'bout every three weeks. Never him. Always sends somebody. The contact is rotated between three different bars and I tell tell 'em if I got somethin' for him. That's all I know, man. I swear. BJ never lets nobody get close to him."

"How do you know which bar to go to?"

"His goon calls and tells me. I don't know which one until I get the call."

Jed let go another blast from the pistol into the ceiling for effect, which resulted in Breakers doing a little hopscotch kind of dance. "You wouldn't be BS'n me on not knowing where he keeps My Girl, would you?"

"No, no, no, man. Look, I told you true and I never want nothing to do with the dude ever again. You gonna let me go now?"

As Jed was about to answer, he heard tires on gravel and saw lights coming toward the cabin. A quick peek through the curtains confirmed that Landfill was back. "On your knees, Breakers," Jed ordered.

"Hey, I told you what you wanted and you said you'd let me go."

"No. I just said I wouldn't kill you." And Jed took a quick step toward Breakers, swinging the barrel of the .357 full force into his left temple. He crumpled like a sad sack of potatoes. Jed waited at the side of the door and Landfill imitated the same potato sack after experiencing a capoeira chop to the back of the neck. Finding a length of hemp rope in the back of the Wrangler, Jed bound their hands and feet and tied them securely back to back.

After wiping down anything he might have touched in the cabin, he used the long driveway and roadway to find the way back to his vehicle. Making his way west on Renton-Maple Valley Road, he tossed the wiped Smith and Wesson over the railing as he crossed the Cedar River, and then called Mercy.

"Better get someone out to the cabin at the end of 174th on the south side of Cougar Mountain Park," Jed said.

"What's up?"

"Breakers and some other scumbag are going to die of thirst if someone doesn't eventually get to them."

"Good job, Jed. Is everybody in one piece?"

"Not exactly. There are a few minor pieces of Breakers scattered about. The other guy might need a neck brace for a couple of weeks."

"Wish I'd have been there to see that. How do I explain my finding them?"

"How about an anonymous tip from one of your informants? You can honestly claim total ignorance about how they got busted and tied up, and most likely no one's going to care. Since Breakers has no idea who I am, he can make up any story he wants about who did what to him. If you get someone from the sheriff's office to meet you there, they should be happy to hand him over to you. You've got the personal cred and the authority of WashACT behind you."

"OK, I'll give that a try and hope no one pushes too hard on the issue. The fact that he's a known perp with an APB out on him for kidnapping doesn't give him a lot of weight with the system. By the way, did you get any useful info in the process of teaching him proper manners?"

"Got at least a direction to pursue. Call tomorrow when you have time and I'll fill you in."

My Girl, Jed ran through his mind. *I think we're going to meet, Sweetheart.*

Chapter 55

May 2005 - Tatoosh Island, Washington

My Girl was anchored on the leeward side of Tatoosh Island off the northwestern tip of Washington's Olympic Peninsula. The uninhabited island, or rather small group of almost-touching islands, is the westernmost point in the lower forty-eight, and home to the Cape Flattery Lighthouse since 1857. It is part of the Makah Reservation and is used only for seasonal fishing camps. On a misty, overcast day no one was putt-putting around to ask what a seventy foot luxury yacht was doing resting in open ocean waters.

The previous evening, just as dusk snuffed out the light of day, My Girl was DIW some five miles due west of Washington's Cape Disappointment State Park, and BJ had the yacht's Zodiac with a 90 horse Honda 4-stroke outboard lowered into the sea. Two men jumped in and headed the craft toward the mouth of the Columbia River.

One of them was Big Sally, the nick-name coming from his Columbian birth certificate's given name, Salvador. But you didn't call him that if you wanted to keep all your teeth. It had something to do with childhood teasing about being an altar boy making him a sissy Christian. Besides, at this point in life if he was going to be anybody's savior, the only candidate was the fellow who stared back at him in the mirror each morning. The Big came from his six-foot-seven, two hundred-and-eighty-five-pound frame. The other big thing about him was the fourteen-inch, perfectly honed hunting knife which always hung from his belt. A time or two it had been Sally's savior, and often someone who found himself facing the business end of the blade would utter a blasphemous, *Jesus*. The only time anyone ever saw him smile was right before he ripped someone's head off, so pains were taken to keep him frowning. The only person Big Sally was afraid of was BJ, for whom he had been a sidekick bodyguard for a little over two years.

The second person in the Zodiac was a man of average size and nondescript looks. Nobody seemed to know his real name, calling him only Buddy. Buddy was into firearms in general and pistols in particular. Heading up the Columbia

River he had on his person a side-belt-holstered .460 S&W Magnum with eight inch barrel, a shoulder-holstered 9mm CZ 75 Tactical Sport Pistol, a middle-of-the-back belt-holstered Rossi Double Action R35202 38 Special, a Taurus PT-22 in a right ankle holster, and a Bond Arms USA Defender derringer with .22 Winchester Mag Rifle (WMR) barrel in a left ankle holster. In a waterproof neoprene bag at his feet was a genuine, beautifully functional and fully automatic Chinese A-47 he had acquired from a dying veteran who had smuggled it home from Vietnam. He loved it because of the firepower and because the 7.62 ammo was available anywhere. Buddy thought Big Sally's knife was something to respect, but, remembering Indiana Jones and the turbaned joker with the two-foot sword, he knew it was no contest against his walking armory.

The two were on their way to pick up Konrad Hotchkins, one of BJ's sycophants who managed the latter's sex traffic in the Portland area. They were to pick up Hotch at a little-used beach on Reeder Road at the unpopulated end of the dirt-road artery on 26,000-acre Sauvie Island, one of the largest river islands in the U.S. Two armed guards sat in front of the GMC Yukon Denali, and Hotchkins was in the back seat sedated, gagged, and arms securely duct-taped to his torso. The Zodiac gently ran up the shallow beach and Hotch was transferred into it. The driver, very happy that it was the Hotch on the deck of the Zodiac instead of him, waved goodbye as he and his partner headed back down-island. Buddy expressed disappointment that he didn't get to shoot at anybody, but Big Sally told him to buck up and then headed back down-stream to hook up with My Girl.

Hotch had a problem. A big problem. He had taken charge of a little Chinese-Vietnamese gal that had been shipped down from Canada, not a particular knockout but an innocent-looking youngster nonetheless. She would be a significant money-maker for at least the first year or so since there seemed to be no shortage of johns who were anxious to demonstrate their virility to the pure and defenseless. After it was obvious that she was no longer a first-timer, she could still command an inflated fee as an early adolescent. Later, if some vicious client or drugs or suicide didn't get her first, she might still have some value to BJ as a common street whore who could keep some modicum of income flowing. When completely used up and useless, she would be dropped off somewhere in the middle of nowhere with a *have a nice day*.

Hotch's problem was that he had screwed things up. Literally. Before putting her into the fresh meat escort service, the pimp thought he'd better give the new little one an introductory lesson. Who would know the difference? What he didn't anticipate was the girls' violent reaction. Namely, screaming, biting, kicking, spitting, scratching and generally flailing all over the place. Hotch, not known for his cool demeanor, popped his cork and lit into the girl like a pit bull shaking a rag doll. She ended up with a broken arm, broken ribs, her vagina torn to shreds, and a knife slash across her face from the right eyebrow to the left corner of her mouth. In short, she was a wreck. Which meant BJ's investment was a wreck. And one simply did not do that to BJ.

By 4 a.m. Sally and Buddy had hoisted Hotch to the deck of My Girl. BJ, who had been having a restful night's sleep sandwiched between two bimbos, one a peroxide blonde and the other shaven bald, was awakened per instructions. Once the Zodiac was back on board, My Girl set a course due west on a gentle sea. BJ addressed the captive on the fantail.

"Feeling OK, Hotch?" No comment from Konrad. He didn't know exactly what was coming, but he couldn't really figure any way to get out of whatever it was.

"Cat got your tongue, my man? I'd like to know if you have anything to say for yourself . . . if you can conjure up any justification whatsoever for what you did. Or any way you can make it up to me."

"Hey, Boss. I blew it, I know. But I can . . . I *will* make it up to you," Hotch blurted out as the direness of his predicament started to sink in.

"Will you now?" BJ stated dispassionately. "My low estimate is that the little bitch would have brought in fifty grand the first half year as a newbie and then another fifty the following year as an experienced teen. You got a hundred Gs, Hotch? You figure you can come up with that kind of dough within, say, two weeks? Because if you can't . . . well, game's over."

Hotch simply lowered his eyes and said nothing.

"Besides, even if you handed over the hundred right this very minute, it wouldn't change a thing. I need people I can trust to get the job done, and done right. You flunked this one royally, you big oaf, and I don't give second chances."

Soiling himself and trembling all over, Hotch knew BJ well enough that saying anything else would probably just inflame him. And he didn't want to do that because he'd rather just get it over and done with rather than experience BJ's legendary cat-with-a-mouse games.

"Dress him up, boys," BJ commanded, and they knew

what to do. They un-duct-taped him, put a life jacket on, and secured his hands in front of him with heavy duty zip ties. A rope was passed underneath his armpits and tied in front with a bowline knot and two half hitches. The trailing end of the long rope was affixed to a stanchion on the starboard side of the fantail. Hotchkins was stood at the extreme stern of the fantail while My Girl accelerated to a steady twenty knots. (BJ loved using nautical terms.) Coming face to face with the now-terrified Hotch, BJ said, "Let's see if you can set a new record. The last one went for just over twenty minutes." And he kicked him in the middle of the chest, sending Hotch cartwheeling backwards into the foaming wake.

The rope was, give or take, a hundred feet long, with the man at the end of it being pulled in the middle of the widening wake. The life jacket kept him from deep-sixing, but the contest was to see how long the one being dragged could keep his head above water before the neck and chest muscles gave out to the inrushing water. BJ always delighted in the panicked thrashing of arms and legs as the drowning one fought the buildup of lactic acid that eventually incapacitated muscle movement. When it was evident that the show was over, and he didn't break the record, the waterlogged body was dragged to the ship and cut loose for the tiger sharks, orcas, or whatever. Hotch was now truly swimming with the fishes. Or, rather, in the fishes.

By noon, My Girl was moored off Tatoosh and BJ was sipping a cool Chardonnay while his bimbos massaged his shoulders and feet. The loss of the little girl was no big deal in the scheme of things, but he was sorry to lose Hotch. Yet he couldn't let a lapse like that go unpunished. People would think he was losing control. Big Sally and Buddy were sleeping off some heavy drinking after Hotch had left them, which was fine. They had done their job and they'd get their new orders later in the day. Life was good and a new shipment of itty-bitty bitches was due to leave Da Nang tomorrow.

Chapter 56

June 2005 - Port Townsend, Washington

BJ arranged to meet Gunnar, known to him as Bolo, at a coffee bar in Port Townsend. My Girl was moored at the Port Townsend Boat Haven, but he didn't want to reveal his floating home and work base at this point. There was some definite research to be done, and Bolo had a serious test to pass before BJ would remotely consider him part of the team.

As the ship's captain, BJ showed up looking like a ship's captain: cream colored chinos, blue blazer over a French silk pearl shirt complemented with Mephisto Felix boat shoes. Bolo wore faded black Levi's, a black cotton turtleneck covered by a black Gor-Tex windbreaker, brand new black Nike cross-trainers, mirrored sunglasses and a navy watch cap. Sitting behind BJ was Big Sally looking like, well, a pimp's bodyguard, and Buddy looking like a gangster wearing a bulky raincoat to hide a plethora of firearms that would excite any NRA executive. Since it was late evening when most people had been coffeed-out for the day, there were only a couple other patrons at hand and Bolo had no trouble spotting his quarry. If Tuyen was in fact dead and Gunnar had known it, he would have blown BJ's head off on the spot and plied his luck with the two swine with him. But something deep inside, maybe simply hope, told him his daughter was alive, and he had to keep this world-class child predator alive until he knew one way or the other. BJ was his one hope for locating Tuyen, and once she was found, BJ had no hope of staying alive.

After Gunnar sat down across from him, BJ began the dialogue. "Bolo, I presume."

"You presume correctly."

"Take off your glasses," BJ said.

"I never take off my shades."

"My reputation must not have preceded me," BJ responded. "When I tell people something, they do it."

Bolo stood up and said, "Might have been nice working together, Mr. Whoever-You-Are. I guess my talents will be better used by Billy Dee." And he proceeded toward the door.

He only took six steps when BJ said, “Excuse me, please. Let’s try starting over.”

Pausing for effect and then walking back and sitting down, Bolo said quietly and with steel in his voice, “Maybe you’re used to dealing with retards and cowards, but I’m neither. We talk with that understanding or we don’t talk at all.”

Gunnar was gambling, but he was pretty confident that BJ was seriously interested in eliminating the competition, namely, Billy Dee. And if he thought Bolo could do it, there was a basis for an ongoing discussion.

“I like a man with self-confidence and ability. But you do know, I hope, that either of my associates could end your life with a flick of my finger.”

Drawing back one side of his windbreaker with his left hand, Gunnar gave BJ a peak at his right hand resting on the butt of his Ruger. “Jack, or whatever your name is, if either of them telegraph any hint of movement toward a weapon, I’ll blow their head off before they got their hands out of their pockets. And that would signal the abrupt end of our budding relationship, and maybe your ability to walk out of here as well.”

Nobody talked to BJ that way. On one hand he was mildly affronted, and on the other he respected it. He didn’t get all emotional over confrontations such as this. Not like Sally or Buddy, both of whom would have been ready to explode if they could have overheared the conversation. There was something he liked about this Bolo guy, and he began to get the feeling that if he really could and did take out Billy Dee, a working relationship might just be a consequence that could benefit both of them. But he also knew that he had to be careful. He hadn't lived this long by being sloppy.

After staring at the reflection of himself in Bolo's sunglasses for a few moments, BJ said, "Point well taken, and I assume you've got the will and the talent to back up your words. If you in fact take out Billy, what's your fee?"

"Not asking for money," Bolo replied. "I get rid of him, pair up with you, and move in to control his territory. We'd then have it covered from Canada to Mexico. Word would spread that I was responsible for the early demise of Jord and Billy, and with the help of some of your experienced personnel we'd make it one profitable system instead of two competing ones. You could lend me some people, like your two duty experts over yonder, to help put the run on anyone else who might try to muscle into Billy's shoes. You'd take the north and I'd take the south, but we'd pool resources for our mutual benefit. I figure that's gotta beat losing pimps and bitches in a war with each other. We'd not really be working together, but coordinating recruitment, transport, price-setting, and so on. Plus, any outsiders who might try to move in on our whole coastal operation would face a united front that we'd make invincible."

"This makes some sense. But I need to know who you are."

"Who I am is who you're looking at. My past life is nobody's business but mine. You go with what you see, the results I deliver, and your gut feeling. If that's not good enough, we don't go anywhere."

BJ sensed that Bolo meant business, so he decided to see if they could do business. "OK, Bolo. Let's start with this. I don't know or care how you do it, but you eliminate Billy Dee within the week and we can talk. If it happens, I'll know within hours."

"How do I get ahold of you after Mr. Dee's demise?"

"You don't. Keep the same cell phone number you gave my guy in Tacoma and I'll get a message to you shortly after."

"I'll be waiting," Bolo said.

They both rose and BJ motioned to his goons that everything was cool. BJ extended his arm for a parting handshake, but Gunnar simply turned and walked out the door.

With the information willingly supplied by the now very dead Jord, Gunnar dispatched a message to Billy Dee noting that he was the one responsible for Mr. Sampson's resting in peace. If he wanted to know why and possibly discuss an attractive business proposition, the man who identified himself as Bolo offered to meet. This was a one-time opportunity, and if he wished to take advantage of it he should come to the Martin Luther King Jr. Memorial Grove at the corner of Doolittle Drive and Swan Way across from the Oakland International Airport at 11 p.m. on Thursday. He noted that his rental car would be in the small 17-space parking lot, and he would be sitting at a picnic table just off the left side of the walking path. Billy could bring as many men as he wanted, but he, Bolo, would be alone. The message said he was confident that Mr. Dee would want to participate in a very lucrative addition to his business interests. The venue was picked not only because of the good line-of-sight to the target, but also because of the jets constantly landing and taking off on runways only several hundred feet away. The noise would easily blanket any returning fire from the entourage's unsuppressed guns.

Dee was furious and interested at the same time. He thought it might be interesting to hear what this Bolo had to say before using him for target practice with his AR-15 automatic rifle.

Gunnar's preparations were complete. He had placed a rental car in the parking lot, and positioned a clothed balloon dummy seated at the picnic table with its back to the walking path. He placed himself on the southwest corner of the roof of Swan Way, a three story office building with a direct line of sight to the Memorial Grove parking lot. He cradled a SR-25 sniper rifle with suppressor and ATN Aries MK 410 night vision scope, and a twenty-round magazine filled to capacity with 7.62x51mm rounds. This was his preferred rifle of those included in his firearms crash course, one with which he had fired some five hundred rounds. He thought he would be able to pick Billy Dee out of the bunch, but didn't care if he had to gun down the whole crowd in order to get him.

At precisely 11 p.m. a Jeep Cherokee pulled into the parking lot followed by a forest green Suburban. Four men piled out of the Jeep and placed themselves at the corners of the Suburban. Two men exited the Suburban and, after perusing the lot and southside treeline, sent two of the Jeep guys to recon the picnic table. A few steps onto the walking path, the lead man stopped and held up one hand while pointing with the other to the figure hunched over the table with his back to them. He shouted for the man to not move or he'd take a bullet, and then waved to the Suburban. A man stepped out of the passenger side back door and was immediately surrounded by the four gunmen still in the parking lot. That was Gunnar's cue.

The first shot hit Billy's left shoulder, spinning him around and into the side of the Suburban. One of his henchman stepped in front of him and, not having heard any shot, frantically looked around to see from where it might have come. One of the other three scurried around to the safe side of the vehicle and the remaining two went into a crouched position with guns drawn. Gunnar was as safe as if he were in a steel-plated bunker since they had only a fuzzy idea of from what direction the shot came and, even if they did return fire, their pea-shooter pistols didn't have a chance over the three hundred yards that separated them. The second shot grazed the standing guard's neck and plowed into the back of Billy's head. By now the other two, who had simultaneously exploded the balloon dummy with bullets, ran to the Suburban and the five of them, minus the one who had been grazed and who now lay on top of Billy, surmised that the only reasonable position for the shooter was the office building kitty-corner from them. They blasted away with their .38s and .44s, nary a bullet coming near Gunnar's position.

Gunnar fired ten more rounds into the group, only a fraction of a second between each shot, resulting in two blown windows, a blown tire, and two more wounded men, one with a shattered forearm and another with a waistline flesh wound. He then calmly walked back to the fire escape and made his way down to the ground. He left the car, rented under a different fictitious name and credit card, in the Grove parking lot and retrieved the one rented to Gaar Houtman which he had parked behind The Independent Institute directly to the east. It was an ironic choice since said institute was renowned for researching and informing the public on the roots and rights of American liberty. If Gunnar had known that, he might have wondered why they didn't put some effort into researching and informing the public about the liberty of little girls sex-marketed to demented American males.

As the survivors in the Memorial Grove parking lot manhandled the very dead Billy Dee and their wounded buddies into the vehicles, one of them noticed something stuck under one of the windshield wipers on the rental car: an ace of spades.

Three days later Bolo got a call from BJ.

Chapter 57

June 2005 - Salsbury Point Park, Kitsap County, Washington

"Need one more test to see if this guy's faking it or not."

BJ slung a frown in Buddy's direction. "You really think so? I mean, he did knock off our main competition."

Buddy replied, "Yeah, Boss, but even the fuzz wouldn't 'ev shed no tears over Dee's bitin' the bullet. This Bolo guy, who we really know nutt'n about, could be happy pulling the trigger while coverin' up what he's really trying to do."

"The cops can't do that, Buddy," BJ said. "Granted, he could be a renegade, but there's no way he'd be sanctioned by the authorities."

"Yeah, well, how'd he know so much 'bout you and Billy Dee both?"

"That stuff's public info, pal. Read the papers, ask around the clubs . . . it's not that the cops or anyone else doesn't know what's going on. They just can't get the goods on us."

"Ya' think maybe that's what this Bolo guy's tryin' to do?"

"Your point is well taken, but I don't quite share your skepticism. Maybe one more little job will convince you. Or convince the both of us."

"What'cha thinkin', Boss?" Buddy asked with arched eyebrows.

"Foxtrot."

"Hey, there ya go. We been kicking 'round how to get rid of that bitch anyhows. If Bolo cashes in her chips, it'll solve two problems at once. Maybe."

"We're meeting tomorrow," BJ said. "I'll put the proposition to him and see if he takes it on. If he carries this off with as much enthusiasm and efficiency as Billy Dee then I think we'll be ready for the next step."

It was a bright day that harkened the end of the rainy season and promised a few months of glorious sunshine to nourish the water-primed foliage. Washington wasn't called the Evergreen State for nothing. BJ and Bolo walked side by side at Salsbury Point Park on the north side of the Hood Canal Floating Bridge. BJ had anchored My Girl out of sight off Hansville on the northern tip of the Kitsap Peninsula, and Big Sally had boated him down the coastline to the park in the Zodiac. He still wasn't ready just yet to reveal his floating headquarters. Bolo had been instructed to park in the lot by the small dock that jutted due north like a compass needle. As they strolled along the shallow beach that fronted the entrance to Puget Sound proper, Sal trailed about fifty yards behind. The big guy had demanded that Bolo consent to a frisk before sending him on a walk with his boss. Couldn't be too cautious was one of BJ's mottos.

"So this new job . . . what? This another test?" Bolo said with a hint of irritation in his voice.

"Matter of fact, yes. You got a problem with that?" BJ responded.

"Look, BJ. I've taken care of my end of the business. What more do you want"

"Look, yourself. This *business* is highly competitive and always being chased by the law. A man simply can't be too careful or it could all go up in flames in a heartbeat. I like what I've seen so far, but if you really want in on a life-changing opportunity it shouldn't bother you that I'm cautious to a fault. We're always concerned about being infiltrated by the cops, so to dispel that idea, your doing this little job should put the icing on the cake.

The job, or test, was something no bona fide law enforcement officer would take on. While BJ knew there were some that pushed the line pretty hard, he also knew that this would be too far over the line for a copper.

“So what are we talking about here” Bolo asked.

“There’s this used-up, spent piece of trash who’s starting to cause problems. Kind of like space junk that’s no good for anything, but dangerous as long as it’s still in orbit. Goes by Foxtrot. She pulled her weight for about three years, but meth and booze have spoiled what little she had to start with. Normally we’d just let her fade away, but she’s starting to harass some of our other workers and, worse, shooting off her mouth. One of my boys said that last week she was in a stupor and babbling about going to cops unless we upped her weekly dope supply. Long and short of it is, we need her disappeared.”

“I’m assuming you mean,” Bolo responded, “permanently.”

“Correct. And the sooner the better.” A pause, then, “This something you can do?”

“I thought you were going to come up with something difficult. Tell me when and where and it’s a done deal.”

BJ was a bit surprised that there was no hesitation whatsoever, but it was a good surprise. He knew that terminating a street whore, a so-called victim, was something anyone within any law enforcement agency would not be able to do. Certainly not jump at like Bolo did. “We want her shut up, like, yesterday. This is where you find her.” And BJ proceeded to give Bolo the particulars.

Bolo memorized the information and then said, “This is it, BJ. I take care of this little task for you and we start doing serious business. No more tests. If you’re not convinced after this then we’re done and I take my skills elsewhere.”

“Agreed. And I hope you understand why this extra step. If you were in my position I’d assume you would do the same thing."

Gunnar produced a slight smile and said, "We're on the same page. But I gotta act at least a little bit pissed off about it. As for the job, sounds like fun to me."

If this guy was for real, BJ was impressed. He gave Bolo the info on when and where to get ahold of him after the fact.

"By the way, your big guy behind us missed something," Bolo said. "Tell him to cool his jets and I'll show you."

Curious, BJ motioned to Big Sally that all was OK and to stand fast, and said, "So what's to show?"

Sally had frisked his arms, side torso, beltline, and legs inside and out, but failed to pat the top of his back. The loose turtleneck he was wearing concealed a thin thread around his neck from which a stiletto hung down his back. "Well, if he knew his job," Bolo said while scratching the top of his head, and then like lightening reached down the back of his neck, pulled the knife out and spun BJ around with it pressed against his Adam's apple. Sal fell to one knee as he drew his Glock 9 and aimed it in the direction of the pair, aware that Bolo was fully protected by BJ's body.

After a brief moment, Bolo laughed, turned BJ around and handed him the knife. BJ didn't know whether to pat him on the back or plunge the knife into his heart. Bolo said, "Just a demonstration, my friend. You need to know who you're working with . . . and that once we're in this together that my loyalty can be counted on."

His heart rate moving back toward normal, BJ said, "That was slick. And a lesson. Me and the boys are going to do some serious reviewing of what a pat-down means," glancing sideways at Sally.

“Maybe a good lesson, huh?” And then Bolo abruptly disengaged, walking across the park toward the car lot and saying over his shoulder, “You’ll hear from me within forty-eight hours.”

As he traversed the small field, Gunnar was thinking about the day he would finish the knife job on BJ.

June 22nd, the day after the full moon. But clouds had moved in and at 1:30 a.m. it was black as an inkwell. Gunnar counted three vehicles parked outside Shorty’s Ship Shop on south Cloverdale Street, interestingly, three blocks from the Seattle Bartending College. The regulars called it Shorty’s Shitshop. Shorty tried hard for a nautical décor, complete with his collection of twenty-seven ships-in-a-bottle. He was a beat-up old merchant mariner himself who fantasized about attracting personnel from the many ships that docked in the Seattle/West Seattle port area. As it was, due to his minimal start-up funds, the place was a drag inside and out, and he was just a bit too far from the docks for the visibility and accessibility needed to attract sailors visiting from around the world. Hence, while he kept the doors open, it was a marginal proposition perpetuated by a stream of locals who couldn’t care less about atmosphere as long as the drinks were less expensive than the nicer places that really didn’t want their patronage anyway. Over time it also became an acquisition point between White Center, to which the locals referred as Rat City, and the industrial area in the southern Seattle metro environs. Acquisition being for a cheap piece of ass. It was Foxtrot’s home port.

Gunnar/Bolo had peered through the grimy side window to ascertain that Foxtrot was still in place. Shorty was wiping down the bar, eyeing the clock's steady ticking toward the 2:00 a.m. closing time and dripping cigar ashes behind the filthy rag he was using to simulate cleaning action. In addition to the target, all four other patrons were fighting to stay conscious, polluting the room with world-record levels of collective smoke and nursing watered-down whiskey that, in their state, they couldn't have distinguished from two-hundred-dollar-a-bottle Sullivan's Cove American Oak. Foxtrot was wobbling at one end of the bar trying to decide what to do first, slam the shot of whiskey or guzzle the tiger piss draft beer. She had on a knee-length black trench coat, guaranteed-to-stumble four inch spike heels, and gigantic oblong plastic sunglasses with green-streaked peroxide bangs obscuring the upper halves.

Bolo had parked his car right in front of the door. There were no worries about identification because it was a stolen junker he had bought the day before for a hundred dollars from a meth-head who thought seventy-five would have been nice, and it was just for this one-night use. He wore black head to toe, including the Navy watch cap, but had no concern to cover his face because he knew that with what was about to happen, no one in the place would remember anything but crapping their drawers. His black-market, no-serial-number AR-15, set to fully automatic, was in his right hand, locked and loaded with a hundred-round drum magazine. A 9mm Sig Sauer P225 pistol was tucked in his belt, and he held a cell phone camera in his left hand.

He hit the video record button on the camera and kicked in the flimsy door, tearing the upper hinge out of the doorframe in the process. Before anyone even had a chance to look up from their drinks Bolo started spraying the interior of the dive with the rifle. He aimed roughly six feet high and shattered anything that looked like glass, all the while screaming, "Run, get out, run!" The ensuing pandemonium made the Keystone Cops look like amateurs. Amidst rounds splintering ships-in-bottles, chairs and tables, and the mirror behind the bar, the four drunks jumped up, fell down, banged into each other, and eventually stampeded out through the kitchen door squealing and shrieking as they tripped over each other. Shorty stood stock still, dumb-founded. As the terrified Foxtrot turned to face Bolo, he dropped the AR-15, pulled the Sig Sauer and fired twice directly at her chest. She wheeled and crashed to the floor. Bolo then centered the pistol on Shorty's forehead and said, "Either you beat it out of here now or join the little lady on the floor." Shorty's quick exit brought to mind that he had in fact moved that fast once, somewhere back in his teenage years. Bolo walked over to Foxtrot where the video captured a shot of her face down, inert body on the shadowed floor before he flicked the phone-camera off. Later he took a fifteen-second video clip of stuffing the body along with some rocks in a 55-gallon, heavy-duty contractor plastic bag, and then one last shot of sliding it into the Duwamish Waterway at the South Park Marina.

In the frenzy and fear of the event, no one would have guessed that the Sig Sauer was loaded with rubber bullets. The two shots both knocked Foxtrot down and knocked the wind out of her lungs. As Shorty turned tail and sprinted out the kitchen door, Gunnar ran to the woman and took a short video shot while she was still inert. As she began to moan, he whispered in her ear that she was to not move a muscle if she wanted to live. He then carried her limp body to the trunk of his car, fairly sure that one of BJ's minions might be watching. After coaching a panicked and peplexed Foxtrot, Gunnar, pausing the camera, removed her from the garbage bag before filming its slip into the salty depths. He had also paid a woman's shelter big money to take her in and facilitate a transfer to a sister organization in the Midwest for treatment and rehabilitation.

The shootout at the bar was major local news, and BJ's extensive information network had added details not accessible to the King 5 or Komo 4 locals. Word was that two of the stampeded patrons turned up at emergency rooms with broken or sprained body parts from their hasty escape, and both needed a change of underwear. Shorty himself was proud to publicize that he held his bowels even when seeing Foxtrot buy the farm. He kept to himself the yellow streak that ran down his left pant leg. A stationed observer in the shadows reported seeing Bolo stuff the prostitute's limp body in the trunk of his car.

They met three days later at 4:00 p.m. in the parking lot of Marine Beach Park adjacent to the Port of Edmonds Marina. Gunnar looked at the sailboats gliding over unusually calm Puget Sound and thought of a similarly beautiful day when he, Thanh, and Tuyen had spirited across the South China Sea's protected Da Nang Bay in their Telstar 28 Trimaran. Laugher and love had filled their family life, a life that the man with whom he now walked had a major part in taking away.

This time when Big Sally moved to frisk Bolo, the latter extended his arm with palm out and a don't-even-think-about-it facial expression.

"If you think this is necessary, we're done," he growled.

"Cool it, Sal," BJ said to the frowning bodyguard. "The guy's earned it."

While the so-called *honor among thieves* was a myth, even when you trusted nobody you had to take some risks. BJ wasn't about to jump naked into bed, so to speak, with Bolo, but he needed the man's cooperation and obvious skills to manage what would now be the southern half of his criminal empire. Since he had to work with him, BJ loosened the reigns to a necessary degree, but without throwing all caution to the wind. Time would either confirm and cement the partnership or provide cause to terminate it.

"You move around a lot, don't you?" Bolo commented.

"You know as well as I do," BJ responded, "that staying in one place is an invitation to disaster. Besides, you'll understand even better when you see what I move around in."

BJ had already confirmed that he knew of Foxtrot's demise, but for added emphasis Bolo showed him the video on his cell phone of both the shooting and the dumping of her body.

"I must say you work both efficiently and effectively," BJ exclaimed. "You've got balls showing your face at Shorty's, but then after seeing your handiwork I don't suppose any of them would be willing to finger you in a lineup."

"Not to worry. You will never, and I mean never, find me in a lineup." The steel in Bolo's voice and the fire in his eyes even gave BJ a small tingle. He was beginning to like this guy more and more. "I need to get back south sooner rather than later. So what's it going to be? Are we going to be cooperating or competing?"

BJ put his hand on his new partner's shoulder, and it took every ounce of will power for Bolo to keep from pulling the Buck hunting knife from the belt sheath beneath his jacket and slitting the man's throat from ear to ear. "Let's talk it over at Anthony's Home Port. A great halibut steak in a fine dining establishment is a much better atmosphere to conduct business than a smelly beach." And they walked the seven hundred feet to one of the west coast's finer seafood restaurants.

They talked in generalities in the restaurant, Big Sally sitting watchfully at the bar sipping rum-laced Cokes. Following the meal, BJ took Bolo to the slip in the marina where My Girl was moored. Bolo had seen a Viking 70 before, but had never been on one. As BJ gave him a tour, Bolo expressed appropriate awe and appreciation, stating that he hoped it wouldn't be long before he could acquire something similar. While they were on the enclosed bridge, BJ's cell phone chirped and he walked to the aft portion to take the call, speaking with his back to Bolo. During that interlude Bolo made a show of sitting in the captain's chair, as if he was driving the sleek craft. When BJ returned he found Bolo with a big grin on his face as he said, "I like."

"So do I, but I'm seriously thinking about trading up. Looking at a Leopard ninety-footer if the price is right. This baby's treated me well, but I'm thinking of expanding to both Alaska and Hawaii, which will mean something more substantial and with longer range. When I do, you might be interested in this little honey."

"A boat does seem ideal," Bolo replied. "No address to pin a fellow down and great mobility for a coastal operation."

"I've also taken the precaution of changing the name and registration every other year. Another way to keep the righteous brothers guessing. Right now I'm back to the original. Anyway, let's get down to business."

They spent the next half hour discussing territorial boundaries, human stock acquisition, price setting, and profit sharing. Publicity wasn't an issue since the network of pimps seemed to have no shortage of clients seeking young virgins. BJ had no intention of sticking to any of their agreed proposals if circumstances dictated otherwise, but might as well make it look good for the new kid. The whole thing made Gunnar sick to his stomach, but he put up an admirable front, even playing the hard guy from time to time to flaunt his dirty colors and business acumen.

As part of the tutorial foisted upon Bolo, BJ opened a computer file, adjuring Bolo that it was important to keep accurate track of the pimps under their control and of the monetary flow that each one was supposed to generate. Every now and then one of the minions down the chain tried to either shortchange BJ or go out on his own, his body eventually being found in pieces on some beach or in some alleyway. He pointed out the program used to create the file, offered Bolo a CD with a copy of the pirated system, and recommended that he utilize it for ease of information sharing between them. Of course, BJ had no intention of giving Bolo any real figures, but hoped the latter was gullible enough to pass on his own statistics.

They were in the lower deck office area and drinking limed Perrier on top of the beer that had accompanied the halibut. “Excuse me, I’ll be right out,” BJ said as he headed for the bathroom aft of their meeting room. As soon as the door clicked shut, Bolo jumped to the computer and began reading. He had scanned three pages in thirty seconds when he heard the toilet flush. He returned the file to the page where BJ had left it and quickly returned to his seat on the leather sofa.

While there were certainly no contractual agreements on paper, they took another fifteen minutes to finish up outlining the final details pertaining to their business relationship. BJ gave Bolo his personal cell phone number, one which he said he changed every two weeks but would inform him of the new number each time. Bolo said he thought that was a good idea and indicated that he would adopt the same practice. There was no handshake, but Bolo understood that in BJ’s world to break an agreement such as the one they just made meant meeting Jesus sooner than expected. Bolo told BJ he was heading to the Bay Area the next day and would contact him with developing news within a week or two.

Two weeks was Gunnar’s outside time limit. He figured that’s all he would need to get the information about Tuyen. In fact, a week would be even better. Having no idea where she was or what she was experiencing at this point, haste was a serious concern. But quick action based on careful planning and controlled execution. It was obvious to Gunnar that BJ’s computer files were the nexus for locating his daughter. He knew he might have only one chance to find out what he needed. In his mind, it was a life-or-death chance.

Late that night Gunnar put down on paper, word for word, the information he had viewed on BJ’s computer file.

Chapter 58

June 2005 - Seattle, Washington

With his ear to the door, the man dressed in black, including balaclava, could hear muffled cries within. The Orca Shores was a mid-range motel on Aurora Avenue a bit north of Lake Union. Not really sleazy lodging, but also not an establishment a couple would pick for their wedding night. It was 1:30 a.m., the neighborhood was quiet, and the room was on the backside of the motel. A keycard, obtained from the night clerk who was now bound and gagged on the floor in the staff room behind the reception desk, was quietly inserted in the scan lock. When the green light blinked, the man in black eased the handle down, slowly opened the door and tiptoed into the short entranceway.

A short, pudgy, buck-naked fellow was standing with his back to the door and looking down at the bed. He held a short homemade whip in one hand. On her back, with arms and legs bound to the four corners, was a young girl. She was also naked and had something stuffed in her mouth with a strip of cloth tied around her head to keep it there. She was obviously an adolescent, certainly well shy of legal adult age, slim of body but with a good start on well-developed breasts. There was a terrified look in her mascara-smeared eyes, which were leaking a stream of teardrops. There was also a swollen lump in the middle of her forehead.

Occupied with his captive and intended pursuits, Whipman was not aware that anyone had entered the room. When man-in-black kicked the door shut with appreciable force, the naked guy uttered something between a squawk and a scream and jumped so high he would have hit his head on the ceiling had he been a foot taller. He wheeled around to reveal a beer belly hanging over an undersized penis at half-mast. When the dark figure approached him he gave another squeaky cry and raised the pitiful little whip above his head. A kick to the solar plexus followed by a chop to the back of his neck as he doubled over rendered him motionless on the floor.

The assailant grabbed a blanket from the other bed and covered the trembling girl. As he cut her bonds and removed the gag, he told the youngster in a gentle voice that he was here to rescue her. Wrapping her in the blanket, he carried her to the door, opened it and gave a soft whistle. Another man appeared, who she vaguely recognized, took her and carried her to a vehicle parked behind the row of trees on Winslow Place behind the motel.

Man-in-black went back into the room to complete his task. When finished, he hiked to his car four blocks away and on his throwaway cell phone called the night desk of the Seattle Post-Intelligencer with the necessary information. Within minutes a reporter and photographer were on their way. They beat the cops, who had been called fifteen minutes later, to the Orca Shores. They went directly to room ninety-seven around back and found the door propped open.

"Well, at least the guy's consistent," said the photographer. She had been on two other such calls within the past month.

The pudgy fellow was still naked, but now he was tied spread-eagle on the bed with penis totally flaccid. As it would remain for the rest of his life. As in the previous instances, two shallow semicircular cuts had been made at the base of the penis, severing the dorsal penal nerve in two places, almost guaranteeing that repairing it to a functional status was impossible. This nerve was necessary for an erection, which Whipman would never experience again. The same computer-printed note was duct-taped to his forehead: STAY AWAY FROM THE LITTLE ONES OR THIS WILL BE YOU. The police arrived to usher the news team out of the crime scene just as the photographer snapped the last of her many-angle shots.

The story and accompanying picture, with the unmanly vitals fuzzed out, hit the streets the next morning. It also, of course, went viral on the World Wide Web. Whoever was doing this needed to be stopped, so said the cops. The general populace disagreed, rooting for the urological surgeon as the papers noted that it appeared in every case that the emasculated predators had been preying on little girls. So far the law enforcement establishment did not have a single lead as to who the vigilante might be.

Well, maybe one. The night clerk at Orca Shores said that as the man was gagging him, the former's black windbreaker shifted and he saw what might have been a clerical collar. The interviewing patrolman, a relative rookie who thought he'd heard everything, chuckled and wrote off the comment as from a delusional man in shock. All the clergymen he'd ever encountered had trouble handling a butter knife properly.

Earlier, Tats had been clearly agitated, and this was not normal. That night, around 12:45 a.m., he had found Jed at one of his favorite haunts, an all-night diner which looked like its interior designer was Boris Karloff but had the best breakfast deals in town, buying pancakes and eggs for some raggedly-looking drifter.

"Gotta talk to you, Father Jed," Tats had panted. "Like, right now."

Jed gave the drifter a twenty, patted him on the back and told the fellow where to find him if he wanted help looking for work. He then followed Tats a block down to a deserted urban park where they had their choice of empty benches. "What's up, big buddy?" Jed asked.

Tats had been mining the streets for intel, which was followed by tactical assistance on a couple of night raids. He was solid, trustworthy, generally unflappable, and had values and concerns that coincided with Jed's. But his disturbed countenance this night was because of something personal. Turns out he was involved in a budding relationship with a nurse at Harborview Medical Center. The nurse had an older sister with a 14-year-old daughter who lived in the Capitol Hill area. The daughter was in the rebellious *I'm-my-own-boss* stage, and spent an appreciable time on the streets of the Emerald City . . . without Mom's approval. The girl wasn't slutty, but she dressed that way and consorted with a fair number of gals, mostly older, who were. Tats knew who a fair share of the town pimps were, and it had worried him that one unsavory predator, whose *nom de guerre* was Diamond Jim, had been stalking his girlfriend's niece with dollar signs in his eyes.

Just an hour or so before he had been watching the girl in Occidental Park when Diamond Jim came up to her and initiated an animated conversation. He kept pointing to a Lincoln Continental parked at the curb and she kept shaking her head. Finally Jim grabbed one of her arms, put his other arm around her shoulders, and forcefully guided her to the open passenger door. While her protestations became louder, folks on the street knew better than to get involved. You work the streets, you take your chances. As she was pushed into the car and was about to let out an ear-splitting scream, a lead pipe bashed into her forehead and her world went dizzy.

As all this happened within roughly thirty seconds, Tats' brain was trying to catch up with his eyes. When the synapse-circuit finally closed and he sprinted for the Lincoln, what he got was the unpolished Diamond's .38 Special pointed at his nose. Strong and self-confident, as the Continental started north on Occidental Tats sprinted for his rust-bucket '95 Dodge Neon parked a half block away and then headed east on Washington with the Lincoln's taillights a block and a half ahead. Keeping his distance, he followed it to where it turned northwest on 5th and then to Battery Street where it turned due north, eventually arriving at Orca Shores on Aurora. Not at all sure what course of action to follow, Tats went looking for Father Jed and found him at the second place he tried.

The big guy related what had happened and pleaded to Jed for immediate assistance. He had helped Jed the first two times, always being the lookout and then transporter of the rescued one. He impressed upon Jed the need to act quickly, hoping that they were not too late. Jed jumped in his car two blocks away and they coordinated via cell phones as they sped north. They agreed that the modus operandi for the two previous capers worked well, the only change being that Tats would take the young girl home rather than to a safe house. Unlike the first two, this was a spur-of-the-moment operation which was called for by Tats' chance spotting and the imminent danger to the child.

It worked. No clues were left and news began spreading faster and farther that raping a minor in these environs could cost one the rest of his sex life.

One of the readers of the news was particularly displeased, and set a few things in motion to attempt to ferret out the offending self-appointed vigilante. The reader's name was BJ.

Chapter 59

June 2005 - Seattle, Washington

With steam rising from their mugs of jet-black coffee as the dawn sun struggled to overcome the competing clouds over the city, the two partners against crime sat in Jed's otherwise deserted office/reception center.

"I'm feeling really conflicted, Jed."

"We all gotta do what we gotta do, Mercy. You've

made the case repeatedly that the system leaves uncountable women treading water in an ocean filled with sharks. The *justice for all* slogan looks good on paper, but tell that to all the little girls being repeatedly ravaged with no one coming to their rescue. Well, I'm coming . . . even if just for one at a time. And once I get to BJ it could put a serious dent in the whole west coast industry."

"I know, I know. And I'm not abandoning either the system or your efforts. But you must be able to understand the inevitable emotional bind I'm caught in."

"Of course I do," Jed responded. "And you gotta believe I wrestle with similar issues. I've had forms of this struggle all my life, but as it is I've been pushed over the line."

"I didn't think anyone ever pushed you, Jed."

"OK, let me rephrase that. Circumstances have prevailed on my conscience and emotions. To do nothing is simply to affirm the status quo, and in this case that is simply unacceptable to me. So *pushed over the line* is simply a way of saying that after putting all the weights on the scale, one side went down. Right or wrong, good or bad, God will judge."

"So will the King County Superior Court judge if you end up standing in front of one."

"I'm willing to take that risk, Mercy. You can bail anytime you want."

"I'm on your side, Jed. On the side of the victims of these vicious perps. The only reason I've been doing what I've been doing all these years, including this new twist in tactics, is because of the women, the little girls."

"And you've seen lots more than I have. But viewing

Isis' little daughter's battered body and seeing that terrified teenager strapped to a bed a couple of days ago, and knowing there's scores more caught in the same terrible cesspool . . . I cannot just sit around waiting for the system to get its act together. As I've affirmed many times, I commend you and your colleagues for all that you're trying to do. But given the magnitude of the situation, I'm going to do what I can from outside official channels. And you know I've got my limits."

"I take some comfort from that. Chances are, if I had been in on that last one, the perp would have been carried away sans pecker. So you see, Father Jed, you're a moderating influence on me," she said with a twinkle in her eye.

"We're watching each other's backs, Mercy. You also help me define my limits and exercise some needed self-control. Which leads me to the next question: How are we doing on locating BJ?"

Mercy was about to answer when her cell phone began chirping. Glancing at the screen she said, "Hang a minute. It's Staples." Jed stepped outside to give her some privacy. When he saw her motion him back in, he returned, refilling his mug on the way to the sitting area.

"Just got a partial answer to your question."

"And . . .?" Jed replied.

"Remember this new guy, Bolo?"

"I remember your mentioning that someone with that handle apparently has joined BJ's gang. Don't know much about him yet, I believe you said."

"Well, we now know a bit more. One of our informants found out that he's the guy that blew Shorty's all to hell a couple of weeks ago. Looks like he's an enforcer or something of the sort who's becoming a fixture in the exploitation network. Staples says his guy thinks this Bolo isn't local. Someone told someone else that someone heard Bolo bragging about hits down in Eugene and Oakland not too long ago. I knew about Billy Dee going down in the Bay Area but nothing about Eugene. Turns out the cops were never notified about anything there. But the grapevine says that one of Dee's organizers in Oregon was put down by the same guy."

"Any clue why they'd think that?"

"Pretty strong one."

"Which is?"

"Remember what was found on Shorty's bar with a smiley face drawn on it?"

"Sure. An ace of spades."

"Bingo. Oakland and Eugene . . . same thing. Apparently Bolo's calling card. Like he wants it known who you're messing with."

Jed scratched his chin and took a big swig of his getting-too-cool coffee. "So we want this guy on our radar too, yes?"

"For sure. Since it looks like he moves around a lot, his base of operations probably isn't in our jurisdiction. Plus, this is BJ's territory. I'm guessing they might be working together. Maybe even Bolo taking over Billy Dee's sector. From all appearances, the competition down south might not want to mess with this guy."

"Why wouldn't they just waste him?" Jed asked.

"Most pimps are just pimps. They talk big and act tough, but very few of them are willing to pull a trigger. So guys like BJ and Bolo, that's how they maintain control. If you know someone has no qualms about blowing your head off, most think it's smart to say 'Yes, sir' and cash in on the system for whatever they can."

"OK, so anything else on BJ himself?"

"Just that My Girl seems to be constantly on the move. It was sighted at Edmonds a few days ago but then disappeared in the mist a day later."

"If we could just pin down a location where he stayed long enough for us to get there."

"For *you* to get there, Jed. Don't forget that I'd need a warrant to nab him, and so far all we've got is rumor and speculation. We both know what he's doing, but so far we've got nothing concrete that a judge would sign on."

"Well, good for the judge. I don't need him. After I have a little talk with Mr. BJ, he'll be seriously looking at other business enterprises. Like maybe cleaning toilets at the Black Bar Hotel. In the meantime, our street people need to keep their eyes and ears open for this Bolo."

"Right. I'll keep priming my informants with greenbacks and I'll let you know if we get any leads worth pursuing. If we can get our hands on him for a nice walk in the park, I'm guessing he'll be happy to tell us where we can find the elusive BJ."

As Mercy left for her day's duties, Father Jed's cell phone blared out Bow Down to Washington, the UDub Huskies fight song. It was Tats calling from the emergency ward at Harborview. He was there with his girlfriend and her sister, the latter needing some critical pastoral care. Her fourteen year old daughter, Tatiana, had slit her wrists and was barely clinging to life.

Jed raced for his car.

Jed spent a good share of the day with Tatiana's mother. The girl was in intensive care and they were waiting to see how much damage her oxygen-starved brain might have incurred from the time her heart stopped beating until revived by on-the-scene med techs. She had also lost a fair amount of blood and they were scratching to find enough of her rare blood type, AB Rh negative, to replace it. As late afternoon approached, Jed headed the short distance to his old haunt, the Cathedral Kitchen run by St. James Cathedral in the First Hill area, where a few of the street people from the Pioneer Square neighborhood were generally there for a hot meal. Sure enough, he found Bo Jangles and Tallulah, street mates for quite some time, and had a pleasant meal discussing the advances in developing non-fossil fuel energy sources. Brother Abelard gratefully received Jed's regular fifty-dollar donation after he had thanked the whole kitchen staff for their dedicated service.

On his way back downhill to the Harborview parkade, the UDub marching band again tickled his hip. It was Mercy.

"Some new info, Jed, which might be worth pursuing."

"I'm all ears," he answered.

"Our office picked up a Coast Guard report today which could be an important piece of the puzzle."

She then proceeded to relate that early in the morning a cutter's radar had picked up a container ship with a smaller vessel, both Dead in the Water, southwest of Kunghit Island in the Charlottes. They were some miles west of the fifty-mile contiguous zone that Canada claims, so by U.S. reckoning, in international waters. Attempts at radio contact went unanswered, so the Coast Guard began an approach to see if either vessel was in distress. When the cutter was yet some ten miles away, the smaller vessel fired up and headed at top speed southeast into protected Canadian waters where the Coast Guard could not follow. The container ship set a course for Tacoma and was intercepted by the cutter. The ship captain's story was that the smaller vessel was a private Canadian boat that had lost power and appealed for assistance. It was claimed that one of the ship's engineers helped get it running again. The name of the yacht they provided was not on any of the lists of private pleasure craft in the Canadian Coast Guard's digital inventory. Since there was no probable cause to search the ship, it was permitted to continue its way to Tacoma. The port authorities there had been alerted to keep an eye out for any suspicious activity, and to use drug-sniffing dogs to check the off-loaded containers.

"Was the name of the smaller craft reported?" Jed asked.

"I'll give you three guesses and the first two don't count."

"My Girl?"

"My, you're sharp. You have a college degree or something?" Mercy teased.

"How about the name of the container ship. Did you get that?"

"Indeed I did. It's registered in Indonesia but home port's in Da Nang. Called the *Keindahan.*"

Chapter 60

July 2005 - Tacoma, Washington

It shouldn't be a surprise anymore, but Jed was always amazed at what people would do for money. It was also fortuitous that, thanks to Darrell, he had substantial funds available. In the grand scheme of things, the amount required for his current venture was chicken feed. But not to a Vietnamese seaman who might have previously been making five hundred dollars a month fixing jalopies in Saigon. Being offered the equivalent of five month's pay in one shot for maybe an hour's work would pique the interest of any sane crew member.

The *Keindahan* was docked at Slip #1 in the Sitcum Waterway. Viewed through binoculars from the parking lot of the Port of Tacoma administrative offices, the ship looked rather innocuous to Jed. A simple lower-tonnage container vessel showing its age but apparently still sea-worthy. The fact that it had rendezvoused with My Girl off the coast cast to the winds any doubts about its innocence. The first of Jed and Tats' rescue missions involved a very under-aged Laotian girl, and if this vessel was the one used to transport her for the sex slave industry, he was going to do what he could to disrupt operations. But not being one to initiate action on a target, especially in this situation, without some credible information, his first task was some intelligence gathering.

It was late afternoon when Jed watched a bevy of seamen come down the *Keindehan*'s gang-plank jabbering and laughing as they headed for some long-awaited shore leave. Studying them through the binoculars, he focused on one of the grubbiest-looking ones who, standing with two other companions at a vehicular pickup point, looked like he was waiting for a ride. It wasn't long before a cab pulled up and the three piled in. Jed ran for his car and, in his nondescript little Honda Civic which he was still nursing along with its two hundred and thirty-five thousand miles, fell in behind the cab as it traveled southwest on 11th Street toward the heart of Tacoma. It eventually stopped at the Anchor Down, a non-descript tavern on 6th Avenue, where the three seamen sent the cab on its way and entered the pub. Jed parked on a side street a couple of blocks away and donned his black windbreaker and watch cap.

He gave them a bit over half an hour to down at least a couple of beers and then went in and took a seat on a bar stool from where he could see the seamen in the facing mirror. He singled out the grimy one because of the good chance that he was with the engineering crew. While it wasn't guaranteed, grease on his coveralls and grit-encrusted hands and fingernails pointed toward one whose job entailed working with the propulsion plant. Jed nursed a beer while the three ordered and ate. They were on another round of beers when Mr. Engineer got up and headed toward the men's room. Making sure that the other two took no particular notice, Jed strolled down to the crapper, which was fortunately around a turn in the hallway.

He entered the restroom to find the man washing his hands. Jed said, "*Ban be buoi toi tot.*" The man looked up startled to see a Caucasian saying "Good evening, friend" in his native Vietnamese. Jed continued, "*Ban nói tieng Anh*?" asking him if he spoke English.

Somewhat wary, but also curious, the man said, "Little. No very good."

"OK," Jed replied. "My Vietnamese is not too good either. I need some help."

"No can help you? I go now, thank you."

Jed blocked his path to the doorway with his considerably larger physique, but he strove to appear as non-threatening as possible when he continued. "Please. I have much money for your help."

The man's eyebrows went up. The conversation was moving to an international language understood by everyone. "What you want? How much money?"

When Jed said two thousand dollars in cash, it was as if a jolt of electricity lit up the man's visage. The wariness was not altogether gone, but Jed sensed the man converting the figure to Vietnamese *dong* in his head with an accompanying warm feeling beginning to pervade his whole body. Jed went on to relate that the money would be his if he answered two questions. He told the man that he was asking because the daughter of a good friend of his had been kidnapped in Vietnam and he was trying to find her, and Vietnamese friends told him a container ship was being used to transport girls to the U.S. For added effect, he noted that the U.S. Coast Guard had suspicions that the *Keindahan* had transferred people to a smaller boat several nights before and was preparing to arrest the entire crew. Since the seaman knew much more about the Vietnamese legal system than the one in America, this information initiated a stream of fear alongside the dollar-induced warm fuzzies.

First, Jed wanted confirmation that the *Keindahan* was indeed ferrying human cargo across the seas for transfer to private craft before entering U.S. waters. After placing ten hundred-dollar bills in the man's hand and assuring him that he had no desire to hold him responsible for whatever the captain was doing, the seaman acknowledged the fact, protesting, "No me! No me! Captain do."

As the man stuffed the money into his pocket, Jed said the remainder of the sum would be his for information on the fastest way to get to the engine spaces from the gangplank and what the night security entailed. When the seaman asked, "What you do?" Jed explained truthfully that he simply wanted to disable the ship until his friend's daughter could be found. When he asked and the sailor replied in the affirmative that he was Buddhist, Jed swore to The Awakened One that he would never reveal from where this information came, and committed to memory the route to the engine compartments communicated by the seaman. He showed the remaining ten hundreds to the seaman, the latter's eyes bulging ever greater with each crisp hundred dollar bill, put it into a sealed envelope on which he printed the man's name, Sang. He told him that he would call the bar at noon tomorrow with instructions on where to find it if his information proved trustworthy.

It was Jed's good fortune to choose this particular sailor. Sang hated shipboard life. Two thousand dollars, over forty-two million Vietnamese *dong*, would enable him to return to Vietnam and begin some sort of other new life. He really didn't care what this wealthy white man wanted to do to the accursed boat.

In the early morning pitch-darkness Jed approached the *Keindahan*. The port security patrol had passed the slip and he knew from observation that it wouldn't be back for at least half an hour. Sang had told him that there was only one unarmed seaman on watch at the ship side of the gangplank, and Jed's educated guess was that he would be snoozing. His guess was right, and as Jed vaulted over the waist-high gate he coldcocked the guard into unconsciousness as he sleepily started to rise from the chair that held his dozing body.

Jed's backpack held one pound of the plastic explosive C-4, thirty feet of detonation cord, and several blasting caps with timed fuses. These materials cannot be purchased at the local hardware store, but, as usual, it's not what you know but who you know. A couple of years previously Jed had rescued a sixteen-year-old runaway from the streets and helped her get in a treatment program. In the process he had become friends with her grateful parents who owned a road construction company in the eastern part of Washington. The eternally-grateful father told Jed that if he could ever do anything for him, just ask. Knowing that the company had a shot-rock and gravel pit where they blasted regularly for building materials, Jed had asked for and received the needed explosives. The father's operating principle was don't-ask-don't-tell. Jed was also no amateur, easily recalling the basics in demolition techniques from his Force Recon training.

Jed made his way to the aft engine compartment per the route perfectly described by Sang without encountering any other living thing. He suspected that this would be the case since who would think there would be any threat to a sleeping cargo ship in the sleepy port of Tacoma? Once there, Jed placed two shaped charges. One of the beauties of C-4 was that the elastic material could be molded to cause the force of the explosion in a specific direction. In this case, having no grudge against crew members who were just doing their jobs, Jed did not wish to puncture the side of the ship and possibly sink it, perhaps causing deaths. So he took half of the C-4 and shaped it to blast upward to sever the main propeller shaft, and the other half was positioned to blast into the main diesel engine at the head gasket. The two charges were connected by det cord, which would facilitate virtually simultaneous detonation. He had fashioned a three minute fuse, which he lit off, and ran for the ladder leading topside.

Hiding behind a stack of containers a hundred yards

away, Jed watched the explosion, muffled in the bowels of the ship, rock the *Keindahan* roughly. Within thirty seconds alarm sirens began screaming, and shortly thereafter two port security jeeps screeched to a halt at the bottom of the gangplank as crew members mimicked rats deserting a sinking ship. In the ensuing confusion and growing crowd, Jed threaded his way through the shadowy piles of containers on the storage grounds and disappeared into the industrial complex fronting the waterway.

Jed was fairly sure that this evil ship would be out of commission for quite a while, maybe even scrapped if the repair costs exceeded the appraised worth of the vessel. At the least, a message would have been sent to whoever was running the show on the Vietnam side. Perhaps whoever that was might just get the message and decide to terminate the west coast operation.

Chapter 61

July 2005 - Da Nang, Republic of Vietnam

Boa had not been idle. But for all his efforts over four months he had not the slightest idea who had invaded his kingdom and carved up Lanh. He had quizzed the office staff repeatedly, and one day, mistaking Nhu's fear for purposely hiding information, wrapped his lariat around her neck and came within a few seconds of ending her life. When she did not show up for work the next day and was discovered to have left the city, Boa flew into another rage.

Never mind that he had enough income from other illicit sources to live like a king in his country. In a way he could not have consciously grasped, someone had injured him. Violated him. Beaten him. He felt again like the little boy being viciously abused by his stepfather. And he could not let it go.

Then came the message that the *Keindahan* was dead in the water and possibly a good candidate for scrapping. He went on a rampage felt throughout the city of Da Nang. Police stations were bombed. Restaurants were sprayed with bullets. Cars were set afire. Street prostitutes and business executives were killed. It made no difference to Boa. Everybody in the world simply needed to die, and he'd do what he could to hasten the process.

Duc knew Boa was out of control, but he was not smart or brave enough to counter the tirades. Boa was both his meal ticket and his friend, to whatever degree friendship was a concept to him. So he basically did what he was told and tried to be inconspicuous the rest of the time.

Boa's countryman in the U.S. who had set up the initial connection between him and BJ was not answering the phone number that was used previously, and Boa knew of no other way to contact BJ. The increasingly hotter fire burning within him overwhelmed any semblance of rational thought. In Boa's mind it was impossible to just write off what happened as lost overhead and lick his wounds. Nobody did this to Boa, no matter what side of whatever ocean he was on. Someone needed to do something to right this wrong, and Boa was that someone.

Flashing a bundle of cash that almost made the skipper gag, Boa booked passage on a freighter leaving for the States in two days. He would figure out how to avoid customs and immigration when he got there. He knew that what happened to Lanh and to the *Keindahan* were connected, and that retribution would have to be meted out in America. Justice, or Boa's perverted sense of it, was on the way.

Chapter 62

July 2005 - Seattle, Washington

It came fast and unexpectedly. Up to this point Gunnar had maintained a measure of self-control that held his rage-fueled impulses in check. But walking back to his rental vehicle in the Port of Edmonds Marina parking lot, it took every ounce of will he could summon to keep from returning to My Girl and breaking every bone in BJ's body . . . slowly, one at a time. But he could not speed up BJ's date with Dante until he knew for sure about Tuyen. And BJ might still be needed for that.

The new sense of urgency was engendered primarily by a feeling that if he didn't find Tuyen soon, he never would. This was not a rational thought process, any more than his conviction that his daughter was still alive. He simply felt in his bones that something had to happen . . . and fast. Who knew to what Tuyen had been subjected or was currently experiencing? All Gunnar knew was that he needed to speed things up measurably and immediately.

The computer data that he had hand-printed in his motel room on old Highway 99 made no sense to him. It was some kind of code he could not decipher, but which he felt held a possible key to Tuyen's whereabouts. With a fifteen-hour difference in time, he waited until five p.m. the next day when it was early morning Da Nang time.

"Ted, how goes it?"

"Gun! Where are you buddy? I've been waiting for weeks to hear from you. Where the hell are you?"

"Sorry, friend, but I've been busy beyond words following anything I thought was a lead. I'm still on the west coast working with both local authorities and the FBI," Gun lied.

"Anything at all positive turning up?" Ted replied.

"Yes and no. First off, my situation isn't exactly at the top of their case priority list. Second, the few leads they did follow turned into dead ends and there doesn't seem to be anything hot on the table."

"OK, that's the no. What about the yes."

"That's one of the reasons I'm calling, Ted. I found

this computer printout in a trash can behind one of the suspect's houses. It might not have anything to do with anything, but I've got to check it out, meaning, I need it translated."

"Translated? What language are we talking about?" Ted said.

"No language. It's some kind of code on an Excel table. A stat record of some kind, but I can't make any sense of it. So I thought you might be able to get Mike to crank up his IT skills and figure out what it's a record of. You happen to know if he's had any experience with codes?"

"Not a clue, although I can sure find out. But why don't you just give it to the FBI to decipher?"

"Well, for one thing, it could just be nothing and they'll think I'm meddling when I shouldn't be. Matter of fact, they'd likely be ticked off that I was even rooting through suspects' trash cans. You know how cops are about outsiders keeping their noses out of cop business, and I sure don't want to piss them off."

"That's what you see on the TV shows. I guess it's like that in real life too, huh?"

"Absolutely. But if Mike can make any sense out of the gobbledygook and it looks like it might be helpful, I'll be talking to the men in blue quicker than you can blink."

"Sounds like it's worth a try. How you going to get it to me?" Ted asked.

"I'll scan it into my laptop and send it to you within a couple of hours. Do you think Mike can get to it soon . . . like, today?"

"Probably. We're at a bit of a lull in our projects so I expect he'll be able to jump at it. Especially when I tell him who it's for."

"Again, might be nothing, but I'm anxious to find out. You can send the results to the email address it came from. And, Ted, because of the sensitive nature of this whole business, I'd appreciate it if you keep this between you, me, and Mike."

"Absolutely, Gun. If this has any chance of helping at all, we're on your team. By the way, it's going on four months and some are wondering when you might be coming back. You're missed here."

"Nice to know, Ted. Thanks. San Diego has given me indefinite leave up to a year. I don't expect to stay away that long, but a lot depends on if and what we find out about Tuyen."

"Well, we all wish you well, especially with Tuyen. Maybe getting back to work in another couple of months would take your mind off everything that's happened."

To Gunnar that sounded like Ted didn't realistically expect Tuyen to be found. Which caused bile to begin to rise in his throat. "We'll see. Right now I sincerely appreciate your help with this printout. I'll look forward to the results as soon as someone there can figure it out."

"OK, buddy. I'll do what I can to expedite it. By the way, how are your parents doing?"

"Fine, fine. Well, as fine as possible given what's happened. They like having me this close."

"So check your inbox in, say, eight hours and chances are something useful will be there."

"You don't know how much I appreciate this, Ted. Hopefully see you soon," Gun said without much optimism.

Realizing it had been a while since he'd communicated with his folks, Gunnar whipped off a quick email stating that he was just doing some needed R&R while waiting to hear if law enforcement authorities came up with anything pertaining to Tuyen. Not to worry, he wrote, and indicated that he did not keep a cell phone because of not wanting the distraction. He wasn't sure about the time frame for a visit, but please keep him in their thoughts and prayers.

Gun purposely did not reveal his location, hoping that his mom and dad would simply respect his need for rejuvenating solitude. And he did not phone them because he didn't trust his ability to lie to them without his voice giving him away.

After transferring his handwritten copies of BJ's tables to an Excel document, he saved it to his laptop and emailed it to Ted. An idea had germinated which began to assume more and more validity in Gun's consciousness. It was becoming obvious to him that some help in his quest was getting close to necessary, although it would have to be solicited carefully since he had no desire to face the legal system for his actions once Tuyen had been found. The semblance of a plan began to form, but it would depend on what the document revealed, if anything.

He wasn't all that hungry, but forced down a salad at a local mom-and-pop café before crashing into bed for some much needed sleep. He had read in a book somewhere in his past that sleep was one of a soldier's weapons, so he grabbed what he could when he could. As the light in his eyes dimmed, Gun's fading mental picture was of holding a deciphered document that pointed to exactly where Tuyen was.

Gunnar awoke at 5 a.m., unable to sleep any longer. He figured it to be mid-afternoon in Da Nang, so he fired up the laptop to see if by chance anything had come back from Ted. It had.

In the body of the email Ted explained that Mike wasn't able to figure out what the confusing array of mixed letters meant. But he knew that one of the techs at company headquarters in San Diego with whom he had worked was a retired squid NCO who had done some work with code-breaking for Navy intelligence. Mike emailed the Excel document to him and it took about ten minutes for the fellow to figure out the system. It was a variation of the Caesar Cipher, one of the simplest and most widely known encryption techniques, labeled such because of Julius Caesar supposedly using the method to send confidential messages. To the average Peter, Paul, or Mary, a text would be totally unreadable and, unless the reader was extremely sharp, the coding system difficult to deduce. But to one with even a bit of schooling in encryption techniques, it was easily identifiable and decodable.

Gunnar opened the attachment and couple of sheets of names, dates, and figures stared him in the face. And his face felt on fire. His heart rate and blood pressure both began to spike, and only his steel self-discipline kept him from screaming at the top of his lungs. There, at the bottom of the second page, was the name "Angel." Even though her captors very likely did not know her name, Tuyen, and that it meant "angel," every cell in his body knew that this was a reference to his daughter. There was another name there as well which he did not know. But as God – or the devil – was his witness, he would find out.

"Phone for you, Mercy."

"Who?"

"Wouldn't say. Just that he needed to talk to someone in vice, and you'd want to talk to him."

Curious, Mercy punched her talk button. "This is Officer Mercedes Gutierrez. How may I help you?"

There was silence on the line, although Mercy could hear breathing. She decided to wait it out at least for fifteen or twenty seconds before she hung up. Finally, "I wasn't expecting a woman."

"What? You don't like women? You gay or something?" Mercy spoke with practiced irritation.

"No, no. Sorry. Just a surprise. I need some assistance."

"First, may I ask who's calling."

Another short silence, then, "They call me Bolo."

That sat Mercy straight up in her chair. "Well, Bolo, we've heard you've been lurking around our neighborhoods. I indeed would like to assist you." Although not in the way for which Bolo might be asking.

"Look, I'm trying to help you folks as well. It would be to our mutual benefit to put BJ out of business, so do you want to talk about that or not?"

Mercy's brain was on high processing speed. This could be the break for which they had been looking. "Depends on what you want to talk about."

"You want BJ. I want something else. Nothing's going to happen unless we speak face-to-face. You've got fifteen seconds to tell me if you want to pursue this or not. I'm counting."

A very brief pause. "When and where."

"There's a little sidewalk bistro on Green Lake Drive just at the north end of the lake. It's on the east end of the mall. I'll be waiting for you there at one o'clock. I realize you could bring a posse and try to nab me, but I guarantee that then you won't get your hands on BJ. It's alone or not at all."

"How will I recognize you?"

"I'll have on a Hawaiian shirt and khaki jeans. I'll be at the table closest to Wallingford. And listen, do I have your word that you'll be alone?"

"What meaning does a person's word have in your world?" Mercy asked, regretting it as soon as she said it.

"Ma'am, I'm not what you think I am. I'll let you judge for yourself when we meet, but it has to be just you and me. And it has to be sooner rather than later because this is a matter of life and death."

Something about the caller's voice and earnestness aroused her curiosity and overrode her normal cautionary instincts. Not that she would be cavalier about it, but a drive to Green Lake was the most promising prospect yet in her determination to bring this BJ-whoever down.

"OK. One o'clock, and you have my word that I'll be alone. But this better not be a wild goose chase."

"It's indeed a chase, Officer Gutierrez. And the goose we're after is a wild one. Again, please hold judgment until after we've met. See you in a few hours." And the connection was broken.

Mercy checked her watch and saw that she had about three hours until their meeting. Resisting the impulse to tell anyone else about the upcoming tête-à-tête, she finished about an hour's worth of paperwork and then sent Justin to interview a prostitute admitted to Swedish Hospital who had been allegedly beaten to a pulp by her pimp. She then headed for Green Lake to reconnoiter the meeting place prior to the arranged hour. She wasn't about to go in cold, or first.

At one o'clock, Mercy was obscured in the treeline across Green Lake Drive from the bistro. A couple who occupied the designated table conveniently got up and left at 1:03. Immediately a man wearing khaki jeans and a Hawaiian shirt walked out of the bistro and headed for the table. Mercy didn't have a clear picture at first due to unfocused binoculars and only a profile view of the fellow. When he sat down with his back to the restaurant, Mercy got the glasses in focus and zoomed in on his face.

Mercy thought nothing in the world could surprise her anymore. But what she saw scrambled her brain and weakened her knees. She was looking at Father Jed.

Chapter 63

July 2005 - Seattle, Washington

An oft-used expression when relating a surprise is, *I couldn't believe my eyes*. Which Mercy couldn't. She refocused the binoculars, wiped her eyes, and looked again. She surreptitiously changed location so as to get a view from a different angle. Something was amiss, in more ways than one. Studying the image with her 20x magnification Bushnell glasses, she began to realize that the man in the picture, though appearing identical to Jed, looked appreciably younger by some ten to fifteen years.

It is postulated that everyone has a double somewhere in the world. Whether that was true or not across the board, it certainly was in this case. The man who called himself Bolo could have been Jed's younger brother. And not just sharing a resemblance, but virtually identical in appearance. A waiter brought Bolo a glass of water as he kept scanning the sidewalk for signs of someone looking at him. Mercy kept staring at him through the lenses, eventually making the decision that she was not going to make contact this day. Years of developed cop sense kept prodding the not-everything's-kosher feeling, and there was something she wanted checked out before sitting down with this man.

By 1:30, Bolo's anxiety was at the stretching point. The officer's no-show give rise to his doubts about her veracity. He got up and went back into the bistro, and a few minutes later Mercy observed him coming out of the entrance to Lakeside Place and disappearing into the congestion of people heading west. She reasoned he must have exited the bistro through their back door into the mall. She sprinted across the street to the table on the bistro patio and grabbed the empty water glass from which Bolo had been drinking. She almost missed it, but saw and picked up what was underneath the glass: an ace of spades. Quickly returning to her car in the parking lot on Densmore, she bagged the glass and card and headed for Jed's place.

Arriving at his office, Mercy entered to find Jed on the phone and two ragged-looking female teenagers with soda pops and fries on the well-worn couch. Jed motioned that he'd be right with her and pointed to the coffee maker, holding up his mug with fingers indicating that just a couple of inches would do. She took his mug, added the coffee, and filled a mug halfway for herself. She chatted with the teens until Jed hung up, and he motioned her over to his desk.

"Hey, Mercy. What's going on today?"

"Nothing much," she responded. "Haven't seen you for a few days. Whatcha been up to?"

Glancing at the two gals who were giggling at some private joke, Jed leaned closer and in a near whisper said, "A bit of progress, but now's not the time to tell you about it. Besides, I'm just about to leave to deposit those two runaways in a safe house to wait for their parents. That was just one of the mothers I was talking to."

"Don't let me hold you up. I was just in the area and stopped by to say hi. If you don't mind, I need to use your computer for some research before my next visit. You can lock the door and I'll just pull it tight behind me when I leave if that's OK."

"Of course it's OK. I shouldn't be gone that long so I might even be back before you're done."

"Super. If not, let's try to fit in some time tomorrow. Go, go. I'll be fine."

Jed left with the girls and Mercy made a show of fiddling with the computer for ten minutes or so. When she was sure Jed wasn't coming back for something he might have forgotten, she headed for her car. With Jed's coffee mug in a plastic bag.

It occurred to Mercy that this might be just a little bit

crazy, but not so crazy that she was going to back out. She arrived at Codex Labs on Boren Avenue where Jeffrey, whom she had called from her car, was waiting for her. Codex was one of the primary DNA testing labs in the greater Seattle area, and Jeffrey was one of the owner/managers. He had a PhD in genetics and had been working in the field for some twenty years.

Three years earlier his then-fifteen-year-old son, Otto, had been a spectator at one of his school's football games when a large multi-party fight broke out after the visiting team experienced a humiliating drubbing by the home team Bearcats. Shots were fired, knives came out, and every available cop within ten miles was called to help quell what had become an out-and-out riot. Blood began seeping out of more than one teenager and plaintive cries for help were mixed with the curses and threats still being shouted by juiced-up warrior-wannabes on both sides.

By the time Mercy and Justin had arrived, there were enough law enforcement personnel on the scene that things had begun to simmer down in general, but pockets of angry youth were still attacking one another. Otto was with two buddies who at that point just wanted to quit the area. As they skirted the stadium parking lot looking toward a residential street where they could melt into the darkness, two things happened almost simultaneously. Four toughs from the other school raced out from between cars in the parking lot and knocked down all three Bearcats, the latter identified by their school jackets. The attackers flashed hunting knives and two of the boys were cut, one of them being Otto whose brachial artery was severed just above the elbow. At that precise moment, Mercy's car screeched to a halt fifteen yards from the melee. When Justin fired into the air, two of the knifers bolted back into the packed parking lot but the other two, at his command, froze with their hands in the air.

Mercy, who had seen more than one knife wound in her experience both in prisons and the SPD, yelled at Jeremy's son to lie still while she grabbed the well-equipped first aid kit from behind her seat. Thankful that just the previous week she had checked to make sure all the elements were there, she yanked out the tourniquet and applied it to Otto's upper arm just below the armpit. She told him it was going to hurt like hell but he either had to take it like a man or die like a man. Otto opted for the former. Meanwhile, Justin had cuffed the other two ruffians and called in their location to the coordinating officer on the scene so he could direct one of the ambulances to them. Because Otto's injury was life-threatening, he was immediately attended to by med techs and whisked to the hospital. The docs later told Jeffrey that without Mercy's quick action he could easily have lost his son. From that point on he would have done just about anything for Mercy.

Jeffrey took the glass and mug in plastic evidence bags from her and listened to her instructions. Normally, due to the average processing load and with nothing necessitating warp speed, the results from DNA testing took two to three weeks. Mercy told Jeffrey that speed was vitally important in this case, and he said that he could have the results in two to three days. She thanked him profusely, asking him to not forward the information to the department but to contact her personally and she would come by for it.

Two days later she held in her trembling hands an earthshaking surprise. Struggling to keep her composure,

Mercy headed for the SPD's crime lab to talk to Bruce Springson. Notwithstanding that he was married, Bruce had had a thing going for Mercy for several years, and even though he had become convinced that it wasn't going anywhere serious, he still enjoyed any opportunity to rub shoulders, so to speak, with her. He was the lab rat who made contact with the FBI CODIS unit when needed. This unit managed the Combined DNA Index System (CODIS) and the National DNA Index System (NDIS) to provide support to federal, state, and local crime laboratories with regard to forensic DNA evidence. There was a huge data bank of DNA records that could be searched for comparison with an agency's sample. While some advocacy groups jumped up and down about the right to privacy, DNA profiles from a myriad of sources were funneled into the bank. The FBI being what it is, very few people knew just how extensive the data base was. But due to the volume of information, it was becoming increasingly common for a sample to turn up a match in the system.

Mercy gave Bruce a copy of Bolo's profile and, with her sexiest smile and brushing her right breast against his shoulder, asked if he could get his buddies at the local FBI office to push the data through the national system ASAP, meaning yesterday. It is very important, she whispered. Struggling to hold down the growing bulge in his pants, Bruce panted an affirmative.

In twenty hours she had a name. After several hours of computer research and numerous phone calls to authorities in Washington, Pennsylvania, Indiana and California, she sat confused and dazed. Stating that it involved an active criminal investigation, she asked the National Adoption

Agency in Philadelphia to email her a copy of the history they had related verbally.

Someone else might have pondered the situation for days before taking action. Mercy, who believed that decision-making was a vital part of leadership, was more programmed for coming to conclusions based on information at hand, and then acting on them. She called Jed.

They sat alone late Friday night in his reception center with the door locked, the shades drawn, and the lights low. Mercy was obviously nervous but Jed didn't have a clue as to why. He was hoping it didn't have anything to do with her probing again for some kind of romantic relationship.

Not being one to beat around the bush, she filled two mugs with java and asked Jed to sit down facing her. There was an intensity in her eyes that would light up any man, but the set of her jaw told him that something very serious was about to be communicated.

"You know this Bolo fellow who we've been looking for?" Mercy asked.

"Sure. Right. I'm hearing more and more rumors about his status in the BJ apparatus. Have you got something solid on him?"

"Matter of fact I have. I don't know what to make of it and I'm guessing you're not going to like it."

"I don't have a clue what that might be, but try me," Jed said with a hint of nervousness.

Mercy took a deep breath, looked him square in the eyes and said, "Jed, Bolo is your son."

Chapter 64

July 2005 - Seattle, Washington

Jed's initial reaction was a chuckle, knowing Mercy couldn't be serious. He knew she liked to poke people in the ribs, but his second reaction was that this poke was irritatingly inappropriate instead of funny. It didn't help matters that her countenance and tone of voice in no way indicated that she was anything but serious.

Without a clue as to why she would say something so absurdly ludicrous, not to mention imprudent, he said, “OK, Mercy. I know you meant this as a joke, but I’m not that amused and I kinda think it’s not something to joke about.”

Taking an extra deep breath, Mercy said, “I wouldn’t joke about this, Jed. If you’re willing to listen, I’ll tell you what I found that leads me to this conclusion.”

Knowing that Mercy had undoubtedly jumped to some preposterous understanding based on erroneous information, Jed responded with a combination of trepidation and vexation in his voice, “Go ahead, but be prepared to be dead wrong.”

Another deep breath and Mercy simply said, “Angela Wyatt.”

For the first second or two it didn’t register. Like a bird that flashes by so quickly that one doesn’t have an opportunity to identify the species. This was followed by another few seconds of confusion that Angela’s name would come out of Mercy’s mouth. Then he felt like he had taken a center-chest shotgun blast. There was hardly a day that went by that she didn’t still enter his consciousness at some point, but the only other person in the world that he thought knew of his relationship with her was Darrell. A kaleidoscope of thoughts resembling the ball bearing in a pinball machine being whapped this way and that raced through his mind. He found himself literally speechless.

“This could be hard, Jed, but please stick with me. When I tell you what I discovered, you can figure out what you might want to do with it.”

Jed massaged his forehead and then squeezed the bridge of his nose. All of his background, training and self-discipline didn't seem much to draw upon with this surprise of surprises . . . if, in fact, it was actually true. Only hearing Angela's name made him want to hear the rest. "This is truly unbelievable, but go ahead, Mercy."

"A few days ago I received a call from the man we know as Bolo. He told me that he wasn't what I thought he was, and that he could help us bring BJ down, and that he needed my help with something else. I agreed to meet him at a sidewalk cafe on Green Lake Drive, but hid in a treeline with glasses so I could get a look before actually approaching him. And I saw you. Or someone who looks exactly like you. I'm not kidding, Jed. He was you, although, on closer look, a few years younger. It was so unnerving that I froze on the spot until he eventually left. After watching him disappear down the street, I bolted to the table where he had been sitting and snatched the water glass he'd been drinking from."

As she stopped to gather her thoughts on what she did next, she could see Jed's wheels turning a mile a minute. "The glass gave me two things: DNA from his saliva and his fingerprints. I copped one of your coffee mugs and took it along with Bolo's to a friend who runs a DNA lab here in town. The results, which my friend said was 99.9% sure, revealed father and son. Through a colleague in the department, Bolo's DNA profile was forwarded to the FBI's data bank. Because of security clearances needed for overseas contract work, he was in the bank and the profile confirmed an identity."

Mercy took his hands in hers and continued. "His name is Gunnar Torkelson. He was adopted by a couple in Indianapolis named Sonny and Linn. They still live there. I'm sure none of them have the slightest clue that you exist."

"How did you find all this out?" Jed asked.

"It took a little digging, but once I had the name it was just a matter of time. I ended up talking to the National Adoption Center in Philadelphia, and after they confirmed my status with the Seattle Police Department they passed on information that is normally not shared. They said their records were sketchy but that your name is on the birth certificate. When it was discovered that at the time you were MIA in Southeast Asia and with no other family found, they put the baby up for adoption, hence, the Torkelsons. From there it was easy to track Gunnar's life. I don't know all the in-between details, but he's employed by a company called Linden Technologies which does major reconstruction work in Vietnam. When I called their corporate headquarters in San Diego the only thing they would tell me was that he was on an extended leave of absence and unavailable."

While the evidence seemed incontrovertible, it was a bit more than Jed could process all at once. Mercy let the silence continue for as long as it took. After pacing slowly around his office for some time, Jed finally said, "I don't know what to do with this, Mercy. Even though I'm only his biological dad, *supposedly*, it's tough to swallow that a child I might have fathered could end up doing what he's doing."

"But that's just it, Jed. We don't know what he's doing because I broke off contact and have no way to get ahold of him. All I can do is hope he tries again."

"And if he does?"

"I've got to meet with him. There's something more than meets the eye going on here. A guy doesn't just up and leave a good professional job with an internationally recognized company to start pimping little girls. Now that I'm over the initial shock, and now that we know something about who he really is, I'm dying to have that conversation. After all, it's BJ we want to put out of business, and Gunnar appears to want the same thing."

"I see your point, but I think I should opt out of the proceedings. It's probably for the best that he never even learns of my existence."

"Let's hold judgment on that. First thing is, he has to contact me again. If he does, I'll go see what I can see."

"Well, you go ahead and do whatever. I've got to try and wrap my head around this . . . this . . . revelation. Give me some time, eh?"

"Of course, Jed. I hope you're not upset with me about what I did. These things have a way of working themselves out."

Memories of his wonderful intimacies with Angela raced through his mind, but it had never occurred to him that she had been pregnant when he left for Vietnam. "No. No. It's OK. I'm still just reeling from the shock. Who would have ever dreamed . . . " and his voice trailed off as it couldn't get past the lump in his throat.

"I'll be in touch, Jed, every step of the way." And she gave him a giant bear hug, which he gratefully received.

Mercy wasn't the praying type, at least not on a regular basis. But walking back to her car she did shoot up a dart prayer that Gunnar a.k.a. Bolo would contact her again.

Jed picked up the phone and dialed Darrell's number.

Chapter 65

July 2005 Saturday - Seattle, Washington

Gunnar was feeling confused, pressured, and fighting a rising anxiety level. While in general it seemed so-far-so-good, he knew that it wouldn't take much to either blow his cover with BJ or for the cops to connect various dots and start pursuing him in earnest. Plus that intuitive feeling, fostered only by a premonition not based on any discernable facts, that time was running out kept pushing his blood pressure up.

The crux of the confusion was the lady cop's failure to show at Green Lake. On one hand he wanted to just forget the projected course of action, but on the other he still felt like it was a necessary outreach. Besides, in the police business it was entirely possible that some higher priority concern waylaid Ms. Gutierrez and, after all, she had no way to contact him with an explanation. So, after jettisoning half a dozen good reasons to drop it, two days later and after some procedural rigmarole, he found himself again talking to what sounded like a rather self-assured female cop.

Trying to cover his apprehensiveness with a gruff, irritated tone, Gunnar said, "So I hope you have some good explanation for standing me up."

"Bolo, I sincerely apologize for the no-show. Two minutes after you called we had a major emergency in Pioneer Square that required my presence. I'd have called you back if it had been possible." During the ensuing prolonged silence Mercy disciplined herself to say nothing until Bolo responded.

Finally, "OK. Let's do it."

"Question," Mercy said.

Silence

She asked anyway. "What's in this for you? If bringing BJ down just opens it up for you to take over his organization, I'm not interested."

"Officer Gutierrez, I'll say it again: I'm not what you think I am. It's way too complicated to explain on the phone, so you're either going to take a chance by listening or throw away the possibility of eliminating a walking bucket of scum."

Mercy had every intention of meeting with him, and was simply probing. "When and where?"

"Tomorrow, ten a.m. Go to Waterfall Garden Park at Main and 2nd. There are several cafe tables there and taped to the underside of one will be a phone number. Call it and I'll give you further instructions. If you try to track the number or if I sense there is anybody else covering you, that's that last you'll ever hear from me."

"Bolo, what if . . . " But the line was already dead.

It was a brilliant Saturday morning. Seattle has cloudy, rainy weather so much of the year that when strings of consecutive warm, sunny days arrive they motivate a plethora of crazy notions in a fair percentage of the citizenry. Like inviting strangers to join an impromptu group rendition of the *Hallelujah Chorus*. Or calling the boss to say, "I feel too good to work today," and then strolling the city streets in Speedo beach wear. Mercy did not sing and she kept her clothes on.

Seattle's nearby mountains offer many vistas of waterfalls, but one can experience a twenty-two-foot transcendent waterfall garden hidden in the Pioneer Square area. If you did not know it was there, you would miss it but for the sound of the rushing waters beyond a high wall. Step through a tall gateway at the sidewalk and you are transported to a green and peaceful garden setting of Japanese maples and pots of bright flowers amidst cafe tables and chairs that beckon one to sit and enjoy the quiet, unexpected beauty. The sixty feet by eighty feet Waterfall Garden Park was built in 1977 to honor the workers of the United Parcel Service, which was formed originally as the American Messenger Service in a saloon at that site on 2nd Ave. Mercy wore blue jeans and Brooks Adrenaline GTS running shoes. Her Seahawks polo shirt was tucked in to demonstrate the fact that she carried no sidearm.

As she entered from Main Street she counted six café tables, three of which were occupied. She casually strolled to one nearest the cascade and sat down. The tables were small enough, two chairs allotted to each, that her hand could cover the entire underside from her seat. Except for a hardened piece of gum, there was nothing else stuck there. Mercy rose and meandered around the small park attempting to look interested in the greenery. After several minutes she sat down at one of the other two unoccupied tables and, after a surreptitious examination, came up empty-handed again. Just as she was about to move to the only other empty table, two young men came in arm-in-arm and sat down with their Starbucks insulated mugs. With her frustration level rising, she was about to pull her badge and start giving orders when a mother and teenage daughter at one of the other tables got up and left the park. This time, watching the clock and with no pretense, she went directly to the table, knelt on one knee, and tipped it until she could observe the bottom. Staring at her was an obviously recently placed folded piece of paper taped in place. She carefully pried it off, unfolded it, and found ten hand-printed digits.

After punching the numbers on her cellphone, Mercy hear Bolo say, “It’s quarter after. I was beginning to wonder,”

“I wasn’t the only one in the park,” Mercy replied. “But here I am. What now.”

“Walk south on 2nd Avenue to King. Cross it and enter

the Century Link parking lot on Stadium Place. Keep walking slowly straight toward the stadium and I'll let you know when I see you. What are you wearing?"

"Jeans and a navy blue polo with Seahawks logo. My black hair's in a ponytail."

"Start now. If I don't see you in five minutes, I'm gone."

"How will I . . . " but the connection had been broken.

Mercy half-walked, half-trotted south for the two blocks and then crossed King into the humungous parking lot. There being no game that day, the lot was largely empty except for a smattering of vehicles likely belonging to stadium crew personnel. She made it all the way to the entrance to the stadium itself and stopped, wondering what to do now. Her cell phone chirped.

"Yes?"

"Look back toward King. On the left in the third row, do you see the grey panel van?"

"Yes."

"Walk straight to it and get in the front passenger door and wait." Disconnect.

Which she did, to find no one was in the van. Bolo was in the treeline on the west side of the parking lot watching with binoculars. He waited to see if this officer was playing straight with him or whether other cops surrounded the vehicle. Fifteen minutes later Mercy's phone rang again.

"Looks like you're alone," he said.

"My word is my word, Bolo. Whether I give it to the chief of police or a scumbag drug dealer."

"A guy can't be too careful though," he responded. "Sit tight."

Three minutes later he appeared at the driver's door, opened it and slid in.

Mercy still couldn't believe what she saw. It was Jed twenty years ago, made all the more startling by the fact that Jed looked at least fifteen years younger than his actual age. She pictured adding another twenty-two years to this fellow and she'd be looking at Jed actual.

Sensing something in the way she looked at him, Bolo said, "What? I'm not dressed for the occasion or something?" He was wearing baggy tan cargo pants and the same Hawaiian shirt from several days back.

"You just look a lot like someone I know. An astounding resemblance actually. Maybe I'll introduce you some day. But let's get down to business. What's this all about?"

"First, Officer Gutierrez, you need to know that we're on the same side."

"Interesting," Mercy interjected. "I didn't realize BJ and I were working together." At this point she had a heightened curiosity over just what this character was all about, and tried to keep any animus out of her voice since she didn't want to antagonize him.

"And neither are BJ and I. I don't expect you to approve of my methods, but I have a twofold goal, one of which is to destroy the bastard and anybody associated with him. The man wrecks lives, and mine is one of them."

With her curiosity level now raised to nine point five, Mercy said, "You care to tell me about it?"

"I'll give you the short version, and only because I want you to understand what has brought me to this point. If you don't sympathize, or if you find it impossible to cooperate, we'll go our separate ways."

"I'm listening," Mercy said.

"I'm an American who has been living and working in Da Nang, Vietnam, since 1993. I married a Vietnamese woman, one of the most wonderful people to walk this planet. We had a little girl who will be ten years old in a few days. Her name is Tuyen and if there was ever a gift of God to the world, she was it." Mercy saw his eyes begin to tear up. "Four months ago while I was out of town on a business trip, a gang that specializes in abducting little girls for the sex trade kidnapped Tuyen and murdered my wife. I was able to learn that my little girl was shipped here to the west coast and sold to BJ. Until a few days ago I no idea if she was alive or where she was, but now I have what I believe is reliable information that could lead me to her." Bolo started to say something else, but was overcome with emotion and had to look away.

Mercy let a bit of silence hang as she processed this information. Realizing that they were talking about Jed's granddaughter, she had to take a couple of deep breaths herself. Finally, "I can't believe you're making this up. And I gather that you somehow wormed your way into BJ's organization as a way to try to find your daughter."

"Exactly. I've done some things I don't expect your approval of, but I don't really give a damn. They were actions necessary to get where I am . . . and to find Tuyen. But I can't keep up the charade much longer, which is why I'm talking to you. To get back my little girl I need help."

Call it woman's intuition, cop instinct, whatever . . . but Mercy knew on the spot that his story was the real thing. "Bolo, I can't help but think that any man would feel the way you do. But not too many would be able to pull off what you've done. We've been trying to nab BJ for years, but he is one slippery dude. It's rather amazing that you've been able to dupe him, and if he finds out, you're probably going to end up on the breakfast table next to his eggs. I'm guessing the kind of tradecraft you've been using wasn't part of your day job in Vietnam. How were you able to pull all this over on BJ?"

"I'm a quick study, Ma'am, and when the heat is on, you do what you gotta do."

"Well, you certainly took the right precautions to arrange this meeting. And by the way, let's disburse with the ma'am and officer stuff. Call me Mercy. Everybody else does."

"If you don't mind my saying so, you don't look like the merciful type," Bolo replied.

"Yeah, well, I came by the handle honestly. My full name is Mercedes and my cohorts thought an antithetical nickname might hoodwink some of the foolhardy."

"Well, Mercy, I don't consider myself foolhardy. So can we talk about working together to find my Tuyen or not?"

"Before I can answer that I need you to tell me what you have in mind."

"I've got a hazy idea of how to go about it, but you need to know that along with rescuing my daughter, I want BJ put out of business . . . permanently."

"If talking about the latter you mean within the confines of the law, we're on. I cannot be a party to assassination, but if we can get him off the streets legitimately, I'm all ears. I also have some cooperating allies outside of the department that might be able to help, depending on what you might be planning."

"Look, I'm going at this pretty much by the seat of my

pants. I've got some ideas, but the reason I'm here with you now is that I'm at the point where it feels like I can't do it all by myself."

"Keep talking," Mercy said.

"OK, here's the deal. I have a fairly extensive list of BJ's organization: his pimps, his buyers, even some of his sales. I also have the name of the man who I think has Tuyen, but I need help locating him, and then getting her away without her being killed. To do this we need to draw BJ into some kind of trap. He operates on this yacht named My Girl, but it's always on the move, which is probably one of the reasons you folks haven't been able to pin him down. We need to get it docked somewhere, and then neutralize BJ and his henchmen so I can access his computer for additional info."

"This list of his organization would be a great help in bringing the whole shebang down. You'd be willing to share that with me?"

Bolo pulled some sheets of paper out of one of his cargo pants pockets. "Here's what I got off of his computer, although it's just a short list." Mercy looked at the sheets which had the following portions highlighted:

ILHKUAAO

OPNAAP/WYPQWH	XEPYD	OPWNP ZWPA	IKJPD-HU EJY-KIA	PKPWH IKJPD-HU ZQA
XAWJO/FKA LAJOGA				
	BKTPNKP	03/03	5000	
	NQXU	11/04	4000	

BKN OWHA

JWIA	OKHZ ZWPA	WIKQJP	XQUAN
XQJJU	08/03	150G	WDIAZ OWHWOOE

<u>LNKOLAYPERA XQUANO</u>

“This is nothing but nonsense. What does it tell us?” Mercy asked.

Bolo handed her additional sheets with the same portions highlighted and said, “Here’s the

translation.”

EMPLOYEES

STREET/ACTUAL	BITCH	START DATE	MONTHLY INCOME	TOTAL MONTHLY DUE
BEANS/JOE PENSKE				
	FOXTROT	03/03	5000	
	RUBY	11/04	4000	

FOR SALE

NAME	SOLD DATE	AMOUNT	BUYER
BUNNY	08/03	150G	AHMED SALASSI

PROSPECTIVE BUYERS

AHMED SALASSI

“What the hell? How’d you get from that mess of letters to real words?”

“A fellow who works in the corporate headquarters of my company knows something about decoding stuff and he figured it out. It’s simple as can be once you learn. It’s a variation of what’s called the Caesar Cipher. In this case, for each letter of the alphabet you simply move four letters forward. For instance, for an ‘a’ you go four letters to the right and you get an ‘e.’

For an ‘i’ you go four to the right and you get an “m.’ and so on. Without a program to automatically decode it, which I don’t have, it’s a bit cumbersome but doable. What you have here is the result of the three pages I was able to access from his computer on My Girl.”

“That’s certainly getting it directly from the source. Assuming you weren’t there alone, how were you able to print them out with BJ on the boat?"

"I didn't. He had to make a quick run to the john and I memorized them."

Mercy looked down at the coded pages again. "Wait a minute. There's no way that . . . " and then stopped. Remembering a few similarly remarkable memorizing feats Jed had demonstrated, such as looking at a restaurant menu for thirty seconds and then being able to reproduce it verbally word-for-word, she mentally made the connection. Like father like son.

"Believe it or not. But if BJ knew I had this, I'd likely be swimming around inside some shark instead of talking to you. Take a look at this."

He showed her a particular line in the For Sale column:

BKN OWHA

JWIA	OKHZ ZWPA	WIKQJP	XQUAN
WJCAH	08/03	1 IEH	CWNYEW-ECHAOEWO

and its translation:

FOR SALE

NAME	SOLD DATE	AMOUNT	BUYER
ANGEL	05/05	1 MIL	GARCIA-IGLESIAS

"And the significance?" Mercy queried.

"Tuyen. Her name means angel."

Mercy pondered this for a moment and then asked, "Would her kidnappers have likely known her Vietnamese name and passed on its meaning to BJ?"

"Could be. I have no way of verifying it one way or the

other. All I know is that I'm willing to bet my life that this is her. My problem is that I don't know who this Garcia-Iglesias is. Google that name and you'll be blasted with thousands of possibilities. That's why I need to get back into BJ's system and hopefully find specifics on who and where he is."

The name jogged something in the back of Mercy's head but she couldn't put her finger on it. "Sounds familiar, but then, like you said, there's a ton of Hispanics with that name."

"Which is why we need to get deeper into his computer. BJ hasn't gotten as far as he has by being dumb, and it appears he's a stickler for keeping records of all his transactions. He's got to have more in there on this Iglesias guy."

"And what if this proves to be a dead end?" Seeing his startled reaction, she added, "Sorry, I didn't mean it that way."

"This is what I've got. Sure, I'm grabbing at straws, but this is the best and most obvious straw available. If I don't grab it I'd never forgive myself."

Mercy had some serious questions about how to proceed, but she was interested enough to hear what Bolo was thinking. "So do you have any kind of plan in mind?"

"Matter of fact I do. First, you need to identify as many of the pimps as you can, those listed as 'employees' on the spread sheets, and locate the ones operating in the greater Seattle area. If you can pull in, say, a dozen, fifteen or so, all at once, BJ's going to want to come in to see what's going on. When we locate My Girl, then I get on, hopefully with your help, and go to work on his computer. Since I know his system, I can make short work of decoding his records. I'm betting we'll get the specifics we need on Garcia-Iglesias."

"Bolo, it seems to me that we don't have enough to convince a judge to sign a search warrant for the boat. All we've got are some unfounded suppositions based on stolen computer files, and any judge I know would laugh me out of the office if this was all I offered."

Emotion-pumping thoughts coursed through Gunnar's brain. "Mercy, please! I don't care what any judge does or doesn't do. I need help getting on that boat, legitimately or otherwise."

With her own mind racing, Mercy replied, "Assuming we draw BJ in, how would we find the boat in any event. He can moor or anchor anywhere."

"I know where My Girl is every minute of every day," Bolo said.

"And how in the world . . . " Then she stopped as it dawned on her. "Transponder," she said as a statement rather than a question.

"Correct. I was able to place one on the underside of the dash on the bridge. Using the Micro Systems IRIDIUM Satellite Datalink I've got on my laptop, I can pinpoint its position almost exactly. It shows the speed and compass direction when sailing, and where it is within twenty-five yards when not moving. When BJ comes ashore to investigate, we'll find it stopped at some moorage on the north coast. And then we'll have to move."

Mercy took note of Bolo's use of the term "we" in the conversation. He seemed to be moving on the assumption that Mercy was committing to aid him. She said, "Let me do some research, Bolo. I want to help, but I've got to figure out the best way to do it. I'm certainly not at the point where I want to bring you in, not to mention that I don't have evidence of any specific crimes you've committed, so I've got to keep my conversations with colleagues somewhat masked. I've got a couple of ideas in mind, and there's one fellow in particular that might be able to help. Do I call this same cell number to reach you?"

"No, that phone will be toast as soon as you walk away. But I've got your number, so look for a call from me at 8:00 tonight. If we're going to do this, we've got to move pretty fast. Right now BJ thinks I'm in the Bay Area rebooting Billy Dee's organization, and as soon as he finds out I'm not, he's going to start getting nervous."

"Billy Dee?" Mercy's eyebrows went up. "Was that your hit?"

"No comment. Let's just say I took advantage of an opportunity to gain some of BJ's trust, if that's a concept in his slug-brain. We can talk more about that later, but right now we need to move on My Girl fast." A pause, then, "Do you have kids, Mercy?"

"Nope. Never been married."

"Well, try to imagine that you had a daughter and this happened to you. The standard law enforcement processes aren't exactly going to kick into high gear for one missing little Vietnamese girl, and in the meantime, who knows what hell she's being put through. So please have your phone on at 8:00."

"I'll see what I can cook up between now and then. No promises, but you've convinced me that I have to see what might be done. Call me tonight," Mercy said as she got out of the van.

As she walked by the end of the vehicle she glanced down at the license plate and memorized the number, but she didn't really anticipate that Bolo would be driving it around long after their meeting. He appeared too smart for that. Nevertheless, she had been drawn into the sad saga of his predicament. There wasn't a whole lot of time, but there were several courses of action that needed to be put into motion sooner rather than later if she was going to be part of saving a little girl's life.

Talking to Jed again immediately was one of them.

Chapter 66

July 2005 - Newport Beach, California

Although thinking daily about escape or rescue, Tuyen spent most of her time in studies and forced family activities. Juan Pablo recognized the innate intelligence of his new "daughter," as well as the excellent education she had obviously been given. A telling mark of his character was that thoughts of her former parents and the life she had had with them never crossed his mind. He willingly accepted, not that it made any difference, BJ's explanation that she was an orphan who needed someone to love her. That explanation was all the more ludicrous due to the fact that while BJ knew there was a word *love*, he had no idea what it was to experience it.

Juan Pablo was withholding judgment on whether to enroll Angel in a prestigious private school the coming September. But in preparation for that possibility, he employed a squad of private tutors to both assess her ability levels and foster growth in subject areas where she was deemed deficient in academic skills for her age. In virtually all categories, she demonstrated the knowledge and expertise of an average twelve- or thirteen-year-old. In addition to applying herself diligently to more advanced studies of mathematics and the sciences, she also began Spanish lessons mandated by her doting "father." Having an elementary facility with the language due to Gunnar's carry-over competence from his time in Mexico, and with her inherited capacity for memorization, after three weeks of study she was able to have rudimentary conversations with Juan Pablo in his native tongue. This delighted the man beyond description and convinced him even more that *los dioses* smiled upon him.

Tuyen was never without supervision. The few times she was taken off the grounds of Gloria de Dios she was kept by the side of either Juan Pablo or Adoria. While she was eventually given free run of the estate's walled-in grounds, one of the servants always had her in sight. Even though his inherent distrust of almost everything and everybody dictated hyper-vigilance, the ever self-confident Señor García-Iglesias felt more and more that his precious Angelita was growing in her love for him. Tuyen was an excellent little actress.

Having coaxed the July thirty-first date out of her, the sleazy father-wannabe planned a fabulous birthday party for her. This would be one more way that he felt his love would be indelibly impressed upon Tuyen, nurturing what he thought to be her growing adoration of him. Bands, dancers, food prepared by the best Mexican chef in Orange County, a ten-foot-high pink and chartreuse cake, and a four foot wide piñata were all ordered. Some fifty thousand dollars of presents were selected which included a $20,000 mini Electric Roadster built by the Morgan Motor Company of Worcestershire, England. The top speed of six mph would be perfect for Angel's motoring around the estate. The select list of guests was fashioned to make sure a handful of girls close to Angel's age would be present.

The luxury, the attention, the blandishment, and the catering to her every need or whim worked diametrically opposite to their intended effect. Instead of inducing gratitude and appreciation, the multitude of niceties showered upon Tuyen strengthened her resolve to somehow extricate herself from her captors. Which is exactly how she felt . . . like she was in prison. A nice jail, but nevertheless a jail. She maintained a cheerful outward disposition, knowing it was a necessary prelude to whatever escape plan she would be able to fashion. Although escape would not be needed when her real daddy came to rescue her. That would, she thought, be the best birthday present of all.

Chapter 67

July 2005 - Redwood City, California

After gliding beneath the Golden Gate, the San Francisco-Oakland Bay, and the San Mateo bridges, the *Sea Queen*, owned by the Australian company Outback Oversea Transport but registered in the Marshall Islands under a flag of convenience, slid gently into her berth at wharf number four at the Port of Redwood City. Not something of which the average tourist would want a picture, the medium-sized cargo ship was designed to be functional with no concern for aesthetics. The function on this particular voyage was to convey a full hold of raw gypsum, which had been picked up at the port of Laem Chabang, Thailand, to an American port to feed California's growing appetite for drywall and building plasters. The topside deck was stacked with shipping containers full of leather footwear cheaply produced in Vietnam to be sold at bargain basement prices in west coast big-box stores. The Port of Redwood City was equipped to handle both. The footwear was loaded at Da Nang, which is where Boa had boarded for his sea crossing.

The International Labor Organization had created an identity document for crew traveling aboard seafaring vessels entering another country's designated seaports. This was a universally recognized credential known as a Seafarer's Identity Document, or SID, which replaced the requirement for a crewmember to present an entry or transit visa for shore leave. Every seaman had to possess a SID before being allowed off the ship by the host country. Boa did not have one.

The *Sea Queen* docked late in the afternoon, and within twenty-four hours had divested itself of the shipping containers, and the gypsum was more than half off-loaded. By four bells of the First Dog Watch only a skeleton crew was left for unloading the remaining gypsum. The rest had been verified by Port Security and were out and about on shore leave. Boa had waited patiently until off-loading ceased at three bells of the First Watch. As darkness shrouded the bow of the ship, he shinnied down the forward hawser, made his way to the fence bordering the wharves, and crept silently toward the sentry gate. It would have been possible to either climb or otherwise breach the fence, but Boa's twisted and irrational mind, fueled by his growing rage, drove him to seek some measure of relief with his well-used leather ligature.

In the comfortable night air, the so-called security guard, supposedly protecting cargo on the dock and saving America from unsavory, unauthorized land-of-opportunity wannabees, sat in a canvas camp chair outside of the cramped guard shack. His back was to Boa while he perused an old copy of Hustler magazine and smoked an Egytian Kyriazi Freres cigarette from a tin he had won in an impromptu international poker game the week before. His two double chins would make constricting his windpipe a bit more arduous, but Boa was always up for a challenge. The guard never knew what hit him, and although he outweighed the little Vietnamese by some eighty pounds, the latter's wiry muscles and tenacity brought the guard's life to a turbulent end within two minutes. Boa was feeling better already.

Although nighttime work on the docks was largely suspended, having alien sailors from around the globe coming to and from their ships at all hours made Boa's presence on Seaport Boulevard nothing out of the ordinary. He walked about a mile to the bus stop at Bloomquist Avenue. Having queried the ship's captain about distances and transportation, and having exchanged Vietnamese *dong* for U.S. dollars to the trading sailor's benefit, he waited patiently for a local bus to take him to the Redwood City Transit Center where, at 1:30 a.m., he caught the SamTrans 397 bus for the late night ride to downtown San Francisco. Arriving a little over an hour later at 18th and Market, Boa walked the few blocks to Corona Heights Park and found a comfortable patch of grass in which he dozed while awaiting the sun. With the dawn's early light he arose, found an early morning café for tea and toast, and headed for Little Saigon, some two miles northeast.

Over the years, San Francisco's Tenderloin district had become home to a growing Vietnamese populace. By 2004 over two hundred and fifty businesses in the Tenderloin – tailors, dentists, travel agents, jewelers, restaurants, acupuncturists, doctors' offices and such – were owned by Vietnamese-Americans, The city eventually officially designated as "Little Saigon" a two-block stretch of Larkin where eighty percent of the establishments were owned by Vietnamese. It was here that Boa sought Frankie Nguyen. This was the only name and location Boa had in addition to the unanswered phone number previously used by one of Frankie's underlings. He did not know that the holder of the number had died four months earlier of a massive heart attack. In any event, Frankie was a long-time U.S. resident with ties to both Ho Chi Minh City's crime syndicate and the U.S. west coast mafia. Boa figured that if anybody could put him in touch with BJ, Frankie could.

It didn't take long. The owner/bartender doing early morning setup at the Good Fortune Bar was somewhat reticent at first to become involved. But Boa's scary visage and imposing demeanor motivated a phone call. He instructed the man to tell Frankie that the Ghost Snake was waiting for him. Ninety minutes later Frankie showed up at the bar where Boa obtained the information he needed. BJ's Vietnamese underling in Washington State operated out of Olympia, and Boa was given the contact information. He and Frankie drank on-the-house Gambrinus Dopplebock to their respective successes, and Boa headed for the terminal to catch a bus for the thirteen-hour ride to the capital of the Evergreen State.

Thanks to Frankie's forewarning, Chopper was expecting the call. His birth name was Công, but that seemed to elicit painful memories for too many Americans. Having once been proficient with an AK-47 in his homeland as a teenager, and now with his preferred mode of travel being an immaculately kept 2003 Big Dog bike with a genuine 24k gold metal flake paint job, *Chopper* seemed an appropriate sobriquet. Once a long-past-his-prime Hell's Angels thought he was being cute when he had called the man Chopsticks and ended up with a pair of them shoved halfway up his rectum. Chopper owned a legitimate dry cleaning business, but gleaned significantly more income from operating a string of streetwalkers and call girls in Olympia and on the Olympic Peninsula. Most people unthinkingly assumed that prostitution was largely confined to larger centers like Seattle and Spokane. Little did they imagine that it also thrived in mid-size and smaller communities like Port Angeles and Aberdeen. Querying the National Human Trafficking Resource Center or the FBI Child Exploitation Task Force would reveal the prevalence of the problem in towns like Bismarck, North Dakota; Fort Collins, Colorado . . . and Olympia.

Chopper's influence covered much of the Asian community in western Washington south of Tacoma. By dint of shrewdness and ruthlessness he had established himself as a valuable associate of the venerable BJ. They scratched each other's backs, BJ supplying the product and Chopper managing them on the street. The latter currently had control over half a dozen girls age ten to twelve who brought in significant profits as long as they stayed healthy and maintained that little-girl-virgin look. Because of this, the two dirtbag pimps were in relatively regular contact.

Boa arrived at the Olympia bus terminal mid-morning after a thirteen-hour red-eye night trip up the I-5 corridor. He had picked up a burner phone before leaving the Bay Area which he now used to arrange a meeting with Chopper. After the lunch crowd dispersed, the two Vietnamese men sat together at a waterside cafe overlooking West Bay of Budd Inlet. A combination of camaraderie and wariness characterized their discussion.

"So, tell me why you need to contact BJ," Chopper said. Although he was vaguely aware of Boa's exploits and reputation in Da Nang, he was also necessarily protective of his partner in crime.

Always short on words, Boa replied, "That between him and me."

"I'm afraid," Chopper continued, "that I need to know more before sharing any information about Mr. BJ."

Boa's icy eyes narrowed to barely discernable slits, his cross-face scar pulsated red with blood, and his voice communicated dead seriousness. "What you need to know, asshole, you and BJ in business because me, and unless you want shaking hands with Buddha before breakfast tomorrow, you give me number." That was the longest sentence Boa had spoken within the past year.

Something in the man's aura communicated to Chopper that he was not dealing with an equal, and that Boa had both the mettle and means to carry out whatever he deemed necessary to accomplish his purpose. And he also knew that a portion of his livelihood came from a supply of Asian youngsters provided by BJ who acquired them from . . . probably this fearsome character sitting across the table from him. So he gave Boa the most recent cell phone number he had for BJ. Not offering a dime to pay for their lunch, Boa simply got up and walked away. Something about the whole encounter left Chopper feeling lucky that he did.

Within the hour BJ found himself on My Girl talking on his cell phone, the number of which only a handful of people had access, to Boa. It was with great surprise that he learned that Boa was in Washington State and wanted a meeting sooner rather than later.

"Tell me when and where," Boa growled. "We meet now or our business through."

BJ wasn't sure what this was all about, but Boa's earnestness was evident. BJ also had some amount of concern over possibly losing this lucrative source of income, so he figured compliance was in good order. "I'm happy to meet with you, but can you give me some idea why you needed to make this surprising journey?"

"*Keindahan*," was all Boa said.

"Hey, I heard about that. Not my fault."

"I no care who fault. You Americans make happen. Now you make up for it."

Did the little joker actually believe he was going to pay for the damage to his ship, BJ thought? Best to humor him though. He'd rather not, but if worse came to worst he could simply make him disappear and cultivate another source in Southeast Asia. He had to come ashore in any event to investigate who was giving numerous of his good clients a limp-dick-for-life. So he gave Boa a time and place. After all, as long as Buddy and Big Sally were with him, the little squirt wouldn't be able to try anything untoward.

Boa hung up and something between a smile and a sneer crossed his face. He would be paid back. Money for money. Blood for blood.

Chapter 68

July 2005 - Seattle, Washington

A warm summer late afternoon bathed Pier 57 with red-orange rays of the downward-drifting sun and temperatures in the long-awaited high eighties. A northwesterly breeze off Elliott Bay created a cooling effect appreciated by the tourists enjoying an open-air seafood meal at Fisherman's Restaurant. Mercy and Jed leaned against the railing on the far northwest corner of the wharf, far enough away from any listening ears so as to ensure privacy. They met here because Saturday nights were somewhere between a zoo and a circus at Jed's reception center and they needed time alone. Jed commissioned Tats to hold down his desk and take notes for action upon his return.

"So?" Jed began.

"So I met with Gunnar. He's got quite a story."

"And now we're calling him Gunnar instead of Bolo?"

"Jed, I'm betting a fair share of the farm that he's what he says he is. The Bolo business was only to conceal his real identity from BJ."

Jed was motivated to at least explore further options based on the seemingly incontrovertible facts Mercy had presented and what, over time, had evolved into an implicit trust in her instincts and professional judgments. In addition, Jed was simply not programmed to run away from a problem. And a progeny of the love relationship between him and Angela roaming around Seattle was a problem. "OK, what did you learn?"

Mercy spelled out the whole story, everything: Gunnar's background, what happened to his family, how he obtained BJ's computer data and decoded them, his planting the transponder on My Girl, his competent tradecraft, and his plan to lure BJ ashore. Everything she knew.

"He sounds like an amateur who picked up professional skills in a hurry," Jed said.

"Well, I don't know all the details, and maybe sometime he'll be willing to share them with you. But right now he's feeling tremendous time pressure, both in terms of his Bolo cover being blown and whatever might be happening to his daughter. If in fact this Garcia-Iglecias has Tuyen, who knows what he might be doing with her and for how long?"

Jed's gray matter was working overtime trying to assimilate and process all this information. One side of him leaned toward giving all this over to law enforcement authorities for action, and the other side gravitated toward taking the bull by the horns as was characteristic of his whole life. Leaning over the railing and looking deep into the waters of Puget Sound, he also looked into the deep waters of his soul. He knew what would be the likely pace of the bureaucratic mechanisms, not to mention the lack of legally-obtained sufficient evidence to act in the first place. If Gunnar was indeed his son, and Tuyen indeed his blood granddaughter, it seemed to Jed an abrogation of his moral duty to not assist if he could. Perhaps it was his Ndebele upbringing which imbued his psyche with this value orientation. Perhaps it was the Corps' engrained dictum that you didn't abandon a member of the team. All the factors considered, he subconsciously crossed the Rubicon.

"So what's the next move?" Jed tendered.

"The three of us need to meet and flesh out a plan. You know I can't be involved physically in any independent action you and Gunnar might take, but perhaps I can provide supportive resources on the side while staying within the confines of my sworn oath as a police officer."

"Does Gunnar know about me?"

"No. At least I didn't say anything and my guess is that he never did any serious research to find out who his biological parents are."

"If we meet, would you tell him about me ahead of time?

"I don't think so. It might really confuse things and I think he'd deal with it better finding out from you face-to-face. I sense a growing desperation, and once he learns something of your background and skills I believe he'll be more than happy to accept your assistance. After all, he'll then know that your efforts will be to help recover your granddaughter."

"What about his parents and what happens with me in the mix if and when Tuyen is rescued?"

"Hey, let's not jump too far ahead here. Everyone will find a way to sort all that out, but we've got a situation on our hands that demands immediate action. Both you and Gunnar need to focus on that first rather than trying to figure out what the future holds."

"Is he waiting for your call?"

"He's more cautious than that. I've got no number for him but he's calling me at 8:00 tonight. I told him I had a good resource outside of the SPD, so I'll simply say we're willing to roll on My Girl and getting to BJ's computer. I don't think he'll hesitate meeting with us."

"Where should we meet?"

"Middle of the night at your office. Hopefully there'll be no heart-of-darkness emergencies."

"And there's someone else," Jed added. "Darrell arrives at SeaTac at 9:45 tonight. As well as moral support, he can hold down my office for however long it takes for us to pull off whatever plan we come up with."

"That's super. I know what a strong friendship you have with him, and he'll be a great sounding board for you to bounce thoughts off of as you and Gunnar take some baby steps in your relationship."

Jed marveled again at Mercy's wisdom and aplomb, and his gratitude was increasing for all that she had done leading up to this point. As they headed down the pier back toward her car, he asked her to call him immediately after her conversation with Gunnar. Anticipating the meeting with his maybe-son, the world-wise, tough old Marine's stomach was a butterfly battleground. After Mercy dropped him off, to calm his jangled nerves he changed into shorts and took off on a long run before heading for the airport to pick up Darrell.

Chapter 69

July 2005 - Seattle, Washington

Her cell phone rang at sixteen seconds after 8:00 p.m.

"Mercy here."

Gunnar jumped right into it with no introduction. "We in business or not?"

"If the business you're talking about is taking BJ down, then I'm willing to see how we might cooperate to get that done. I'd also like to involve that fellow I mentioned who could be a definite asset."

"He a cop too?"

"No. But solid as a rock and definitely wants to see BJ put away. I've known him for a long time."

"Is this guy willing to take some risks outside of . . . well, not exactly working with the law enforcement system?"

Mercy knew she was treading on soft shoulders here, but being a risk-taker, she responded, "Bolo, you'll have to judge for yourself, but I have confidence both that he'll want to help you and that you'll want his help."

"OK. But we've got to meet soon. As in tonight."

"My thoughts as well. Jed, that's his name, has a storefront office on south Main. Let's get together there at midnight tonight."

Gunnar wanted to trust Mercy, thought he could trust her. But what was at stake was too high to throw all caution to the winds, so he responded, "Better idea. There's a parking lot on the southwest corner of Yesler and 6th. You pull in there at midnight, park right next to Yesler. The two of you get out of the car and have your cell phone on."

Mercy understood what he was doing. She didn't blame him, and figured that in his shoes she'd probably do the same thing. "OK. Your call. Let's make this work."

"I'll be there. Just keep your cell on." And he was gone.

At precisely midnight Mercy and Jed pulled into the parking lot in his little Honda. The heavens were mostly clear with a few wispy clouds floating on and off the waning gibbous moon. The pair exited the vehicle and waited, Mercy's cell phone in hand. By 12:10 the phone had not chirped and by 12:20 they began to wonder. They had no idea that Gunnar was watching them from his perch on the roof of the King County Metro Transit building. The roof provided a vantage point from which Gun could survey the surrounding streets for SPD cars or other vehicles that looked like they shouldn't be there. If anything looked even slightly suspicious, he would simply hunker down until the coast was clear and then split.

Mercy had second-guessed Gunnar's apprehensiveness and was determined to wait it out. At 12:33 an SPD patrol car pulled into the parking lot, the officer got out and commanded Mercy and Jed to keep their hands where he could see them. Mercy thought, *Holy crap; just what we need.* When the cop recognized who it was, and after a stern admonition from Mercy to be on his way pronto, he exited the scene with appropriate dispatch. Guessing that Gunnar was glassing them, Mercy held her hands out in a shrug and did a three-sixty. Sixty seconds later the phone, set for silence, began vibrating against her hip.

"What was that?" Gunnar inquired.

"Routine check on two suspicious looking dudes. He recognized me and went his way," Mercy responded. "I figured it might give you the jitters, but, Gunnar, I gave you my word and my word is good."

Something about her tone and determination reaffirmed that it was worth taking the risk. "OK. Get in your car, head down Yesler to City Hall Park and pull into one of the parking stalls.

When you see the headlights of a white Chevy sedan

blink twice, take off for your guy's office on Main. I'll follow."

"We'll leave right away. There's parking on the street right in front of Jed's storefront office. We'll open it up and go inside and wait for you. And, Gunnar, on my mother's grave, it will only be the three of us."

After seeing the blinking lights, Jed headed for his office. The middle-of-the-night traffic was almost non-existent and Gunnar kept about a block and a half behind them. After parking, Jed unlocked the office and turned on a corner floor lamp. Mercy stayed on the sidewalk to greet Gunnar, who did a U-turn and parked facing east across from the office. He was wearing black Levis, a dark short-sleeved navy blue shirt, and a Seahawks baseball cap with the bill pulled down low.

"Hey, Bolo," Mercy said. "I don't blame you for being cautious, but it's just Jed and me. I need to tell you something before we go in."

A bit nervous, "OK, what?"

"You're going to be surprised when you see Jed. Please just go with the flow for a few minutes and he'll explain the situation."

"What situation?" Gun replied, ready to bolt.

"It just has to do with who Jed is. You'll understand when you meet. And he is not, I repeat, not a cop."

Gun's mild anxiety was balanced by his curiosity. If Mercy wasn't true to her word, he'd find out in a few seconds. "Lead the way."

When they walked in, Jed was about ten feet away in the middle of the room. The space was semi-dark and his face was in more shadow than light, but seeing him, Gunnar immediately sensed something odd.

"Bolo, Jed. Jed, Bolo," Mercy said.

"Please take off your hat, sir," Jed requested. Albeit hesitantly, Gunnar did so and Mercy hit the overhead light switch.

Time froze. Jed was looking at himself twenty years ago. Gunnar was looking at himself twenty years from now. Even having been forewarned, Jed was shocked to the core. Gunnar was simply stunned into a catatonic stance. Both felt more or less like they were looking into a mirror and neither was sure what to do next. Finally, Jed stepped forward and said, "I'm Jedediah and I think it'd be a good idea for us to have a talk."

Gunnar said, "I thought that's why we're here. But Mercy was right when she said there was a surprise inside."

As Gunnar said "I think I'm glad to meet you," he extended his hand. Jedediah grasped it and for the first time felt the touch of his son. Holding the handshake for somewhat longer than normal, something passed between them. Even through his confusion, Gunnar sensed that something important was up. And some inner sense alerted him to the fact that it would be something good.

Mercy, perceiving their need for privacy, said, "I'm going to give you two fellows a bit of time to get acquainted. I'll be right outside the door to head off any visitors." And she left.

"Please come and sit down," Jed said as he moved to seating directly under the floor lamp. "By the way, there will be a big guy we all call Tats joining Mercy outside on the sidewalk simply to head off any possible late night visitors. But before we figure out the BJ business, there's something I need to explain."

Gunnar did as requested and was affected to an even greater degree when seeing Jed in full light. "Does this have something to do with why we look so much alike?" Gunnar asked.

"Yes it does. I know your real name, and what I'm about to tell you was as big a shock to me as it's going to be to you."

Now Gunnar's curiosity level was off the charts. His mind raced at warp speed to try to imagine what he was about to hear.

"You know, I presume, that your parents adopted you," Jed went on.

"How the hell did you know that?" Gunnar blurted, several antennas going up searching for a signal that wasn't registering on his radar.

"I'll explain that in a minute. But I need to ask you if you have any idea who your biological parents are."

Without taking time to process the probable meaning of the question, Gunnar replied, "All I know is that my biological mother died in the delivery room. My parents told me that her husband went MIA in Southeast Asia and died somewhere over there. I've never felt the need to pursue any additional information."

"Do you know your biological mother's name?"

"Angela something or other. I was told a long time ago and forgot. It isn't really of any importance to me."

"Her name was Angela Wyatt, Gunnar. And I am your biological father."

The brain does interesting things when faced with new life-changing information. If this information portends a crisis, the natural reaction can be to fight or take flight.

New and unexpected data can also cause so many synaptic reactions that inaction is the consequence. Confronted with this statement, Gunnar's mind raced to and fro trying to sort out the likelihood of its veracity and, if true, what bearing it would have on the situation at hand. The fact that Jed mentioned the name Wyatt, which called forth a long-buried memory, and with the physical resemblance – resemblance, hell; he was looking at his double – the rational side of Gunnar's makeup said that this fellow named Jedediah was the real deal. The emotional side was trying to figure out Tuesday from apples.

After a prolonged silence because Jed didn't want to say anything else until Gunnar did, the latter said, "Son of a bitch."

"Not hardly," Jed responded. "She was one of the most wonderful women to ever walk this planet."

"I'm sorry. I didn't mean that. I . . . I just don't know what to say. I'm guessing you believe in the certainty of this revelation or you wouldn't be saying it. But how do you know? How did you find out?"

"Gunnar, it's a long story which I hope to be able to share with you someday. For now, suffice it to say that a DNA match and adoption records are undeniable. Until forty-eight hours ago I didn't even know you existed, and the fact that we're sitting together in this room is a truly miraculous happening. But I want to assure you of one thing. I in no way want to intrude on the relationship you have with your parents. To what degree our relationship might develop in the future remains to be seen, and I will respect whatever your desires are in that regard. From what Mercy has told me, we have a much more pressing concern on our hands at the moment. I believe her name is Tuyen."

The name snapped Gunnar's mind back to the real reason he was here. What might happen in the future between Jed and him could wait. His focus was instantly back on finding and rescuing his daughter, although it did register that, assuming that all this was true, they were talking about Jed's biological granddaughter.

"Before we get to that, what is your last name, may I ask?

"It's Bazo. B-A-Z-O."

"Never heard that as a surname. Where does it come from?"

"It's an Ndebele tribal name from Zimbabwe. It was called Rhodesia when I grew up there. But that's a much longer story for another day. What do we need to do to find your daughter?"

"May I first ask how you think you might be of assistance." Even as he asked this question Gunnar noted that he was talking to a large, perfectly proportioned man in prime physical shape.

"Let's just say that I have a skill set that could be useful in a physical confrontation. I'm a man of peace, but if it boils down to rescuing Tuyen or not, I have no problem with doing whatever it takes to get her back. I've wanted to put BJ out of business for quite some time, but what we've learned about each other makes it much more personal for me. So let's move. Mercy says you have something in mind."

First, with a sense that time was running out, Gunnar felt that he had to take a chance with Mercy and Jed. Second, while he would likely seek later confirmation of Jed's claim, he had a gut-level feeling that he was in fact looking at his birth father. Looking at a painting on the office wall which a street artist had crafted and labeled, he said, "OK, *Father* Jed. Tell me what you think."

Jed invited Mercy in and Gunnar proceeded to outline a course of action.

When Gun left around 3:00 a.m., his dog-tired brain felt like the playing surface for a world championship table tennis match. Thoughts bounced back and forth at what seemed to him Mach 3 speed, and he was having trouble even keeping some on the table. He felt tremendously encouraged by having a team to work with; one that, justifiably or not, gave him some much-needed confidence. But the meeting of his probable biological father was startling, to say the least. It seemed to add several extra ping pong balls to the game. Yet this was not a game; neither his quest to find Tuyen nor the existence of the look-alike that was supposedly his progenitor.

With regard to the latter, he told himself that pursuing a relationship with a man, bio-dad or not, who had never been and would likely not be a part of his future life was not worth much time or effort. On the other hand, what is generally a universal desire to connect with one's biological roots had been awakened and was difficult to simply dismiss. While this was now reality in the flesh that was part of the play, his overriding concern was how it might augment the effort to recover his daughter. The more he thought about it, the more he became convinced that Jed's conviction that Tuyen was his blood granddaughter would result in determined efforts that could only aid his own. He also found not small comfort in the fact that Jed's reaction wasn't simply to call in the cops full-force. Mercy, of course, was a cop, but one who knew both her place within the organization, and also the limits of that same system.

The plan called for communicating at 10:30 the next morning, so Gunnar gratefully took the opportunity for a few hours of sleep. As he drifted off in the rented Malibu stationed in the back of a crowded industrial area parking lot, all other thoughts were blasted off the table save one: *Tuyen, Daddy's coming*.

When Mercy and Gunnar left, Jedediah headed back to his lodgings for a welcome conversation with his old friend, Darrell. They were both tired, but sleep was out of the question until they had processed this new turn of events. After accepting a mug of fresh coffee that Darrell had made, Jed plopped down in the rocking chair with an enigmatic look on his face.

"Feel like telling me how it went?" Darrell prompted.

Jed took a long sip of the hearty brew and then tried to process what had happened with the image of Angela dominating his mental picture. Darrell was sharp enough to simply wait until Jed proffered a reply.

After a time, Jed said, "A lot happening all at once here, my friend. At this point I'm just trying to keep my wits about me and take one step at a time."

"From the little you told me beforehand, I'm guessing whatever might happen between you and this Gunnar is going to be put on hold until the mystery of his daughter is solved."

"Yeah, that's certainly the top priority. If I thought putting BJ out of business was imperative before, the fact that Angela's and my child is in the mix adds another whole dimension."

Darrell responded, "But every child is important. Isn't that why you got involved in this crusade to begin with?"

"C'mon, Darrell. You know I feel that way, but you can also try to imagine what it might feel like to know your own granddaughter is one of the victims. She's not any more or less important than any of BJ's captives, but you know as well as I do that when a personal stake is involved . . . well, something just cuts closer to the bone."

"I'm just playing devil's advocate, Jed. Of course I know that. What I don't want it to do is cloud your judgment."

"About what?"

"About what you might be willing to do to save Gunnar's daughter."

Jed paused, thinking, and then asked, "Can you tell me where you'd draw the line?"

"That's a tough one to answer objectively, but I'll try to put myself in your shoes. My convictions say that I'd resort to the absolute least amount of violence possible, but my emotions say that I'd do whatever is necessary to get the job done. And I believe there's an important distinction between getting the job done, which in this case is rescuing a little girl, and exacting retribution for whatever she's been put through. Gunnar might have a problem distinguishing between the two."

Jed rolled that around in his head for a few moments and then said, "Seems like a lot of the discussions we've had over the years are coming to a head. I guess for me it boils down to the old what's-going-to-do-the-least-harm. I know two wrongs don't make a right, but if I'm forced to pick one or the other I'm going to try to pick the lesser of the two. Taking down some evil men, if that's what it comes to, is the preferable option to letting them continue to sell little girls into sex-slavery, whether it's my granddaughter or not."

Coming at it from another angle in an attempt to plumb the ethical depths involved, Darrell asked what could be construed as a loaded question. "What about Jesus' turn-the-other-cheek admonition? We've also kicked that one around several times over the years."

"Yes we have. And if you remember, we basically came to the conclusion that there was a specific context for those words, and that writing them in stone as an absolute for any and every situation goes beyond the original intent." After a pause, "Let me ask you this, Darrell: would you be willing to tell Tuyen to turn the other cheek?"

"Of course not. She's simply an innocent victim."

"And what choice does she have in any of this?"

"Not much, I'd say. In fact, none at all."

"Right. And there's the difference: I do. And I believe Isaiah was on the same page as Jesus when he said to seek justice and rescue the oppressed."

"I'd have a hard time arguing against that. Listen, you've got my support, Jed, for doing what you have to do, but within the limits of reasonable restraint. You might have to watch Gunnar in that regard."

"I appreciate that, Darrell. It does seem rather propitious that all this came together like it did. Miraculous even. I'll work hard to keep my wits about me, but I'm determined to see this BJ's reign of terror put to an end."

"Again, hard to argue with that. By the way, why is it that you can't just call in the cavalry in full force?"

“No probable cause. That’s been SPD’s problem all along. They’ve got nothing solid on BJ that any judge would issue a search warrant for. All Gunnar really wants is to get his hands on BJ’s computer for more information about who has Tuyen. If BJ tries to make that impossible, that’s when the fireworks might start. But my hope is that we can avoid that.”

“Well, as they say in Tijuana-town, *buena suerte*. Or, in our parlance, God bless.”

“Right. Also, Darrell, I’d be much obliged if you could man the office for a few days. I’m not sure how long this is going to take, but it’d be nice to have you there to field emergencies in the interim. I can pretty much guarantee you that some interesting things will happen . . . and that you’ll enjoy the folks who stumble in and out.”

“No problem. Watching your ministry all these years, I’d be privileged to be part of it.”

Notwithstanding the strong coffee, both men conked out within five minutes of hitting the pillow. Jed still believed in sleep as one of the arrows in his quiver, and three or four hours of it would be enough to top up his battery.

As Jed and Darrell chatted and then slumbered, Mercy began putting her part of the plan into operation. While she would work within the law enforcement structures to which she was committed, her actions would likely lead to consequential circumstances in which she could not in good conscience take part. While she knew that expecting the law of the land to result in justice was often a non sequitur, the oath of office she had taken meant at least trying to make it work. She wrestled a bit with the fact that distancing herself from what was to come could simply be a self-preserving rationalization. But when she thought of Marissa's dead little body pulled from a dumpster or Gunnar's daughter possibly being raped numerous times per day, the mental wrestling match ended. BJ had beat the system long enough. It was his turn to pay the piper.

Chapter 70

July 2005 - Cape Charles, Quimper Peninsula, Washington

As My Girl sailed toward Cape Charles, the meeting place given to Boa, BJ mulled over this new development. Was something else going on here other than the disabling of the *Keindahan*? In fact, no one seemed to have a clue who was responsible for the sabotage of Boa's ship. One of the Tacoma cops acquiring some extra income from BJ as a source of information relayed that there wasn't a single lead to follow. But BJ had been around long enough to deduce that an act of aggression on that particular ship wasn't a coincidence. Someone was likely trying to home in on his territory, if not put him out of business. There was nothing concrete to connect it to Bolo, but BJ's innate distrust of every human being, including his mother, impelled him to keep a sharp and close eye on the newcomer.

Maybe I should just ignore Boa and let the little shit hang out to dry. After all, this is my country, my neighborhood. What could one pissed-off little Vietnamese do against my whole organization? Then again, he was curious. And if whatever troubled Boa could be smoothed over, he would continue to be a supplier of needed goods rather than BJ having to somehow drum up another source. All these thoughts ran through BJ's mind when his cell phone started playing Jimmy Hendrix' "Purple Haze."

"Hey boss, Utah Kidd here," the voice said.

"Thanks for telling me what I already knew," BJ said, looking at the caller ID. "What's so important that you need to bother me on my day off?"

"Somethin' I thought you'd wanna know," Utah responded. "Crackerjack, Red Ball, Mohawk, and a bunch more all been rounded up."

"What do you mean, rounded up?" BJ said with a mixture of anger and apprehension.

"Carted off by the cops. A dozen, fifteen, I'm not sure. All of 'em our boys. Cuffed and stuffed into patrol cars. They missed Wolfman and Frenchy, but somebody's got a list and they're hitting us one by one. I'm on the run 'til we figure out what's going on, and I thought you might be the one to do the figuring."

"Stay cool, Kidd. I'd be surprised if they had anything solid to hold any of 'em for long. But someone's trying to shake us up and I'm damn sure going to find out who."

"OK, boss. You got my number so let me know if I can help."

BJ knew that Utah Kidd could hardly help himself, let alone anyone else, but he replied, "Thanks, my man. I'll be in touch if I need you."

BJ had no way of knowing that Mercy had organized the coordinated several-county raid based on the list Gunnar had given her, many of the names and address on the list already known to her. Her respected reputation, along with calling in a few favors, resulted in the busts that Kidd had reported to BJ. From a legal standpoint it was all exploratory stuff based on "anonymous tips," and virtually all of them would be released with no charges within a couple of days. But the objective was to rattle BJ's cage and bring him ashore to investigate. Which is exactly what it did. Between the *Keindahan* and now this, it seemed obvious to him that, as opposed to busting the odd john and/or whore, a major assault on the very foundation of his business was at hand. Perhaps Boa thought the same thing, or was even the perpetrator. He told Big Sally to make haste for Cape Charles.

Cape Charles was a quiet little community on the western side of the Quimper Peninsula, a small, upside-down boot-shaped extension on the extreme northeast corner of the Olympic Peninsula. The bustling east side of the peninsula, if anything bustled on the Quimper, was the Port Townsend/Fort Worden State Park area. BJ chose Cape

Charles for its more secluded situation, not to mention the open water providing direct access to the Strait of Juan de Fuca. A route of egress for a quick getaway was always a good thing to have at hand.

Under cover of darkness My Girl pulled into a reserved slip at the marina. Gunnar's computer satellite program had the boat's GPS position pinpointed on his computer even as Buddy and Big Sal tied up to the dock.

Since the late July sunset at that latitude wasn't until a bit after 9:00 p.m., Boa had told BJ he would arrive sometime after 10:00. Boa didn't want to be walking around in broad daylight, especially with what he had in mind. His conveyance was an old but serviceable Harley Sportster which Chopper had provided. With some amount of consternation Chopper had heard Boa's voice on the line again, and with some amount of reticence offered the Sportster in light of Boa's promise of enough cash to buy a new one when he returned it. Chopper had done some checking within the west coast Vietnamese crime family and was told, "It would be an excellent idea to aid Boa in whatever way possible, if you know what I mean." Given that, and the promise of cold, hard cash, he gave Boa the bike, directions, and a full-face helmet. He wondered if he'd ever see the bike again, or the cash, but, hey, a fellow's gotta take some risks, eh?

Motorcycles being a primary mode of transportation in Vietnam, Boa had been a rider for many years. He deftly handled the curvy Highway 101 along the east side of the Olympic Peninsula, being careful to stay inconspicuously within the speed limits. By the time he arrived at the Highway 20 turnoff to the Quimper Peninsula, dusk was on its way and he pulled off the road to study the map and memorize the turns on the maze of roads leading to the west side. By 10:15 he had sequestered the bike in a grove of trees bordering a park-like area and proceeded on foot toward the marina. Once there, it took but a minute to identify My Girl as the standout in the small crowd. While there was some noise and movement at the clubhouse a hundred and fifty yards away, there was no apparent human activity on the docks.

When Boa arrived at the short gangplank to My Girl, Big Sally met him. It was like the Jolly Green Giant looking down on Willie Shoemaker. Boa was not intimidated by size, and his aura and demeanor ironically put the big man on edge. Sal escorted the Ghost Snake below decks to the luxurious cabin spaces where BJ waited with a drop-dead gorgeous blonde on each arm. Sally then retreated to his watch post topside.

"Well, well, my friend. It's been a long time," BJ drawled with manufactured pleasure.

"Girls leave," Boa said. "We do business."

Knowing that loquaciousness was not Boa's strong point, BJ smiled at the bimbos and said, "Head down to the clubhouse, girls. Put whatever you want on my tab and don't come back until you get the word." Boa couldn't care less how they wiggled their cute little cheeks as they climbed the ladder to the stern deck.

Once he heard the gals' chattering fade away down the dock, BJ said with a smile, "Please tell me to what I owe the pleasure of this unexpected visit."

"You owe me money to fix *Keindahan*," Boa said with characteristic terseness.

Attempting a lighthearted lilt in his voice, BJ said, "As I said before, Boa, that was not my fault and I do not think it is reasonable to ask me to pay for it."

"It happen here in your America. You want girls, you pay."

BJ expected this threat, and had reckoned that offering the haughty little bastard something would put him off guard as he unfolded his plan. "How much are we talking about?" he asked.

"One million. You pay now."

Playing the game with the endpoint in sight, BJ responded, "Half million. And I think that's a fair offer since, as I've repeatedly said, the damage to your ship was not my fault."

"OK, half million. You pay now," Boa said to BJ's surprise. If BJ had been in Boa's shoes he would have pressed harder for the first figure, especially since the latter controlled the product flow. Then he remembered the relative value of a half million bucks in Vietnam vis-à-vis the U.S., and Boa's quick acceptance made more sense.

"Then we've got a deal. After all, we do need to get the ship sailing again in order to continue doing business. Follow me."

BJ then walked into the humongous master bedroom, pulled aside a curtain, and knelt down to open the safe as Boa stood behind him. As the tumblers slid into place and BJ cranked the handle to open the door, Boa slipped his leather garrote around BJ's neck and, thinking of Lanh, yanked it tight. It didn't really matter to him whether BJ had anything to do with Lanh's death or not. Someone along the food chain was obviously out to get him, and BJ was as good a candidate as anyone. Again, bloodlust was the operative mode rather than any rational thought.

Although the attack was totally unexpected, BJ pulled a three inch custom-made Randy Lee skinner from under his shirt and slashed backwards, managing to open up Boa's midsection. Even though he was shocked and blood poured out, Boa furiously tightened his grip. Normally BJ would have been unconscious in about fifteen seconds and dead in under three minutes. What saved him was Buddy stepping out of the closet to Boa's left and smashing the butt of his S&W Magnum into the side of Boa's head. He went down like a rag doll and lay in an enlarging pool of blood. BJ, gasping for breath, ripped the ligature off, stood up and kicked Boa over onto his back. Gingerly lifting the hem of his shirt, he saw that the knife wound was wide but did not seem to have severed anything vital. The greatest danger was that he would simply bleed to death with no medical attention.

With his typical lack of emotion, BJ told Buddy to zip-tie Boa's wrists behind him and wrap him up with the spread from the king-size bed. He would likely dump him overboard as shark food when they headed back to sea. Before that, he had to investigate what was happening with his pimps and maybe get some clues as to who was attacking their valuable clients. Rubbing the bruises on his throat, he tromped back into the main room for a stiff drink. Early in the morning he would be on the horn to several key players in his organization.

There was nothing to prompt any suspicion that his career might be coming to an end.

Chapter 71

July 2005 - Cape Charles, Quimper Peninsula, Washington

They had been in position since ten o'clock. Jed had dropped Gunnar off on the road just east of the trees that separated it from the marina. Even though the last vestige of twilight had faded into the west horizon, it wouldn't help much if someone spotted him carrying a hard-to-conceal rifle down a peaceful country road. Especially a long-barrel SR-25 sniper rifle with suppressor and night scope. Jed then drove back a mile east and parked Gun's rental car in a deserted little park next to a small lake on Cape Charles Road. He kept to the trees lining the road as he walked back to join Gun. They were concealed in bushes on a small rise overlooking the marina. In spite of the warm, humid night, both were wearing all-black long sleeves and pants with watch caps and blackened faces.

The Cape Charles Marina consisted of three piers and My Girl was at the far end of the center one with bow pointed seaward. A club house, tennis courts, and swimming pool were located at the north end of the facility, approximately two hundred yards from the subject yacht. Numerous other smaller craft filled about three quarters of the available slips, but it was a clear line of sight from where they sat to BJ's boat, their Simmons 600 Laser Rangefinder marking it at two hundred and seventy-four feet. Jed utilized his EOTech X320 thermal imager monocular to scope the entire marina area. While there was no discernable activity on the dock itself, they decided to wait until closer to midnight before putting their plan into action.

They were just settling in for the wait when they heard movement in the same tree line in which they were concealed, Jed guessed some twenty or thirty yards away. They froze, and a couple of minutes later watched a man emerge onto the marina property and head for the center pier. He strode purposefully to the far end and turned to face My Girl. A very large man came across to the dock, spoke briefly with the new arrival, and then escorted him aboard the boat. They disappeared below decks, but the Hulk reappeared in short order and assumed what Jed took to be a sentry position.

Jed and Gunnar waited. And waited. Hulk had gone back aboard for a short time, but then came back to resume his post astern. While they had no idea who the unexpected arrival might be, by 11:45, and with things appearing to be all-quiet-on-the-western-front, Gun said he thought it was time to act. Jed advised waiting fifteen more minutes, to which Gunnar agreed. At midnight Jed donned his ragged coat and wide-brimmed scrubby hat, grabbed his wine bottle, and crossed the beach road to the marina.

As soon as his feet hit the floating concrete dock he started staggering and singing softly with slurred words. Jed would never have passed muster for the Mormon Tabernacle Choir, which was OK since he needed to sound drunk. But he thought his massacre of "The Sloop John B" was passable, although the Beach Boys probably wouldn't agree. As he swayed to and fro, Big Sally, dozing in a stern deck chair, came to a fuzzy semblance of consciousness and looked to see who in the hell was disturbing his dreams of beautiful naked women. When he saw the boozer wobbling toward the end of the dock, his greatest hope was that he would simply topple off singing the curren hit, Totally Underwater, by Shelly Poole. Not so lucky. Almost abreast of My Girl's berth, the plastered idiot fell to his knees and started dry-heaving with great gusto. Thoroughly disgruntled with this intrusion, Sally made haste across the gangplank with the intention of knocking the joker out and stuffing him into the dumpster at the far end of the pier. As he bent over to deliver a blow to the head, Jed put a 9.5 million volt mini stun gun to his neck and hit the send button. Holding it there for two seconds destroyed Sally's mental and physical world, and he fell to the deck with the ability to do nothing other than mimic the old alligator dance moves of the 80's.

A series of swine-like grunts, accompanied by scuffling sounds on the pavement, reached Buddy, who was on the skybridge and a much lighter sleeper. He grabbed his beloved AK-47 and with the illumination from the dock lighting saw what was happening below. At this point Jed had zip-tied the still twitching Big Sal's hands behind his back and stood erect for Gunnar to see. There was enough light for Buddy to put the crosshairs of his custom-mounted scope in the center of Jed's back. His brain told him to begin the slow trigger-squeeze of death, but it stopped short when five ounces of lead passed through it and closed down all circuits. Jed turned just in time to see him crumple to the deck. It occurred to him how close a call that was, and how it was a world-class paradox that his son had just saved his life.

Gunnar joined Jed on the pier in short order. "How long have you been shooting?" Jed asked with discernable admiration in his voice.

"Several months, but I'm a fast learner. I figure I've put some five thousand rounds in targets during that time."

"Hmmmm. When I saw your sniper rifle I thought it must have been considerably longer than that. But whether it was luck or skill, thanks for watching my back." It crossed Jed's mind that maybe there was even something genetic in the use of firearms.

They dragged the subconscious Sally into the shadows, made sure no one on other boats had been roused, and quietly discussed their next move. They knew there was at least one other man aboard in addition to BJ, along with the likelihood of several females, the latter of which BJ was rarely without.

Chapter 72

July 2005 - Cape Charles, Quimper Peninsula, Washington

The bottom trough of BJ's sleep stages was about a quarter of an inch under consciousness. He virtually never went below Stage 1 of non-REM slumber. Therefore when Buddy and his AK-47 hit the deck on the Skybridge, the noise brought him to full alertness in roughly four seconds. By-passing the other bedroom where the inert Boa was wrapped up in a bloody quilt, he tiptoed through the living room, picking up his Glock 9 on his way to the ladder leading up to the bridges. On the enclosed bridge he glanced down at the stern deck and noted that Big Sally was nowhere to be seen. When he called in an almost-whisper to Buddy on the upper level and was greeted with silence, he crept up the ladder just far enough for his eyes to rise above deck level. Even in the quasi-darkness he could see the expanding puddle of blood around Buddy's destroyed head.

While true psychopaths feel little or no emotion, the closest they come to one is fear. Perhaps not the kind of spine-tingling sensation a normal person might experience if, for instance, being charged by a grizzly bear. Rather, varying degrees of apprehension over the possibility of losing control. With Big Sally gone and Buddy out of the picture, BJ felt some measure of control slipping away. The heft of the powerful pistol in his hand gave him a dollop of confidence as he went quietly down the two ladders and stepped through the hatchway onto the stern deck.

He saw movement in the shadow created by the yacht moored diagonally from My Girl, and moved closer to the gunnel for a better look. Squinting, he could make out two dark figures huddled over a prone body which had to be Sal. Not caring who they were and figuring he could claim self-defense, he lined up his sights center-chest on the one holding what appeared to be a big rifle. But he did not get to take the shot because all motor functions cease when one's spinal cord is severed. No sound came from BJ's mouth as he dropped the gun and collapsed onto the deck. Boa remained standing, at least for a few seconds.

Although he had feigned being dead to the world,

Boa was semi-conscious shortly after Buddy cold-cocked him in the bedroom. When his hands were being zip-tied he had purposefully twisted his wrists slightly outward but not enough to be noticeable. This provided a little bit of slack in the ties when he rotated his hands back to a full-facing position. After being wrapped in the quilt and carried into another room, he had truly passed out from lack of blood and a mild concussion. Sounds awoke him in the middle of the night, and with concerted effort, aided by the somewhat-loosened zip-ties, he was able to free his hands. His weakened condition and the severe pain from his abdominal wound had made rolling himself out of the quilt a challenging task. But he did it. He peeked into the main cabin area just in time to see BJ exit onto the stern deck. As Boa staggered across the room he pulled a four-inch blade skinning knife from his boot, something for which Buddy had never thought to check. He followed BJ outside and, as he saw the latter raise his Glock, used every last ounce of strength to plunge the knife into BJ's neck. Shortly after watching Benny Jepson's last twitch, Boa lost consciousness again and fell across him.

Jed and Gun heard the commotion on My Girl some forty feet away. The murkiness of the shaded deck revealed only a mass of something lying in a heap. Jed used his glasses to discover that the clump was two inert bodies.

"Cover me," Jed said, and, pulling his SIG Sauer P320 from a belt holster, began a slow, careful traverse of the dock toward the boat. He was ready to sprint at the first hint of movement or sound. Gunnar started sweeping the yacht and the dock area on either side with the thermal imaging monocular Jed had handed him.

When Jed attained the stern deck and ascertained that the two bodies were disabled, he called out for Gunnar to join him. They cleared the yacht room by room, deck by deck, to ensure no unwanted surprises. Other than the very dead Buddy on the skybridge, they found no one. Gunnar's primary objective was BJ's laptop, which he found exactly where he had last seen it. He also found a miracle of miracles. The computer was booted up and running, with all files open and not requiring a password. For BJ to leave it like that he had to have been either roaring drunk or a gold-medal imbecile. Whichever way mattered not to Gun; the treasure trove of info was staring him in the face.

After seeing the bodies on the stern, Gunnar thought he might find the confirmation he was looking for on the computer. Designating the "find" function for all of the accounting files, he typed in "Vietnamese." Within seconds one of the files that appeared was labeled "Boa." It even included a crude picture, which matched the body on the boat. He knew that name from Lanh. He knew the gutted creep lying a few feet away was the man responsible for everything that happened . . . for destroying his family. Looking at both the picture and the scar-crossed face of the unconscious Boa, Gunnar thought: *You are one ugly sonofabitch . . . and one dead sonofabitch.*"

Gun then inserted a 128GB flash drive into the laptop, copied all the files he could access, and pocketed the mobile storage device. He checked to see that the battery was on full charge, and then confiscated the computer for the trip to Seattle. Looking around at the luxurious pleasure craft, and wondering if Tuyen had ever been aboard, he knew what needed to be done.

Handing the laptop to Jed, Gunnar said, "Please go get the car and I'll meet you on the road in fifteen or so."

"What's the plan?" Jed asked.

"They're all dead except for Big Sally. Let's just leave him tied up on the dock with the message that if we ever see his face again he'll be joining his buddies in hell. I don't care what happens to him. I'll take care of disposing of the boat and bodies."

"Gunnar, you know what you're doing?"

"We both knew what could happen the minute we headed the car in this direction. There's nothing whatsoever to connect us to this time or place, so please just get the car while I take care of this pile of trash. But I'm not going to blow it, if that's what you're worried about. We certainly wouldn't want to damage this beautiful marina and the other nice boats here."

Jed saw the fire in Gun's eyes and heard the determination in his voice. And, yes, he did know what might happen in the quest to find Tuyen. So he took the laptop and started trotting toward the car, wondering what Gunnar might have done if he had resisted.

After seeing Jed disappear through the trees across the road from the marina, the first thing Gunnar did was go to the bridge to familiarize himself with the controls. After learning what he needed, he went back down to the stern deck where he found a fifty-foot section of marine rope in a side locker. He could feel no discernable pulse on Boa, but it wouldn't have mattered to him if he did. Tying one end of the rope to Boa's feet and the other end to a cleat on the stern gunnel, he dragged Boa's body across the gangplank to the dock. He then went back to the bridge, started the yacht's engines, keeping them at low idle, and pushed the gear lever to the forward position. He could feel the craft straining against the lines that held it to the dock.

Back on the stern deck he found a short axe in the locker. Jumping to the dock, he severed first the forward and then the aft lines. As My Girl slowly pulled away, the rope attached to Boa eventually became taut and pulled Boa's body into the dark waters of Discovery Bay. He had set the automatic pilot for a heading of 315°, which put it on a due course for Protection Island. If it missed that uninhabited wildlife refuge, the next stop would be Vancouver Island. In any event, there would be nothing left on the end of the rope.

The two blood relatives said nothing for a good while as they headed back down Highway 101 for Olympia and then north to Seattle. Finally Jed proffered, "How are you feeling?"

"Tell the truth, I'm trying not to feel. If anything, it's hope over what is in that computer. When we find out just who has Tuyen and where she is, then we go to work again. Assuming, that is, that you're still with me."

"Gunnar, I know you don't know me, but you don't have to ask that. The life of your daughter, my blood granddaughter, is at stake here. I just wish she knew we were coming."

A few miles passed before Gunnar responded. Then, "Maybe she does."

Chapter 73

July 2005 – Seattle, Washington

The first blush of the mid-summer day began announcing its arrival with the chirping and trilling of Seattle's menagerie of feathered critters as Jed and Gun staggered from the car to Jed's digs. Exhausted from so few hours of sleep, from the adrenaline spike that always accompanies a risk-filled endeavor, and from the drive back to the city in the wee hours, both were sawing proverbial logs within seconds of getting horizontal. Even though Gunnar could have used twice as much battery-charging, after a mere four hours the subconscious riot of thoughts brought him to sudden alertness. His Zodiac Seawolf told him it was only 8:30 a.m., but he found the makings for coffee, started a pot and went to wake up Jed.

Amidst the thoughts of what they had done several hours before and the need for immediate consequent action, he was still trying to wrap his mind around the fact that somehow his birth father was now involved in all of this. It was his intention to later check in depth the veracity of the claim, but the more time he spent with Jed the more he experienced the paranormal perception that he indeed was the offspring of this man. What that might mean for his future, and how it would figure into the relationship with his parents, would play out later. At present he had a much more immediate concern. And he needed Jedediah's help to deal with it.

They sat in Jed's apartment because there was too much activity at his office for any privacy. Jed mused that perhaps later in the day he would be posting an "Unavailable Until Further Notice" sign on the door. By 9:30 a.m. Mercy had joined the men, bringing a box of sugar-fix donuts and pastries to accompany the fresh pot of java. Jed had told Gunnar about Darrell on the way north, and had made a howdy-see-you-later introduction as they had hit the sack five hours earlier. Sharing the first cup of strong, dark brew with him while Jed performed morning ablutions, Gunnar somehow felt that Darrell's presence lent credence to both the paternal claim and the course of action being pursued. He wasn't thinking about evidence that would stand up in a court of law. More the old gut-feeling phenomenon.

Mercy was, of course, more than a little anxious to learn what had transpired. Jed related the happenings concisely, noting in particular that the only death for which they were responsible was Buddy's, and that this was an act of bona fide self-defense to save his life. It was anybody's guess where My Girl was at present, and Mercy noted that she hadn't heard on any state police channels of a runaway boat being found with dead guys on it. Gunnar hadn't said anything to Jed about My Girl's tow package; no one needed to know. He did note that there was no physical evidence of their having been on the craft, and, due to their watch caps and black face paint, Big Sally wouldn't be able to pick them out of lineup if his life depended on it. Besides, more than likely he felt that his life depended on simply disappearing over the horizon. Mercy related that one of the pimps caught in the dragnet, an ex-con whose last desire in the world was to return to Walla Walla, offered to turn state's witness against BJ in exchange for immunity. But, of course, that was a moot offer now. She guessed that most, if not all, of those nabbed would likely be released later in the day.

Gunnar pulled BJ's laptop out from under the couch on which he had been sleeping and said, "There's got to be something more on this Iglesias guy in here. I know someone in my company who could probably find it, but I'm thinking we should hold this as close to our chests as possible. Is there anybody in SPD who could do this for us? Preferably on the Q.T."

Darrell asked, "Why the Q.T.? Why can't the police

find out where she is, assuming the info is in that laptop, and charge in full force?"

"A couple of reasons," Mercy said. "To begin with, unless we find something much more specific – which I doubt because BJ is, or, I should say, was, no dummy – what we've seen so far wouldn't take a judge fifteen seconds to throw out the window. All we have is the name Angel, which isn't her real name to begin with, and only the buyer's last name, one which only about a zillion Hispanics have. Secondly, if Angel is in fact Tuyen and the buyer handed over a million, it's a sure bet he's got his ass covered with the best paper money can buy. He'll likely have all the proper documents for whatever bullshit explanation he's cooked up for having the little girl with him. And even if they were to be challenged, you can also bet that a gaggle of lawyers would string out the process for who knows how long, with the disappearance of Tuyen probably taking place somewhere along the line. Another complicating matter would be finding out she's maybe located in some other state, which would mean coordinating both interstate police agencies along with the FBI jumping in and . . . well, you can guess how balled up cross-jurisdictional so-called cooperation can get. I really hate to say it fellows, but with the knowledge of the system and the relatively unlimited funds at the disposal of these dirtbags, the chances of rescuing her with conventional law-and-order means is pretty slim."

"Which means," Gunnar cut in, "that if I find out where my daughter is, I'm going to get her NOW, and not wait for some BS bureaucratic process that might or might not happen. And like you said, Mercy, if this Iglesias guy realizes that all of a sudden he's under a magnifying glass, he could make Tuyen disappear forever."

"I'm with Gunnar on this," Jed added. "There's no record of her ever having entered the country, and with Iglesias' resources, he could laugh us out of court and then disappear Tuyen before we even have a chance to prove who she really is. I think we need to ID who this guy is fast, and without him knowing. Then we locate him and do the recon for an extraction."

"Whoa with the Jarhead talk, Jed," Darrell jested. "Us poor civilians might not all understand that military jargon."

Jed smiled and retorted good-naturedly, "OK, how about this. We scope out where she is, develop a plan, and then go get her."

The innocent poke-in-the-ribs brought a momentary, alleviative lightheartedness to what was a deadly serious conversation. Even a small break in the tension was beneficial as all four of them were operating with little sleep and nerves on edge.

"Thinking it over," Mercy said, "there's something else here that's outside the normal."

"We're all ears," Jed responded.

"The data on the initial stat sheets that Gunnar decoded indicates that Iglesias paid a million bucks for Tuyen, assuming that's who Angel is. No prostitute, not even a young one peddled off repeatedly as a virgin, would ever come close to turning a profit on that investment."

"Whoa again," Darrell exclaimed. "You mean she could have been purchased for some other reason than the sex trade?"

"Doing the math certainly says so," Mercy responded.

"Like what?" Jed asked.

"The question of the hour, isn't it?" said Mercy. "Maybe identifying the perp will give us a clue."

Gunnar, who had been silent during the last exchange, said, "Which is what we have to do, like, yesterday."

"To answer your question of a few minutes ago, Gunnar, yes I have a pretty good relationship with the IT forensics guy in our department. In fact, he owes me a favor. As soon as we're finished here I'll see if he's available to do some digging for us in that laptop."

"I trust you'll impress on him the urgency of the situation," replied Gunnar.

"Gun, you haven't seen Mercy turn on the charm. She's irresistible," Jed chimed in.

The way Jed looked at her caused her a momentary blush, but she answered, "You can bet a fair chunk of change that if there's anything in there to find, we'll know by sundown."

"Thanks," said Gunnar. "And here's what I'm going to do. I copied all the files I could find onto a flash drive. Forget what I said a minute ago about not going outside the system. Our computer guru – *our* being my company, LinTech – is in San Diego. He's helped me out some already, and knowing my situation I'm sure he'll drop whatever he's doing to see what he can find. Having two guys working on it doubles the chance of someone turning up what we need."

"And when we get a location," Jed offered, "we'll have to do some serious reconnaissance before forming a plan. Gunnar and I will talk about what might be needed for that depending on time and distance. I mean, she could be anywhere in the country or, God forbid, on the other side of the globe."

As soon as he said the last part, Jed wished he hadn't. Gun didn't need any negative thinking at this point. His hope meter was hitting the high mark and Jed didn't want to do anything to diffuse it. But at the same time he wanted to stay close to him as a control, or at least moderating, element. He'd seen too many men panic under pressure, and he hoped he could exert enough confidence and influence to keep the father from rushing in pell-mell and precipitating a situation where either he or his daughter, or both, got hurt. Jed still retained enough of his knowledge and skills to plan, prepare, and then execute in a way most likely leading to success. For these reasons, Jed was going to be right by Gunnar's side in any advance recon they would be doing prior to an actual rescue operation. It did boost his confidence somewhat when he marveled at his son's – *Did I really think that? My son?* – acquired abilities and what he had accomplished thus far.

"Well, let's get to work," Jed went on. "Darrell, I'd appreciate if you'll hold down the office again for a while. A few of the regulars are getting used to seeing you now and then anyway. Think up something creative if people ask where I am."

"My pleasure, Jed. You might call Tats and ask him to come around so we can chat. I'd like to have him as an available resource if needed."

"Will do. Mercy and Gunnar, you go get cracking on those computer files. I'll start assembling the gear Gun and I will need, plus make a few important phone calls. Let's all meet at my office at, say, 5:00 p.m. I'll put a closed-for-business sign on the door. If something's holding you up, give me a call on my cell. Otherwise, see you then."

Mercy, Gunnar, and Darrell all headed for their respective tasks. Jed had naturally assumed leadership of the impromptu task force, and the other three seemed comfortable with that. For Gunnar to not feel all alone in his quest was a huge boost, and, father or not, his confidence in Jedediah was growing measurably.

Gunnar called LinTech in San Diego and solicited the willing assistance of the IT tech who had broken the code for BJ's records, and who said he'd get right on it when the files were emailed to him. He said that, given the unsophisticated nature of BJ's attempts at coding, he thought he'd be able to have something – assuming there was something to be had – by late afternoon. Gun gave him his current cell phone number and told him he'd be checking his email inbox every half hour.

Then he dialed Indianapolis. It had been a couple of months since he had communicated with his folks directly by voice, and he figured they were probably somewhat worried.

"Hi, Mom," he greeted, trying to sound cheerful.

"Gunnar!" Linn exclaimed. "Sonny," she yelled, "get on the phone. Quick!"

Before Linn could say anything else, Sonny almost shouted, "Son, where are you? We haven't heard anything for so long we started worrying that something had happened." Privately, the parents had some serious concern that their son would sink into depression, or already had. They didn't think he would do anything rash, but when someone's mind is tortured, well, you never knew.

"Hi, Dad. I'm fine. I'm actually in the States. I've been travelling up and down the coast trying to work out the mental kinks." Not altogether a falsehood. "Things are OK, considering."

Hesitating somewhat to ask, Linn said, "Any news at all about Tuyen? Is anyone making any progress on finding her?"

"Nothing concrete, Mom," he lied. "They think they might have a lead or two, but they keep telling me to not have too much hope. I don't think *they* have much hope, and just don't want me to get too built up."

Gunnar was trying to walk the tightrope between half-truths and downright lies. He couldn't tell his folks what he had been doing, and he also didn't want to enliven their hopes by telling them that he thought they were homing in on what could be her actual location.

"Son," Sonny went on, "why don't you just come home for a bit and let us pamper you. There's really not much you can do anyway but let the police continue their investigations. We've got to trust that they'll do their jobs and find her."

If only you knew, thought Gunnar. "I'm not quite ready for that yet. I just wanted to touch base and let you know that things are OK. I mean, they're not OK, but I'm dealing with it."

They chatted for another ten minutes about life in Indianapolis, everyone's health, and their love for each other before Gunnar said he'd keep in more regular touch and ended the call. There was no way he could reveal Jedediah's existence at this point. When he was reunited with Tuyen and the dust settled on all of this, he would figure out then how to break the news, and what they all might do with it. For the time being, he was checking his email about every fifteen minutes, and watched the clock hands tick their way around toward five o'clock.

They would know who had his daughter. And on this day, July thirty-first, her tenth birthday, he willed her to know: *Daddy's coming*.

Chapter 74

August 2005 - Seattle, Washington

Finding Tuyen's buyer being the first order of business, the group waited with an almost palpable individual and collective anxiety. By 4:30 they were all back at Jed's office with the door locked, windows covered, and the only light being what filtered through the worn curtains. It was as if some undefinable yet ambient force had bound them together for the coming mission. A parent ready to move heaven and earth; a cop who had seen too much to walk away; a retired pastor whose compassion was born of faith; a former Marine, street priest, vigilante, and now grandfather whose whole life was characterized by action instead of apathy. Their singular and common focus was a beautiful little girl who had been wrenched from her family and carted off to a foreign country for a life of captive servitude. The implicit assumption was that she would be found. The agreement that did not require articulation was that they would do whatever was necessary to rescue her.

Mercy's phone rang at 5:04. It was Chet, the SPD Information Tech guy, and he had found what he thought they needed. Mercy thanked him profusely and said she would be by the next morning to go over the rest of the data he was mining from BJ's records.

"Chet says sorry it took him so long, but BJ had encrypted some of his files with something other than the primitive Caesar Cipher used in the pages Gunnar had memorized. I don't pretend to understand it all, but he said it didn't take much to determine that the system being used was a built-in encryption tool for Windows systems called Encrypting File System, or EFS. The problem was that a specific cryptographic key is needed to read the encrypted data which, of course, Chet didn't have but figured was embedded in the system somewhere. This being a bit above his skill level, he called in an old high school buddy who went from hacker-for-hire to software developer for Microsoft. Once the guy could break free and get over to Chet's lab, he found the key within fifteen minutes."

"And?" the others exclaimed almost in unison.

"The records refer to a Juan Pablo García-Iglesias in California."

"This is our man, yes?" Gunnar forcibly exclaimed. "Where is he?"

"Hold on," Mercy responded. "Chet did a cursory check and found seven fellows with that name in the state. But full Spanish names include other surnames between the first and last one. We're bound to find a Fernandez, Hernandez, Gomez, probably even my name, Gutierrez, or whatever between the Juan Pablo and the Garcia-Iglesias. The task is to identify which one did business with BJ."

"How do we go about doing that?" Jed asked.

"I don't know any other shortcut to getting the list of names and tracking them down one by one."

"That could take forever," Gunnar exclaimed.

"Maybe not. There's been something in the back of my mind about that name, but I can't put my finger on it." Even as she said this, a faded memory started to come into focus and Mercy experienced a spine-tingling hunch. "Hang tight while I make a phone call or two to check on something."

As she said that, Gunnar's laptop sounded the tone for an incoming e-mail. He quickly brought it up and it was indeed the anticipated one from San Diego. Gunnar read it with the other three all trying to look over his shoulder.

"Looks like my guy found the same thing, but he tacked on something additional: a list of the seven Juan Pablo García-Iglesiases in California that includes their full Hispanic names."

"OK," Jed began, "Mercy, if you've got someone on the force or know someone in another agency who can get us any kind of current information on all the names, please try to put that in motion and then make your hunch call. Gunnar, can you see if your guy has the time and resources to do the same? Addresses, work places, family history, anything . . . any bio information that will help us narrow down the search."

"Done." Gunnar said. "He knows what's at stake here, and his computer tracking skills are world-class. I'll call him right away. Let's put our heads together here again around, say, eight."

Mercy left for her SPD office and Gunnar stayed at the street ministry center. Jed headed for his apartment with Darrell for a quick bite and maybe even an hour's snooze. At this point he knew any catnap would help bolster his physical and mental resources. A couple of prayers floated up to do the same for his spiritualty.

The distant memory prodding Mercy came from her three years working at the California Institution for Women outside Chino. She knew the name García-Iglesias figured in there somewhere, but it wasn't coming into clear enough focus. It was fifteen or so years before that she had worked the Chino facility, but she had maintained a now-and-then relationship with one of the other correctional officers who had stayed in the system. Her name was Carolee Allerdice. She had attained a Bachelor's in Law Enforcement degree, and was now a mid-level executive with the California Department of Corrections and Rehabilitation in Sacramento. It took Mercy a while to run the gauntlet of phone menus and just-a-moment-while-I-transfer-you-to, but eventually she had the live person on the other end.

"Mercedes, my goodness, it's been a long time. How in

the world are you?" Carolee said cheerfully.

"Good. Very good." Mercy answered. "Indeed it has been too long, and we should just get together on purpose one of these days."

"Love it if we could. I imagine you're as busy as I am, but all too often we let this career stuff get too much in the way of friendships. So let's not forget our desire to work something up, but I'm guessing that's not why you called."

"You're sharp as ever, Carolee," Mercy commended. "I'm working on a case where a name came up that rings some bells from the past, and I think it's from our time together at Chino."

"OK, gal. Who you talking about?"

"Does the name Juan Pablo García-Iglesias ring any bells?"

"You kidding me? His capital "B" bells are still echoing through the halls of justice. I didn't know you could pour bullshit into a suit and then watch it walk and talk, but he's living proof it can be done."

"Refresh me, please. All I have is a hazy memory about a murder charge and him having something to do with getting somebody off."

"Pretty good, honey. You're in the ball park. You remember Lita Rios?"

"Wasn't she the one who killed her pusher and a couple of kids?"

"Hey, it's coming back. Good for you! Yeah, Lita was totally pissed on some combination of juice and pills. Went to this gal's house to get more, except she was outta cash and her pusher wouldn't give her any credit. So she pulled out a .38 Special and plugged her right in front of her kids. Both still in grade school, I think. Buzzed up and thinking she couldn't have any witnesses, she summarily executed them, a boy and a girl, and hightailed it with the drugs she wanted."

"But she was convicted, right?"

"Sure was. She claimed innocence, like everyone else in here, but the DA got a guilty verdict along with a sentence for life without parole."

"So how does this Juan Pablo factor in?"

"This dude was some kind of bigwig in one of the Columbian cartels, maybe the head guy. But they could never get enough solid evidence on him, either there or here, to even indict the turd. By the time the Rios caper happened, he had amassed millions, maybe billions, and eased out of the drug world into supposedly legitimate businesses."

"So, OK, what's this got to do with Lita?"

"Turns out he had an interesting relationship with her. She's not only his half-sister, but he's banging her. Apparently there's some soft spot for her in his perverted heart, so he hires two of the most experienced, and I might add, dirtbag defense lawyers in the western U.S. and, to make a long story short, they get a re-trial based on some flimsy technicality, I can't remember exactly what it was. And guess what?"

"She's acquitted."

"Pretty sharp yourself, Mercy. She gets out, and four months later, driving in a drugged stupor, runs head-on into a van with a family inside. Both vehicles go up in flames. Mom, dad, and three kids are toast, pardon the expression."

"It's coming back now," Mercy said. "I remember the corrections community up in arms over the stupid system that would let something like this happen."

"Yeah, and times haven't changed much. I could give you several more stories along the same line if you were interested."

"Carolee, I see enough of that with the system here in Washington. Disconcerting, but we both know it's something we've got to live with. But Juan Pablo . . . what happened to him?"

"Very respected retired businessman. Millionaire, philanthropist, community supporter. Loved by all, except those of us who know the whole story."

"How come somebody doesn't expose him?" Mercy asked.

"One journalist tried that about five years ago. Because nothing could be proved, he was sued for libel, went bankrupt, lost his job, and disappeared."

"And where is this Juan Pablo today?"

"Might I ask why the interest?

"It's a criminal investigation. Has to do with the sex-trafficking task force I'm on."

"Hmmmm. Sounds like something that turd would be doing. I believe he's somewhere in southern California. Can't remember the exact location."

"Anyway. you could find out and e-mail me? And also his full Hispanic name if you can get it."

"Sure, honey. Gimme your address and I'll get what I can for you."

"Thanks, Carolee. This is really important. And the time factor is kinda crucial."

"Check your e-mail within an hour or two. Should be something there for you."

"You're a peach, Carolee. Thanks a mil. And let's really

do try to hook up sometime before too long."

"I'd like that. In the meantime, take care of yourself."

Ten minutes before heading back to Jed's office she received an e-mail from Carolee with the following message: Juan Pablo Fernández de Aguiniga y García-Iglesias, Pelican Crest, Newport Beach, California.

Target acquired. Maybe.

Gunnar juggled the emotions of excitement, fear, and rage as he hung up the phone. He had given Ralph, the Lin-Tech IT resource, his cell phone number and asked him to call when he had anything to report.

Ralph relayed that six out of the seven Juan Pablo García-Iglesiases were quite unlikely candidates. One was in an old folk's home with Alzheimer's, one was a corporate VP with Google, one played for the Oakland Raiders, one was a sophomore at UCLA, one was a homeless fellow currently in the Sacramento County lockup for shoplifting, and one was a vascular surgeon operating out of San Francisco General.

"We'll still probably have to check them all out, Ralph. But what about number seven?" Gunnar asked.

"This could be your guy, Gunnar. Juan Pablo Fernández de Aguiniga y García-Iglesias. Lives in Newport Beach, California."

"What makes you think he's the one?"

"He's originally from Columbia and, you guessed it, has been associated with a major drug cartel there for years but no one could ever get the goods on him. He had a reputation for being a ruthless butcher. Problem is, after stockpiling enough of the green stuff for you and me to live ten lifetimes, he left the trade and is now a so-called respected businessman who built a palatial estate on a hill overlooking Newport Beach. Lives a pretty private life, but contributes liberally to local charities, apparently liking the aura of a kind and generous do-gooder."

"So why does this point to him being involved with a sex-trafficking ring?"

"OK, stick with me. He's married to a Columbian beauty queen and they had a child who became the light of his life. A year ago his 9-year-old daughter died and apparently he became unhinged with grief. Add to that the fact that several months later his wife had a total hysterectomy."

"Which meant no more children," Gunnar murmured.

"Exactly. And here's the kicker: in the past couple of months he's been seen with his wife and a newly adopted little girl."

Gunnar stopped breathing and the room started spinning momentarily. There was absolutely no doubt in his mind that Ralph was talking about Tuyen.

"Gun, you still there?" Ralph asked after a protracted silence.

"Yeah, yeah. Just reacting to the fact that we could be on to something."

"So do you think," Ralph asked, "this is enough for the cops to go take a look?"

"Maybe. Probably." *Sure*, he thought. "You've been a great help, Ralph. This is the kind of lead the police are looking for. I'll follow up on it and let you know if anything comes of it. Can't thank you enough."

"My pleasure, pal. I just hope this is what you think it is."

"It is, Ralph. It is. By the way, how'd you find all this

info?"

"Remember, it's magic with me and the keys. Lots of it, anyway, is public record, but I've got some contacts up and down the coast who are fountains of info if the price is right."

"Hey, if this cost you anything I . . . "

"No, no. I meant that figuratively. We scratch either other's backs and it all evens out."

"Well, OK. I'm indebted to you beyond words. We'll see what the authorities can do with this and I'll be in touch."

"Ciao, my friend. Take it easy."

The picture that materialized in Gunnar's mind was of some fat-cat drug lord pretending to be Tuyen's father, and his blood pressure headed skyward again. It indeed was comforting to learn that she wasn't a sex-slave in some untraceable location, but just thinking of the fact that she had been kidnapped and her mother killed brought to the surface the fury that had dominated his life since that fateful day in Da Nang. But now, knowing exactly where she was, he realized that cool-headed control was an absolute necessity for the action to come. Of course, he didn't make the connection, but that was exactly the attitude Jed had embodied all his life.

With the summer sun still high enough at 8:30 p.m. to read a book on a park bench, they met back at Jed's office. After comparing what both Mercy and Gunnar had learned and reviewing all the pieces of the puzzle, they mutually and confidently concluded that everything pointed to Newport Beach. The next step was to determine the next step.

After making a phone call, Jed took the lead. "There's a 10:30 flight tonight leaving for LA. Gunnar and I will be on it. It's only about an hour from there to Newport Beach. We'll rent a car and grab a room down there for some shut-eye before beginning our recon of Iglesias' place. The key is to somehow positively identify Tuyen. An eyeball sighting would obviously be best, but hopefully you've got a picture or two, Gunnar, that we can print off and take to show people."

"Absolutely. There's some on my laptop. Can we print them here?"

"Mine's not a color printer," Jed replied, "but there's a 24/7 print shop up on 5th where we can get some good copies on our way to the airport. Mercy, you mind dropping us off at SeaTac?"

"Wouldn't miss it. But you fellas better get what you need because we've got to be hitting the road as soon as possible."

"I'll hold down your office, Jed," Darrell said. "You've got my cell number if we can do anything on this end."

"OK, we can't proceed any further until we have total intel on this guy's location, schedule, and so forth. Gunnar and I will see what we can find out and let you know what kind of support we need. Mercy, there's one thing you might explore. If you can figure out a way to get us the gear down there that we're going to need, that'd be a great help. I've got an old buddy who might be able to assist, but what he can't get, maybe you can. The kind of stuff I'm talking about we can't take on a plane."

"I think that's doable, Jed. Give me a call when you have a list. I've got some ideas, so I'll make a few preliminary inquiries."

"So that's it for now. I've got a call to make, Mercy, and you can pick Gunnar and me up in about twenty minutes."

"Gunnar," Mercy said, "if you've got a flash drive to put the pictures on that you want printed, I can get that done on my way to pick you guys up." Gunnar did. He put the images on the drive and gave it to Mercy.

Jed, Gun, and Darrell headed to Jed's apartment. As they threw a few things together in bags that would fit in the overhead compartments, Darrell said to his long-time friend, "This could get dicey, Jed."

"You're telling me."

"Rescuing Tuyen unharmed, keeping Gunnar under control, not killing anybody, and not getting nabbed by the cops . . . that's a tall order."

"You see any other way?" Jed queried.

"Not really. Especially with what Mercy had to say. But take it easy, or keep your cool, or something like that."

"I hear what you're saying, Darrell." And looking him square in the face, Jed added, "But we're going to do whatever is necessary to get Gunnar's daughter back. You know me well enough to know that I won't go off capriciously with guns blazing. But you also know that we're coming back with Tuyen."

With no further words needed, Darrell squeezed both of Jed's shoulders with affection.

As Gunnar threw his traveling kit together, two words overwhelmed his brain again and again: *Daddy's coming. Daddy's coming*!

Chapter 75

August 2005 - Newport Beach, California

Gloria de Dios is a six-acre estate in the Pelican Crest development south of Newport Beach, California. The southern boundary of the property was the edge of a precipice that sloped seaward in a jumble of forested terraces toward the oceanfront community below. Its relative isolation was occasioned by it being the singular dwelling on a wide bench, with nothing to the east between it and Crystal Cove State Park except uninhabited rocky forest. A U-shaped eight-foot fence topped with electrified barbed wire surrounded the property from the drop-off on the west curving around to the same on the east.

The acreage was trapezoidal in shape, gently sloping downhill with the seaward side measuring roughly a third again as long as the northern edge. Juan Pablo had spared no expense to establish a hilltop kingdom where he could spend the rest of his days securely and luxuriously. A long lane off of Newport Coast Drive led to an ornate gatehouse at the northwest corner of the estate. Along the short, or northern, border was a regulation-size soccer field and a wooded section with walking trails to its east. The forty-room mansion sat on the edge of the cliff with an Olympic-size pool behind it. Between the pool and the soccer field was a child's play area equipped with custom-designed swing and jungle gym sets, a wading pool with cascading waterfall, and a covered picnic area that included snow cone and popcorn machines. The dwelling was located in the southwest corner with a Frank Lloyd Wright-designed California Redwood gazebo next to it which overflowed with a mixture of purple and white bougainvillea. Extending eastward from the party area were extensive formal gardens that would cause world-class envy in any floral horticulturist. Some fifty thousand dollars worth of topsoil had been trucked in to ensure a prime growing environment.

This was Juan Pablo's little fiefdom, and Tuyen's prison.

Jed had the location, and now needed to create a workable plan for liberating Gunnar's daughter. To do so first required thorough observation accompanied by determining and acquiring the tactical gear needed for the mission. Hopefully, the latter could be facilitated by an old friend of Jed's, a retired USMC gunnery sergeant who lived in San Clemente and with whom Jed had maintained occasional contact over the years. Marine gunnies were some of the best military scroungers on the planet, and Gunny Omdahl appeared to carry the skill into retirement with a military surplus store and who-knows-what available under the counter.

Because their arrival at the White Sands Inn was in the middle of the night, father and son, who secured the room under false ID's, didn't rise and shine until a bit after 8:00 a.m. The roughly five hours was enough to revive both of them, not to mention that their anxiousness prevented further sleep in any event. As the in-room coffee brewed, Gunnar took a shower and Jed ran a quick three miles to get the blood flowing and the kinks out of his joints. It was a crystal-clear, blue-sky day with the high temperature promised in the seasonal low-70's.

Toward the middle of their second mug of coffee, Jed prepped Gun for what lay ahead. A nascent plan was forming in his mind, but a requirement was that Gun knew the rules and was committed to follow them. He began, "Gunnar, there are a couple of things where we really need to be on the same page."

"I'm listening," Gun replied.

"The first is that today is observation only. We're here for nothing unless we absolutely and positively identify Tuyen. And I mean absolutely. We can't go charging into this guy's life and end up finding some other little girl."

"I hear you, Jed. I don't want to waste time and effort any more than you do."

"Besides," Jed added, "going in might easily mean some serious damage to life and limb, and I'm talking about theirs, not ours. If it's the wrong place, we could be creating a whole lot of havoc that might even hamper any future efforts."

"Makes all the sense in the world. But I know that's my little girl up there."

Jed knew how desperate Gunnar was to find and rescue Tuyen . . . how every cell in his body was on high alert and ready for action. But Jed also knew how that state of mind can play tricks with one's perception and judgment, and the last thing they needed was for Gun to go off half-cocked if the situation wasn't what they thought it was.

"Well, I think it is too, and I'll tell you why. On my run this morning I took one of Tuyen's pictures. I popped into a children's clothing boutique on the main drag and asked if they recognized the picture. Told them I was a scout for a modeling agency and she would be perfect for a shoot on swimwear for youngsters. Said one of my colleagues saw this picture with Newport Beach written on the back, but we don't have a clue where we might find her. The young clerk said she couldn't be positive, but that it looked a lot like Señor Garcia-Iglesias' daughter."

Gunnar stood up and looked out the window at the rolling waves with saltwater dripping down his cheeks. Jed sat still until Gun eventually turned around and said in a husky voice, "When do we leave to do the reconnaissance?"

"We'll leave shortly to do a drive-by. But, Gunnar, I need to know that you're under control. We absolutely cannot try to storm in and demand he give Tuyen over, assuming again that it really is her. Both of us are really keyed-up, but this isn't going to work unless we get a look at the complete situation and then develop a plan that'll actually work. We'll do this, but we'll do it with the right kind of preparation and with ironclad discipline. That's how things get accomplished."

Bringing his breathing under control, Gun looked him in the eye and said, "Jed, I've never been more in control in my life. Every waking minute since March twentieth has been focused on this moment. I do not want to, *I will not*, blow it. You're way ahead of me on the skills needed to make this happen, and I have come to the point of trusting your judgment completely. Just let me know what to do . . . and trust that I'll do it."

Jed, fighting to overcome the frog in his throat, replied, "OK. I've got a couple of calls to make first and then we'll take that drive."

With a preliminary list in mind, Jed contacted Gunny Omdahl to see what was available. He then placed a call to Dub, who was both surprised and delighted to hear from him.

After acquiring both a road map and satellite images from Google maps, they took their morning drive. While the estate itself could not be seen from Newport Coast Road, they noted the entrance to the driveway. Most importantly, they found a secluded pullout off of Vista Ridge Road several benches higher up the slope than Gloria de Dios. Parking their rental car there would make it invisible from the road at night.

Returning later in the day, by 9:30 p.m. they had navigated on foot the downhill terrain in the twilight and were perched on a narrow shelf above the mansion. They found a spot that provided a direct line of sight to the front of the house, and the hope was for Tuyen to appear either outside or in one of the windows. Their objective was two-fold: to positively ID Tuyen, and to observe the complete estate layout and whatever security personnel might be utilized.

There were no indications that they had been observed, either parking the car or on their downward traverse to their hidden perch. The stars were out in full force in the clear night, and the biggest hazard had been stumbling on the rocky hillside. Jed had timed their arrival for after sundown so that there was no chance of light reflecting off their optical lenses. He used his thermal imager monocular for the unlit areas, and Gunnar had his tripod-mounted 20x80 binoculars. With the latter, Gun had a one hundred and seventy-five foot field of view at a thousand yards. The rangefinder indicated just under five hundred yards from their position to the mansion.

Since it was after dark and not knowing what might be a regular bedtime for Tuyen, the two were wondering what the odds might be that the girl would actually wander into Gun's field of view. It was nearing 10:00 p.m. when someone in a second story window opened the curtains. Seeing that it was a maid who did so and then promptly left the room, Gunnar could make out that it was a rather extensive playroom, and a little girl stood in the middle of the room with her back to the window. His heart almost stopped when the girl started across the room toward the door. He willed her with all his might to turn around. As she came to the door and reached up for the light switch, she turned around as if to look for something she had forgotten.

Gunnar felt as if all his vital functions came to a screeching standstill. He was unmistakably looking at Tuyen.

No words were spoken. Jed knew what he had seen. He gave Gunnar a supportive arm squeeze, which was also a gently communicated "cool it," and they spent another two hours scrutinizing the layout of the grounds, including timing the security guards. Jed scanned the fence line arduously from several angles for any signs of motion detectors or security cameras, and could find neither. After observing all that they figured they could without risking detection, they picked their way back up the slope by moonlight.

Early the next morning Jed made the necessary calls. The first one was to Gunny Omdahl who confirmed that he could supply most of the required items. He gave Jed the address of a house in Laguna Beach where he'd meet him with the gear around 7:00 p.m.

The next call was to Mercy.

"You're absolutely sure?" she asked.

"Not my call. Gunnar says there's no question that it's her and he ought to know," Jed responded.

"Then this is it. You able to get what you need to pull this off?"

"Almost all," Jed told Mercy. "But we're a couple of items short which I hope you can line up." He then proceeded to give her a brief synopsis of the physical setup, his operational plan, and the items he would need her to procure for him.

After listening to Jed, Mercy paused to run the picture

through her mind. Finally Jed said, "Hey, you still there?"

"Yeah, yeah. Just thinking. Sounds to me like this is a little ambitious for just two guys."

"Risky but doable. Not much choice when it comes to available manpower."

"What about womanpower?"

It took a couple of seconds for what she was proposing to sink in. "I don't think so, Mercy."

"Really? Might that have something to do with your thinking I can't keep up with you guys?"

"No, no. That's not even remotely an issue. I'm thinking more of your need to keep your copper hands clean. If we somehow muffed this, your whole career would be down the tubes."

While it might have been more of a subconscious rather than a conscious thought, Jed also was feeling a bit protective. Serious injury, or even death, was always a chance in a situation like this. His platonic friendship with Mercy had deepened to the point where caring about her safety, and her career, went appreciably beyond what it would have been with a less personal relationship.

"Well, with only the two of you, the whole enterprise could go south. Besides, while I genuinely appreciate your concern, it's my decision to make. I'm not going to sit this one out. I'll be on the late flight to LA tonight."

Jed knew her well enough to not try to change Mercy's mind. But even with any misgivings he might have, he was relieved to have a three-person team. It gave him a much better feeling about the chance for his plan's success.

Letting an appropriate silence lapse, Jed finally replied, "OK. Let's do it." He then gave her some instructions about what to do when she landed, and told her how to find the White Sands in Newport Beach.

Then he called Dub again to confirm times and locations.

Around noon, when all the calls had been made, the two sat in beach chairs facing the ocean. "Gunnar, let's talk this through one more time."

"Fine with me. I want every detail imprinted on my brain."

"I can only imagine the emotions running rampant in you right now. They're real and they're powerful. Which is all the more reason to focus on control when we go in. It's always hard, but self-discipline, or the lack of it, can make or break an operation like this."

"You're worried about me?"

"Gunnar, I don't know you well enough to make that kind of judgment. From what I've heard and seen, you seem to have some good skills which you've put to use carefully. The only concern I'm expressing has to do with the focus being your daughter. Any normal father would be over-hyped in this situation. So I'm just saying that you need to be aware of it and factor it in to what we've planned."

"OK, but what does it mean in a practical sense?"

"First, you take directions from me. You've gotta trust that I know what I'm doing and have the ability to get it done. Second, if something unexpected happens that forces a change in plans, take a deep breath, although not too long a one, to assess what a new move might be. Again, chances are I'll be able to give directions, but you never know. I guess what I'm lobbying for is using your best judgment even given the emotional aspect."

"I think I see what you're getting at, and I appreciate the counsel."

"Remember, the two things we're going to accomplish are to rescue Tuyen and to get all of us out of there alive."

After a brief silence, Gunnar asked, "Are you glad Mercy's coming along?"

"The more I think about it, the better I feel about it. Having three of us will simplify some things and increase our chance of pulling this off."

"Can she really pull her weight?"

"Stick around and watch," Jed said with a hint of a smile.

"One more thing, if you don't mind my asking," Gun hesitantly voiced. "Back in Seattle you said your last name was from an African tribe. How'd you get an African name and does it have a meaning?"

"It's somewhat complicated and someday I hope to have time to tell you the whole story. But it's an Ndebele word that means 'axe.'"

"What? Were they loggers?" Gun said with a teasing lilt to his voice.

Jed smiled and responded, "Has to do with martial arts and singing contests going way back. It was known that my clan always cut down the competition."

Gunnar thought about that and looked forward to the day he could learn more about this interesting man's history. In the meantime, he hoped Jed would live up to his name in the coming hours.

Gazing at the pounding surf along with the lack of sleep began to induce a drowsiness in both men. Jed suggested they get a few hours of shuteye before he headed to Laguna Beach to pick up the gear from the Gunny Omdahl. They would then sort it out back at the motel and wait for Mercy's arrival.

Chapter 76

August 2005 - Newport Beach, California

Mercy arrived around 4:00 a.m. The late-night flight from Seattle had been delayed due to mechanical problems, and then the SUV she had reserved under a false ID was not at the airport and she had to wait for it to be delivered from another location. She was beat from the lack of sleep, but didn't want to lie down until learning the details of the plan

Jed had devised. She confirmed that the items he had requested were available, and her source, a friend of a friend in Long Beach, was going to meet her at 3:00 p.m. at a Park-n-Ride just off I-405 in Fountain Valley. Darrell had provided her with the cash needed to complete the transaction.

They also inventoried the gear that Omdahl had provided. When Jed knew Mercy would be joining them, he had called the gunny and added a number of items to his initial list. Jed and Gun would each have an ATN Viper Night Vision goggle headset since their initial approach would be in the dark. Jed would carry a USMC officer's standard issue Colt .45 on his hip with Remington 230 grain SJHP High Terminal Performance bullets in a 7-round mag and one in the chamber. Two extra full magazines would be in one of his cargo pockets. Gunnar's weapon would be the lighter Ruger LC380 loaded seven-plus-one with 100 grain RNFP 380 Auto cartridges and two extra mags. Due to the role she would play, Mercy would have a reconditioned surplus M16 with four 30-round mags filled with NATO 7.62 FMJ cartridges. If she had to use it, disciplined shooting would need to prevail since the M16 could fire 60 rounds per minute on semi and 700 rounds per minute on fully auto. In other words, even if she used only the semiautomatic setting she could expend one complete magazine in a half a minute unless a controlled fire discipline was observed.

Although they were fairly spendy, Jed had the gunny provide Inmarsat satellite phones for all three. He would have preferred in-ear wireless walkie-talkies, but most of the time they would not have the line of sight required for that mode of communication. The sat phones were reliable, and they'd simply have to hand-hold it when there was a need to talk. They also carried duct tape and flex cuffs. Jed and Gun would wear cargo pants and long sleeve cotton shirts, both black. Mercy would wear black jeans and a tight-fitting cotton blouse that, according to the plan, showed an admirable amount of cleavage. All three would be wearing tight, thin leather gloves.

Jed, ever the military tactician, proffered the professional judgment that what he and Gunnar had observed was surely not all of the drug lord's support group. They did not know what extra people might be in the mansion itself, and surely there were additional security personnel close at hand, both to switch shifts with those whom they'd observed and as reserves to call up in the unlikely case of an emergency. For this reason, Mercy had acquired the material needed in the event of unexpected troops. He also told them about the extraction once Tuyen was safely in their hands. This was where Dub would come in.

As they reviewed the plan one more time, Jed expressed the viewpoint that, both in terms of the task at hand and the equipment acquired for it, they were likely overestimating the difficulty. Even though Juan Pablo had armed security guards, he probably felt no significant risk in his protected palace since he had left the drug trade behind years ago. Time has a way of subconsciously sweet-talking heretofore heightened alertness into lackadaisical inattention, and several years of respectable and respected community life accompanied by no perceived or realized threats had, in fact, resulted in exactly the laissez-faire outlook for which Jed was hoping. The alertness level of the guards themselves, due to night after night of boringly plodding around the premises, would probably be low-to-very-low. Besides, who in their right mind would think of attacking Juan Pablo Garcia-Iglesias in the first place?

With several hours to go, Mercy and Gunnar hit the sack for some needed sleep while Jed hit the beach for a five-mile run to calm his nerves. He didn't really feel like he was getting too old for this stuff, but he also knew his body couldn't quite do what it could twenty or even ten years ago. Nevertheless, the coming action was perhaps one of the most critical ones in his life, certainly from a personal perspective, and he had an abundance of confidence that success was in the offing. By the time he returned and showered there were still a few hours left before they went into action.

Although the official sunset was a bit before 8:00, they waited until the waning light faded to darkness. The sky was clear and the waxing moon was halfway from new to full. Very little was said as Jedediah, Gunnar, and Mercedes suited up and double-checked their equipment. They had previously put brand new batteries in their sat phones, and, placing themselves a mile apart from each other, made sure they were all operating properly. They each squeezed one another's hands and then got into their respective vehicles. Jed and Gun headed their car for the pullout on Vista Ridge Road. Mercy would slowly cruise up and down coastal Highway 1 in the SUV until getting the call from Jed to motor up Newport Coast Drive to the estate.

Somewhat surprising but also gratifying, Jed and Gun did not see a single vehicle on their way to the pullout. After they parked out of sight from the road and exited the car, they checked to make sure nothing was left in it that could in any way point to them. Then with a wet washcloth from the motel Jed carefully wiped down every square inch of the vehicle, inside and out, that they might have touched. With an understanding of each other's tasks, they started downhill on roughly the same tack they had used two nights previously. Both had their night vision goggles on and took extra care to not dislodge any rocks or snap any branches as they crept toward the fence encircling the estate.

Due to their previous observations, they knew that the perimeter guards travelled in opposite directions, usually pausing for a smoke when they met at either the gatehouse or the opposite side halfway point. They also knew from their timing of the guards' routes that it took roughly thirty minutes for each one to complete his half of the circuit. This meant that Jed and Gun had about three quarters of an hour, maybe a few minutes more depending on how long the guards might linger at the gatehouse, from the time they passed each other at the east end of the circuit until they were halfway back again. Jed reckoned this would be plenty of time for Gun and him to get in position.

Fifteen minutes after the guards had passed each other and headed back toward the gatehouse, the two interlopers approached the fence on the east end at a point largely obscured by brush on both sides. The bolt cutters they had brought made light work of cutting a man-sized hole through which they both scrambled, then they set the chain link back in place. Jed was gratified that only the barbed wire on top was electrified and not the whole fence. He wondered if the people Juan Pablo had hired to provide a secure environment had ever heard of bolt cutters. Then again, perhaps they simply figured the threat level was small enough not to worry, or else the primary function of the fence was to keep coyotes, bobcats, and mule deer out of the manicured enclosure. Wordlessly, Jed headed to the right, or north, and secreted himself in a clump of bushes at the northeast corner of the wooded area. Gun went south and fortunately found a stand of California lilac at the end of the formal gardens which provided a good hiding place.

Jed had stuffed the night vision goggles in his fanny pack to let his eyes adjust to the dark. About twenty minutes after he was in place he heard the light scuffling of boots on the trail, and he could both smell and see the glow of a dangling cigarette as the guard approached. When the man was one step past, Jed calmly stepped onto the trail and delivered a chop to his neck that resulted in instant unconsciousness. He then flex-cuffed the fellow's hands behind his back, duct-taped both his ankles and mouth, and with a section of light twine ran a line from his wrists to his feet. The latter was done to prevent the man from somehow getting to his feet and hopping his way back down the trail. Jed then headed back toward Gunnar.

Gunnar basically duplicated what Jed had done except for a slight glitch. Not having the martial arts skill of Jedediah, Gunnar used the butt of his pistol to knock out the guard on his side of the compound. Except his first blow only stunned the man, who fell only to his knees. So as he was groggily reaching for his sidearm Gunnar had to deliver another blow, which he did with significantly more conviction. This time the man crumpled and the flex cuffs, duct tape and twine were applied in like fashion.

Jed slowly and carefully approached the area designated for Gun just in case things hadn't gone as planned. He was relieved when he heard a *pssst* from amongst the lilacs and Gunnar's face appeared. Figuring that they were about a ten-minute brisk walk to the east side of the house, Jed gave Mercy the call to action. She would buzz him back when she was in place, which would indicate the next step for Gun and him. They headed for the west side of the formal gardens to await Mercy's call back.

The GMC Yukon Mercy was driving made it from Highway 1 to the Gloria de Dios drive-way in a matter of minutes. She turned in and drove slowly toward the gate house, stopping about twenty yards short when it came into view. The guard on duty, who had been engrossed in the latest issue of *Guns & Ammo*, hustled outside to see who this visitor might be. He had not been informed of any expected guests, but unannounced vehicles showed up from time to time. Generally they were either the curious or the lost, although it was unusual for such a happening this late in the evening. The pole lighting emitted enough for the ex-drug mule to see a gorgeous woman step out of the SUV, and his first thought was that this could be his luckiest day of the month. As Mercy headed toward the gate house with the swagger of a fashion model, she said, "*Buenas tardes, señor. Estoy muy perdida y me pregunto si usted me puede ayudar.*" The guard thought that if this babe needed assistance she had indeed come to the right place. Noting that she was alone, he said, "*Estaré encantado de ayudarle señorita. Tal vez le gustaría una bebida primero de hablar sobre las posibilidades, ¿no?*" hoping she would take up his offer for a friendly drink while they discussed possibilities. Assuming a manly pose, his feet a bit wider than shoulder width and hands on hips, it appeared to him as if this lost gal was almost falling out of her bra particularly for his enjoyment.

Mercy was now three feet in front of him when she smiled and asked what possibilities he might have in mind. Just as his male hormones began to kick in big time, Mercy kicked in big time with the boot on her right foot swinging forcefully up into his genitals. If it had been on the pistol range, she would have scored a direct bullseye. The man doubled over as if struck by lightning, and the last thing he felt before the lights went out was the woman's clasped hands coming down on the back of his neck. Mercy then went to work with the flex cuffs and duct tape, and dragged the lecherous jerk into the gatehouse. *Ah, how men will be men*, she thought. She followed instructions by parking the Yukon sideways across the drive about a hundred yards back down the driveway from the gate, effectively blocking any vehicular access to the estate. When that was done, she called Jed and simply said, "Go."

The only remaining obstacle between Jed and the house interior was the guard that casually sauntered around the dwelling's exterior, generally taking a leisurely twenty minutes or so for one round. Jed waited until he passed the seaward side around to the west wall before he moved into position between some bushes and the west end of the gazebo. Gunnar crouched unseen at the east end of the gazebo. When the guard eventually came back into view, Jed made some discernable scratching sounds on the side of the gazebo with a stick he had picked up for this purpose. The guard, most likely thinking an animal of some sort had entered the property, strode toward the sound with a hand on his holstered pistol. Since this was a frontal confrontation instead of a stealthy attack from the rear, when the man was three feet away Jed simply stood up. Jed wasn't sure if the fellow actually jumped out of his boots, but before his surprise resulted in anything coming from his vocal cords, Jed's right fist connected with his left temple and the heretofore conscious guard started seeing a different set of stars. More flex cuffs and duct tape left the man a non-threat as Jed and Gun slid over to the side of the mansion and began creeping around the corner toward the front door.

Chapter 77

August 2005 - Newport Beach, California

There were two rooms designated as servants quarters on the ground level, and all of the family bedrooms in the mansion were on the second floor. Dual spiral staircases curved upward from each side of the large entrance foyer and connected to a hallway with bedrooms to the right and left. In between was a spacious south-facing lounge area with floor-to-ceiling windows framing the rolling and sometimes roiling Pacific Ocean. Turning into the east wing at the top of the stairs one came to the seven-hundred-square-foot master bedroom in which Juan Pablo and Señora Marmolejo used to sleep together. Of late, due to both his increased sleeping difficulties and an increasing estrangement from his wife, the master of the house relegated Adoria to a west wing bedroom right next to Angelita's. Being placed right next door to what she considered a growing nemesis and commanded to the east wing only when her husband wished to exercise his manhood was a palpabul burr under Adoria's saddle. Actually more like a pineapple.

On this particular night they had turned in a bit earlier than usual. Juan Pablo had forced Adoria to read a bedtime story to Angelia while he listened with a look of rapture on his face. The "mother's" expression was less comely. A maid was then detailed to tuck the little one into bed while husband and wife consumed the better part of a nine-hundred-dollar magnum of Schrader Cellars Old Sparky Beckstoffer. *All the better for sleeping, my dear*. Juan Pablo departed for bed first while Adoria sat gazing at the lights of the ships cruising the coast. Finally, when she could no longer stand to listen to his sonorous breathing waft down the hallway, she staggered to her own room and fell on top of the bed fully clothed.

Pancho had been with Juan Pablo for the better part of a decade. If he had a last name, it had been long forgotten. Although his IQ was opposite the genius side of the scale, this was counter-balanced by his tenacity in fighting with fists or weapons, and his proven loyalty. In the past drug-dealing years, much of his boss' ruthlessness had been meted out by Pancho and his cohorts. He particularly enjoyed hanging adversaries by their arms until both shoulders dislocated, and then using them as targets to test various new ballistic combinations. Getting up in age and plagued by arthritis in the majority of his joints, he was now a household manager of sorts for *Gloria de Dios*, with supervision of the kitchen and cleaning staffs his primary billet. Nobody could say Juan Pablo didn't take care of his own.

It just so happened that Pancho was making his last round of ground floor check-ups when he glanced out of an east end window just in time to see two crouched, dark figures glide by. His knee-jerk reaction was to make haste to a foyer closet where a Stoeger's Condor Outback over-and-under 12 gauge was kept. Just as he reached the closet, the front door opened and two men dressed in black walked in. While he couldn't make out detailed features due to the muted foyer night lights, he knew they were not part of the security detail, hence, they were intruders. Jed pushed Gunnar to his right and he dove to his left just as Pancho swung the short-barrel weapon around and pulled the trigger on the first barrel causing a horrendously loud sound in the small enclosure. They were close enough that the No. 6 Winchester double-o buckshot didn't have time to reach much of a spread. The sideways dive saved both of them from the blast's killing zone, nevertheless, two pellets caught the outside of Gun's left thigh, and another one grazed Jed's right triceps. Pancho then leveled the second barrel at Jed's chest and pulled the trigger. *Click* was the only sound. A dud. Bad primer, unserviced firing pin, whatever. Unusual, but it did happen, and this time it saved Jed's life. As Pancho opened the breech, extracted the two shells and turned to the closet to grab more ammunition, Jed jumped up and took two steps toward Pancho, some ten feet away, who was simultaneously reloading and turning toward the unwanted guests. Jed launched himself through the air in a practiced capoeira move. A second before Pancho was ready to bring the shotgun up, Jed's right foot with a hundred and ninety flying pounds behind it crashed into his sternum. An audible pop was heard as its center portion snapped and perforated the left lung. The lower portion, the xiphoid process, also broke and was propelled backwards into the liver. Pancho dropped the shotgun and fell to the floor writhing in pain and incapacitated.

Only a few moments had passed, but the commotion woke everyone in the house. Whatever servants were there stayed in their quarters when they heard gunfire. Adoria came running out of the west wing with Tuyen close on her heels and unthinkingly flipped the switch to fully light the entranceway. A few seconds later Juan Pablo stumbled out of the east wing to investigate why anyone would be discharging firearms in his house. For some reason he would never understand, he did not grab the Glock 9 in the nightstand drawer, but did have the presence of mind to hit the panic button next to the light switch on the way out.

As everyone's eyes adjusted to the light, Juan Pablo saw the three men below, Pancho holding his midsection and having difficulty breathing, and he bellowed at the two men in black, "You are muerto! You hear me? You are DEAD!"

At that same moment Gunnar looked up to the right side of the balcony and Tuyen looked down at him. "DAAAAAADDY!" she screamed and darted for the stairs. As inconceivable facts began to click into place in his head,

Juan Pablo lunged for Tuyen and caught her just before she reached the first step.

"*Sucios bastardos. Voy a matarte.* You will never get out of here alive." he roared.

Seeing the mighty Pancho disabled and eyeing the pistols on both men's hips below, Adoria's racing mind calculated a way to both save their lives and rid herself of the child's intrusion in her life. As Jed and Gunnar contemplated their next move, with a strength she didn't know she had Adoria grabbed Tuyen's other arm and yanked her away from Juan Pablo. "Let her go, Pablito." she shrieked. "She is nothing. Let her go!"

Not caring if he killed his wife, Juan Pablo swung his arm backward with as much force as he could, and with spittle flying snarled, "Shut up, bitch. Barren whore! You give me no children and I should give up Angelita?" She had ducked just enough that his hand gave her a glancing blow on her cheek, although it knocked her backwards and she reflexively released Tuyen as she put out her arms to catch her fall. Juan Pablo stood glaring with his back to the stairs while Tuyen cowered behind the ornate woodwork on the doorway to the west wing. Years of pent up rage overflowed, and Adoria, with no forethought or sense of reason, charged with outstretched arms and plowed into him with all her might. The totally unexpected retaliation caught Juan Pablo with so much surprise that he had no opportunity to grab the staircase railing. He fell straight backwards and did two somersaults, ending up motionless at the bottom of the stairs.

Everything had happened within a matter of seconds. As Gunnar leapt over the unconscious figure and started up, Tuyen raced past a dazed Adoria and into her father's arms.

At the moment of their embrace, Jed's sat phone buzzed.

"Jed, we've got company. Could be a problem."

"What's up, Mercy? Quickly!"

"A Jeep with five armed men just pulled up to the Yukon. They look a bit hesitant to proceed this way. Maybe they're worrying about an ambush."

"OK. If anyone starts to come around it and toward you, send some fire in their direction. I'm calling Dub right now and when I hear his approach I'll call you to pull the plug and meet up with us. Any problems with that?"

"Should be OK. If they advance, which they probably will, I'll pop off a quick full-auto burst or two to let 'em know what's waiting on this end. What's our time frame?"

"I'm thinking five minutes. He's only coming from John Wayne airport. Figure you can hold that long?"

"Piece of cake, boss. But don't dawdle."

Jed then called Dub, who had been on standby.

Gunnar and Tuyen embraced mid-stairs, both sobbing uncontrollably. Adoria was nowhere to be seen and Juan Pablo was breathing but still motionless.

"Gunnar, let's move now! We gotta vacate before any of the other staff call in the local posse." Seeing the blood dripping down his pant leg, Jed asked, "You OK on that leg?"

"Doesn't feel the best," Gun replied, "but it appears to be superficial. I'll motor OK."

He then proved so by bounding down the stairs with his daughter in his arms. Jed did a quick but thorough sweep to make sure they had not dropped anything that might be traceable to them, and then they headed out the door and northward alongside the swimming pool. It took about three minutes to reach the soccer field. Jed told Gunnar and Tuyen to wait in the changing hut at the southeast corner while he quickly ran and placed white phosphorous flares at each corner of the field.

The new arrivals keeping Mercy busy were security guards that rotated shifts with the ones that Jed and Gunnar had rendered moot. The panic button in the master bedroom had set off an alarm in their quarters at the base of the hill and just off El Camino Real. They knew it meant to get up to *Gloria de Dios* fast. With guns. Far from being professionally trained, they were mostly hoodlums who had worked for Garcia-Iglesias in the past and had been recruited as personnel for a supposedly legitimate security company. Still, a man with a gun was a man with a gun. Mercy was succeeding at making them keep their distance, but as time elapsed she thought she heard movement among the trees on both sides of the driveway. They were obviously trying a flanking movement. As she was contemplating which flank to take out first, her sat phone came alive with a four-word message from Jed: "Fire in the hole."

Spraying the trees lining the road one last time, as she rounded the gate house and headed for the soccer field she heard it: *Whomp-whomp-whomp-whomp*. Sounded like Dub was on time. Some hundred and fifty yards away and glancing back at the Yukon, she hit the button on the transmitter which sent a signal to the electronic detonator buried inside a pound of C4 plastic explosive on the floor behind the driver's seat. The initial explosion blew all the windows out and all four doors off. As the doors were settling to earth, a secondary explosion, namely, the gas tank, lit off and the concussive force leveled everything within a twenty-five yard radius. This would not only deter the attackers, perhaps some permanently, but would prevent any other vehicles from accessing the estate until the wreckage was cleared.

Just as Mercy came to the west edge of the soccer pitch, the Bell UH-1 Iroquois, better known as a "Huey," settled down at center field. Jed, Gunnar and Tuyen came running from the changing hut and they all met underneath the still churning rotors. Jed jumped in the open door and Gunnar handed up Tuyen. Then Gun and Mercy dove in and Jed gave the pilot a thumbs-up. With the chopper gaining altitude fast, Jed climbed into the co-pilot's seat and said, "Long time no see, Dub."

Dub looked over and grinned. "'Bout time, ol' buddy."

As the pilot headed toward the drop-off point, Jedediah offered a short prayer of thanks to his God. At the same time he grasped the mahogany African fish eagle that hung around his neck which his father had carved for him so long ago.

Chapter 78

August 2005 - Newport Beach, California

Just off the northwest corner of Crystal Cove State Park was a short, ridgetop road that was an offshoot of a housing project not yet fully developed. Someday Seawatch Drive would likely have multimillion-dollar homes flanking it, but at the moment it was an ideal place for a chopper to drop off Jed. It took the helicopter less than a minute from the soccer field to deposit him there. He had previously reconned the area via road maps and satellite photos, and plotted a compass route from Seawatch to where his rental car sat secluded off Vista Ridge Road. As the crow flies it was only a little over a quarter of a mile, but the route was uphill through lightly forested, rocky terrain. Jed watched the helicopter's lights fade to the west as it headed for Temecula and then he beelined for the vehicle. Enough of his night vision had returned that he could pick his way by the available light, but, if needed, his NVGs were at hand.

Temecula was a moderately-sized community about sixty miles due north of San Diego in the grape-growing, wine-producing country along Interstate 15. Dub's home was out of town on the west side of Riverside County. His isolated acreage on the north border of the Santa Margarita Ecological Reserve fit well with his penchant for flying his chopper without disturbing neighbors. Because of his affection for the cocktail of the same name, Dub thought it providential that he was only about a mile's hike from the Margarita River. A Huey pilot who lost track of how many missions he had flown in two tours in Vietnam, he had purchased the surplus helicopter ten years before and rehabilitated it. He could practically take apart and reassemble the aircraft blindfolded. He had been known in Nam for his daredevil flight antics, which he claimed he did only to save American lives. The exploit most talked about happened during Operation Dewey Canyon, the last major USMC operation which took place in the A Shau Valley early in 1969. An infantry squad had been pinned down by a superior NVA force in a narrow defile north of the valley. Heedless of friendly artillery fire in support of the trapped Marines, Dub flew his Huey between canyon walls which observers said gave him about three feet of leeway on each side. Only when every man was on board did he lift off in a straight vertical maneuver. The squad leader later swore the rotors lightly caressed one of the walls on the way up.

His full name was Hugh Clairmont Daniels. Because of the chopper he piloted it was natural to call him Huey Hugh. That sounded much too fancy-pants for a Jarhead air jockey, so some of his comrades-in-arms mutated it to "Double H." That being considered a somewhat unimaginative mouthful, someone else shortened it to "Dub," which stuck. When Jed had been stationed at Camp Pendleton after returning from Vietnam, First Reconnaissance Battalion often did training exercises with the Marine Air Ground Task Force Training Command from Twenty-nine Palms where Dub was stationed. Jed had flown on Dub's Huey more than once and they struck up a friendship that continued through the years. Dub had put in his twenty, eventually flying every type of helicopter the Marine Corps owned, and in retirement did contract flying jobs for fun. When Jed had called about the rescue mission, Dub couldn't get his flight suit on fast enough.

Completing the forty-mile straight shoot to the country abode in short order, Gunnar, Tuyen, and Mercy were welcomed into the rustic home by Dub's wife, Gabriela. Gabby, as Dub affectionately called her, had steaming coffee ready and hot chocolate for Tuyen. The father and daughter were still in a state of shock and had said very little to each other. Mercy shared a bit with Dub and Gabby about what had transpired at *Gloria de Dios* while Gunnar sat back in an overstuffed recliner with Tuyen hanging onto his neck as if for dear life. She eventually dozed off, feeling safe for the first time in five months. The adults eventually lapsed into a kind of exhausted stupor and drifted off on couches and chairs as they awaited Jed's arrival.

After thankfully finding his car still there and unmolested, Jed wound his way north to the Corona del Mar Freeway and then headed northwest to where he would pick up the Costa Mesa Freeway. This would curve north and east around the Santa Ana Mountains to hook up with I-15 where he would turn south to Temecula. It was only seventy miles and change from Newport Beach to Dub's ranch, but Jed took it easy both because of night animals on the road and not wanting to bring any attention to himself. Once the group was rejoined, their next task would be to exit the state undetected and with nothing left behind to indicate they had been there. Although Jed and company were unaware of it, this task was not as critical as they might have thought it would be since Juan Pablo had no desire to involve law enforcement authorities in any part of his life or business.

Jed arrived in the middle of the night and, after hugs all around, the group decided to try for a few hours of sleep before firming up the next day's plans with the rising sun. Shortly after first light, Jed was awakened by the heavenly smell of strong coffee and buttermilk flapjacks. As he showered and shaved, the rest of the crew came to life and they met around the dining room table, with large windows providing a view of the Peninsular Ranges stretching southward. On a clear day Palomar Mountain with its famous observatory could be seen some twenty five miles to the southeast.

They were feeling relatively refreshed and, even more so, relieved that they all had gotten out with only minor injuries. Before getting horizontal earlier, Jed and Gun had doctored their flesh wounds, thankful that the buckshot had done unpleasant but not serious damage.

While the adults talked about next steps, Tuyen sat next to her daddy and clung to his arm as if she never wanted to let it go. They had had no conversation yet about either what she had experienced or what had happened to her mother, which Gunnar knew would come in time. For now, the only thing that seemed to matter to either of them was that they were with each other. They looked as if they would have liked to duct-tape their arms together, and Gun was having some difficulty keeping his eyes dry.

It was necessary to go back to Newport Beach to retrieve the belongings they had left in the motel. Instead of retracing Jed's route, they decided to continue south on I-15 to Highway 76 which would take them southwest to pick up I-5 at Oceanside. From there it would be a straight shoot up the coast highway to Newport, the total driving distance being only slightly longer than going back the northern route. Once they had cleared out and sanitized the motel room, they had another drive ahead of them.

Jed was as meticulous as possible in erasing any evidence of their presence in Newport Beach. For the quick trip in and out Tuyen was fitted with a hoodie and huge sunglasses that hid most of her face. Even with that, she stayed in the car and hunkered down in the back seat unobservable to anyone looking at the passing vehicle. The motel room had been secured by Gunnar with cash paid in advance and one of his fake IDs. They made sure nothing of theirs was left in the room, and Jed scrubbed for fingerprints every surface that they could possibly have touched, even though he couldn't see anyone connecting what happened at *Gloria de Dios* with their room rental. As an undercover cop with access to fake names and documents, Mercy had rented the blown-up Yukon with cash. This meant there was no way to trace it to her. Jed didn't feel good about the rental agency or the insurance company taking a hit for its loss, but perhaps he could find a way later to anonymously recompense them for it. Since they would pass through Laguna Beach on the drive north, Jed had called Gunny Omdahl to meet them there so he could return the weapons and other gear. Thanking him profusely, Jed told the gunny that he would be making good on the financial end soon. Omdahl nodded an acknowledgement and, looking over at the hooded little girl in the back seat, smiled. It had never crossed his mind that Jed's mission wouldn't succeed.

It was early afternoon by the time they made the trip from Temecula, cleansed the motel, and headed north out of Newport Beach. They had made the decision to make the seven-hour drive and fly out of San Francisco instead of Los Angeles. While there was no paper or credit card trail, Jed wanted all of them out of Southern California, farther away from the scene of the action the night before. The only thing confirming their presence would be a visual identification, but no one had any valid names for their faces since Gunnar and Mercy had both used false IDs in L.A. and Newport. Also, of the thousands of motel and resort rooms in Newport Beach, there was no reason for anyone to suspect that their rental of one had any connection with a vehicle explosion on a ridge south of the city.

They made it through the traffic maelstrom of L.A. slowly but without difficulty. By the time they reached Santa Clarita, they agreed to stop for the night. Gunnar paid for a room at a nondescript Super 8 Motel just off the freeway with a different bogus-name ID and credit card. Once they were ensconced in the room with take-out meals from the El Semental Real Mexican restaurant adjacent to the motel, Gun opened up his laptop to explore and hopefully book flights for the next day.

Jedediah said, "What about Tuyen? They're going to be examining documents for her at airport security, you know."

"I thought about that," Gunnar replied. He pulled a piece of paper out of a compartment in his laptop case. "I've had her birth certificate with me since the day I left Vietnam. I'll be using my real name and passport, so there won't be any question about who belongs to who."

"Good thinking," Jed responded. "So see what's available and we'll put it on my card. Try to find a flight to SeaTac with the two of you seated across the aisle from Mercy and me."

"I'll see what I can find. But it's going to be two different flights, Jed."

Mercy looked over at Jed to see a surprised expression materialize. Jed asked Gunnar, "Why two different flights?"

Gunnar answered, "Because Tuyen and I aren't going to Seattle."

Chapter 79

August 2005 - Indianapolis, Indiana

The phone call to Sonny and Linn left them dumb-founded, to say the least. All Gunnar wanted to convey from the airport was that Tuyen was with him and they would arrive at Indianapolis International that evening. He said he would tell them the story when they were all together at home. After hanging up, he reflected on using the term "home," and how much it felt like that. In the days to come he would have to make some significant decisions about vocation, location, and about life in general. At the moment, all he felt was a desperate need to be sheltered safely within the family womb in America's heartland. Tomorrow would bring what tomorrow would bring.

The Seattle flight left about an hour before Gunnar and Tuyen's. Just before they boarded, as Gun attempted to thank Jed and Mercy he came close to a total breakdown. Jed simply held him. His son. Gunnar gave him his parents' contact information with the assurance that he would be in touch before too long. Both of them were aware that their knowledge of each other and what they had experienced together would lead to something else in the future. Jed also knew that the revelation of his existence would be a bombshell of sorts to the Torkelsons, and he resolved to let Gunnar guide whatever the future might hold for involvement with his family.

All four of them embraced one more time in a group hug, little Tuyen in the middle of the three adults. The look of fear in her eyes had significantly decreased, although she asked several times about Mommy. Until he was in a safer and more secure environment, all Gun replied was that her mother was back in Vietnam, and all she needed to know at the moment was what Gunnar said to her about every ten minutes: "You are with Daddy now, and I will never leave you." They waved goodbye to Mercy and Jed as they headed for their boarding gate, and then walked hand in hand toward the gate for United Airlines Flight 317 to Indianapolis.

The reunion at the Indianapolis airport included more

tears than one would have thought possible. The few passersby at the late hour knew something out of the ordinary was happening, and gave warm smiles as they walked around them. It immediately increased Tuyen's sense of well-being to be cuddled in Grandma's and Grandpa's comforting embraces. By the time they arrived at the Torkelson residence, Tuyen was somewhere between dead-tired and exhausted, but she didn't want to be put in a bedroom alone. She curled up on a couch with her head on Gunnar's lap, and after she fell into a deep sleep he covered her with an afghan as the three adults moved to the dining room table. Gunnar made sure he was in Tuyen's line of sight in case she woke up.

"What can you tell us, Gunnar?" Sonny began.

"Mom, Dad, I'm going to ask you to trust me on this. I am not at liberty to share many details, but the police were not involved in locating or rescuing Tuyen. I did some things I wish I wouldn't have had to. I suppose you'd call it vigilante stuff. But it became apparent that the chances of law enforcement agencies finding her were poor to nothing. Please understand that the only goal was to find my daughter, and the only thing that really matters is lying over there on the sofa."

Sonny gave Linn a knowing glance that indicated they needed to honor the position their son had taken both with respect to his course of action and to his felt need to withhold information. In light of the tragic events of the past March in Da Nang, having their son and granddaughter back was enough for them.

Sonny did venture one question. "I know you're a capable man, son, but thinking of the almost impossible odds of your doing this all alone, I'm wondering if you had any help. I heard Tuyen say something to you on the way from the airport about Jed somebody. You shushed her at the time, and if it's best to keep that under wraps, I'll understand. But you can't blame me for being curious."

Gunnar was quiet for a time and then took a deep breath. "I guess now is as good a time as ever to share the news. Again, I need to keep the details of Tuyen's rescue confidential, but it couldn't have been done without Jed."

"We're all ears. Who is this Jed?"

Another deep breath. "He's my biological father."

Silence. Prolonged, absolute silence. Both parents were dumbstruck, not because they had any immediate doubts about Gunnar's feelings or loyalty as their son, but simply because the news was a categorical surprise of the first order. You might as well have told them Jesus was at the front door.

All Linn, who was known for her aplomb and level-headedness, could finally say was, "My goodness."

Sonny added, "I'll ditto that. Uh . . . how . . . what . . . uh, I mean . . . help us out here, son."

The first thing Gunnar did was go around to their side of the table and give them both reassuring hugs. Then he sat back down and told them an ultra-simplified story about someone in Seattle recognizing him as an almost double of Jed. He showed them a picture of the latter that he had taken on his cell phone and his parents immediately understood how someone would have made the connection. With a bit of concoction, he related how a meeting was arranged and how they both had DNA tests to confirm what looked obvious. Then Gunnar went on to describe what he had learned about Jed's background and skill set, and his offer to help find Tuyen. Apologizing again for not being able to share details, suffice it to say, Gun said, that without Jed's help – especially with the friends he had that were able to provide resources – he and Tuyen wouldn't be here in Indianapolis. He also told what he knew about his birth mother, Angela, to help fill in the picture of how he had become lost in the adoption shuffle after his birth. He purposefully kept Mercy out of the story due to her position with the Seattle Police Department.

Gunnar shared a bit more about Jedediah, where he was and what he did, and then Sonny asked, "Do you know what Jed's feelings are about all of this? Does he want to stay in contact? Does he want to meet us? Is this going to complicate anything for you?"

"Whoa, Dad. That's a lot of questions all at once. Tuyen and I need to readjust to our new situation in life first. Time will bring what it will bring, but I'm pretty sure Jed will want to meet you and you'll be happy to meet him. After all, he helped save Tuyen's life. I know he has every intention of not wanting to in any way come between us, not that he could anyway. But let's just let the revelation sink in for a bit and talk down the line about where we might want to go with it. By far my first priority is help for Tuyen, and figuring out what we're going to do with our lives."

"Do you know," Linn hesitantly asked, "if she was . . . well, how bad it might have been?"

"From what I can tell, Mom, she was not violated or mistreated. She was lucky, if you can call it that, to be sold to a man who simply wanted a daughter to replace one he lost. Although the whole experience was without question tremendously traumatic for her, it could have been much worse."

"In all likelihood she'll need some professional counseling to deal with both her experience and her mother's . . . " Sonny said as he looked over at the couch.

"That'll come in time," Gunnar replied. "First things first, which, to me, means at least for a while staying in this protected environment here with you."

Sonny and Linn almost simultaneously assured Gun that staying with them for as long as he wished was a given. Gunnar knew that would be their response and he acknowledged his gratitude. They also asked about his slight limp and he told them it was a minor injury sustained while rescuing Tuyen that he'd get looked at in a day or two.

"Son, have you thought much about your position with LinTech?" Sonny asked. "They've been very gracious with all that's happened, but I'm surmising that soon or later they're going to need you back in Da Nang."

Gun looked over at Tuyen for reassurance that she was deep in slumberland before saying, "Not going back to Vietnam. I think you understand why. I like the company and they've been more than good to me over the years. Not too far down the line I'm going to have to fly to San Diego to discuss the possible options face to face. Parts of the company's operations are sprinkled throughout the western states, R&D, regional offices, and the like. There's actually one of the latter in Portland that might fit my skills and experience, but whether the head honchos see it that way is anybody's guess. If we can't come to some agreement on an assignment for me here in America, I'll just have to start looking elsewhere. But I'm getting ahead of myself. The immediate concern is to nurture Tuyen's sense of security and well-being after all that she's been through. I'll contact the company when I'm satisfied that we've got a good start on that."

"Just to reiterate, Gunnar, use us and our home – heavens, *your* home – in any way you see fit. We're here for you for anything . . . and for the long haul." As Gun went to check on Tuyen, Sonny and Linn looked at each other with conjoint nods of mutual understanding. They were communicating their tremendous relief that their son would not be going back halfway around the globe. To their mind, it would be a whale of a lot easier to be supportive parents and grandparents being only, say, a four hour plane ride away.

After the folks retired for what remained of the night and he picked up Tuyen to carry her into his old bedroom where she would sleep curled up against him, he drifted off with two thoughts. First, how his panicky hatred seemed to have largely abated, if not disappeared. Feeling the warmth of his daughter next to him, he wasn't sorry for all that he had done, but regretted that he had had to do it. Yet he knew he needed to recover the person he used to be instead of the killer he had become. The world in which he had lived for the past five months was not his world, but he realized that there were other little ones like Tuyen still out there, and what that might mean for his future he did not know. Second, with his wife's death and what he had subsequently done, he would probably, as well as Tuyen, need some professional counseling for himself in time.

While he hadn't been thinking much about God in the past few months, the last thought to cross his fading mind before sleep took over was, "Thank You."

Chapter 80

August 2005 - Seattle, Washington

A week after Jed's return to Seattle, he and Darrell were strolling side by side walking the trails of Jefferson Park in the southeast part of the city. It was a gorgeous summer day with dahlias and hydrangeas in full bloom and Stellar jays rasping at them from the trees. In the previous days, Jed had related some bare bones details about the California operation, but Darrell was sharp enough to be satisfied with only what Jed was willing to share. It appeared to him as they ambled that the latter had something on his mind, so Darrell ventured a query.

“At this point are you feeling OK with all that’s transpired in the past few months?” He well knew Jed’s psychological makeup and how he had wrestled over the years with the huge grey area that is the context for most of life’s decisions.

“It’s occurred to me that some of the discussions we’ve had in the past were preparation for what I had to do.”

“I suppose that’s the key: you felt like you had to do whatever you did.” Darrell could fantasize about actions his friend had taken, but he was not privy to many specific details.

They walked another fifty yards before Jed responded. “Life’s experiences, at least for me, have shrunk the list of absolutes to a pretty narrow band. I remember all the debates back at seminary about the pros and cons of so-called situational ethics, but they don’t seem to me to have much relevance to a twelve-year-old girl enslaved by pimps and daily savaged by perverted johns. I still believe that very careful consideration and self-disciplined restraint are part of the equation, and all too often people leap into action without either. I also believe in respecting all life, all of God’s creation and God’s creatures. But if a child falls into the ocean and a shark is cruising in for an attack and I have the means to take out the shark, I wouldn’t hesitate doing so.”

“Don’t have any argument with that. But doesn’t it get a bit fuzzier when human beings are involved on both sides?” Darrell was playing his familiar role as devil’s advocate.

"Of course it does. But when those on one side are acting like rabid hyenas preying on the innocent, who're you gonna go to bat for?"

"Are you kind of saying Robin Hood had a point?"

"Yeah. Whatever. All I know is that my faith and life's experiences have led me to the point of standing up for the oppressed and marginalized. If that sometimes means using harsh methods, so be it."

"Sounds to me like you've worked a fair bit of this out in your head, Jed. We're pretty much on the same page. The big difference is that you've got some personal skills to apply in various extreme situations that I don't have. But I admire you and sometimes wish I could be more involved at the nitty-gritty level than I've allowed myself to be."

"Well, you already are to some degree."

"What do you mean?"

"I never would have been able to begin and sustain my street ministry here without your financial support. And, in fact, the funds you bankrolled for me paid for the rescue op. Which wasn't cheap, by the way."

Not having specifically thought of that dimension before Jed's comment, Darrell said, "I'm OK with that. We haven't talked much about the fund lately. Was there enough for both that and your continuing needs here?"

"More than enough. I'll show you the figures tomorrow on how it's multiplied. Which reminds me, though, I've got to get payments to Dub and the gunny. And I've also got to figure out an anonymous way to make up for the rental Yukon we blew up."

"Well, whatever it took, the money was well spent for Tuyen and Gunnar."

After a short pause, Jed proffered, "As for a deeper involvement on, to use your words, the nitty-gritty level, it's never too late, Darrell."

"What do you mean?"

"You've mentioned a time or two on your visits that this kind of ministry holds some appeal for you. Ever think of joining me here?"

They sat down on a park bench and the older man rubbed his chin for a while. Jed remained quiet until Darrell finally spoke. "Got to admit that filling in for you those days you were off saving Tuyen made me kick the idea around. I'm getting up there in age, but still feel like I've got lots of energy and enthusiasm. I don't know. It's an intriguing idea that we should talk about after I've given it more thought."

"First of all," Jed added, "you're a doggone young seventy-one, and I know you've got a heart for the kinds of folks we're surrounded with here. And aren't you getting tired of those Minnesota winters? The old saying is that *the grass is greener on the other side* . . . well, it truly is greener here, at least you can see it all year round."

"Let's keep that on the back burner. But I'll surely give it some thought."

Jed intelligently left it at that for the moment. The idea had crossed his mind ever since Darrell had retired from parish ministry. Now that the subject had been broached, he even got a bit excited about the actual possibility. Time would tell.

Another week passed. Darrell had flown back to Minneapolis with the promise to do even more thinking about their discussion in the park. It was late evening after they finished the Chinese takeout meal that Mercy had brought by Jed's apartment.

"Any news yet?" Jed asked.

"Checking the state crime reports I haven't come across a thing about local or California state agencies investigating a kidnapping in Newport Beach. In fact, there doesn't seem to be any crime report on what happened up the hill. Just a notice a couple of days afterwards about a vehicle explosion off of Newport Coast Drive. All it said was "investigation ongoing."

"Looks like we're in the clear. Any questions from your office?"

"None. As far as they're concerned I just took a few earned days off. Back at it now full steam, and a few of the cases I had hanging need some full attention."

After cleaning up the dishes, they moved to the living room area and sipped their favorite Malbec as they sat on Jed's old couch. "I want to thank you again, Mercy, for your support in all of this. We work pretty well together, don't we?"

She seemed to be weighing something in her mind and Jed recognized the pensive look on her comely face. Thinking it prudent, he just sat quietly sipping his wine waiting for her response. As he observed her expression seeming to change to one of decision or determination, Mercy put her glass on the coffee table. She then took Jed's and did the same. Turning back to him, she drew his face to hers and kissed him gently but passionately. They held the kiss for considerably longer than one that would have characterized a salutary friendship peck. When Mercy sat back she was somewhat unsure what Jed's reaction would be. She was encouraged by the fact that after the initial surprise, he did seem more than willing to let it happen.

He said with a winsome smile, "I guess that means you agree with me."

"Jed, I know what you've told me about your past, your commitment to celibacy and all. But I need to be honest with you about my feelings. I'll understand if you feel we can't explore our relationship on a deeper level. But I can't go on pretending this isn't something that's real for me."

Attempting to choose his words carefully, Jedediah said, "Mercy, meeting you has touched off something I thought was lost forever. When thoughts or feelings about you came up, I purposefully pushed them out of my mind. I don't know . . . maybe I thought I needed to do that to be true to Angela. Then finding Gunnar and all the memories that has evoked . . . it's all set my mind churning with a fair bit of confusion."

"Jed, if you don't . . ."

"No, wait. Please let me finish. Angela is long gone. I've known that intellectually, but have never seemed to accept it emotionally. In some way, Gunnar's presence has been a catalyst for self-examination . . . some re-thinking about what I've been carrying all these years."

"But Jed, if I'm presuming too much, or if I'm not the woman who . . ."

Jed put his finger to her lips to hush her again. "There's lots of dimensions to this, Mercy. Our age difference, our . . . well, our . . ."

"Yes?" she said with her own Cheshire cat smile. "What other dimensions were you thinking of?"

Jed put his hands on her shoulders and said, "I have

immense affection and appreciation for you, Mercy, but let's take it slow and easy. It's all new to me after so many years, but let's walk down this road one step at a time." And the next step was that he kissed her again.

Epilogue

September 2005 - Newport Beach, California

Juan Pablo Fernández de Aguiniga y García-Iglesias used a walker most of the time. On his better days he could get along with a cane for short periods. The doctors said that this would likely be a permanent disability due to his several broken vertebrae and nerve damage.

Immobile at the foot of the stairs down which Adoria had pushed him, Juan Pablo had regained consciousness just in time to hear the helicopter *whomp-whomping* off to the east. He had no conscious memory of hearing the explosion outside the estate gate. Looking over at Pancho who, with a punctured lung and bleeding liver, could do nothing but lie in a fetal position and wait for help to arrive, Juan knew that something serious had happened to his own back.

When the Yukon and surrounding area became a scene out of Dante's Inferno, all five of the wannabe relief force, three on one side of the drive and two on the other, were sent tumbling with singed hair and clothing, and ears buzzing like a nest of angry hornets. The one closest to the gate house, therefore farthest away from the blast, composed himself enough to half-walk, half-crawl to the mansion. Moments before he burst into the entrance foyer, one of the cooks came from her quarters and was clucking around the area like a panicked chicken.

Although in great pain, Juan Pablo called both over to him and commanded that no, absolutely no police were to be allowed on the grounds. Unavoidably, calls from overlooking neighbors would obviously have sent fire trucks on the way, and he instructed them to call for two ambulances, one for Pancho and one for himself. But absolutely no police.

When standard operating procedure required questioning by authorities at the hospital, Juan Pablo related that he had stumbled at the top of the stairs and when Pancho grabbed him in an attempt to assist him they had both tumbled pell-mell all the way down. This was corroborated by the cook, although not by Señora García-Iglesias since she was out of the country visiting relatives at the time.

As for the remnants of what used to be a GMC Yukon, its demise was explained as a leaky gas line ignited by sparks from faulty wiring under the hood. The lazy employee, who should have had the gas line fixed, had been approaching the gate house when he saw smoke coming from under the hood. Fearing an explosion, he exited the vehicle and ran like a scared rabbit, getting just far enough away that he received only light burns when the big blow came. The police, having no reason to doubt the esteemed member of the community, who was also a generous contributor to the Riverside County Police Benevolent Association, accepted his version of events and wished him a speedy recovery. The recoverable burned parts of the Yukon were gathered and sent to a salvage yard within days.

Adoria had disappeared, along with all her jewelry and a hefty suitcase full of cash taken from the house safe. Juan Pablo had to give her some credit; he'd had no idea she knew the safe's combination. But wherever she was, he would track her down eventually to repay all the kindness she had showered upon him.

Pancho spent ten days in intensive care and some were surprised he had even survived. Now living in an assisted care home, albeit a nice one, he was operating on one smoked-out lung and a failing liver damaged by years of who-knows-how-many barrels of tequila and aguardiente. Due to his newfound mobility problems, an inability to visit Pancho as much as he would like increased Señor García-Iglesias' growing level of frustration.

For virtually all of Juan Pablo's life, revenge had been sweet nectar to his demented palate, healing balm for his troubled soul. The fact that there seemed to be no ready access to it after Angelita's kidnapping fired his growing rage. The three disabled security guards could tell him nothing, and the consequence of their incompetence was a test to see how long they could tread water five miles off the coast with cinder blocks attached to each leg.

With regard to determining who had initiated all this misery in his life, Juan Pablo knew the only possible avenue of investigation was to discover his Angelita's biological parentage. He truly believed that she was his child and that whoever brought her into this world had, for whatever rationalized reasons Juan Pablo might manufacture, forfeited their rights as parents. But the only possible source for this information was BJ, and his investigators had learned of the man's unfortunate demise.

Brooding alone day after day in his magnificent *Gloria de Dios*, giving anything but glory to God, one objective, and only one, dominated virtually every waking minute. He swore on his mother's grave, his father's grave, the graves of the saints, *anybody's grave*, that he would find little Angelita. He would bring her back home to love him, and utterly destroy the evil beings who had wrenched her from him. To whatever gods might be listening, his solemn pledge was to find these people and cut them up into little pieces with the sharpest axe he could find.

ACKNOWLEDGEMENTS

First and foremost I want to thank my wife, Betsy, for her immeasurable and enduring support from the story's conception until going to press. The never ending pot of coffee was combined with her affirmation of my determination and her constant words of encouragement. Our children, David and Katherine, also provided much moral support along with critical analysis of the text from time to time. Inestimable gratitude goes to David Faro for the manuscript conversions and cover design.

Words are inadequate to express my appreciation to sisters, Donna Rae Cintora and Pamela Faro. They spent endless hours proofreading the manuscript and offering valuable content editing counsel. The novel is eminently better for the application of their expertise.

For an awareness of the human trafficking problem, particularly in Washington State, I am indebted to members of the Seattle Police Department's Vice and High Risk Victims Unit, Megan Bruneau, Jaycin Diaz, Maurice Washington, and Stefanie Hanley, for sharing their time and experience. They provided information and knowledge of law enforcement structures that contribute to the novel's authenticity.

Bear Tracks Press
2017

Olympia, Washington

Made in United States
Troutdale, OR
01/26/2024

17173471R00428